The Freedom Trap

Bahama Crisis

The Enemy

Desmond Bagley

Diamond Books
An Imprint of HarperCollins*Publishers*,
77–85 Fulham Palace Road
Hammersmith, London W6 8JB

This Diamond Books Omnibus edition first published 1994

ISBN 0 261 66276 7

Printed in Great Britain by
BPCC Hazells Ltd

The Freedom Trap

To Ron and Peggy Hulland

1

I

Mackintosh's office was, unexpectedly, in the City. I had difficulty in finding it because it was in that warren of streets between Holborn and Fleet Street which is a maze to one accustomed to the grid-iron pattern of Johannesburg. I found it at last in a dingy building; a well-worn brass plate announcing innocuously that this Dickensian structure held the registered office of Anglo-Scottish Holdings Ltd.

I smiled as I touched the polished plate, leaving a smudged fingerprint. It seemed that Mackintosh knew his business; this plate, apparently polished by generations of office boys, was a sign of careful planning that augured well for the future – the professional touch. I'm a professional and I don't like working with amateurs – they're unpredictable, careless and too dangerous for my taste. I had wondered about Mackintosh because England is the spiritual home of amateurism, but Mackintosh was a Scot and I suppose that makes a difference.

There was no lift, of course, so I trudged up four flights of stairs – poor lighting and marmalade-coloured walls badly in need of a repaint – and found the Anglo-Scottish office at the end of a dark corridor. It was all so normal that I wondered if I had the right address but I stepped forward to the desk and said, 'Rearden – to see Mr Mackintosh.'

The red-headed girl behind the desk favoured me with a warm smile and put down the tea-cup she was holding. 'He's expecting you,' she said. 'I'll see if he's free.' She went into the inner office, closing the door carefully behind her. She had good legs.

I looked at the scratched and battered filing cabinets and wondered what was in them and found I could not possibly guess. Perhaps they were stuffed full of Angles and Scots. There were two eighteenth-century prints on the wall – Windsor Castle and the Thames at Richmond. There was a Victorian steel engraving of Princes Street, Edinburgh. All very Anglic and Scottish. I admired Mackintosh more and more – this was going to be a good careful job; but I did wonder how he'd done it – did he call in an interior decorator or did he have a pal who was a set dresser in a film studio?

The girl came back. 'Mr Mackintosh will see you now – you can go right through.'

I liked her smile so I returned it and walked past her into Mackintosh's sanctum. He hadn't changed. I hadn't expected him to change – not in two months – but sometimes a man looks different on his home ground where he has a sense of security, a sense of knowing what's what. I was pleased Mackintosh hadn't changed in that way because it meant he would be sure of himself anywhere and at any time. I like people I can depend on.

He was a sand-coloured man with light gingery hair and invisible eyebrows and eyelashes which gave his face a naked look. If he didn't shave for a week probably no one would notice. He was slight in build and I wondered how he would use himself in a rough-house; flyweights usually invent nasty tricks to make up for lack of brawn. But then Mackintosh would never get into a brawl in the first place; there are all sorts of different ways of using your brains.

He put his hands flat on the desk. 'So you are,' he paused, holding his breath, and then spoke my name in a gasp, 'Rearden. And how was the flight, Mr Rearden?'

'Not bad.'

'That's fine. Sit down, Mr Rearden. Would you like some tea?' He smiled slightly. 'People who work in offices like this drink tea all the time.'

'All right,' I said, and sat down.

He went to the door. 'Could you rustle up another pot of tea, Mrs Smith?'

The door clicked gently as he closed it and I cocked my head in that direction. 'Does she know?'

'Of course,' he said calmly. 'I couldn't do without Mrs Smith. She's a very capable secretary, too.'

'Smith?' I asked ironically.

'Oh, it's her real name. Not too incredible – there are plenty of Smiths. She'll be joining us in a moment so I suggest we delay any serious discussion.' He peered at me. 'That's a rather lightweight suit for our English weather. You mustn't catch pneumonia.'

I grinned at him. 'Perhaps you'll recommend a tailor.'

'Indeed I will; you must go to my man. He's a bit expensive but I think we can manage that.' He opened a drawer and took out a fat bundle of currency. 'You'll need something for expenses.'

I watched unbelievingly as he began to count out the fivers. He parted with thirty of them, then paused. 'We'd better make it two hundred,' he decided, added another ten notes, then pushed the wad across to me. 'You don't mind cash, I trust? In my business cheques are rather looked down upon.'

I stuffed the money into my wallet before he changed his mind. 'Isn't this a little unusual? I didn't expect you to be so free and easy.'

'I daresay the expense account will stand it,' he said tolerantly. 'You are going to earn it, you know.' He offered a cigarette. 'And how was Johannesburg when you left?'

'Still the same in a changing sort of way,' I said. 'Since you were there they've built another hundred-and-sixty-foot office block in the city.'

'In two months? Not bad!'

'They put it up in twelve days,' I said drily.

'Go-ahead chaps, you South Africans. Ah, here's the tea.'

Mrs Smith put the tea tray on to the desk and drew up a chair. I looked at her with interest because anyone Mackintosh trusted was sure to be out of the ordinary. Not that she looked it, but perhaps that was because she was disguised as a secretary in a regulation twin-set – just another office girl with a nice smile. Yet in other circumstances I thought I could get on very well with Mrs Smith – in the absence of Mr Smith, of course.

Mackintosh waved his hand. 'Will you be Mother, Mrs Smith?' She busied herself with the cups, and Mackintosh said, 'There's no real need for further introductions, is there? You won't be around long enough for anything but the job, Rearden. I think we can get down to cases now.'

I winked at Mrs Smith. 'A pity.'

She looked at me unsmilingly. 'Sugar?' was all she asked.

He tented his fingers. 'Did you know that London is the world centre of the diamond business?'

'No, I didn't. I thought it was Amsterdam.'

'That's where the cutting is done. London is where diamonds are bought and sold in all stages of manufacture from uncut stones to finished pieces of jewellery.' He smiled. 'Last week I was in a place where packets of diamonds are sold like packets of butter in a grocer's shop.'

I accepted a cup of tea from Mrs Smith. 'I bet they have bags of security.'

'Indeed they have,' said Mackintosh. He held his arms wide like a fisherman describing the one that got away. 'The safe doors are that thick and the place is wired up with so many electronic gimmicks that if you blink an eyelash in the wrong place at the wrong time half the metropolitan police begin to move in.'

I sipped the tea, then put down the cup. 'I'm not a safe cracker,' I said. 'And I wouldn't know where to begin –

you need a peterman for that. Besides, it would have to be a team job.'

'Rest easy,' said Mackintosh. 'It was the South African angle that set me thinking about diamonds. Diamonds have all the virtues; they're relatively anonymous, portable and easily sold. Just the thing a South African would go for, don't you think? Do you know anything about the IDB racket?'

I shook my head. 'Not my line of country – so far.'

'It doesn't matter; perhaps it's for the better. You're a clever thief, Rearden; that's why you've stayed out of trouble. How many times have you been inside?'

I grinned at him. 'Once – for eighteen months. That was a long time ago.'

'Indeed it was. You change your methods and your aims, don't you? You don't leave any recurring statistics for a computer to sort out – no definite *modus operandi* to trip over. As I say – you're a clever thief. I think that what I have in mind will be just up your street. Mrs Smith thinks so, too.'

'Let's hear about it,' I said cautiously.

'The British GPO is a marvellous institution,' said Mackintosh inconsequentially. 'Some say ours is the best postal system in the world; some think otherwise if you judge by the readers' letters in the *Daily Telegraph*, but grousing is an Englishman's privilege. Insurance companies, however, regard the GPO very highly. Tell me, what is the most outstanding property of the diamond?'

'It sparkles.'

'An uncut diamond doesn't,' he pointed out. 'An uncut stone looks like a bit of sea-washed bottle glass. Think again.'

'It's hard,' I said. 'Just about the hardest thing there is.'

Mackintosh clicked his tongue in annoyance. 'He's not thinking, is he, Mrs Smith? Tell him.'

'The size – or the lack of it,' she said quietly.

Mackintosh pushed his hand under my nose and curled his fingers into a fist. 'You can hold a fortune in your hand and no one would know it was there. You could put diamonds worth a hundred thousand pounds into this matchbox – then what would you have?'

'You tell me.'

'You'd have a parcel, Rearden; a package. Something that can be wrapped up in brown paper with enough room to write an address and accept a postage stamp. Something that can be popped into a letter-box.'

I stared at him. 'They send diamonds through the *post*!'

'Why not? The postal system is highly efficient and very rarely is anything lost. Insurance companies are willing to bet large sums of money on the efficiency of the GPO and those boys know what they're doing. It's a matter of statistics, you know.'

He toyed with the matchbox. 'At one time there was a courier system and that had a lot of disadvantages. A courier would personally carry a parcel of diamonds and deliver it to its destination by hand. That fell through for a number of reasons; the couriers got to be known by the wide boys, which was very sad because a number of them were severely assaulted. Another thing was that human beings are but human, after all, and a courier could be corrupted. The supply of trustworthy men isn't bottomless and the whole courier system was not secure. Far from it.

'But consider the present system,' he said enthusiastically. 'Once a parcel is swallowed into the maw of the Post Office not even God can extract it until it reaches its destination. And why? Because nobody knows precisely where the hell it is. It's just one of millions of parcels circulating through the system and to find it would *not* be like finding a needle in a haystack – it would be like searching a haystack for a particular wisp of hay. Do you follow me?'

I nodded. 'It sounds logical.'

'Oh, it is,' said Mackintosh. 'Mrs Smith did all the necessary research. She's a very clever girl.' He flapped his hand languidly. 'Carry on, Mrs Smith.'

She said coolly, 'Once the insurance company actuaries analysed the GPO statistics regarding losses, they saw they were on to a good thing providing certain precautions were taken. To begin with, the stones are sent in all sizes and shapes of parcel from matchbox size to crates as big as a tea chest. The parcels are labelled in a multitude of different ways, very often with the trade label of a well-known firm – anything to confuse the issue, you see. The most important thing is the anonymity of the destination. There are a number of accommodation addresses having nothing to do with the diamond industry to which the stones are sent, and the same address is never used twice running.'

'Very interesting,' I said. 'Now how do we crack it?'

Mackintosh leaned back in his chair and put his fingertips together. 'Take a postman walking up a street – a familiar sight. He carries a hundred thousand pounds' worth of diamonds but – and this is the interesting point – he doesn't know it and neither does anyone else. Even the recipient who is eagerly awaiting the diamonds doesn't know when they'll arrive because the Post Office doesn't guarantee delivery at any specific time, regardless of what they say about first-class post in their specious advertising. The parcels are sent by ordinary post; no special delivery nonsense which would be too easy to crack open.'

I said slowly, 'It seems to me that you're painting yourself into a corner, but I suppose you have something up your sleeve. All right – I'll buy it.'

'Have you ever done any photography?'

I resisted the impulse to explode. This man had more ways of talking around a subject than anyone I had ever known. He had been the same in Johannesburg – never talking in a straight line for more than two minutes. 'I've clicked a shutter once or twice,' I said tightly.

'Black-and-white or colour?'

'Both.'

Mackintosh looked pleased. 'When you take colour photographs – transparencies – and send them away for processing, what do you get back?'

I looked appealingly at Mrs Smith and sighed. 'Small pieces of film with pictures on them.' I paused and added, 'They're framed in cardboard mounts.'

'What else do you get?'

'Nothing.'

He wagged his finger. 'Oh yes, you do. You get the distinctive yellow box the things are packed in. Yes, yellow – I suppose it could be described as Kodak yellow. If a man is carrying one of those boxes in his hand you can spot it across a street and you say to yourself, "That man is carrying a box of Kodachrome transparencies."'

I felt a thrill of tension. Mackintosh was coming to the meat of it. 'All right,' he said abruptly. 'I'll lay it out for you. I know when a parcel of diamonds is being sent. I know to where it is being sent – I have the accommodation address. Most important of all, I know the packaging and it's unmistakable. All you have to do is to wait near the address and the postman will come up to you with the damn thing in his hand. And that little yellow box will contain one hundred and twenty thousand quid in unset stones which you will take from him.'

'How did you find out all this?' I asked curiously.

'I didn't,' he said. 'Mrs Smith did. The whole thing is her idea. She came up with the concept and did all the research. Exactly *how* she did the research is no concern of yours.'

I looked at her with renewed interest and discovered that her eyes were green. There was a twinkle in them and her lips were curved in a humorous quirk which smoothed out as she said soberly, 'There must be as little violence as possible, Mr Rearden.'

'Yes,' agreed Mackintosh. 'As little violence as possible commensurate with making a getaway. I don't believe in violence; it's bad for business. You'd better bear that in mind.'

I said, 'The postman won't hand it to me. I'll have to take it by force.'

Mackintosh showed his teeth in a savage grin. 'So it will be robbery with violence if you get nabbed. Her Majesty's judges are hard about that kind of thing, especially considering the amount involved. You'll be lucky to get away with ten years.'

'Yes,' I said thoughtfully, and returned his grin with interest.

'Still, we won't make it too easy for the police. The drill is this; I'll be nearby and you'll keep on going. The stones will be out of the country within three hours of the snatch. Mrs Smith, will you attend to the matter of the bank?'

She opened a folder and produced a form which she pushed across the desk. 'Fill that in.'

It was a request to open an account at the *Züricher Ausführen Handelsbank*. Mrs Smith said, 'British politicians may not like the gnomes of Zürich but they come in handy when needed. Your number is very complicated – write it out fully in words in this box.'

Her finger rested on the form so I scribbled the number in the place she indicated. She said, 'That number written on the right cheque form in place of a signature will release to you any amount of money up to forty thousand pounds sterling, or its equivalent in any currency you wish.'

Mackintosh sniggered. 'Of course, you'll have to get the diamonds first.'

I stared at them. 'You're taking two-thirds.'

'I did plan it,' Mrs Smith said coolly.

Mackintosh grinned like a hungry shark. 'She has expensive tastes.'

'Of that I have no doubt,' I said. 'Would your tastes run

to a good lunch? You'll have to suggest a restaurant, though; I'm a new boy in London.'

She was about to answer when Mackintosh said sharply, 'You're not here to play footsie with my staff, Rearden. It wouldn't be wise for you to be seen with either of us. Perhaps when it's all over we can have dinner together – the three of us.'

'Thanks,' I said bleakly.

He scribbled on a piece of paper. 'I suggest that after lunch you . . . er . . . "case the joint" – I believe that is the correct expression. Here is the address of the drop.' He pushed the paper across the desk, and scribbled again. 'And this is the address of my tailor. Don't get them mixed up, there's a good chap. That would be disastrous.'

II

I lunched at the Cock in Fleet Street and then set out to look up the address Mackintosh had given me. Of course I walked in the wrong direction – London is the devil of a place to get around in if you don't know it. I didn't want to take a taxi because I always play things very cautiously, perhaps even too cautiously. But that's why I'm a success.

Anyway, I found myself walking up a street called Ludgate Hill before I found I'd gone wrong and, in making my way into Holborn, I passed the Central Criminal Court. I knew it was the Central Criminal Court, because it says so and that surprised me because I always thought it was called the Old Bailey. I recognized it because of the golden figure of Justice on the roof. Even a South African would recognize that – we see Edgar Lustgarten movies, too.

It was all very interesting but I wasn't there as a tourist so I passed up the opportunity of going inside to see if there was a case going on. Instead I pressed on to Leather Lane behind Gamage's and found a street market with people selling all kinds of junk from barrows. I didn't much like the look of that – it's difficult to get away fast in a thick crowd. I'd have to make damned sure there was no hue and cry, which meant slugging the postman pretty hard. I began to feel sorry for him.

Before checking on the address I cruised around the vicinity, identifying all the possible exits from the area. To my surprise I found that Hatton Garden runs parallel with Leather Lane and I knew that the diamond merchants hung out there. On second thoughts it wasn't too surprising; the diamond boys wouldn't want their accommodation address to be too far from the ultimate destination. I looked at the stolid, blank buildings and wondered in which of them were the strongrooms Mackintosh had described.

I spent half an hour pacing out those streets and noting the various types of shop. Shops are very useful to duck into when you want to get off the streets quickly. I decided that Gamage's might be a good place to get lost in and spent another quarter-hour familiarizing myself with the place. That wouldn't be enough but at this stage it wasn't a good thing to decide definitely on firm plans. That's the trouble with a lot of people who slip up on jobs like this; they make detailed plans too early in the game, imagining they're Master Minds, and the whole operation gets hardening of the arteries and becomes stiff and inflexible.

I went back to Leather Lane and found the address Mackintosh had given me. It was on the second floor, so I went up to the third in the creaking lift and walked down one flight of stairs. The Betsy-Lou Dress Manufacturing Co. Ltd was open for business but I didn't trouble to introduce myself. Instead I checked the approaches and found them reasonably good, although I would have to observe the postman in action before I could make up my mind about the best way of doing the job.

I didn't hang about too long, just enough to take rough

bearings, and within ten minutes I was back in Gamage's and in a telephone booth. Mrs Smith must have been literally hanging on to the telephone awaiting my call because the bell rang only once before she answered, 'Anglo-Scottish Holdings.'

'Rearden,' I said.

'I'll put you through to Mr Mackintosh.'

'Wait a minute,' I said. 'What kind of a Smith are you?'

'What do you mean?'

'Don't you have a first name?'

There was a pause before she said, 'Perhaps you'd better call me Lucy.'

'Ouch! I don't believe it.'

'You'd better believe it.'

'Is there a Mr Smith?'

Frost formed on the earpiece of my telephone as she said icily, 'That's no business of yours. I'll put you through to Mr Mackintosh.'

There was a click and the line went dead temporarily and I thought I wasn't much of a success as a great lover. It wasn't surprising really; I couldn't see Lucy Smith – if that was her name – wanting to enter into any kind of close relationship with me until the job was over. I felt depressed.

Mackintosh's voice crackled in my ear. 'Hello, dear boy.'

'I'm ready to talk about it some more.'

'Are you? Well, come and see me tomorrow at the same time.'

'All right,' I said.

'Oh, by the way, have you been to the tailor yet?'

'No.'

'You'd better hurry,' he said. 'There'll be the measurements and at least three fittings. You'll just about have time to get it all in before you get slapped in the nick.'

'Very funny,' I said, and slammed down the phone. It was all right for Mackintosh to make snide comments; he wasn't going to do the hard work. I wondered what else he did in that shabby office apart from arranging diamond robberies.

I took a taxi into the West End and found Austin Reed's, where I bought a very nice reversible weather coat and one of those caps as worn by the English country gent, the kind in which the cloth crown is sewn on to the peak. They wanted to wrap the cap but I rolled it up and put it into the pocket of the coat which I carried out over my arm.

I didn't go near Mackintosh's tailor.

III

'So you think it's practicable,' said Mackintosh.

I nodded. 'I'll want to know a bit more, but it looks all right so far.'

'What do you want to know?'

'Number one – when is the job to be?'

Mackintosh grinned. 'The day after tomorrow,' he said airily.

'Christ!' I said. 'That's not allowing much time.'

He chuckled. 'It'll be all over in less than a week after you've set foot in England.' He winked at Mrs Smith. 'It's not everyone who can make forty thousand quid for a week's not very hard work.'

'I can see at least one other from here,' I said sarcastically. 'I don't see that you're working your fingers to the bone.'

He was undisturbed. 'Organization – that's my forte.'

'It means I've got to spend the rest of today and all tomorrow studying the habits of the British postman,' I said. 'How many deliveries a day?'

Mackintosh cocked his eye at Mrs Smith, who said, 'Two.'

'Have you any snoopers you can recruit? I don't want to spend too much time around Leather Lane myself. I might get picked up for loitering and that would certainly queer the pitch.'

'It's all been done,' said Mrs Smith. 'I have the timetable here.'

While I was studying it, she unrolled a plan on to the desk. 'This is a plan of the entire second floor. We're lucky on this one. In some buildings there's a row of letter-boxes in the entrance hall, but not here. The postman delivers to every office.'

Mackintosh put down his finger with a stabbing motion. 'You'll tackle the postman just about here. He'll have the letters for that damnably named clothing company in his hand ready for delivery and you ought to see whether he's carrying the package or not. If he isn't you pass it up and wait for the next delivery.'

'That's what's worrying me,' I said. 'The waiting bit. If I'm not careful I'll stick out like a sore thumb.'

'Oh, didn't I tell you – I've rented an office on the same floor,' said Mackintosh blandly. 'Mrs Smith went shopping and all home comforts are installed; an electric kettle, tea, coffee, sugar and milk, and a basket of goodies from Fortnum's. You'll live like a king. I hope you like caviare.'

I blew out my breath sharply. 'Don't bother to consult me about anything,' I said sarcastically, but Mackintosh merely smiled and tossed a key-ring on the desk. I picked it up. 'What name am I trading under?'

'Kiddykar Toys Limited,' said Mrs Smith. 'It's a genuine company.'

Mackintosh laughed. 'I set it up myself – cost all of twenty-five quid.'

We spent the rest of the morning scheming and I didn't find any snags worth losing any sleep over. I found myself liking Lucy Smith more and more; she had a brain as sharp as a razor and nothing escaped her attention, and yet she contrived to retain her femininity and avoid bossiness, something that seems difficult for brainy women. When we had just about got everything wrapped up, I said, 'Come now; Lucy isn't your real name. What is?'

She looked at me with clear eyes. 'I don't think it really matters,' she said evenly.

I sighed. 'No,' I admitted. 'Perhaps not.'

Mackintosh regarded us with interest, then said abruptly, 'I said there was to be no lally-gagging around with the staff, Rearden; you just stick to doing your job.' He looked at his watch. 'You'd better leave now.'

So I left the gloom of his nineteenth-century office and lunched again at the Cock, and the afternoon was spent in the registered office of Kiddykar Toys Ltd, two doors away from the Betsy-Lou Dress Manufacturing Co. Ltd. Everything was there that Mackintosh had promised, so I made myself a pot of coffee and was pleased to see that Mrs Smith had supplied the real stuff and not the instant powdered muck.

There was a good view of the street and, when I checked on the timetable of the postman, I was able to identify his route. Even without the telephone call Mackintosh was to make I ought to get at least fifteen minutes' notice of his arrival. That point settled, I made a couple of expeditions from the office, pacing the corridor and timing myself. There really was no point in doing it without knowledge of the postman's speed but it was good practice. I timed myself from the office to Gamage's, walking at a fair clip but not so fast as to attract attention. An hour in Gamage's was enough to work out a good confusing route and then work was over for the day and I went back to my hotel.

The next day was pretty much the same except I had the postman to practise on. The first delivery I watched from the office with the door opened a crack and a stopwatch in my hand. That might seem a bit silly; after all, all I had to do was to cosh a man. But there was a hell of a lot at stake so I went through the whole routine.

On the second delivery of the day I did a dummy run on

the postman. Sure enough, it was as Mackintosh had predicted; as he approached Betsy-Lou's door the letters for delivery were firmly clutched in hand and any box of Kodachromes should be clearly visible. I hoped Mackintosh was right about the diamonds; we'd look mighty foolish if we ended up with a photographic record of Betsy-Lou's weekend in Brighton.

Before I left I telephoned Mackintosh and he answered the telephone himself. I said, 'I'm as ready as I'll ever be.'

'Good!' He paused. 'You won't see me again – apart from the hand-over of the merchandise tomorrow. Make a neat job of that, for God's sake!'

'What's the matter?' I asked. 'Got the wind up?'

He didn't answer that one. Instead, he said, 'You'll find a present awaiting you at your hotel. Handle with care.' Another pause. 'Good luck.'

I said, 'Give my sincere regards to Mrs Smith.'

He coughed. 'It wouldn't do, you know.'

'Perhaps not; but I like to make my own decisions.'

'Maybe so – but she'll be in Switzerland tomorrow. I'll pass on your message when I next see her.' He rang off.

I went back to the hotel, picked up a small package at the desk, and unwrapped it in my room. Nestling in a small box was a cosh, lead-centered and rubber-padded with a non-skid grip and a neat strap to go round the wrist. A very effective anaesthetic instrument, if a bit more dangerous than most. Also in the box was a scrap of paper with a single line of typescript: HARD ENOUGH AND NO HARDER.

I went to bed early that night. There was work to do next day.

IV

Next morning I went into the City like any other business gent, although I didn't go so far as to wear a bowler and carry the staff of office – the rolled umbrella. I was earlier than most because the first postal delivery of the day was before office hours. I arrived at Kiddykar Toys with half an hour in hand and immediately put on the kettle for coffee before inspecting the view from the window. The stallholders of Leather Lane were getting ready for the day's sales and there was no sign of Mackintosh. I wasn't worried; he'd be around somewhere in the neighbourhood keeping an eye open for the postman.

I had just finished the first cup of coffee when the phone rang. Mackintosh said briefly, 'He's coming.' There was a click as he hung up.

In the interests of his leg muscles the postman had put in a bit of time and motion study on this building. It was his habit to take the lift to the top floor and deliver the letters from the top down on the theory that walking downstairs is easier than climbing them. I put on my coat and hat and opened the door a couple of inches, listening for the whine of the lift. It was ten minutes before I heard it go up, and then I stepped out into the corridor, carefully drawing the office door closed but not quite shut so that the least push would swing it open.

It was very quiet in the building at that hour and, as I heard the postman clattering down the stairs to the second floor, I retreated down the flight of stairs to the first floor. He hit the second floor and turned away from Betsy-Lou's door to deliver the post to other offices. That was his usual routine and so I wasn't worried.

Then I heard him coming back a few steps at a time, the

intervals punctuated by the metallic bangs of swinging letterbox flaps. Just at the right time I came up the stairs and headed for the Kiddykar office which brought me facing him. I stared at his hands but there was no little yellow box to be seen.

'Morning,' he said. 'Lovely day, isn't it?' He went past at a quick pace and I fumbled my way into the office, faking the opening of the door with a key. As I closed it behind me I found that I was sweating slightly; not much but enough to show that I was under tension. It was ridiculous, I suppose – I had only to take a little box away from an unsuspecting man, which should have been the easiest thing in the world and no occasion for nerves.

It was the contents of that box which set up the tension. A hundred and twenty thousand quid is a hell of a lot of money to be at stake. It's rather like the man who can walk along a kerbstone unconcernedly and never put a foot wrong, yet let him try the same thing with a two-hundred-foot drop on one side and he'll break into a muck sweat.

I walked over to the window and opened the casement, not so much to get fresh air as to signal to Mackintosh that the first delivery was a bust. I looked down into Leather Lane and saw him in his appointed place. He was standing before a fruit and vegetable stall prodding tomatoes with a nervous forefinger. He flicked his eyes up at the window then swung around and walked away.

I lit a cigarette and settled down with the morning papers. There was quite a while to wait before the second post.

Two hours later the telephone rang again. 'Better luck this time,' said Mackintosh, and hung up.

I went through the same routine as before – there was no harm in it as this would be a different postman. I waited on the landing just below the second floor and listened intently. It would be more difficult now that the building was inhabited and a lot depended on whether I could catch the postman alone in the corridor. If I could then it was easy, but if there was anyone else present I would have to grab the box and run for it.

Steady footsteps warned me that he was coming and I trotted up the stairs at the critical moment. I swung my head back and forwards like someone about to cross a street, and found that all was clear – no one in the corridor except for me and the postman. Then I looked at his hands.

He was carrying a bundle of letters and right on top of the bundle was a little yellow box.

I stepped right in front of him as he drew abreast of the Kiddykar office. 'Have you anything for me?' I asked. 'I'm in there.' I pointed to the door behind him.

He turned his head to look at the name on the door and I hit him behind the ear with the cosh, hoping to God he hadn't an unusually thin skull. He grunted and his knees buckled. I caught him before he fell and pushed him at the door of the office which swung open under his weight, and he fell over the threshold spilling letters before him. The Kodachrome box fell to the floor with a little thump.

I stepped over him and hauled him inside, pushing the door closed with my foot. Then I grabbed the yellow box and dropped it into the innocuous brown box that Mackintosh had had specially tailored to fit it. I had to pass it on to him in the street and we wanted no flash of that conspicuous yellow to be seen.

In less than sixty seconds from the time I greeted the postman I was outside the office and locking the door on him. As I did so someone passed behind me in the corridor and opened the door of the Betsy-Lou office. I turned and went downstairs, not moving too fast but not dawdling. I reckoned the postman wouldn't come round for two or three minutes, and then he still had to get out of the office.

I came out on to the street and saw Mackintosh staring at me. He averted his eyes and half-turned away and I strode across the street among the stalls in his direction. It was easy enough, in the throng, to bump him with my shoulder, and with a muffled 'Sorry!' I passed the packet to him and continued in the direction of Holborn.

I hadn't gone far when I heard the smash of glass behind me and a confused shouting. That postman had been smart; he had wasted no time on the door but had broken the window as a means of drawing attention to himself. Also he hadn't been unconscious for as long as I had hoped – I hadn't hit him nearly hard enough.

But I was safe – far enough away not to be spotted by him and moving farther all the time. It would take at least five minutes to sort out the confusion and by that time I intended to get thoroughly lost – and I hoped Mackintosh was doing the same. He was the hot one now – he had the diamonds.

I ducked into the rear entrance of Gamage's and made my way through the store at an easier pace, looking, I hoped, like a man who knows where he's going. I found the men's room and locked myself into a cubicle. My coat came off and was reversed – that so carefully chosen coat with the nicely contrasting colours. The natty cap came from my pocket and the hat I was wearing was regretfully screwed into a shapeless bundle. It wouldn't do it much good to be jammed into my pocket but I didn't want to leave it lying around.

Clothes make the man and a new man left that men's room. I wandered casually about the store, drifting towards the front entrance, and on the way I bought myself a new tie just to have a legitimate reason for being in Gamage's, but that precaution was unnecessary. I emerged on to the pavement of Holborn and set off to walk west. No taxis for me because taxi-drivers would be questioned about pick-ups in the area at that time.

Half an hour later I was in a pub just off Oxford Street near the Marble Arch and sinking a thankful pint of beer.

It had been a good smooth job but it wasn't over yet, not by a hell of a long way. I wondered if I could trust Mackintosh to do his half of the job properly.

V

That evening, as I was preparing to go out on the town, there came a firm knock at the door of my room. I opened it and was confronted by two very large men dressed very conservatively and in the best of taste. The one on the right said, 'Are you Joseph Aloysius Rearden?'

I didn't have to bend my brain too far to realize that these two were coppers. I gave a twisted grin. 'I'd rather forget the Aloysius.'

'We are police officers.' He flipped a wallet in front of me negligently. 'We hope you can assist us in our enquiries.'

'Hey!' I said. 'Is that a warrant card? I've never seen one of those before.'

Reluctantly he flipped open the wallet again and let me read the card. He was Detective-Inspector John M. Brunskill and indubitably the genuine article. I babbled a bit. 'You see these things happening at the bioscope; I never thought it would happen to me.'

'Bioscope?' he said dubiously.

'The films – we call a cinema a bioscope in South Africa. That's where I'm from, you know. I don't know how I can help you in any enquiries, Inspector. I'm a stranger to London – in fact, I'm a stranger to England. I've been here only a week – less than that, really.'

'We know all that, Mr Rearden,' said Brunskill gently.

So they'd checked on me already. These boys moved fast – the British police are wonderful.

'May we come in, Mr Rearden? I think you *will* be able to help us.'

I stood on one side and waved them into the room.

'Come in and take a seat. There's only one chair so one of you will have to sit on the bed. And take your coats off.'

'That won't be necessary,' said Brunskill. 'We won't be staying long. This is Detective-Sergeant Jervis.'

Jervis looked an even harder nut than Brunskill. Brunskill was polished and had the suavity that maturity brings, while Jervis still had his sharp corners and was all young, rock-hard cop. But Brunskill would be the more dangerous – he'd be tricky.

I said, 'Well, what can I do for you?'

'We are making enquiries about the theft of a package from a postman in Leather Lane this morning,' said Brunskill. 'What can you tell us about it, Mr Rearden?'

'Where's Leather Lane?' I asked. 'I'm a stranger here.'

Brunskill looked at Jervis and Jervis looked at Brunskill and then they both looked at me. 'Come, Mr Rearden,' said Brunskill. 'You can do better than that.'

'You've got a record,' said Jervis suddenly.

This was the shot across the bows. I said bitterly, 'And you johns will never let me forget it. Yes, I've got a record; I did eighteen months in Pretoria Central – eighteen months of stone cold jug – and that was a long time ago. I've been straight ever since.'

'Until perhaps this morning,' suggested Brunskill.

I looked him straight in the eye. 'Don't pull the old flannel on me. You tell me what I'm supposed to have done, and I'll tell you if I did it – straight out.'

'Very good of you,' murmured Brunskill. 'Don't you think so, Sergeant?'

Jervis made a nasty noise at the back of his throat. Then he said, 'Mind if we search your room, Rearden?'

'It's Mr Rearden to sergeants,' I said. 'Your boss has better manners than you. And I most certainly do object to you searching my room – unless you have a warrant.'

'Oh, we have that,' said Brunskill calmly. 'Go ahead, Sergeant.' He took a document from his pocket and slapped it into my hand. 'I think you'll find that in order, Mr Rearden.'

I didn't even bother to look at it, but just tossed it on to the dressing-table and watched Jervis do an efficient overhaul of the room. He found nothing – there wasn't anything for him to find. At last he gave up, looked at Brunskill and shook his head.

Brunskill turned to me. 'I must ask you to come to the police station with me.'

I was silent and let the pause lengthen for a long time before I said, 'Well, go ahead and ask.'

'We've got ourselves a joker here, sir,' said Jervis. He looked at me with dislike.

'If you do ask I won't come,' I said. 'You'll have to arrest me to get me anywhere near the nick.'

Brunskill sighed. 'Very well, Mr Rearden; I arrest you on suspicion of being involved in an assault on a postman on premises in Leather Lane at about nine-thirty this morning. Does that satisfy you?'

'It'll do to be going on with,' I said. 'Let's go.'

'Oh, I almost forgot,' he said. 'Anything you say will be noted and may be used in evidence.'

'I know the form,' I said. 'I know it only too well.'

'I'm sure you do,' he said softly.

I expected them to take me to Scotland Yard but I found myself in quite a small police station. Where it was I don't know – I don't know London at all well. They put me into a small room unfurnished except for a deal table and two bentwood chairs. It had the same institutional smell of all police stations anywhere in the world. I sat in a chair and smoked one cigarette after another, watched by a uniformed copper who stood with his back to the door, looking undressed without his helmet.

It was nearly an hour and a half before they got around to doing anything and it was tough boy Jervis who started the attack. He came into the room and waved abruptly at the uniformed john who did a disappearing act, then he sat down at the other side of the table and looked at me for a long time without speaking. I ignored him – I didn't even look at him and it was he who broke first. 'You've been here before, haven't you, Rearden?'

'I've never been here before in my life.'

'You know what I mean. You've sat on hard wooden chairs with a policeman the other side of the table many, many times. You know the drill too well – you're a professional. With another man I might pussyfoot around – use a bit of psychology, maybe – but that wouldn't work with you, would it? So I'm not going to do it. There'll be no tact, no psychology with you. I'm going to crack you like a nut, Rearden.'

'You'd better remember Judges' Rules.'

He gave a sharp bark of laughter. 'See what I mean? An honest man wouldn't know Judges' Rules from Parkinson's Law. But you know, don't you? You're a wrong 'un; you're bent.'

'When you're finished with the insults I'll go,' I said.

'You'll go when I say you can,' he said sharply.

I grinned at him. 'You'd better check with Brunskill first, sonny.'

'Where are the diamonds?'

'What diamonds?'

'That postman is in a bad way. You hit him a bit too hard, Rearden. The chances are he'll cash in his chips – and where will that put you?' He leaned forward. 'You'll be inside for so long that you'll trip over your beard.'

I must say he was trying hard but he was a bad liar. No dying postman could have busted that window in the Kiddykar office. I just looked him in the eye and kept my mouth shut.

'If those diamonds aren't found it'll go hard for you,' said

Jervis. 'Maybe if the diamonds turn up the judge will be a bit easier on you.'

'What diamonds?' I asked.

And so it went on for a good half-hour until he got tired and went away and the uniformed man came back and took up his old stance in front of the door. I turned and looked at him. 'Don't you get corns? Isn't this job bad for your feet?' He looked at me with a bland face and expressionless eyes and said exactly nothing.

Presently a bigger gun was brought to bear. Brunskill came in carrying a thick folder bulging with papers which he put on the table. 'I'm sorry to have kept you waiting, Mr Rearden,' he said.

'I wouldn't like to bet on it,' I said.

He gave me a pitying, though understanding, smile. 'We all have our jobs to do, and some are nastier than others. You mustn't blame me for doing mine.' He opened the folder. 'You have quite a record, Mr Rearden. Interpol have a fat dossier on you.'

'I've been convicted once,' I said. 'Anything else is not official and you can't use it. What anyone might have to say about me isn't proof of a damned thing.' I grinned and, pointing at the folder, quoted: '"What the policeman said isn't evidence."'

'Just so,' said Brunskill. 'But it's interesting all the same.' He mused over the papers for a long time, then said, without looking up, 'Why are you flying to Switzerland tomorrow?'

'I'm a tourist,' I said. 'I've never been there before.'

'It's your first time in England, too, isn't it?'

'You know it is. Look here, I want an attorney.'

He looked up. 'I would suggest a solicitor. Have you anyone in mind?'

From my wallet I took the scrap of paper with the telephone number on it which Mackintosh had given me with this eventuality in mind. 'That'll find him,' I said.

Brunskill's eyebrows lifted when he read it. 'I know this number very well – he's just the man to tackle your type of case. For a man who's been in England less than a week you know your way around the fringes.' He put the paper on one side. 'I'll let him know you're here.'

My throat was dry from smoking too many cigarettes. 'Another thing,' I said. 'I could do with a cup of tea.'

'I'm afraid we can't run to tea,' said Brunskill regretfully. 'Would a glass of water be all right?'

'It'll do.'

He went to the door, gave instructions, and then came back. 'You people seem to think that we spend all our time in police stations drinking tea – running a continuous cafeteria for old lags. I can't think where you get it from unless it's from television.'

'Not me,' I said. 'We have no TV in South Africa.'

'Indeed!' said Brunskill. 'How curious. Now, about those diamonds. I think that . . .'

'What diamonds?' I broke in.

And so it went on. He shook me more than Jervis because he was trickier. He wasn't stupid enough to lie about something I knew to be true, as Jervis had done, and was better at the wearing down process, being as persistent as a buzzing fly. The water came – a carafe and a tumbler. I filled the tumbler and drank thirstily, then refilled it and drank again. Brunskill watched me and said at last, 'Had enough?'

I nodded, so he reached out and took the tumbler delicately in his fingertips and carried it out. When he came back he looked at me sorrowfully. 'I didn't think you'd fall for that chestnut. You know we can't fingerprint you until you're booked. Why did you let us have them?'

'I was tired,' I said.

'Too bad,' he said sympathetically. 'Now, to get back to those diamonds . . .'

* * *

Presently Jervis came into the room and beckoned to Brunskill and they stood by the door and talked in low voices. Brunskill turned around. 'Now, look here, Rearden; we've nailed you. We have enough evidence now to send you up for ten years. If you help us to get back those stones it might help you when the judge sentences you.'

'What diamonds?' I asked tiredly.

His mouth shut with a snap. 'All right,' he said curtly. 'Come this way.'

I followed, the meat in a sandwich between Brunskill and Jervis. They escorted me to a large room occupied by a dozen men lined along one wall. Jervis said, 'No need to explain what this is, Rearden; but I will because the law says I must. It's a line-up – an identification parade. There are three people coming in to see you. You can insert yourself anywhere in that line, and you can change your position in the intervals if you like. Got it?'

I nodded and walked over to the wall, putting myself third in line. There was a pause in the action and then the first witness came in – a little old lady, someone's darling mother. She went along the line and then came straight back to me and pointed at my chest. 'That's the one.' I'd never seen her before.

They took her out, but I didn't bother to change position. There wasn't any point, really; they had me nailed just as Brunskill had. The next one was a young man of about eighteen. He didn't have to go all the way along the line. He stopped in front of me. 'That's 'im,' he said. ' 'E did it.'

The third witness didn't have any trouble either. He took one look at me and yelled, 'This is the boyo. I hope you get life, mate.' He went away rubbing his head. It was the postman – not nearly as dead as Jervis would have me believe.

Then it was over and Jervis and Brunskill took me back. I said to Jervis, 'You'd make a good miracle-worker; you brought that postman back to life pretty smartly.'

He gave me a sharpish look and a slow smile spread over his face. 'And how did you know that was the postman?'

I shrugged. My goose was cooked whichever way I looked at it. I said to Brunskill, 'Who is the bastard of a nark that shopped me?'

His face closed up. 'Let's call it "information received", Rearden. You'll be charged tomorrow morning and you'll go before a magistrate immediately. I'll see that your solicitor is in attendance.'

'Thanks,' I said. 'What's his name?'

'By God!' he said. 'But you're a cool one. Your solicitor is a Mr Maskell.'

'Thanks again,' I said.

Brunskill whistled up a station sergeant who put me in a cell for the night. I had a bite to eat and then stretched out and went to sleep almost immediately.

It had been a tiring day.

2

I

Maskell was a short, stout man with shrewd brown eyes and an immense air of dignity. He was introduced to me just before the charge was laid and did not seem at all perturbed at the prospect of acting for a criminal. The law is a strange profession in which ordinary morality goes by the board; a well liked and generally respected barrister will fight like a tiger for his client, who may well be a murderer or a rapist, and will receive well-merited congratulations on an acquittal. Then he will go home and write a letter to the editor of *The Times* fulminating about the rise in crime. A schizophrenic profession.

I said as much to Maskell once when I knew him better. He said gently, 'Mr Rearden, to me you are neither guilty nor innocent – the people who decide that are the twelve men in the box. I am here to find out the facts in a case and to present them to a barrister who will conduct the argument – and I do it for money.'

We were in court at the time and he waved his hand largely. 'Who says crime doesn't pay?' he asked cynically. 'Taking all in all, from the court ushers to his Lordship up there, there are at least fifty people directly involved in this case, and they're all making a living out of it. Some, such as myself and his Lordship, make a better living than others. We do very well out of people like you, Mr Rearden.'

But at this time I didn't know Maskell at all. It was a hurried introduction, and he said hastily, 'We will talk in more detail later. First we must find what this is all about.'

So I was taken and charged. I won't go into all the legal

language but what it all boiled down to was robbery with violence – an assault on the person of John Edward Harte, an employee of the GPO, and the theft of diamonds, the property of Lewis and van Veldenkamp Ltd, valued at £173,000.

I nearly burst out laughing at that. It had been a bigger haul than Mackintosh had expected, unless Mr Lewis and Meneer van Veldenkamp were trying to sting their insurance company. But I kept a straight face and when it was over I turned to Maskell and asked, 'What now?'

'I'll see you in the Magistrates' Court in about an hour. That will be a mere formality.' He rubbed his chin. 'There's a lot of money involved here. Have the police recovered the diamonds?'

'You'd better ask them. I know nothing about any diamonds.'

'Indeed! I must tell you that if the diamonds are still – shall we say *at large*? – then it will be very difficult for me to get you out on bail. But I will try.'

The proceedings in the Magistrates' Court were brief, lasting for about three minutes. They would have been even briefer but Brunskill got on his hind legs and argued against the granting of bail. 'The diamonds have not yet been recovered, your Honour, and if the prisoner is released on bail I fear they never will be. Further, if the prisoner had not been apprehended last night he would have been in Switzerland this morning.'

The magistrate flapped his hand. 'You think the prisoner will jump bail?'

'I do,' said Brunskill firmly. 'And there is one thing more, the prisoner is in the dock on a charge of violence and he has a police record in which violence figures largely. I fear the intimidation of witnesses.'

He nearly overreached himself. 'You think he will leave the country *and* intimidate witnesses?' asked the magistrate with polite incredulity. 'I doubt if his violent arm would reach so far. However, on the balance of evidence and especially in respect of the missing property I am inclined to agree with you. Bail is denied.'

Brunskill sat down and Maskell shrugged and stuffed some papers back into his briefcase. And so I was remanded for trial at the Central Criminal Court. I was going to see the inside of the Old Bailey, after all.

Maskell had a few words with me before I was taken away. 'Now I can find out the strength of the police case against you. I'll have a word with the prosecution and then you and I can sit down together and discuss this whole thing. If you want anything ask that I be informed, but I shall probably see you tomorrow, anyway.'

A prisoner on remand is theoretically an innocent man. Practically, he is regarded neutrally as neither guilty nor innocent. The food was good, the bed soft and there were no irksome restrictions – except one. I couldn't get out of the nick. Still, you can't have everything.

Maskell came to see me the following afternoon and we sat in one of the interviewing rooms. He regarded me thoughtfully, then said, 'The case against you is very strong, Mr Rearden; very strong, indeed. Unless you can prove conclusively and without equivocation that you could not have committed this crime, then I fear you will be convicted.'

I was about to speak, but he raised his hand. 'But we can go into that later. First things first. Now, have you any money?'

'About a hundred and fifty pounds. But I haven't paid my hotel bill – I wasn't given the chance. I don't want hotel bilking to be added to the charge sheet, so it'll be nearer a hundred pounds I have to play around with.'

Maskell nodded. 'As you may know, my own fee has been taken care of. But I am not the man who will fight your case in court; that will be done by a barrister, and barristers come even more expensive than I do, especially barristers of the calibre needed to win this case. A hundred pounds would come nowhere near the amount necessary.'

I shrugged. 'I'm sorry; it's all I've got.' That wasn't exactly true but I could see that even the best barrister in the business couldn't get me out of this one and there wasn't any point in throwing my money away.

'I see. Well, there is provision for a case like yours. A barrister will be appointed by the Court to act for you. The trouble is that he will be not of your choice; yet I am not without influence and I will see if I have any strings to pull that will get us the best man.'

He took a folder from his briefcase and opened it. 'I want you to tell me exactly what you did on the morning in question.' He paused. 'I already know you did not have breakfast at your hotel.'

'I didn't sleep well that night,' I said. 'So I got up early and took a walk.'

Maskell sighed. 'And where did you walk to, Mr Rearden?'

I thought it out. 'I went into Hyde Park and walked up as far as the Round Pond. There's a famous building up there – Kensington Palace – but it was closed. It was very early in the morning.'

'I shouldn't imagine there would be many people in Hyde Park or Kensington Gardens so early. Did you speak to anyone – make enquiries – at Kensington Palace? Did you ask the time of opening, for instance?'

'There wasn't anyone around to ask.'

'Very well; what did you do then?'

'I walked back through the park to Hyde Park Corner and over into Green Park. Then up Bond Street into Oxford Street. I was doing a bit of window shopping, you see.'

'And what time would this be?'

'Oh, I don't know. Say, about nine-fifteen. I was dawdling a bit. I had a look at a place called Burlington Arcade, then I went on up Bond Street looking at the shops, as I said. It's marvellous – nothing like it in South Africa.'

'And you didn't speak to anyone at all?'

'If I'd known I needed an alibi I would have,' I said bitterly.

'Just so,' said Maskell. 'So you arrived at Oxford Street – what did you do then?'

'Well, I hadn't had breakfast and I felt a bit peckish so I found a pub and had some sandwiches and a pint. I was chatting to the barman, an Irishman. He ought to remember me.'

'And what time was this?'

'It must have been after ten o'clock because the pub was open. Say, half past ten.'

'That alibi comes a little late,' said Maskell. 'It's not relevant.' He consulted a sheet of paper from the folder. 'I must tell you that the police version differs from yours substantially – and they have a great deal of evidence to show.' He looked me in the eye. 'Do I have to point out the dangers of lying to your lawyer?'

'I'm not lying,' I said indignantly.

He spoke gravely. 'Mr Rearden, let me say that you are in deep trouble. I gather you want to enter a plea of not guilty at your trial, but I must warn you that, on the evidence now extant, you are likely to lose the case. Public concern about crimes of violence of this nature has been increasing and this concern is reflected by the heavy sentences imposed by the courts.'

He paused to collect his thoughts and then went on in measured tones. 'Now, as your solicitor I cannot prejudge this case, but I would like to say this: If the diamonds were to be returned, and if you entered a plea of guilty, then the court would be inclined to leniency and, in my opinion, your sentence would be not more than five years and possibly as little as three years. With a remittance of sentence for good behaviour you could be out of prison in as little as two years.

'On the other hand, if the diamonds are *not* returned and if you enter a plea of not guilty then your sentence is going to be very heavy – assuming you are convicted, an assumption which on the evidence I have is very likely. If I may use slang I would say that his Lordship is going to throw the book at you; he'll lock you up and throw away the key. I doubt if you would get away with much under fourteen years, and I assure you that I have great experience in these forecasts and I do not speak lightly.'

He cleared his throat. 'Now, what do you say, Mr Rearden? What shall we do about this?'

'The only diamonds I saw that morning were in the shop windows of Bond Street,' I said distinctly.

He looked at me in silence for a long time then shook his head. 'Very well,' he said quietly. 'I will go about my business – and yours – but with no great hope of success. I ought to warn you that the police have such evidence that will be very difficult for defence counsel to refute.'

'I'm innocent,' I said obstinately.

He said no more but collected his papers and left the room without a backward glance.

II

So there I was in the dock of the Central Criminal Court – the Old Bailey. There was much pomp and circumstance, robes and wigs, deferences and courtesies – and me popping up from the bowels of the earth into the dock like the demon king in a pantomime, the centre of attraction. Of course, I had competition from the judge. It seems that when a man gets to sit on the Bench he feels that he's entitled to be a licensed jester and he loves nothing more than to have the audience rolling in the aisles at his witticisms. I've seen worse music hall turns than a Criminal Court judge. Still, it does lighten the atmosphere – a court would be a pretty grim place without the comic bits – and the Chief Comic isn't prejudiced; he aims his barbs at prosecution and defence alike. I found that I quite enjoyed it and laughed as much as anyone else.

Maskell was there, of course, but in a minor role; defence counsel was a man called Rollins. Maskell had tried again, just before the trial, to get me to alter my plea of not guilty. He said, 'Mr Rearden, I want you to consider once more the consequences of losing this case. You will not only receive a long sentence but there are certain other implications. Long-term prisoners are invariably regarded as high risk prisoners, especially those who are regarded as having financial backing. In the absence of diamonds to the value of £173,000 you would undoubtedly come into that category. A high risk prisoner is treated very differently from the ordinary prisoner and I understand that the circumstances can be rather unpleasant. I would think of that if I were you.'

I didn't have to think of it. I hadn't a hope in hell of getting the diamonds back and that was the crux of the matter. Even if I pleaded guilty I'd get a stiff sentence in the absence of the diamonds. The only thing to do was to put on a brave face and make the best of it. It struck me that Mackintosh was a very smart man and that maybe Mrs Smith was even smarter.

I said, 'I'm sorry, Mr Maskell, but I'm innocent.'

He looked puzzled. He didn't believe a word I said but he couldn't figure out why I was keeping my mouth shut. But then a wintry smile came to his face. 'I hope you don't think the investment of so many years of your life is worth the money. Too much time in prison is apt to change a man for the worse.'

I smiled at him. 'I thought you said you wouldn't prejudge the case.'

'I think you are a very foolish young man,' he said. 'But you have my best wishes in your unfortunate future.'

The trial got under way laboriously. First the jury details were settled and then the action began, the prosecution getting first crack. The prosecuting counsel was a tall, thin man with a face like the blade of a hatchet, and he fairly revelled in his job. He led off with a rather skimpy introduction and then began to lay on the prosecution witnesses, while Rollins, my counsel, looked on with a bored expression on his face. I had met Rollins only twice and he had been offhanded on both occasions. He knew this was one he wasn't going to win.

The prosecution witnesses were good – very good, indeed – and I began to see why the prosecuting counsel was looking so cheerful despite the misfortune of his face. Expert police witnesses introduced photographs and drawings of the scene of the crime and, that groundwork laid, the pressure was applied.

There was the motherly old soul who had identified me at the police station line-up. 'I saw him strike the postman,' she testified, the light of honesty shining from her eyes. 'I was standing in the corridor and saw the accused hit the postman with his fist, grab a yellow box from him, and push him into an office. Then the accused ran down the stairs.'

The prosecutor offered her a plan of the second floor. 'Where were you standing?'

She indicated a place in the corridor and looked across the court straight at me as guileless as you please. The sweet old lady was lying like a flatfish, and she knew that I knew she was lying. She couldn't have been standing in the corridor because I'd checked, and the details of her evidence were all wrong, anyway. There wasn't a thing I could do about it, though.

Another highlight was a man from Fortnum and Mason who testified to having sent a packed picnic basket to a certain hotel. The order was telephoned in by a Mr Rearden. Questioned by the defence he said he couldn't be certain that the Mr Rearden who ordered the basket was the accused.

A hotel employee testified that the accused stayed at his hotel and that a basket had been delivered addressed to Mr Rearden. Asked what had happened to it he said he didn't know but presumably the accused had collected it. There was a bit of argument about that and part of his answer was struck out.

A detective produced a picnic basket in court and testified that he had found it in the office of Kiddykar Toys Ltd. It had been identified as coming from Fortnum's. Another police witness testified that the basket was liberally covered with the accused's fingerprints, as were other items in the room; to wit – an electric kettle, a coffee pot and several pieces of crockery and cutlery.

The jury drew its own conclusions.

Then there was the police witness who said he had been interested in tracking down the ownership of Kiddykar Toys Ltd. Apparently it was a genuine company but not doing any business. The lines of ownership were very tangled but he had finally cracked it with the helpful assistance of the South African police. The owner proved to be a Mr Joseph Aloysius Rearden of Johannesburg. No, he had no means of knowing if the Joseph Aloysius Rearden of Kiddykars was the Joseph Aloysius Rearden who stood in the dock. That would be taking him further than he was prepared to go.

Again the jury drew its conclusions.

The postman gave his evidence fairly. I had hit him and he had recovered consciousness in the Kiddykar office.

There was nothing in that which contradicted the perjured evidence of Old Mother Hubbard. The third eye-witness was the office boy from Betsy-Lou; he said he saw me lock the office door and run downstairs. I remembered him vaguely as the person who had walked behind me at that time. But I hadn't *run* downstairs – that was his imagination working overtime.

Brunskill was a star witness.

'Acting on information received I went, with Detective-Sergeant Jervis, to see the accused at his hotel. His answers to my questioning were such that I arrested him on suspicion of having been concerned in this crime. Subsequently I obtained his fingerprints which matched prints found in the office of Kiddykar Toys Ltd. Further enquiries were made which resulted in three witnesses coming forward, all of whom identified the accused. More extensive enquiries led to the further evidence that has been presented to the Court relating to the picnic basket and the ownership of Kiddykar Toys Ltd.'

The prosecutor sat down with a grin on his face and Rollins bounced to his feet for cross-examination.

Rollins: You spoke of 'information received', Inspector. How did this information come to you?

Brunskill: (hesitantly) Must I answer that, my Lord? The sources of police information may be prejudicial to . . .

Rollins: (quickly) This goes to the malice of a person or persons unknown which may prejudice the case for the accused, my Lord.

Judge: (in Churchillian tones) Mr Rollins; I don't see how your case *can* deteriorate much further. However, I am inclined to let the question go. I am as interested as anybody. Answer the question, Inspector.

Brunskill: (unwillingly) There was one telephone call and one letter.

Rollins: Both anonymous?

Brunskill: Yes.

Rollins: Did these communications indicate that the accused had committed this crime?

Brunskill: Yes.

Rollins: Did they indicate where he was to be found?

Brunskill: Yes.

Rollins: Did they indicate that the basket found in the Kiddykar office had been purchased by the accused at Fortnum and Mason?

Brunskill: er . . . Yes.

Rollins: Is it a crime to purchase foodstuffs from that eminent firm of retailers?

Brunskill: (sharply) Of course not.

Rollins: Did these anonymous communications indicate that the firm of Kiddykar Toys Ltd was owned by the accused?

Brunskill: (uncomfortably) Yes.

Rollins: Is it a crime to own such a firm as Kiddykar Toys Ltd?

Brunskill: (with ebbing patience) No.

Judge: I am not so sure. Anyone who so maltreats the English language as to arrive at so abominable a name ought to be treated as a criminal.

(Laughter in court)

Rollins: Inspector, would you not say it was true that all your work had been done for you in this case? Would you not say it was true that without these malicious communications the accused would not be standing in the dock at this moment?

Brunskill: I cannot answer that question. He would have been caught.

Rollins: Would he? I admire your certitude.

Brunskill: He would have been caught.

Rollins: But not so speedily.

Brunskill: Perhaps not.

Rollins: Would you not characterize your mysterious communicant as someone who 'had it in' for the accused at worst – or a common informer or stool pigeon at best?

Brunskill: (smiling) I would prefer to think of him as a public-spirited citizen.

Very funny! Mackintosh – a public-spirited citizen! But, by God, the pair of them had been infernally clever. The first time I had laid eyes on that picnic basket had been in the Kiddykars office, and I certainly hadn't telephoned Fortnum's. Mrs Smith had done her shopping to good effect! Nor did I own Kiddykar Toys Ltd – not to my own knowledge; but I'd have a hell of a time proving it. They had delivered me to the law trussed up like a chicken.

There wasn't much after that. I said my piece, futile though it was; the prosecutor tore me into shreds and Rollins half-heartedly tried to sew up the pieces again without much success. The judge summed up and, with one careful eye on the Appeal Court, directed the jury to find me guilty. They were out only for half an hour – just time enough for a much-needed smoke – and the answer was predictable.

Then the judge asked if I had anything to say, so I spoke up with just two words: 'I'm innocent.'

Nobody took much notice of that – they were too busy watching the judge arrange his papers and gleefully anticipating how heavy he'd be. He fussed around for a while, making sure that all attention would be on him, and then he began to speak in portentous and doomladen tones.

'Joseph Aloysius Rearden, you have been found guilty of stealing by force diamonds to the value of £173,000. It falls to me to sentence you for this crime. Before I do so I would like to say a few words concerning your part in this affair.'

I could see what was coming. The old boy couldn't resist the chance of pontificating – it's easy from a safe seat.

'An Englishman is walking the streets in the course of his usual employ when he is suddenly and unexpectedly assaulted – brutally assaulted. He is not aware that he is carrying valuables which, to him, would undoubtedly represent untold wealth, and it is because of these valuables that he is attacked.

'The valuables – the diamonds – are now missing and you, Rearden, have not seen fit to co-operate with the police in their recovery in spite of the fact that you must have known that the court would be inclined to leniency had you done so. Therefore, you cannot expect leniency of this court.

'I have been rather puzzled by your recalcitrant attitude but my puzzlement abated when I made an elementary mathematical calculation. In the normal course of events such a crime as yours, a crime of violence such as is abhorrent in this country, coupled with the loss to the community of property worth £173,000, would be punished by the heavy sentence of fourteen years' imprisonment. My calculation, however, informs me that for those fourteen years you would be receiving an annual income of not less than £12,350 – tax free – being the amount you have stolen divided by fourteen. This, I might add, is considerably more than the stipend of one of Her Majesty's Judges, such as myself – a fact which can be ascertained by anyone who cares to consult Whitaker's Almanack.

'Whether it can be considered that the loss of fourteen years of freedom, and confinement to the hardly pleasant environs of our prisons, is worth such an annual sum is a debatable matter. You evidently think it is worth while. Now, it is not the function of this court to make the fees of crime worth while, so you can hardly blame me for endeavouring to reduce your annual prison income.

'Joseph Aloysius Rearden, I sentence you to twenty years' detention in such prison or prisons as the appropriate authority deems fit.'

I'd bet Mackintosh was laughing fit to bust a gut.

III

The judge was right when he referred to 'the hardly pleasant environs of our prisons'. The one in which I found myself was pretty deadly. The reception block was crowded – the judges must have been working overtime that day – and there was a lot of waiting about apparently pointlessly. I was feeling a bit miserable; no one can stand in front of a judge and receive a twenty year sentence with complete equanimity.

Twenty years!

I was thirty-four years old. I'd be fifty-four when I came out; perhaps a bit less if I could persuade them I was a good boy, but that would be bloody difficult in view of what the judge had said. Any Review Board I appeared before would read a transcript of the trial and the judge's remarks would hit them like a hammer.

Twenty long years!

I stood by apathetically while the police escort read out the details of my case to the receiving officer. 'All right,' said the receiving officer. He signed his name in a book and tore out a sheet. 'Here's the body receipt.'

So help me – that's what he said. 'Body receipt.' When you're in prison you cease to be a man; you're a body, a zombie, a walking statistic. You're something to be pushed around like the GPO pushed around that little yellow box containing the diamonds; you're a parcel of blood and guts that needs feeding at regular intervals, and you're assumed not to have any brains at all.

'Come on, you,' said the receiving officer. 'In here.' He unlocked a door and stood aside while I walked in. The door slammed behind me and I heard the click of the lock. It was a crowded room filled with men of all types, judging by their clothing. There was everything from blue jeans to a bowler and striped trousers. Nobody was talking – they just stood around and examined the floor minutely as though it was of immense importance. I suppose they all felt like me; they'd had the wind knocked out of them.

We waited in that room for a long time, wondering what was going to happen. Perhaps some of us knew, having been there before. But this was my first time in an English gaol and I felt apprehensive. Maskell's words about the unpleasant circumstances that attend the high risk prisoner began to worry me.

At last they began to take us out, one at a time and in strict alphabetical order. Rearden comes a long way down the alphabet so I had to wait longer than most, but my turn came and a warder took me down a passage and into an office.

A prisoner is never asked to sit down. I stood before that desk and answered questions while a prison officer took down the answers like the recording angel. He took down my name, birthplace, father's name, mother's maiden name, my age, next-of-kin, occupation. All that time he never looked at me once; to him I wasn't a man, I was a statistics container – he pressed a button and the statistics poured out.

They told me to empty my pockets and the contents were dumped on to the desk and meticulously recorded before being put into a canvas bag. Then my fingerprints were taken. I looked around for something with which to wipe off the ink but there was nothing. I soon found out why. A warder marched me away and into a hot, steamy room where I was told to strip. It was there I lost my clothes. I wouldn't see them again for twenty years and I'd be damned lucky if they'd be in fashion.

After the bath, which wasn't bad, I dressed in the prison clothing – the man in the grey flannel suit. But the cut was terrible and I'd rather have gone to Mackintosh's tailor.

A march up another corridor led to a medical examination, a bit of bureaucratic stupidity. Why they can't have a medical examination while a man is stripped after his bath is beyond me. However, I undressed obligingly and dressed again, and was graded for labour. I was top class – fit for anything.

Then a warder took me away again into an immense hall with tiers of cells lining the walls and with iron stairs like fire escapes. 'I'll tell you once,' said the warder. 'This is "C" Hall.'

We clanked up some stairs and along a landing and he stopped before a cell and unlocked it. 'This is yours.'

I went inside and the door slammed with a cold sound of finality. I stood for some time, not looking at anything in particular. My brains had seized up – gone on strike. After, maybe, fifteen minutes I lay on the bed and damn near cried my eyes out.

After that I felt better and was able to bring some intelligence to bear on the situation. The cell was about twelve feet by seven, and perhaps eight feet high. The walls were distempered – institutional cream and Borstal green – and in one of them was a small barred window set high. The door looked as though it could withstand artillery fire and there was a Judas hole set in it.

The furnishing was sparse; an iron-framed bed, a wooden table and a chair, a washstand with a jug, basin and chamber-pot, and a bare shelf. Exploring a prison cell is one of the quickest tasks a man can set himself. Within three minutes I had checked everything there was to find – three blankets, two sheets, a lumpy mattress, another shirt, a pair of felt slippers, a thin non-absorbent towel, a spoon and a mug. Hanging on a nail in the wall by a loop of string was a copy of the Rules and Regulations governing HM Prisons together with an informational pamphlet.

Three minutes and I knew practically everything there was to know about that cell. I wondered what I was going to do for the next twenty years. Right there and then I decided I'd have to ration my curiosity – shut down the dampers on thought. There would be too much time and not enough happening, and every new experience would have to be jealously hoarded.

The walls of that prison suddenly had physical meaning. I felt them looming all about me, thick and strong. It was a claustrophobic quarter-hour before the feeling receded and I was able to stop shivering.

I immediately broke my promise about rationing curiosity by beginning to read the informational pamphlet, but that was absolutely necessary. I was a new boy in this school and the sooner I learned the ropes the better. There were too many tricks that could be played on the newcomer by the old hands and I didn't want to fall for any of them.

It was an interesting compilation of data. I discovered that the spare shirt in the cell was to be used as a night shirt, that lights-out was ten-thirty, that the waking call was six-thirty in the morning, that I was to be issued with a razor blade to be returned after shaving. There were other helpful hints even to the point of finding a way out of prison.

For instance, I could refer my case to the Court of Criminal Appeal and, if that failed, I could apply to the Attorney-General to put the case before the House of Lords. At any time I could petition the Home Secretary and I was permitted to write to my Member of Parliament.

I couldn't see myself doing any of those things. I wasn't pally enough with the Home Secretary to enter into any kind of extended correspondence and my Member of Parliament was a shade too far away to do any good – 6,000 miles away.

I read the booklet through and then started on it again from the beginning. I had nothing else to do so I decided to memorize the whole goddamn thing. I was still reading it when the light went out.

IV

The bell clanged and I opened my eyes and was confused until I remembered where I was. I dressed hurriedly and made the bed, then hoisted it up so that it stood on end in a corner of the cell. I sat on the chair and waited. Presently there was a slight metallic sound from the door and I knew someone was watching through the Judas hole.

There was a sharp snap from the lock and the door opened. I stood up and the warder came in. He looked appraisingly around the cell and then fixed me with a hard eye. 'You're new here. You've been reading that thing, haven't you?' He nodded to the booklet on the table.

'Yes, I have.'

'Your bed's in the wrong corner, and the book should be hanging on the wall where you found it. You'll learn. Take a tip from me; do just what you're told and you'll be all right. Now, pick up your chamber-pot and get ready for slopping out.'

'I haven't used it,' I said.

'It gets slopped out whether you've used it or not,' he said curtly. 'Remember what I told you – do as you're told with no arguments. That's lesson number one.'

I picked up the chamber-pot and followed him on to the landing which was full of men, all lined up and each holding his pot. 'All right,' someone shouted. 'Move along.'

There was mephitic stink in the air. I trudged along and found that I was expected to empty the pot into one sink and wash it in another. I went through the motions and returned to my cell, taking my cues from what the others were doing.

The warder came back. 'You can eat in your cell if you like. You'll be served with the others down in the hall, but you can bring your tray up here if you don't feel like joining the party just yet.'

I didn't feel like talking to anyone at all right then. I was too busy trying to keep a firm hold on myself. 'Thanks,' I said, and heard my voice crack.

He was ironic. 'Don't thank me; it's regulations for new prisoners. And another thing, you'll be seeing the Governor this morning. A trusty will take you to his office.'

The trusty came just before ten o'clock and I went with him out of 'C' Hall. 'You're Rearden,' he said. 'I've heard about you.'

'Have you?'

'I'm Simpson.' He nudged me in the ribs with a sharp elbow. 'You're going before the Reception Board. Don't volunteer anything – that's my tip.'

'What happens?'

'Oh, it's just the big boys giving you the once-over. The Governor, the Bible-Slapper, the Senior Screw, the Welfare Officer – people like that. The Governor's not too bad if you keep on the right side of him, but Gawd help you if you don't. Some of the others'll try to feed you a load of old cod's wallop – a crowd of flaming do-gooders. But watch out for Hudson – he's a right bastard.'

'Who's he?'

'The Chief Screw.'

Simpson took me into a waiting room in which half a dozen other prisoners were sitting. They all looked dispirited. Simpson chuckled. '*You* won't have to wait your turn, mate. You're on first; you're someone special.'

I stared at him. 'What's so special about me?'

'You'll see. The Governor'll explain it all very nicely.'

I was about to pursue that a bit further but a warder came into the room. 'Rearden, come this way. Simpson, get back to "C" Hall.'

There were five men seated around a large table, two of them prison officers in uniform. It's a funny thing about prison officers – they never take off their caps, not even when sitting in the Governor's office. Perhaps it's a tradition of the service. One of the civilians wore a dog-collar, so he'd be Simpson's Bible-Slapper – the Prison Chaplain.

The military-looking man in the middle spoke up first. 'Rearden, I'm the Governor of this prison. You are here because you have committed a crime and society has decided that you cannot be allowed to remain at large. How you get on in this prison is your own affair. There are two ways of looking at a prison – as a place of punishment and as a place of rehabilitation. The choice is up to you; we have ample facilities for both modes of operation. Do I make myself clear?'

'Yes, sir.'

He picked up a paper from the table. 'It is normally my practice to treat all prisoners alike. However, I have received notification from the Home Office that you are to be treated as a high risk prisoner and that entails certain restrictive modifications of your treatment here. For instance, you were brought to this office by a Star Class trusted prisoner, that will never happen again. In future, if you have to move about inside the prison you will be escorted by a prison officer. You will also wear coloured patches upon your clothing. I have prepared a list here of all the other restrictions appertaining to a high risk prisoner which you will study and to which you will conform.'

He handed me the paper and I folded it and put it into my pocket.

He cleared his throat. 'You must understand, Rearden, that whether you remain in the high risk category depends entirely upon yourself. The position is reviewed at regular intervals and my recommendations are forwarded to the Home Office. You must also understand that the Home Office is at liberty to disregard my recommendations. The fact that you are a high risk prisoner is entirely of your own doing, and if there is any way you can convince the police authorities that you are not a risk then I strongly recommend that you do so.'

He meant the diamonds, of course. They still wanted those bloody diamonds. 'Yes, sir,' I said woodenly. 'I'll try to think of something, sir.'

The Governor turned his head. 'Anything from you, Padre?'

The chaplain smiled. 'My name is Clark. I note you claim to have no religion.'

'That's right, sir.'

'I'm not one for pushing religion down a man's throat,' said Clark. 'But do you mind if I come to see you from time to time?'

'No, sir.'

The Governor said, 'This is Mr Anderson, our Welfare Officer. He can do a lot for you if you let him. Any time you want to see him ask your landing officer. Have you anything you would like to ask him now?'

'Yes, sir. How do I get writing material and books?'

Anderson said easily, 'The writing materials – pens and paper – you will buy in the canteen shop with money you will earn by doing work in the prison. You will be paid a minimum of one shilling and eightpence a day, but you can improve on that if you choose to. Books you can obtain from the prison library.'

'Thank you, sir,' I said. 'Is it possible to get books from outside?' I hesitated. 'I'll be here for a long time – I want to study. I want to improve myself.'

Anderson started to speak but checked himself and looked at the Governor, who said, 'Very commendable, but we'll have to see about that. That will depend upon your general conduct and, as you say, you'll be here a long time.' He nodded to the uniformed officer at the end of the table. 'This is Mr Hudson, the Chief Officer responsible for prison discipline. Have you anything to say, Mr Hudson?'

'Just one thing, sir,' said Hudson. He had a hard face and eyes like chips of glass. 'I don't like high risk prisoners, Rearden. They upset prison routine and cause trouble among the other prisoners. Don't give me any trouble, that's all. If you do it will be the worse for you.'

I kept my face studiously blank. 'I understand, sir.'

'I sincerely hope you do,' said the Governor. 'You have a visitor – a police officer from Scotland Yard.' He signalled to a warder standing by the door. 'You know where to take him.'

I expected to see Brunskill but it was another detective. 'Detective-Inspector Forbes,' he said. 'Sit down, Rearden.'

I sat down, facing him over the table, and he said pleasantly, 'I expect the Governor has broken the news that you have been classified as a high risk. Do you know what that means?'

I shook my head. 'Not really.'

'You'd better find out,' Forbes advised. 'The Governor must have given you a copy of the high risk rules. I'll give you five minutes to read it.'

I took the sheet of paper from my pocket and smoothed it out on the table. It was immediately apparent after a cursory reading that life was going to be made quite a bit tougher. The light in my cell was going to be on all night, for one thing. All my clothes, except for shirt and slippers, were to be deposited outside the cell door each night. Any letters I wrote I would have to hand to a prison officer – copies would be made and only photostats would be sent to the ultimate destination, the originals to be filed in the prison. Any conversations with visitors were to be monitored by a prison officer.

I looked up at Forbes. He said, 'Those are only the rules which concern you directly, of course. There are other things. You'll be moved from cell to cell without warning;

your cell will be searched – and so will you – at a moment's notice. It will all be very harassing.'

'And what is it to you?' I asked.

He shrugged. 'Nothing really – except that I feel sorry for you. If you weren't so stupid you could get yourself out of this jam.'

'Out of this nick?'

'I'm afraid not,' he said regretfully. 'But the Review Board would look upon you very kindly if you co-operated with us.'

'What sort of co-operation?'

'Come off it, Rearden,' he said tiredly. 'You know what we want. The diamonds, man; the diamonds.'

I looked him in the eye. 'I've never seen any diamonds.' Which was the exact truth – from the start to the finish of the caper. I never saw the diamonds at all.

'Look, Rearden; we know you did it, and we've proved it conclusively. Why try to act the innocent? My God, man; you've been sentenced to a quarter of a lifetime in prison. Do you think you'll be good for anything when you come out? The judge was right – the game isn't worth the candle.'

I said, 'Do I have to sit here and listen to you? Is that part of my punishment?'

'Not if you don't want to,' Forbes said. 'I don't understand you, Rearden. I don't understand why you're taking all this so calmly. All right, let's try another tack. How did you know the drop? How did you know where the diamonds were being sent? That's of some interest, too.'

'I don't know anything about it.'

'You don't know anything about it,' he repeated. 'Do you know – maybe that's true. You could be telling the truth.' He leaned back in his chair, opened his mouth and shut it again and stared at me. After a few moments he began to laugh. 'Oh, no!' he said. 'It couldn't be as simple as that!

You couldn't have been double-crossed, could you, Rearden?'

'I don't know what you're talking about.'

Forbes tapped the table. 'You arrive in England out of the blue, and four days later you do the snatch. It must have been set up for you – you couldn't have laid it all on in three days. Then we pick you up and there are no diamonds. So where are they? Obviously, someone else must have them.'

He chuckled. 'Could it be the same someone who made a telephone call and wrote an anonymous letter? You passed on the diamonds and then got shopped, Rearden. Your brainy pal who planned all this made a patsy of you – isn't that the truth?'

I sat mute.

'What!' he said. 'Honour among thieves? Don't be as big a fool as you make out to be. Your friend sold you to the law for a few thousand lousy quid and you're standing for it.' He sounded disgusted. 'Don't think you're going to get out of here to go looking for him; it's not going to be as simple as that. I'm to make recommendations to the Home Office, too, you know; and I'm going to report a total lack of co-operation. And that will mean that you'll be a high risk prisoner for a hell of a long time – no matter what the Governor may recommend. You can be a good boy in here – you can be the perfect prisoner – but it will cut no ice with the Review Board after they read my report.'

I said hesitantly, 'I'll think about it.'

'You do that,' he said forcibly. 'Any time you want to see me just pass word to the Governor. But don't try to play the fool with me, Rearden. Don't waste my time. You give us what we want and we'll nail your friend for you. We'll crucify him. And *you'll* be off the hook as far as high risk is concerned. What's more, I'll see to it personally that the Review Board gives your case every favourable consideration. I can't do more than that, can I?'

Privately, I doubted if he could do as much. A detective-inspector is pretty small fry at Scotland Yard and if he thought I couldn't see what he was up to he must have thought I was a dumb bunny. All that Forbes wanted was to clear the case and get a good conduct tick on his card – the man who recovered the unrecoverable. And once he'd done it then I could go to hell as far as he was concerned. I wouldn't count; I was just another bent villain, and you don't have to keep promises to crooks. Talk about honour among thieves!

I said slowly, 'Twenty years is a long time. I'll think about it very seriously, Mr Forbes.'

'You won't be sorry,' he said expansively. 'Here, have a cigarette.'

3

I

I suppose a man can get used to anything. They tell me the Jews even got used to living – and dying – in Belsen and Dachau. Well, this was no Dachau, crummy though it was.

At the end of the first week I no longer had my meals in the cell but joined with the others in eating in the Hall. It was then I discovered that I was a personality. There's a very strong caste system in a prison largely based on criminal achievement and, oddly enough, on the lack of achievement which results in a long sentence. Roughly speaking, the long-term prisoners, such as myself, were at the top of the heap with the high risk boys as the élite. They're looked up to and respected; they hold their little courts and can command the favour of many parasites and hangers-on.

That is one classification. Another is by type of crime. The brainy boys – the con men and professional frauds – are on top with safe breakers running them close. At the bottom of this heap are the sex criminals whom nobody likes. The honest burglar is a much respected man, more for his workmanlike and unassuming ways than anything else.

I was in a position to command a lot of respect, had I so wished it. My status stemmed from the fact that not only was I a long-term man but that I'd diddled the johns and hadn't grassed on my mysterious pal. You can't keep a secret in prison and everyone knew the facts of my case. Because I kept my mouth shut about the diamonds and because everyone knew what pressure Forbes was exerting I was reckoned to be one of the all right boys; an oddity, but one to be respected.

But I steered clear of all entanglements and alliances. I was being a good boy because I didn't want my high risk status to continue for any longer than it had to. The time would come when I was going to escape and I had to get rid of the constant surveillance – the singling out of attention on Rearden. Not that I was the only high risk prisoner – there were others – about half a dozen in all. I steered clear of the lot of them.

Because I was high risk they gave me the job of looking after the tidiness of 'C' Hall where I was under the eye of the Hall screw permanently on duty. Otherwise they would have had to provide a warder to escort me to the workshops instead of going with the others in a gang supervised by a trusty. They were short-staffed and this was a convenient arrangement. I didn't object; I mopped the floors and scrubbed the tables and worked with a will. Anything to be a good boy.

Homosexuals are the bane of prison life. One of them rather fancied me and pursued me to the extent that the only possible way of dissuading him was to give him a thump on the nose which I didn't want to do because that would have been a black mark on my record sheet. It was Smeaton, my landing screw, who got me out of that predicament. He saw what was happening and warned off the queer with a few choice and blasphemous threats, for which I was thankful.

Smeaton was typical of the majority of prison officers. He hadn't interfered because he particularly wanted to prevent my corruption. He'd done it for the sake of a quiet life. The screws looked upon us neutrally for the most part and to them we were just a part of the job. Over the years they had learned a technique – stop it before it starts; keep the temperature down; don't let trouble spread. It was a very effective technique.

So I kept to myself and out of trouble. Not that I didn't mix with the others at all; if I drew attention as a loner then the prison psychiatrist would fix his beady eye on me. So, during the free association periods, I played a few games of cards and improved my chess considerably.

There were others to talk to besides one's fellow criminals. There were the unofficial visitors. Why these were called unofficial I never found out because they had to be authorized by the Governor. They were the prison visitors, the do-gooders and penal reform crowd, and a mixed bag they were. Some of them thought the way to reform a criminal was to moralize at him solemnly by the hour as though a steady drip of predigested religious pap would wash away the canker of the soul. Others were better than that.

Fortunately they weren't obligatory and one could pick and choose to some extent. I discarded a couple before finding a good one. He used to come and chat with me about all sorts of things without ever once trying to fill me up with a lot of guff or trying to convert me. He, also, had lived in South Africa and so we had something in common. Of course, since I was a high risk prisoner, all these conversations were under the watchful eye and listening ear of a screw. Once I popped in a sentence in Afrikaans to which my visitor replied in the same language. The screw soon put a stop to that and we were both reprimanded by the Governor. But no black mark for Rearden, thank God.

Clark, the Prison Chaplain, also came to see me occasionally. He, also, was no toffee-nose and we got on together quite well. Basically, he was a very religious man and so found himself in a dilemma. He found it hard to reconcile the Christian precept of 'Love thy enemies' with the task of ministering to his flock who were locked up in a big cage. I think it was wearing him down a bit.

The best of the lot was Anderson, the Welfare Officer. He did quite a lot for me and I think his reports to the Governor were encouraging. It was through him that I got the radio, something for which I had worked assiduously. I had been going to the library once a week, as per regulations, and each visit needed the supervision of a screw. I asked Anderson why I couldn't take out a double ration of books and halve the number of library visits, thus taking a bit of strain off the overworked staff.

He saw the point and quickly agreed. I think I managed successfully to give him the notion that I was playing along and trying to help. When I applied for permission to have a radio there was no opposition and, soon after that, I was given permission to start correspondence courses through the prison educational system. After all, if you are doing twenty years' bird you have to fill in the time somehow.

I chose English Literature and Russian. There was a bit of doubt about the Russian but it went through all right in the end. I had no intention of finishing either course if I could help it; it was all a bit of wool-pulling to make them think Rearden was reconciled to his fate. Still, I buckled down and worked hard. It had to look good and, besides, it was something to do.

The only other prisoner I got close to at this time was Johnny Swift who was doing a 'cut' for burglary. In prison jargon a 'sleep' is a sentence of from six months to two years; a 'cut' is from two to four years, and a 'stretch' is anything over four years. Johnny had been sent up for three years for having been found on business premises after closing time, so he was doing a cut and I was doing a stretch.

More shrewd than intelligent, he gave me lots of tips about the minor rackets that go on in prison and the best ways of keeping out of trouble. Once, when I had changed cells for the umpteenth time, I was a bit grouchy about it. He laughed. 'The penalty of being famous,' he said. 'I know one cell you'll never be put in.'

'Which is that?'

'That one over there in the corner. Snooky's cell.'

Snooky was an odd little man with a permanent smile;

he also was in for burglary. 'And why shouldn't I go in there?'

Johnny grinned. 'Because the main sewer runs under there – right across the corner of the Hall. It's big enough to crawl through if you could dig down to it.'

'I see,' I said thoughtfully. 'But they'll trust your burglar mate, Snooky.'

'Burglar!' said Johnny in disgust. 'He's no more a burglar than my Aunt Fanny. He's nick-struck – that's what he is. Every time he's discharged tears roll down his cheeks as they push him through the gate. Then he goes and does a job and bungles it so he can get back in here.'

'He *likes* it here!'

'If you'd been brought up like Snooky you'd find this place a home from home,' said Johnny soberly. 'But I agree he's not all there.'

Another time Johnny said, 'Be careful who you talk to in here. I wouldn't trust a bloody soul myself.'

'Even you?'

He chuckled. 'Especially me, mate. But seriously, watch out for Simpson – he's a proper arse-creeper. If you find him hanging around, clip his bloody earhole.'

He pointed out others I should beware of, and some of them surprised me. 'That gang would peach on anyone if they thought it would get them in good with the Governor so he'll put in a good word to the Review Board. But they're wasting their time; he's too fly for them. He knows what goes on in here without those narks helping him.'

Johnny was philosophical about doing time. To him, his work was his profession and prison an occupational hazard. 'I've done two sleeps and a cut,' he said. 'Next time it'll be a stretch.'

'Aren't you worried about that?'

'A bit,' he admitted. Like an economist discussing the effect of government legislation on industrial activity he began to analyse the situation. 'It's these bloody do-gooders,' he said. 'They've knocked out capital punishment and they've got to put something in its place. So you get long terms for murderers. But a bloke serving a long term doesn't like it and wants to get out, so they class him as a high risk.'

He grinned. 'And they've got to find a special place to put him. Nicks like this are no good – you could get out of here with a bent pin – so they're building high risk nicks special like. But when you've got a place like that there aren't enough killers to fill it – there's a bit of space going to waste – so they begin to get a bit harder on the sentences. That's where you felt the draught, chum.'

I said, 'But why put me in here to do my bird if it isn't safe?'

'Because the special nicks aren't ready yet. You wait until they've built those places on the Isle of Wight that Mountbatten's been going for. You'll be whizzed out of here in no time. In the meantime they spread you high risk blokes around thin, a few in each nick, so you can be watched easy.'

I looked around 'C' Hall. 'If this place is so easy to get out of why haven't you tried?'

He looked at me incredulously. 'Think I'm a mug, mate? I'm only doing a cut, and that means I'm out of here in just over two years from start to finish – if I don't lose me temper and clobber that bastard, Hudson. You got no idea what it's like when you go over the wall and you know that every blue-bottle in England is looking for you. It ain't worth it, chum; not with all those bloody dogs. They use helicopters, too, and radio. It's like a bloody army exercise.'

He tapped my arm. 'Could be different for you, though. You ain't got as much to lose. But it wouldn't be as easy for you to go over the wall as it would be for me, 'cause they're watching you all the time. They're on to you, mate. And if you *did* get over the wall you'd get nowhere without an organization.'

That sounded interesting. 'Organization! What organization?'

'You got to have planning on the outside,' said Johnny. 'You don't want to be like those mugs who find themselves on the Moor running in circles and eating raw turnip and listening for the dogs.' He shuddered slightly. 'Those bloody dogs! No, you got to have an organization that'll get you clean away. How do you suppose Wilson, Biggs, and the others did it?'

'All right,' I said. 'I'll buy it. How did they get away?'

He rubbed the side of his nose. 'Like I said – organization and outside planning. But it takes the shekels; you got to have a lot of money.' He looked around to see if there was anyone within earshot, and lowered his voice. 'You ever hear of the Scarperers?'

'*Scarperers?*' I shook my head. 'Never heard of them.'

'Well, it's only a rumour and I could be wrong, but the griff is that there's a mob specially set up for it – helping you long-term blokes.' He chuckled. 'Could call it a new kind of crime. But you got to have the bees.'

That didn't need much working out; the bees and honey – the money. 'How do I contact them?'

'You don't,' said Johnny bluntly. 'They contact you. This is a very exclusive mob; very picky and choosy. But I hear on the grapevine that they do a guaranteed job – you get clear away or no pay – barring expenses. Course, they don't bother about blokes like me because they know it ain't worth me while, but you could be different.'

I hesitated. 'Johnny, this isn't my country and I don't know the ropes. I was in England for less than a week before I was picked up. But if you put it out on the grapevine that there's a bloke in this nick who could do with a bit of help it might do me some good. No names, mind!'

'Think I'm a mug?' he asked. 'No names it is.' He looked at me speculatively. 'Can't say that I blame you, chum. Twenty years' bird would send me round the twist. Trouble with you is that you didn't cough up nicely when asked; you slapped 'em in the face with it and they didn't like it.'

He sighed heavily. 'As I said, next time I'm up before the beak it'll be a stretch. Time was when I could reckon on five or seven years, but that was before the beaks got bloody-minded. Now I don't know what they'll do – could be ten, twelve or even fifteen years' bird. I don't know if I could do fifteen years. It unsettles a man, it really does, not having a dependable stretch to rely on.'

I said, 'Maybe you'd better call it a day when you get out of here.'

'What else can I do?' he said despondently. 'I'm not brass-faced enough to go on the con; besides, I ain't got the voice – you need to be la-di-da for that. And I'm too old to learn how to dip. And I hates the protection bit – too soft-hearted to beat anybody up. No, I'm an inside man – up the old drainpipe, that's me.'

'You could turn honest,' I suggested.

He looked at me incredulously. 'That's for peasants. Can you see me as a nine-to-five? Can you see me working in the corner garage getting me hands black?' He was silent for a while. 'Not that I'm *relying* on getting boobed, you understand. I'm not like Snooky, you know. But I know it's in the cards and I got to face it.'

He stared blindly into the middle distance as though seeing a very bleak future. 'And the scarperers won't do nothing for me,' he said softly. 'I ain't got the bees – I never have had.'

As far as I could see there wasn't much difference between Snooky and Johnny Swift – they both faced the same end.

II

The months went by.

I mopped and scrubbed and polished 'C' Hall in a continual round of endeavour; it was like cleaning out the Augean stables because of some of the pigs who lived in it. I had one or two arguments on that score but nothing serious enough to get me a black mark.

Forbes tried to con me a couple of times into narking about the diamonds but when he saw he wasn't getting anywhere he gave it up. I suppose I was written off as incorrigible.

Maskell came to see me a couple of times. The first time he asked if I wanted to appeal against my sentence. I said, 'Is there any point?'

'A technicality,' he said. 'You may remember that the judge told Rollins that he didn't see how your case could deteriorate much further. That was an unfortunate remark and could be construed on appeal as having undue influence on the jury. On the other hand, your attitude about the missing property has not been an encouraging feature.'

I smiled at him. 'Mr Maskell, if I knew nothing about the diamonds then I couldn't help in the way I'm expected to, could I?'

We did nothing about the appeal.

The second time he came I saw him in the Governor's office. The Governor said, 'Your solicitor is asking that you should sign a power of attorney.'

Maskell broke in smoothly. 'Mr Rearden had certain assets in South Africa which have now been liquidated and transferred to England. It is natural that he had an advisor to handle the investment of these funds since he is incapable of doing it himself.'

'How much is involved?' asked the Governor.

'A little over £400,' said Maskell. 'A safe investment in trustee funds should turn it into over £1,000 in twenty years – something for Mr Rearden to look forward to, I hope.' He produced a document. 'I have Home Office approval.'

'Very well,' said the Governor, so I signed the power of attorney. Someone had to pay for the radio I had been granted permission to have – they aren't supplied free of charge. And it was nice to know I hadn't been forgotten. I thanked Maskell warmly.

The time came when I was able to strike day number 365 from my calendar – only another 19 years to go. I had heard nothing from Johnny about the so-called scarperers and was becoming despondent about my chances.

I was still classified as high risk with all the attendant irritants. By now I had got used to sleeping with the light on and it had become an automatic and unthinking reaction to put my clothes outside the cell door before Smeaton locked up for the night. I changed cells irregularly and kept a record, wondering if I could detect a pattern but there were no regularities as far as I could see, either in the timing or in the particular cell I was transferred to next. I think they randomized it by pulling numbers out of a hat or some such method. That kind of thing is unbeatable.

It was about this time that I first met Slade. He was a new boy inside for a first offence and he'd got forty-two years, but I don't believe the First Offenders Act covers espionage. I had heard about him before, of course; the news broadcasts had been full of the Slade Trial. Since most of the juicy bits had been told *in camera* no one really knew what Slade had been up to, but from all accounts he was the biggest catch since Blake.

He was a pallid man and looked as though he had been bigger at one time but had shrunk, so that his skin was baggy and ill-fitting, something like the skin of a bloodhound. He walked with two sticks and I later learned that he'd been shot through the hips and had spent eight months in hospital before being put on trial. A spy leads an interesting life – sometimes too interesting.

At the trial it had come out that he was really Russian but to speak with him you wouldn't think so because his English was perfect, if a little too public school. His forty-two year stretch should have made him the doyen of the prison but it didn't work out that way. Surprisingly, the most hardened criminal can be patriotic and, to a large extent, he was given the cold shoulder.

Not being English that didn't worry me too much. He proved to be a most interesting conversationalist, cultured and knowledgeable, and was instantly prepared to help me with my Russian lessons when I asked him. He looked at me blandly when I put the question. 'Certainly I speak Russian,' he said. 'It would be very odd if I didn't under the circumstances.' A faint smile played about his lips.

My Russian improved spectacularly after Slade's arrival.

It was nearing the end of Johnny's sentence and he had been transferred to the hostel. That meant he was employed on jobs outside the prison, the theory being that it would acclimatize him gradually to the rigours of the outside world – a part of the rehabilitation process. I didn't see it would make much difference to Johnny Swift.

But it meant I didn't see him as often. Sometimes we had a few words in the exercise yard but that was as far as it went. I looked around in 'C' Hall for someone else to chum up with, someone who was a likely prospect for contacting an escape organization – if the damned thing existed. At any moment I could be transferred without notice to another nick – possibly a high security prison – and that didn't suit my book at all.

It was fifteen months to a day before anything happened. I was breathing the lovely smog-laden air in the exercise yard when I saw Johnny Swift signal that he wanted to talk. I drifted over to him and caught the football that he threw, apparently by accident. I bounced it a couple of times and took it to him and handed it over. 'You still want to get out?' he asked, and kicked the ball up the yard.

I felt my stomach muscles tense. 'Had an offer?'

'I been approached,' he admitted. 'If you're still interested it could go further.'

'I'm bloody interested. I've had enough of this.'

'Fifteen months!' he scoffed. 'That's nothing. But have you got the lolly? That's important.'

'How much?'

'Five thousand nicker and that's just a starter,' said Johnny. 'It's to be put up before anything happens – before they even think about getting you out.'

'Christ! That's a lot of money.'

'I been told to tell you that this is the expense money – and it's non-returnable. The real payment will be more than that.'

'How much?'

'I dunno. That's all I been told. They want to know how soon you can spring the five thousand quid.'

'I can get it,' I said. 'I have funds tucked away in South Africa that no one knows about.' I looked along the exercise yard. Hudson was at the bottom end, making his way up slowly. 'I'll want a cheque form on the Standard Bank of South Africa, Hospital Hill Branch, Johannesburg. Got that?'

He repeated it slowly, then nodded. 'I got it.'

'I'll sign it, and they cash it. It'll have to be cashed in South Africa. That shouldn't be too difficult.'

'It'll take some time, mate,' said Johnny.

I laughed humourlessly. 'I've got nineteen years. But tell them to hurry. I'm getting nervous about being moved out of here.'

'Watch it – here's Hudson,' Johnny said. 'You'll be

contacted.' He ran forward and intercepted the football and both he and I joined in the game.

The cheque form came ten days later. A new arrival brought it in and it was passed to me surreptitiously. 'I was told to give you this. Pass it to Sherwin when you've done with it.'

I knew Sherwin; he was due for release. I said quickly, 'Wait a minute; anything else?'

'I don't know nothing else,' the man muttered, and shuffled away.

That night I settled my correspondence course books on the table and started work as usual. I'd been plugging away at the Russian and I reckoned I was pretty good – my pronunciation had improved vastly since Slade's arrival although that makes no difference to the examiner's marks in a correspondence course. I carried on for half an hour and then dug out the cheque form and smoothed it out.

It had been quite a while since I'd seen that familiar sight, and I could almost smell the dust blowing off the Johannesburg mine dumps. The amount had been filled in – R10,000 – Ten Thousand Rand – and I thought the mob was laying it on a bit thick; since devaluation the value of the pound sterling had deteriorated relative to the Rand, and this cheque was for about £5,650. The payee line was blank – I wasn't supposed to know about that yet, and when I did find out it would be too late to do anything about it.

I filled in the date and added my signature – and it wasn't J. A. Rearden, either – then stuck the cheque between the pages of the Russian grammar, wondering if I was a wise man or the prize chump of all time. Someone could be conning me – it could even be Johnny Swift – and if he was I was over £5,000 in the red and all for nothing. But I had to rely on cupidity; if it was realized that there was more loot where that came from then someone would be back for more, but this time it would be payment by results – after the results had been achieved.

Next morning I passed the cheque on to Sherwin who palmed it expertly and I knew he wouldn't have any trouble in getting it out unseen. Sherwin was a card sharp and no one in 'C' Hall would dream of playing nap with him; he could make a deck of cards sit up and talk, and concealing a cheque would be no trouble at all.

Then I settled down to wait, wondering what expenses the mob would have that could run to five thousand quid.

The weeks went by and again nothing happened. I had figured out the time needed to cash the cheque and get word back to England and had estimated it at just over a week. When five long weeks had gone by without result I began to get edgy.

Then it broke very suddenly.

It was at free association time. Smeaton was giving me a minor dressing down for a small infraction; I'd not been cleaning up as well as I should have done – a sign that I was slipping. Cosgrove came up carrying a chess board. He waited until Smeaton had finished, then said, 'Cheer up, Rearden; what about a game?'

I knew Cosgrove; he'd been the brains behind a hi-jacking mob – cigarettes and whisky mostly – and someone had squealed on him and he'd been pulled in and got ten years. He was in his sixth year and, with a bit of luck, he'd be out in another two. He was also the 'C' Hall chess champion, a very astute and intelligent man.

I said abstractedly, 'Not today, Cossie.'

He glanced sideways at Smeaton who was standing two paces away. 'Don't you want to win out?'

'Win out?' I said sharply.

'The big tournament.' He held up a box of chessmen. 'I'm sure I can give you a few tips if you play with me.'

We found a table at the other end of the Hall away from

Smeaton. As we set out the pieces I said, 'Okay, what is this, Cossie?'

He put down a pawn. 'I'm your go-between. You speak to me and no one else. Understand?' I nodded briefly and he carried on. 'To begin with I'm going to talk money.'

'Then you can stop right now,' I said. 'Your mob already has over five thousand quid of mine, and I've yet to see a result.'

'You're seeing me, aren't you?' He looked around. 'Play chess – it's your first move.' I moved to QP3 and he laughed softly. 'You're a cautious man, Rearden; that's a piano opening.'

'Quit being subtle, Cossie. Say what you have to say.'

'I don't blame you for being cautious,' he said. 'All I'm saying is that it's going to cost you a hell of a lot more.'

'Not before I'm out of here,' I said. 'I'm not that much of a sucker.'

'I don't blame you,' said Cossie. 'It's like taking a jump in the dark. But the fact is we've got to talk money or the deal's off. We've both got to know where we stand.'

'All right. How much?'

He moved his king's knight. 'We're a bit like tax collectors – we take *pro rata*. You made a killing of £173,000. We want half – that's £86,500.'

'Don't be a bloody fool,' I said. 'There are too many things wrong with that calculation and you know it.'

'Such as?'

'There was only supposed to be £120,000 in that parcel. I think the owners were laying it on a bit.'

He nodded. 'Could be. Anything else?'

'Yes. Do you suppose we could sell for the full value? It's not like selling legitimate – you ought to know that more than anyone.'

'Play chess,' he said calmly. 'That screw's watching us. You could sell for full value with uncut diamonds if you were clever enough and I think you are clever. That wasn't a stupid job you pulled. You'd have got clean away if you hadn't been shopped.'

'They *weren't* uncut diamonds,' I said. 'They'd been cut in Amsterdam and were being brought back for setting. Diamonds of that value are X-rayed, photographed and registered. They've been recut and that means a hell of a drop in value. And another thing – I wasn't alone. I had a mate who's in on a fifty-fifty split. He planned it and I did it.'

'The boys were wondering about that,' said Cossie. 'They can't quite make you out. Did your mate shop you? Because if he did you've not got a bean, have you? And that means you're no good to us.'

'It wasn't my mate,' I said, hoping to make it stick.

'The buzz is going around that it was your mate.'

'The buzz couldn't have been started by a busy called Forbes – or another called Brunskill? They have their reasons, you know.'

'Could be,' he said thoughtfully. 'Who is your mate?'

'Nothing doing,' I said firmly. 'I didn't give him to the busies, and I'm not giving him to your mob. That, in itself, ought to prove he didn't shop me. My friend and I move along very quietly; we mind our business and we don't want anyone else minding it for us.'

'We'll let that one lie for a bit,' said Cossie. 'I'll put it to the boys. But that brings us back to the boodle – what was *your* take?'

'We estimated it at forty thousand nicker,' I said calmly. 'And it's out away safely. You get it through me – not my mate.'

He smiled slightly. 'In a Swiss numbered account?'

'That's right. It's quite safe.'

'So it's still half,' he said. 'Twenty years at a thousand a year – cheap at half price. We take you over the wall and deliver you *outside* the United Kingdom, and if you come back that's your trouble. But let me tell you something –

you'd better not welsh on us; you'd better have the boodle for us because, if you don't, nobody will ever hear of you again. I hope that's quite clear.'

'It's very clear,' I said. 'You get me out of here and you'll get your money. I'll still be up on the deal, anyway.'

'I'll put it up to the boys,' he said. 'It's up to them whether you're accepted as a client.'

I said, 'Cossie, if your mob is as good as you say it is, what the hell are you doing in here? That puzzles me.'

'I'm just the contact man,' he said. 'I was recruited in here. Besides, I only have another two years' bird, then I'm out, anyway. Why make trouble for myself? I've got a good business waiting for me outside and I'm not going to throw that away.' He looked up. 'It'd be dicey for you if you came back to England.'

'That doesn't trouble me,' I said. 'I was only on the loose for a week in England – I know nothing about the place and I don't care to know any more.'

Cossie moved a piece. 'Check. There's another thing. You've been matey with Slade lately, haven't you? You do a lot of talking together.'

'He's helping me with my Russian,' I said, moving my king.

'That stops,' said Cossie flatly. 'You keep clear of Slade or the deal's off no matter how much money you have.'

I looked up, startled. 'What the hell . . .'

'That's the way it is,' he said equably, and moved his bishop. 'Check!'

'Don't tell me your mob is patriotic,' I said, and laughed. 'What's the idea?'

Cossie gave me a pained look. 'You ought to know better than to ask questions. You just do as you're told.' He turned to Smeaton who was walking past. 'What do you know?' he said. 'Rearden nearly beat me.' And that was a damned lie. 'He's got a good chance in the tournament.'

Smeaton looked at him with expressionless eyes and moved on.

III

So the game was on. I felt the tension rising in me and this time it was the tension of hope and not hopelessness. I even began to sing a bit as I scrubbed the tables in the Hall and I didn't slip up on a thing. Smeaton looked on me with approval, or as near to it as he could show. I was proving to be a model prisoner.

I obeyed Cosgrove's orders and dropped Slade who glanced at me reproachfully from time to time. I didn't know why Cossie wanted me to do that but this wasn't the time to argue it out. All the same, I felt a bit sorry for Slade; he hadn't too many friends in this nick.

I kept my eye on Cosgrove unobtrusively and watched who he talked to and who his pals were. As far as I could see he was as relaxed as usual and there were no changes in his normal pattern, but since I hadn't studied him especially before it was difficult to tell.

After a couple of weeks I went up to him during free association time. 'What about a game of chess, Cossie?'

He looked at me with blank eyes. 'Keep away from me, you silly bastard. I don't want to be involved with you.'

'You *are* involved,' I snapped. 'Smeaton was just asking if I wasn't going to enter the chess tournament, after all. He wanted to know if I'd given up my lessons. He also wanted to know if I'd given up Russian.'

Cosgrove blinked. 'Okay,' he said. 'Let's go over there.'

We set up the board. 'Any news?'

'I'll tell you when there's any news.' He was in a bad temper.

'Look, Cossie; I'm worried,' I said. 'I've just heard that

the top security nick is finished – the one on Wight. I'm scared of being transferred. It could happen any time.'

He looked around the Hall. 'These things can't be rushed – it's a complicated set-up. What do you suppose you've paid five thousand quid for? Just a jump over a wall? There's a whole escape line to be laid on.' He moved a chess piece. 'I don't know much about that side of it, but I hear it's a different set-up every time. No pattern, see? You ought to know that, Rearden, of all people.'

I stared at him. 'I see someone's been checking up on me.'

He looked at me with cold eyes. 'What do you think? A part of that five thousand nicker went towards checking you out. The boys are very security-minded. You have an interesting record; I can't see why you slipped up this time.'

'It happens to all of us,' I said. 'I was shopped – same as you, Cossie.'

'But I *know* who shopped me,' he said savagely. 'And the bastard is going to regret it to his dying day once I get out of here.'

'Better have it done before you get out,' I advised. 'You have the perfect alibi – you're in the nick; and enough time has gone by so that the busies aren't likely to think of you.'

He smiled reluctantly. 'You have interesting ideas, Rearden.'

'And what makes you think I don't know who shopped *me?*' I asked. 'Trouble is I don't have contacts on the outside to arrange an accident.'

'I can arrange it,' he offered.

'Forget it. I'll be out myself soon enough if your mob comes up to scratch. So they had me investigated in South Africa, did they? I hope they were satisfied.'

'You passed. You've got some good friends out there.' Smeaton was passing close by. Cossie said, 'Not that move, stupid; it gives me mate in three moves.' He looked up at

Smeaton. 'He's not as good as I thought he was; he'll never make it in the tournament.'

Smeaton sneered at him without moving a muscle of his face.

IV

Cossie was right – I didn't make it in the tournament – but it wasn't because of my lousy chess. Two days later he came to me instead of *vice versa*. 'It's set up.'

'They changed my cell yesterday,' I said.

'Doesn't matter. You'll be taken out in daylight – from the exercise yard on Saturday. Three o'clock exactly – remember that.'

There was a sudden tightening in my belly. 'What's the drill?'

'Have you ever seen them putting up the Christmas lights in Regent Street?' Cossie asked. He snapped his fingers in annoyance. 'Of course, you haven't. Anyway, they have this truck, see, with a platform on a long articulated arm – to hoist up the electricians.'

'I know what you mean,' I said. 'They use them at Jan Smuts Airport at Jo'burg to service the big jets. They call them cherry-pickers.'

'Do they?' he said interestedly. 'I see why they might. Anyway, there'll be one of those coming over the wall on Saturday. I'll show you where to stand, and when it comes over you jump in quick. There'll be a bloke on the platform to help you, and you'll be out in two ticks. That's going over the wall in style.'

He turned to survey the Hall, then continued rapidly. 'There'll be a hell of a lot of other things going on at the same time, but you won't take any notice of all that. Just keep your mind on the big platform.'

'Okay,' I said.

'And I've been asked to tell you something – if you're taken out and you can't find the twenty thousand quid, then God help you because no one else will. You'll not live to regret it – and that's not a slip of the tongue. I was specially asked to tell you that in case you want to change your mind.'

'The mob will get its money,' I said shortly.

'All right; I'll see you on Saturday then.' He turned away, then paused and turned back. 'Oh, I nearly forgot,' he said casually. 'Someone else is going with you, and you're going to help him.'

'Who?'

Cosgrove looked at me blandly. 'Slade!'

4

I

I stared at Cosgrove unbelievingly. 'Are you out of your mind?'

'What's the matter?' he asked. 'Don't you believe in freedom for others?'

'The matter!' My voice rose. 'The man walks with *sticks*, Cossie. He's a bloody cripple.'

'Keep your voice down,' he warned.

In a low voice I said savagely, 'How in hell is Slade supposed to make a break for it? He can't run.'

'You'll be there to help him, won't you?' said Cosgrove smoothly.

'Like hell I will.'

'Well, I'll tell you something, Rearden. Those sticks of his are a bit of a fake – he's been putting it on a bit ever since he came out of hospital. He can run well enough. Oh, I don't say he could break the four-minute mile, but he can toddle along enough for what we want.'

'Then he can bloody well toddle along by himself,' I said forcibly. 'Christ, if he obstructs my escape and I'm nabbed, I'll spend six months in solitary – and I'd certainly be sent to the new nick in Wight or to "E" Wing in Durham. I'd *never* get out of there.'

'The same applies to Slade,' said Cosgrove easily. 'And don't forget he's in for over forty years.' His voice tautened and a rasp entered into it. 'Now you listen to me, Rearden; Slade is a bloody sight more important to us than you are. You wouldn't believe how much money we have riding on him. So you'll bloody well do as you're told. As for going to Durham, you're due to be transferred there on Sunday, anyway.'

'Oh, boy!' I said. 'You play rough.'

'What's the matter? Is it that Slade is a spy? Has a sudden wave of patriotism overcome you?'

'Hell, no! I wouldn't care if he's inside for kidnapping the Queen, the Prime Minister and whole damned Cabinet. It's just that he's going to be a flaming liability.'

Cosgrove assumed a placatory tone. 'Well, now; maybe we can compensate you for that. Our agreement is that when we get you out then you pay us twenty thousand quid. Right?'

I nodded wearily. 'Right.'

'Suppose we cut that in half and make it ten thou'. With the live body of Slade as makeweight for the other ten thou'. How would you feel about that?'

'It has its points,' I conceded.

'I don't think it's at all bad considering you're going to be lumbered with Slade anyway,' said Cosgrove.

'Do you have authority for that offer?' I asked suspiciously.

'Of course I have,' he said, and smiled thinly. 'Of course, it has its converse side. If you get over the wall and Slade doesn't, then you get the chop. That's just so you remember that Slade is more important than you are.'

I said, 'This is just getting him over the wall?'

'That's it. Once the pair of you are on the other side my pals will look after you both.' He shrugged. 'It's a certainty Slade couldn't make it on his own so that's why we're doing it this way. I'll give it to you straight; he *can't* run very well. Neither could you if you had a stainless steel peg through each hip joint.'

'How is he at climbing?'

'His arms are strong but you might have to give him a bunk-up when that platform comes over.'

'All right,' I said. 'I'd better have a talk to him.'

'No!' said Cosgrove. 'You don't go near him. That's part of the deal. He's been talked to already and he knows what to do. I'm the one who tells *you* what to do.' A bell rang stridently signifying the end of free association time. He flipped his hand at me. 'See you in the yard on Saturday.'

Saturday was a long time coming. I was in a muck sweat when they changed my cell again – two changes in three days – and I wondered if someone guessed that an escape was in the wind. It took all my will power to carry on with my studies in the evenings and my Russian suffered and I turned to the course on Eng. Lit. but found *Finnegans Wake* hardly more relaxing in the circumstances.

I kept my eye on Slade and noted with glumness the obvious weakness of his legs. It wasn't going to be at all easy to get him over the wall, cherry-picker or no cherry-picker. Once he saw me watching him and his eyes casually swept past me without a flicker. I didn't see Cosgrove talking to him and came to the conclusion that he might have a different contact. It was possible that the whole damn prison was riddled by the hirelings of the Scarperers.

I scrubbed the tables and swept the Hall during the day and made sure I did a good job – even on the Saturday morning. I wanted no sign of abnormality to appear at all. But I hadn't much appetite for the midday meal and left most of it. At a table across the Hall I saw Slade polishing his tin plate with a slice of bread.

At two-thirty we were marched into the yard for free exercise. Some of the boys were kicking a ball about, but most strolled up and down enjoying the sun and the sky and the air. I drifted over to Cosgrove and we walked the length of the yard. He said, 'I'll tell you where it's coming over and then we walk right past, see? Then I'll take you to the place you have to wait. You stay there and you keep one eye on me and one on the wall – but don't stare at it as though expecting something to happen.'

'I'm not stupid.'

He grunted. 'That's as maybe. All right, we're coming to it now. See that chalk mark?'

'I see it,' I said, and almost laughed. It was a crudely phallic scrawl more likely to be found in a run-down public lavatory.

Cossie wasn't laughing. 'That's where it comes over. Now we carry on to the end of the yard.' We walked on and turned in unison, just like the teachers who supervised the playground at school used to do when I was a kid. 'You might have to jump for it, but there'll be a bloke to help you.'

'Jump!' I said. 'What about Slade?'

'You give him a bunk-up first. There'll be ropes hanging from the platform. He'll be all right once he grabs those – he has strong arms.'

I saw Slade watching the football match with evident appreciation. 'He'll be leaving his sticks behind then.'

'That's obvious,' said Cosgrove impatiently. We strolled back to a point on the other side of the yard facing the chalk mark. Slade was leaning against the wall quite close to the mark and wouldn't have to move more than a few feet when the action started.

Cosgrove said, 'Now you just stay here and wait for it.' He consulted something he held in his fingers and I saw it was a very small ladies' watch. 'Nearly twenty minutes to go.'

The watch vanished. 'Where did you get that?' I asked.

'That doesn't matter,' he said with a sour grin. 'And I won't have it at all in twenty-five minutes. The screws'll act as though someone lit a fire under them when this comes off and they'll turn the whole bloody place upside down. They won't find this watch, though.'

I leaned against the wall and looked at the faint chalk mark on the other side of the yard. I could hear the traffic on the other side of that exterior wall but not much because it was Saturday afternoon and there wasn't much commercial stuff on the roads.

Cosgrove said, 'I'll leave you now, and this is what you do. At two minutes to three a fight will start over in that corner. There'll be a lot of noise. As soon as you hear it you start walking – slowly, mind you – across the yard towards that mark. Don't make a fuss about it and, for God's sake, don't run. Slade will see you move and he'll get ready.'

'I could have done with talking to him about it myself,' I grumbled.

'Too dangerous,' said Cosgrove. 'Now, don't be surprised by anything else that happens around you, no matter what it is. Just keep your mind on your job and head for that mark. By the time you get there the platform will be coming over. You hoist Slade up on your shoulders and then you jump for it yourself. It should be easy.'

'I'll be all right, Cossie.'

'Okay,' he said. 'Good luck, Rearden.' He grinned crookedly. 'Under the circumstances we won't shake hands. I'm going now; I'll be talking to Paddy Colquhoun until this thing's all over.' The watch appeared again. 'Fifteen minutes exactly.'

'Wait a minute,' I said. 'What about the closed circuit TV outside the wall?'

'That'll be taken care of,' he said patiently. 'Goodbye, Rearden.'

He walked away across the yard leaving me leaning against the wall alone. My hands were sweating and my mouth was suddenly dry as I looked at the barbed wire on top of the exterior wall. God help me if I got snagged on that. I wiped my wet hands on my trousers and squatted down on my heels.

Slade was standing next to the chalk mark and he, too, was alone. Probably everyone had been warned to keep clear of us; they wouldn't know why but they'd obey, especially if the warning had been given by the strong-arm boys. Accidents can be arranged, even in prison, and it's awfully easy to get a broken arm, or worse.

Cosgrove was talking to Paddy and they appeared to be enjoying a huge joke. I hoped the joke wasn't on me. I was taking a hell of a lot on faith, but if Cossie was conning me – if he was pulling a practical joke – I'd have his lights for a necktie. The prison wouldn't be big enough for both of us. But I looked across at Slade and knew, deep in my bones, that this was the real thing.

There were four screws in the yard, walking up and down with set, expressionless faces. And I knew there were two more watching from the high windows above my head. From there they could see into the street outside the exterior wall. God in heaven, surely they'd ring the alarm as soon as they saw that mechanical lift drive into the street. They couldn't be as stupid as all that.

The minutes went by. I found myself losing track of time. Fifteen minutes had already gone by – or was it only five? Again I could feel the sweat on the palms of my hands, and again I rubbed them dry. If I had to jump for a rope I didn't want any chance of slipping.

I looked at Cosgrove again. He was standing with his head cocked on one side listening to what Paddy had to say, and I saw him flick an eye towards me before he burst into a guffaw of laughter and slapped Paddy on the back.

I didn't see him give the signal but suddenly there were raised voices at the other end of the yard, so perhaps the slap on Paddy's back had been the signal. I got to my feet and began to walk slowly forward as though hypnotized by that distant chalk mark. Slade pushed himself away from the wall and came forward, hobbling on his sticks.

The men all around me were looking towards the disturbance which had grown noisier. Some of the prisoners were running in that direction and the screws had begun to converge on the fight. I glanced to my right and saw

Hudson, the senior screw, who had apparently sprung from nowhere, making his way across the yard. He wasn't running but walking at a smart pace, and he was on a collision course with me.

Something astonishing happened behind. There was a sharp crack, like a minor explosion, and a billow of dense, white smoke erupted from the ground. I kept going but Hudson turned and stared. There were more explosions in the yard and the smoke grew thick and heavy. Somebody was being liberal with the smoke bombs that were being tossed over the wall.

Hudson was now behind me, and I heard his anguished bellow. 'Escape! Escape! Sound the alarm.'

Frantically he blew on his whistle but I kept going to where Slade was waiting. His face was set in lines of strain and as I approached he said urgently, 'Where the hell is that damned contraption?'

I looked up and saw it coming over through the wreaths of smoke, looming over the wall like the head and neck of a prehistoric monster with slimy weeds dripping from its jaws. As it dipped down I saw that the weeds were four knotted ropes dangling from the platform on which stood a man who was, so help me, talking into a telephone.

I bent down. 'Come on, Slade; up you go!'

He dropped his sticks as I heaved him up and he made a grab at one of the ropes as it came within reach. He was no lightweight and it was not easy for me to hold him up. He caught on to the rope and I was thankful when his weight eased from me.

The man on the platform was looking down at us and when he saw that Slade had a secure hold he spoke urgently into the telephone and the platform began to rise. The only trouble about that was it was leaving me behind. I made a frantic leap and grasped the last knot on the same rope that Slade was climbing. He was going up fast but his legs were flailing about and he caught me under the jaw with the tip of his shoes. I felt dizzy and nearly let go but managed to tighten my grip at the last moment.

Then somebody grabbed my ankle and I looked down and saw it was Hudson, his face contorted with effort. The man had a grip like iron so I lifted my other leg and booted him in the face. I was learning from Slade already. He let go and tumbled to the ground which, by that time, seemed to be a long way down. I carried on up the rope, my shoulder muscles cracking, until I could grasp the edge of the platform.

Slade was sprawled on the steel floor, gasping with the effort he had made, and the man with the telephone bent down. 'Stay there,' he said. 'You'll be all right.' He spoke into the mouthpiece again.

I looked down and saw the barbed wire apparently moving away underneath as the great articulated arm swept me over the wall. Then it began to drop and the man bent down again, directing his words at both of us. 'Do exactly as I do,' he said calmly.

We were swept dizzily over the street and then stopped dead. A small open delivery truck came from nowhere and pulled up beneath the platform. The man swung over the railings of the platform and dropped lightly into the back of the truck and I thankfully let go of the rope and followed him. Slade came after and fell on top of me and I cursed him, but then he was thrown off me by a sudden surge of acceleration as the little truck took off and went round the first corner with a squeal of tyres.

I looked back along the street and saw the big cherry-picker move ponderously into view and the great arm fell forward, completely blocking the street. Men tumbled from the cab and ran, and then we turned another corner and I saw no more of that.

Slade leaned against the side of the truck with his head lolling on one side. His face was grey and he seemed thoroughly exhausted. I remembered that he had been in hospital not long before. The man with us thumped his elbow into my ribs. 'Pay attention!' he said sharply. 'You'll be transferring into a little black mini-van. Get ready to move.'

The truck was moving fast but there was little traffic to hinder us on that Saturday afternoon. Suddenly we swooped to a stop behind a mini-van which stood at the kerb with its rear doors open. 'That's it. Into there – quickly.'

I jumped out of the truck and took a header into the mini-van, and heard the doors slam shut behind. I lifted my head and, looking through the windscreen between two broad-shouldered men in the front seats, saw that the truck I had left was already on the move with Slade still in it. It turned ahead to the right and at high speed.

The mini-van took off more sedately, well within the speed limit, and turned to the left. I felt absolutely breathless. My lungs were strained and my heart was thumping as though it was going to burst in my chest. I lay there panting until I felt better and then raised myself and poked at the passenger in front with my finger. 'Why were we separated?'

He made no answer to that, so I tried again. 'Where are we going?'

'Shut up and keep down,' he said without turning. 'You'll find out soon enough.'

I relaxed as much as I could, sitting there on the hard metal floor of the van. From what I could gather from the brief glimpses I saw from the rear windows we were covering a complicated course among the streets, stopping properly at all the traffic lights and not moving fast enough to excite attention.

The van turned into a side street and swung up an alley. I leaned up on my elbow and looked forward cautiously. Ahead were two big wooden doors which were open, and inside the building was a huge moving-van with the tail-gate down. Without hesitation the driver headed right for it in low gear, bumped up the ramp formed by the tail-gate and drove right inside the pantechnicon. Behind us something came down from the roof, enclosing the van completely, and I heard the slam of the tail-gate as it was closed.

We were in complete darkness when the rear doors of the mini-van were opened. 'You can get out now.' It was a woman's voice.

I scrambled out and bumped into her, steadying myself on a soft arm. The front door of the mini-van slammed. 'For God's sake!' she said. 'Turn on a light.'

A light came on in the roof and I looked around. We were in a cramped compartment just big enough to take the van with a little space left over. The woman was a tall blonde dressed in a white overall and looking like a doctor's receptionist. One of the men pushed past me and bent down; I saw he was attaching a shackle to the rear bumper of the mini-van.

I heard the throb of a heavy diesel engine and the whole compartment lurched. The man straightened up and gave me a grin. He patted the side of the van. 'We don't want this to get loose, do we?'

There was another lurch and a grinding of gears. The big pantechnicon was travelling, taking me to – where?

The blonde smiled at me. 'We haven't much time,' she said practically. 'Take your clothes off.' I must have gaped at her because she said sharply, 'Strip, man! Don't be prudish – you won't be the first man I've seen bollock-naked.'

I took off the grey flannel jacket – the uniform of servitude – and watched her unpack a suitcase, producing underwear, socks, a shirt, a suit and a pair of shoes. 'You can start to get dressed in these,' she said. 'But don't put on the shirt yet.'

I took off the prison uniform and dressed in that lovely soft underwear, then balanced uneasily against the rocking motions of the moving pantechnicon to put on the socks. One of the men said, 'How does it feel to be out, chum?'

'I don't know. I'm not sure I'm out, yet.'

'You are,' he assured me. 'You can bank on it.'

I put on the trousers and then the shoes. Everything was a perfect fit. 'How did you know my measurements?' I asked.

'We know *everything* about you,' the man said. 'Except maybe one thing.'

'And what's that?'

He struck a match and lit his cigarette, then blew a plume of smoke in my face. 'Where you keep your money. But you'll tell us, won't you?'

I zipped up the trousers. 'At the proper time,' I said.

'Come over here,' said the blonde. She had pulled up a stool in front of a basin set on a shelf. 'Sit down. I'm going to give you a shampoo.'

So I sat down and she lathered my hair, digging her fingers deep into my scalp. She rinsed and then shampooed again before giving a final rinse. Then she took me by the chin and tilted my head. 'That'll do. Now for the eyebrows.' She got to work on my eyebrows and when she had finished she handed me a mirror. 'How do you like yourself now?'

I looked at my reflection in the mirror. Gone was the black hair and I was now middling blond. I was surprised at the difference it made; even Mackintosh wouldn't recognize me now. I felt her fingers on my cheek. 'You'll have to shave twice a day. That dark five o'clock shadow would give you away. You'd better shave now – you'll find the kit in your suitcase.'

I opened the case and found it very well fitted out with everything a man would normally travel with. There was a small battery-powered shaver which I put into use immediately. As I shaved she began to lay objects on the shelf. 'Your name is Raymond Cruickshank,' she said. 'Here are your initialled cuff-links.'

'Do I have to be that kind of a man?' I asked lightly.

She wasn't amused. 'Don't be funny,' she said coldly. 'The same initials are on the suitcase. All this is your insurance, Rearden; insurance against getting caught – treat it seriously.'

'Sorry,' I said.

'You've been to Australia, Rearden. You were mixed up in something in Sydney a few years ago, so we've made you an Australian. People over here can't tell the difference between a South African and an Australian accent, so you should get away with it. Here's your passport.'

I picked it up and flipped it open. It had a photograph of a blond-haired me.

She produced a wallet and opened it for my inspection. 'This is all pure Cruickshank; you'd better check it to make sure you know what's in it.'

So I did, and was very surprised. This mob was super-efficient – no wonder Cossie had said it needed time to set up. There were membership cards of Sydney clubs, an odd Australian two-dollar note among the British currency, an Australian AA card together with an Australian driving licence and an International driving licence, a dozen business cards announcing where I lived and what I did – it seemed I was the managing director of a firm importing office machinery. All very efficient, indeed.

I held out a dog-eared photograph. 'What's this?'

'You and the wife and kids,' she said calmly.

I looked at it more closely in the dim light and, by God, she was right! At least, it was a blond-haired me with my arm around a brunette's waist and with a couple of kids in front. A nice tricky photograph.

I put it back into the wallet and felt something else at the bottom of the pocket which I dug out. It was an old theatre stub, dated two months previously – the theatre, naturally enough, was in Sydney. Apparently I had been to see *Fiddler on the Roof*.

I put it back carefully. 'Very nice,' I said admiringly. 'Very nice indeed.' I laid down the wallet and began to put on my shirt. I was just about to fasten the sleeves with the cuff-links when she said, 'Mr Cruickshank, I said all this stuff was your insurance.'

I paused. 'Well?'

'Hold him, boys,' she said sharply, and I was grabbed from behind and held cruelly tight.

'What the hell . . . ?'

'Mr Cruickshank,' she said clearly. 'This is *our* insurance.' Her hand came from behind her back holding a hypodermic syringe which she held up to her eyes and squirted professionally. With one movement she rolled up the unfastened shirt sleeve. 'No hard feelings,' she said, and jabbed the needle into my arm.

There wasn't a damned thing I could do about it. I just stood there helplessly and watched her face go all swimmy. And then I didn't know any more about anything.

II

I woke up with the feeling of having been asleep for a long, long time. I didn't know why this should be, but it seemed a hundred years since I had gone to sleep in my cell, the new cell into which I had just been moved. I certainly didn't feel as though I had wakened from a normal night's sleep; after all, by now I had got used to the light being on all night.

And I had a hangover!

Hangovers I don't mind when there has been a cause for

them; one takes one's pleasures and pays the consequences. But I strongly object to the consequences when the pleasure has been missed. I hadn't had a drink for eighteen months and to have an unaccountable hangover was abominable.

I lay there in bed with my eyes closed stickily. My head felt as though there was a red-hot iron bar wrapped around it and it throbbed as a blacksmith beat lustily on it with his hammer. I also had the old familiar dehydrated feeling and my mouth tasted, as a friend once inelegantly put it, like the inside of a Greek wrestler's jockstrap.

I turned over slowly and groaned involuntarily as the blacksmith gave an extra hard thump. Then I opened my eyes and looked at the ceiling vacantly. With care I traced the elegant moulding of the cornice which was picked out in gilt, being careful not to go too quickly in case my eyeballs fell out. 'Funny!' I thought. 'They've given me a nice cell this time.'

With grudging movements I leaned up on one elbow just in time to see someone leave. The door closed with a gentle click and there was the sound of a key turning in a lock. That was familiar enough, anyway, which was more than the cell was.

As I stared uncomprehendingly at the dove-grey walls and the gilt rococo panelling, at the Dolly Varden dressing-table and the comfortable armchair standing on the thick-piled carpet, it hit me suddenly. My God, I made it! I got out of the nick!

I looked down at myself. I was dressed in silk pyjamas and the last time I had seen those was in the bottom of a suitcase in a moving-van.

A moving-van?

Slowly and painfully it all came back. The frantic grab at the rope; the wild swing over the barbed-wired wall; the jump into the truck, then into the mini-van, then into the pantechnicon.

The pantechnicon! That was it. There was a blonde who

had dyed my hair and who gave me a wallet. My name was Cruickshank and I was an Australian, she said. And then the bitch doped me. I put my hand to my arm and rubbed it where it felt sore. Now, why the hell had she done that?

I threw back the bedclothes and swung out my legs. No sooner was I standing upright than I felt violently ill, and so I staggered to the nearest door which gave at a push and I fell into a bathroom. I lurched to my feet and over to the water-closet where I retched up my guts, but nothing came forth but a thin brown mucus. Still, when it was over I felt fractionally better, so I got to my feet and swayed towards the wash basin which I clutched hard as I stared into the mirror at the unfamiliar face.

She was right, I thought; the five o'clock shadow does give the game away. The blond hair with the black-bearded face looked incongruous and the whole ensemble wasn't improved by eyes which looked like burnt holes in a blanket. I rubbed my arm again and, on impulse, rolled up the pyjama sleeve to see *five* red pinpricks.

Five! How long had I been unconscious? I fingered my beard which rasped uncomfortably. That felt normal for about thirty-six hours, or maybe a bit longer. Unless they'd shaved me when I was dead to the world – which was a distinct possibility.

I turned on the cold tap and ran some water into the basin, then gave my face a thorough dousing, spluttering a bit. There was a clean towel at hand and, as I wiped myself dry, I began to feel better but the feeling tended to ooze away when I caught sight of the bathroom window. There were thick steel bars on the inside and, although the glass was frosted, I could see the outline of similar bars on the outside.

That was going one better than the nick. Even in there they had but one set of bars to a window.

I dropped the towel on to the floor and went back into the bedroom. Sure enough the bedroom window was also barred inside and out, although here the glass was clear. I looked through the window and saw a courtyard surrounded by buildings. Nothing moved except a blackbird foraging for worms on a neatly mown lawn.

I watched the courtyard for five minutes but nothing happened, so I turned my attention to the bedroom. On the dressing-table by the window was the toilet case and the shaver that the blonde had provided. I opened the case, took out a comb and combed my hair. Shaving could wait a while. I looked into the mirror and stuck out my tongue at the changed man who faced me. He did the same and I hastily pulled it in again as I saw the coating on the tongue.

Then I stiffened as I looked over his shoulder, and I whirled about to face the room. There were *two* beds; the one I had occupied had rumpled sheets, but the other bed was occupied. I strode over and found Slade breathing heavily through his mouth and totally unconscious. I slapped his cheeks and prised open his eyelids all to no avail; apart from the breathing he was a reasonable facsimile of a dead man.

So I left him to it, principally because I had seen a newspaper lying by the side of the armchair. Whoever had been waiting for me to wake up hadn't taken his *Sunday Times* with him.

We were front page news. The headlines blared in a most uncharacteristic *Sunday Times* manner, but I'd bet the *News of the World* outdid them in that respect. There was a photograph of the outside of the nick with a thick, pecked line to show the course of events – there was a photograph of the cherry-picker with its neck collapsed across the entrance to a street, looking a bit like a dead Disney dinosaur from *Fantasia*; there was a photograph of someone being carried to an ambulance on a stretcher – Senior Prison Officer Hudson had unaccountably broken his leg!

The front page news story was pretty factual and they hadn't got much wrong as far as I could see. I read with interest that the exterior closed-circuit TV cameras had been rendered inoperable by having paint sprayed on to the lenses. That was a nice touch. It was also interesting to read that the small open truck had been found abandoned near Colchester, and the black mini-van near Southampton. Police had established road blocks around both areas.

Slade captured most of the limelight. What was a jewel thief compared with a master spy? But Brunskill had a go at me. 'This man is dangerous,' he said, with a straight face. 'He was convicted for a crime of violence and has a record of violence extending back for many years. The public should be wary of him and should on no account try to tackle him unaided.'

That was the most libellous thing I've ever read. Two convictions for violence over twelve years and I was being described as a Jack the Ripper. All Brunskill was trying to do was to build up the original arrest. I hoped his bosses threw the book at him for talking out of turn.

Insight had nothing to say about it, but they would, they would – I'd have to wait until next week's issue to get the inside story on how we'd escaped. But the editorial went off pop! The escape was described as a colossal piece of impudence and that if criminals were going to use such methods as mortar-fired smoke bombs then it was time that the prison authorities should also use military means to defend the integrity of the prisons.

I thought so, too.

Lord Mountbatten was not available for comment, but lots of other people were, whether they had anything relevant to say or not. One man especially fulminated about it – a Member of Parliament called Charles Wheeler who spoke bitterly about gangsterism in our English streets and swore he'd put a question to the House at the first available opportunity. I wished him luck. The mills of government grind slowly and it takes a hell of a long time to close even a stable door.

I quite enjoyed reading that Sunday paper.

I had just finished when the door clicked open and a man in a white coat wheeled in a trolley on which were several silver covered dishes. Behind him followed a tall man with a balding head fringed with silvery hair. 'Ah,' he said. 'I'm sure you would relish a light meal.'

I looked at the trolley. 'I might,' I said cautiously. 'If my stomach will stand it.'

He nodded gravely. 'You feel a little ill; that I can understand. You will find two bottles on the table. One contains aspirin and the other a stomach preparation. I had assumed you would find them.'

'I didn't,' I said, and held up the paper. 'I was more interested in this.'

He smiled. 'It does make interesting reading,' he agreed, and tapped the white-coated man on the shoulder. 'You can go now.' He turned back to me. 'You don't mind if I stay for tea?'

'Not at all,' I said magniloquently. 'Be my guest.'

White Coat had laid the table and pushed out the trolley; he closed the door behind him and again I heard the snap of the lock. They weren't taking any chances even with one of their own in the room. I looked with attention at the tall man; there was something incongruous about him which I couldn't put my finger on – and then I had it. He was tall and thin but had a curiously pudgy face, ill-suited to his build. It was as though the face of a fat man had been grafted on to a thin man's body.

He gestured. 'You'll find a dressing-gown behind the bathroom door.'

I crossed to the table and found the two small bottles, then went into the bathroom. The stomach preparation I ignored but the aspirin was very welcome. I put on the dressing-gown and returned to the bedroom to find Fatface in the act of pouring himself a cup of tea. 'You don't mind if I'm Mother?' he asked sardonically.

I sat down and picked up the glass of chilled tomato juice. Fatface pushed over the Worcestershire sauce. This improved it. I laced the juice liberally, added pepper, and drank it quickly. Almost immediately I felt better, but not so much better that I could face the breakfast that faced me when I lifted the silver cover from my plate. I looked down at the yellow eyes of eggs, with sausages for eyebrows and a bacon moustache, and shuddered delicately. Pushing the plate away distastefully I picked up a slice of toast and buttered it sparingly.

I said, 'If you're being Mother you can pour me a cup of tea.'

'Certainly – anything to oblige.' He busied himself with the teapot.

I crunched on the toast and said indistinctly, 'Anything? Then perhaps you can tell me where I am.'

He shook his head regretfully. 'Then you'd know as much as me – and that would never do. No, Mr Rearden; that is one of the things I can't tell you. You realize, of course, that because of that particular restriction your movements must be, shall we say, circumscribed.'

I'd already figured that out; the double bars at the windows weren't there for nothing. I jerked my head at the bed behind me. 'Slade is a bit too circumscribed right now.'

'He'll be all right,' said Fatface. 'He's older than you and takes longer to recover.' He passed me a cup of tea. 'You will be confined to these two rooms until the time comes to move you again.'

'And when will that be?'

'That depends entirely on you. We hope to make your stay here as comfortable as possible. If you have any special preferences at meals – grapefruit juice instead of tomato juice, for instance – we will do our best to please you.' He rose to his feet and crossed to a cabinet which he opened. It was well stocked with bottles. 'You can help yourself to a drink at any time. By the way, what cigarettes do you prefer?'

'Rothmans filter.'

He produced a notebook and made an entry like a conscientious *maître d'hôtel*. 'That we can manage easily.'

I grinned at him. 'I'd like a half-bottle of wine with lunch and dinner. White, and on the dryish side; a hock or moselle, preferably.'

'Very well.' He made another note. 'We try to run a top-class establishment. Of course, our expenses being what they are, our charges are high. In fact, there is a standard charge no matter how long you stay here. In your case I think it has been agreed already – twenty thousand pounds, wasn't it, Mr Rearden?'

I picked up my tea-cup. 'It wasn't,' I said economically. 'Ten thousand pounds is lying on that bed over there. That was the deal.'

'Of course,' said Fatface. 'I forgot.'

'No, you didn't,' I said amiably. 'You were trying it on. Your tea is getting cold.'

He sat down again. 'We would prefer to settle the account as soon as possible. The sooner it is settled the sooner you will be able to go on the next stage of your journey.'

'To where?'

'I think you can leave that to us. I assure you it will be outside the United Kingdom.'

I frowned at that. 'I don't like buying a pig in a poke. I want a better guarantee than that, I want to know where I'm going.'

He spread his hands. 'I'm sorry, Mr Rearden; but our security arrangements preclude your knowing in advance. You must understand the importance of this. We cannot take any chances at all on the penetration of our organization by . . . er . . . undesirable elements.'

I hesitated, and he said impatiently, 'Come, Mr Rearden;

you are an intelligent man. You must know that we have a reputation that rests entirely on our ability to keep our promises. Our good faith is our stock-in-trade and it would need but one dissatisfied client to do us irreparable harm.' He tapped gently on the table with his teaspoon. 'In any case, I believe you were informed of what would certainly happen to you if you did not keep your side of the bargain.'

The threat was there again – veiled but unmistakable. I had to play for time, so I said, 'All right; get me a cheque form of the *Züricher Ausführen Handelsbank.*'

Fatface looked pleased. 'And the number – the account number?'

'You'll know that when I put it on the cheque,' I said. 'I have security precautions, too, you know.' I did a quick calculation. 'Make it out for 200,000 Swiss francs. You take your share and let me have the balance in the currency of the country in which I'm being dropped.'

He nodded. 'A wise precaution. The sensible man never leaves himself short of liquid funds,' he said sententiously.

I looked down at myself. 'Do I *have* to live in pyjamas?'

He looked shocked. 'Of course not. I apologize for not telling you sooner. Your clothes are in the wardrobe.'

'Thanks.' I crossed the room and opened the wardrobe. Hanging up was a business suit and, next to it, a more sporty and informal outfit. Underwear was neatly laid out on the shelves and two pairs of highly polished shoes – black and brown – nestled in the shoerack.

I went through the pockets of the suits quickly and found them empty, then I clicked open the suitcase which stood at the bottom of the wardrobe and found it as empty as Mother Hubbard's cupboard. I swung on Fatface. 'No passport,' I said. 'No wallet – no identification.'

'We let you look at those to show our good faith, Mr Rearden – or should I call you Mr Cruickshank? We wanted you to see the lengths to which we would go to ensure a successful outcome of this enterprise. But there is no necessity for you to have them just yet. They will be returned to you prior to the next stage of your journey.' He wagged his finger at me solemnly. 'Security – that's the watchword here.'

That I could well believe. This mob considered all the angles.

Fatface said, 'If you want anything, all you have to do is to press this button – like this.' He waited, looking expectantly at the door, and White Coat arrived within two minutes. 'Taafe will look after you, Mr Rearden; won't you, Taafe?'

White Coat nodded, but said nothing.

'I must be going now,' said Fatface regretfully, as though he desired nothing more in the world than to stay and chat. 'We have to get on with our business.' He looked at me closely. 'I advise you to shave; you look most uncivilized. I daresay that while you are attending to your toilet Taafe will tidy up the room.' He gave me a brief nod and departed.

I looked curiously at Taafe who was busying himself with the breakfast crockery and leaving only his broad back for my inspection. He was a big man with the battered face of a small time bruiser – small time because good boxers don't get hit about like that. After a while I shrugged and went into the bathroom. It was a good idea, no matter who had suggested it.

I ran a bathful of hot water and settled down to soak and think. The mob was good – there was no doubt about that. Provided I could come up with the money I would undoubtedly be released in some foreign country with adequate, if fraudulent, identification and enough money to see me right. Of course, the converse wasn't too good – if I couldn't provide the funds required then I would probably occupy a cold hole in the ground in an isolated place and my bones would be discovered to mystify some rural copper in the distant future.

I shook my head. No – this mob was too efficient for that. They would leave no bones to be discovered. I would probably be encased in a block of concrete and tipped over the side into the deepest part of the sea available. It would be an act of charity if they killed me *before* pouring the concrete.

I shivered a little in spite of the hot water and thought glumly of the *Züricher Ausführen Handelsbank* and that cold-minded bastard, Mackintosh. I had better begin making plans to break out of this luxurious nick.

That brought me to another question. Where the hell was I? Fatface had played safe on that one, but maybe he had slipped up, after all. I thought about Taafe. That wasn't an English name at all – so could I be already out of England? It hadn't been smart of Fatface to let that name slip out.

As I mused, a little rhyme came into my head:

Taffy was a Welshman,
Taffy was a thief;
Taffy came to my house
And stole a side of beef.

I had learned that one at my mother's knee. Apart from being libellous to Welshmen did it mean that I was somewhere in Wales – still in the United Kingdom?

I sighed and splashed water. Time would tell, but time was something I hadn't much of.

5

I

They looked after us like an international hotel looks after a couple of Greek shipping magnates. Nothing was too good for Mr Slade and Mr Rearden – nothing except immediate freedom. We asked for newspapers and we got newspapers; I asked for South African brandy and I got it – Oude Meester, too – something I had found unobtainable during my few days in London. Slade looked askance at my South African brandy; his tipple was 15-year-old Glenlivet which was also hospitably provided.

But when we asked for a television set or a radio we drew a blank. I said to Slade, 'Now why is that?'

He turned his heavy face towards me, his lips twisted with contempt for my minuscule intelligence. 'Because the programmes would tell us where we are,' he said patiently.

I acted dumb. 'But we get the newspapers regularly.'

'Oh, God!' he said, and stooped to pick up *The Times*. 'This is dated the fifth,' he said. 'Yesterday we had the issue of the fourth, and tomorrow we'll have the issue of the sixth. But it doesn't follow that today *is* the fifth. We could be in France, for example, and these newspapers are airmail editions.'

'Do you think we are in France?'

He looked from the window. 'It doesn't look like France and neither does it . . .' He twitched his nose '. . . smell like France.' He shrugged. 'I don't know where we are.'

'And I don't suppose you care very much,' I said.

He smiled. 'Not really. All I know is that I'm going home.'

'Your people must think you're important,' I said.

'Moderately so,' he said modestly. 'I'll be glad to get home. I haven't seen Russia for twenty-eight years.'

'You must be bloody important if my help in getting you out was worth ten thousand quid.' I turned to him and said seriously, 'As a sort of professional what do you think of this mob?'

He was affronted. 'A *sort* of professional! I'm good in my work.'

'You were caught,' I said coldly.

'After twenty-eight years,' he said. 'And then by sheer chance. I doubt if anyone could have done better.'

'Okay, you're good,' I said. 'Answer my question. What do you think of this crowd?'

'They're good,' he said judiciously. 'They're very good. Their security is first class and their organization impeccable.' He frowned. 'I didn't think ordinary criminals could retain that kind of cohesion.'

That thought had occurred to me and I didn't like it. 'You think they're in your line of work?'

'It's unlikely but just barely possible,' he said. 'To run a network takes a lot of money. The West Germans had the Gehlen *Apparat* just after the war – that was more-or-less private enterprise but it was supported by American money.'

'Who would support this kind of outfit?' I asked.

He grinned at me. 'My people might.'

True enough. It seemed as though Slade was home and dry; instead of growing his beard in the nick he'd be knocking back vodka in the Kremlin with the boss of the KGB before very long, and dictating his memoirs as a highly placed member of British Intelligence. That much had come out at his trial; he'd infiltrated the British Intelligence Service and got himself into quite a high position.

He said, 'What do you think of me?'

'What am I supposed to think?'

'I spied on your country . . .'

'Not my country,' I said. 'I'm from the Republic of South Africa,' I grinned at him. 'And I come of Irish stock.'

'Ah, I had forgotten,' he said.

Taafe looked after us like Bunter looked after Lord Peter Wimsey. The meals were on time and excellently cooked and the room kept immaculately tidy, but never a word could I get out of Taafe. He would obey instructions but when I sought to draw him into conversation he would look at me with his big blue eyes and keep his mouth tightly shut. I didn't hear him say one word the whole time I was imprisoned in that room, and I came to the conclusion he was dumb.

There was always another man outside the bedroom door. Sometimes I would catch a glimpse of him as Taafe came into the room, a dim and shadowy figure in the corridor. I never saw his face. I thought hard about him and came to a swift conclusion. It would be impossible for one man to keep up a twenty-four hour guard duty, so there would be three of them, at least. That meant at least five in the house, and maybe more.

I didn't see any women; it was a purely masculine establishment.

I checked on the bars of the windows, both in the bathroom and the bedroom, and Slade watched me with a sardonic amusement which I ignored. It seemed that to get out that way was impossible; it was the double-barred arrangement, inside and out, that was the trouble. Besides, Taafe checked them, too. I came out of the bathroom once to find him on a tour of inspection, making very thoroughly sure they hadn't been tampered with.

Fatface came to see us from time to time. He was affability itself and spent time by the hour discoursing on world affairs, the situation in Red China and the prospects for South Africa in Test Cricket. He would join us in a drink but took care not to take too much.

That gave me an idea. I took care to appear to drink a

lot, both in his presence and out of it. He watched me swig the brandy and made no comment when I became maudlin. Luckily I have a hard head, harder than I allowed to appear, and I took damned good care not to drink too much in Fatface's absence, although I contrived to fool Slade as well. I didn't know that I could trust Slade very much if things came to the crunch. It was with regret that I poured many a half-bottle of good hooch into the lavatory pan before pulling the chain for the night.

I've always found it good policy to appear to be what I'm not, and if Fatface and his mob thought I was a drunk then that might give me a slight edge when I needed it. There was certainly no attempt to stop me drinking. Taafe would take away the dead soldiers every morning and replace them with full bottles, and not a smile would crack his iron features. Slade, however, came to treat me with unreserved contempt.

Slade didn't play chess, but all the same I asked Fatface if he could rustle up a set of chessmen and a board as I wanted to work out chess problems. 'So you play chess,' he said interestedly. 'I'll give you a game, if you like. I'm not a bad player.'

He wasn't a bad player at all, though not as good as Cossie, but Cossie had more time to practise. He was certainly better than me, and after the first couple of games he gave me two pawns' advantage and I still had to battle to beat him.

Once, as we finished a game, he said, 'Alcohol and the type of concentration needed in chess don't mix, Rearden.'

I poured another slug of Oude Meester. 'I don't intend to take it up professionally,' I said indifferently. 'Here's to you . . . er . . . what the hell is your name, anyway?'

He kept a blank face. 'I don't think that matters.'

I giggled drunkenly. 'I think of you as Fatface.'

He was miffed at that and inclined to take umbrage. 'Well, I have to call you *something*,' I pointed out reasonably.

'What do you expect me to do? Whistle or shout "Hey, you!"'

But that crack lost me a chess partner.

The *Zürich Ausführen Handelsbank* cheque came a week after I had woken up in that room, and it was long enough for Slade and I to get on each other's nerves. I thought of the Swiss numbered account, of Mackintosh and of the slim chances of escape. What Slade thought about I don't know but he also became increasingly restless.

Once he was taken out of the room under guard, and when he returned an hour later, I said, 'What was that about?'

'A business conference,' he said enigmatically, and lapsed into silence.

My turn came the next day. I was taken downstairs and into a pleasant room which had just one fault – the curtains were drawn. The Scarperers were too bloody efficient for my own good; even here they were taking no chances of me finding out where I was.

Fatface came in and laid a cheque on the table. He unscrewed the cap of a fountain pen and put the pen down next to the cheque. 'The account number,' he said briefly.

I sat down and picked up the pen – and hesitated. Numbered accounts are funny things, and the number is something you guard as jealously as the combination of your safe.

I had to make this look good because he would be expecting it. I put down the pen, and said, 'Look, Fatface; any jiggery-pokery with this account and you'll wish you'd never been born. You take out of the account exactly the amount set out on this cheque – 200,000 Swiss francs and not a centime more. If you clean out this account I'll find you and break your back.'

'Finding me might prove impossible,' he said suavely.

'Don't bank on it, buster; don't bank on it.' I stared at

him. 'You've had me checked pretty thoroughly so you know my record. People have tried things on before, you know; and I have a reputation which you ought to know about by now. The word has got about that it's unprofitable to cross Rearden.' I put a lot of finality in my voice. 'You'd get found.'

If he was nervous, he didn't show it, except that he swallowed before speaking. 'We have a reputation to keep up, too. There'll be no tampering with your account.'

'All right,' I said gruffly, and picked up the pen again. 'Just so we understand each other.' Carefully I wrote the number – that long sequence of digits and letters which I had memorized at Mrs Smith's insistence – and put a stroke on the uprights of the sevens in the continental manner. 'How long will it take?'

He picked up the cheque and peered at it, then flapped it in the air to dry the ink. 'Another week.'

I watched the cheque fluttering in his hand and suddenly felt cold. Now I was totally committed.

II

Three days later they took Slade away and he didn't come back. I missed him. He had become an irritant but once he had gone I felt lonely and oddly apprehensive. I did not like at all the idea of us being separated and I had assumed that we would be going along the escape route together.

Fatface had taken a dislike to me and had stopped his social visits so I spent long hours at the window, screening my face behind the pot plants, and watched the courtyard through rain and sunshine. There wasn't much to see; just the unused gravel drive to the house and the trim lawn, much blackbird-pecked.

There was one peculiar thing that happened every morning at about the same time. I would hear the *clip-clip* of hooves; not the heavy *clip-clop* of a horse, but the lighter sound as of a pony, and accompanied by a musical clinking noise. It would stop and there would be more clinks and clanks and sometimes the faint piping whistle of a man pleased with himself. Then the *clip-clip* would begin again and fade away into the distance. And once, at this time, I saw the shadow of a man fall athwart the entrance to the courtyard, although I did not see him.

On an occasion when Fatface made a rare appearance I tried to talk my way out. 'Christ, I wish I could get some exercise,' I said. 'What about letting me stretch my legs in the courtyard?'

He shook his head.

'You can have a couple of your goons watching me,' I said, but then gave up as I saw I was making no impression. 'I should have stayed in the nick,' I grumbled. 'At least there was an exercise yard.'

Fatface laughed. 'And look what happened when you used it,' he pointed out. 'You got away. No, Rearden; if you want exercise do some physical jerks in this room.'

I shrugged and poured another drink. Fatface looked at me contemptuously. 'You'll rot your liver, Rearden. You'd better do some exercise if only to sweat the booze out of your system.'

'There's damn-all to do except drink,' I said sullenly, and took a swallow of brandy. I was glad he'd fallen for the line I was feeding him, even though it was becoming a strain to keep up. Reckoning by the dead soldiers Fatface would think I was getting through a bottle and a half a day, and when he was in the room I had to drink heavily in order to keep up the pretence. On this occasion I had drunk a quarter of a bottle in under an hour. I'm a fair drinker but my head was beginning to spin.

'What's the matter?' he asked. 'Getting edgy?' He smiled

mirthlessly. 'Could it be there's nothing in that bank account? Could it be there is no bank account at all?' He stretched out his legs and looked at me thoughtfully. 'We know you were shopped, Rearden; and the story is that it was your partner who shopped you. I know you deny it, but it won't do you any good at all if your partner has skipped with all the loot leaving you holding the bag. I had my doubts about you when I heard Cosgrove's report.'

'You'll get your money,' I said. 'My mate will have seen me right.'

'I sincerely hope so,' he said. 'For your sake.'

But Fatface was right – I *was* getting edgy. I snapped at Taafe irritably when he brought my meals. It made no difference; he just looked at me with those baby blue eyes set in that battered face, said nothing and went about his business leaving me to pace the room and ignore the food.

The hours and days slipped by. Every morning I heard the *clip-clip* of the pony and the pleasantly fluting whistle; every day my chances became slimmer.

At last it happened.

Fatface came into the room. 'Well,' he said in an unusually jovial voice. 'You've surprised me, Rearden.'

'I have?'

'Yes. I rather think you've been playing fast and loose. We cashed your cheque.'

'I'm glad to hear it,' I said. 'I hope there was enough in the account to cover it.'

'Quite enough,' he said. 'You've been trying to lead me up the garden path, haven't you?'

'My God!' I said. 'I *told* you the money would be there.' I laughed a little uncertainly. 'You're like the man in Moscow who said, "Schmuel, you told me you were going to Minsk so I would think you were going to Pinsk, and you fooled me by going to Minsk, anyway. I can't believe a thing you say."'

'A very interesting illustration,' said Fatface drily. 'Anyway, the money was there – all we needed.'

'Good!' I said. 'When do I leave?'

He gestured. 'Sit down. There's something we have to discuss.'

I walked around him to the liquor cabinet and poured a drink. This time I really needed it – I never *had* been absolutely sure of Mackintosh. I splashed water into the glass and sat down at the table. 'I'll be bloody glad to get out of this room.'

'I daresay you will,' said Fatface. He regarded me in silence for a long time, then said at last, 'There's just one snag. It's only a small detail, but it may prove to be an insuperable obstacle. Still, if you can explain it satisfactorily – and I don't mean explain it *away* – I see no reason why we can't carry on as planned.'

'I don't know what in hell you're talking about,' I said bluntly.

He lifted his eyebrows. 'Don't you? I'm sure you do. Think hard.'

'Don't play games, Fatface. If you've got anything to say, then spit it out.'

'All right,' he said. 'But *I'm* not playing games.' He leaned forward. 'Now, I know you're not Rearden but, for the record, I would like to know who the devil you are.'

It was as though a giant had gripped me hard and squeezed me in the belly, but I think I kept my face straight. 'Are you crazy?' I said.

'You know I'm not.'

I took a deep breath. 'Well, I think you are. What is this? Are you trying to welsh now you've got the loot?' I stuck my finger under his nose. 'I wouldn't try that, my friend; you'll come unstuck so bloody fast.'

'You're at a disadvantage,' said Fatface calmly. 'You're in no position to threaten anyone about anything. And I'd stop playing the innocent if I were you. You're not Rearden and we know it.'

'I'd like to see you prove it,' I said tightly.

'Don't be a damned fool – we *have* proved it.' He leaned back in his chair. 'You surely didn't think we pass a man on the escape line without checking him thoroughly – turning him inside out? We had you checked in South Africa and you failed the test. No police force is incorruptible – not the British police and not the South African police. If you are Rearden you must know John Vorster Square – you've been bounced in and out of there often enough.'

'But they never could prove anything,' I said.

'Yes, it's police headquarters in Johannesburg, isn't it?' He waved his hand. 'Oh, I'm sure you know the geography of Johannesburg well enough – but that doesn't prove that you are Rearden.'

'You haven't proved otherwise yet.'

'We have a friend in John Vorster Square, a brave policeman who does occasional odd jobs for us. He checked the files on Rearden and sent us a copy of Rearden's fingerprints. You've had it, chum, because they certainly don't match your dabs – and don't think we haven't tried over and over again, just to make sure.' He pointed to the glass I was holding. 'We've had plenty of chances to get your prints, you know.'

I stared at him for a long time. 'I know what a John Vorster Square dab-sheet looks like,' I said. 'I ought to – I've seen enough of them. You bring yours to me and I'll put my dabs anywhere you like for comparison.'

A veiled look filmed his eyes. 'All right,' he said abruptly. 'We'll do that. But I'll tell you something – you'll not leave this house alive until we know exactly who you are and what the hell you're doing here.'

'You know what I'm doing here,' I said tiredly. 'You

bloody well brought me here. You've got your boodle, now keep your side of the bargain.'

He stood up. 'I'll be back tomorrow bright and early. That will give you plenty of time to think up a good story.' He pressed the service button. 'It had better be a true story.'

The door clicked unlocked and he stalked out.

I sat and looked at the amber liquid in the glass before me. Fatface was full of good ideas. Perhaps it would be better to think up not one story but two – the true story and a plausible false one. It would be difficult; I'm a pretty good liar when the need arises, but I never was much good at sustained fiction.

III

Where does a thing like this begin? I suppose one might be logical and say it began at birth, but that's the trouble with logic – it leads to silly conclusions. Again, one might say it began in Johannesburg but it was only because of who I was – and what I was – that led to me being chosen, and so the roots go further back. Anyway, Johannesburg seemed to be a convenient point to begin, so I started to think of Jo'burg, that overgrown mining camp where the streets are paved with gold.

It was a bright sunny morning with not a cloud in the sky, something which might lighten the spirits of an Englishman but doesn't do a damn thing for a South African because most mornings are bright and sunny and clouds in winter are as rare as hens' teeth. I lived in Hillbrow in a flat in one of the towering blocks of concrete overlooking the city – the city which, at that moment, was covered with its usual layer of greasy smog. On and off, for twenty years, the City Fathers have been thinking of introducing the smokeless zone system, but they haven't got round to it yet.

A man living on his own either lives like a pig or develops certain labour-saving knacks, short-cuts like the egg in the coffee percolator. Within twenty minutes of getting up I was on my way down to the street. In the foyer I opened my personal letter-box and collected the day's mail – three of those nasty envelopes with windows in them which I stuck into my pocket unopened – and a letter from Lucy.

I looked at it a little blankly. I hadn't heard from Lucy for over six years – six slow and uneventful years – and I couldn't really believe it at first. I read the letter again. It was just a quickly scrawled note really; green ink on expensive, deckle-edged writing paper.

> Darling,
>
> I'm in Johannesburg for a quick visit. Could I see you again for old times' sake? I'll be at the Zoo Lake restaurant at midday. I've changed, darling, I really have – so I'll be wearing a white gardenia. I don't want you to put your foot in it by accosting the wrong girl.
>
> Please come, darling; I'm looking forward to seeing you so much.
>
> Ever yours,
> Lucy.

I sniffed the sheet of paper and caught a delicate fragrance. Lucy was up to her old tricks again. I put the note into my breast pocket and went back to my flat to telephone the office. I forget what excuse I used but I really couldn't tell the boss I wanted the day off to see an old girl friend. Then I took the car for servicing; it could be I would need it in a hurry and it had better be in good shape.

At a quarter to twelve I was drifting along the road towards the Zoo Lake. The expanses of winter-yellowed grass were dotted with black nannies looking after their young charges and, in the distance, the lake twinkled under the hot sun. I put the car in the restaurant car park and wandered slowly down to the water's edge where people were feeding the birds.

There was nobody around who looked like Lucy. At least no one was wearing a gardenia. I looked across the lake at the people boating inexpertly then turned to go back to the restaurant where, just outside, a sand-coloured man sat on a bench fanning himself with his hat. He wore a white gardenia.

I walked over and sat beside him. 'Lucy?'

He turned and looked at me with curiously naked eyes. 'Lucy!' he said venomously. 'Ever since that Russian operation in Switzerland during the war the security clots have gone nuts on the name.' He put on his hat. 'I know who you are – I'm Mackintosh.'

'Glad to know you,' I said formally.

He cast a speculative eye at the lake. 'If I happened to be a crackerjack secret service man I'd suggest that we hire a boat and row into the middle of that bit of water so we could talk privately. But that's nonsense, of course. What I suggest is that we have an early lunch here. We'll be just as private, providing we don't shout, we'll be a bloody sight more comfortable, and I won't run the risk of making a damned fool of myself in a boat.'

'Suits me,' I said. 'I didn't have much breakfast.'

He arose and took the gardenia from his lapel to drop it into a convenient waste basket. 'Why people have this fetish for the sexual organs of vegetables is beyond me,' he said. 'Come on.'

We found a table in a corner in the outside court where a vine-covered trellis protected us from the heat of the sun. Mackintosh looked around and said appreciatively, 'This is a nice place. You South Africans know how to live well.'

I said, 'If you know who I am then you know I'm not a South African.'

'Of course,' he said, and took a notebook from his pocket. 'Let me see – ah, yes; Owen Edward Stannard, born in Hong Kong in 1934, educated in Australia.' He reeled off a string of schools. 'At university specialized in the study of Asiatic languages. Was recruited by a department that it is better not to mention while still at university. Worked in the field in Cambodia, Viet-Nam, Malaysia and Indonesia under a variety of covers. Was captured in Indonesia during the upheaval which disposed of Sukarno and cover badly blown.'

He looked up. 'I understand you had a nasty time there.'

I smiled. 'There are no scars.' That was true – no scars that were visible.

'Umph!' he said, and returned to his notebook. 'It was considered that your usefulness was at an end in the Far East so you were pulled out and sent to South Africa as a sleeper. That was seven years ago.' He snapped the notebook closed and put it back into his pocket. 'That would be while South Africa was still in the Commonwealth.'

'That's right,' I said.

'Our masters are not very trusting folk, are they? Anyway, you're here as a sleeper; you say nothing and do nothing until you're called upon – is that right?' He wagged a finger. 'Forgive the recapitulation but I'm from a different department. All this secret service stuff strikes me as being a bit comic opera, and I want to see if I've got it right.'

'You've got it right,' I assured him.

Serious conversation stopped then because a waiter came to take our order. I ordered crayfish cardinal because it wasn't often that someone stood me a lunch, while Mackintosh had something with a salad. We shared a bottle of wine.

When the dishes were on the table and it was safe to talk again Mackintosh said, 'Now I want to get this absolutely straight. Are you known to the police here – or to the security forces?'

'Not that I know of,' I said. 'I think my cover is safe.'

'So you've never had a prison sentence?'

'No.'

'What about civil cases?'

I considered. 'Just the usual things. I've had a couple of parking tickets. And a couple of years ago I had a legal barney with a man who owed me money; it came to a court case.'

'Who won?'

'He did, damn it!' I said feelingly.

Mackintosh smiled. 'I've been reading your record so I know most of these things. I just wanted to see your reactions. So what it comes to is that you have a clean record here as far as the local coppers are concerned.'

I nodded. 'That sums it up.'

'Good,' he said. 'Because you are going to be working with the South African police and it would never do if they knew you to be a British plant. I couldn't see them co-operating in those circumstances.' He nibbled on a lettuce leaf. 'Have you ever been to England?'

'Never,' I said, and hesitated. 'You ought to know that I've built up my cover with a slightly anti-British bias. It's a quite common thing here for even English-speaking people to be anti-British – especially since Rhodesia blew up. In the circumstances I thought it inadvisable to take a holiday in England.'

'I think we can forget your cover for a moment,' said Mackintosh. 'I'm authorized to pull you out if I find it necessary. The job I'm considering you for will be in England.'

It was very strange. All my adult life had been spent in the service of Britain and I'd never even seen the place. 'I'd like that,' I said.

'You might not like it when you hear what the job is,' said Mackintosh grimly. He sampled the wine. 'Very nice,' he said appreciatively, 'if a touch acid.' He put down the glass. 'What do you know about the British prison system?'

'Nothing.'

'I'll let you have a copy of the Mountbatten Report,' he said. 'You'll find it fascinating reading. But I'll give you the gist of it now. Lord Mountbatten found that the British prisons are as full of holes as a Swiss cheese. Do you know how many escapes there are each year?'

'No. There was something about it in the papers a couple of years ago, but I didn't read it up closely.'

'More than five hundred. If it's any less than that they think they've had a good year. Of course, most of the escapees are picked up quite soon, but a small percentage get clean away – and that small percentage is rising. It's a troublesome situation.'

'I can imagine it would be,' I said. I couldn't see his point; there was nothing in this to concern me.

Mackintosh wasn't a man to miss a nuance in a tone of voice. He looked me in the eye and said quietly, 'I don't give a damn how many murderers or rapists, homicidal maniacs or ordinary small time thieves get out of gaol. That's the worry of the prison officers and the police. My field is state security and, as far as I'm concerned, the situation is getting out of hand. The Prime Minister thinks likewise and he's told me to do something about it.'

'Oh!' I said uncertainly.

'Oh!' he echoed disgustedly. 'Look at it this way. We put Blake away for forty-two years, not altogether as a punishment but to keep him out of the hands of the Russians. Within five years he flies the coop and pops up in Moscow where he chirps his head off.'

He looked broodingly into his glass. 'Suppose Blake hadn't got clean away – suppose he'd been picked up in a month. The police would be happy and so would the prison officers, but damn it all to hell, I wouldn't! I'd want to know what the devil he'd been doing that month – who he'd been talking to. See my point?'

I nodded. 'If that happened the major reason for gaoling him would disappear. To slap him back in chokey for another forty years would be like closing the stable door after the horse has gone.'

'The horse being the information in Blake's head – not the man himself.' Mackintosh moved restlessly. 'They're building a high security prison on the Isle of Wight. Mountbatten wants to call it Vectis which shows that, among other things, he's had a classical education. A very able man, Mountbatten. He took one look at the plans of this high class chicken coop and demonstrated how easy it would be to get a man out.'

He looked at me expectantly as though he wanted me to say something, so I obliged. 'To *get* a man out?'

He grinned. 'I'm pleased to see you live up to the good things your dossier records of you.' He held out his glass. 'I rather like this wine.'

I gave him a refill. 'It's nice to know I'm appreciated.'

'If you read the Mountbatten Report – particularly the bits towards the end where he discusses this new prison – you'll find yourself wondering if you haven't come across a major work of science fiction. Closed-circuit television with delay lines and electronic logic circuits which trigger an alarm if anything moves in the field of vision is one nice idea – that's for the defence, of course. For the attack there are helicopters and rocket-powered jump suits, for God's sake! Very James Bondery. Do you get the drift of it?'

'Yes,' I said slowly. 'Organization.'

'Right!' said Mackintosh. 'For the first time in years someone has come up with a brand new crime. Crime is just like any other business – it's conducted only for profit – and someone has figured a way to make a profit out of getting people out of prison. I suppose it started with the Great Train Robbery; those boys were given exceptionally heavy sentences – Biggs and Wilson got thirty years each – but they had money and were able to buy an organization.'

He sighed. 'Sometimes I wonder if the judges know what the devil they're doing. A murderer can be out in ten years or less, but watch your step if you commit a crime against property. Anyway, an organization was set up, dedicated to springing long-term prisoners who could pay enough, and you'd be surprised how many of those there are. And once such an organization gets going, like any other business it tends to expand, and whoever is running it has gone looking for custom – and he doesn't care where the money comes from, either.'

'The Russians?'

'Who else,' said Mackintosh sourly. 'I don't care if all the train robbers fly the coop and live the life of Riley on the Riviera, but when it comes to state security then something must be done.' He frowned. 'If I had my way such security risks would be collected together in a special prison and guarded by the army – military police empowered to kill if necessary. But our masters prefer not to do it that way.'

I said curiously, 'Where do I come into all this?'

'I haven't finished putting you in the picture,' he said irritably. 'The PM wanted something done about it – so something was done. The police had a crack at it, and so did the Special Branch and the more shady and esoteric counter-intelligence units. They all got nowhere. There was one occasion when they did get a bit close to it; a prisoner already in gaol expressed a willingness to talk. Guess what happened to him.'

I'm a realist, so I said flatly, 'He died suddenly.'

'Oh, he was killed, all right,' said Mackintosh. 'But this gang sprung him from prison to do it. Can't you see the flaming impudence of it? This organization is so bloody sure of itself that it can take a man out of one of Her Majesty's prisons who doesn't want to go. One cheep from him and he'd still be alive – but they were still able to spring him. His body was found three days later; he'd been shot through the back of the head.'

'I didn't see any reports on that,' I said.

'It was put under security wraps immediately,' said Mackintosh a little tiredly. 'Nobody wanted a thing like *that* to be aired publicly. There's a veiled reference to it in the Mountbatten Report – look at paragraph 260.'

'Where do I come in?' I asked again.

'I'll come to you when I'm good and ready. Now, my business is state security, and you can put out of your head any guff about counter-intelligence cloak-and-dagger stuff. I work on a quite different plane, at Cabinet level, in fact – responsible and reporting to only the Prime Minister. Since everybody else has fallen down on this job he has given me the sole and total responsibility of getting the job done in my own peculiar way – but not in my own time.' He rubbed the top of his head. 'Of course, time is a relative thing, as I explained to the PM and he agreed. But let's hope there are no more security escapes while I'm in charge, because it's my head that's on the block.'

He looked around and waved at a waiter. 'Let's have coffee – and I think I'll have a van der Hum; I believe in sampling the wine of the country. Will you join me?'

'I'll have a Drambuie,' I said drily.

He ordered the coffee and the liqueurs, then said abruptly, 'Ever heard of a man called Rearden – Joseph Rearden?'

I thought about it for a while. 'No.'

'I didn't think you would. Rearden is – or was – a criminal. A very good one, too. Clever, intelligent and resourceful; somewhat like you, I'd say.'

'Thanks for the compliment,' I said. 'He's dead?'

'He was killed three weeks ago in South-West Africa. No funny business suspected – just a plain ordinary car crash. The God of Motorists sacrifices good and bad alike. The point is that no one knows he's dead, except you, me and a few highly placed South African coppers. When the PM gave me this Godawful job certain facilities were placed at my disposal, and I immediately began to look for someone like Rearden – a newly dead rotten egg whose death could be hushed up. He could have been found in Canada, Australia, New Zealand, the States or, even, South Africa. The fact is that he turned up in South Africa. Here's his photograph.'

I laid it face down on the table as the waiter served the coffee and only turned it up when we were alone again. Mackintosh watched me approvingly as I scanned the picture. He said, 'As soon as I had Rearden I began to look for someone who looked like Rearden, someone who could pass for a South African. Computers are marvellous gadgets – one came up with you in twenty minutes.'

'So it's going to be a substitution,' I said. 'I've done that kind of thing before, but it's risky. I could be spotted very easily.'

'I don't think so,' said Mackintosh confidently. 'To begin with, you'll be in England where Rearden has never been and, even so, you won't be moving about England much so it's unlikely you'll bump into any of his old pals.'

I said, 'What happened to Rearden's body?'

'He was buried under another name. I pulled some strings.'

'Tough luck on his family,' I said. 'Did he have a wife?'

'No wife – and his parents will get along without him.'

I looked at this spare man with the thinning sandy hair and the colourless eyelashes and thought that he was a pretty ruthless bastard. I wondered how I would get along with him in this peculiar arrangement he was planning. 'So I'm Rearden,' I said. 'And I'm in England. What then?'

'Not so fast,' said Mackintosh. 'Although Rearden was clever he lost – once only. He served a prison sentence in Pretoria quite a while ago. Do you know anything about South African prisons?'

'Not a thing, thank God!'

'You'd better learn. I'll have a man give you a course on prison conditions and the slang – especially the slang.' He offered me a twisted smile. 'It might be a good idea if you did time for a month to get the right idea. I can arrange that.' I could see him turning the idea over in his mind and rejecting it. He shook his head. 'No, that won't do. It's too risky.'

I was glad of that; I don't particularly like gaols. He drained his coffee cup. 'Let's leave here; the place is filling up and I'd like to discuss the rest of it in greater privacy.' He paid the bill and we left the restaurant and strolled into the middle distance to sit under a gum tree where there were no ears within fifty yards.

He took out a pipe and started to fill it. 'All the people who have tried to crack this organization have failed. They've tried it from the outside and failed, and they've tried penetration and failed. They've tried to ring in fake gaolbirds – and failed. The organization has fantastically good security because we know as much now as we did at the beginning – and that's only one thing. The organization is known to the underworld as the Scarperers, and that doesn't get us very far.'

He struck a match. 'Stannard, this is a volunteer's job, and I'll have to ask you to make up your mind now. I can't tell you anything more – I've already told you too much. I suppose I must tell you that if anything goes wrong it'll go badly for you – and your death may not be the worst thing that can happen. Not in my book, at any rate. It's a tricky and dangerous task and, I don't mind telling you, I wouldn't volunteer for it myself. I can't be more honest than that.'

I lay back on the grass and looked up at the sky, leaf-dappled through the branches of the gum tree. My life in South Africa had been calm and uneventful. Seven years before I had been in pretty bad shape and I'd sworn I'd never do that kind of thing again. I suppose my bosses had seen that frame of mind and had given me the job of a sleeper in South Africa as a sort of sinecure – a reward for past services. God knows, I had done nothing to earn the retainer that was piling up quite nicely in that British bank account and which I had never touched.

But time heals everything and of late I had been restless, wishing that something would happen – an earthquake – anything. And here was my earthquake in the person of this insignificant-looking man, Mackintosh – a man who hob-nobbed with the Cabinet, who chit-chatted about security with the Prime Minister. I had a vague idea of what he was getting at and it didn't seem difficult. Risky, perhaps; but not too difficult. I wasn't afraid of a gang of English crooks; they couldn't be worse than the boys I'd been up against in Indonesia. I'd seen whole towns full of corpses there.

I sat up. 'All right; I volunteer.'

Mackintosh looked at me a little sadly and thumped me gently on the arm. 'You're a lunatic,' he said. 'But I'm glad to have you. Perhaps we need a little lunacy on this job; orthodox methods haven't got us anywhere.'

He pointed at me with the stem of his pipe. 'This is top-secret. From now on only three people will know about it; you, me and one other – not even the PM knows.' He chuckled sardonically. 'I tried to tell him but he didn't want to know. He knows how my mind works and he said he wanted to keep his hands clean – he said he might have to answer questions in the House and he didn't want to be put in the position of lying.'

I said, 'What about the South African police?'

'They know nothing,' said Mackintosh flatly. 'It's a *quid pro quo* – a favour returned. They might do a bit of digging into your background, though. Can it stand it?'

'It should,' I said. 'It was designed by experts.'

Mackintosh drew gently on his pipe and blew out a plume of smoke. 'Other people have tried to penetrate this damned organization and they've failed – so we start from there and ask, "Why did they fail?" One of the more promising gambits was to ring in a fake prisoner and wait for advances to be made. At one time there were no less than eight of these decoys scattered through the British prisons. Not one of them was contacted. What does that suggest to you?'

'The Scarperers have a good intelligence service,' I said. 'I'll bet they do a preliminary check before contact.'

'I agree – and that means that our bait, which is Rearden, must stand up to rigorous scrutiny. There must be no cracks in the cover at all. Anything else?'

'Not that I can think of off-hand.'

'Use your loaf,' said Mackintosh with an air of disgust. 'The crime, man; the crime! Rearden – or, rather, you – is going to commit a crime in England. You'll be caught – I'll see to that – you'll be tried and you'll be jugged. And it has to be a particular form of crime; a crime which involves a lot of money and where the money isn't recovered. The Scarperers have to be convinced that you can pay hard cash for your escape. Now, what does that suggest to you – in view of what I've already told you?'

'Nothing much,' I said. 'It shouldn't be too difficult to arrange.'

'No, it shouldn't be too difficult,' said Mackintosh in an odd voice. 'Look here, Stannard; this is going to be a genuine crime – don't you understand that? Nothing else will do. I am going to plan, and you are going to execute, a crime of some magnitude. We are going to steal a considerable sum of money from some inoffensive British citizen who will scream to high heaven. There's going to be no fake about it because . . .' He spaced his words very distinctly. '. . . I . . . will . . . not . . . risk . . . breaking . . . security.'

He turned and said very earnestly, 'If this is so then when you are tried and gaoled you will be in the jug for a perfectly genuine crime, and if anything goes wrong there will be nothing that I, or anyone else, can do about it. If you get fourteen years then you'll rot in prison for your sentence if the Scarperers don't contact you. And the reason for that is because I *cannot* compromise security on this operation. Are you willing to risk it?'

I took a deep breath. 'Christ! You're asking a hell of a lot, aren't you?'

'It's the way it's got to be,' he said doggedly. 'A trained man like you should be able to get out of any leaky British prison without half trying. But you won't, damn you! You'll sit on your backside and wait for the Scarperers to get you, no matter how long they take to make up their minds. You'll bloody well wait, do you hear?'

I looked into his fanatical eyes and said very gently, 'I hear. Don't worry; I'm not going to back out now. I gave you my word.'

He took a deep breath and relaxed. 'Thanks, Stannard.' He grinned at me. 'I wasn't worried about you – not *too* worried.'

'I've been wondering about something,' I said. 'Mountbatten investigated the prisons when Blake flew the coop. That was quite a long time ago. Why all the sudden rush now?'

Mackintosh reached out and knocked out his pipe on the trunk of the tree. 'A good question,' he agreed. 'Well, for one thing, the effect of Mountbatten is wearing off. When the Report came out and the prisons tightened security every sociologist and prison reformer in Britain let out an outraged howl – and I'm not saying they were wrong, either. There are two ways of regarding prisons – as places of punishment and as places of rehabilitation. The suddenly tightened security knocked rehabilitation right out of the window and the penal reformers say it did ten years of damage in six months.'

He shrugged. 'They're probably right, but that's outside

my field. I'm not interested in civil prisoners – it's the Blakes and Lonsdales of this world who are my meat. When you catch them you can either put them up against a wall and shoot them, or you can put them in chokey. But you imprison them not to punish and not to rehabilitate, but to keep them out of circulation because of what they know.'

There was nothing in this to explain the question I had asked, so I prompted him. 'So what now?'

'There's a big fish coming down the line,' he said. 'The biggest we've caught yet. God knows, Blake was big enough, but this man is a shark to Blake's tiddler – and he must not escape. I've pleaded with the PM to establish a special prison for this type of prisoner but he says it's against policy, and so Slade goes into the general prison system, admittedly as a high risk man.'

'Slade!' I said thoughtfully. 'Never heard of him.'

'He's in hospital,' said Mackintosh. 'He was shot through the hips when he was caught. When he's fit he'll stand trial, and if we handed out sentences like the Texans he'd get five thousand years. As it is, we must keep him secure for the next twenty – after that it won't matter very much.'

'Twenty years! He must know a hell of a lot.'

Mackintosh turned a disgusted face towards me. 'Can you imagine that a Russian – and Slade is a Russian – could get to be second-in-command of an important department of British Intelligence concerned with counter-espionage in Scandinavia? Well, it happened, and Sir David Taggart, the damned fool who put him there, has been kicked upstairs – he's now Lord Taggart with a life peerage.' He snorted. 'But he won't be making any speeches or doing any voting. If he knows what's good for him he'll keep his mouth permanently shut.'

He blinked his colourless eyelashes and said in a passionately suppressed voice, 'The man who caught Slade was a man whom Taggart had fired for inefficiency, for God's sake!' He rapped his pipe against the tree with such force that I thought it would break. 'Amateurs!' he said in a scathing voice. 'These bloody amateurs running their piddling private armies. They make me sick.'

'How do I relate to Slade?' I asked.

'I'm going to try to put you next to him,' he said. 'And that will mean breaking the law. What Slade knows is sheer dynamite and I'd break every law in Britain, from sodomy upwards, to keep that bastard inside where he belongs.' He chuckled and thumped my arm. 'We're not just going to bend the laws of England, Stannard; we're going to smash them.'

I said a little shakily, 'Now I *know* why the Prime Minister wouldn't listen to you.'

'Oh, yes,' said Mackintosh matter-of-factly. 'It would make him accessory to the crime, and he's too much the gentleman to get his hands dirty. Besides, it would lie heavily on his conscience.' He looked up at the sky and said musingly, 'Funny animals, politicians.'

I said, 'Do you know what kind of a tree this is?'

He turned and looked at it. 'No, I don't.'

'It's a gum tree,' I said. 'The thing I'll be up if this operation doesn't pan out. Take a good look at it.'

IV

I suppose you could call Mackintosh a patriot – of sorts. There don't seem to be many avowed patriots around these days; it has become the fashion to sneer at patriotism – the TV satire programmes jeer at it, and to the with-it, swinging set it's a dead issue. So with patriots so few on the ground you can't pick and choose too freely. Certainly, to a casual eye Mackintosh bore a remarkable resemblance to a dyed-in-the-wool fascist; his God was Britain – not the Britain of green fields and pleasant country lanes, of stately buildings and busy towns, but the *idea* of Britain incorporated in the State. He took his views directly from Plato, Machiavelli and Cromwell who, if you think about it, aren't all that different from Mussolini, Hitler and Stalin.

But there was more to him than that as I found out later – much later.

There was a lot of work to be done and not a great deal of time in which to do it. I studied South African prison conditions with a prison officer, temporarily donning the guise of a sociologist for the occasion. He advised me to read the works of Herman Charles Bosman which was a superfluity as I had already done so. Bosman, possibly the best writer in English South Africa has produced, knew all about prison conditions – he had done a stretch for killing his step-brother and he wrote illuminatingly about his experiences in Pretoria Central Prison – Pretoria Tronk, in the vernacular – which conveniently was where Rearden had served his sentence.

I also studied Rearden's record, culled from the files of John Vorster Square. There was not much fact and a hell of a lot of conjecture in that file. Rearden had been imprisoned only once and that for a comparatively minor offence, but the conjecture was lurid. He was suspected of practically every crime in the book from burglary to drug-smuggling, from armed robbery to illicit gold buying. He was a many-faceted character, all nerve and intelligence, whose erratic and unexpected switches in criminal activity had kept him out of trouble. He would have made a good intelligence agent.

I smiled at that. Perhaps Mackintosh had been right when he said that Rearden was like me. I had no illusions about myself or my job. It was a dirty business with no holds barred and precious little honour, and I was good at it, as would have been Rearden if anyone had had the sense to recruit him. So there we were – birds of a feather – Mackintosh, Rearden and Stannard.

Mackintosh was busy on the upper levels of the job in South Africa – pulling strings. From the way people danced to his tune like marionettes I judged he had been right when he said the Prime Minister had given him 'certain facilities'. This was counter-espionage work at diplomatic level and I wondered what was the *quid pro quo* – what the hell had we done for the South Africans that we should be given this VIP treatment with no questions asked?

Gradually I was transformed into Rearden. A different style of haircut made a lot of difference and I took much trouble with the Transvaal accent, the accent of the Reef towns. I studied photographs of Rearden and copied his way of dress and his stance. It was a pity we had no films of him in action; the way a man moves means a lot. But that I would have to chance.

I said to Mackintosh once, 'You say I'm not likely to run into any of Rearden's pals in England because I'm not going to be at large for very long. That's all very well, but I'm a hell of a lot more likely to run into his mates when I'm in the nick than when I'm walking up Oxford Street.'

Mackintosh looked thoughful. 'That's true. What I can do is this; I'll have a check done on the inhabitants of the prison you're in, and any that have been to South Africa I'll have transferred. There shouldn't be too many and it will minimize your risk. The reason for transfer shouldn't become apparent – prisoners are being transferred all the time.'

He drilled me unmercifully.

'What's your father's name?'

'Joseph Rearden.'

'Occupation?'

'Miner – retired.'

'Mother's name?'

'Magrit.'

'Maiden name?'

'Van der Oosthuizen.'

'Where were you born?'
'Brakpan.'
'The date?'
'28th May, 1934.'
'Where were you in June, 1968?'
'. . . er . . . in Cape Town.'
'Which hotel did you use?'
'Arthur's Seat.'

Mackintosh stuck his finger under my nose. 'Wrong! That was in November of the same year. You'll have to do better than that.'

'I could get away with it if I had to,' I said.

'Maybe. But this has to be a seamless job – no cracks which need papering over. You'd better get down to studying again.'

Again I pushed my nose into the files, if a little resentfully. My God, a man wasn't supposed to remember and account for every minute of his life. But I knew Mackintosh was right. The more I knew about Rearden, the safer I'd be.

At last it was over and Mackintosh was due to return to England. He said, 'The local coppers are a bit worried about you; they're wondering why you've been picked for this job. They're wondering how I was able to lay my hands on an Australian immigrant to impersonate Rearden. I don't think you'll be able to come back here.'

'Will they talk?'

'There'll be no talk,' he said positively. 'There are only a few of the top brass who know about you, and they don't know *why* – that's why they're becoming curious. But it's all top-secret, diplomatic-level, hush-hush stuff and that's something the South Africans are good at. They understand security. As far as the middle and lower levels of the police are concerned – well, they'll be a bit surprised when Rearden gets nabbed in England, but they'll just heave a sigh of relief and cross him off the books for a few years.'

I said, 'If you're right about the Scarperers they'll be doing some extensive checking here in South Africa.'

'It'll stand up,' he said with certainty. 'You've done a good job on this, Stannard.' He smiled. 'When it's all over you'll probably get a medal. There'll be a few private words with the people concerned – insurance company, whoever we rob, and so on. The Home Secretary will probably issue a free pardon and you won't have a stain on your character.'

'If it comes off,' I said. 'If it doesn't, I'll be up that bloody gum tree.' I looked straight at him. 'I want a bit of insurance on this. I know you're nuts on security – and rightly so. As you've organized it there'll be only three people who know about this operation – you, me and one other. I'd like to know who this "other" is, just in case anything happens to you. I'd be in a hell of a mess if you got run over by a bus.'

He thought about that. 'Fair enough,' he said. 'It's my secretary.'

'Your secretary,' I said expressionlessly.

'Oh, Mrs Smith is a very good secretary,' he said. 'Very efficient. She's hard at work on this case now.'

I nodded. 'There's something else,' I said. 'I've been going over possible eventualities. What happens if I'm sprung and Slade isn't?'

'Then you go for the Scarperers, of course.'

'And if Slade is sprung and I'm not?'

Mackintosh shrugged. 'That wouldn't be your fault. We'd have to leave it to the ordinary authorities. Not that I'd like it very much.'

'Try this on for size,' I said. 'Supposing both Slade and I are sprung. What then?'

'Ah,' he said. 'I see what you mean.'

'Yes; I thought you would. Which is the more important? To smash the Scarperers or to take Slade back to the jug?'

He was silent for a moment. 'Slade is obviously the more important, although ideally I'd like you to pull off both jobs should that eventuality arise. As far as taking Slade back to prison goes you may use your own discretion. If he turned up dead I wouldn't shed a single tear. The important thing about Slade is that he must not get loose – he must not communicate any information to a third party.' He flicked his pale blue eyes in my direction. 'Dead men tell no tales.'

So that was it. Orders to kill Slade – at my discretion. I began to understand the Prime Minister's reservations about Mackintosh. A tame hatchet man must be an uncomfortable asset to have around the house. He went to England next day and I followed two months later in response to another letter from Lucy. The crime had been set up.

6

I

I stared at the brandy in the glass. I had been thinking for a long time and I hadn't touched a drop. The time for drinking had gone and the time for thinking had arrived. And I had a hell of a lot to think about.

Everything had gone as Mackintosh had planned. The crime, the trial, the nick, Slade – and the Scarperers. Then things turned sour. They were a clever mob and as keen on security as any professional espionage ring. Here I was, injected into their organization like a drug, and I was no nearer to cracking it than I had been in South Africa.

It was that damned hypodermic syringe in the moving-van that had turned the trick in their favour. I hadn't expected that, nor had I expected this imprisonment. Still, I could see their point; they worked on the 'need to know' principle, and an escapee didn't need to know how he had escaped – just that he had done so. This mob was too bloody professional to be true.

And I had lost Slade.

That was the worst bit, and Mackintosh would rip open my guts for it if ever I got past Fatface. His instructions had been oblique but clear; if there was any possibility of Slade getting clear then I was to kill him. I could have cut his throat with a blunt table knife while he slept, or strangled him with a length of electrical wire from the table lamp. I had done neither.

Of course, if I had killed Slade one night then next morning I would have been a dead man, but that wasn't why I'd refrained. I had weighed the odds and made a number of assumptions – that Slade and I would be going out together; that I still had a chance of escape, taking Slade with me; that my cover was still secure. Not one of those assumptions had proved valid and now things were in one hell of a mess.

I lay on the bed with my hands clasped behind my head and wondered how they had tumbled to the substitution. Fatface was trying to convince me that he knew I wasn't Rearden because of Rearden's fingerprints extracted from his file at John Vorster Square. I knew that to be a damned lie because I had personally substituted my own fingerprints for Rearden's in that very file, with Mackintosh looking on, and any prints coming from that file would match mine.

If Fatface knew I wasn't Rearden it certainly wasn't on account of fingerprints – so why in hell was he trying to kid me?

I thought hard, trying one hypothesis after another. For instance supposing Fatface only suspected I wasn't Rearden – he might try to pull a bluff in the hope that I'd crack. I hadn't cracked, and I'd put him in the position of having to produce those fingerprints which I knew damned well he hadn't got or, if he had, would certainly match mine.

That was one hypothesis among many, but they all boiled down to the same thing – that either Fatface knew for a certainty I wasn't Rearden, or he merely suspected it. And in both cases the problem was how the devil had he done it? Where had I slipped up?

I went back over my actions since my arrival in England and found no flaw. I had done nothing, in either word or deed, to break my cover, and that led me to the nasty suspicion that there had been a leak – a flaw in security.

I thought about Mackintosh. Now there was a tough, ruthless, conniving bastard who would sell his grandmother to boil down for soap if that soap would grease the runway of the Ship of State. I shook my head irritably. That was straining a metaphor pretty far which showed I was tired –

but it was true, all the same. If Mackintosh thought it would serve his purpose to break security on me he would do it without hesitation.

I thought about it hard then rejected the possibility for the time being because I could see no purpose to it. And that left the super-efficient Lucy Smith whom Mackintosh trusted so much and about whom I knew damn-all. There were other possibilities, of course; either of them could have inadvertently broken security, his office could have been bugged by an interested third party, and so on.

I went into the bathroom and doused my face in cold water. To hell with Mackintosh's devious ways! What I had to do now was to find a way out of this trap. There must be less thinking of how I had got into it and more on how to get out.

I wiped my face dry, went back into the bedroom, and sat at the table to review my armoury of weapons. A trained man in my position assembles his weapons as and when he can from the materials at hand. For instance, I had three meals a day at which pepper was on the table. In my pocket was a twist of paper containing enough pepper to blind a man, which could come in useful on an appropriate occasion.

After a few minutes' thought I went to the wardrobe and took out a sock which I half-filled with earth from the row of pot plants on the window ledge, taking a little from each. I hefted the sock, whirled it, and swung it against the palm of my hand. It made a satisfying thump. It wasn't as good as a sandbag – it wasn't all that heavy – but it would do.

There are many ways of getting out of a locked room. You can shoot your way out – if you have a gun. You can set fire to the place, but that's risky; there's no guarantee you'll get out, and it can have disastrous consequences – I've always kept in mind Charles Lamb's story of burnt pig. You can use deception in its many forms but I didn't think these boys would be deceived easily; I'd already tried to con Fatface into letting me walk in the courtyard and he hadn't fallen for it.

That led me to think of Fatface and what he did when he came into the room. He was very careful; the door would click open and he would walk in, closing it behind him and always facing into the room with his back to the door. The man outside would then lock it. Fatface always kept his front to me. I had experimented a bit – trying to get behind him – but he'd never let me. He also carried a gun. When your life may depend on it you notice little details like that, and, no matter how carefully tailored the suit, the bulge shows.

So I had to get behind Fatface and club him with a sockful of wet leaf mould. And that involved a conjuror's trick – he had to believe I was in front of him when I was really behind him. Short of hypnosis I didn't see how I could do it but I tackled the problem.

Presently I went into the bathroom and flushed the water closet. It had no chain being one of those low cistern contraptions operated by a short lever. Then I hunted around for a cord. What I really needed was a ball of string, but that I hadn't got, so I had to improvise.

The light switch in the bathroom was operated, as good buildings regulations insist, by a ceiling pull-switch from which a strong cord hung to a convenient hand level. That gave me four feet. The bedside lamp was wired to a plug on the skirting board behind the bed, and the wire was two-strand, plastic coated, the strands spiralling around each other. When I separated the strands I had a good bit more cord.

There was another lamp on the dressing-table which contributed more, but still not enough, so I was forced to consider other sources. My dressing-gown was of terry-towelling and had a cord which went around the waist. This cord unravelled into several strands which I plaited and, at last, I had enough. In fact, there was enough wire to make a garrotting loop – not as efficient as piano wire, it's true – but I was in no position to complain.

I made a loop on the end of my long cord and slipped it over the lever of the cistern, then ran the cord from the bathroom, around the walls of the bedroom and right up to the door. I could have done with some small pulleys but, instead, I used the insulated staples which had held down the electric wiring and hoped they would hold.

They didn't.

A gentle tug and nothing happened. A harder tug gave the same result. A very hard tug and a staple sprang from the skirting board.

This wasn't working at all.

I went back to the bathroom and flushed the water closet again, using as little pressure on the lever as possible. It was obviously too stiff to be pulled down by my improvised cord, so I had to think of something else. I studied the cistern for a while, and then removed the top, revealing its guts – the ball valve and associated gimmickry invented by that unsung genius, Thomas Crapper. The action of the lever downwards resulted in the movement of a plunger upwards, and I figured it was the friction involved in this mechanism that stiffened the lever action. If I could disconnect that lever and work on the plunger directly I thought I could do it.

Half an hour later I was ready to try again. I had lengthened my cord by means of a stip torn from the sheet; it would show, but that didn't matter in the bathroom. I left the bathroom door ajar and returned to my post at the other end of the cord. I picked it up, crossed my fingers, and pulled with a steady pressure.

The toilet flushed with a welcome and loud squirt of water.

I dropped the cord and carefully surveyed the room, making sure that nothing was out of place, that nothing would give the game away to Fatface when he entered.

Everything was neat and tidy except for the bed I had stripped. I took the sheet I had ripped and tore it into long lengths. I would have a use for those. Then I remade the bed.

There still remained a few things to do. I opened the wardrobe and considered the contents. There was a suit of a decent dark grey, and there was a sports coat with non-matching trousers and brown shoes. I didn't know where I was – country or town – and if I emerged into a town then the suit would be more appropriate; but if I was in the heart of the country the suit would stick out a mile whereas the more informal dress would not be out of place in a town. So I plumped for the sports coat and associated trimmings. I'd also take the hat and the raincoat.

I'd been on the run before and I knew that one of the most difficult things to do is the apparently simple act of washing and the general idea of keeping clean. If my beard grew out a different colour than my hair I'd be an object of attention – that blonde had warned me to shave twice a day. This question of cleanliness is something of which the police are well aware, and in searching for a man on the run a check is routinely made on all public washrooms in railway stations and large hotels.

So I was taking the shaver, a tablet of soap, a face cloth and a hand towel – all of which would fit conveniently into the pockets of the raincoat without bulging too much. I coiled my garrotting wire loosely and fitted it into the sweatband of the hat. Any copper worthy of the name knows one of those when he sees it, and if I was searched I didn't want it to be obvious – I'd be thrown in the nick immediately if it were found.

That also went for the gun – if I could get hold of Fatface's artillery. Which brought me to another question. How far was I justified in using a gun if the occasion arose?

The cult of James Bond has given rise to a lot of nonsense. There are no double-o numbers and there is no 'licence to kill'. As far as I knew I didn't have a number at all, except perhaps a file number like any other employee; certainly no one ever referred to me as number 56, or whatever it was – or even 0056. And agents don't kill just for the hell of it. That doesn't mean that agents never kill, but they kill strictly to order under carefully specified conditions. Elimination by death is regarded with distaste; it's messy and irretrievable, and there are usually other ways of silencing a man which are almost as effective.

Yet sometimes it has to be done and an agent is detailed to do it. Whether this constitutes a licence to kill I wouldn't know; it certainly doesn't grant a general licence to commit unrestricted mayhem. You leave too many unexplained bodies lying around and the secret service stops being secret.

Now, Mackintosh hadn't told me to kill anyone apart from Slade and that meant, generally speaking, no killing. Such unordered deaths are known in the trade as 'accidental' and any agent who is crass enough to cause such an accidental death quickly gets the chop as being unreliable and inept. For an agent to leave a trail of corpses in his wake would cause untold consternation in those little hole-in-the-corner offices in Whitehall which have the innocuous and deceptive names on the doors.

In fact, it came back to the old moral problem – when is a man justified in killing another man? I resolved it by quoting the phrase – 'Kill or be killed!' If I were in danger of being killed then I would kill in self-defence – and not until them. I had killed only one man in my life and that had made me sick to my stomach for two days afterwards.

That settled in my mind, I began planning arson. An inspection of the liquor cabinet showed a bottle and a half of South African brandy, the best part of a bottle of Scotch, ditto gin, and a half-bottle of Drambuie. A few tests showed the brandy and the Drambuie as being most inflammable, although not as fiery as I would have wished.

I was sorry I hadn't developed a taste for rum – there's some nice 100° stuff on the market which would have suited me fine – although God knows what it does to the lining of the stomach.

Then I went to bed and slept the sleep of the morally just.

II

There was no breakfast next morning. Instead of Taafe trundling his trolley before him he came in empty-handed and jerked his thumb at the door. I shrugged and walked out. It seemed as though the party was over.

I was taken downstairs and across the hall into the closely curtained room where I had signed the cheque. In the hall I passed an elderly couple, Darby and Joan types, who were sitting nervously on the edges of their chairs as though they thought it was a dentist's waiting room. They looked at me incuriously as I walked past them into the room where Fatface was waiting for me.

There was a bleak look on his face. 'You've had a night to think about it,' he said. 'Your story had better be very good, Mr Whoever-you-are.'

I went on the attack. 'Where's that dab-sheet?'

'We don't keep it here,' he said shortly. 'In any case, it isn't necessary.'

'I still don't know what you're talking about,' I said. 'And if you think I've spent all night cooking up a cock-and-bull story just to satisfy you then you're crazy. I don't have much to do with my time, but I've better things to do than that.' I was telling him the exact truth.

He made a noise expressive of disgust. 'You're a liar. Can't you get it into your thick skull that the gaff has been blown? There's just one little detail missing – your identity.' He shook his head pityingly. 'We *know* you're not Rearden. All we want to know is who the devil you really are.'

Now, why did he want to know that? I had a fair idea, and I didn't like it at all. If I wasn't Rearden then he'd want to know if I'd be seriously missed. That's an important thing to know if you're contemplating murdering anyone. Was I important? Did I have important connections? For whom was I working? And why? All those were questions he would want answering.

And he was too damned certain that I wasn't Rearden, which was faintly alarming. I heaved a deep sigh. 'I'm Joseph Rearden. From what Cosgrove told me before you got me out of the nick you've done a thorough check on me. Why this sudden switch, Fatface? Are you trying to slip out of your obligations?'

'Don't call me Fatface,' he snapped. 'I don't need fingerprints to tell me you're not Rearden because you've just proved it yourself. Out there in the hall you passed a couple of old people, Mr and Mrs Rearden from Brakpan, South Africa. Your dear old father and your sainted old mother, you son of a bitch. You didn't recognize them and they didn't recognize you.'

There wasn't much to say to that, so I kept my mouth shut. But my stomach did a back flip.

Fatface showed his teeth in a savage grin. 'I said the gaff has been blown, and I meant it. We know about Mackintosh and there's no point in you denying you know him. We know all about that tricky little set-up, so you'd better get ready to tell the truth for a change.'

This time I really was jolted – and badly. I felt as though I'd just grabbed a live wire and I hoped it didn't show on my face. For my cover to be blown could have meant any number of things; for Mackintosh's cover to be blown sky-high was bloody serious.

I said, 'For God's sake – who is Mackintosh?'

'Very funny,' said Fatface acidly. He looked at his watch. 'I can see we'll have to take stronger measures but, unfortunately, I have an appointment and I don't have the time now. I'll give you two hours to think about those stronger measures. I can assure you they will be most unpleasant.'

Depressed as I was I nearly laughed in his face. He was acting like the villain in a 'B' picture. He had no appointment and the two hours were intended to break me down thinking of very imaginable tortures. And he wouldn't be away for two hours, either; he'd be back in an hour, or possibly three hours. It was supposed to add to the uncertainty of the situation. Fatface was an amateur who seemed to get his ideas from watching TV. I think he was too soft-centred to get down to the torture bit and he was hoping I'd break down more-or-less spontaneously.

'All right,' I said. 'If you want me to cook up a story, then I'll cook up a story. It will take me two hours to think it up.'

'We don't want a story – as you put it. We want the truth.'

'But you've got the truth, damn it!'

He merely shrugged and waved to the man behind me who took me upstairs again. The Reardens – if that's who they were – had vanished from the hall. It struck me that Fatface might very well have been bluffing about them. But he still knew about Mackintosh.

Once locked in the bedroom I got on with what I had to do. I shaved quickly and put the shaver and the rest of the stuff into the pockets of the raincoat. I dressed and put on the tweed sports coat, grabbed my weighted sock and took up position behind the door, the end of the improvised cord held in my fingers.

It was a long wait and it seemed to be hours, but I had to stay there, exactly in that place, because in this thing timing was everything. I looked about the bedroom, checking to see that all was in order, and found it good. The bathroom door was ajar, but looked closed; the cord going around the room was invisible and wouldn't be noticed by the casual eye. All I had to do was to stay behind that door and wait.

Although it seemed a long time he was back on the hour – I'd been right in predicting that. I heard the murmur of voices on the other side of the door and tightened my fingers on the cord. As soon as I heard the key in the lock I began to pull, exerting a steady and growing pressure on the piston in the cistern.

As the door opened the cistern flushed noisily.

Fatface came into the room alone and cautiously, but relaxed visibly as he heard the noise from the bathroom. He took a step forward, pushing the door closed behind him, and I heard the key turn as the outside guard locked it. He took another step forward without looking behind him. He could easily have seen me by a half turn of his head but the thought never came to him. After all, wasn't I in the bathroom?

I wasn't! I hit him with the weighted sock very hard, much harder than I'd hit the postman in the Kiddykar office. He gasped and his knees buckled but he kept his feet and he twisted his head slightly so that I could see his mouth was open and he was gasping for air and struggling to shout. I knew the sock wasn't too efficient – not like a proper sandbag – so I hit him even harder, and then again, pounding unconsciousness into his skull.

I caught him as he fell. I didn't want him thumping on the floor with a noise which might be heard outside. Even then, the repeated thud of the sock hitting his head had seemed to echo around the room and I paused for a moment, holding him in my arms, and waited to see if anything would happen.

Nothing did, so with a sigh of relief I lowered him to the

floor. The first thing I did was to go for his gun. It was a neat flat automatic with nine rounds in the magazine but nothing in the chamber. I had been right; the man was an amateur, after all! To carry a gun with nothing up the spout is to carry a piece of junk metal. What's the use of a gun which can't be fired at a split second's notice?

I put back the magazine, worked the action to jump a round into the breech, saw the gun was on safety, and put it into my pocket. And all the time I was talking aloud. The guard outside must not hear dead silence.

I stripped off Fatface's jacket and took off the shoulder holster he wore. Then I trussed him like a fowl, using the strips of sheeting I had prepared, and not forgetting to stuff his mouth with a gag. He was breathing heavily through his mouth and I wondered for a moment if the gag would suffocate him, but he began to breathe through his nose rather noisily and I knew I hadn't hit him too hard. Apart from the moral aspect of murder I wanted him alive. I had a use for him.

Swiftly, I went through the pockets of his jacket. There was a wallet, which, when flicked open briefly, displayed the edges of many bank notes. That was very good – I'd need money. I didn't investigate it further, but stowed it away, together with a small notebook I found, and got on with the search. I found a handful of loose change which went into my pocket and a couple of spare magazines for the pistol, also well worth confiscating. Everything else I left, except for a penknife and a fountain pen, both of which could prove handy to have.

Then I went about the next part of the plan. I tossed the mattress on to the floor just by the door and ripped open the ticking, using Fatface's useful penknife. There was a lot of beautifully inflammable cotton wadding which I piled in a heap ready for the conflagration, and I set the bottles of brandy and Drambuie close to hand.

Then I turned my attention to Fatface who was just

coming round. He stirred a little and a heavy snoring noise came from his nose which would have been a groan if he hadn't been gagged. I went into the bathroom, filled the tooth glass with cold water, went back and dumped the lot on his face. He snorted again and his eyes flickered open.

It must have been quite a shock for him to see the muzzle of his own gun held not a foot from his head. I waited until full comprehension came to him, then said casually, 'If you think there isn't one up the spout, you're wrong. If I want to blow your brains out all I have to do is pull the trigger.'

He flinched and arched his neck, trying to pull his head away, while muffled noises came from behind the gag. 'Take it easy,' I counselled. 'That way you won't get hurt.' I could see the muscles of his arms working as he tested the bindings on his wrists which were pinioned behind his back. When he had finished struggling, I said, 'I'm going out of here – and you are going to help me. You can help voluntarily or involuntarily; take your pick. I have to warn you that one mistaken move on your part might mean your death. You'll be in the middle and if any shooting starts you'll probably stop a bullet.'

I didn't wait to see his reaction to that – it didn't really matter – but took the raincoat and hat and put them on, and checked the pockets to see if I had everything. Then I doused the mattress wadding with the spirits, pouring liberally until the room smelled like a distillery.

I returned to Fatface and cut his ankles free. 'Get up – slowly!'

He staggered to his feet, hampered by the bonds on his arms. He stood quite passively, just looking at me, and I could read no expression in his eyes. I jerked the gun. 'Walk forward to the door and stop a yard in front of it. I wouldn't kick it, though; that could be fatal.'

He shuffled forward obediently, and I took his jacket and draped it across his shoulders so that the empty sleeves hung loose. Apart from the gag and the lack of hands he looked quite normal – normal enough to give me a fraction of a second's advantage when that door opened. The trick is to keep the opposition off balance, and the guard would have other things to do with his eyes just at that moment.

I struck a match and dropped it on the pile of wadding, and blue flames ran over the surface. It wasn't much of a fire but it was the best I could do under the circumstances. I kept an eye on it until the first yellow flames appeared, then pressed the bell-push – the signal that Fatface wanted to be let out.

When the lock snapped I was right behind him, prodding him with the pistol to make sure he understood the spot he was in. The door swung open and I pushed him forward, the flat of my hand in the middle of his back, and yelled at the top of my voice. 'Fire!'

I followed up fast as he staggered into the corridor and, over his shoulder, saw the startled face of the guard who was slow in reacting. He had some kind of a weapon in his hand but he dithered as he saw Fatface lurch towards him and the flickering glow of the flames from the room. With the opening of the door a draught had swept into the bedroom and the fire really got going. I don't think the guard saw me at all.

I gave Fatface another mighty push so that he collided heavily with the guard and they both went down in a tangled heap. A gun went off and someone screamed; it must have been the guard because Fatface had a gag in his mouth.

I jumped over the sprawl of wriggling bodies and ran down the corridor, the pistol in my hand with the safety catch off. The corridor was wood-panelled with doors on either side which I ignored. At the end was a stair landing with stairs going both up and down. I went *up*. I had made my decision on that one the previous evening. It's a curious thing, but people escaping from a house always try to get immediately to the ground floor – which is why they're usually caught. I suppose it's an instinctive reaction, but the department that trained me worked hard to eradicate it.

The floor above was not so fancy – no wood-panelled walls – so I figured I was in the servants' quarters, which meant I had to look out for Taafe, if he was that kind of servant, which I doubted. I moved fast, trying to make no noise, and heard an increasing uproar from downstairs. It was becoming too dangerous to stay in the corridors so I ducked into the nearest room – gun first.

It was empty of occupants, thank God, and I'd done it just in time because someone ran down the corridor with a heavy thumping tread. I shot the bolt and crossed to the window and found I was on the other side of the house away from the courtyard. For the first time I could see the surrounding country and it was very pleasant to view – rolling fields and areas of woodland with blue-green mountains beyond. About half a mile away a car sped along a road. There lay freedom.

For over a year and a half I had seen nothing but stone walls and my eyes had focused on nothing further away than a few yards. This glimpse of countryside caused a sudden lump to come to my throat and my heart thumped in my chest. It didn't matter that dark clouds were lowering and that a sudden shift of wind sent a spatter of raindrops against the window. Out there I would be free and nobody was going to stop me.

I returned to the door and listened. There was a slice of chaos downstairs and it seemed that the fire I had started had got out of hand. I unbolted the door and opened it a crack, to hear Fatface shout, 'To hell with the fire – I want Rearden. Taafe, get downstairs to the front door; Dillon, you take the back door. The rest of us will search the house.'

A deep voice said, 'He's not upstairs. I've just come down.'

'All right,' said Fatface impatiently. 'That leaves just this floor. Taafe was at the bottom of the stairs and didn't see him. Get moving.'

Someone else said, 'Mother of God, will you look at it! It'll burn the house down.'

'Let it burn. We're done for here, anyway, if Rearden escapes.'

I stepped out into the corridor and hastened away from the staircase and, turning a corner, came upon the back stairs. I trotted down quickly, depending on speed to get to the ground floor before the searchers spread out. And I made it, too, only to find the back door wide open and a man standing before it. That would be Dillon.

Fortunately, he was not looking in my direction as I came down the back stairs, but was staring up the wide passage which led to the front of the house. I oozed my way into a side passage and out of his line of sight and then let out my breath inaudibly. No doubt I could have overcome Dillon, but not without noise, and noise would have brought the lot on top of me.

The first door I opened led into a broom closet – useless because it had no window. But the second door led into a well-stocked larder and there was a sash window. I closed the door gently and tackled the window which evidently hadn't been opened for years because it was very tight. As I forced it open it groaned and rattled alarmingly and I stopped to see if Dillon had heard it. But there was no sound apart from a few heavy thumps upstairs.

I attacked the window again and got it open at last, a mere nine inches or so, but enough to take me. I went through head first and landed in a bed of nettles, but fortunately screened from the back door by a large water-butt. As I rubbed my stinging hands I looked about and felt a bit depressed as I noted the high stone wall which seemed to encircle the house. The only gate within view was directly opposite the open back door and if I tried to leave that way Dillon would certainly spot me.

A trickle of water ran down my neck. It was beginning to rain really hard, which was in my favour. The wind was strong and blowing sheets of rain across the kitchen garden. If I could get into the open countryside I stood a chance of getting clean away because the low visibility was in my favour. But it wasn't as low as that – Dillon could certainly see from the back door to the garden gate.

The water-butt wasn't going to collect much rain; it was rotten and useless, and a stave had come away from the hoops. I picked it up and hefted it thoughtfully. No one, least of all Dillon, would expect me to go back *into* the house, and one of the major arts of warfare is the attack from the unexpected direction. I grasped the stave in both hands, sidled up to the back door, and then stepped through boldly.

Dillon heard me coming and must have noticed the dimming of the light as I blocked the entrance. But he was very slow in turning his head. 'Found him?' he asked, and then his eyes widened as he saw who it was. He didn't have time to do much about it because I swung the stave at him and caught him on the side of the head. His head was harder than the stave which, rotten as it was, splintered in two – but it was hard enough to lay Dillon out.

Even as he fell I turned and ran for the gate, dropping the remnant of the stave as I went. The gate wasn't locked and within seconds I was through and walking in a dampish country lane. That wasn't good enough because it was too open, so I ran to the left until I found a gate leading into a field, over which I jumped and then sheltered in the lee of a hedgerow.

Rain dripped on to my face from the brim of my hat as I looked across the field, trying to remember the layout of the land as I had seen it from that upstairs window. If I went across that field I would come to a wood beyond which was the road I had seen. I set off at a brisk pace and didn't look back.

Only when I was sheltered in the wood did I stop to check on my tracks. There was no sign of pursuit and, over the house, I thought I saw an eddying streamer of black smoke, although I could have been wrong because of the wind-driven rain.

I reached the other side of the wood and left by a gate and came out on to the road. But before I got to the gate I heard again the light *clip-clip* of hooves, together with a clinking sound and that pleasant fluting whistle. I opened the gate and looked up the road. A flat cart was just passing, drawn by a donkey, and a man was sitting holding the reins and whistling like a blackbird. A couple of cans which might have held milk clinked behind him on the cart.

I watched it go and tried to figure out which country I was in. The donkey cart looked as though it could be Spanish but, surely to God, it never rained like this in Spain except, maybe, in the plain. I watched the cart recede into the distance and found I couldn't even tell which side of the road he was supposed to be on because he drove dead centre.

I turned and looked up the road the other way. In the distance I could see an approaching bus and, on the other side, a man was waiting by a bus stop. I noted that the bus was coming up on the left of the road so it was pretty certain I was still in England. I was surer of it still when I crossed the road and the man turned a shining red countryman's face towards me, and said, ''Tis a grand, soft morning.'

I nodded, and the rain dripped from the brim of my hat. 'Yes.'

Then my self-confidence received a sudden jolt because when I looked up at the sign above my head I found it was written in two languages, English and another, and the second wasn't even in Roman script but in some weird characters I had never seen before, although they were vaguely familiar.

The bus was coming along the road very slowly. From where I was standing I could see the roof and the top storey of the house, from which a column of black smoke was rising. I switched my gaze back to the bus and wished the bloody thing would get a move on. I felt terribly vulnerable.

On impulse I put my hand into my pocket and fished out some of the loose change I had looted from Fatface. The first coin I examined was apparently a penny, but certainly not an English one. It depicted a hen and chickens and underneath was a single word in that odd script – a word I couldn't even read. I turned the coin over in my fingers and nearly dropped it in surprise.

On this side was a harp and the inscription in the strange script, but this time it was readable. It said: 'Eire – 1964'.

My God, I was in Ireland!

7

I

The bus drew up and because I was now screened from the house, some of the tension left me. However, so preoccupied had I been with my discovery, I had neglected to look at the destination board of the bus. Damn silly omissions of that kind can be the death of one, and I felt a bit of a fool as I sat down. I took Fatface's wallet from my breast pocket and riffled through the bank notes. Most of them were British Bank of England fivers but there were some Irish pound notes, so I took one of those as I didn't know if British currency was acceptable in Ireland.

The conductor came up and I held out a pound note. 'All the way,' I said casually.

'Right you are,' he said. 'That'll be two-and-tuppence.' He gave me the ticket and counted the change into my hand. I hung on to it until he had moved away and then examined it. It was interesting to see that half the coinage was British, so it seemed as though all the currency in Fatface's wallet would be readily negotiable.

So here I was, going 'all the way' and with not a notion in my head about where I was going. It was bloody ridiculous! I looked at the passing scene and found nothing to tell me where the devil I was. Ireland! What did I know about Ireland?

The answer came without much thought – practically nothing! Ireland was a page in the atlas I hadn't bothered to study, and Irishmen were comic characters given to fighting. There were also vague ideas of revolution and civil war – the Black and Tans and armed insurrection – but that had been a long time ago, although I had read of recent trouble in Northern Ireland.

The bus stopped to take on passengers and before it started again a fire engine went by with a clanging bell, going the other way at a hell of a clip. Necks were craned to follow its passage and I smiled. During my getaway a gun had gone off and someone had screamed, so there was probably someone in the house with a gunshot wound, a circumstance which Fatface might have difficulty in explaining away.

The bus trundled on, going God knows where. We passed a place called Cratloe which didn't sound particularly Irish, but there was a sign pointing the other way to Bunratty, which did. A big jet came over – a commercial air liner, not a military job – and circled widely, losing altitude and obviously intending to land somewhere nearby. From nowhere a name clicked in my mind – *Shannon Airport*. That was the Irish international airport, but I hadn't a clue where in Ireland it was.

I mentally added an item to the list of things urgently required – maps.

We pressed on and the sun came out, shining through the rain to make a rainbow. There were more houses here, and a racecourse – and then a magic word – Limerick. So that's where I was! It didn't make a great deal of difference; all I knew of Limerick was the one about the girl from Khartoum. But it was a big, busy city and that was something to be thankful for; I could get lost in a town of this size.

I got off the bus before it reached the centre of town and the conductor looked at me in a puzzled way – but that might have been my imagination. The reason I dropped off was that I had seen a biggish bookshop which could give me what I wanted most of all – information. I walked back the hundred yards to the shop and went inside, drifting casually from counter to counter until I found what I wanted.

It was there in plenty. There were a score of guidebooks to choose from, and any number of maps from folded sheets to bound volumes. I disregarded the antiquarian and literary guides and settled for a closely printed compendium of information. I also bought a single sheet motoring map which would fold for the pocket, a writing pad, a packet of envelopes and a newspaper, paying with one of Fatface's fivers. I took this booty into a tea-shop next door and settled to examine it over a pot of weak tea and a few stale buns – it was that kind of tea-shop.

The map told me that Limerick was at the head of the Shannon estuary and, as I had suspected, not very far from Shannon Airport. The house from which I had escaped was to the north of Limerick, somewhere between Sixmilebridge and Cratloe, very handily placed for Fatface and his crew, a mere fifteen minutes' drive from the airport.

I poured another cup of lukewarm tea and opened the newspaper to find that Slade and Rearden were still very much in the news and even on the front page, but that might have been because Detective-Inspector Brunskill had arrived in Dublin, which would make for local interest. There was a photograph showing him getting off the aircraft and when questioned about what he expected to find, he said, tight-lipped, 'No comment.' Detective-Inspector Forbes was just back in London from Brussels where he reported, 'No joy!'

Of course, Slade made the running in the newspaper much more than I did; a spy has more glamour than a jewel thief. But, from the way Brunskill and Forbes were running around, I wasn't being neglected. Those two had been picked because they could identify me by sight, and it seemed they had a lot of travelling still to do because Rearden had been seen in the Isle of Man, Jersey, the Côte d'Azur, Ostend, Manchester, Wolverhampton, Regent

Street, Bergen and Middle Wallop. I wondered if Detective-Sergeant Jervis was just as busy.

The tea-shop was empty so I pulled out the wallet and opened it. First I counted the money; it was important and I couldn't get far without it. There was a total of £78, mostly in British fivers, which was most welcome. There was also a British driving licence which was even more welcome. I wanted to be mobile which meant hiring a car, something I couldn't do without producing a driving licence. It was made out in the name of Richard Allen Jones, which sounded phoney on the face of it, although the name could have been genuine. There *are* a few Joneses around; there must be for the rest of us to keep up with.

There was a letter which made no sense at all because it was written in an unknown language. I tasted the words on my tongue and thought I detected faintly Slavic overtones but I could have been wrong; eastern languages are my strong point. I pondered over it for some time then carefully put it away without becoming any the wiser.

The thin notebook was of more interest because it contained a few addresses scattered through the pages – some in Ireland, some in England and others in France, Italy and Spain. It gave me a jolt to find the address of Anglo-Scottish Holdings Ltd, in London; Mackintosh's cover was blown wide open.

There were two Irish addresses, one in the Irish Republic at a place called Clonglass in Connemara, and the other in Belfast. Both places were a hell of a long way from Limerick, and Belfast was across the frontier in Northern Ireland. It was thin stuff to work on but it was all I had and it would have to do.

I paid for the tea and asked for, and got, a handful of loose change; then I went to look for a telephone box, which I found difficult until I discovered that the Irish paint them green. I didn't make a call from the first box I found but took a note of the number and then went in search of another from which I put a call through to Anglo-Scottish in London. It was only a few minutes before I heard the voice of Mrs Smith: 'Anglo-Scottish Holdings Limited.' Her voice was warm and friendly, but that might have been an illusion on my part – I hadn't spoken to a woman for a year and a half, apart from the one who doped me.

I said, 'Your telephone might be tapped – I think it is. Find a safe phone and ring this number as soon as possible.' I gave her the number of the other box and rang off before she could answer.

Ultra-cautious maybe, but I'm still around to prove it's the best method. Besides, if she rang me I wouldn't have to keep stuffing small coins in the slot during what might be a lengthy conversation. I trudged back to the first telephone kiosk and found it occupied, so I sneered at the woman through the glass until she went away, then I went inside and fiddled with the directory while waiting for the ring.

All things considered she was prompt; the bell rang within ten minutes. I picked up the telephone, and said, 'Stannard.'

'What are you doing in Limerick?' Her voice wasn't as warm as it had been.

'What the hell do you think I'm doing?' I said grumpily. 'I want to speak to Mackintosh.'

'He's not available.'

'Make him available,' I snapped.

There was a pause. 'He's in hospital,' she said. 'He was in a car accident.'

'Oh! How serious?'

'The doctors don't expect him to live,' she said flatly.

A yawning cavity opened in the pit of my stomach. 'Christ!' I said. 'That's bad. When did it happen?'

'The day before yesterday. It was a hit-and-run.'

Bits of a deadly jigsaw began to fall into place. That was about the time that Fatface Jones had become so certain I wasn't Rearden – and he'd had Mackintosh's address in his notebook. 'That was no accident,' I said. 'His cover was blown.'

Mrs Smith's voice sharpened. 'Impossible!'

'What's so impossible about it?' I demanded.

'Only the three of us knew.'

'That's not so,' I contradicted. 'I've just hammered one of the Scarperers and he had the Anglo-Scottish address written down in a notebook. That's why I thought you might have a tap on your phone.' I took a deep breath. 'Take very good care of yourself, Mrs Smith.'

I had every reason for saying that, even apart from natural humanity. If Mackintosh died and the Scarperers also killed Mrs Smith then I'd be well and truly up that gum tree. The very best that could happen was that I'd be taken back to gaol to serve the rest of the sentence.

And there would be more. They would nail me for an assault on a prison officer; I had kicked the Chief Screw in the face and caused him to break his leg and they'd put me away for another five years because of that.

With Mackintosh and Mrs Smith gone I wouldn't have a hope of proving anything. Mackintosh's tight security system had just blown up in my face. I had lowered the telephone and a quacking noise came from the ear piece. I raised it again, and said. 'What was that?'

'How *could* they have known the address?'

'That doesn't matter right now,' I said. 'This whole operation has gone sour on us and the best we can do is to cut our losses.'

Her voice sharpened. 'What happened to Slade?'

'He got away,' I said wearily. 'God knows where he is now. Probably stowed away in the hold of a Russian freighter bound for Leningrad. It's a bust, Mrs Smith.'

'Wait a minute,' she said, and there was an abrupt silence which lasted a full five minutes. I became aware of a man standing outside the kiosk tapping his foot impatiently and glaring at me. I gave him the stony stare and turned my back on him.

Mrs Smith came back on the line. 'I can be at Shannon Airport within three hours. Is there anything you need?'

'By God there is,' I said. 'I need money – lots of it; and a new identity.'

'There's no reason why you shouldn't resume your real identity,' she said. 'I have your suitcase here with your clothing and passport. I'll bring them with me.'

'Stay away from the Anglo-Scottish office,' I warned her. 'And watch out for strange men on your tail. Do you know how to shake surveillance?'

Her voice was cold. 'I wasn't born yesterday. Meet me at Shannon in three hours.'

'That's not on. Airports aren't for men on the run. They're apt to be full of men in my line of business. Don't forget I'm on the run from the police and that Brunskill has just arrived in Ireland.' I turned and looked past the queue that was forming. 'Take a taxi to the St George Hotel – I'll meet you outside. I might even have a car.'

'All right – and I'll bring the money. How much do you want?'

'As much as you can lay your hands on conveniently. Can you really make it in three hours?'

'If I'm not held up talking to you,' she said acidly, and rang off.

I put down the telephone and pushed open the door. The first man in the queue said sarcastically, 'And where would it be you'd be telephoning to? Australia?'

'No,' I assured him blandly. 'Peking.' I pushed past him and walked up the street.

II

Hiring a car proved to be easy – the British licence was good enough. A hired car is not notoriously speedy but I managed to get a Cortina 1500 which would be enough to get me out of trouble – or into it – reasonably quickly.

I arrived at the St George Hotel early and parked on the other side of the road and about a hundred yards along. Several taxis drew up but no Mrs Smith appeared but finally she arrived and only fifteen minutes late. She stood on the pavement when the taxi departed with two suitcases at her side and the hall porter from the hotel dashed out to succour her. I saw her shake her head and he went back into the hotel, a disappointed man, while she looked uncertainly about her. I let her stew for a while because I was more than curious to see if anyone was taking an undue interest in her.

After ten minutes I came to the conclusion that if I didn't pick her up then someone else would because she looked too damned fetching in stretch pants, open-neck shirt and short jacket, so I entered the traffic stream and swung around to pull up in front of the hotel. I wound down the nearside window, and said, 'Give you a lift, ma'am?'

She leaned down to look into the car, and her green eyes were snapping. 'Where have you been?' she said curtly. 'I've been standing here like a fool. I've already slapped down three passes.'

'It's the Irish,' I said. 'They can't resist a pretty girl. Get in; I'll put the bags into the boot.'

Three minutes later we were rolling on our way out of Limerick and towards Cratloe. I said, 'You made good time. You must have just caught the plane at the right moment.'

She stared ahead through the windscreen. 'I flew in my own plane.'

'Well, well!' I said. 'The intrepid aviatrix. That might prove useful – but for what, I don't know.'

'I didn't like something you said on the telephone,' she said.

'What was that?'

'You were talking about cutting losses. I didn't like that at all.'

'I don't like it much,' I said. 'But there are precious few leads to follow and I have no great hopes.'

'Why did you let Slade get away?'

'I didn't,' I said. 'He was taken.'

'There must have been *something* you could have done.'

I glanced sideways at her. 'Would you have relished cutting his throat while he slept?'

She gave me a startled glance. 'Why, I . . .' She fell into silence.

I said, 'It's easy criticizing from the sidelines. These Scarperers are efficient – more efficient than any of us realized. Slade thought they might be a Russian outfit – Russian subsidized, anyway; possibly Russian trained. One thing is certain; they're no gang of ordinary criminals.'

'You'd better tell me about it,' she said. 'But first tell me where we're going now.'

'I want to have a look at the house in which we were incarcerated. We may be able to pick up something, but I doubt it; the last I heard the boss man was shouting about abandoning the place. Anyway, this is the way it went.'

One thing about Irish roads is that they're traffic free and we made good time, so much so that I was only halfway through my tale of woe by the time I saw the first fire engine. 'This is it,' I said, and pulled off the road well away from the scene of action.

It was a shambles. Mrs Smith took one look at the smoking shell of the house, and said, 'I don't know about the boss abandoning the house, it looks as though it abandoned him. Why should he burn it down?'

'He didn't,' I said immodestly. 'I did.' I stuck my head out of the window and hailed a passing cyclist coming from the scene of the crime. 'What's happened here?'

The cyclist, a gnarled old man, wobbled across the road and lurched to a halt. 'A wee bit of a fire,' he said, and gave me a gap-toothed grin. 'Reminds me of the Troubles, it does.'

'Anyone hurt?'

'Indeed there was. They found a poor gentleman in the middle of it all – burnt to a crisp.'

'That's dreadful,' I said.

The old man leaned forward and peered at me. 'A friend of yours, could he be?'

'Oh, no,' I said. 'I was just passing and saw the fire engines.'

'A natural curiosity,' he agreed. 'But there's a mystery going on, there is. There were other men in that house and they've all run away. The *garda* are wondering why.'

'The *garda*?'

'The natural enemies of good men,' said the ancient. 'The men in blue.' He pointed up the road. 'In England you call them the police.'

About a hundred yards away was a police car – they're unmistakable – with a policeman walking towards it. I glanced at Mrs Smith. 'Should we be on our way, darling? We have to be in Roscommon tonight.'

'Roscommon, is it?' said the old man. 'But it's on the wrong road you are.'

'We're calling in to see friends in Ennis,' I said. The man was as sharp as a tack.

'Ah, then it's straight ahead.' He took his hand from the side of the car. 'May you have luck in Ireland – you and your beautiful lady.'

I smiled at him and let out the clutch and we drove

slowly past the police car. I looked at the mirror and checked that it showed no inclination to follow before I said, 'If they do a thorough autopsy of that corpse they're likely to find a bullet.'

'Did you kill him?' asked Mrs Smith. Her voice was as cool and level as though she had asked if I had slept well.

'Not me. It was an accident, more-or-less; he shot himself in a scuffle.' I checked the mirror again. 'He was right, you know.'

'Who was?'

'The old man. You *are* beautiful.' I gave her no time to worry about it but went straight on. 'How's Mackintosh?'

'I telephoned the hospital just before I left London,' she said. 'There was no change.' She turned to me. 'You don't think it was an accident?'

'How did it happen?'

'He was crossing a street in the City late at night. A man found him by the side of the road. Whoever hit him didn't stop.'

'The man Jones knew I wasn't Rearden about the same time,' I said. 'I don't think it was an accident.'

'But how did they know?'

'I didn't tell them so it must have been either you or Mackintosh,' I said.

'It wasn't me,' she said quickly. 'And why should it have been him?' I shrugged and she was silent for a while before she said slowly, 'He's always been a good judge of men but . . .' She stopped.

'But what?'

'But there was £40,000 in that Swiss numbered account and you had the number.'

I glanced at her. She was staring straight ahead, her body held rigid, and a pink spot glowed on her cheek. 'That's all we need,' I said. 'So you think I sold out to the Scarperers, is that it?'

'Can you think of any other explanation?'

'Not many,' I admitted. 'Talking about money – how much did you bring?'

'You're taking this too damned coolly.' Her voice had an edge to it.

I sighed and drew the car to a halt by the roadside. I put my hand beneath my jacket and brought out the gun I had taken from Jones – butt first. I offered it to her on the palm of my hand. 'If you're so certain I sold out then we may as well get it over with quickly,' I said. 'So take this and let me have it.'

Her face whitened when she first saw the pistol, but now she flushed pink and lowered her eyelids to avoid my gaze. 'I'm sorry,' she said quietly. 'I shouldn't have said that.'

'It's just as well you did,' I said. 'Or you might be still thinking it. There are only the two of us, and if we can't trust each other we'll get nowhere. Now, you're sure you couldn't have let fall even a hint of the operation?'

'I'm positive,' she said.

I put away the gun. 'I didn't,' I said. 'So that leaves Mackintosh.'

'I don't believe it,' she said.

'Who did he see just before this so-called accident?'

She thought about it. 'He saw the Prime Minister and the Leader of the Opposition. They were both worried about the lack of news of Slade. There's an election coming up and the PM thought the Leader of the Opposition should be informed of developments.'

'Or the lack of them,' I said. 'I suppose he might do that – it's not a party issue. Anyone else?'

'Yes; Lord Taggart and Charles Wheeler. Wheeler is a Member of Parliament.'

'I know of Taggart,' I said. 'He was Slade's boss at one time.' The name, Wheeler, rang a faint bell. 'What did he talk to Wheeler about?'

'I don't know,' she said.

'If Mackintosh were to tell anyone of the operation would you expect him to inform you?'

'He never kept anything from me that I know of.' She paused, then said, 'But he had the accident before he could get to me.'

I mulled it over and got nowhere. I sighed, and said, 'I'm damned if I'm going to keep calling you Mrs Smith and neither am I going to call you Lucy. What *is* your name?'

'All right,' she said resignedly. 'You may call me Alison.'

'What do we do now, Alison?'

She said decisively, 'We check on the Irish addresses you found in Jones's notebook. First, at Clonglass, and then at Belfast if necessary.'

'That might not be too easy. The Clonglass reference wasn't as much an address as a mention – just a scribbled memorandum; "Send Taafe to the House at Clonglass".'

'We'll try it anyway,' she said. 'It's not far.'

III

We booked in for the night at a hotel in Galway, but pushed on immediately to Clonglass which was about 25 miles further west along the coast. From the bare look of the map there didn't seem to be any likelihood of finding an hotel west of Galway, especially late at night, so we played safe.

Clonglass proved to be a wide place in the road overlooking a small inlet from the main bay. The houses were scattered, each with its thatched roof tied down against the advent of the western gales, and each with its peat stack handy to the door. It didn't look too promising.

I drew the car to a halt. 'What do we do now? I wouldn't know where to start in a place like this.'

She smiled. 'I do,' she said, and got out of the car. An old woman was toiling up the road, swathed in black from head to foot and with a face like a frost-bitten crab apple. Alison hailed her and damned if she didn't proceed to jabber away in a strange language.

As always when one eavesdrops on a conversation in a foreign language it seemed as though they were discussing everything from the current price of potatoes to the state of the war in Viet-Nam and it seemed to go on interminably, but presently Alison stepped back and the old woman resumed her trudge up the road.

I said, 'I didn't know you could speak Irish.'

'Oh, yes, I have the Gaelic,' she said casually. 'Come on.'

I fell into step. 'Where are we going?'

'To the place where the gossip is,' she said. 'The local shop.'

The shop was instantly familiar. I had seen many like it in the back-blocks of Australia and the more remote parts of the African veld. It was what I used to call as a child an 'anything shop' selling anything and everything in minute quantities to a small population. This shop had an added attraction; it had a bar.

Alison went into her Irish routine again and the words washed around my ears without penetrating, and then she turned to me, and asked, 'Do you drink whiskey?'

'Indeed I do.'

I watched with fascination as the bartender did his best to empty the bottle into a glass. In Ireland a glass of whiskey is a tenth of a bottle and the men are noble drinkers. Alison said, 'One of them is for him – his name is Sean O'Donovan. You talk to him and I'll join the ladies at the other end of the shop. Men can talk to each other better over a drink.'

'Talk to him!' I said. 'That's easy, but what do I do when he talks back?'

'Oh, Sean O'Donovan speaks English,' she said, and drifted away.

'Yes,' said O'Donovan in a soft voice. 'I have the English. I was in the British army during the war.' He put the glasses on the counter. 'You'll be here for a bit of a holiday?'

'Yes,' I said. 'Having a look around – a travelling holiday. You have a beautiful country, Mr O'Donovan.'

He cracked a grin. 'You English have always shown a fancy for it,' he said sardonically. He lifted his glass and said something in Irish which I didn't catch but the action was obvious so I returned the toast in English.

We talked for a while about the things a man talks about to a bartender in bars, and finally I got down to the meat of it. 'All over Ireland I've been crossing the tracks of a friend of mine,' I said casually. 'But I haven't caught up with him. I was wondering if he's been here. His name is Jones.' That sounded silly, but I said it all the same.

'Would he be a Welshman?' asked O'Donovan.

I smiled. 'I doubt it. He's English.'

O'Donovan shook his head. 'I have not heard of the man. He may be at the Big House, but they keep to themselves entirely.' He shook his head. 'They buy their provisions in Dublin and not a thought do they give to the local trader. My father, now, who had this place before me, supplied the Big House all his days.'

That sounded promising. I said sympathetically, 'Stand-offish, are they?'

He shrugged. 'Not that Himself is here often. He comes only once or twice a year – from the Other Island, you know.'

It took me a good twenty seconds to realize that O'Donovan meant England. 'So the owner is English?'

O'Donovan gave me a sidelong glance. 'It would seem he is another Englishman who has taken a fancy to a piece of Ireland.' I looked at O'Donovan's tough face and wondered if he was an active member of the IRA; he appeared to like

Englishmen only in so far as they stayed in England, although he chatted pleasantly enough to me.

He held up his hand. 'I said "seems" and that is what I meant, for I was reading in the paper only the other day that the man is not English at all.'

'So he gets his name into the newspapers?'

'And why wouldn't he? He speaks in the Parliament of the Other Island. Now isn't that a strange thing, and him not an Englishman.'

'It is, indeed,' I said. My acquaintanceship with members of the British Parliament was limited, to say the least of it, and I didn't know the rules of entry. 'So what is he if he isn't English?'

'Ah, now; that I forget entirely. Some small place far away in Europe he comes from. But it's a rich man he is. He has all the money in the world that the American Kennedys haven't laid their fists on already. He comes here in his big yacht which is now anchored in the bay and it's as big as the British royal yacht, if not bigger. Such a pleasure boat has never been seen in these waters before.'

A wealthy and foreign Member of Parliament! It wasn't as promising as I had thought, although it had its curiosity value.

O'Donovan shook his head. 'Maybe Mr Wheeler is richer than the Kennedys, after all.'

Wheeler!

Every nerve cell in my cerebrum sprang to attention simultaneously. That was the name of the MP Mackintosh had seen the day before being hit by the car. I put down my glass slowly. 'I think we'll have another, Mr O'Donovan.'

'And that's a kindly thought,' he said. 'I'm thinking you'll be from the newspapers yourself.' I opened my mouth to speak, and he winked at me. 'Hush, now; you've no need to fear I'll give you away. We've had other London reporters here – ay, and one American – all trying to find out things about the Wheeler man to publish in their papers but not one of them had the wit that you have – to bring an Irish girl with you to do a bit talking in the Gaelic.'

'I thought it might smooth the way,' I said prevaricatingly.

He leaned over the counter and looked into the shop where Alison was talking animatedly to a group of black-shawled women. 'Ah, but she did not learn her tongue in the West; in Waterford, maybe.'

'I believe she mentioned that she lived there,' I said guardedly. 'But she lives in Dublin now.'

O'Donovan nodded in satisfaction, pleased to have been proved right. He picked up the glasses, and then paused, looking over my shoulder. 'Look, now; here comes Seamas Lynch from the Big House. I'll not tell him what you are.'

I turned and looked at the man who was walking up to the bar. He was a black Irishman, dark as a Spaniard, and tall, lean and muscular. O'Donovan put our whiskey on the counter, and said, 'And what will you have, Seamas?'

'I'll have a half,' said Lynch.

O'Donovan picked up a glass and turned to fill it, throwing a question over his shoulder. 'Seamas, when is Himself leaving in his big boat?'

Lynch shrugged. 'When he takes it into his head to do so, Sean O'Donovan.'

O'Donovan put the glass in front of Lynch. I observed that half an Irish single whiskey was about as big as an English double. 'Ah, it's nice to be rich,' he said. 'And have all the time in the world.'

I said, 'Maybe the House of Commons isn't sitting.'

'Then he should be talking to his constituents – and he has none here,' said O'Donovan. He turned to Lynch. 'This gentleman is having a fine time seeing Ireland.'

Lynch looked at me. 'So you think Ireland is a fine place, do you?'

It wasn't what he said but the way he said it that made

my hackles rise; his tone of voice held a thinly veiled contempt. I said, 'Yes; I think it's very nice country.'

'And where are you going next?' asked O'Donovan.

I had an inspiration and told a true story. 'I believe my grandfather on my mother's side was harbourmaster at Sligo many years ago. I'm going up there to see if I can trace the family.'

'Ach,' said Lynch. 'Every Englishman I meet tells me of his Irish ancestry.' His contempt was now open. 'And they all claim to be proud of it. You'd think from the way of it that the British Parliament ought to be in Dublin.'

I nearly lost my temper but kept my voice even. 'Maybe it's true. Maybe it's because your Irish girls can't find good husbands at home so they have to cross the Irish sea,' I said coolly.

Lynch's face darkened and his hand tightened on his glass. As he straightened up from leaning on the counter O'Donovan said sharply, 'Seamas, that's enough, now. You've got as good as you've given, which does not happen too often, so put your glass back in your mouth or on to the counter. I'll have no breakages in my house unless it's your head with a bottle I'll be holding.'

Lynch sneered at me and turned his back. O'Donovan said, not very apologetically, 'You'll understand the English are not well liked hereabouts.'

I nodded. 'And with good reason, from some of the things I've heard. As it happens, I'm not English – I'm Australian.'

O'Donovan's face lightened. 'Are you, now? I ought to have known from your pleasant ways and your good manners in the face of provocation. That's a great country – it is, indeed.'

I finished my drink as I saw Alison giving me a come-hither look. O'Donovan watched approvingly as I sank the full Irish measure in four seconds flat. I put down the empty glass. 'It's been nice talking to you, Mr O'Donovan,' I said. 'I'll be back.'

'And you'll be welcome,' he said.

I went to join Alison at the door. As I passed Lynch he stuck his foot out backwards but I neatly evaded it and carried on. I wasn't looking for a fight. Alison opened the door and went outside. I was about to follow her but stood aside as a big man entered. He walked past me and then paused uncertainly.

I ran for it. It was Taafe, and while his thought processes might have been slow they hadn't stopped altogether. While he was making up his minuscule mind about what action to take I dashed outside and grabbed Alison's arm. 'Run for the car!' I said urgently. 'We've found trouble.'

What I liked about Alison was her quick comprehension. She wasted no time insisting on having an explanation, but immediately took to her heels and ran. She must have been in superb physical condition because she could cover the ground faster than I, and within a hundred yards she was ten yards ahead.

Behind I heard boots thumping the ground as someone chased behind and I reckoned the someone was Taafe. It was now dusk and the light was ebbing from the western sky which is why I didn't see the fishing net spread out to dry about twenty yards from where we had left the car. I got my feet tangled in the netting and pitched forward to the ground.

That made it easy for Taafe. I heard the crunch of his boots as he ran up, and then the rasp of the engine as Alison started the car. The next thing I knew was Taafe had put the boot into me good and solid. He had boots like a skinhead, probably steel-tipped, and one of them crunched into my side with terrifying force. He made no sound apart from a heavy breathing.

I rolled over, desperately trying to free my feet, and his foot whistled past my head so closely that I felt the draught.

If he kicked me in the head it would be lights-out for Stannard – maybe permanently. The engine of the car roared and then we were illuminated as Alison switched on the headlights.

I looked up and saw Taafe loom over me, his teeth drawn back over his lips in a snarl as he manœuvred for another kick. I rolled frantically and saw a stab of light from the direction of the car, and heard a report as from a dud firecracker. Taafe made a gargling sound in his throat and suddenly collapsed on top of me. He made horrible noises as I heaved him off and then he writhed on the ground clutching his left knee.

I ripped the netting from my feet and ran to the car. The passenger door was open and Alison was revving the engine impatiently. As I tumbled in she was putting a small pistol into the glove compartment and, before I got the door closed, she was away, swinging the car around and barely avoiding Taafe who still wriggled on the ground.

I gasped, 'Where did you shoot him?'

'In the kneecap,' she said. Her voice was as steady and cool as though she was discussing a shot on the target range. 'It seemed the best thing to do. He was going to kill you.'

I turned and looked back. Although it was dark I could see someone bending over Taafe. It was someone tall and lean and it could very well have been Seamas Lynch.

IV

'Wheeler,' I said thoughtfully. 'What can you tell me about him?'

It was next morning and we were having breakfast in my bedroom. If the management thought this an irregular procedure they showed no sign of it, and, in view of the previous evening's brouhaha, I didn't feel like being pinned down to a static and open position in the public dining room.

She spread marmalade on toast. 'MP for Harlingsdon East, very wealthy, not too popular with fellow Commons members, so I understand.'

'And a foreigner?'

She wrinkled her brow. 'I believe he is. But he must have arrived in England a long time ago. He'll be naturalized, of course.'

'Can a foreign-born person become an MP?'

'Oh, yes; there have been quite a few,' Alison said indistinctly past the toast.

'An American President must be American born,' I said. 'What about an English Prime Minister?'

'I don't think there's any rule about it,' she said. 'We'd have to look it up in Erskine May.'

'What's his standing? In politics, I mean? Is he a Minister or anything like that?'

'He's a very vociferous back-bencher.'

I snapped my fingers. 'That's where I saw his name before. He was blowing off steam after Slade and I escaped. Going on about "gangsters in our English streets". I read about him in the *Sunday Times*.'

'Yes,' said Alison. 'He made quite a noise about it in the House. The PM put him down quite firmly.'

I said, 'If what I'm thinking is correct then he's got a hell of a nerve. Try this on for size. Mackintosh sees Wheeler and he's hit by a car – a hit-and-run car. I take a notebook from Jones which mentioned Clonglass. In Clonglass we run across Wheeler; we also run into Taafe – and too bloody hard, if I might say so – and I know that Taafe is one of the Scarperers. Wouldn't you think it would be too much of a coincidence for Wheeler *not* to be implicated with the Scarperers?'

Alison buttered another piece of toast; the girl had a

healthy appetite. 'I'd say he's in it up to his neck,' she said concisely. She paused. 'What I don't understand is why Taafe didn't shout; he didn't make a sound even when I shot him.'

'I don't think he *can* shout,' I said. 'I think he's dumb. I've never heard him speak. Let me have a look at that pistol of yours.'

She leaned over, picked up her bag, and produced the pistol. It was a very natty little weapon, only .22 in calibre and with a total length of less than four inches – hardly the gun for accurate shooting in uncertain light at any range over twenty feet. I said, 'Did you intend to hit Taafe in the kneecap?'

'Well,' she said. 'He had one foot off the ground but even then these bullets are so small that if I'd hit him anywhere else it wouldn't bring him down. I could have gone for a head shot, of course, but I didn't want to kill him.'

I looked at her with respect. As I had thought, Mackintosh gathered around him people with talents. 'So you *did* intend to hit him where you did.'

'Oh, yes,' she said, and put the ridiculous little gun away.

I said, 'Let's get back to Wheeler. What kind of a foreigner is he? Or was he? Where did he come from?'

'I don't know. I haven't taken much interest in him. But the details ought to be in *Who's Who*.'

'I'm thinking of Slade,' I said. 'He was taken out of the house near Limerick four days ago. That yacht is very convenient. If it has been anchored at Clonglass for more than four days *and* Wheeler decides to take off on a Baltic cruise this summer then there'll be a bloody good chance that Slade is on board. It's just a hypothesis, mind you.'

'I like it.'

'I've got a few more. What about this one? Let's say there's a man called X who is either a Russian or favours the Russian philosophy; and let's say he devotes his time to springing Russian spies from British gaols. He'd need assistance and where would he get it?' Alison opened her mouth to answer but I ploughed on. 'There's a fair amount of anti-British feeling in Ireland, especially now that Northern Ireland has blown up, and the IRA is still an active force. I detected a bit of that ill feeling last night.'

'Was that the man you were talking to at the bar?'

'He was Seamas Lynch and he seemed to hate my guts on principle. What's more, he works for Wheeler and I think I saw him helping Taafe when we left last night. But I digress. Let's say Mr X organizes the Scarperers from elements of the IRA. He has the money to get it started but from then on it's self-financing because the Scarperers don't confine their attention to spies. The IRA need the money and it's a better way of getting it than holding up banks, so they're happy. Mr X is also happy because the IRA are doing a good job for him. How does that strike you?'

She raised her eyebrows. 'Mr X being Wheeler?' She shook her head sadly. 'Self-made millionaires aren't usually enthusiastic communists.'

'How did he make his money?'

'I think he made his first fortune in the property boom of the 1950s and early '60s. Then he got into the property market in the United States and made another fortune. *Time* had a front cover article about him; they called him "Wheeler-Dealer". Since then he's diversified into nearly everything you can think of that makes money.'

'And he still has time to be a Member of Parliament! He's a busy little man.'

'Too busy to be a Russian spy,' said Alison.

'Maybe.' I had my own reservations about that. I said, 'I'd like to know how Mackintosh is getting on. Will you telephone?'

'I was going to,' she said. 'I think we ought to get rid of the car. It will have been seen at Clonglass.' She hesitated.

'I'll go out and get another. I don't think you ought to walk the streets of Galway just now.'

'But . . .'

'They're not likely to know much about me yet,' she said. 'We weren't conspicuously together last night.'

'Providing Sean O'Donovan has kept his mouth shut,' I said.

'I'll have to chance it,' she said, and picked up the telephone.

She put a call through to London and talked to someone at the hospital. Her words were brief and she did more listening than talking but I knew what was happening by the expression of her face. She put down the handset and said bleakly, 'Still no change. He's fighting hard – but he would.'

I lit a cigarette. 'Have you known him long?'

'All my life,' she said. 'He's my father.'

V

That led to an argument. My immediate reaction was to say that I'd get on with the job myself while she went back to London.

'Damn it!' I said. 'You *ought* to be there. You'll never forgive yourself if he dies in your absence.'

'And he'd never forgive me if Slade gets away because I'm too damned sentimental,' she said. 'You don't know my father very well, Owen, if you think he'd want that. He's a hard man.'

'And you're a hard woman,' I said. 'A chip off the old block.'

She said tautly, 'An unnatural daughter?'

'I think you ought to go back,' I said stubbornly.

'And I'm staying,' she said, equally stubbornly. 'I have

two jobs to do here. One is to help you to get Slade. You can't run up against this crowd by yourself.'

'And the other?'

'To stop you getting yourself killed, you damned fool!'

I was turning that over in my mind while she opened her suitcase and impatiently ripped open a brown-paper parcel, revealing more money than I've seen anywhere outside a bank. For a moment that diverted me. 'How much have you got there, for God's sake?'

'Five thousand pounds,' she said, and tossed me a bundle of fivers. 'There's five hundred. We might get separated and you'll need the money.'

I said drily, 'Her Majesty's Treasury is becoming unreasonably reckless. Do I sign a receipt?'

'I'm going to find out what I can about Wheeler,' she said. 'Don't move out of this room.'

She stuffed the rest of the money into one of those oversized bags women carry and stormed out of the room before I could say another word. I sat down bonelessly on the bed and looked at the bundle of notes, one hundred sheets thick, and the only thought in my head was the irrelevancy that she had called me by my given name for the first time.

She was away for two hours and came back with news – Wheeler's yacht was on the move, heading south. She didn't know if Wheeler was on board or not.

She pulled a piece of paper from her pocket, a printed page from a book. 'I bought an old copy of *Who's Who*. It was a bit too big to lug around so I tore out the relevant page.'

She passed it to me and pointed out the paragraph. Charles George Wheeler, aged 46, was born in Argyrokastro, Albania. *Albania!* He was a Member of Parliament with three honorary doctorates, a member of this, an associate of that, a fellow of the other. A flat in London, a country house in Herefordshire; clubs so-and-so and such-and-such – my eye skipped down the page until I was suddenly arrested by an entry – Interests – penal reform, for God's sake!

I said, 'How does he come by the name of Charles George Wheeler?'

'He probably changed it by deed poll.'

'Do you know when he arrived in England from Albania?'

'I know nothing about him,' said Alison. 'I've had no occasion to study him.'

'And his yacht has gone south. I'd have thought he'd have gone north – to the Baltic.'

'You're still assuming that Slade is aboard.'

'I have to,' I said grimly.

Alison frowned. 'He might be going to the Mediterranean. If so, he'll refuel somewhere in the south, perhaps Cork. I have a friend in Cork: an old lady – an honorary aunt. We can fly to Cork from Shannon.'

'There'll be more coppers than tourists at Shannon Airport,' I said. 'I can't risk it.'

'Airports are big places. I can get you through,' Alison said confidently.

'And how will you account for me to your old aunt?'

Alison smiled. 'I could always twist Maeve O'Sullivan around my little finger.'

VI

We sneaked into Shannon Airport quite easily and unobtrusively. It seemed to me that their security was lousy, but the places are so big and the perimeters so extensive that to make them leakproof would swallow all the profits. Within fifteen minutes, after a bit of radio natter, we were in the air heading for Cork while I watched Alison's expert handling of the controls. She flew the plane – a Piper

Apache – like she did everything else – with an economy of movement and a total lack of showmanship. I wondered what it was like to have Mackintosh as a father. Some girls might have found it a traumatic experience.

Maeve O'Sullivan lived in Glanmire on the outskirts of Cork. She was very old, but still quick and sharp-eyed and shrewd as the proverbial barrel-load of monkeys. She crowed with delight as she saw Alison and gave me a glance which stripped me to the bone in two seconds. 'You've been away too long, Alison Mackintosh.'

Alison smiled. 'Smith,' she said.

'And so it is – so it is. A sassenach name for a Celt, more's the pity.'

'This is Owen Stannard,' said Alison. 'He's working for my father.'

The wise old eyes regarded me with renewed interest. 'Is he, now? And what devil's business is that young rip up to now?'

The idea of a man as hard-bitten as Mackintosh being referred to as a young rip made me want to smile, but I manfully repressed it. Alison gave me a warning glance. 'Nothing that should concern you,' she said tartly. 'He sends you his love.' I mentally agreed with her that it would not be a kindness to tell the old lady of his condition.

'You're just in time for your tea,' said Mrs O'Sullivan, and went off in a bustle into the kitchen with Alison close behind her. I sat down in a big armchair which swallowed me in comfort, and looked at my watch. It was six-thirty – early evening – less than twenty-four hours had passed since Alison had punctured Taafe in the kneecap.

'Tea' proved to be an enormous meal with many dishes thrust upon us, interspersed with brisk and depreciatory comments on the poor appetites of young folk these days. When I called the old lady Mrs O'Sullivan she laughed and said, 'You call me by my name, young man, and I'll feel easier,' so I called her Maeve, but Alison called her Aunt Maeve.

'There's something I must tell you, Aunt Maeve,' said Alison. 'Owen, here, is wanted by the *garda*, so no one must know he's here.'

'The *garda*, is it?' cried Maeve. 'It'll not be dishonest, I know; but is this Alec's doing?'

'In a way,' said Alison. 'It *is* important.'

'I've held my tongue about more things than you've ever spoken in your life, girl,' said Maeve. 'You don't know what it was like here in the old days, and now the crazy men are at it again in the North.' She looked up with sharp black-button eyes. 'It's nothing to do with that, is it, now?'

'No,' I said. 'Nothing to do with Ireland at all, really.'

'Then I'll keep my peace,' she said. 'You are welcome in this house, Owen Stannard.'

After tea we washed up and Maeve said, 'I'm an old woman and I'm wanting my bed. Make yourselves easy, the pair of you.'

'I'd like to use the telephone,' said Alison.

'It's there when you want it. Put your sixpences in the box – I'm saving up for my old age.' Maeve shouted with laughter.

'It'll be more than sixpences, Aunt Maeve,' said Alison. 'I'll be telephoning to England and more than once.'

'Rest easy, girl. If you talk to Alec, ask him why he never comes to Ireland these days.'

'He's a busy man, Aunt Maeve.'

'Aye,' said Maeve. 'And when men like Alec Mackintosh get busy it's time for normal folk to find a deep hole. But give him my love, and tell him he doesn't deserve it.'

She went off and I said, 'She's quite a character.'

'I could tell you stories about Maeve O'Sullivan that would make your hair curl,' said Alison. 'She was very active during the Troubles.' She picked up the telephone. 'Let's hear what the Harbourmaster has to say.'

The Harbourmaster was most obliging. Yes, *Artina* was expected. Mr Wheeler had arranged for refuelling. No, he didn't really know when she would arrive but if previous visits by Mr Wheeler were anything to go by then *Artina* would be staying in Cork for a couple of days.

As Alison put down the telephone I said, 'Now I have to think of a way of getting aboard. I wish I knew more about Wheeler's craft.'

'Give me a few hours and I'll have all you need to know,' said Alison. 'The telephone is a wonderful invention. But first I must ring the hospital.'

It was a time for rejoicing because Alec Mackintosh was fighting his way through to life again. Alison was radiant. 'He's better! The doctor said he was better! His condition has improved and they think there's a chance now.'

'Is he conscious? Is he able to speak?'

'No, he's still unconscious.'

I thought back. If Mackintosh had been unconscious all this time it would be quite a while before the doctors let him speak to anyone, even if he was able and willing. I'd have given a lot to be able to hear what he'd said to Wheeler the day before the hit-and-run.

'I'm glad he's better,' I said sincerely.

Alison picked up the telephone again, suddenly all businesslike. 'And now to work.'

I left her to it, only answering her questions from time to time. I was busily engaged in developing my hypothesis which was beginning to blossom into a very strange shape indeed. If I was right then Wheeler was a most odd fish and a very dangerous man – more dangerous to state security, even, than Slade.

I was deep in thought when Alison said, 'I've done all I can now; the rest will have to wait for morning.'

She flipped open the notebook which was full of shorthand notes, page after page. 'What do you want first – Wheeler or the yacht?'

'Let's have the yacht.'

She leafed through the pages. 'Here we are. Name – *Artina;* designed by Parker, built by Clelands on Tyneside; she was two years old when Wheeler bought her. She's a standard design known as a Parker-Clelands which is important for reasons I'll come to later. Overall length – 111 feet, beam – 22 feet, cruising speed – 12 knots, speed flat out – 13 knots. She has two Rolls-Royce diesel engines of 350 horse-power each. Is this the sort of stuff you want?'

'Just right.' I could begin to build up a picture. 'What's her range?'

'I haven't got that yet, but it's coming. A crew of seven – skipper, engineer, cook, steward and three seamen. Accommodation for a maximum of eight passengers.'

'How is the accommodation arranged?'

'That will be coming tomorrow. The plans of her sister ship were published a few years ago. They're being photographed and sent by wire to the Cork *Examiner* where we can pick them up tomorrow, together with some photographs of the ship.'

I regarded Alison with admiration. 'Wow! Now that's something I wouldn't have thought of doing.'

'The newspaper is a very efficient information gatherer and transmitter. I told you I could pull strings.'

'What about Wheeler?'

'There's a detailed account coming to the *Examiner* on the telex, but this is the meat of it. He fought the Italians when they moved into Albania before the war.' She looked up. 'He'd be about 14 years old then. He fled with his family into Jugoslavia and again fought against the Italians and the Germans during the war both in Jugoslavia and Albania towards the end of the war. He left Albania in 1946 when he was somewhere in his early twenties and settled in England. Was naturalized in 1950. Started to deal in property just about that time and that was the beginning of his fortune.'

'What kind of property?'

'Offices. That was about the time they first began to put up the big office blocks.' She wrinkled her brow. 'I talked to a financial editor; he said there was something funny about the first deals Wheeler made.'

'That's interesting,' I said. 'Tell me more.'

'According to this editor it wasn't easy to see how Wheeler had made a profit. He evidently had made a profit because he suddenly had the money to go bigger and better, and he never looked back right from the early days.'

'I wonder how he paid his taxes,' I said. 'It's a pity we can't subpoena his tax inspector. I'm beginning to see the light. Tell me, when he was fighting in the war – did he fight for the Cetniks or the Partisans? The Nationalists or the Communists?'

'I don't have that here,' said Alison. 'It will be coming by telex, if it's known at all.'

'When did he enter politics?'

She consulted her notes. 'He fought a by-election in 1962 and lost. He fought in the general election of 1964 and got in by a fair margin.'

'And I suppose he lashed out generously for party funds,' I said. 'He'd do that, of course. Any known connections at present with Albania.'

'Nothing known.'

'Russia? Any communist country?'

Alison shook her head. 'He's a dinkum capitalist, mate. I don't see it, Owen. He's always popping off with anti-communist speeches in the House.'

'He's also against prisoners escaping from gaol, if you remember. What about this prison reform bit?'

'He used to be a prison visitor, but I suppose he's got too big for that now. He's generous in his subscription to various prison reform societies, and he's a member of a House Committee studying prison reform.'

'My God, that would come in useful,' I said. 'Did he visit prisons in that capacity?'

'I suppose he might.' She put down the notebook. 'Owen, you're building up quite a structure on a weak foundation.'

'I know.' I stood up and paced the room restlessly. 'But I'll add another layer on my hypothesis. I once talked to a multi-millionaire, one of the South African variety; he told me that the first quarter-million is the hardest. It took him fifteen years to make £250,000, three years to bring it up to the round million, and in the next six years he reached the five million mark. The mathematicians would say he was riding an exponential curve.'

Alison was getting a little impatient. 'So what?'

'The first quarter-million is hardest because our potential millionaire has to make all his own decisions and has to do his own research, but once he has money he can afford to hire regiments of accountants and platoons of lawyers and that makes decision making a lot easier. It's the starting of the process that's the snag. Go back to your financial editor – the one who smelled something funny in Wheeler's first deals.'

Alison picked up her notes again. 'I haven't anything more than I've already told you.'

'Let's take our man X,' I said. 'He's not a Russian – let's call him an Albanian – but he still favours the Russians. He comes to England in 1946 and is naturalized in 1950. About that time he starts dealing in property and makes money at it, but at least one man can't see how he did it. Let's assume the money was fed to him from outside – perhaps as much as half a million. X is a sharp boy – as sharp as any other potential millionaire – and money makes money. So he begins to roll in the time-honoured capitalistic way.'

I swung around. 'In 1964 he entered politics and got himself a seat in the Commons where he's now an enthusiastic and keen back-bencher. He's forty-six years old and still has another twenty-five years of political life in him.'

I stared at Alison. 'What would happen if he were to attain high position in the Government? Say, Chancellor or Minister of Defence – or even Prime Minister – in 1984, which seems to me to be an appropriate date? The boys in the Kremlin would be laughing their heads off!'

8

I

I slept badly that night. In the dark hours my hypothesis began to seem damned silly and more and more unlikely. A millionaire and an MP could not possibly be associated with the Russians – it was a contradiction in terms. Certainly Alison found she could not accept it. And yet Wheeler was associated with the Scarperers, unless the whole series of assumed links was pure coincidence – and that possibility could not be eliminated. I had seen too many cases of apparent cause and effect which turned out to be coincidence.

I turned over restlessly in bed. Yet assume it was so – that Wheeler actually was controlling the Scarperers. Why would he do it? Certainly not to make money; he had plenty of that. The answer came out again that it was political, which again led to Wheeler as a Member of Parliament and the dangers inherent in that situation.

I fell asleep and had dire dreams full of looming menace.

At breakfast I was still tired and a shade bad-tempered. My temper worsened rapidly when Alison made the first phone call of the day and was told by the Harbourmaster that *Artina* had arrived during the night, refuelled quickly, and left for Gibraltar in the early hours.

'We've lost the bastard again,' I said.

'We know where he is,' said Alison consolingly. 'And we know where he'll be in four days.'

'There are too many things wrong with that,' I said glumly. 'Just because he has clearance for Gibraltar doesn't mean he's going there, for one thing. For another, what's to prevent him from transferring Slade to a Russian trawler heading the other way through the Baltic? He could do it easily once he's over the horizon. And we don't even know if Slade is aboard *Artina*. We're just guessing.'

After breakfast Alison went out to collect the stuff from the *Examiner*. I didn't go with her; I wasn't going anywhere near a newspaper office – those reporters had filled up their columns with too much about Rearden and too many photographs. A sharp-eyed reporter was the last person I wanted to encounter.

So I stayed in the house while Maeve tactfully busied herself with the housework and left me alone to brood. Alison was away for an hour and a half, and she brought back a large envelope. 'Photographs and telex sheets,' she said, as she plopped the envelope in front of me.

I looked at the photographs first. There were three of Wheeler, one an official photograph for publicity use and the others news shots of him caught with his mouth open as the news photographers like to catch politicians. In one of them he looked like a predatory shark and I'd bet some editor had chortled over that one.

He was a big man, broad-shouldered and tall, with fair hair. The photographs were black-and-white so it was difficult to judge, but I'd say his hair was ash-blond. His nose was prominent and had a twist in it as though it had been thumped at some time or other, and the cartoonists would have no trouble taking the mickey if he ever attained a position of eminence. I put the photographs of Wheeler aside – I would recognize him if I saw him.

The other photographs were of the *Artina*, and one was a reproduction of the plans of her sister ship. Sean O'Donovan had exaggerated – she was not nearly as big as the royal yacht, but she was a fair size for all that, and it would take a millionaire to buy her and to run her. There was an owner's double cabin forward of the engine room and aft were three double cabins for six guests. The crew lived forward, excepting the skipper who had the master's cabin just behind the wheelhouse.

I studied that plan until I had memorized every passage and door. If I had to board her I would want to know my way around and to know the best places to hide. I checked off the aft peak and the room which held the air conditioning equipment as likely places for a stowaway.

Alison was immersed in reading the telex sheets. 'Any joy there?'

She looked up. 'There's not much more than I told you last night. It's expanded a bit, that's all. Wheeler fought for the Partisans in Jugoslavia.'

'The communists,' I said. 'Another strand in the web.'

I began to read and found that Alison was right; there wasn't much more solid information. The picture was of a bright young man who became a tycoon by the usual clapper-clawing methods and who now had a solid base in society built up by saying the right things at the right times and by contributing largely to the right causes. The picture of a successful man now looking for new worlds to conquer – hence the politics.

'He's not married,' I said. 'He must be the most eligible bachelor in England.'

Alison smiled wryly. 'I've heard a couple of rumours. He runs a mistress who is changed regularly, and the story goes that he's bisexual. But no one in his right mind would put that on the telex – that would be publishing a libel.'

'If Wheeler knew what was in my mind libel would be the least of his worries,' I said.

Alison shrugged unenthusiastically. 'What do we do?'

'We go to Gibraltar,' I said. 'Will your plane take us there?'

'Of course.'

'Then let's chase the wild goose. There's nothing else to do.'

II

We had time to spare and in plenty. An inspection of the plans of *Artina's* sister ship and a reading of the description that went with it made it quite certain that she was no high speed craft and she certainly couldn't get to Gibraltar in less than four days. We decided to play it safe and to be in Gibraltar in three days so we would be there when she came in.

That gave Alison time to fly back to London to see how Mackintosh was managing to survive and to dig up more dirt on Wheeler. We decided it would be most unwise for me to go back to London. Ducking in and out of Cork Airport was one thing – Gatwick or Heathrow was quite another. Every time I smuggled myself incognito through the airport barriers I took an added risk.

So I spent two days cooped up in a suburban house in Cork with no one to speak to but an old Irishwoman. I must say that Maeve was most tactful; she didn't push and she didn't question, and she respected my silences. Once she said, 'Och, I know how it is with you, Owen. I went through it myself in 1918. It's a terrible thing to have the hand of every man against you, and you hiding like an animal. But you'll rest easy in this house.'

I said, 'So you had your excitement in the Troubles.'

'I had,' she said. 'And I didn't like it much. But there are always troubles – if not here then somewhere else – and there'll always be men running and men chasing.' She gave me a sidelong glance. 'Especially men like Alec Mackintosh and whoever concerns himself with that man.'

I smiled. 'Don't you approve of him?'

She lifted her chin. 'Who am I to approve or disapprove? I know nothing of his business other than that it is hard and dangerous. More dangerous for the men he orders than for him, I'm thinking.'

I thought of Mackintosh lying in hospital. That was enough to disprove that particular statement. I said, 'What about the women he commands?'

Maeve looked at me sharply. 'You'll be thinking of Alison,' she said flatly. 'Now that's a bad thing. He wanted a son and he got Alison, so he did the best with what he had and made her to his pattern; and it's a strong pattern and a hard pattern, enough to make a girl break under the burden of it.'

'He's a hard man,' I said. 'What about Alison's mother? Didn't she have a say in the matter?'

Maeve's tone was a little scornful, but the scorn was intermingled with pity. 'That poor woman! She married the wrong man. She didn't understand a man the like of Alec Mackintosh. The marriage never went well and she left Alec before Alison was born and came to live here in Ireland. She died in Waterford when Alison was ten.'

'And that's when Mackintosh took over Alison's education.'

'It is so,' said Maeve.

I said, 'What about Smith?'

'Has Alison not told you about him?'

'No,' I said.

'Then I'll not be telling,' said Maeve decidedly. 'I've gossiped enough already. When – and if – Alison wants you to know, then she'll tell you herself.' She turned away, and then paused, looking over her shoulder at me. 'I'm thinking you're a hard man yourself, Owen Stannard. I doubt if you'll be the one for Alison.'

And I was left to make of that what I could.

Alison rang up late the first night. 'I flew out to sea when I left,' she said. '*Artina* was on course for Gibraltar.'

'You didn't make the inspection too obvious, I hope.'

'I overtook her flying at five thousand feet and climbing. I didn't turn until I was out of sight.'

'How is Mackintosh?' I still called him that, even to her.

'He's better, but still unconscious. I was allowed to see him for two minutes.'

That wasn't too good. I could have done with Mackintosh being awake and talkative; he wasn't alive enough yet for my liking. Which brought me to another and delicate subject. 'You might be under observation in London.'

'No one followed me. I didn't see anyone I know, either, except one man.'

'Who was that?'

'The Prime Minister sent his secretary to the hospital. I saw him there. He said the PM is worried.'

I thought of Wheeler and the man who had been taken out of prison to be killed, and then I thought of Mackintosh lying helpless in a hospital bed. 'You'd better do something,' I said. 'Ring the secretary chap and ask him to spread the word around that Mackintosh is dying – that he's cashing in his chips.'

She caught on. 'You think they might attack Father in hospital?'

'They might if they think he's going to recover. Ask the PM's secretary to drop the unobstrusive word, especially to any of Wheeler's known associates in the House. If Wheeler rings London to have a chat with one of his mates the news might get through – and that could save your father's life.'

'I'll do that,' she said.

'Anything on Wheeler?'

'Not yet; not what we want, anyway. He lives a blameless public life.'

'It's not his public life we're interested in,' I said. 'But do your best.'

Alison came back two days later, arriving in a taxi in mid-afternoon. She looked tired as though she had not had much sleep, and Maeve clucked at the sight of her but relaxed as Alison said, 'Too much damned night-clubbing.'

Maeve went away and I raised my eyebrows. 'Been living it up?'

She shrugged. 'I had to talk to people and the kind of people I had to talk to are in the night club set.' She sighed. 'But it was a waste of time.'

'No further dirt?'

'Nothing of consequence, except maybe one thing. I checked the servant situation.'

'The *what* situation!'

She smiled tiredly. 'I checked on Wheeler's servants. The days of glory are past and servants are hard to come by, but Wheeler does all right even though he needs a large staff.' She took her notebook from her pocket. 'All his staff are British and have British passports excepting the chauffeur who is an Irish national. Do you find that interesting?'

'His contact with Ireland,' I said. 'It's very interesting.'

'It gets better,' she said. 'As I said, the rest of his servants are British, but every last one of them is naturalized and they've all had their names changed by deed poll. And what do you think was their country of origin?'

I grinned. 'Albania.'

'You've just won a cigar. But there's an exception here too. One of them didn't take a British name because it would be peculiar if he did. Wheeler has taken a fancy to Chinese cooking and has a Chinese cook on the premises. His name is Chang Pi-wu.'

'I see what you mean,' I said. 'It would seem bloody funny if he changed his name to McTavish. Where does he hail from?'

'Hong Kong.'

A Hong Kong Chinese! It didn't mean much. I suppose it was quite reasonable that if a multi-millionaire had a taste for Chinese food then he'd have a Chinese cook; millionaires think differently from the common ruck of folk and that would be part of the small change of his life. But I felt a tickle at the back of my mind.

I said carefully, 'It may be that Wheeler is doing the charitable bit. Maybe all these British Albanians are his cousins and his cousins' cousins, nieces and nephews he's supporting in a tactful sort of way.'

Alison looked up at the ceiling. 'The problem with servants is keeping them. They want four nights a week off, television in their rooms and a lie-in every morning, otherwise they become mobile and leave. The turnover is high, and Wheeler's turnover in servants is just as high as anyone else's.'

'Is it, by God?' I leaned forward and peered at Alison closely. 'You've got something, damn it! Spit it out.'

She grinned cheerfully and opened her notebook. 'He has thirteen British Albanians working for him – gardeners, butler, housekeeper, maids and so on. Not one had been with him longer than three years. The last one to arrive pitched up last month. They come and go just like ordinary servants.'

'And they take holidays in Albania,' I said. 'He's got a courier service.'

'Not only that,' said Alison. 'But someone is supplying him with a regular intake.' She consulted her notebook again. 'I did a check with the local branch of the Ministry of Social Security in Herefordshire; in the last ten years he's had fifty of them through his hands. I can't prove they were all Albanians because they had British names, but I'll take a bet they were.'

'Jesus!' I said. 'Hasn't anyone tumbled to it? What the hell is the Special Branch doing?'

Alison spread her hands. 'They're all British. If it's come to anyone's attention – which I doubt – then he's doing the charitable bit, as you said – rescuing his compatriots from the communist oppressors.'

'Fifty!' I said. 'Where do they all go when he's done with them?'

'I don't know about the fifty – I've only had time to check on two. Both are now in the service of other MPs.'

I began to laugh because I couldn't help it. 'The cheek of it,' I said. 'The brazen nerve! Don't you see what he's doing? He's getting these fellows in, giving them a crash course on British mores and customs as well as the finer points of being a gentleman's gentleman, and then planting them as spies. Can't you imagine him talking to one of his mates in the Commons? "Having servant trouble, dear boy? It just happens that one of mine is leaving. Oh, no trouble like that – he just wants to live in Town. Perhaps I can persuade . . ." It beats anything I've ever heard.'

'It certainly shows he has present connections with Albania,' said Alison. 'I wasn't convinced before – it seemed too ridiculous. But I am now.'

I said, 'Do you remember the Cicero case during the war? The valet of the British Ambassador to Turkey was a German spy. Wheeler has been in the money for twenty years – he could have planted a hundred Ciceros. And not only at the political end. I wonder how many of our industrial chieftains have Wheeler-trained servants in their households?'

'All with English names and all speaking impeccable English,' said Alison. 'Wheeler would see to that.' She ticked off the steps on her fingers. 'They come to England and while they're waiting for naturalization they learn the language thoroughly and study the British in their native habitat. When they're British they go to Wheeler for a final gloss and then he plants them.' She shook her head doubtfully. 'It's a very long-term project.'

'Wheeler himself is a long-term project. I don't see him packing his bags and returning to his native land. Look at Slade, for God's sake! He was worming his way in for *twenty-eight* years! These people take the long view.' I paused. 'When do we leave for Gibraltar?'

'Tomorrow morning.'

'Good,' I said. 'I want to catch up with this incredible bastard.'

III

I went into Cork Airport the hard way, as usual. I was beginning to forget what it was like to use the front door. Maeve O'Sullivan had been uncharacteristically emotional when we left. 'Come back soon, girl,' she said to Alison. 'It's an old woman I am, and there's no telling.' There were tears in her eyes but she rubbed them away as she turned to me. 'And you, Owen Stannard; take care of yourself and Alec Mackintosh's daughter.'

I grinned. 'She's been taking care of me so far.'

'Then you're not the man I thought you were to let her,' replied Maeve with asperity. 'But go carefully, and watch for the *garda*.'

So we went carefully and it was with relief that I watched the city of Cork pass under the wings of the Apache as we circled to find our course south. Alison snapped switches and set dials, then took her hands from the control column. 'It will be nearly six hours,' she said. 'Depending on the wind and the rain.'

'You're not expecting bad weather?'

She smiled. 'It was just a manner of speaking. As a matter of fact, the weather report is good. The wind is northerly at 24,000 feet.'

'Will we be flying that high? I didn't think these things did that.'

'The engines are supercharged, so it's more economical to fly high. But this cabin isn't pressurized, so we'll have to go on oxygen soon – as soon as we reached 10,000 feet. You'll find the mask by your side.'

The last time I had seen the Apache it had been a six-seater but in Alison's absence in London the two rearmost seats had been removed and had been replaced by a big plastic box. I jerked my thumb over my shoulder, and said, 'What's that?'

'An extra fuel tank – another seventy gallons of spirit. It increases the range to 2,000 miles at the most economical flying speed. I thought we might need it.'

The capable Alison Smith thought of everything. I remembered what Maeve had said: *Made to a hard pattern, enough to break a girl under the burden of it*. I studied Alison; her face was calm as she checked the instruments and then tested the oxygen flow, and there were no lines of stress to substantiate Maeve's remark. Alison glanced sideways and caught me looking at her. 'What's the matter?'

'A cat may look at a king,' I said. 'So a dog may look at a queen. I was just thinking that you're lovely, that's all.'

She grinned and jerked her thumb backwards. 'The Blarney Stone is back there, and I know for a fact you never went near it. You must have Irish in your ancestry.'

'And Welsh,' I said. 'Hence the Owen. It's the Celt coming out in me.'

'Put on your mask,' she said. 'Then you'll look as beautiful as me.'

It was a long and boring flight. Although the masks had built-in microphones we didn't do much talking, and presently I put down the back of the seat to a reclining position. We flew south at 200 miles an hour – fifteen times faster than Wheeler in *Artina* – and I slept.

Or, rather, I dozed. I woke up from time to time and found Alison alert, scanning the sky or checking the instruments or making a fine adjustment. I would touch her shoulder and she would turn with a smile in her eyes and then resume her work. After nearly four hours had passed she nudged me and pointed ahead. 'The Spanish coast.'

There was a haze of heat below and a crinkled sea, and ahead the white line of surf. 'We won't overfly Spain,' she said. 'Not if we're landing at Gibraltar. It's politically inadvisable. We'll fly down the Portuguese coast.'

She took out a map on a board and worked out the new course, handling the protractor with smoothly efficient movements, then switched off the auto-pilot and swung the aircraft around gently. 'That's Cape Ortegal,' she said. 'When we sight Finisterre I'll alter course again.'

'When did you learn to fly?' I asked.

'When I was sixteen.'

'And to shoot a pistol?'

She paused before answering. 'When I was fourteen – pistol and rifle and shotgun. Why?'

'Just wondering.' Mackintosh believed in teaching them young. I found it hard to imagine a little girl of fourteen looking past the sights of a rifle. I bet she knew the Morse code, too, and all the flag semaphore signals, to say nothing of programming a computer and lighting a fire without matches. 'Were you a Girl Guide?'

She shook her head. 'I was too busy.'

Too busy to be a Girl Guide! She'd have her head down at her books studying languages when she wasn't practising in the air or banging away on the target range. I wouldn't have put it past Mackintosh to make certain that she was at home in a submarine. What a hell of a life!

'Did you have any friends in those days?' I asked. 'Girls of your own age?'

'Not many.' She twisted in her seat. 'What are you getting at, Owen?'

I shrugged. 'Just the idle thoughts of an idle man.'

'Has Maeve O'Sullivan been filling you up with horror stories? Is that it? I might have known.'

'She didn't say a word out of place,' I said. 'But you can't help a man thinking.'

'Then you'd do better to keep your thoughts to yourself.' She turned back to the controls and lapsed into silence, and I thought it would be as well if I kept my big mouth shut, too.

As we turned the corner and flew up the Strait of Gibraltar Alison took the controls and we began to descend. At 10,000 feet she took off her oxygen mask and I was glad to do the same. And then, in the distance, I saw the Rock for the first time, rising sheer from the blue water. We circled and I saw the artificial harbour and the airstrip jutting into Algeciras Bay like the deck of an aircraft carrier. Apparently, to Alison who was busy on the radio, it was all old hat.

We landed from the east and our small aircraft did not need all that enormous runway. We rolled to a halt and then taxied to the airport buildings. I looked at the military aircraft parked all around, and said grimly, 'This is one airport which will have good security.' How was I going to smuggle myself through this one?

'I have something for you,' said Alison, and took a folder from the map pocket from which she extracted a passport. I flicked it open and saw my own face staring up from the page. It was a diplomatic passport. She said, 'It will get us through customs in a hurry, but it won't save you if you are recognized as Rearden.'

'It's good enough.' Even if I was recognized as Rearden the sight of that diplomatic passport would be enough to give my challenger cause to wonder if he could possibly be right. I said, 'My God, you must have pull.'

'Just enough,' she said calmly.

The passport officer smiled as he took the passport, and the civilian with the hard face who was standing next to him ceased to study me and relaxed. We went right through within three minutes of entering the hall. Alison said,

'We're staying at the Rock Hotel; whistle up a taxi, will you?'

If Wheeler's trained Albanians made the perfect servants then Alison Smith was a God-given secretary. I hadn't thought for one moment of where we were going to lay our heads that night, but she had. Alec Mackintosh was a lucky man – but, perhaps, it wasn't luck. He'd trained her, hadn't he?

We had adjoining rooms at the Rock Hotel and agreed to meet in the bar after cleaning up. I was down first. Alison Smith was no different in that respect from any other woman, I was glad to observe; the female takes fifty per cent longer to prink than the male. It *is* only fifty per cent even though it seems twice as long. I had sunk my first cold beer by the time she joined me.

I ordered her a dry Martini and another beer for myself. She said, 'What will you do when Wheeler arrives?'

'I have to find if Slade is aboard *Artina* and that will mean a bit of pirate work.' I grinned. 'I promise not to have a knife in my teeth when I go over the bulwarks.'

'And if he is on board?'

'I do my best to bring him off.'

'And if you can't?'

I shrugged. 'I have orders covering that eventuality.'

She nodded coolly, and I wondered briefly if Mackintosh had ever given his own daughter similar instructions. She said, 'Wheeler being what he is and who he is will probably anchor off the Royal Gibraltar Yacht Club. I wouldn't be surprised if he's a member – he comes here often enough.'

'Where is it?'

'About half a mile from here.'

'We'd better take a look at it.'

We finished our drinks and strolled into the sunshine. The yacht basin was full of craft, sail and power, big and small. I stood looking at the boats and then turned. 'There's a convenient terrace over there where they serve cooling drinks. That will be a nice place to wait.'

'I'm just going to make a telephone call,' said Alison, and slipped away. I looked at the yachts and the sea and tried to figure how I could get aboard *Artina* but without much success because I didn't know where she would be lying. Alison came back. 'Wheeler is expected at eleven tomorrow morning. He radioed through.'

'That's nice,' I said, and turned my face up to the sun. 'What do we do until then?'

She said unexpectedly, 'What about a swim?'

'I forgot to pack trunks; I didn't expect a semi-tropical holiday.'

'There *are* shops,' she said gently. So we went shopping and I bought trunks and a towel, and a pair of German duty-free binoculars, smooth, sleek and powerful.

We went across the peninsula and swam at Catalan Bay which was very nice. That night we went night-clubbing, which was even nicer. Mrs Smith seemed to be human and made of the same mortal clay as the rest of us.

IV

At ten o'clock next morning we were sitting on the terrace overlooking the yacht basin and imbibing something long, cold and not too alcoholic. We both wore sun-glasses, not as much to shade our eyes as to join the anonymous throng just as the film stars do. The binoculars were to hand and all that was lacking was *Artina* and Wheeler, and, possibly, Slade.

We didn't talk much because there wasn't anything to talk about; we couldn't plot and plan in the absence of *Artina*. And Alison had loosened the strings of her personality the previous night as near as she had ever got to letting her hair down, and possibly she was regretting it. Not that she had let me get too close; I had made the expected pass and she evaded it with practised ease. But now she had returned to her habitual wariness – we were working and personal relationships didn't matter.

I soaked up the sun. It was the thing I had missed in England, especially in prison, and now I let it penetrate to warm my bones. Time went on and presently Alison picked up the binoculars and focused them on a boat making its way to harbour between the North Mole and the Detached Mole. 'I think this is *Artina*.'

I had a glass to my lips when she said it, and I swallowed the wrong way and came up for air spluttering and choking. Alison looked at me with alarm. 'What's the matter?'

'The impudence of it!' I gasped with laughter. '*Artina* is an anagram of Tirana – and that's the capital of Albania. The bastard's laughing at us all. It just clicked when you said it.'

Alison smiled and proffered the binoculars. I looked at the boat coming in with the dying bow wave at her forefoot and compared what I saw with the drawings and photographs of her sister ship. 'She could be *Artina*,' I said. 'We'll know for sure within the next five minutes.'

The big motor yacht came closer and I saw the man standing at the stern – big and with blond hair. '*Artina* it is – and Wheeler.' I swept the glasses over her length. 'No sign of Slade, but that's to be expected. He wouldn't parade himself.'

She anchored off-shore and lay quietly in the water and I checked every man who walked on deck, identifying five for certain without Wheeler. There was a crew of seven apart from an unknown number of guests, but the men I saw didn't seem to be guests. Two were on the foredeck by a winch and another was watching the anchor chain. Two more were lowering a boat into the water.

I said, 'Count the number of men who come ashore. That might be useful to know.'

The two men by the winch moved amidships and unshipped the folding companionway and rigged it at the side of the yacht. One of them went down the steps and tethered the boat. Presently Wheeler appeared with a man in a peaked cap and they both descended the companionway into the waiting boat. The engine started and it took off in a wide curve and then straightened, heading for the yacht club.

Alison said, 'Wheeler and the skipper, I think. The man at the wheel is a crewman.'

They stepped ashore at the club and then the tender took off again and returned to *Artina* where the crewman tethered it to the bottom of the companionway and climbed up on board again. Alison nudged me. 'Look!'

I turned my head in the direction her finger indicated. A big work boat was ploughing across the water towards *Artina*. 'So!'

'It's a fueller,' she said. '*Artina* is taking on diesel fuel and water already. It seems that Wheeler isn't going to waste much time here.'

'Damn!' I said. 'I was hoping he'd stay the night. I'd much rather go aboard in darkness.'

'He doesn't seem to have any guests,' she said. 'And he's in a hurry. From our point of view those are encouraging signs. Slade might very well be on board.'

'And a fat lot of use that is if I can't go aboard to find him. How long do you think refuelling will take?'

'An hour, maybe.'

'Time enough to hire a boat,' I said. 'Let's go.'

We bickered with a Gibraltan longshoreman for the hire of a motor launch and got away with him charging not more than twice the normal rate, and then launched out into the harbour. The fueller and *Artina* were now close-coupled on the port side, with hoses linking them. Another crew member in a peak cap was supervising – that could be the engineer.

I throttled down as we approached and we drifted by about fifty yards from the starboard side. Someone came into view, looked at us incuriously and then lifted his head to look up at the Rock. He was Chinese.

I said, 'That, presumably, is Chang Pi-wu. Wheeler must like Chinese cooking if he takes his Chinese chef to sea. I hope the crew like Chinese food.'

'Maybe they have their own cook.'

'Maybe.' I studied the Chinese covertly. Many occidentals claim that all Chinese look alike. They're wrong – the Chinese physiognomy is as varied as any other and I knew I'd recognize this man if I saw him again. But I'd had practice; I'd lived in the East.

We drifted to the stern of *Artina*. The ports of the rearmost guest cabin were curtained in broad daylight, and I had a good idea of where Slade was lying low. It was exasperating to be so close and not be able to get at him.

Even as I opened the throttle and headed back to the shore I saw a crewman drop into the boat moored at the bottom of *Artina's* companionway and take off. He was faster than we were and as we handed our launch to the owner I looked out and saw him returning with Wheeler and the skipper. They climbed aboard and the companionway was unshipped and stowed.

An hour later I was burning with a sense of futility as *Artina* moved off and headed out to sea. 'Where the hell is she going now?' I demanded.

'If he's going east into the Mediterranean to the Greek islands he'll refuel at Malta,' said Alison. 'It would be the logical thing to do. Let's go and find out where he's cleared for.'

So we did, and Alison was right – not that it made me feel any better. 'Another four days?' I asked despondently.

'Another four days,' she agreed. 'But we might have better luck at Valletta.'

'I'd like that yacht to have an accident,' I said. 'Just enough to delay her for one night. You don't happen to have any limpet mines about you?'

'Sorry.'

I stared moodily at the white speck disappearing into the distance. 'That Chinese worries me,' I said. 'He ought to worry Slade even more.'

'Why ever should he?'

'Communist Albania has ceased to hew to the Moscow line. Enver Hoxha, the Albanian party boss, has read the Little Red Book and thinks the thoughts of Mao. I wonder if Slade knows he's in the hands of an Albanian?'

Alison wore a half-smile. 'I was wondering when you'd get there,' she said.

'I got there a long time ago – probably before you did. It would be very nice for the Chinese if they could get hold of Slade – a top British intelligence man and a top Russian intelligence man in the same package. They'd squeeze him dry in a month and they wouldn't care how they did it.'

I shrugged. 'And the damned fool thinks he's going home to Moscow.'

9

I

Limpet mines we didn't have but, in the event, I got hold of something just as good and a lot simpler. That was in the Grand Harbour of Valletta and four days later. In the meantime we paid the bill at the Rock Hotel and flew to Malta where that diplomatic passport got me through the barriers at Luqa Airport just as easily as it had done at Gibraltar.

With nearly four days to wait we suddenly found ourselves in holiday mood. The sky was blue, the sun was hot and the sea inviting, and there were cafés with seafood and cool wine for the days, and moderately good restaurants with dance floors for the nights. Alison unbent more than she had ever done.

I found there was something I could do better than she, which did my mauled ego a bit of good. We hired scuba equipment and went diving in the clear water of the Mediterranean and I found I could out-perform her at that. Probably it was because I had lived in Australia and South Africa where the ambient waters are warmer and skin-diving is a luxury and not a penance as it is in England.

We swam and lazed the days away and danced the nights away for three days and three nights until, on the morrow, Wheeler was due to arrive. It was nearly midnight when I brought up the subject of Mr Smith. Alison took no umbrage this time but, perhaps, it was because I had been plying her with the demon alcohol. Had it been the opposition tipping the bottle she would have been wary but the hand that filled her glass was the hand of a friend and she was taken unaware. Sneaky!

She held up the wine glass and smiled at me through liquid amber. 'What do you want to know about him?'

'Is he still around?'

She put down the glass and a little wine spilled. 'No,' she said. 'He's not around any more.' She seemed sad.

I lit a cigarette and said through the smoke, 'Divorce?'

She shook her head violently and her long hair flowed in heavy waves. 'Nothing like that. Give me a cigarette.'

I lit her cigarette and she said, 'I married a man called John Smith. There *are* people called John Smith, you know. Was he an intelligence agent? No. Was he even a policeman? No. He was an accountant and a very nice man – and Alec was horrified. It seemed I hadn't been designed to marry an accountant.' Her voice was bitter.

'Go on,' I said gently.

'But I married him, anyway; and we were very happy.'

'Had you been with your father before then?'

'With Alec? Where else? But I didn't stay on – I couldn't, could I? John and I lived in a house near Maidenhead – in the Stockbroker Belt – and we were very happy. I was happy just being married to John, and happy being a housewife and doing all the things which housewives do, and not having to think about things I didn't want to think about. Alec was disappointed, of course; he'd lost his robot secretary.'

I thought of John Smith, the accountant; the nine-to-fiver who had married Alison Mackintosh. I wondered how he had regarded the situation – if he ever knew about it. I couldn't see Alison cuddling up on his knee, and saying, 'Darling, you're married to a girl who can shoot a man in the kneecap in impossible light, who can drive a car and fly a plane and kill a man with one karate chop. Don't you think we're going to have a delightful married life? Look how handy it will be when we're bringing up the children.'

I said, 'And then?'

'And then – nothing. Just a stupid, silly motorway

accident on the M4.' Her face was still and unsmiling and she spoke through stiff lips. 'I thought I'd die, too; I really did. I loved John, you see.'

'I'm sorry,' I said inadequately.

She shrugged and held out her glass for more wine. 'Wanting to die didn't help, of course. I brooded and moped for a while, then I went back to Alec. There wasn't anything else to do.' She sipped the wine and looked at me. 'Was there, Owen?'

I said very carefully and noncommittally, 'Perhaps not.'

She gave me a wry look, and said, 'You're pussyfooting, Owen. You don't want to hurt my feelings by saying what you think. Well, that's commendable, I suppose.'

'I'm not one to make casual judgements.'

'Without knowing the facts – is that it? I'll give you some. Alec and my mother never got on very well. I suppose they were basically incompatible, but he was away so often, and she didn't understand his work.'

'Was he in the same work as now?'

'Always, Owen; always. So there was a legal separation just before I was born, and I was born in Waterford where I lived until I was ten when my mother died.'

'Were you happy in Waterford?'

Alison became pensive. 'I don't really know. I can't seem to remember much about those days; there has been so much overlaid on top since.' She stubbed out her cigarette. 'I don't know if anyone would ever call Alec an ideal father. Unorthodox, maybe, but not ideal. I was a bit of a tomboy – never one for frilly frocks and playing with dolls – and I suppose he took advantage.'

I said slowly, 'You're a woman now.'

'I sometimes wonder about that.' She plucked at the tablecloth with tapering fingers. 'So Alec trained me to be – I didn't know what. It was fun at the time. I learned to ride a horse, to ski on snow and water, to shoot, to fly – I'm qualified on jets, did you know that?'

I shook my head.

'It was damned good fun, every bit of it – even grinding at the languages and mathematics – until he took me into the office and I learned what it was all for. Then it wasn't fun any more.'

'Did he send you out on field jobs?'

'I've been on three,' she said evenly. 'All very successful – and most of the time I was sick to my stomach. But that wasn't the worst of it. The worst was being in the office and sending others out into the field, and watching what happened to them. I planned too many operations, Owen. I planned yours.'

'I know,' I said. 'Mackintosh . . . Alec told me.'

'I became the one person whom he could trust absolutely,' she said. 'A very valuable consideration in the profession.'

I took her hand. 'Alison,' I said. 'What do you really think of Alec?'

'I love him,' she said. 'And I hate him. It's as simple as that.' Her fingers tightened on mine. 'Let's dance, Owen.' There was a hint of desperation in her voice. 'Let's dance.'

So we went on to the dimly lit floor and danced to the sort of music that's usually played in the early hours of the morning. She came very close and rested her head on my shoulder so that her lips were by my ear. 'Do you know what I am, Owen?'

'You're a lovely woman, Alison.'

'No, I'm a Venus Fly Trap. Vegetables – like women – are supposed to be placid; they're not supposed to be equipped with snapped jaws and sharp teeth. Have you ever watched a fly alight on a Venus Fly Trap? The poor beastie thinks it's just another vegetable plant until the jaws snap closed. Most unnatural, don't you think?'

I tightened my arm about her. 'Take it easy.'

She danced two more steps and then a deep shudder

went through her body. 'Oh, God!' she said. 'Let's go back to the hotel.'

I paid the bill and joined her at the door of the restaurant and we walked the two hundred yards to our hotel. We were both silent as we went up in the lift and along the corridor, but she held my hand tightly as we came to the door of her room. She was trembling a little as she held out her key.

She made love like a maniac, like a savage, and I had the deep scratches on my back to prove it next morning. It seemed as though all the pent-up frustrations of a warped life were loosed on that night-time bed. But when it was over she was relaxed and calm, and we talked for a long time – maybe two hours. What we talked about I'll never remember; just inconsequentialities too meaningless to take note of – she had had time for few trivialities in her serious life.

The second time was better and she was all woman and, when it was over, she fell asleep. I had sense enough to go to my own room before she woke; I thought she would not be too pleased with herself in the sober light of day.

II

Wheeler was due that morning and we had plans to make. When she came down to breakfast I was on my first cup of coffee and rose from the table to greet her. She was a little self-conscious as she came up and tended to avoid my eye. I sat down, and said, 'What do we use instead of a limpet?'

When I leaned against the back of the chair I felt the pain as the pressure impinged on the scratches she had inflicted. Hastily I leaned forward again and took a piece of toast.

I looked up and saw she had snapped back into professionalism as she took in what I said; personal relationships were one thing and the job was quite another. 'I'll check with the Port Captain when *Artina* is due.'

'We don't want to have a repetition of Gibraltar,' I said. 'One jump from here and Wheeler and Slade will be in Albania – home and dry. What do we do if *Artina* arrives in daylight and leaves in daylight?'

'I don't know,' she said.

'There's one thing certain,' I said. 'I can't invade her in the middle of the Grand Harbour in daylight and take Slade off. So what remains?' I answered the question myself. 'We have to make sure she stays all night.'

'But how?'

'I've thought of a way. We'll go shopping after breakfast. Can I butter some toast for you?'

So the pair of us ate a hearty breakfast and sallied forth into the hot streets of Valletta, a heat seemingly intensified by the warm golden limestone of the buildings. The Port Captain expected *Artina* at midday and that was sad news. Sadder still was the information that the fuelling ship had been booked in advance and was to go alongside as soon as *Artina* anchored.

We went away, and I said, 'That does it. Let's do my bit of shopping.'

We found a ship's chandlery and went inside to find all the usual expensive bits and pieces that go towards the upkeep of a yacht. I found what I was looking for – some light, tough nylon line with a high breaking strain. I bought two hundred feet of it and had it coiled and parcelled.

Alison said, 'I suppose you know what you're doing.'

'It was the scuba gear we've been using that gave me the idea.' I pointed towards the harbour. 'How would you get to the middle of there without being seen?'

She nodded. 'Underwater. That's all very well, but doesn't help you to get aboard.'

'It will – eventually. You're included in this operation. Come and get the gear. We want to be back on the spot when *Artina* arrives.'

We went to the place we had hired the scuba gear and I made absolutely certain we were issued with full bottles. Then after a brief test in the swimming pool of the hotel, we went back to the harbour. At the swimming pool Alison suddenly drew in her breath and I turned to find that she was blushing deeply. She was looking at my back.

I chuckled. 'They ought to issue a bottle of Dettol with you,' I said. 'You're quite a woman.'

Unaccountably she became angry. 'Stannard, you're a . . . a . . .'

'Buck up,' I said sharply. 'We have a job to do.'

That brought her back fast and the awkward moment was over. We went down to the harbour and settled down to wait for *Artina*. Alison said, 'What's the plan?'

'If you've read my record you'll know I was in Indonesia,' I said. 'One of the diciest moments I ever had out there was when I was in a small launch being chased by a fast patrol boat which was popping off with a 20mm cannon. There was a mangrove swamp nearby so I nipped in there for shelter – that was a big mistake. There was too much seaweed and it got wrapped around the propeller shaft and the launch came to a dead stop. That seaweed was nearly the end of me.'

'What happened then?'

'That doesn't matter.' I nodded towards the harbour. '*Artina* is a lot bigger than the launch I had, but this nylon line is a hell of a lot stronger than strands of seaweed. When she comes in we're going to swim out and wrap the lot around both propeller shafts. It might immobilize her and it might not, but I'm betting it will. And the beauty of it is that even when they find it there'll be no suggestion of foul play. It's something that could happen to any boat. Anyway, they'll have a devil of a job freeing it once the engines have tightened it up, and I'm hoping it will take all night.'

'It could work,' agreed Alison, and then continued evenly, 'I'll do something for those scratches. This water is dirty and they might become infected.'

I looked at her and she met my eye without a tremor. 'Good enough,' I said, and took great pains not to laugh.

She went away briefly and returned with a bottle of something-or-other which she applied to my back. Then we sat and waited patiently for *Artina* to show up.

It was a long hot day. *Artina* was late and I began to wonder if she hadn't by-passed Malta and headed straight for Albania. She came in at two-thirty and dropped anchor well off-shore. Again she lowered a boat but this time only the skipper came ashore. Wheeler wasn't to be seen.

I stubbed out my cigarette. 'This is it,' I said, and tightened the straps of the scuba gear. 'Can you swim as far as that?'

Alison splashed water into her mask. 'Easily.'

'Just stick close to me.' I pointed. 'We're not going to swim right for it. We'll pass by about twenty yards from the stern and then come in from the other side. The fueller might be there – I hope it is – so keep your head down.'

I had the skein of nylon rope strapped to my thigh; I tested to see if it was secure and then slipped into the water. I doubt if skin-divers are encouraged in the Grand Harbour, not that they would want to make a habit of swimming there – the water is none too clean and decapitation by the churning propellers of passing traffic a constant hazard. I had chosen a quiet spot where we could go into the water unobserved.

We went deep right from the start, going down to about twenty-five feet before heading on course. I knew my speed and I had estimated the distance so I kept a steady count of the seconds and minutes. The problem in this sort of exercise was to keep swimming in a straight line. Occasionally I looked back and saw Alison swimming strongly in echelon, behind and to the left.

When I estimated we had arrived at the point I had chosen I waved Alison to a halt and we swam lazily in circles while I looked about. There was an oncoming rumble and a shadow overhead as a vessel passed, her propellers flailing the water and causing eddies which jerked us about. The propellers stopped and presently there was an audible clang transmitted through the water. That would be the fueller coupling to *Artina*.

I waved to Alison and we went on in the new direction. As we went on towards the two boats I hoped that no one was looking over the side to see the line of bubbles breaking on the surface. But we were coming in at the side of the fueller and all the action would be where they were coupling up the fuel and water lines. If anyone had time to look over the side then that fueller was over-manned.

The light diminished as we swam underneath the two boats and I paused again before heading aft and rising to trail my fingers along *Artina*'s keel. We came to the stern and I stopped with my left hand on one blade of the port phosphor-bronze propeller, hoping that no damned fool in the engine room would punch the wrong button and start the engine. If those three blades started to move I'd be chopped into bloody mincemeat.

Alison swam up on the starboard side as I fumbled with the strap holding the rope to my thigh. I got it free and began to uncoil it with care. The propeller was about four feet in diameter, and the shaft was supported by struts before it entered the stern gland in the hull. I slipped the end of the rope in between the strut and the hull and coiled it around the shaft and then passed a loop around the shaft in between the propeller and the strut. When I tugged gently it held firm, so that was a start.

That rope was the damnedest stuff. At times it was like

wrestling with a sea serpent – the coils floated around in the water dangerously, threatening to strangle us or bind our legs, and Alison and I must have closely resembled that remarkable piece of antique statuary, the Laocoön.

But we finally did it. We entangled those two propellers in such a cat's cradle that when the engines started and the ropes began to tighten all hell would break loose. Most probably everything would grind to a sudden halt, but a shaft could bend and, at worst, one of the engines might slam a piston through the cylinder casing. It was a good job.

We slipped away and swam back to shore, emerging from the water quite a distance from where we had gone in. My sense of direction had become warped, but then it always does underwater. An unshaven character leaning on the rail of a tramp steamer looked at us with some astonishment as we climbed up to the quay, but I ignored him and Alison and I walked away, our back packs bumping heavily.

We went back to our original position and I lit a cigarette and looked across at *Artina*. The fueller had finished and was just casting off, and the skipper was returning in the tender. It seemed as though they intended a faster turn-around than Gibraltar. I wondered where the skipper had cleared for – it wouldn't be Durazzo, the port for Tirana, although I'd be willing to bet that was where he intended to go.

The skipper climbed aboard and the companionway was unshipped immediately. There was a lot of movement on deck and even as the tender was hoisted clear of the water someone was at the winch on the foredeck ready to lift anchor.

Alison said, 'They're very much in a hurry.'

'It seems so.'

'I wonder why.'

'I don't know – but I expect they'll be very annoyed within the next few minutes.'

The anchor came up and *Artina* moved off slowly. I hadn't expected her to move at all and it came as a shock. Apparently 700 horse-power was more than a match for a few coils of nylon line. Alison drew in her breath. 'It isn't working!'

Artina turned and headed for the open sea, picking up speed so that a bow wave showed white. I lowered the binoculars, and said, 'It was a good try.' I felt gloomy. Albania was only 450 miles away and *Artina* could be there in less than two days. The only way I could think of stopping her was by a kamikaze attack in the Apache.

Alison was still watching through her monocular. 'Wait!' she said urgently. 'Look now!'

Artina had swerved suddenly and unnaturally as though someone had spun the wheel fast, and she was now heading straight for the shore. She slowed and water boiled at her stern as the engines were put into reverse. Then the bubble of white water stopped and she drifted helplessly, right into the path of a big Italian cruise liner which was leaving harbour.

There was a deep *booom* as the liner peremptorily demanded right of way but *Artina* did not react. The liner altered course fractionally at the last moment and her sheer side might have scraped *Artina*'s paintwork. From the bridge of the liner an officer in whites was looking down and I guessed that a string of choice Italian imprecations was being directed down at the hapless skipper of *Artina*.

The liner went on her way and *Artina* bobbed inertly in the waves raised by her wake. Presently a little tug put out and went to her aid and she was towed back to where she had come from and dropped anchor again.

I grinned at Alison. 'For a moment there I thought . . . Well, it's done and she'll be staying the night. When they find out what's happened they'll be cursing the idiot who carelessly dropped a line in the water.'

'There's no chance they'll guess it was done deliberately?'

'I shouldn't think so.' I looked over the water at *Artina*. The skipper was at the stern looking down. 'They'll soon find out what it is, and they'll send down a diver to cut it free. It'll take a hell of a lot longer for him to free it than it did for us to tangle it – those engines will have tightened the tangle considerably.' I laughed. 'It'll be like trying to unscramble an omelette.'

Alison picked up her gear. 'And what now?'

'Now we wait for nightfall. I'm going to board her.'

III

We went into Marsamxett Harbour from Ta'Xbiex to where *Artina* was anchored in Lazzaretto Creek. A tug had moved her during the afternoon and put her with the rest of the yachts. We went out in a fibreglass object that resembled a bathtub more than a boat, but Alison seemed to find no difficulty in handling it and she used the oars as though she'd been trained as stroke for Oxford. More of Mackintosh's training coming to the surface.

It was a moonless night but the sky was clear so that it was not absolutely pitch-black. Ahead loomed Manoel Island and beyond a light flashed at Dragutt Point. To our left Valletta rose, clifflike and impregnable, festooned with lights. There were no lights on *Artina*, though, apart from the obligatory riding lights; since it was 2.30 a.m. this was not surprising. I hoped everyone on board was in the habit of sleeping soundly.

Alison stopped sculling as we approached and we drifted silently to *Artina*'s stern. The rope ladder which the diver had been using was not there but I hadn't been counting on it even though it was nine feet from the water to the stern rail. What I wanted was a grapnel, but those are hard to come by at a moment's notice, so I had improvised. A shark hook is shaped like a grapnel, being three big fish-hooks welded together. I had wrapped it in many layers of insulating tape, not only to prevent myself from being nastily hooked but also for the sake of silence.

I looked up and saw the ensign-staff silhouetted against the sky and used that to mark the position of the rail. Holding a coil of the rope I threw up my grapnel so it went over the rail. There was a soft thud as it landed on the deck and, as I drew the line back, I hoped it would hold. It did; it caught on the rail and a steady pull told me it would be not unreasonable to climb the rope.

I bent down and whispered, 'Well, this is it. I may come back with Slade or I may not. I may come over the side in a bloody hurry so stick around to fish me out of the drink.' I paused. 'If I don't come back then you're on your own and the best of British luck to you.'

I swarmed up the rope and managed to hook my arm round the ensign-staff, taking the strain off the shark hook. The pistol thrust into the waist of my trousers didn't help much; as I twisted like a contortionist to get a foot on deck the muzzle dug into my groin agonizingly and I was thankful that I'd made sure there wasn't a bullet in front of the firing pin.

I made it at last and in silence. At least nobody took a shot at me as I looked back at the water. Alison was nowhere to be seen and there was just a suspicious looking ripple where no ripple should have been. I stayed there quietly for a moment and strained my ears listening to the loud silence.

If there was a man on watch he was being quiet in his watching. I hazarded a guess that anyone on watch would stay up forward, perhaps in the wheelhouse or comfortably in the dining saloon. To get to the stern cabins I didn't have to go forward; the entrance to the cabin deck was by a staircase in the deck lounge, and the door to the lounge was just in front of me if the ship plans I had studied were correct.

I took out a pen-light and risked a flash. It was lucky I did so because the deck immediately in front of me was cluttered with diver's gear – I could have made a Godawful clatter if I hadn't seen that. I managed to navigate the booby traps safely until I got to the deck lounge door and was thankful to find it unlocked; which was just as expected because who locks doors on a ship?

The lounge was in darkness but I saw light gleaming through a glass-panelled door on the starboard side. There was just enough light spilling through to illumine the hazards of furniture so I stepped over to look through the door and I froze as I saw movement at the end of a long passage. A man came out of the dining saloon and turned into the galley and out of sight. I opened the door gently and listened; there was the slam of something heavy followed by the clink of crockery. The man on watch was enlivening the night hours by raiding the refrigerator, which suited me very well.

I crossed the lounge again and went below to the cabin deck. There were three cabins down there, all for guests. Wheeler's master cabin was amidships, the other side of the engine room, so I didn't have to worry about him. The problem that faced me was if he had any guests, apart from Slade, occupying any of the three guest cabins.

The cabin that had been curtained in broad daylight at Gibraltar was the big stern cabin, and that was my first objective. This time the door *was* locked, and this raised my hopes because Slade would certainly be kept under lock and key. I inspected the lock with a guarded flash of the light. It wasn't much of a problem; no one installs Chubb triple-throw locks on a cabin door and I could have opened one of those if I had to – it would have taken longer, that's all.

As it was I was inside the cabin inside two minutes and with the door locked again behind me. I heard the heavy breathing of a sleeping man and flicked my light towards the port side, hoping to God it was Slade. If it wasn't I was well and truly up that gum tree I had shown Mackintosh.

I needn't have worried because it was Slade all right and I cheered internally at the sight of that heavy face with the slightly yellowish skin. I took the gun from my waist and pushed a bullet up the spout. At the metallic sound Slade stirred and moaned slightly in his sleep. I stepped forward and, keeping the light on him, I pressed gently with my finger at the corner of his jaw just below the ear. It's the best way to awaken a man quietly.

He moaned again and his eyelids flickered open, and he screwed up his eyes at the sudden flood of light. I moved the pen-light so that it illumined the gun I held. 'If you shout it'll be the last sound you make on earth,' I said quietly.

He shuddered violently and his adam's apple bobbed convulsively as he swallowed. At last he managed to whisper, 'Who the hell are you?'

'Your old pal, Rearden,' I said. 'I've come to take you home.'

It took some time to sink in, and then he said, 'You're mad.'

'Probably,' I admitted. 'Anyone who wants to save your life must be mad.'

He was getting over the shock. The blood was returning to his face and the self-possession to his soul – if he had one. 'How did you get here?' he demanded.

I let the light wander to the nearest port. It wasn't curtained, after all; plates of sheet metal had been roughly welded over the oval scuttles so that it was absolutely impossible for Slade to see outside – more security expertise on the part of the Scarperers. I grinned at Slade, and asked softly, 'Where is here?'

'Why – on board this ship,' he said, but his voice was uncertain.

'I've been following you.' I watched with interest as his eyes shifted sideways to look at a bell-push by the side of his berth, and I hefted the gun so that it came into prominence again. 'I wouldn't,' I warned. 'Not if you value your health.'

'Who are you?' he whispered.

'I suppose you could say that I'm in the same business as yourself, but in the other corner. I'm in counter-espionage.'

The breath came from him in a long, wavering sigh. 'The executioner,' he said flatly. He nodded towards the gun. 'You won't get away with it. You have no silencer. Kill me with that thing and you're dead, too.'

'I'm expendable,' I said lightly, and hoped I wouldn't have to make that statement stick. 'Use your brains, Slade. I could have slid into this cabin and cut your throat in your sleep. It would have been messy, but silent. A better way would have been to stick a steel knitting needle through the nape of your neck and into the medulla oblongata – there's not much blood. The fact that we're talking now means I want to take you out alive.'

He frowned slightly and I could almost see the wheels spinning as he thought it out. I said, 'But don't have any misconceptions. I either take you out alive or you stay here dead. It's your choice.'

He had recovered enough to smile slightly. 'You're taking a big chance. You can't keep me under the gun all the time. I could win yet.'

'You won't want to,' I said. 'Not when you've heard what I have to say. My guess is that you were taken from that room we shared, given a shot of dope, and woke up in this cabin where you've been ever since. Where do you think you are?'

That set the wheels going round again, but to no effect. At last he said, 'There's been no temperature change, so I couldn't have been taken very much north or south.'

'This hooker has a very efficient air-conditioning plant,' I said. 'You wouldn't know the difference. Do you like Chinese food?'

The switch confused him. 'What the hell! I can take it or leave it.'

'Have you had any lately?'

He was bemused. 'Why, yes – only yesterday I . . .'

I cut in. 'The ship has a Chinese cook. Do you know whose ship it is?' He shook his head in silence, and I said, 'It belongs to a man called Wheeler, a British MP. I take it you haven't seen him.'

'No, I haven't,' said Slade. 'I'd have recognized him. I met him a couple of times in . . . in the old days. What the devil is all this about?'

'Do you still think you are going to Moscow?'

'I see no reason to doubt it,' he said stiffly.

'Wheeler was born an Albanian,' I said. 'And his Chinese cook does more than rustle up sweet and sour pork. They're not your brand of communist, Slade. Right now you're in Malta and the next scheduled stop is Durazzo in Albania; from there I guess you'll be shipped by cargo plane straight to Peking. You'd better acquire a real taste for Chinese cooking – always assuming they give you any food at all.'

He stared at me. 'You're crazy.'

'What's so crazy about the Chinese wanting to get hold of you? What you have locked up inside that skull of yours would interest them very much – the secrets of two top intelligence services. And they'd get it out of you, Slade – even if they had to do it by acupuncture. The Chinese *invented* the term "brainwashing".'

'But *Wheeler*?'

'What's so odd about Wheeler? You got away with it for over a quarter of a century – why shouldn't someone else be as smart as you? Or smarter? Wheeler hasn't been caught – yet.'

He fell silent and I let him think it out. Yet I hadn't much time to waste so I prodded him again. 'It seems to me that your choice is simple. You come with me willingly or I kill you right now. I think I'd be doing you a favour if I killed you because I'd hate to see you after you'd been in the hands of the Chinese for a month. I think you'd better come with me and retire to a nice, safe, top-security wing in one of Her Majesty's nicks. At least you won't be having your brains pulled out through your ears.'

He shook his head stubbornly. 'I don't know if I believe you.'

'For God's sake! If Wheeler wanted you to go to Moscow then why didn't he transfer you to one of those ubiquitous Russian trawlers? In the Atlantic they're as thick as fleas on a mangy dog. Why bring you to the Mediterranean?'

Slade looked at me cunningly. 'I've only your word for that, too.'

I sighed, and lifted the gun. 'You don't have much of a choice, do you?' I was getting mad at him. 'If ever I saw a man looking a gift horse in the mouth it's you. I haven't followed you from Ireland to . . .'

He cut in. 'Ireland?'

'That's where we were held together.'

'Lynch is Irish,' he said thoughtfully.

'Seamas Lynch? He works for Wheeler – he's an IRA thug with a dislike of the English.'

'He looks after me here,' said Slade. 'He's my guard.' He looked up and I saw that the strain of uncertainty was beginning to tell. 'Where are we now – exactly?'

'Anchored in Marsamxett Harbour.'

He made up his mind. 'All right, but if I get on deck and I don't recognize it then you might be in big trouble. You'll be wanting silence and I might take my chances on the gun in the darkness. Remember that.'

'How long is it since you've been in Malta?'

'Five years.'

I smiled humourlessly. 'Then I hope to God you have a good memory.'

Slade threw back the bedclothes and then paused, looking at me questioningly. There had been a creak which was not one of the usual shipboard noises. I listened and it came again.

Slade whipped the covers back over his chest. 'Someone's coming,' he whispered.

I held up the gun before his eyes. 'Remember this!' I backed off and opened the door of the lavatory and even as I did so I heard a key snap metallically at the cabin door. I closed the lavatory door gently and used my pen-light in a quick flash to see what I'd got into. As usual in lavatories there was no back door, just the usual paraphernalia of toilet, wash basin, medicine cabinet and shower. The shower was screened off by a semi-transparent plastic curtain.

I switched off the light, held my breath, and listened. Lynch's voice was unmistakable. 'I heard voices – who the devil were you talking to?'

This was the crunch. If Slade was going to give me away he'd do it now, so I listened with care to what was arguably the most important conversation I was ever likely to hear.

'I must have been talking in my sleep,' said Slade, and my heartbeat slowed down to a mere gallop. 'I've been having bad dreams and I've got the makings of a headache.'

'Ach, it's no wonder, and you being cooped up in here all this while,' said Lynch. 'But rest easy, you'll soon be home.'

'Why have we been stopped all this time?'

'Something's gone wrong with the propellers,' said Lynch. 'But I didn't get the exact hang of it.'

'Where are we?'

'Now you know better than to ask that, Mr Slade. That's top secret.'

'Well, when will we be moving again and when do I get my feet on dry land?'

'As to the first,' said Lynch, 'maybe it'll be tomorrow. As to the last, I couldn't rightly tell you. I'm not one of the bosses, you know; they don't tell me everything.' He paused. 'But you're looking so white and peaky, Mr Slade. Could I get you the aspirin?'

The hairs on the nape of my neck stood up and did a fandango as Slade answered. 'No, don't worry; I'll be all right.' It was borne heavily upon me that although I could hear Slade's voice I couldn't see what he was doing with his hands. He might be saying one thing and pointing out to Lynch that he had an unwanted visitor.

Lynch said solicitously, 'Ach, it's no trouble at all. We promise to get you home in good condition; that's part of the deal. I'll get the aspirin for you.'

I ducked into the shower stall and drew the plastic curtain just as Lynch opened the lavatory door. He switched on the light and I saw his outline quite clearly through the curtain as he stepped forward to open the medicine cabinet. I had the gun trained on him all the time and I thought that I could dispose of him and Slade, too, if it came to the push. Getting out would be another matter.

I heard the rattle of pills in a bottle and then the rush of water as a tap was turned on. It was a relief to know that Lynch actually was getting aspirin and that Slade had not sold me out. Lynch filled the glass and turned to leave – he was so close that I could have touched him by only half-extending my arm and only the curtain was between us. Fortunately he was back-lit and I wasn't or he would have seen me had he glanced my way.

He went out, switching off the light and closing the door. 'Here, you are,' he said. 'This should clear up your headache.'

'Thanks,' said Slade, and I heard the clink of the glass.

'Man, but you're sweating,' said Lynch. 'Are you sure it's not the fever you've got?'

'I'll be all right,' said Slade. 'You can leave the light on. I think I'll read for a while.'

'Surely,' said Lynch. 'Have a quiet night, mind.' I heard the cabin door open and close, and then the snap of the lock as the key was turned.

I was doing a fair amount of sweating myself as I waited for the trembling of my hands to stop. My stomach felt all churned up as the adrenalin sped on its appointed rounds gingering up my muscle tone and twanging my nerves like harp strings. At last I stepped out of the shower and gently opened the lavatory door.

Whether his sweating was due to a fright or fever Slade had used his wits when he had asked Lynch to leave on the main cabin light. It meant that I could see at a glance if the place was safe. Slade certainly didn't want to be shot by accident.

He lay in bed with a book held between slack fingers and his face was the yellow colour of old newsprint. 'Why didn't he see you?' he whispered.

I flapped a hand at him to keep him quiet and went to the door, still keeping the gun pointing in his general direction. I heard nothing so presently I turned and strode over to Slade. 'Where does Lynch live? Do you know?'

He shook his head and tugged at my sleeve. 'How the hell did he miss you?'

He found it difficult to believe that in a narrow space the size of two telephone booths one man could miss seeing another. I found it hard to believe myself. 'I was taking a shower,' I said. 'How was Lynch dressed?'

'Dressing-gown.'

That meant he hadn't come far and he probably had been allocated one of the cabins next door to be conveniently close to his charge. 'Have you any clothes?' Slade nodded. 'All right; get dressed – quietly.'

I watched Slade carefully while he dressed, principally to make sure he didn't slip a blunt instrument into his pocket. When he had finished I said, 'Now get back into bed.' He was about to expostulate but I shut him up fast with a jab of the gun. 'I want to give Lynch time to get back to sleep.'

Slade got back into bed and I retreated into the lavatory, leaving the door ajar. Slade had pulled the sheet up high and was lying on his side apparently reading his book. Everything would appear normal if Lynch took it into his head to come back. I gave him half an hour by my watch and during that time heard nothing out of the ordinary.

I stepped into the cabin and signalled Slade to rise. While he was disentangling himself from the bedclothes – it's really surprising how difficult it is to get out of bed when fully dressed because the sheet wraps itself round one's shoes – I jimmied the lock on the door. I had to turn my back on Slade at this point but it couldn't be helped.

I turned and found him walking towards me slowly. When he approached he put his mouth to my ear and whispered, 'When I get on deck I'd better see Valletta.'

I nodded my head impatiently, switched off the light, and opened the door on to the darkness of the passage. The staircase was immediately to the left and I prodded Slade up it with the gun in his back, holding his right arm. I stopped him before we got to the top and cautiously surveyed the deck lounge. All was quiet so I urged him on his way and we went out on the afterdeck.

I shone the light to give Slade some idea of the obstacle race he must run to get the twenty feet to the stern rail, and off we went again. Half-way across the afterdeck he stopped and looked around. 'You are right,' he whispered. 'It *is* Valletta.'

'Quit chattering.' I was edgy as I always am on the last lap. Once ashore I could turn Slade in to the Maltese

Constabulary and the job was done, apart from wrapping up Wheeler and his mob, but we still had to get ashore.

We got as far as the stern rail and no further. I groped for the grapnel alongside the ensign-staff and couldn't find it. Then shockingly a blaze of light split the darkness as the beam of a powerful lamp shone vertically down on us from the boat deck above, and a voice said, 'That's far enough.'

I dug my elbow into Slade's ribs. 'Jump!' I yelled, but neither of us was quick enough. There was a rapid tattoo of feet on the deck as a small army of men rushed us and we were both grabbed and held. There wasn't a damned thing I could do – two of the three men who tackled me were trying to tear my arms off so they could use them as clubs to beat me over the head, and the other was using my stomach as a bass drum and his fists weren't padded as drumsticks are.

As I sagged and gasped for breath I was vaguely aware of Slade being dragged forward, hauled by two seamen with his feet trailing along the deck. Someone shouted and I was also hustled forward and thrust headlong through the doorway of the deck lounge. A burly black-bearded man whom I recognized as the skipper issued orders in a language whose flavour I couldn't catch. I was unceremoniously dropped to the deck and my assailants began to draw the curtains to the windows.

Before the last of them was drawn I saw a searchlight from the bridge forward begin to search the water around *Artina* and I hoped Alison had got clear. Someone handed my pistol to the skipper; he looked at it with interest, made sure it was cocked, and pointed it at me. 'Who are you?' His English was accented, but with what I didn't know.

I pushed myself up with wobbly arms. 'Does it matter?' I asked wearily.

The skipper swung his eyes to Slade who sagged against a chair, and then beyond him to the staircase which led below. 'Ah, Lynch!' he said, rumbling like a volcano about to explode. 'What kind of a guard are you?'

I turned my head. Lynch was looking at Slade with shocked amazement. 'How did he get here? I was with him not half an hour ago, and I made sure the door was locked.'

'The door was locked,' mimicked the skipper. '*Te keni kujdes;* how could the door be locked?' He pointed to me. 'And this man – he brought Slade out of the cabin.'

Lynch looked at me. 'By God, it's Rearden. But he *couldn't* have been in the cabin,' he said stubbornly. 'I'd have seen him.'

'I was in the shower, standing right next to you, you silly bastard.' I turned to the skipper. 'He nearly got himself killed. Not much of a guard, is he?'

Lynch made for me with blood in his eye, but the skipper got to me first, warding off Lynch with an arm like an iron bar. He dragged my head up by my hair and stuck the gun in my face. 'So you are Rearden,' he said, caressing my cheek with the barrel. 'We're very interested in you, Rearden.'

A cool voice said, 'He's not Rearden, of course.'

The skipper swung away and I saw the Chinese, Chang Pi-wu, who looked at me expressionlessly. Next to him stood a tall man with ash-blond hair, who, at that moment, was fitting a cigarette into a long holder. He dipped his hand into the pocket of his elegant dressing-gown, produced a lighter and flicked it into flame.

'Stannard is the name, I believe,' said Wheeler. 'Owen Stannard.' He lit his cigarette. 'So thoughtful of you to join us, Mr Stannard. It saves me the trouble of looking for you.'

10

I

'How did you get hold of him?' Wheeler asked the skipper.

'Mehmet found a hook on the stern rail and a rope leading to the water. He removed it and told me. I set up a watch.'

Wheeler nodded. 'You didn't know whether someone was going to come on board or leave,' he commented.

The skipper waved his hand at me and Slade. 'We caught these two leaving. This idiot . . .' He stabbed his finger at Lynch. '. . . let them go.'

Wheeler regarded Lynch frostily. 'I'll talk to you later. Now get below.'

Lynch looked as though he was about to expostulate but he caught the cold glare from Wheeler's eye and promptly turned on his heel and went away, giving me a look of dislike as he went. I was beginning to improve physically; my shoulders no longer felt totally dislocated and although my belly was one massive ache I could now breathe more or less normally.

Wheeler said, 'Well, Mr Stannard; how did you expect to take Slade ashore? By boat? Where is it?'

'I swam out,' I said.

'And you were going to swim back,' he said incredulously. 'With Slade a cripple? I don't believe you.' He swung around to the skipper. 'Make a search for the boat.'

The skipper didn't move. 'It's being done.'

Wheeler nodded approvingly and crossed to Slade who had now sagged into a chair. 'My dear chap,' he said anxiously. 'What possessed you to leave with this man? Do you know who he is? If you had left the ship he would have put you in the hands of the police. And you know what that would mean – forty years in a British gaol. What sort of tale could he have told you?'

Slade wearily lifted up his head. 'I know you,' he said. 'We've met before.'

'Yes – in happier circumstances,' said Wheeler. 'Once at an EFTA conference and again, if my memory is correct, at a dinner given by some industrial organization or other – I forget which.'

'Your name is Wheeler; you're a Member of Parliament. Why should you want to help *me*?'

'A good question,' I said. 'Answer him, Wheeler. Tell Slade why you are willing to commit treason.' I rubbed my sore stomach tentatively. 'As far as I know treason still carries the death penalty – it isn't covered by the Act of Parliament which abolished hanging for murder.' I grinned at him. 'But who should know that better than you?'

Wheeler didn't rile easily. He smiled, and said coolly, 'I am helping you because I don't recognize British law; because, like you, I'm fighting for a better world.' He put his hand on Slade's shoulder. 'Because, also like you, I'm a good communist.'

'Then why didn't I know about you?' asked Slade. 'I should have known.'

'Why should you have known? You didn't *need* to know, and therefore you weren't told. It was safer that way.' Wheeler smiled. 'You might have been important, Slade, but you were never as important as I am.'

I corrected him. 'As important as you *were*. You're finished, Wheeler.'

Apart from gently shaking his head he ignored me. With his eyes fixed on Slade, he said, 'What nonsense has Stannard been filling you up with? You're a fool if you believe the enemy.'

Slade said, 'What are we doing here in Malta?'

Wheeler straightened and laughed. 'So that's the maggot he's put in your mind. I'm taking you home, of course. I spend my annual holiday in the Mediterranean; it would have looked damned suspicious if I'd gone to the Baltic this year. Even for you I wouldn't risk that.'

I said to Slade, 'Ask him if he's read any good thoughts lately – from the Little Red Book.'

'You're an Albanian,' said Slade flatly. 'I don't trust you.'

'So that's it,' said Wheeler softly. 'Does it make any difference?'

Slade nodded towards the silent Chinese who stood behind Wheeler. 'He does.'

I chipped in again. 'He makes a hell of a difference. Wheeler says he's taking you home. Home is where the heart is, and his heart is in Peking.'

That got to Wheeler. He said venomously, 'I think I'll have to shut you up – permanently.' He relaxed again and struck his hands lightly together. 'Not that it makes much difference whether you know or not, Slade. It made things easier as long as you believed you were going to Moscow – a willing prisoner is easier to handle. But we've got you and you'll still get to your destination intact.'

From the look in Slade's eyes I doubted it. It wouldn't be beyond his capabilities to commit suicide somewhere along the way, and death would be far preferable to the information-extracting process awaiting him in China. Besides, under the circumstances it was his duty to commit suicide. Any man in his position knew that when it came to this sort of crunch he was expendable.

But Wheeler was ahead of us on that one. 'Your confinement will be more rigorous, of course. We can't have you hanging yourself by your braces.'

'Do I get to go along?' I asked.

Wheeler looked at me reflectively. 'You?' He shook his head. 'I don't think my friends would be interested in you. You've been out of the game too long to know much about recent developments in British Intelligence. A South African sleeper is of no consequence.' He half turned his head and said over his shoulder, 'What do you think?'

The Chinese spoke for the first time. 'He is of no use, but he is dangerous because of what he knows,' he said dispassionately. 'Kill him.'

I said something indescribably rude in Mandarin, and he opened his mouth in surprise. Orientals aren't all that inscrutable.

'Yes, Stannard; we must kill you. But how to do it?' Wheeler asked himself pensively. 'I have it. We discover a stowaway on board – an armed stowaway. There is a scuffle on his discovery and a shot is fired – the stowaway is killed with his own gun. We notify the police here and he turns out to be none other than Rearden, the British gaol-breaker.' He smiled. 'That would do a lot for my image; think of the headlines in the British press. What do you think of it?'

'Not much,' I said. 'If you turn me in to the police they'll want to know about Slade, too. He's a hell of a sight more important than I am. They'll want to search this ship, and they'll take it apart. You wouldn't want them to do that with Slade still aboard.'

Wheeler nodded. 'True. I'm afraid I must forgo that charming theatricality; my image must do without it. Besides, before you die there are some questions to be answered, such as what accomplices you have. That reminds me.' He turned to the skipper. 'What result of the search for his boat?'

'I'll find out,' said the skipper, and left the lounge.

I sighed. 'I came aboard alone.'

Wheeler nodded. 'You were alone at the beginning – I know that. But you might have picked up someone along the way. You realize that I must be certain.' He indicated the Chinese. 'My friend has ways of making sure, but you won't want to hear about that.'

I looked about the lounge casually. The departure of the skipper had reduced the odds against me, but not by much. There were two seamen behind me, one covering me with my own gun, and Wheeler and the Chinese were in front. The Chinese held his hand in his pocket and I was certain he also had a gun. I looked at Slade and wondered if he'd join me if it came to putting up a fight.

I said, 'I'd like to know how you got on to Mackintosh and me so fast. You seem to know all about me – including my South African history.'

Wheeler chuckled. 'You British are a nation of amateurs – and that goes for your intelligence services. I was told about you, of course.'

I was genuinely bewildered. 'Who could have told you? There was only Mackintosh and me.'

'Precisely. And you didn't tell me.'

My jaw dropped and I stared at Wheeler incredulously. 'Mackintosh?'

'Who else could – as you point out. He was a little drunk and very indiscreet. I had no difficulty in flattering the fool. Towards the end he realized he was saying too much and shut up, but I got enough out of him.' He laughed. 'We were having a discussion on prison reform at the time.'

I was bewildered. Wheeler's description didn't fit the Mackintosh I knew, who was not a fool and certainly not susceptible to flattery. What in hell had Mackintosh been doing to blow things like that?

'He's dead, of course,' said Wheeler casually. 'I saw to that immediately as soon as I was certain we had you safe in Ireland. But we didn't have you safe, did we? Those IRA clowns are also amateurs. Never mind; here you are and all is well, after all.'

I felt chilled to my bones. Whether Mackintosh was dead or not – and that was a moot point because I had told Alison to spread the word of his impending demise – I felt betrayed and utterly alone. Like a man who treads on a stair that isn't there. I felt jolted. I had to believe Wheeler because nothing else made sense, and yet Mackintosh's betrayal didn't make sense, either. Unless . . .

The skipper returned, breaking my chain of thought. 'No boat found,' he said.

Wheeler was fitting another cigarette into his holder. 'You may have been telling the truth, after all,' he said. He turned his head to the skipper. 'I want safe places for these two separately. What do you suggest?'

'Slade can go back to the cabin,' said the skipper.

'After what has just happened?' Wheeler lifted his eyebrows.

The Chinese said, 'He must be manacled to the bed, and a man must stay *in* the cabin all the time. He must not be permitted to make noise.'

Wheeler thought about it. 'All right; what about Stannard?'

'The forepeak; there's a steel bulkhead with a watertight door. He won't get out of there.'

Wheeler nodded curtly, then said to me, 'I'm afraid your interrogation will have to be postponed until we're away from land. The sound of a man screaming travels a long way.' He waved his hand and I found my arm held. 'By the way, were you responsible for what happened to our screws?'

'What's happened to your screws?' I managed to grin. 'Are they loose?'

'Very stiff-upper-lipped,' commented Wheeler. 'A quip in the face of death – very British. Take him away.'

I was hustled out of the lounge, a man on each side of me. I passed Slade whose face was yellowy-grey and who looked absolutely defeated and then I was thrust out on to the stern deck. There were now lights aboard *Artina* and, as we went forward along the side-deck, I saw that the man on my right still carried my gun. I didn't like the sound of that forepeak; from what I had seen of it on the plans of *Artina*'s sister ship it was only four feet high – a hermetically-sealed steel box. The odds were I'd die of heat-stroke or suffocation.

But relish the prospect or not, the man next to me had a gun. The fact that he wasn't pointing it directly at me made not a ha'porth of difference – not while he gripped my arm and the man on the other side held me in a hammer-lock.

They pushed me along the deck until we were amidships and then there was a noise like a dud firecracker and the man with a gun gave a yelp and dropped it on to the deck. He stopped and looked at the blood oozing from the hole in the back of his hand, and let go of me. I'd heard that dud firecracker go off before.

I heard it go off again and saw a brief flash of light from the top of the deckhouse. The seaman who had me in the hammer-lock stumbled slightly and his grip loosened. He went down in apparent slow motion and I saw there was a dark red spot in the middle of his forehead.

'Jump, you damned fool,' yelled Alison, and I went over the side in an inelegant dive, arms and legs going every which way. I landed in the water with a hell of a splash and heard, two seconds later, another neater and more ladylike splash as Alison joined me.

I wasted no time in getting under the surface and swam in a circle searching for her. My hand touched her leg and she twisted in the water and grabbed my wrist. I pulled, leading her, and we swam deep and under *Artina*. It would be natural for anyone to look for us from the side of the ship from which we had jumped and I wanted to get away from there.

Matters were complicated by the fact that I was running out of air. Things had happened so fast that I hadn't had time to prepare myself by taking a good lungful of air, and that wasn't so good. I didn't want to come up within shooting distance of the ship. I compromised by coming up for air under *Artina*'s stern, hanging on to her rudder with just my nose and mouth above water. Alison joined me.

I took a few deep breaths and then allowed an ear out of the water. Things were going pop on deck; men ran along the deck in a seemingly confused way and the deep rumble of the skipper's voice held a note of menace. I prodded Alison under the chin so that her head came out of the water and whispered into her ear. 'Swim to Ta'Xbiex – under water as far as possible. I'll meet you at the place we left.'

She wasted no time in answering but sank under water and vanished. I took a last breath and followed her. Normally I like swimming but this was getting to be a bit too much; I like to swim in water I know to be clean. I took it easy, letting the air dribble from my mouth as the strain grew intolerable. When it finally became impossible to stay under any longer I surfaced face upwards, letting only my nose and mouth break the surface.

I cleared my lungs in four breaths and then risked a glance back at *Artina*. A searchlight was probing the water again but not in my direction. As I was about to go under again I heard a roar and ducked under just in time as a fast launch came hurtling in my direction. I struck out strongly to gain depth and the launch passed directly overhead, the disturbance of the wake buffeting me in the water.

Three times I had to surface before I came to the shore or, rather to the long line of yachts moored stern on to the wharf of the Lazzaretto Creek Marina. I came up under the bows of a floating gin palace, puffing and panting in an attempt to get my breath back, but I soon stopped that when I heard the pad of naked feet on the deck above.

Whoever it was seemed irritable. 'More uproar – everyone rushin' about in the middle of the night. What the hell do they think they're doin'?'

A woman said, 'I thought I heard fireworks earlier.'

'Fireworks be damned – they're tomorrow night. And who the hell lets off fireworks at this time in the mornin'?'

The launch came by again, going at a hell of a clip, and the boat I was holding on to rocked heavily in the swell of its passage. This provoked an outburst of rage from above. 'What the hell do you think you're doin'?' the man screamed, and I pictured him as a peppery, curry-voiced retired colonel.

His wife said, 'You're making more noise than anyone else, George. Come back to bed!'

There was the slap of bare feet on the deck as they padded away. 'All right; but a fat lot of sleep I'll get,' he grumbled. 'I'll see the manager tomorrow. We can't have this happenin' at night.'

I grinned and swam a couple of boats down the line before climbing ashore. Then I dog-trotted towards the place I'd assigned to meet Alison, hoping that she'd made it. I was worried about Alison for a number of reasons. Back in Ireland she had been distrustful of me and had wondered out loud if I hadn't sold out to the Scarperers. Now I was distrustful of her.

If what Wheeler had said was true – that Mackintosh had blown the gaff – then I was really in trouble because Mackintosh wouldn't do a thing like that unheedingly. But why should I believe Wheeler? What incentive did he have to tell me the truth? In that case there was only one other person who could have sold out – Alison!

What brought that line of thought up short with a jerk was the recent episode on *Artina*. If Alison had sold out then why did she rescue me? Why did she pop off with that natty pistol of hers to wound one man, kill another, and get Stannard off the hot spot? That made even less sense. But I determined to keep a careful eye on Mrs Alison Smith in the future – providing she hadn't been run down by that launch.

II

I waited for fifteen minutes before she arrived. She was exhausted – so weary she couldn't pull herself from the water. I hauled her out and waited for a while until she recovered sufficiently to speak. Her first words were, 'That damned boat – nearly ran me down twice.'

'Did they see you?'

She shook her head slowly. 'I don't think so – they were just lucky.'

'They nearly got me,' I said. 'What happened to our boat?'

'I saw a man find the grapnel,' she said. 'And I knew you'd be in trouble. I went to the bows and climbed the anchor cable, and just let the boat drift.'

'Lucky for me you did. You're pretty handy with that pop-gun.'

'Six yards – no more. Anyone could do that.'

'Anyone wasn't there,' I said. 'You were.'

She looked about her. 'We'd better move. We could be picked up if we stay here.'

I shook my head. 'We're pretty safe. This harbour has so many inlets and creeks that Wheeler and his boys would have to search ten miles of coastline. But you're right – we'd better move on. It's a long walk back to the hotel and I want to get there before it's light. Do you feel fit?'

Alison got to her feet. 'I'm ready.'

It would take us, I estimated, a good hour to walk back to the hotel. We walked silently; I don't know what Alison was thinking but I was busy wondering what the hell to do next. At last I said, 'Well, I've fallen down on this one – my instructions were to bring Slade back or to kill him. I've done neither.'

'I can't see that you could have done differently,' said Alison.

'Yes, I could – I could have killed Slade on that yacht but I tried to bring him out.'

'It isn't easy to kill a sleeping man,' she said, and shivered. 'It isn't easy to kill anyone.'

I gave her a sideways glance and wondered about her. All that training must have produced something. 'How many men have you killed?'

'One,' she said, and her voice caught. 'To . . . night.' She started to shake violently.

I put my arm around her. 'Take it easy. It's a bad reaction, but it wears off in time. I know.' I damned Mackintosh for what he had done to his daughter. Yet at least he had made her into a professional and she would respond to the right stimulus just like one of Pavlov's dogs. To take her mind off what she had just done I said, 'We must leave the hotel.'

'Of course,' she said. 'But what then?'

'I'm damned if I know,' I admitted. 'It all depends on how much damage we've done to Wheeler's yacht. If she moves we're finished.'

'And if she doesn't?'

'We have another chance.'

'You can't go on board again – that won't work twice.'

'I know,' I said. 'I must think of something else.' We fell into a dispirited silence as we trudged along. We were both wet and it was cold in the early hours of the morning. We were also tired, and none of this helped us to think straight.

The sun was rising as we came into Floriana and there were a few people stirring in the streets. During our long walk our clothes had pretty well dried out and we didn't attract undue attention. Presently we passed workmen with ladders who were stringing up rows of gay bunting across the street. 'Those boys have started early,' I said. 'What's the celebration?'

'There's a *festa* today,' said Alison. 'They're always having them here.'

I remembered the disgruntled man who had complained about noise in the harbour. 'They'll be having fireworks tonight, then.'

'Inevitably. The two go together in Malta.'

Something prickled at the back of my mind – the first stirrings of an idea. I left it alone to grow in its own good time. 'How much money have we got?'

'About three thousand pounds – including the five hundred I gave you.'

At least we were well equipped with the sinews of war. The idea burgeoned a little more, but I'd have to study the plans of *Artina*'s sister ship a little more closely before I could bring it into the open.

A sleepy porter gave us our keys at the hotel and we went up to our rooms. At my door, I said, 'Come in here for a minute.' When we were inside I poured a big lump of scotch into a tooth-glass and gave it to Alison. 'Put that inside you and you'll feel better. Get yourself a hot shower and a change of clothing, but make it fast. We're evacuating – I want us to be out of here within a half-hour.'

She gave a wan smile. 'Where are we going?'

'We're going to ground – just where I don't know. But Wheeler will have his men checking the hotels; he might have started already. Just bring essentials – the money, passport and aircraft documents.'

When she had gone I followed my own advice. I knocked back a fast scotch and took a three-minute hot shower which chased away some of the aches and put some warmth in my bones again. My stomach was black with bruises. I dressed quickly and began to assemble the things I needed, not that there was much.

Then I sat down and began to study the ship plan. Fortunately it was scaled and I was able to measure distances fairly accurately. Not only was the idea burgeoning but blossoms were appearing. It all depended on whether Wheeler was immobilized in Marsamxett Harbour for another night.

Alison came back carrying one of those big bags which magically hold about six times more than they appear to. We left the hotel by a rear entrance and five minutes later we were at Kingsgate boarding a bus for Senglea.

Alison seemed brighter and said, 'Where are we going – and why?'

I paid the fare. 'I'll tell you when we get there.' The bus was crowded and I didn't want to talk about how I was going to kill Slade and Wheeler in public. The driver of the bus laboured under the misapprehension that his name was Jack Brabham, or perhaps he thought that the little shrine to the Virgin, so gaily decked in flowers, was a reasonable substitute for brakes. We got to Senglea in a remarkably short time.

Senglea is a peninsula jutting out into the Grand Harbour between Dockyard Creek and French Creek. Since the run-down of the Royal Navy and the demilitarization of the Naval Dockyard in Malta it seemed to be a reasonable place to find what I wanted – a boatshed, preferably with its own slipway.

It was still too early to do anything about that but the cafés were already open so we had breakfast, and very welcome it was. Over the bacon and eggs I said, 'Were you seen last night – seen to be recognized again?'

Alison shook her head. 'I don't think so.'

'Wheeler appeared to be uncertain about whether I had assistance,' I said. 'Of course, he knows now – but he doesn't know who. I think you're elected to do the shopping; it might not be safe for me on the streets.'

'What do you want?' she asked concisely.

'I want a boatshed. I only want it for twelve hours but we can't say so – we'll probably have to take it on three months' lease. I'm a boat designer and I'm working on a new type of . . . er . . . hydrofoil. I don't want anyone – my rivals, for instance – looking over my shoulder while I'm doing it, so I want discretion and security. That's the story.'

'Then what?'

'Then you push off and buy us a boat. Something about twenty feet overall and hellish fast, with big engines.'

'Outboard or inboard?'

'Doesn't matter. Outboards will be cheaper, but they must be powerful. You bring the boat round to the shed.' I looked through the window of the café. 'Over there is a scrap metal yard; I should be able to get most of what I want over there, including the hire of a welding outfit.'

Alison's brow wrinkled. 'So you have a fast boat and a welding outfit.' She waited patiently.

'Then you hire a truck. Can you drive a truck?' She gave me a look of silent contempt, and I grinned. She had probably passed her driving test with flying colours – in a Chieftain tank. I said, 'You take the truck and you buy enough fireworks to fill the boat.'

Now I had got her attention. 'Fireworks!'

'Big ones – especially the ones that go bang and throw out a shower of pretty lights. None of your paltry penny bangers; I want the big professional stuff. If they're so keen on fireworks here there should be quite a stock somewhere in this island. Think you can do that?'

'I can do it,' she said. 'Now tell me why the hell I should.'

I pulled out the ship plan and laid it on the table. 'I've been on board *Artina* and everything I saw fitted in with this plan, so I think we can trust it.' I tapped with my finger. 'The engine room, containing two 350 hp Rolls-Royce diesels which gulp a hell of a lot of fuel. Under the engine room a supply of fresh water and the ready use fuel tank which holds 1,200 gallons.'

My finger moved on the plan. 'Forward of the engine room is Wheeler's cabin, and farther forward are the crew's quarters. Under that, extending for twenty feet, is a double bottom containing the main fuel supply – 5,350 gallons of fuel oil. We know she's just taken on fuel so the tanks are full.'

I did a bit of measuring with my finger nail. 'To penetrate that tank we have to ram a hole at least three feet below the water line – preferably deeper. Her plating is mild steel, five-sixteenths of an inch thick – to punch a hole through that will need a hell of a lot of power.'

I looked up. 'I'm going to build a ram on the boat you're going to get me. At one time ramming was an orthodox naval tactic – all naval vessels had rams. But this is going to be a little different; it's going to be a combination ram and fireship. The boat will be full of fireworks. When we ram the tank we let out the oil. It floats. The fireworks go off pop and set the oil on fire.'

'So you're going to smoke out Wheeler?'

I looked at her in silence for a moment, then I said, 'Don't be silly, I'm going to burn the bastard out.'

III

It all took time, and we had little enough of that. I was right in thinking that I could get a suitable boatshed in Senglea, but moving in quickly was something else again. A few enquiries made in the district soon turned up just what I wanted but the dickering promised to be protracted and it was ten-thirty that morning before the deal went through and only then because of the production of a hundred pounds in crisp, British fivers.

As time was getting short I sent Alison off to buy the boat, which I hoped wouldn't prove to be as difficult and time-consuming as renting the shed. In the meantime I went to the scrap metal yard and rummaged about until I found what I wanted. I selected a few lengths of angle-iron, a lot of nuts and bolts and a steel bar, eight feet long and an inch and a half in diameter. I was also able to hire a welding outfit there, together with two full bottles of oxygen and acetylene and a pair of goggles.

As I paid out for this lot I reflected that the expense account for this lark was going to raise some Treasury official's hair. I could imagine him querying the purchase of perhaps a quarter of a ton of fireworks and acidly scratching out a memo asking Mrs Smith for further verification. But perhaps Mrs Smith also had training in cooking the swindle sheet.

I got all my equipment to the shed and waited around for Alison. I stared across the Grand Harbour to Valletta and wished I could see through it and into Marsamxett Harbour where *Artina* was still anchored – I hoped. At one-thirty I was still waiting and coming to a slow boil. Time was wasting and I had a hell of a lot to do.

It was nearly two o'clock before she arrived and the steam was blowing out of my ears. I caught the painter she tossed, and said curtly, 'What kept you?'

'I had to go to Sliema. Is she what you wanted?'

I studied the boat. She was a sleek, Italian-built job with two 100 hp Kiekhaefer Mercury outboard motors. Her lines looked good and those big engines would push her along at a fair lick. Alison said, 'I got more than thirty knots out of her on the way here.'

'You brought her from Sliema? You must have passed *Artina*.'

'She's still there.' I sagged a little in relief. 'They're doing a lot of work on her stern. When I passed they were hoisting out one of the propellers.'

'Were they, by God?' I laughed. 'Then it will be an all day job.' I jerked my thumb at the shed. 'There's a cradle in there. Help me get this thing up the slip and out of sight.'

We ran the cradle down the slip, floated the boat into it, and then winched the lot into the shed. Alison looked at her watch. 'I've arranged for the fireworks, too. They'll be ready to be picked up at three.'

'Then you'd better push off.'

She hesitated. 'Can you manage alone?'

'I should be able to. There's a block and tackle up there – I can use that to take the engines out.'

'There's a flask of coffee and a packet of sandwiches in the boat. And a bottle of whisky. I'll be back as soon as I can.'

She turned to go, and I said, 'Alison, there's just one more thing; see if you can get a big axe. A felling axe used for cutting down trees.'

She looked puzzled and then doubtful. 'I'm not sure they use those on Malta – there are not too many trees.'

'Do your best.' She left and I rescued the victuals before the bottle got broken, and then I uncoupled the steering cables on the boat and hoisted out the engines. I also used the block and tackle to turn the boat out of the cradle so that it lay upside down on trestles. I ate the sandwiches and drank the coffee while studying the problem; the whisky I left strictly alone because there was a job to be done, although I'd probably be glad of a stiff jolt before I set out.

I proceeded to get my hands dirty. The hull was of glass fibre and I began to ruin it by drilling holes in carefully selected places. The idea was to position the ram so that it was at least three feet below the water line when the boat was planing at speed, and it had to be fixed to the hull firmly enough so that it wouldn't come adrift on impact. If that happened then the momentum given by those big engines would be lost and the ram wouldn't penetrate *Artina*'s steel shell.

I cut up lengths of angle-iron and bolted them to the hull and through to steel cross-members which ran athwartship. Then I started to weld it up. It wasn't pretty welding and would have won no prizes at a craft school but, by God, it was strong – I made sure of that. When I had got that far there were two steel triangles built into the hull, the apexes of which were a little over three feet below the bottom. I took the long steel bar and welded it to the apexes of my steel triangles so that it was parallel to the bottom of the hull and projecting two feet in front.

Alison was back long before I had got that far and gave me a hand. It was hot and sweaty work and it took time. It was seven in the evening when I put the finishing touch to it. 'Did you get the axe?'

She produced just what I needed – a long-handled felling axe. I didn't need the handle and wasted no time in fiddling but cut it off with the welding torch. Then I took the blade and welded it vertically to the end of the steel bar – that was the cutting edge of my ram.

I stood back and looked at what I had done. Oddly enough it did look like a weird kind of hydrofoil, but I didn't like to think of what all that heavy ironmongery hung under the boat would do to her planing characteristics. I began to worry about the speed I was going to lose and if I could get her to plane at all.

'I could use a drink,' I said.

Alison poured some whisky into the cup from the vacuum flask and gave it to me. She looked at the boat, and said, 'It's going to be dangerous. I was wondering . . .'

'Wondering what?'

She turned to face me. 'I was wondering if this can't be done more simply – by the police.'

'That's a great idea,' I said sardonically. 'Can you imagine the local coppers believing us? Christ, Wheeler comes here every year and he's a respected figure, a British MP and an eminent capitalist. He's probably given prizes to the yacht club and I wouldn't be surprised if he's the sole support of a local orphanage. By the time we managed to convince anyone both he and Slade would have flown the coop.'

'There's still a body on *Artina*,' said Alison. 'That would take a lot of explaining away.'

'Same objection,' I said. 'Forget it. Let's have a look at the fireworks.'

There were a lot of them and they were big; rockets that would go up under their own power and maroons designed to be fired from mortars. 'This lot should add to the festivities,' I said in satisfaction. 'We must get the boat on to the cradle.'

I had to cut bits away from the cradle to accommodate our strange craft and it was forever ruined for handling normal boats. More expense for the Treasury. I installed the engines and hooked up the steering cables and tested them. When I jumped to the ground the boat, now right way up, looked a bit more practicable.

'How much did you pay for her?' I asked curiously.

'Fifteen hundred pounds,' said Alison.

I grinned. 'Guided missiles always are expensive. Let's put the cargo aboard.'

We filled up every spare inch of the hull with the big fireworks. Alison, as foreseeing as ever, had brought along a jerrican full of petrol and, after topping up the tanks, there was still half a gallon left, more than enough to start a fire to get things going. I now had a new worry; I had drilled a dozen holes in the hull to take bolts and had caulked them with putty, and I was wondering if I had sealed her tight. That couldn't be tested until we put her in the water and that wouldn't be until it was good and dark.

'When do they start shooting off the fireworks for the *festa*?' I asked.

'Two hours after sunset.'

'I'd like to ram *Artina* when the official fireworks are going full blast. It'll help to confuse the issue.' I sat down wearily and pulled out my ship plan; it was becoming worn and tatty and dirty at the creases, but it was still legible. 'The trouble is that I might hit one of the main frames,' I said. 'In that case I doubt if I'll get enough penetration.'

The frames were about two feet apart; statistically I had a good chance of missing – the odds were on my side.

Alison said, 'If we're going to do more underwater swimming we might as well do it comfortably.' She got up and dragged some scuba gear from the corner. 'I took the precaution of hiring this.'

'That slipped my mind.' I wondered what else I'd forgotten. I looked at the gear – there were two sets. 'I'm going to do the swimming,' I said. 'Not you.'

'But I'm coming with you,' she expostulated.

'For what? I don't need you.'

She flinched as though I had slapped her face. I said, 'You're right – it's a dangerous operation, and there's no point in both of us going. Besides, I need you for something else.' I thumped the side of the boat. 'Whether this works or not there's going to be ructions when these fireworks explode. If I don't get back someone must be around to have another crack at Wheeler – and you're elected.'

I reached out for the bottle and poured some more whisky. 'You can try going to the police; they might be interested enough by then to take you seriously.'

She saw the point, but she didn't like it. She set her face in a stubborn mould and prepared to argue. I forestalled her. 'All right; this is what you do. You wait here until nightfall and help me to get the boat into the water. Then you hop over to Ta'Xbiex and hire another boat – if you can get anyone to trust you.' I smiled. 'Looking as you do now I wouldn't trust you with a kid's bath toy.'

She rubbed her smudged face and distastefully inspected her fingertips. 'Thanks,' she said. 'I'll clean up.'

'If you can't hire a boat, steal one. There are plenty of

loose boats at the Marina. Meet me at the seaward point of Manoel Island and then follow me in, but not too closely. When the balloon goes up watch out for Slade and Wheeler – they should be doing their best to jump overboard if all goes well. See they don't get ashore.'

'I lost the gun last night,' she said.

'Well, bat them over the head with an oar,' I said. 'I'll be around somewhere so keep your oar away from me.' I looked at my watch. 'It'll be dark enough for launching in about an hour.'

That hour seemed to stretch out interminably rather like I'm told it does in an LSD trip; I wouldn't know about that – I haven't tried it. We didn't talk much and when we did it was of inconsequentialities. The sun set and the light slowly ebbed from the sky until at last it was dark enough to take the boat down the slip without anyone seeing it. Once it was in the water it wouldn't appear too abnormal.

I patted the wickedly gleaming steel axe-head which formed the tip of the ram and went to open the big double doors of the shed, and we steered the cradle down the slip and into the water. I released the boat and we took the cradle away and I turned to see how my handiwork had turned out.

It wasn't too bad; she was down by the head but not by too much considering the weight of iron under her bows, and she appeared quite normal apart from the bits of angle-iron which showed above water on each side of the hull. In another ten minutes it would be too dark to see even that, but even if I was picked up by a light in the harbour I doubt if anyone would notice anything particularly odd about her.

'That's it,' I said wearily. I was bone-tired; no sleep, a beating-up and a hard day's work did nothing to improve me.

'I'll go now,' said Alison quietly. 'Good luck, Owen.'

She didn't kiss me, or even touch me. She just walked away, picking up her coat as she went.

I climbed into the boat and rearranged a few of the fireworks to make myself more comfortable. I put the scuba gear handy and checked my primitive system of fuses. Then there was nothing to do but wait another hour before I was due to move off.

Again it was a long wait.

11

I

I checked my watch for the twentieth time in fifteen minutes and decided that time had come. I put on the scuba gear, tightened the weighted belt around my waist, and hung the mask around my neck. Then I started the engines and the boat quivered in the water. I cast off the painter and pushed the boat away with one hand and then tentatively opened the throttles a notch, not knowing what to expect.

At a slow speed she didn't handle too badly although there seemed to be something a little soggy about her response to the wheel. I switched on the lights because I didn't want the harbour patrol to pick me up for running illegally, and went down French Creek into the Grand Harbour. Here, in time past, the British Battle Fleet had lain, line upon line of dreadnoughts and battle cruisers. Now, there was another, but odder, naval craft putting to sea, but this one was in an earlier tradition – more like one of Drake's fireships.

Across the harbour Valletta was all lit up and there were strings of coloured lights spangling Floriana. Tinny music floated across the quiet water punctuated by the thumping of a bass drum. The merry-making was well under way.

I rounded the head of Senglea and steered to the harbour mouth. Nothing was coming my way so I decided to open up and see what the boat would do. The note of the engines deepened as I opened the throttles and I felt the surge of acceleration as 200 hp kicked her through the water. In terms of horse-power per ton of displacement this little boat was perhaps forty times as powerful as *Artina*; that's where the speed came from.

The steering was worse than bad – it was dreadful. The wheel kicked in my hands violently and my course was erratic, to say the least, and I went down the Grand Harbour doing a pretty good imitation of a water boatman, those jerky insects that run across the surface of ponds.

The damned boat wouldn't get on the step and plane and I don't suppose her speed was more than twelve knots, and that wasn't going to be enough. All the power going into the screws was doing nothing more than raising waves and I wasn't supposed to be in the wave-raising business. In desperation I slammed the throttles hard open and she suddenly rose in the water and took off, picking up at least an extra ten knots in as many seconds. But the steering was worse and there was a definite lag between hauling the wheel around and the corresponding reaction.

I throttled down again and she sagged into the water, and her speed dropped as though she'd run into a wall. This was going to be a dicey business. At a pinch I could get the speed, provided the engines didn't blow up, but I didn't know if I could steer her straight enough to hit my target. In spite of the flow of cooling night air I found I was sweating profusely.

If the only way to get her to plane was to run the engines at full bore I'd better not try that again. There would be no more trial speed runs because I was scared of the engines packing up, and next time this boat would be at speed again would be the last time. As for the steering, I'd have to handle that as best I could.

I dropped speed even further and plugged on towards St Elmo's Point. Fort St Elmo reared up starkly against the night sky as I passed between the point and the breakwater. Now I was in the open sea and the boat wallowed sickeningly. That heavy steel bar slung three feet under the water was acting as a pendulum. This lubberly craft was enough to give any self-respecting boat designer the screaming meemies.

I rounded the point and turned into Marsamxett Harbour, glad to get into sheltered waters again, and headed towards Manoel Island. Valletta was now to my left and I wondered from where they shot their fireworks. I checked the time and found I had little to spare.

As I approached Manoel Island I closed the throttles until the engines were barely ticking over, just enough to give me steerage way. Not far away a light flickered and I saw that Alison was in position; she had struck a match and held it so that it illuminated her face. I steered in that direction and made contact.

She was in what seemed to be a small runabout driven by a little outboard motor. 'That's nice,' I said. 'Where did you get it?'

'I took your advice; I stole it,' she said, and laughed quietly.

I grinned in the darkness. 'It's our duty to save government money,' I said virtuously.

'How did you get on?' she asked.

'She's a bitch,' I said. 'As cranky as the devil.'

'She was all right when I brought her from Sliema.'

'That was a different boat. She's damned near uncontrollable at speed. How much time have we got?'

'About ten minutes.'

I looked about. 'I'd better get in position. We don't want to stay here or we'll be run down by the Sliema ferry – she's coming now. Is *Artina* in the same place?'

'Yes.'

'Then I'll be on my way. I'll go right down Lazzaretto Creek and turn around so as to get a good run up. You keep clear on the other side of *Artina*.' I paused. 'The steering is so bloody bad I might even miss her on the first pass. In that case I'll turn around and have a go on the other side. Don't be in my way or you'll get run over.'

'Good luck again,' said Alison.

I said, 'If you see Wheeler give him a good clout with my compliments. He was looking forward to seeing his Chinese friend operate on me. If things work out I'll see you in Ta'Xbiex – at the same place as last night.'

Gently I eased the throttles forward and moved off. I passed *Artina* quite closely; there were three men on deck – Wheeler, the skipper and the Chinese, Chang Pi-wu. I could see them quite clearly because they were illuminated, but I was low on the water in the dark and there was no chance of them recognizing me. I was just another ship passing in the night.

Mentally I made a cross on the place on the hull I intended to hit, and then I carried on down Lazzaretto Creek. At the bottom, near the Manoel Island bridge I turned with idling engines. I switched on the air from the scuba bottle and checked the demand-valve, and then bit on the mouthpiece and put on the mask. If things went well I wouldn't have time to do any of that later.

Behind me traffic passed on the road and presently a procession came by with a band of pounding drums and off-key brass. I ignored it and looked across to Valletta and the forthcoming firework display. There was what I thought to be a heavier thump on a drum but it was a mortar banging off. A maroon burst over Valletta in a yellow sunburst and in the echoing reflection from the water of the harbour I saw *Artina* clearly for a brief moment. The fireworks had begun and it was time for me to add my share to the festivities.

I advanced the throttles and moved off slowly as a rocket soared up and exploded in a shower of red and green fiery rain. I steered with one hand and with the other liberally doused my cargo with petrol from an open can, hoping to God that the sparks from the fireworks were totally extinguished by the time they reached water level. It only needed one of those in the boat and I'd go up in a cloud of glory.

Then I pushed open the throttles wider and by the time I was making any kind of speed the sky was alive with lights as the Maltese spent their fireworks with reckless abandon. *Artina* was clearly silhouetted as, with equal abandon, I jammed the throttles wide open.

The engines roared and the boat reared up in the water almost uncontrollably as she began to plane. The wheel kicked in my hands as I strove to keep her on course and I zig-zagged dangerously close to the line of yachts moored at the marina. I swung the wheel hard over but the bitch was late in responding and there was an outraged cry from the bow of one of the yachts. It sounded like the curry-voiced colonel who must have got the fright of his life as I scraped his paint at twenty knots.

Then I was past him and heading out into the harbour, bucking and twisting and steering a course which would have brought tears to the eyes of any self-respecting helmsman. The fireworks banged and flashed overhead striking dazzling reflections from the water and my heart jumped into my mouth as a small runabout came out of nowhere and cut across my bows. I cursed him and swung the wheel and missed him by a whisker. That made two damned fools at large in Marsamxett Harbour.

As I swung the wheel hard over the other way I looked for *Artina* and I saw that I was going to miss her by a sizeable margin. I cursed again at the thought of having to make another mad sortie. It occurred to me that with the steering being as crazy as it was then I'd better aim at anything but *Artina* and then I might have a chance of hitting her.

I estimated I was going to shoot under her stern but just then the hard-pressed port engine blew up and, with a nasty flailing rattle of a broken connecting rod, it expired. The boat checked a little in the water and her bow came over to aim directly at *Artina*. I hung on as she loomed over me and then, with a satisfying smash, my underwater ram struck her amidships.

I was thrown forward and bruised my ribs on the wheel but it saved me from going into the water. I still had one last thing to do. As I groped for my cigarette lighter I heard a shout on deck and I looked up into the eye-straining alternation of light and darkness and saw a movement as someone peered over the side to see what the hell had happened now. I couldn't see much of him but I must have been clearly visible as another batch of rockets went up.

I flicked the lighter and it sparked but there was no flame. In the rocket's red glare I saw that the boat's bow was smashed and broken with the impact against *Artina*'s side. The ram must have been deeply embedded because she showed no sign of wanting to drift away.

Desperately I flicked the lighter again but again there was no flame. There was a bang from above and a bullet smashed into the instrument panel next to my elbow, ruining the rev counter. I leaned forward and put the lighter right next to a bunch of petrol-soaked fireworks. The boat was making water and I had to start a fire before she went under.

I flicked again and the whole damned lot went up in a brilliant sheet of flame. It was only because I was fully equipped in scuba gear that I wasn't instantly incinerated. It went up, as suddenly ignited petrol does, in a soft explosion – a great *whooof* of flame that blew me overboard. And as I went something hit me in the shoulder very hard.

Whether or not I was actually on fire for a moment I don't know. When I hit the water I was dazed, but the sudden shock brought a reflex into action and I struck for the depths. It was then I found that my right arm was totally useless. Not that it mattered very much; in scuba diving the flippered feet do most of the work. But it worried me because I didn't know what could be wrong with it.

I swam under water for a short while, then stopped because I didn't know where I was going. I was absolutely disoriented and, for all I knew, I could have been swimming out to sea. So I surfaced cautiously and looked around to get my bearings and to see what was happening to *Artina*.

I had not swum as far as I thought – she was about a hundred yards away, too close for comfort, especially in view of the little piece of hellfire that I had established amidships. My fireship was going great guns. With the ram stabbed into *Artina*'s side like a narwhal's tusk she was securely fixed, and the fireworks were exploding like an artillery barrage, showering multi-coloured sparks and great gouts of flame which licked up her side. Already a canvas deck awning was on fire and men were running about the deck every which way.

A big maroon went off like a howitzer shell, sending out a burst of green flame and sparks which reached out to patter on the surface of the water about me, hissing viciously as they were extinguished. I was close enough to be seen if anyone had the time to look, so I sank beneath the surface again after a last glance around, and struck out for the shore.

I had not done a dozen strokes before I knew something was wrong. I felt curiously weak and light-headed and my right shoulder had developed a dull throb which was rapidly sharpening up into a stabbing pain. I eased off and felt my shoulder with my left hand and the pain jabbed me with such intensity that I nearly yelled aloud which is a good way of getting oneself drowned.

So I surfaced again and drifted, becoming more light-headed and feeling the strength ebbing from my legs more swiftly every minute. The fire by *Artina* was still going strong but it all seemed blurred as though seen through a rain-washed window. It was then I knew that I was probably going to die, that I no longer had the strength to swim to the shore which was so close, and that I was drifting out to sea where I would drown.

I think I passed out for a moment because the next thing I knew there was a light flashing in my eyes from very close and an urgent whisper, 'Owen; grab this!'

Something fell across my face and floated in the water next to my head and I put out my left hand and found a rope. 'Can you hold on?' I knew it was Alison.

An engine throbbed and the rope tightened and I was being drawn through the water. Desperately I concentrated all my attention on to holding on to that rope. Whatever strength I had left must be marshalled and pushed into the fingers of my left hand so that they would not relinquish their grip. The water lapped about my head, creating a miniature bow wave as I was towed behind Alison's boat and, even in that extremity, I paid tribute to the efficiency of Alison Smith and Mackintosh's training. She knew she could not haul an almost unconscious man into the boat without either capsizing or, worse, attracting attention.

It was a ridiculously short distance to the shore and Alison brought up at a slipway. She rammed the boat up it, careless of the consequences, and jumped overboard into two feet of water and hauled me out bodily. 'What's wrong, Owen?'

I flopped down and sat into the shallow water. 'I think I was shot,' I said carefully, and my voice seemed to come from miles away. 'In the shoulder – the right shoulder.'

The pain washed over me as her fingers probed, and then I heard the rip of cloth and she bandaged the wound roughly but effectively. I wouldn't have been surprised if she had operated there and then, using a penknife and a hairpin to extract the bullet. I was becoming used to her surprising range of talents.

I said tiredly, 'What's happening to *Artina*?'

She moved away and I saw *Artina* in the harbour beyond. All the sea was on fire about her and above the yellow flames rose the roiling cloud of greasy black smoke that could only come from oil. The ram had done its work. Even as I watched there was a red flash just under the wheelhouse and then the wheelhouse vanished as an oil tank exploded in her vitals and blasted through the deck. A deep boom came across the water, echoed and re-echoed from the cliff-like fortifications of Valletta.

'That's it, then,' I said abstractedly.

Alison leaned over me. 'Can you walk?'

'I don't know. I can try.'

She put her hand under my left arm. 'You've been leaking blood like a stuck pig. You need a hospital.'

I nodded. 'All right.' It didn't really matter now. The job had been done. Even if Slade or Wheeler had survived they were done for. I would be asked why I had destroyed *Artina* and I would tell the truth, and I would be listened to very carefully. People don't wander around blowing up millionaires' yachts for nothing and what I had to say would be heard. Whether it was believed or not would be another matter, but enough mud would stick to Wheeler to make sure that hard, professional eyes would be on him for ever more. As for Slade, I had escaped from prison with him and if I was on Malta and said that Slade was around then he would be picked up in jig time. It's a small island and strangers can't hide easily.

As for myself I didn't know what would happen. Alison might give evidence *in camera* as to my part in the affair, but if Mackintosh was dead I didn't know how much weight that would carry. There was a strong possibility that I would spend the rest of my life in the maximum security wing of Durham Gaol. Right at that moment I was past caring.

Alison helped me to my feet and I staggered like a drunken sailor up the slipway, hanging on to her arm with a flabby grip. We had just reached the top when I paused and stared at the man who was waiting. He looked remarkably like that tough, young copper, Sergeant Jervis, who had taken such a strong dislike to me because I had stolen some diamonds and had not the grace to tell him where they were.

I turned my head and looked in the other direction. Brunskill was there with Forbes just behind him. Already they were striding out and coming towards us.

I said to Alison, 'The end of the line, I think,' and turned to face Brunskill.

He stood in front of me and surveyed me with expressionless eyes, noting every detail of my disarray and the bandage on my shoulder. He flicked his eyes at Alison, and then nodded towards the harbour where *Artina* was going down in flames. 'Did you do that?'

'Me?' I shook my head. 'It must have been caused by a spark from the fireworks.'

He smiled grimly. 'I must caution you that anything you say may be taken down in writing and used in evidence.' He looked at Alison. 'That applies to you, too.'

'I don't think Malta is within your jurisdiction,' she said coolly.

'Not to worry about that,' said Brunskill. 'I have a platoon of the local constabulary on call.' He turned to me. 'If you had as many lives as a cat you'd spend them all inside. I'm going to wrap you up so tight this time that they'll have to build a prison just for you.'

I could see him mentally formulating the list of charges. Arson, murder, grievous bodily harm, carrying weapons – and worse – using them, driving a horse and cart through the Explosives Act. Maybe, with a bit of twisting, he could toss in piracy and setting fire to the Queen's shipyards. Those last two are still capital offences.

He said, 'What in hell did you think you were doing?' There was wonder in his voice.

I swayed on my feet. 'I'll tell you after I've seen a doctor.' He caught me as I fell.

II

I woke up in the nick. It was the prison hospital, to be sure, but still inside thick walls, and they build walls thicker in Malta than anywhere else. But I had a private room and came to the conclusion that the local coppers didn't want the simple, uncomplicated Maltese criminals to be corrupted by contact with such a hard case as myself. This proved to be a wrong assumption.

An uncommunicative doctor performed a simple operation on my shoulder under local anaesthetic and then I lay waiting for the arrival of Brunskill and his inevitable questions. I spent the time thinking out ingenious lies to tell him; there are certain aspects of HM Government it is better for the ordinary copper not to know.

But it was a stranger and not Brunskill who was ushered into the room. He was a tall, middle-aged man with a smooth, unlined face and an air of quiet authority who introduced himself as Armitage. His credentials were impressive; I read a letter of introduction from the Prime Minister and pushed back the rest of the bumf unread.

He pulled up a chair to the bedside and sat down. 'Well, Mr Stannard; how are you feeling?'

I said, 'If you know my name is Stannard then you know most of the story. Did Alec Mackintosh send you?'

'I'm afraid not,' he said regretfully. 'Mackintosh is dead.'

I felt a cold lump settle in my stomach. 'So he never came out of hospital.'

'He died without recovering consciousness,' said Armitage.

I thought of Alison and wondered how she'd take it. The

love-hate relationship she had with her father made it difficult to estimate her reaction. I said, 'Has Mrs Smith been told?'

Armitage nodded. 'She took it quite well.'

How would you know? I thought.

'This is all going to be difficult,' said Armitage. 'Your activities – particularly in the Irish Republic – could put the Government into an awkward position.' He paused. 'Should they be fully disclosed.'

I could imagine that they could. Relations were already strained over what was happening in Ulster and the Press would have a field day with garbled stories of a British agent on the rampage in the sovereign State of Ireland.

I said ironically, 'Not to mention my own awkward position.'

'Just so,' said Armitage.

We stared at each other. 'All right,' I said at last. 'Who blew the gaff? This operation had the tightest security of any I've been on. How did it fall apart?'

Armitage sighed. 'It fell apart *because* of the tight security. It fell apart because Mackintosh was constitutionally unable to trust anyone.' He held me with his eye. 'He didn't even trust you.'

I nodded, and Armitage snorted. 'He didn't even trust the Prime Minister. All through he played a lone hand and deceived everyone regarding his motives.'

I said quietly, 'I have a big stake in this. I think you'd better tell me the story.'

It all started with the spate of prison escapes which worried the people at the top. Mountbatten investigated the prison service and security was tightened, but the vague rumours of the Scarperers' organization kept the worries on the boil and Mackintosh was put in charge of doing something about it.

'I didn't like that,' said Armitage disapprovingly. 'And I

said so at the time. It ought to have been left to the Special Branch.'

'Mackintosh told me they'd tried and failed,' I said.

Armitage nodded impatiently. 'I know – but they could have tried again. Mackintosh was too much the lone wolf – too secretive.'

I could see what stuck in Armitage's craw. He was a top-level civil servant – a Whitehall mandarin – and he liked things to go through channels in an orderly way. In particular, he didn't like the idea of the Prime Minister having a private hatchet man. It offended his sense of what was fitting.

He leaned forward. 'Unknown to anybody Mackintosh already had his eye on Wheeler but he kept his suspicions to himself. He didn't even tell the PM. We'll never know what went through his mind, but perhaps he thought he wouldn't be believed. Wheeler was coming up fast in popularity and influence; in fact, the Prime Minister was on the point of making him a Junior Minister in the Government.'

'Yes,' I said. 'I can see Alec's problem. How did he get on to Wheeler?'

Armitage shook his head. 'I don't know. I believe the Prime Minister reposed full confidence in Mackintosh regarding certain measures of top-level security.' He sounded even more disapproving.

So Mackintosh was running security checks on the élite. That was one answer to the question: *Quis custodiet ipsos custodes?* I could imagine the Prime Minister might expect Mackintosh to turn up some member of the radical Left or Right as a potential risk, but who would suspect a bourgeois capitalist who firmly trod the middle road of being a Maoist? The idea was laughable.

'So Mackintosh had unprovable suspicions,' I said. 'He didn't want them getting back to Wheeler so he kept his mouth shut until he could catch Wheeler in the act.'

'That must have been the size of it,' conceded Armitage. 'He brought you in and put you next to Slade by means of the diamond robbery.' A slight smile mitigated his severe expression. 'Most ingenious. But he didn't tell you about Wheeler.'

'I wouldn't expect him to,' I said flatly. 'At that stage I didn't need to know.' I rubbed my chin. 'But I'd expect him to tell Mrs Smith.'

'He didn't – but I'll come to that later.' Armitage leaned forward. 'When you and Slade escaped Mackintosh went to see Wheeler. We have established that he saw Wheeler at his club. They had a conversation in the course of which Mackintosh disclosed who you were. That's how . . . er . . . the gaff was blown.'

I blinked, then closed my eyes and lay back on the pillow. 'He did it deliberately?' I asked softly.

'Oh, yes. He wanted to stampede Wheeler into ill-advised action. He wanted to catch him *in flagrante delicto.* Apparently you were expendable.'

I opened my eyes and looked at Armitage. 'I always was. It's an occupational hazard.' All the same I thought that Alec Mackintosh was a ruthless son of a bitch.

'Wheeler was stampeded, all right, but I'm not sure that Wheeler's action was ill-advised,' said Armitage reflectively. 'Mackintosh was run down by a car the same day. We've impounded all Wheeler's cars for forensic examination and I'm pretty sure we'll turn up some evidence even at this late date. I think the job was done by his Irish chauffeur.'

'Or his Chinese cook.'

Armitage shrugged. 'So Mackintosh was unconscious in hospital. He was run down on his way to his office where Mrs Smith was awaiting him. Whether he was going to tell her what he'd done we'll never know. At all events, at this time no one in the Government knew about Wheeler. Do you see what I mean about the security of the operation being too tight?'

I said, 'A top-rank Whitehall man, such as yourself, doesn't turn up in Malta out of the blue so opportunely. Something must have come up.'

'It did. Mackintosh died. He'd taken out insurance. He wrote out a full account of his actions and posted them to his lawyer just before he saw Wheeler. The snag about that was that the sealed envelope was inscribed, "Only to be opened in the event of my death."'

Armitage stared at me. 'And Mackintosh was in the hands of the doctors. He wasn't dead, but you'd hardly call him alive although in the legal sense he was. He was a vegetable maintained by modern medical techniques and the doctors' duty by the Hippocratic Oath, and that was something he hadn't calculated for. That damned envelope was in the lawyer's hands for two weeks before Mackintosh died and by then it was nearly too late. It would have been too late were it not for your actions.'

'That's all very well,' I said. 'But how did that lead you to me? Mackintosh didn't know where I was.'

'We went straight for Wheeler,' said Armitage. 'We were just wondering how to tackle him when you took the problem out of our hands.' He smiled slightly. 'Your methods are direct, to say the least. It was thought that you might be around, so we brought along people who could recognize you.'

'Brunkskill and company,' I said. 'So you've got Wheeler.'

He shook his head. 'No; Wheeler is dead, and so is Slade. You saw to that very effectively, if I may say so. The Special Branch is working on the ramifications of Wheeler's organizations – those that are legal and those that are not. I think it will be a lengthy task, but that is none of your concern.' He leaned back in his chair. 'However, you do present a problem to the Government, which is why I am here.'

I couldn't suppress the smile. 'I bet I am.'

'It's no laughing matter, Mr Stannard,' said Armitage severely. 'Already the Press has become alerted to the fact that there is something in the wind.' He stood up and wandered over to the window. 'Fortunately, the worst of your . . . er . . . crimes were committed outside the United Kingdom and to those we can turn a blind eye. But there is the matter of a diamond robbery which may well prove awkward to handle.'

I said, 'Were the diamond merchants paid out by their insurance company?'

Armitage turned and nodded. 'I should think so.'

'Well, why not leave it at that?'

He was affronted. 'Her Majesty's Government cannot connive in the cheating of an insurance company.'

'Why not?' I asked reasonably. 'Her Majesty's Government is conniving in the murder of Wheeler and Slade. What the hell's so sacred about a few thousand quid?'

That didn't sit well with him. Property rights come before human rights in British law. He harrumphed embarrassedly, and said, 'What is your suggestion?'

'Wheeler is dead and Slade is dead. Why shouldn't Rearden be dead, too? He can be killed while evading arrest – it shouldn't be too difficult to stage manage. But you'll have to gag Brunskill, Forbes and Jervis, and you can do that under the Official Secrets Act. Or you can throw the fear of God into them; I don't think any of that gang would relish being transferred to the Orkneys for the rest of his days.'

'And Mr Stannard comes to life again?' he queried.

'Precisely.'

'I suppose it could be arranged. And how do we explain the spectacular death of Wheeler?'

'It must have been those rockets they were shooting over

the harbour,' I said. 'One of them must have gone out of whack and hit the ship. It was being repaired at the time – I'll bet there was some fuel open on deck. I think the Maltese Government ought to be ticked off for not keeping proper control.'

'Very ingenious,' said Armitage, and took out a notebook. 'I'll suggest that the Navy offer a ship and a diver to help lift the wreck. We'll choose the diver, of course.' He made a note with a silver pen.

'You'd better,' I said, thinking of that ram which was probably still embedded in *Artina*'s side. 'A sad end to a popular MP. Most regrettable.'

Armitage's lips twitched and he put away the notebook. 'The organization for which you worked before Mackintosh pulled you out of South Africa apparently thinks highly of you. I am asked to inform you that someone called Lucy will be getting in touch.'

I nodded. How Mackintosh would have sneered at that.

'And the Prime Minister has asked me to pass on his sincere thanks for the part you have played in the affair and for the way you have brought it to a conclusion. He regrets that thanks are all he has to offer under the circumstances.'

'Oh, well, you can't eat medals,' I said philosophically.

III

I sat in the lounge of the Hotel Phoenicia waiting for Alison. She had been whisked to England by the powers-that-be in order to attend Alec's funeral. I would have liked to have paid my respects, too, but my face had been splashed in the pages of the British newspapers with the name of Rearden underneath and it was considered unwise for me to put in an appearance until Rearden had been forgotten in the short-lived public memory. Meanwhile I was growing a beard.

I was deriving much amusement from an intensive reading of an air mail edition of *The Times*. There was an obituary of Wheeler which should put him well on the road to canonization; his public-spiritedness was praised, his financial acumen lauded and his well-known charitableness eulogized. The first leader said that in view of Wheeler's work for the prisons his death was a blow to enlightened penology unequalled since the Mountbatten Report. I choked over that one.

The Prime Minister, in a speech to the Commons, said that British politics would be so much the worse for the loss of such a valued colleague. The Commons rose and stood in silence for two minutes. That man ought to have had his mouth washed out with soap.

Only the Financial Editor of *The Times* caught a whiff of something rotten. Commenting on the fall of share prices in the companies of Wheeler's empire he worried at the question of why it was thought necessary for the auditors to move in before Wheeler's body was cold. Apart from that quibble Wheeler had a rousing send-off on his journey to hell.

Rearden came off worse. Condemned as a vicious desperado, his death in a gun battle was hailed as a salutary lesson to others of his kidney. Brunskill was commended for his perseverance on the trail of the villainous Rearden and for his fortitude in the face of almost certain death. 'It was nothing,' said Brunskill modestly. 'I was only doing my duty as a police officer.'

It was hoped that Slade would soon be caught. There were full security wraps on Slade's death and I had no doubt that in another ten or twenty years any number of criminologically inclined writers would make a fair living churning out books about the Slade Mystery.

I looked up to see Alison coming into the lounge. She

looked pale and tired but she smiled when she saw me. I rose to my feet as she approached and she stopped for a moment to survey me, taking in the cast on my arm and the unshaven stubble on my cheeks. 'You look awful,' she said.

'I'm not feeling too bad; I can still bend my left elbow. What will you have?'

'A Campari.' She sat down and I whistled up a waiter. 'I see you've been reading all about it.'

I grinned. 'Don't believe everything you read in the papers.'

She leaned back in the chair. 'Well, Owen; it's over. It's all over.'

'Yes,' I said. 'I'm sorry about Alec.'

'Are you?' she asked in a flat voice. 'He nearly got you killed.'

I shrugged. 'He miscalculated the speed and direction of Wheeler's reaction. But for that it was a good ploy.'

'Even though he was selling you out?' Her tone was incredulous.

'God damn it!' I said. 'We weren't playing pat-a-cake. The stakes were too great. Wheeler *had* to be nailed down and if the way to do it was to sacrifice a man in the field then there was no choice. Wheeler was striking at the heart of the State. The Prime Minister was considering him for a ministerial position, and God knows where he could have gone on from there.'

'If all statesmen are like Alec then God help Britain,' said Alison in a low voice.

'Don't be bitter,' I said. 'He's dead. He killed himself, not me. Never forget that.'

The waiter came with the drinks and we were silent until he had gone, then Alison said, 'What are you going to do now?'

I said, 'I had a visit from Lucy. Of course I can't do much until the shoulder heals – say a month to six weeks.'

'Are you going back to South Africa?'

I shook my head. 'I think I'm being considered for the active list.' I sipped my drink. 'What about you?'

'I haven't had time to think yet. There was a lot to do in London apart from the funeral. Alec's personal affairs had to be wound up; I spent a lot of time with his solicitor.'

I leaned forward. 'Alison, will you marry me?'

Her hand jerked so that she spilled a few drops of red Campari on to the table. She looked at me a little oddly, as though I were a stranger, then said, 'Oh, no, Owen.'

I said, 'I love you very much.'

'And I think I love you.' Her lower lip trembled.

'Then what's the matter? We're very well suited.'

'I'll tell you,' she said. 'You're another Alec. In twenty years – if you survive – you'll be sitting in a little, obscure office pulling strings and making men jump around, just like Alec. You won't be doing it because you like it but because you think it's your duty. And you'll hate the job and you'll hate yourself – just as Alec did. But you'll go on doing it.'

I said, 'Someone has to do it.'

'But not the man I marry,' said Alison. 'I told you once that I was like a Venus Fly Trap. I want to be a cabbage of a housewife, living, perhaps on the green outskirts of an English country town, all tweedy and *Country Life*.'

'There's no reason why you shouldn't have that, too,' I said.

'And stay behind and be alone when you went on a job?' She shook her head. 'It wouldn't work, Owen.'

I felt a sudden resentment, and said abruptly, 'Then why did you come back here – to Malta?'

A look of consternation crossed her face. 'Oh, Owen; I'm sorry. You thought . . .'

'You didn't say goodbye and Armitage told me you'd be coming back after the funeral. What was I supposed to think?'

'I was flown to England in an RAF transport,' she said quietly. 'I've come back to pick up my plane . . . and to say goodbye.'

'To say goodbye – just like that?'

'No,' she flared. 'Not just like that.' Her eyes filled with tears. 'Owen, it's all going wrong.'

I took her hand in mine. 'Have you ever been to Morocco?'

She looked at me warily, taken wrong-footed by the sudden change of subject. 'Yes; I know it quite well.'

'Could that aircraft of yours fly to Tangier from here?'

'It *could*,' she said uncertainly. 'But . . .'

'I need a holiday,' I said. 'And I have a year and a half of back pay which I need help in spending. I'm sure you'd make an efficient guide to Morocco. I need one – I've never been there.'

'You're trying the blarney again,' she said, and there was laughter in her voice. 'Maeve O'Sullivan warned me about that.'

Maeve had also told me that I wasn't the man for Alison Smith. She could be right, but I had to try.

'No strings and no promises,' said Alison.

I smiled. Six weeks together was all the promise I needed. A lot could happen in six weeks.

Bahama Crisis

To Valerie and David Redhead
with much affection

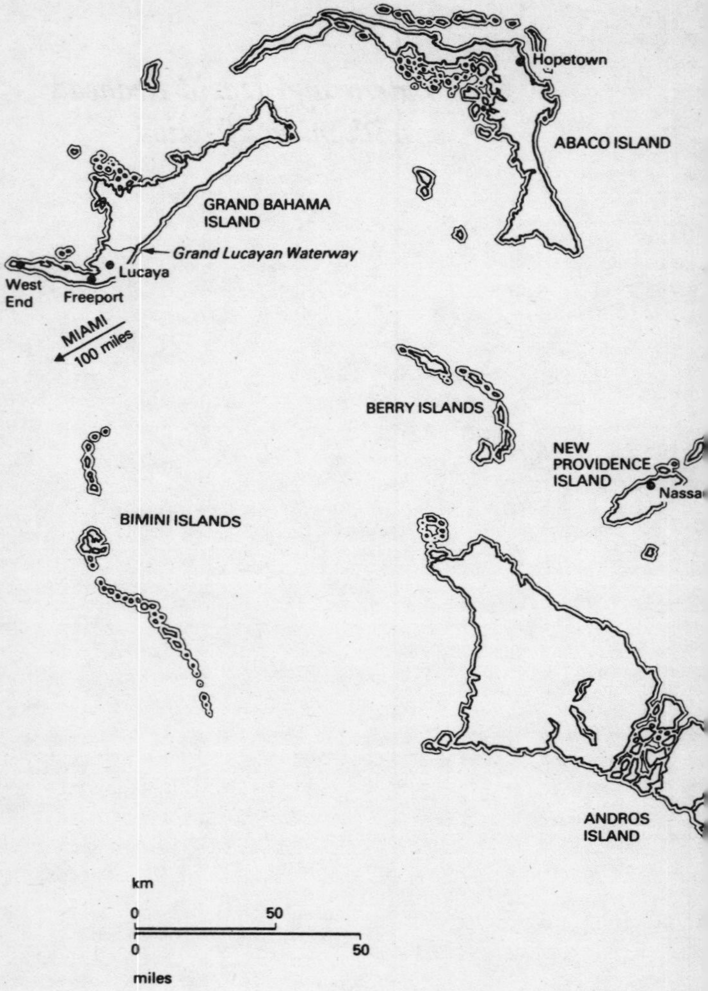
Hopetown
ABACO ISLAND
GRAND BAHAMA
ISLAND
Grand Lucayan Waterway
Lucaya
West
End
Freeport
MIAMI
100 miles
BERRY ISLANDS
NEW
PROVIDENCE
ISLAND
Nassa
BIMINI ISLANDS
ANDROS
ISLAND
km
0
50
0
50
miles

THE BAHAMA ISLANDS

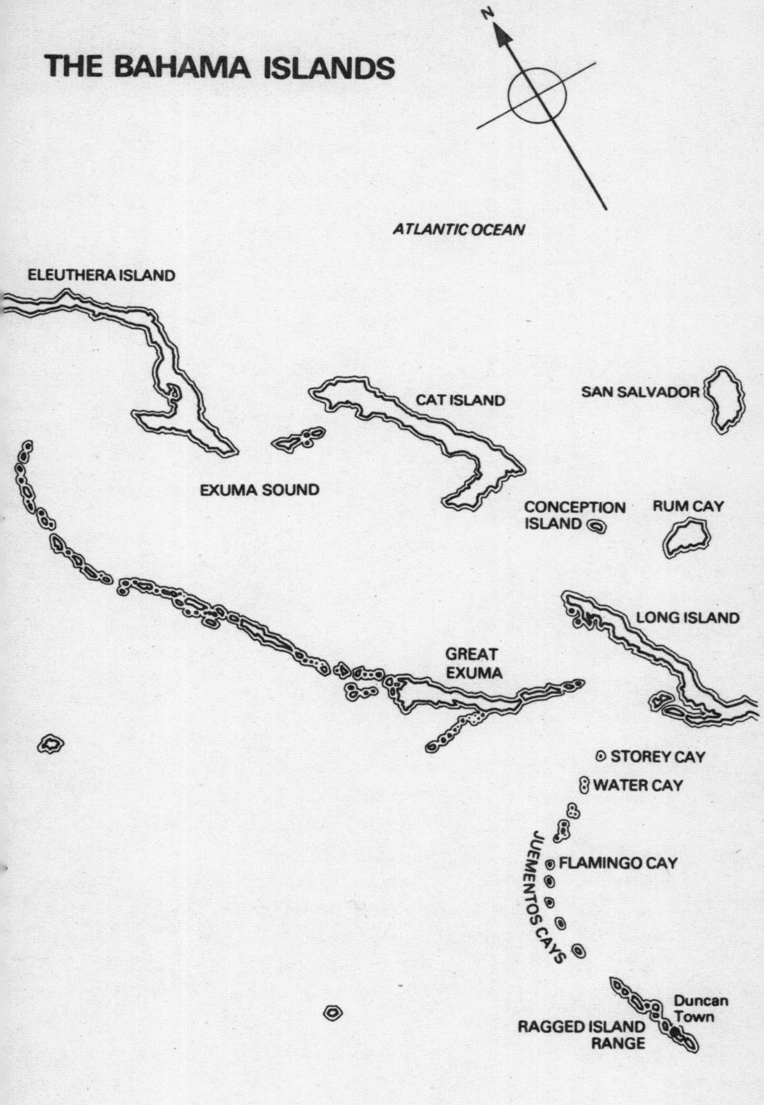

Prologue

My name is Tom Mangan and I am a Bahamian – a white Bahamian. This caused some comment when I was up at Cambridge; it is surprising how ill-informed even supposedly educated people can be about my home islands. I was told that I could not be a Bahamian because Bahamians are black; that the Bahamas are in the Caribbean, which they are not; and many confused the Bahamas with Bermuda or even Barbados. For these reasons and because an understanding of the geographical and political nature of the Bahamas is essential to my story it seems to me that I must describe them and also give a brief account of my family involvement.

The Bahamas are a chain of islands beginning about fifty miles off the coast of Florida and sweeping in an arc 500 miles to the south-east to a similar distance off the coast of Cuba. They consist of 700 islands (called cays locally, and pronounced 'keys') and about 2000 lesser rocks. The name is derived from the Spanish *baja mar* which means 'shallow sea'.

I am descended from one of the Loyalists who fought in the American War of Independence. Surprisingly few people are aware that more Americans fought in that war on the side of the British than ever did under the rebel generals, and that the war was lost more by the incompetence of the British than any superiority on the part of George Washington. Be that as it may, the war was lost by the British, and the American nation was born.

Life in the new United States was not comfortable for the erstwhile Loyalists. Reviled by their compatriots and abandoned by the British, many thought it prudent to leave, the northerners going mostly to Nova Scotia and the southerners to the Bahamas or to the sugar islands in the Caribbean beyond Cuba. So it was that in 1784 John Henry

Mangan elected to settle with his family on the island of Abaco in the Bahamas.

There was not much to Abaco. Shaped something like a boomerang, Great and Little Abaco Islands stretch for about 130 miles surrounded by a cluster of lesser cays. Most of these smaller cays are of coral, but Abaco itself is of limestone and covered with thick, almost impenetrable, tropical bush. Sir Guy Carleton intended to settle 1500 Loyalists on Abaco, but they were a footloose and fractious crowd and not many stayed. By 1788 the total population was about 400, half of whom were black slaves.

It is not hard to see why Carleton's project collapsed. Abaco, like the rest of the Bahamian islands, has a thin, infertile soil, a natural drawback which has plagued the Bahamas throughout their history. Many cash crops have been tried – tomatoes, pineapples, sugar, sisal, cotton – but all have failed as the fertility of the soil became exhausted. It is not by chance that three settlements in the Bahamas are called Hard Bargain.

Still, a man could survive if he did not expect too much; there were fish in the sea, and one could grow enough food for one's immediate family. Timber was readily available for building, the limestone was easily quarried, and palmetto leaf thatch made a good waterproof roof. John Henry Mangan not only survived but managed to flourish, along with the Sands, the Lowes, the Roberts and other Loyalist families whose names are still common on Abaco today.

The Mangans are a thin line because, possibly due to a genetic defect, they tend to run to girls like the Dutch royal family. Thus they did not grow like a tree with many branches but in a straight line. I am the last of the male Mangans and, as far as I know, there are no others of that name in the Islands.

But they survived and prospered. One of my forebears was a ship-builder at Hope Town on Elbow Cay; most of the local ships sailing the Bahamian waters were built on Abaco and the Mangan family built not a few and so became moderately well-to-do. And then there was the wrecking. As the United

States grew in power there was much maritime traffic and many ships were wrecked on the Islands of the Shallow Sea. The goods they contained contributed greatly to the wealth of many an island family, the Mangans not excepted. But the great turning point in the family fortunes came with the American Civil War.

The Confederate south was starved of supplies because of the northern blockade, and cotton rotted on the docks. Any ship putting into Charleston or Wilmington found a ready market for its cargo; quinine costing $10 in Nassau brought in excess of $400 in Charleston, while cotton costing $400 at the dockside was worth $4000 in Liverpool. It was a most profitable, if risky, two-way trade and my great-grandfather saw his opportunity and made the family rich in half a decade.

It was his son, my grandfather, who moved the family from Abaco to Nassau on New Providence – Nassau being the capital of the Bahamas and the centre of trade. Yet we still own land on Abaco and I have been building there recently.

If my great-grandfather made the family rich it was my father who made it really wealthy. He became a multi-millionaire which accounts for the fact that a Bahamian was educated at Cambridge. Again, it was running an American blockade which provided the profit.

On 15 January 1920 the United States went dry and, as in the Civil War, the Bahamas became a distribution centre for contraband goods. The Nassau merchants known as the Bay Street Boys, my father among them, soon got busy importing liquor. The profit margin was normally one hundred per cent and the business was totally risk-free; it was cash on the barrel and the actual blockade-running was done by the Americans themselves. It was said that there was so much booze stacked at West End on Grand Bahama that the island tipped by several degrees. And, for a Bahamian, the business was all legal.

All good things come to an end and the 18th Amendment was repealed by Franklin Roosevelt in 1933, but by then my father was sitting pretty and had begun to diversify his interests. He saw with a keen eye that the advent of aircraft was going to have an impact on the tourist industry and would alter its structure. Already Pan-American was pioneering the Miami-Nassau route using Sikorsky seaplanes.

Bahamian tourism in the nineteenth and early twentieth centuries was confined to the American rich and the four-month winter season. An American millionaire would bring his family and perhaps a few friends to spend the whole season on New Providence. This, while being profitable to a few, was of little consequence to the Bahamian economy, millionaires not being all that plentiful. My father took the gamble that aircraft would bring the mass market and invested in hotels. He won his gamble, but died before he knew it, in 1949.

I was eleven years old when my father died and had as much interest in money and business as any other boy of eleven, which is to say none. My mother told me that a trust fund had been set up for me and my two sisters and that I would come into my inheritance on my twenty-fifth birthday. She then continued to run the family affairs which she was quite capable of doing.

I went to school in Nassau but spent my holidays on Abaco under the watchful eye of Pete Albury, a black Abaconian whom I thought was old but, in fact, was about thirty at the time. He had worked for the family since he was a boy and looked after our property on Abaco. He had taught me to swim – a non-swimming Bahamian being as common as a wingless bird – and taught me to shoot, and we hunted the wild pig which are common on Abaco. He acted *in loco parentis* and tanned my hide when he thought I needed it. He stayed in my employ until his death not long ago.

Those early years were, I think, the most enjoyable of my life. In due course I went to England to study at Cambridge, and found England uncomfortably cold and wet; at least in the Bahamas the rain is warm. I took my degree and then went to the United States for a two-year course in business studies at Harvard to prepare myself for the administration of my inheritance. It was there I met Julie Pascoe who was to become my wife. In 1963 I was back in Nassau where, on my twenty-fifth birthday, there was much signing of documents in a lawyer's office and I took control of the estate.

Many things had changed in the Bahamas by then. My father's hunch had proved correct and the coming of the big jets brought the mass tourist market he had predicted. In 1949, the year he died, 32,000 tourists came to the Islands; in 1963 there were over half a million. It is worth adding that next year the estimated total is over two million. My mother had looked after our interests well, but now she was getting old and a little frail and was glad to relinquish responsibility into my hands. I found that one of the things she had done was to become involved in the development of Grand Bahama. At the time that worried me very much because Grand Bahama was turning sour.

Wallace Groves was an American who had a dream and that dream was Freeport on the island of Grand Bahama. He persuaded Sir Stafford Sands, then Minister of Finance in the Bahamian Government, to sell him over 200 square miles of government land on Grand Bahama upon which he would build a city – Freeport. His intention, not actually realized in his lifetime, was to create a duty-free area for the benefit of American corporations where they could avoid American taxes. In 1963 the scheme was not working; no immediate enthusiasm was being shown by any corporation anywhere. Groves switched the emphasis to tourism, recreation and residential housing, and twisted Sands's arm to allow the building of a casino to attract custom.

Sands was a quintessential Bay Street Boy who could catch a dollar on the fly no matter how fast it went. It was he who was primarily responsible for the vast increase of tourist traffic. Reasoning that the tourist needs much more than mere sun and sand he saw to it that the whole infrastructure of the tourist industry was built and maintained. He acceded to Groves's request and the casino opened in 1964.

It was the worst mistake Sands could ever have made. The shadowy figure supervising the running of the casino was Meyer Lansky who used to run casinos in Havana until he was tossed out of Cuba by Castro. Having put out a contract on Castro for $1 million Lansky looked for somewhere else to operate and found Grand Bahama. The gangsters had moved in.

Politics and economics walk hand in hand, largely revolving around the question of who gets what, and the black Bahamians saw the wealth created by the tourist industry going into the pockets of the white Bay Street Boys who also controlled the House of Assembly and ran the country in the interest of the whites. Something had to give, and in 1967 the largely black Progressive Liberal Party led by Lynden Pindling squeaked into power with a two-seat majority. The following year Pindling unexpectedly held another election and the PLP got in with twenty-nine seats out of the thirty-eight.

This landslide came about because of the mistake made by Stafford Sands. As soon as Pindling came to power he decided to take a closer look at Freeport and, in particular, the casino. He found that Groves and Lansky were giving kick-backs to Sands and others in the form of dubious 'consultancy fees' and that Sands himself was reputed to have taken over $2 million. When this was disclosed all hell broke loose; Sands was discredited and fell, bringing his party down with him.

But Groves had been right – the casino had brought prosperity to Grand Bahama, and Freeport had boomed and was thriving. There were plans for vast residential developments – great areas were already laid out in streets, complete with sewerage and electricity. The streets even had names; all that was missing were the houses on the building plots.

But investors were wary. To them a Caribbean revolution had taken place and what would those crazy blacks do next? They ignored the fact that it had been a democratic election and that the composition of the Assembly now compared with the ethnic composition of the Bahamas; they just pulled out and took their money with them and the economy of Grand Bahama collapsed again and is only now recovering.

And what was I doing while this was going on? I was trying to keep things together by fast footwork and trying not to get my hands too dirty. To tell the truth I voted for Pindling. I could see that the rule of the Bay Street Boys' oligarchy was an anachronism in a fast changing world and that, unless the black Bahamian was given a share in what was going, there would be a revolution and not a peaceful election.

And among other things I got married.

Julie Pascoe was the daughter of an American doctor and lived in Maryland. When I left Harvard we kept up a correspondence. In 1966 she visited the Bahamas with her parents and I took them around the Islands; showing off, I suppose. We married in 1967 and Susan was born in 1969. Karen came along in 1971. The propensity of the Mangans to breed daughters had not failed.

Although I had been worried about the investments on Grand Bahama, three years ago I decided that an upswing was due. I floated a company, the West End Securities Corporation, a holding company which I control and of which I am President. More importantly I moved my base of operations from Nassau to Freeport, and built a house at Lucaya on Grand Bahama. Nassau is an old town, a little stuffy and set in its ways. Brave new ideas do not sprout in an environment like that so I left for Grand Bahama where Wally Groves's dream seems about to come true.

I suppose I could have been pictured as a very lucky man – not worrying where my next dollar was coming from, happily married to a beautiful wife with two fine children, and with a flourishing business. I *was* a lucky man, and I thought nothing could go wrong until the events I am about to recount took place.

Where shall I begin? I think with Billy Cunningham who was around when it happened just before the Christmas before last. It was the worst Christmas of my life.

1

Billy Cunningham was a scion of the Cunningham clan; his father, uncle, brother and assorted cousins jointly owned a fair slice of Texas – they ran beef, drilled for oil, were into shipping, newspapers, radio and television, hotels, supermarkets and other real estate, and owned moderate tracts of downtown Dallas and Houston. The Cunningham Corporation was a power to be reckoned with in Texas, and Prince Billy was in the Bahamas to see what he could see.

I had first met him at Harvard Business School where, like me, he was being groomed for participation in the family business, and we had kept in touch, meeting at irregular intervals. When he telephoned just before Christmas asking to meet me on my own ground I said, 'Sure. You'll be my guest.'

'I want to pick your brains,' he said. 'I might have a proposition for you.'

That sounded interesting. The Cunningham Corporation was the kind of thing I was trying to build West End Securities into, though I had a long way to go. I had a notion that the Cunninghams were in a mind for expansion and Billy was coming to look over the chosen ground. I would rather cooperate than have them as competitors because they were a tough crowd, and I hoped that was what Billy had in mind. We fixed a date.

I met him at Freeport International Airport where he arrived in a company jet decked in the Cunningham colours. He had not changed much; he was tall, broad-shouldered and blond, with a deep tan and gleaming teeth. The Cunninghams seemed to run to film star good looks, those of them I had met. There was nothing about him to indicate he was American, no eccentricity of style which might reasonably be expected of a Texan. Texans are notorious, even in the United States, for their unselfconscious and nostalgic frontier rig. If he ever wore them, then Billy had left his ten-gallon hat, string tie and high-heeled boots at home, and was dressed in a lightweight suit of obviously English cut. Being a Cunningham he would probably order them casually by the half-dozen from Huntsman of Savile Row.

'How's the boy?' he said as we shook hands. 'I don't think you've met Debbie – this is my little cousin.'

Deborah Cunningham was as beautiful as the Cunningham menfolk were handsome; a tall, cool blonde. 'Pleased to meet you, Miss Cunningham.'

She smiled. 'Debbie, please.'

'Tell me,' said Billy. 'How long is the runway?'

That was a typical Billy Cunningham question; he had an insatiable curiosity and his questions, while sometimes apparently irrelevant, always had a bearing on his current train of thought. I said, 'The last time I measured it came to 11,000 feet.'

'Just about handle everything,' he commented. He turned and watched the Cunningham JetStar take off, then said, 'Let's move.'

I drove them through Freeport on my way to the Royal Palm Hotel. I was proud of the Royal Palm; for my money it was the best hotel in the Bahamas. Of course, it had been my money that had built it, and I was looking forward to seeing Billy's reaction. On the way I said, 'Is this your first time in the Bahamas, Debbie?'

'Yes.'

'Mine, too,' said Billy. That surprised me, and I said so. 'Just never gotten around to it.' He twisted in his seat. 'Which way is Freeport?'

'Right here. You're in downtown Freeport.' He grunted in surprise, and I knew why. The spacious streets, lawns and widely separated low-slung buildings were like no other city centre he had seen. 'It shows what you can do when you build a city from scratch. Twenty years ago this was all scrubland.'

'Oh, look!' said Debbie. 'Isn't that a London bus?'

I laughed. 'The genuine article. There seems to be a mystique about those all over the English-speaking world – I've seen them at Niagara, too. I think the London Transport Board makes quite a profit out of selling junk buses as far-flung tourist attractions.'

In the foyer of the Royal Palm Billy looked around with an experienced eye. The Cunningham Corporation ran its own hotels and knew how they ticked. He glanced upwards and gave a long, slow whistle. The foyer rose the entire height of the hotel, a clear eight storeys with the bedrooms circling it on mezzanines. 'Wow!' he said. 'Isn't that a lot of wasted space?'

I smiled; even the Cunninghams had a lot to learn. 'It might be in a city hotel, but this is a resort hotel. There's a difference.'

Jack Fletcher, the hotel manager, was standing by and I introduced him to the Cunninghams. He booked them in with as few formalities as possible, then said, 'Here are your room keys – Mr Cunningham, Miss Cunningham.' He gave Billy another key. 'Your car's in the garage.'

I said, 'Find another car for Miss Cunningham; she might like to do some sightseeing by herself.'

'Hey!' said Billy. 'No need for that.'

I shrugged. 'No sweat; we run a car hire company and the season hasn't topped out yet. We have a few cars spare.'

He took me by the elbow and led me to one side. 'I'd like to talk with you as soon as possible.'

'You always were in a hurry.'

'Why not? I get things done that way. Say, fifteen minutes?'

'I'll be in the bar.' He nodded in satisfaction.

He was down in ten minutes and strode into the bar at a quick clip. After ordering him a drink I said, 'Where's Debbie?'

Billy smiled crookedly. 'You know women; she'll take a while to prettify herself.' He accepted the bourbon on the rocks. 'Thanks.'

'Your room all right?'

'Fine.' He frowned. 'But I still say you're wasting a hell of a lot of space.'

'You're thinking in terms of city downtown hotels. Space is cheap here and the clientèle is different.' I decided to push. 'What are you here for, Billy? You mentioned a proposition.'

'Well, we have a few dollars going spare and we're looking for somewhere to invest. What's your idea of the future of the Bahamas?'

'My God, Billy, but you have a nerve! You want to come in here as a competitor and you're asking my advice?'

He laughed. 'You won't lose out on it. You've already said a couple of things that have set me thinking. We think we know how to run hotels back home, but it might be different here. Maybe we could set up a partnership of sorts and use your local expertise.'

'A consortium?' He nodded, and I said contemplatively, 'A few dollars. How few would they be?'

'About forty million few.'

The bartender was standing close by, polishing an already over-polished glass. I said, 'Let's go and sit at that corner table.' We took our drinks and sat down. 'I think the future of the Bahamas is pretty good. Do you know much of our recent history?'

'I've done my homework.' He gave me a swift and concise résumé.

I nodded. 'That's about it. You Americans are now coming to the realization that Pindling isn't an ogre and that he runs a fairly stable and conservative government. He's safe. Now, let's come to your hotels and the way you run them. Your clientèle consists of businessmen and oil men, fast on their feet and on the move. They want fast service and good service, and they're here today and gone tomorrow. Because your land values in the city are so enormous you pack them in tight and charge them the earth because you have to. If you didn't the operation wouldn't pay; it would be more profitable to sell up and move into some other business. Have I got it right?'

'Just about. Those guys can pay, anyway; we don't get many complaints.'

I waved my arm. 'What do you think of this place?'

'Very luxurious.'

I smiled. 'It's intended to look that way; I'm glad you think it succeeds. Look, Billy; your average tourist here isn't a jet-setter and he doesn't have all that many dollars to spend. He's a man and his wife, and maybe his kids, from Cleveland, Ohio. Perhaps he's done one trip to Europe, but he can't go again because Europe is too damned expensive these days and the dollar is bloody weak. So he comes here because he's going foreign and economizing at the same time. Big deal.'

'What about the Europeans? Lots of those about here.' Billy jerked his thumb towards the lobby. 'Out there I heard German, French and Spanish.'

'The Spanish would be coming from the Argentine,' I said. 'We get lots of those. They, and the Europeans, come for the same reason – because it's cheaper here. But they don't come first class or even tourist. They come on charter flights in package deals organized by the travel agents – mostly German and Swiss. Neither the Americans nor the Europeans, with few exceptions, have a lot of money to throw around. So how do we handle the operation?'

'You tell me.'

'Okay.' I spread my hands. 'We give them the semblance of luxury – stuff they can't get at home. Palm trees are cheap to buy, easy to plant and grow quickly; and you don't get many of those in Cleveland or Hamburg. And they look damned good. We have a few bars dotted about the place; one on the beach, one by the pool, a couple inside. We hire a local guitarist and a singer to give the live mood music – Bahamian and Caribbean calypso stuff – very romantic. We have a discothèque. We have a place to serve junk food and another for gourmet dining – both are equally profitable. We have shops in the lobby; jewellery, clothing, local handicrafts, a news-stand and so on. So far those have been concessions, but now we're tending to operate them ourselves; I've just started a merchandising division. And, as I said, we run a car hire outfit; that's part of the tours division. On the beach we have a few sailboats and wind-surfing boards, and we hire a beach bum to act as life-guard and to show the clients how to use the stuff. That's free. So are the tennis courts. There's also use of an eighteen-hole golf course for a concessionary fee. There's a marina linked to the hotel so we also pull in the boating crowd.'

'It seems a customer can get most of what he wants on his vacation without ever leaving the hotel,' Billy hazarded.

'That's it,' I said. 'That's why they're called resort hotels. But what we *don't* have in the lobby is a liquor store; if a tourist wants his booze he pays bar prices. We want to squeeze as many dollars and cents out of these people as we can while they're in our tender care. And they *are* in our care, you know; they have a good time and they're not cold-decked. We have a crêche and a children's playground – that's more to keep the kids out of people's hair than for anything else – and we have a doctor and a nurse. And there's no drill or razzmatazz – they're just left alone to do as they please which seems to be mostly roasting in the sun.'

Billy grimaced. 'Not the kind of vacation I'd fancy.'

'Neither would I, but we're not tourists. So what happens when our man goes home? His friends look at that deep tan and ask him about it. "Gee!" he says. "I had the greatest time. Free sailboating, free tennis, cheap golf on the most superb course you can imagine. It was marvellous." Then he does a hip shimmy around the office. "And, gee, that calypso beat!" That's what he tells his friends when the snow is two feet deep in the street outside the office, and they like the idea, so they come, too. Maybe the year after.'

Billy mused. 'Fast turnover and small margins.'

'That's the name of the game,' I said. 'That's why room occupancy is critical; we keep filled up or go broke.'

'Any trouble in that direction?'

I smiled. 'We're doing just fine,' I said lightly.

He grunted. 'I'd like to see your profit and loss account and your balance sheet.'

'If you come up with a firm offer I might give you a quick

look.' I thought for a moment. 'I'll introduce you to a few people and you can get a feel of the place. David Butler is a good man to talk to; he's top man in the Ministry of Tourism here on Grand Bahama.' I hesitated. 'There might be a problem there.'

'What problem?'

'Well, you're a southerner. Would you have any problem dealing with a black on equal terms?'

'Not me,' said Billy. 'Billy One might, and Jack certainly would; but they won't be involved out here.' Billy One was Billy's father, so called to distinguish him from Billy. Jack was his uncle and head of the Cunningham clan. 'Is this guy, Butler, black?'

'He is. There's another thing. Any hotels you build here must be Bahamian-built and Bahamian-staffed.'

'The Bahamas for the Bahamians – is that it?'

'Something like that. No one else can hold down a job here if it can be done by a Bahamian.'

Billy jerked his head towards the lobby. 'Your hotel manager – Fletcher; he's white.'

'So am I,' I said evenly. 'We're both white Bahamians. But the manager of the Sea Gardens – that's our hotel on New Providence – is black.'

Billy shrugged. 'It doesn't worry me as long as we have an efficient operation.'

'Oh, we're efficient.' I looked up and saw Debbie Cunningham coming into the bar. 'Here's your cousin.'

She was wearing a halter top and a pair of shorts which were well named – a long-stemmed American beauty. 'I hope this is okay,' she said, and looked down at herself. 'I mean, do you have *rules*?'

'Not so as you'd notice. Our visitors can dress pretty much as they like – up to a point.' I inspected her. 'I don't think you've reached the point yet, though. Will you have a drink?'

'Something soft; a Coke, maybe.' I signalled a waiter and she sat down. 'Isn't this quite a place? Have you seen the pool, Billy?'

'Not yet.'

I checked the time. 'I'm going to be busy for the next hour. Why don't you give the place the once-over lightly and I'll meet you at the desk. We'll have lunch at home. If you need to know anything ask Jack Fletcher.'

'That's fine,' said Billy. 'You've told me enough already so I know what to look for.'

I left them and went to my office to do some hard thinking. When Billy had told me the size of his proposed investment it had given me quite a jolt, although I had tried not to show it. Forty million dollars is a hell of a lot of money and that much injected into West End Securities could provide for a lot of expansion. The problem would be to avoid being swamped by it, and it was going to be quite a puzzle to put together a suitable package which would keep both me and the Cunningham Corporation happy.

If Billy had been surprised by the Royal Palm Hotel he was equally surprised by my home and he showed it. I took him through into the atrium where the swimming pool was. He looked around and said, 'My God!'

I laughed. 'Ever been in Rome in August?'

'Who goes to Rome in August?' He shrugged. 'But yes, I have – once,' and added feelingly, 'Goddamn hot. I got out of there fast.'

'And humid – just like here. When I built this place I had an architect dig into the plans of Roman villas; the ancient Romans, I mean. I had a feeling they'd be building for the climate. This is not a reproduction of a villa – more an adaptation. With modern conveniences, of course; air-conditioning included. But my air-conditioning costs less to run than any of my neighbours' because the building design helps. We used some of that know-how when we built the Royal Palm; that big, tall lobby is a natural cooling tower.'

Billy was about to say something when Julie walked out of the house. I said, 'Here's Julie now. Julie, you've met Billy, but I don't think you know Debbie, his cousin.'

'Hi, Billy, welcome to Grand Bahama. Glad to meet you, Debbie.'

'You have a beautiful home,' said Debbie.

'We like to think so.' Julie turned and called, 'Come out of there, Sue. We have guests; come and meet them.'

My elder daughter emerged from the pool as sinuously as an otter. 'Say "hello" to Mr Cunningham,' commanded Julie.

'To Billy,' I amended.

Sue shook hands gravely. She had an impish look as she said, 'Hello, Mr Billy Cunningham.'

Billy laughed. 'A regular little towhead, aren't you?'

'And this is Debbie.' Sue curtsied, something that would have looked better done in a crinoline instead of a minimal bathing suit.

'How old are you, Sue?' asked Debbie.

'Eleven years, two months, three weeks and six days,' said Sue promptly.

'You swim very well,' said Debbie. 'I bet you swim better than I can.'

Julie looked pleased – Debbie had said exactly the right thing. 'Yes, she swims well. She came second in the Marathon in her class.'

I said, 'It's a two-mile course in the open sea.'

Debbie was visibly startled and looked at my daughter with new respect. 'That's really something; I doubt if I can swim a quarter-mile.'

'Oh, it's nothing,' said Sue airily.

'All right, fish,' I said. 'Back into your natural element.' I turned to Julie. 'Where's Karen?'

'She's running a temperature. I put her to bed.'

'Nothing serious?'

'Oh, no.' Julie looked at Debbie. 'She's been having school problems and might even be faking it. Come and see her; it might buck her up.'

The women went into the house, and I said to Billy, 'I think drinks are indicated.'

'Yeah, something long and cold.'

'A rum punch, but easy on the rum.' As I mixed the drinks I said, 'Air-conditioning in hotels is important if we're to have a year-round season. We don't want the tourists frying even if it is good for the bar trade.'

Billy took off his jacket and sat in a recliner. 'You forget I'm a Texan. Ever been in Houston in summer? You know what Sherman said about Texas?' I shook my head. 'He said, "If I owned Hell and Texas, I'd rent out Texas and live in Hell."'

I laughed. 'Then you'll see the problems, although we're not as bad as Texas. There's always a sea breeze to cut the heat.'

We chatted while Luke Bailey, my general factotum, laid the table for lunch. Presently the women came back and accepted cold drinks. 'You have two very nice girls,' said Debbie.

'Julie must take the praise for that,' I said. 'I get any of the blame that's going.'

Talk became general over lunch and I was pleased to see that Julie and Debbie got on well together. If the womenfolk of business associates are bitchy it can upset things all round, and I have known several sweet deals fall down because of that.

At one point Julie said, 'You know Mom and Pop are coming for Christmas.'

'Yes.' It was an arrangement that had been made earlier in the year.

'I thought I'd do my Christmas shopping in Miami and meet them there.'

I said, 'Why don't you give them a sea trip? Take *Lucayan Girl* and bring them back by way of Bimini. I'm sure they'd enjoy it.'

She said, 'It's a good idea. Would you come?'

'Afraid not, I'll be too busy. But I'll have a word with Pete; he'll need an extra hand for that trip.'

'Still a good idea,' said Julie meditatively. 'I think I'll take Sue – and Karen, if she's better.'

'Take me where?' Sue had joined us draped in a towel. She helped herself to ice-cream.

'How would you like to go to Miami to meet Grandma and Grandpop? We'd be going in the *Girl*.'

Ice-cream went flying and Sue's squeal of delight was an adequate answer.

After lunch Julie took Sue back to school and Debbie went along because Julie said she would show her the International Bazaar where you can walk from France to China in one stride. When they had gone Billy said, 'How big is your boat?'

'Fifty-two feet. Come and look at her.'

His eyebrows lifted. 'You have her here?'

'Sure. This way.' I led him through the house to the lagoon on the other side where *Lucayan Girl* was moored at the quayside. Pete Albury was on board and when he heard us talking he appeared on deck. 'Come and meet Pete,' I said. 'He's skipper, but sometimes he thinks he's the owner.'

'Tom, I heard that,' called Pete, his face cracking into a seamed black grin. 'But I'll allow you on board anyway.'

We went aboard. 'Pete, this is Billy Cunningham, an old friend from the States.'

Pete stuck out his hand. 'Glad to know you, Mr Cunningham.'

I was watching Billy carefully. He did not know it, but this was a minor test; if he had hesitated, even fractionally, in spite of what he had said I would have been worried because no one who is a nigger-hater, even in a minor way, can get along successfully in the Bahamas. Billy grasped Pete's hand firmly. 'Glad to know you, Mr . . . er . . .'

'Albury,' said Pete. 'But I'm just Pete.'

'I'm Billy.'

I said, 'Julie wants to go to Miami next week to do the Christmas shopping and to pick up her parents. She'll be taking Sue and maybe Karen, and you'll be touching in at Bimini on the way home. Is everything okay for that?'

'Sure,' said Pete. 'Are you comin'?'

'Sorry. I can't make it.'

'Then I'll need a hand. Don't worry; there's always youngsters around the marinas. I'll pick a good one who'll be glad of the ride for a few dollars.'

'That's it, then,' I said.

Billy was looking at the lagoon. 'This is artificial,' he said abruptly.

'I hoped you'd notice.' I pointed. 'The channel out to sea is there – by the Lucayan Beach Hotel. That's where the BASRA Marathon begins.'

'BASRA?' he said interrogatively.

'The Bahamas Air-Sea Rescue Association. The Marathon is run by and for BASRA to raise funds. It's a voluntary organization – a good crowd. If you're coming in here it wouldn't do you any harm to donate a few dollars or offer facilities.'

'Do you do that?'

'Yes. We have the company planes . . .' I broke off and laughed. 'Not big jets like yours, but we have four Piper Navajos – seven-seaters we use to take tourists to the Out Islands, part of our tours division. And they're used on other company business, of course. But if a boat is lost and BASRA wants an air search the planes are available.'

He nodded. 'Good public relations.' He switched his attention back to the lagoon. 'So this has been dredged out?'

'That's it. This lagoon, and others like it, stretches for about three miles up the coast.'

Billy looked at the lagoon and then back at the house. 'Not bad,' he said, 'having a house with a water frontage. And it's protected, too; no big waves.'

'You've got it. Now I'll show you something weird. Let's take a drive.' We said farewell to Pete, left the house, and I drove about four miles east into Lucaya. 'Notice anything?'

Billy looked around. 'Just trees –and the traffic is light.'

That was an understatement; there was no traffic. I had not seen a car for the last two miles. But there were many trees. I pointed. 'That's a street. See the name plate? Now keep your eyes open.'

I drove on and presently the trees thinned out and we came on to a plain dotted with mounds of limestone. I said, 'We're coming to the Casuarina Bridge. It crosses the Great Lucayan Waterway.'

'So?'

'So we're going to cross it.'

'I don't get it,' said Billy.

I said, 'We've been passing streets, all named and paved. Those poles carry power lines. Now, I don't know how it is in the States where any wide place in the road can call itself a city, but to me a road is something that goes from one place to another, but a street *is* a place, and it usually has houses on it.'

Billy was momentarily startled. 'Houses!' he said blankly. 'No goddamn houses! Nary a one.'

'That's it. But I've more to show you or, rather, not show you. We'll get a better view from Dover Sound.' I carried on driving, following the signposts to Dover Sound and Observation Hill. It is not really a hill – just a man-made mound with the road leading up and a turning circle at the top. I stopped the car and we got out. 'What do you think of that?'

Billy looked at the view with a lack of comprehension. I knew why because I had been baffled by the sight when first I saw it. There was land and there was water and it was not easy to see where one stopped and the other began. It was a maze of water channels. Billy shrugged helplessly. 'I don't know. What am I supposed to think?'

I said, 'Think of my house and the lagoon. This is the Grand Lucayan Waterway – it cuts right across Grand Bahama, nearly eight miles from coast to coast. But it has forty-five miles of water frontage.' I flapped open the map I held. 'Look at this. You can see where the streets and waterways fit together like fingers in a glove.'

Billy studied the map then took out a calculator and began punching buttons. 'At a hundred feet of water frontage to a house that's nearly 2500 houses. Where the hell are they?'

'There's more. Look at the map.' I swept my hand over an area. 'Twenty square miles of land all laid out in paved streets with utilities already installed – the unfleshed skeleton of a city of 50,000 people.'

'So what happened?'

'An election happened. Pindling got in and the investors ran scared. But they're coming back. Take a man who runs his own business in Birmingham, Alabama, or Birmingham, England, come to that. He sells out to a bigger company at, say, the age of fifty-five when he's still young enough to enjoy life and now has the money to indulge himself. He can build his house on the canal and keep his fishing boat handy, or he can take one of the dry land plots. There's sun and sea, swimming and golf, enough to keep a man happy for the rest of his life. And the beauty of it is that the infrastructure already exists; the power station in Freeport is only working to a tenth of its capacity.'

Billy looked over the expanse of land and water. 'You say the investors are coming back. I don't see much sign.'

'Don't be fooled.' I pointed back the way we had come. 'You can see the landscaping has begun – tree planting and flower beds. And that big parking lot, all neatly laid out. It looks a bit silly, but it's probably earmarked for a supermarket. There are houses being built right now, but you don't see them because they're scattered over twenty square miles. Give this place a few years and we'll have a thriving community. That's one answer to a question you asked – what's the future of the Bahamas?'

He rubbed his jaw. 'Yeah, I see what you mean.'

'Don't take my word for it – look for yourself. I'll lend you a plane and my chief pilot, Bobby Bowen, and you can do some island hopping. Go to Abaco; we have a hotel there –the Abaco Sands at Marsh Harbour. Go on to Eleuthera where we're building a hotel. Have a look at some of the other islands and don't leave out New Providence. I'll give you a list of people you can talk to. Then come back and tell me what you think.'

'Okay,' he said. 'I'll do just that.'

2

Billy went on his tour a couple of days later after looking around Grand Bahama, but Debbie stayed on at the Royal Palm. Billy confided in me that he had brought her along in an attempt to cure a fit of the blues; apparently Debbie had been having man trouble – an affair had turned sour. Anyway, she fell into the habit of going to the house and using the pool, and she and the children became friends in jig time. Debbie would pick up the kids from school and take them home and then stay on to lunch with Julie. Julie must have liked her because she put off her trip to Florida until Billy came back.

As for me, I was damned busy. I rousted Jamieson, the chief accountant, who fairly set the computer smoking as we figured the net worth of the company as at the end of that month. I wanted to have all my ammunition ready and dry for Billy when he came back because I had the notion he would be ready to talk turkey.

One evening after Julie had put the girls to bed I told her about Billy's proposition and asked what she thought of it. She was ambivalent. She saw the possibilities for expansion, but on the other hand she said, 'I don't know if it would be good for you – you're too independently minded.'

I knew what she meant. 'I know I like to run my own show and that's my problem – how to extract forty million bucks from the Cunninghams without losing control. I have a few ideas about that and I might be able to swing it.'

She laughed at me. 'I always knew I married a genius. All right, if you can do that then it won't be a bad thing.'

I had to consult my sisters, Peggy and Grace. Both had stock in the West End Securities Corporation, enough for them to have a say in any decision as big as this. Peggy lived on Abaco with her son and daughter and her husband, Bob Fisher, who ran the Abaco Sands Hotel for the corporation. Grace had married an American called Peters and lived in Orlando, Florida, with their three sons. It seemed that the tendency of the Mangans to produce girls was confined to the males. It meant some flying around because this was not something that could be settled on the telephone, but I had written agreements by the time Billy came back.

He returned to Grand Bahama after eight days, having gone through the Bahamas like a whirlwind. He was armed with so many facts, figures and statistics that I wondered how he had assembled them all in the time, but that was like Billy – he was a quick student.

'You were right,' he said. 'The Bahamas have potential, more than I thought. You didn't tell me about the Hotels Encouragement Act.'

I laughed. 'I left you to find out yourself. I knew you would.'

'My God, it's like stumbling across a gold mine.' He ticked the points off on his fingers. 'No customs duty on anything imported to build or equip a hotel; no property taxes for the first ten years; no company taxes for the first twenty years. And that applies to hotels, marinas, golf courses, landscaping – anything you can damn near think of. It's incredible.'

'It's why we're going to have two million tourists next year.'

He grunted. 'I've been thinking about that. I was talking to that tourism guy, Butler. He told me that eighty per cent of your economy and two-thirds of your population are supported by tourism. That's a hell of a lot of eggs in one basket, Tom.' His voice was serious. 'What if something happens like war breaking out?'

Something told me I had better come up with the right answer. I said lightly, 'If World War III breaks out everybody's eggs get broken.'

'I guess you're right at that.'

'Are you ready to talk business yet?'

'No. I'll be speaking to Billy One and Jack today. I'll let you know the decision tomorrow.'

I grinned. 'I promise I won't bug the switchboard. I won't be coming in to the office tomorrow. Julie is leaving for Miami and I like to see them off. Why don't you come to the house and bring Debbie along?'

'I'll do that.'

So Billy and Debbie arrived at the house next morning at about ten o'clock. Debbie joined the girls in the pool and I winked at Julie and took Billy into my study. He said, 'I think we're in business.'

'You may think so, but I'm not so sure. I don't want to lose control.'

He stared at me. 'Oh, come on, Tom! Forty million bucks swings a lot of clout. You don't want us busting in as competitors, do you?'

'I'm not afraid of competition. I have plenty of that, anyway.'

'Well, you can't expect us to put up all that dough and not have control. That's ridiculous. Are you joking or something?'

'I'm not joking,' I said. 'I'm perfectly serious. But I'd like to point out that there are different kinds of control.'

Billy looked at me speculatively. 'Okay, I'll buy it. What's on your mind?'

'I take it you'd be setting up a corporation here.'

'That's right, we would. I've been talking to some of your corporate lawyers over in Nassau and they've come up with some great ideas, even though they'd be illegal back in the States. This sure is a free-wheeling place.'

'Rest easy,' I said. 'As an offshore tax haven we're positively respectable, not like some others I could mention. What would you call your corporation?'

'How would I know? Something innocuous, I guess. Let's call it the Theta Corporation.'

I said, 'I run three hotels with a fourth building for a total of 650 rooms. That's a lot of bed linen, a lot of crockery and cutlery, a lot of kitchenware and ashtrays and anything else you care to name. Now, if the Theta Corporation is going to build and equip hotels it would be better to consolidate and keep the economy of scale. You get bed sheets a damn sight cheaper if you order by the 5000 pair rather than the 500 pair, and that applies right down the line.'

'Sure, I know that.' Billy flapped his hand impatiently. 'Come to the point.'

'What I'm suggesting is that the Theta Corporation take over West End Securities in return for stock.'

'Ha!' he said. 'Now you're saying something. How much stock?'

'One-fifth.'

'We put in $40 million, you put in West End and take a fifth of the stock. That makes it a $50 million corporation, so you estimate West End as being worth $10 million. Is it? What's the book value?'

I said, 'Jamieson and I have been working it out. I put it at $8 million.'

'So you put in $8 million and take stock worth $10 million. What kind of a deal is that? What do we get for the other two million bucks?'

'Me,' I said evenly.

Billy burst out laughing. 'Come on, Tom! Do you really think you're worth that?'

'You're forgetting quite a few things,' I said. 'If you come in here on your own you come in cold. I know you've picked up your facts and statistics and so on, but you don't know the score – you don't know the way things get done here. But if you come in with me you begin with a firm base ready for expansion, eager for expansion. And you don't only get me, but you get my staff, all loyal to me personally. And don't forget the Bahamas for the Bahamians bit. Call it goodwill, call it know-how, call it what you like, but I reckon it's worth two million.'

Billy was silent for a long time, thinking hard. 'Maybe you're right,' he said at last.

I gave him another jolt. 'And I get to be President of the Theta Corporation,' I said calmly.

He nearly choked. 'Jesus, you don't want much! Why don't you just pick my pocket of forty million bucks and have done with it?'

'I told you. I don't want to lose control. Look, Billy; you'll be Chairman and I'll be President – the Cunninghams retain financial control but I have operational control. That's the only way it can work. And I want a five-year contract of service; not a cast iron contract – that fractures too easily – an armour plate contract.'

Billy looked glum, but nodded. 'Billy One might go for it, but I don't know about Jack.' He drummed his fingers on the desk and said cautiously, 'If we take over West End we get everything? Not just the hotels part of it?'

'You get all the trimmings,' I assured him. 'Tours division, car hire fleet, merchandising division – the lot.'

'Before we go any further into this,' he said. 'I'd like to have your ideas about expansion. Have you given it any thought?'

I pushed a folder across the desk. 'There are a few ideas here. Just a beginning.'

He studied the papers I had put together and we discussed them for a while. At last he said, 'You've obviously been thinking hard. I like your idea of a construction division.' He checked the time. 'I need the telephone. Will you give me half an hour? I might have to do some tough talking.'

I pushed the telephone towards him. 'Best of luck.'

I found Julie holding Karen in her arms and looking faintly worried. Karen was sniffling and wailing. 'But I *want* to go!'

'What's the matter?'

'Oh, Karen's not well,' said Julie. 'I don't think she should come with us. That cold in the head has sprung up again and she's got a temperature.'

'It's not *fair*!' cried Karen. 'Sue's going.'

I put out my hand and felt her forehead; Julie was right

about the rise in temperature, but it was not much. 'Maybe we should cancel the trip,' said Julie.

'Put her to bed and we'll talk about it.' I looked around. 'Where's Sue?'

'On *Lucayan Girl* helping Pete or, rather, getting in his way. I'll be back soon.' Julie walked into the house carrying Karen who had burst into tears.

I found Debbie relaxing by the pool and dropped into a chair next to her. 'Poor kid,' she said. 'She's so disappointed. How ill is she?'

'Not very. You know how kids are; their temperature goes up and down for no apparent reason. She'll probably be all right in a couple of days. But Julie is thinking of cancelling the trip.'

'I've noticed something about this household,' said Debbie. 'Apart from Julie and the girls there are no women in it. If Julie wants someone to look after Karen I could do that.'

'It's a kindly thought,' I said. 'But if it comes to the push I'll take Karen to the Royal Palm. We have a very efficient and charming young nurse there whom Karen knows very well. I've done it before when Julie has been away.'

'Then talk Julie out of cancelling. It would disappoint Sue so much.'

'I'll do my best.' Presently Julie came out of the house, and I asked, 'How is she?'

'Rebellious.'

'You don't have to cancel the trip. I don't want *two* gloomy kids sulking about the house. Debbie has offered to look after Karen, and there's always Kitty Symonette at the hotel.'

'Thanks, Debbie. That's good of you.' Julie thought for a moment. 'Very well – we'll go.' She looked at Debbie. 'Don't let Karen play you up; that little minx is full of tricks.'

I stood up. 'If everything's aboard I'll come and see you off.'

Just then Billy came striding out of the house and beckoned me with a jerk of his head. He said, 'There'll be a squad of lawyers and auditors flying in to look at your books. If everything checks we have a deal.' He laughed and put out his hand.

So it was with a light heart that I saw Julie and Sue away on *Lucayan Girl*. I told Julie about the deal and she was delighted, and then we went out to the lagoon where the *Girl* was ready to cast off, her engines already ticking over. Sue was running about taking photographs with the camera I had given her for her birthday; her teacher had set her the exercise of a photo-essay as her homework for the Christmas vacation. By the look of her both she and her stock of film would be exhausted before the voyage began.

I had a word with Pete who was coiling a rope in the bows. 'Got a crewman?'

'Sure.'

'How is he?'

'He'll do,' said Pete laconically. Knowing Pete that meant the young fellow was pretty good.

'Where is he?'

'Below – greasing the shafts.' Pete raised his voice. 'All right, then; all aboard that's goin' aboard.'

Sue scampered aboard and Julie kissed me and followed more sedately. 'Cast off the after line, Miss Mate,' said Pete. He cast off the forward line and quickly went to the helm on the flying bridge. The engines growled and *Lucayan Girl* moved slowly away.

We watched as the *Girl* went down the lagoon and turned into the channel which led to the open sea and so out of sight. I said to Billy, 'I think we have work to do.' I stooped to pick up Sue's camera which she had left on a chair. 'Sue will be mad enough to bust. When Julie rings tonight I'll tell her to buy another. We mustn't disappoint teacher.'

3

It was late in the day when it went bad – an hour from midnight. Billy and I had worked late, sorting out the details of the proposed merger and outlining future plans, and were having a final drink before he went back to the Royal Palm. Suddenly he broke off what he was saying in mid-sentence. 'What's the matter? You got ants in your pants? That's the third time you've checked your watch in five minutes. I hope I'm not that unwelcome.'

'Julie hasn't telephoned,' I said shortly. 'That's not like her.'

I picked up the telephone and rang the Fontainbleu in Miami where she usually stayed. The call took an annoyingly long time to place and Billy occupied himself with shuffling his papers together and putting them into his briefcase. Finally I got through and said, 'I'd like to speak to Mrs Mangan.'

There was a pause. 'Do you know the room number, sir?'

'No.'

Another pause. 'There's no one of that name in the hotel, sir.'

'Put me through to the desk clerk, please.' Again that took a bit of time but I finally got him. I said, 'My name is Mangan. Has my wife checked in yet?'

A rustle of papers. 'No, sir.'

'But she did make a reservation?'

'Yes, sir; two rooms. Mrs Mangan and Miss Mangan, and Mr and Mrs Pascoe.'

'Have the Pascoes checked in?'

'No, sir.'

'Thank you.' I put down the telephone and said blankly, 'She's not there.'

'What time was she supposed to get into Miami?' asked Billy.

'Before dark; say, eight o'clock. Pete has standing instructions from me to get into port in daylight if possible, especially with the family aboard. She's a fast boat for her type and he'd have no trouble about that.'

'She's only three hours overdue, Tom. Anything could have happened. Engine trouble, perhaps.'

'Boats with Pete aboard don't have engine trouble,' I said sharply. 'Besides, the *Girl* has two engines.'

'If one was knocked out it would slow her down.'

'Not by a lot – not by three hours.' I picked up the telephone again. 'I'll ring the marina in Miami.' Ten minutes later I knew that *Lucayan Girl* had not arrived. I said to Billy, 'I've got a feeling about this. I'm going over to BASRA – they can raise the US Coast Guard.'

'How long will you be?'

'Fifteen – twenty minutes. It's quite close.'

'I'll stick around until you get back. Julie might ring.'

'Thanks. I'll check that Karen's safely asleep before I go.'

BASRA headquarters on Grand Bahama are in the building which also holds the Underwater Exploration Society. Five minutes later I was climbing the stairs to the Tide's Inn, a tavern which supports both the Society and BASRA. The place was noisy with vacationers and I found Joe Kimble of BASRA employed in his favourite occupation – chatting up a couple of nubile females. I crossed to his table. 'Sorry to interrupt, Joe, but *Lucayan Girl* is overdue in Miami.'

He looked up. 'How much overdue?'

'Over three hours now.' I met his eye. 'Julie and Sue are aboard.'

'Oh!' He stood up. 'Sorry, girls, but business comes first.'

We went down to the BASRA office and I said, 'What's the weather like in the Florida Straits?'

'Calm – no problems there.' He sat behind a desk and took a pen. 'When did she leave?'

'Dead on eleven this morning.'

'Give me the number of the marina in Miami.' He scribbled it down, then said, 'You'd better go home, Tom, and stick by your telephone. But don't use it. I'll do any telephoning that's necessary – you keep an open line. I'll ring the marina and tell them to notify BASRA if she comes in.'

'What about the Coast Guard?'

'I'll radio them but there's not much they can do at night – you know that.'

'Can I use the phone here?' At Joe's nod I picked it up and rang Bobby Bowen at his home. I outlined the situation, then said, 'There may be nothing in it, but if there's no report in the next few hours I'll need planes in the air at first light. How many can we raise?'

'Just two here,' said Bowen. 'There's one in Nassau and the other has its engine stripped for the 300-hour check.'

'Get that plane back from Nassau as fast as you can. You'll liaise with Joe Kimble of BASRA who will be coordinator. Unless the order is cancelled you'll rendezvous at . . .' I twitched an eyebrow at Joe who said, 'Lucayan Beach Air Services.'

I passed that on, and added, '. . . at five-thirty a.m.' I put down the phone. 'I'm going home, Joe. Julie might ring.'

He nodded. 'If I'm going to fly tomorrow I'll need some shuteye. I'll get one of the groundlings to stand by here as soon as I've raised the Coast Guard.'

I had an argument with Billy which he won. 'I'll stay by the telephone,' he said. 'You've got to sleep. If anything comes through I'll wake you.' He raided the kitchen and made me warm milk laced with brandy. Afterwards he told me that he had roused Luke Bailey who found Julie's sleeping pills and he dissolved one into the milk.

So it was that when he woke me at five in the morning I felt doped and muzzy. At first I did not know what he was doing there in my bedroom, but then the knowledge hit me. 'Any news?' I demanded.

He shook his head. 'Just a call from BASRA; the Coast

Guard are putting helicopters out of Miami as soon as it's light enough to see.'

I got up and found Debbie in the living-room; Billy had rung her and she had immediately come from the hotel. None of us did much talking because there was nothing much to say, but Debbie insisted that she was going to stay to look after Karen. Luke Bailey made an early breakfast and I drove to the airport feeling like hell.

Joe Kimble was in the office of Lucayan Beach Air Services, allocating areas on a map. Bobby Bowen was there, and Bill Pinder, another Corporation pilot, and there were three other pilots, volunteers from BASRA. Joe said, 'Now, remember we're tying in with the US Coast Guard on this. Stick to your own areas and watch your altitude. And watch for the choppers – we don't want a mid-air collision to complicate things.'

We walked out to the tie-down lines and the sky was just lightening in the east as we took off. I flew with Bobby Bowen and, as we flew west and gained altitude, the panorama in the rising sun was achingly beautiful.

Lucayan Girl was of a type which the Americans call a trawler. Because of recurrent oil crises a demand has arisen for a boat, not particularly fast, but with range and sea-keeping qualities, and light on fuel. These boats, no matter who the designer, all look pretty much alike because they were all trying to solve the same problems and inevitably came up with the same results. And our problem was that in Florida and Bahamian waters they are as thick as fleas on a dog.

Not many people make night passages in power boats in the Islands but we spotted our first twenty miles out and heading our way. We were flying at 2500 feet, adhering strictly to regulations for the course we were on, and Bowen dropped us 1000 feet, again going by the book. I looked at the boat through glasses as we went by and shook my head. Bowen took us up again.

It was a long and futile search. We found six boats but not *Lucayan Girl*. From the intermittent chatter on the radio no one else was having any luck either. Visibility so early in the morning was generally good but, as the sun rose, cloud began to form. Presently Bowen said, 'Got to go back.' He tapped the fuel gauge.

So we went back, the engine coughing as we landed, and found that all the others had already returned. No one had seen the *Girl* and neither had the US Coast Guard. Joe Kimble reamed out Bobby Bowen. 'You cut that too damn fine.'

Bowen managed a tired smile. 'No problem; I emptied my cigarette lighter into the tank.'

'I sure as hell don't want to go out there looking for plane wreckage because some damn fool has run out of gas. Don't do it again.'

I said, 'Refuel, Bobby.'

One of the BASRA pilots stirred. 'I'll take you out again, Mr Mangan. I'm fuelled up.'

So I went out again. They all went out again. They were a good crowd. And we all came back, but not *Lucayan Girl*.

The next few days were grim. People pussyfooted around me, not knowing what to do or say, and work went to hell. I felt as numb as though I had been mentally anaesthetized and I suppose I acted like a zombie, one of the walking dead. I wished I was dead.

Billy said, 'This is no time to talk business, Tom. Let me know when we can get together again.' He went back to Houston, but Debbie refused to go home and stayed on to look after Karen. I was in no mood to argue.

Looking back I can see that this was worse than a normal death in the family. There was no funeral, no assuaging ceremonial – nothing to do. There was the ever-present expectation of a telephone call which would magically solve everything and restore my wife and daughter to me and bring back my old friend, Pete Albury. I jerked every time a phone rang – anywhere.

The house was haunted. Although the pool was mirror-like in its quietness there was still held in the mind's eye the image of a lithe young body, sleek as an otter, breaking the surface with a shout of joy, and I expected, on turning a corner, to find at any moment the dark beauty of Julie, perhaps going about some domestic chore like watering the roses.

I suppose I was a haunted man.

Debbie was very good. At first she sought to cheer me up, but I was impervious so she desisted and contented herself with acting as a barrier between me and the world of the newspapers. And she saw that I ate regularly and did not drink too much or, at least, drink alone. She need not have worried about that; I have never considered that diving into a bottle could solve any problems.

She looked after Karen and played with her and stopped my little daughter from worrying me too much in those awful first days. Once I overheard Karen say to her, 'What's wrong with Daddy?'

'Your father has some problems,' said Debbie. 'Don't bother him now – he'll be all right soon.'

Karen had not been told, but sooner or later I would have to tell her that her mother and sister were dead. I wondered if the idea of death would mean much to a nine-year-old. I sweated at the thought of telling her.

And then there were Julie's parents, Mike and Ellen Pascoe. I did not know how to contact them because they were on the move, driving from Maryland to Miami where they expected to meet Julie at the Fontainbleu. I left a message at the Fontainbleu asking that they ring me immediately on arrival.

The call came two days later and Ellen was on the line. 'Julie isn't here,' she said. 'Has she been held up?'

'Can I speak to Mike?'

'Of course.' Her voice sharpened. 'Is anything wrong, Tom?'

'Just let me talk to Mike for a moment.' Mike came on and I told him what had happened, and I heard his breath hiss in my ear.

He said, 'Is there no . . . hope?'

'Oh, God! Hope is the only thing that's been keeping me

going. But it's been nearly three days, and every hour that goes by . . . Look, I'll send a plane for you. It'll be there this afternoon. Just wait at the hotel for Bobby Bowen. Okay?'

'All right,' he said heavily.

Half an hour after that telephone call Debbie came into my study. 'There are two men to see you. Policemen.'

I jerked around. 'With news?' She shook her head sadly and I sighed. 'All right; show them in.'

Debbie led them into the study and then left. I stood up and looked at Perigord in some perplexity. Deputy-Commissioner Perigord, a black Bahamian, was the top-ranking police officer on Grand Bahama and I knew him slightly, having met him at social functions. His companion was also black but unknown to me. Both were in uniform.

Perigord said, 'I'm sorry to have to intrude at this time, Mr Mangan; I assure you I wish it were otherwise. I put it off for as long as possible but . . .' He shrugged.

'I know,' I said. 'Won't you sit down?'

He took off his uniform cap and laid it on my desk together with his swagger stick. 'This is Inspector Hepburn.'

I nodded in acknowledgement and sat down. Perigord said, 'I knew Mrs Mangan slightly; we met at PTA meetings – our daughters attend the same school. If there is anything my wife and I can do to help then please call on us. However, I am here on a different errand. You must know that in circumstances like this there are questions to be asked.'

'Yes,' I said. 'Just get on with it.'

He took out a notebook. 'The name of your boat is *Lucayan Girl*?'

'Yes.'

'Where did she sail from?'

'Here.' I pointed through the window towards the atrium. 'Her mooring is just through that archway.'

'Would you mind if Inspector Hepburn looks at the mooring?'

'No – but what does he expect to find?'

'I don't know. Police work consists of looking at a lot of

things, most of which turn out to be useless in the end. But sometimes we get lucky.' He nodded to Hepburn who got up and left the room.

'I don't see how the police come into it.' I saw Hepburn walk by the pool and disappear through the arch.

'There is more to police work than crime; we fulfil many social functions. Were you present when *Lucayan Girl* sailed?'

'Yes.'

'Who was on board?'

'Julie, my wife; my daughter, Susan; Pete Albury, the skipper; and a crewman.'

'What is the crewman's name?'

'I don't know.'

Perigord frowned. 'You don't know!' he said with a tinge of perplexity in his voice.

'Pete Albury hired him. I didn't want my wife and daughter to sail with only Pete aboard so I asked Pete to hire a hand just for this trip.'

'I see. But if you hired him you were obviously going to pay him. Was it to be by cash or cheque?'

'I don't know,' I said to Perigord's obvious bafflement. As he made a disapproving clicking sound with his tongue I said, 'That was Pete's business. He ran *Lucayan Girl*; he had a bank account from which to draw funds, and I checked the account monthly. He'd have paid, but whether in cash or by cheque I wouldn't know.'

'You must have trusted Mr Albury,' said Perigord.

'I did,' I said evenly.

'Now, then; what did this man – this crewman –look like?'

'I don't know; I didn't see him.'

Perigord definitely lost his composure. 'You mean you hired a man you didn't even *see*!'

'I didn't hire him,' I said. 'Pete did. I had every confidence in Pete to pick a good man. Look, I run a business. I don't hire personally everyone who works for me, neither do I necessarily know them by name or sight. That's known as delegation of authority.'

'And so you bring your business practices into your household.'

'I trusted Pete,' I said stubbornly.

'How do you know that this . . . this stranger was on board when the boat sailed?'

'Pete told me. I asked him and he said the crewman was below greasing the shafts.'

'But you don't know it of your own knowledge.'

'I can't say that I do.'

Perigord pondered for a moment, then asked, 'Is there anyone else to whom I can refer who would know it from his own knowledge?'

I thought about that, casting my mind back to the scene by the lagoon. Billy, Debbie and I had walked through the archway together and if I had not seen the crewman then neither could they. I shook my head. 'No, I don't think so.'

Inspector Hepburn came back and Perigord glanced at him. 'So what it comes to is this – we have a man, probably dead, whose name we don't know and whom we can't describe. We don't even know his colour. In fact, Mr Mangan; we might even be wrong about the sex – this crew member *could* be a woman for all we know.'

'No,' I said definitely. 'I asked Pete about him, and Pete said, "*He*'ll do."'

'Well, that's something,' said Perigord. 'Where does Mr Albury live?'

'Here,' I said. 'There are some work rooms and store rooms for ship's chandlery with an apartment over. Pete moved in here when his wife died last year.'

'There may be something in the apartment to give us a lead. Do you mind if Inspector Hepburn looks?'

'Of course not.' I opened the wall safe and took out the key to Pete's rooms and gave it to Hepburn, then rang for Luke who appeared with suspicious alacrity. 'Show the Inspector where Pete's rooms are.'

They left and I turned to Perigord. 'There's something here which may possibly be useful.' I took a small book from the safe. 'I record the serial numbers of any important equipment I own, and there's a section for *Lucayan Girl* in here – her engine numbers, radar, radio and so on. Even the binoculars and the cameras we routinely carry aboard.'

'Ah, that's better!' Perigord took the book and flicked through it. 'And the numbers carried on certain documents, I see. Is the boat insured?'

'Of course.'

'And you, Mr Mangan; do you carry life insurance?'

'Certainly.'

'And Mrs Mangan? Was her life insured?'

I stared at him. 'I'm a rich enough man not to want to benefit by my wife's death. What the hell are you getting at?'

He held up his hand in a conciliatory gesture. 'I'm sorry; in my work we are forced to intrude at inopportune moments with questions which may be construed as tactless – tactless but necessary. I did not wish to offend, sir.'

'I'm sorry,' I said. 'I'm under a bit of strain. No apology is necessary.'

There were more questions, the answers to most of which appeared to satisfy him, and presently Hepburn came back and Perigord picked up his cap and swagger stick. 'That will be all for now, sir. There'll be an enquiry; I'll let you know where and when it will be held. May I offer my profound sorrow and my . . . condolences. I did like Mrs Mangan.'

'Condolences!' I said in a choked voice.

'It *has* been two and a half days,' said Perigord gravely.

I took a grip on myself. 'Commissioner, what do you think happened?'

'I doubt if we'll ever know. Perhaps a gas leak in the bilges leading to an explosion – that's rather common. Or the boat could have been run down by a supertanker.'

'In daylight!'

'We don't know that it was daylight,' he pointed out, and shrugged. 'And those ships are so big they could run down a moderately small craft and no one would feel a thing. A ship carrying 300,000 tons of oil has a lot of momentum. We'll do our best to find out what happened, but I offer no certainties.' With that he and Hepburn left.

He had not been gone two minutes when Luke Bailey came in wearing a worried frown. 'I'd like to tell you something.' He jerked his head at the door. 'That policeman . . .'

'Who – Perigord?'

'No, the other one – the Inspector. He's on the Narcotics Squad. I thought you'd like to know.'

4

That evening I had to cope with the Pascoes who, oddly enough, were more philosophical about it than I was. I was in a cold, helpless, miserable rage; wanting to strike out at something but finding nothing to hit – no target. The Pascoes were more equable. Nearing the end of their own days I suppose that death was a not unexpected figure lurking over the horizon, something with which they had come to terms on a personal level. Besides, Mike was a doctor and death had been a factor in his professional life. They did their best to comfort me.

I had a long talk with Mike after Ellen had gone to bed. 'I know how you feel,' he said. 'I lost a boy – killed in Vietnam. Did Julie ever tell you about that?' I nodded. 'It hit me hard. Allen was a good boy.' He wagged his head sagely. 'But it wears off, Tom; you can't grieve for ever.'

'I suppose so,' I said moodily. Deep in my heart I knew he was wrong; I would grieve for Julie and Sue for the rest of my life.

'What are you going to do now?' he asked.

'I don't know.'

'For God's sake, wake up! You can't just let everything slide. You're running a corporation and you have folk depending on you. You're still a young man, too. How old? Forty what?'

'Forty-two.'

'You can get married again,' he said.

'Let's not talk about that now,' I said sharply. 'Julie's not been gone three days. And maybe . . .'

'Maybe she'll come back? Don't set your heart on that, Tom, or you'll drive yourself nuts.' I said nothing to that and there was a long silence. After a while Mike stirred. 'What are you going to do about Karen?'

'I haven't thought about it yet.'

'Then you'd better put your mind to it. Debbie Cunningham's a good girl from what I've seen of her, but she won't be around for ever. You'll have to make some arrangements. Bringing up a daughter aged nine *and* running a corporation could be a mite tough – tough on Karen, I mean.'

'I'll get a woman in to look after her, I suppose.'

'Humph!' Evidently he did not think much of that idea. I did not think much of it myself. He said, 'Ellen and I have been talking. We'd like to take Karen until you've got things settled in your mind.'

'That's generous of you.'

'No; just plain horse sense. Karen should be with her own kin.' He smiled slowly. 'But I thought I'd gotten past the age of child-raising.'

'I agree,' I said. 'I had a call from my sister, Peggy, this morning. She wants to take Karen to Abaco, at least until I get settled and can make other arrangements. She has two kids of her own, and that might be better for Karen.'

Mike looked a shade relieved. 'It would be better,' he said positively. 'Children brought up by old folk sometimes turn out funny. You're starting to think, Tom.'

We talked about it some more and then I changed the subject. 'There's something I can't understand. I don't see why Perigord should be conducting this investigation personally. He's a Deputy-Commissioner, the top cop on the island. I shouldn't have thought this would warrant it.'

'You're running yourself down,' said Mike. 'You're a prominent citizen on Grand Bahama. And you say he knew Julie?'

'So he says. He says he met her at the school, at PTA meetings. I didn't go to many of those.'

'Maybe he feels he has a personal obligation.'

'Perhaps. But then there's Hepburn. Luke Bailey tells me Hepburn is a narcotics officer, and he did give Pete's rooms a good shakedown. There's something behind all this, Mike.'

'Imagination!' he scoffed. 'Probably Hepburn was the only officer handy in the precinct house at the time.' He got up and stretched. 'I'm going to bed; I'm not as young as I was.' He looked down at me. 'Tom, I've been a doctor all my life until I retired three years ago. I've seen a lot of people die and a lot of grief in families. Tell me; have you shed one single tear since Julie went?'

'No,' I said flatly.

He walked to the corner cupboard, poured four fingers of brandy into a glass, and brought it back to me. 'Drink that, relax, and let yourself go. There's no fault in a man crying, and bottling it up can harm you.' He turned and walked out of the room.

Mike was a kindly man and a good man. He had once said that being a doctor made a man a fair jackleg psychologist and he was right about this. I sat for a long time holding the glass and just looking into its brown depths. Then I swallowed the lot in two long gulps. The brandy burned going down and I gasped. Fifteen minutes later I was sprawled on the settee and crying my heart out. I cried myself to sleep and awoke in the early hours of the morning when I went to bed after turning out the lights.

It was acceptance that Julie and Sue were dead; and Pete and an unknown man. The acceptance brought a curious kind of peace; I still felt numbed in my mind, but I felt better and was a functioning man. Mike had known what he was doing.

Four days later I took Karen to Abaco, and Debbie came with us. It was then, in the presence of Peggy and Bob, that I told Karen that her mother and sister were dead and that she would be staying with her aunt and uncle for a while. She looked at me, wide-eyed, and said, 'They won't be coming home? Ever?'

'I'm afraid not. You remember when Timmy died?' Timmy was a pet kitten who had been run over by a car, and Karen nodded. 'Well, it's something like that.'

Tears welled in her eyes and she blinked them away.

'Timmy didn't come back,' she agreed. 'Does that mean I won't see Mommy and Susie – not ever?' Suddenly she bust loose. She burst into tears and tore herself away. 'I don't believe you,' she cried, and began to wail, 'I want my Mommy. I want my Mommy.'

Peggy caught her up in her arms and comforted her, then said over her shoulder to me, 'I think a mild sedative and bed is the best thing now.' She took Karen away.

Bob said awkwardly, 'It's hard to know what to say.'

'I know – but the world goes round as usual. It'll take me a bit of time to get used to this, but I'll pull through. Where's Debbie?'

'On the patio.'

I looked at my watch. 'We'll have to get back; the plane is needed. I'll come across as often as I can – at least once a week.'

Debbie and I did not talk much at first on the flight back to Grand Bahama; both of us were immersed in our private thoughts. It was a long time before I said, 'I suppose you'll be going back to Houston.'

'Yes,' she said colourlessly. Presently she said, 'And I thought I had troubles.'

'What happened?'

She laughed shortly. 'Would you want to know?'

'Why not? We can cry on each other's shoulder.'

'A man happened – or I thought he was a man. I thought he loved me, but he really loved my money. I happened to pick up a telephone at the wrong time and I heard a really interesting conversation about the big deals he was going to make and the life he was going to lead as soon as he'd married me. The trouble was that he was talking to another woman, and she was included in his plans.'

'That's bad,' I said.

'I was a damned fool,' she said. 'You see, I'd been warned. Billy was against it all along because he didn't trust the guy and he made that very clear. But would I listen? Not me. I was grown up – a woman of the world – and I knew it all.'

'How old are you, Debbie?'

'The ripe old age of twenty-five.'

'I had my fingers burned, too, when I was your age,' I said. 'That was before I met Julie. You'll get over it.'

'You think so? But, God, it's taught me something and I don't think I like what it's taught me. Here I am – a poor little rich girl – and from now to eternity I'll be looking at every guy I meet and wondering if he wants me or all that lovely dough. That's no way to have to go through life.'

'Other rich people cope,' I said.

'Yes?' she said challengingly. 'Examined the divorce statistics lately?'

Her voice was bitter and I could see that she had been badly hurt. And coming to Grand Bahama and seeing how happily Julie and I were married could not have helped much. Presently she said quietly, 'But you don't want to be burdened with my problems even though you do seem to have got over the worst of your blues. Was it the talk you had with Mike Pascoe the other day?'

'Yes,' I said. 'He dutch-uncled me, and it helped. It could help you.'

'All right, Tom,' she said. 'What would you do if you were me? I know you can't possibly put yourself in my position, but I've told you enough to know about me. I'd like your advice. You know, Billy thinks a lot of you and I respect Billy's judgement – now.'

I scratched the angle of my jaw and thought about it. 'Well, I wouldn't get rid of your money, if that's what you're thinking about. It's too useful; you can do a lot of good if you have enough dollars.'

'Buying my way out?'

'Not exactly. Are you thinking of being a missionary in Calcutta or something like that?'

Her laugh was rueful. 'You know more about me than I thought.'

'Forget it,' I said. 'It doesn't work. Besides, charity begins at home. Now, you're a Texan. I'll bet there are poor black kids in Texas who have never even seen the sea.'

'That's a thought. What are you getting at?'

'I'm working it out,' I said slowly. 'Starting from the fact that we're in the Bahamas with plenty of black faces around. Your black Texan kids wouldn't stand out if you brought them here, and we've no colour bar to speak of. Teach them to swim, scuba-dive, sail a boat – things they've only been able to dream about back home. If you brought them out of season I could give you cheap rates in the hotels. They could go to Abaco and Eleuthera; real desert island stuff.'

'My God!' she said. 'What a marvellous idea. And there are poor white kids, too.'

'All right, mix 'em up.' I saw she was caught up in enthusiasm, and warned, 'But you'll have to do more than pay for it, Deb, if it's going to work – I mean for you personally. You'll have to participate and bring the kids yourself, with perhaps a couple of assistants. It's something to think about.'

'It surely is.'

My eye was caught by Bill Pinder, the pilot, who was waving at me. I leaned forward and took the piece of paper he held. It was a message that had been radioed through Freeport air control and told me that Perigord wanted to see me urgently in his office.

I took Debbie along to the police station which was on the corner of Pioneer's Way and East Mall. I suppose I could have driven her to the Royal Palm and then gone back, but there was something about Perigord's message which made me want to see him fast, so I asked Debbie if she minded stopping off. It was a hot day and I did not want to leave her sitting in the car so I took her inside with me.

I happened to catch Perigord walking through the entrance hall so I introduced them, and added, 'Miss Cunningham and her brother were present when *Lucayan Girl* left for Miami.'

Perigord looked at her thoughtfully. 'You'd better come into my office – both of you,' he said abruptly, and led the way. In his office he turned to Debbie and asked without preamble, 'Are you a good friend of Mr Mangan?'

She was startled and shot me a swift look. 'I would say so.'

I said, 'I haven't known Miss Cunningham long but I would certainly consider her my friend. Her cousin and I have been friends for many years.'

For a moment Perigord looked undecided, then he waved at a chair. 'Please sit down.' He sat opposite us and said, 'I am not certain that Miss Cunningham should be here at this point, but you might need some support from a friend.'

'You've found them,' I said with certainty.

He took a deep breath. 'A fisherman found the body of a small, female child on a beach on Cat Island.'

'Cat Island!' I said incredulously. 'But that's impossible! *Lucayan Girl* was going south-west to Miami – Cat Island is 200 miles south-east. It *can't* be Sue!'

'I'm sorry, Mr Mangan, but there is no doubt.'

'I don't believe it. I want to see her.'

'I would advise against it.' Perigord shook his head. 'You wouldn't recognize her.'

'Why not?'

Perigord was unhappy. 'I don't have to explain to a fellow Bahamian what happens to a body in our seas in a very short time.'

'If I wouldn't recognize her how in hell can *you* be so sure?' I was becoming angry at the impossibility of all this. 'How could Sue have got to Cat Island?'

Perigord took a card from his desk drawer and laid it flat. 'This is your daughter's dental record; we obtained it from the school. Dr Miller, your daughter's dentist, has done a comparison and it fits in every respect. We took no chances; we had another evaluation from a dentist who does not know your daughter. He confirmed Dr Miller's identification.'

I suddenly felt sick and a little dizzy. It must have shown in my colour because Debbie put her hand on my arm. 'Are you all right, Tom?'

'Yes,' I said thickly. I raised my head and looked at Perigord. 'And Julie? And the others?'

'Nothing, I'm afraid.' He cleared his throat. 'There'll be an inquest, of course.'

'How do you explain Cat Island? You know it's bloody impossible. Anything abandoned in the Florida Straits would be swept north-east in the Gulf Stream.'

'I can't explain it; at least, not to your satisfaction.' He held up his hand as I opened my mouth. 'It might help if you could identify the crewman.'

I said dully, 'I didn't see him.'

Perigord said, 'We have asked questions at the marinas with no luck at all. The trouble is that the marinas have, literally, a floating population.' He repeated that, appreciating the double edge. 'Yes, a floating population – here today and gone tomorrow. Nobody has been reported missing because everybody is missing, sooner or later. It makes police work difficult. We have also checked from the other end by asking Mr Albury's friends if he had been seen talking to a stranger. Again, no luck.'

Debbie said, 'He might not have been a stranger.'

'Oh, yes, I think he was,' said Perigord confidently. 'I think he was a beach bum, one of the young Americans who hitch-hike around the islands on the cheap and are willing to crew for anyone if it gives them a leg further. I think this one was going home.'

'Then he might be on an American missing persons list,' she remarked.

'Why should he be?' asked Perigord. 'He's only been gone a week, and he's probably a footloose young man, a social drop-out. In any case, in which American city do we ask? And with no name and no face how do we operate?'

My brain started to work creakily. Perigord had said something which aroused my ire. 'You said you couldn't explain how Sue came to be on Cat Island *to my satisfaction*. Does that mean that you are satisfied?' I was becoming enraged at Perigord because I knew he was holding something back.

That got to him. 'By God, Mr Mangan, I am not satisfied. It gives me no satisfaction to sit here and pass on bad news, sir.'

'Then what's all the bloody mystery? Is it because I am a suspect? If I am then say so. Am I to be accused of blowing up my own boat?'

My voice had risen to a shout and I found myself shaking. Again Debbie held my arm, and said, 'Take it easy, Tom.'

'Take it easy? There's been something damn funny going on right from the start.' I stabbed a finger at Perigord. 'No one can tell me that a Deputy-Commissioner of Police does his own legwork when a boat goes missing. Especially when he brings a narcotics officer with him. Perigord, I'm well-known in Government circles, and if you don't come across I'll be over in Nassau talking to Deane, your boss, and a few other people and you won't know what hit you.'

Perigord made a curious gesture as though to brush away an irritating fly. 'I assure you that the police are treating this with the utmost seriousness. Further, the Government is serious. And alarmed, I might add. The Attorney General, acting under direct instruction from the Prime Minister, is putting very heavy pressure on me – as much as I can stand – and I don't need any more from you.'

'But you'll damn well get it,' I said. 'Good Christ, this is my family we're talking about!'

He stopped being impervious and his voice softened. 'I know – I know.' He stood up and went to the window, looking out on to East Mall in silence and with his hands clasped tightly behind his back. He stood there for a long time evidently having difficulty in making up his mind about something.

Presently he turned and said quietly, 'I suppose if I were in your position I would feel and act as you do. That's why I'm going to tell you something of what is happening in the Bahamas. But I'll want your discretion. I don't want you going off half-cocked and, above all, I want your silence. You must not talk about what I'm about to tell you.'

Debbie rose to her feet. 'I'll leave.'

'No,' said Perigord. 'Stay, Miss Cunningham.' He smiled. 'Mr Mangan will want to talk to someone about this; he wouldn't be human if he didn't, and his confidante might as well be you. But I'll need the same assurance of your silence.'

Debbie said, 'You have it.'

'Mr Mangan?'

I thought Perigord was every bit as good an amateur psychologist as Mike Pascoe. 'All right.'

He returned to his seat at the desk. 'It is not normal for a well-found boat to vanish in a calm sea, and the enquiries made before I took over the case gave us the assurance that *Lucayan Girl* was a very well-found boat with more than the usual complement of safety equipment. She was very well-equipped, is that not so?'

'I made it so,' I said.

Perigord examined the backs of his hands. 'There have been too many boats going missing these past few years. There has been much ill-informed and mischievous talk about the so-called Bermuda Triangle of which we are in the centre. The Bahamian Government, however, does not believe in spooks – either do the insurance companies. The Government is becoming most worried about it.'

'Are you talking about piracy?' said Debbie unbelievingly.

'Just that.'

I had heard the rumours, as I suppose every other Bahamian had, and it had been a topic in some of the American yachting magazines. I said, 'I know there was piracy around here in the old days, but these boats aren't treasure ships – they're not carrying gold to Spain. I suppose you could sell off bits and pieces – radar, radio, engines, perhaps – but that's chicken feed, and dangerous, too. Easy to detect.'

'You're right. Your boat is probably on the sea bed by now, with all its equipment intact. These people are not going to risk selling a few items for a few dollars. Mr Mangan, I think we're dealing with coke smugglers, and I don't mean Coca-Cola – I mean cocaine. It comes through here from South America and goes to the States. Some heroin, too, but not much because we're not on that route. Some marijuana, also, but again not much because it's too bulky.'

He nodded and gestured towards the large map of the Bahamas on the wall. 'Look at that – 100,000 square miles of which only five per cent is land. If the land were conveniently in one place our task would be easier, but there are thousands of cays. An area the size of the British Isles with a population of 220,000. That's what we have to police.'

He walked over to the map. 'Take only one small group.' His arm slashed in an arc. 'The Ragged Island Range and the Jumentos Cays – 120 miles long with a total population of 200, mostly concentrated in Duncan Town in the south. Anyone could bring a boat in there with a nine nines certainty of not being seen even in daylight. They could land on Flamingo Cay, Water Cay, Stoney Cay – or any one of a hundred others, most of which don't even have names. And that's just one small chain of islands among many. We could turn our whole population into police officers and still not have enough men to cover.'

Debbie said, 'How does piracy come into this?'

'It's not called piracy any more, although it is,' said Perigord tiredly. 'It's become prevalent enough to have aquired its own name – yacht-jacking. They grab a boat and sail it out of the local area, fast. A quick paint spray job of the upperworks takes care of easy identification. They head for the cay where the cocaine is hidden and then run it to the States. Once the cocaine is ashore they usually sink the boat; sometimes they may use it for a second run, but not often. And you know how many we've caught?' He held up a single finger.

'And for that they murder the crew?' I demanded.

'Do you know what the profits are, Mr Mangan? But normally the boats are stolen from a marina and there are no deaths. That's easy enough considering the informality of most boat owners and the laxity of the average marina.'

'*Lucayan Girl* wasn't stolen from a marina.'

Perigord said deliberately, 'When a man like you sends his wife and small daughter to sea with a crewman he has never seen and whose name he doesn't know he's asking for trouble.'

He had not come right out and said it, but he was implying that I was a damn fool and I was inclined to agree with him. I said weakly, 'But who could have known?'

Perigord sighed. 'We hand out circulars, put posters in marinas – watch your boat – know your crew – use your keys – and no one apparently takes a damn bit of notice.' He paused. 'I wouldn't say that the case of *Lucayan Girl* is the norm. Boats *are* lost at sea for other than criminal reasons; storm damage, fire, explosions, run down, and so on. But if they're taken by piracy and then sunk who's to know the difference? That's our problem; we don't *know* how many acts of piracy are occurring. All we know is that too many boats are being lost.'

Debbie said, 'Are you implying that the crewman on *Lucayan Girl* might be alive?'

Perigord spread his hands. 'Miss Cunningham, if this is a simple matter of sinking, which we can't discount, then he's probably dead. If it is piracy, which is more than likely because of what we found on Cat Island, then he is probably alive. And that's why I want your silence. If he's still here I don't want him to know he's being looked for.' He pursed his lips in a dubious manner. 'But without a name or description he's going to be difficult to find.'

I said, 'Commissioner, find the bastard. If it's a matter of a reward to be offered I'll put it up, no matter how much.'

'I mentioned discretion,' said Perigord softly. 'Offering a public reward is hardly being discreet.' He clasped his hands in front of him. 'This is a professional matter, Mr Mangan; a matter for the police. I don't want you butting in, and you did give me your word.'

'He's right, Tom,' said Debbie.

'I know.' I stood up and said to Perigord, 'I'm sorry if I blew my top.'

'No apology is necessary. I understood.'

'You'll keep me informed of developments?'

'Insofar as I can. You must understand that I may not be

able to tell all I know, even to you. Discretion also applies to the police when in the public interest.'

He stood up and we shook hands, and with that I had to be satisfied. But, as Perigord had warned, it was not to my entire satisfaction.

5

And so there was a funeral after all, but before that, the inquest. I attended, but before the proceedings began Perigord had a word with me. 'Regardless of the findings of this inquest we're treating this as a murder case.'

I looked at him sharply. 'New evidence?'

'Not really. But your daughter didn't die by drowning; there was no salt water in the lungs. Of course, in the event of an explosion on the boat she could have struck her head hard enough to kill her before entering the water. The head injuries are consistent with that.' He paused. 'It might help you to know that, in the opinion of the forensic pathologist, death was instantaneous.'

Debbie sat with me at the inquest – she was staying until after the funeral. The inquest was beautifully stage-managed; by Perigord, I suspect. The coroner had obviously been briefed and knew all the questions he was not supposed to ask, and he guided witnesses skilfully. As I gave my evidence it occurred to me that one of the factors in Perigord's decision to tell me what he had was to prevent any awkward questions coming from me at the inquest.

The verdict was death by unknown causes.

The family was at the funeral, of course. Grace came from Florida, and Peggy and Bob from Abaco, bringing Karen with them. Karen had regained most of her spirits but the funeral subdued her a little. In Peggy's opinion it was a good thing for Karen to attend. She was probably right. Also present were some of my Bahamian friends and a surprising number of Corporation employees.

It was sad to see the pathetically small coffin being lowered into the sandy earth. Karen cried, so I picked her up and held her close during the brief ceremony. A few last words were said and then it was all over and the crowd drifted away.

Debbie left for Houston the next day and I drove her to the airport. I picked her up at the Royal Palm and, on the way, she asked me to stop at the International Bazaar as there was something she wanted to pick up. I parked outside, and she said, 'Don't bother to come in; I won't be long.' So I sat in the car and waited, and she was back in five minutes.

At the airport we had coffee after we had got rid of her luggage and were waiting for her flight announcement. I said, 'You can tell Billy I'm willing to talk business as soon as he's ready.'

She looked at me closely. 'You're sure?'

'Mike was right,' I said. 'Life goes on, and the Corporation doesn't run itself. Yes, I'm sure.'

'I've been thinking of what you suggested when we were coming back from Abaco. You know, when I think of it I've lived a pretty useless life.' She smiled wryly. 'The Cunningham family doesn't believe in women in business. They're supposed to be ornamental, be good in bed and make babies – preferably boys to carry on the line. Damned misplaced southern chivalry. So I've been ornamental and that's about all.'

I smiled. 'What about the bed bit?'

'You won't believe this, but I was a virgin until I met that bastard back in Houston.' She shook the thought from her. 'Anyway, I think all that's going to change, and it's going to give a hell of a shock to my father – me mixing with black kids and poor white trash. I think I can get it past Billy One though.'

'Stick at it. It's time the Cunninghams made something besides money. Making people happy isn't a bad aim.'

We talked about it some more, and then she excused herself and walked across the concourse to the toilets. When she came back she was hurrying, her heels clicking rapidly on the hard floor. She stopped in front of me and said, 'There's something I have to show you, Tom. I wasn't going to, but . . .' She stopped and bit her lip nervously, then thrust an envelope into my hand. 'Here!'

‘What is it?’

‘You remember Sue left her camera behind. Well, I took out the film and had it developed. I just picked up the prints at the International Bazaar and I went into the john to have a look at them.’

‘I see,’ I said slowly. I was not sure I wanted to see them. There would be too many memories of that last day.

‘I think you ought to look at them,’ Debbie urged. ‘It’s important.’

I took the prints out of the envelope and shuffled through them. There were a couple of pictures of the *Girl* in one of which Pete posed in the bows, striking a mock-heroic attitude; three pictures of Sue herself, probably taken by Julie, which damn near broke my heart to see; and the rest were of Julie herself in various locations – by the pool, by the boat, and on board supervising the loading of luggage. There was one picture of Debbie and also four duds, out of focus and blurred. Sue had not yet got the hang of the camera and now never would. I got a lump in my throat and coughed.

Debbie was watching me closely. ‘Look again.’

I went through the pictures again and suddenly Debbie said, ‘Stop! That one.’ In the picture where Pete was in the bows there was a dim figure in the stern – a man just coming on deck from below. He was in the shade and his face was indistinct.

‘Well, I’ll be damned!’ I put down the print and took out the negative. A 110 film negative is damned small – it will just about cover your thumbnail – and the bit which showed the man was about as big as a pinhead. ‘The crewman!’ I said softly.

‘Yes. You’ll have something to show Perigord.’

‘But I’ll have it enlarged first. I’m not letting this into Perigord’s hands without having a few copies for myself. His ideas of discretion might get in my way. I have a shrewd idea that once he gets this I’ll never see it again.’

Debbie’s flight was announced, garbled by bad acoustics, and I accompanied her to the barrier where we said our goodbyes. 'I'll write to you about our scheme,' she said. 'Look after yourself, Tom.' She kissed me, a chaste peck on the cheek.

Then she was gone and I went back into Freeport to find a photographer.

Two days later I had what I wanted. I sat in my office and examined the duplicate negative, the copies of the colour print, and the six glossy black-and-white blow-ups of the pinhead-sized area of the negative which was the head of the crewman. The darkroom technician had done a good job considering the size of the image he had to work with. It could not be said to be a good portrait, being very grainy and slightly out of focus, but it was not all that bad.

The man was youngish – I would say under thirty – and he appeared to be blond. He had a broadish forehead and narrow chin, and his eyes were deepset and shadowed. One hand was up by his face as though he intended to hide it, and the head was slightly blurred as though it was in motion when the picture was taken. On the colour print it looked as though he was emerging from below, and perhaps he had suddenly been aware that he was on candid camera. If so, he had not beaten the speed of a camera shutter and a fast film.

I studied the face for a very long time. Was this a callous murderer? What did a murderer look like? Like anyone else, I suppose.

I was about to ring Perigord when the intercom buzzed so I flicked the switch. 'Yes, Jessie?'

'Mr Ford to see you.'

I had forgotten about Sam Ford. I pushed the photographs to one side of my desk, and said, 'Shoot him in.'

Sam Ford was a black Bahamian, and manager of the marina which was attached to the Sea Gardens Hotel on New Providence. He was an efficient manager, a good sailor, and did a lot for the branch of BASRA over there. Ever since the talk in Perigord's office and his expressed views on marina security I had been thinking about ours, and I had a job for Sam.

He came in. 'Morning, Mr Mangan.'

'Morning, Sam. Take a chair.'

As he sat down he said, 'I was real sorry to hear about what happened. I'd have come to the funeral, but we had problems that day at the marina.'

There had been a wreath from Sam and his family. 'Thanks, Sam. But it's over now.' He nodded and I leaned back in my chair. 'I've been reviewing our policy on marinas. We have three, and soon we'll have another when the hotel is finished on Eleuthera. If things turn out as I hope we'll have more. So far the marinas have been attached to the hotels with the marina manager being responsible to the hotel manager. It's worked well enough, but there's been a certain amount of friction, wouldn't you say?'

'I've had trouble,' said Sam. 'I don't know about the other marinas but my boss, Archie Bain, knows damn all about boats. The times he's asked me to put a quart in a pint pot I swear he thinks boats are collapsible.'

I had heard similar comments from other marina managers. 'All right, we're going to change things. We're going to set up a marinas division with the marina managers responsible to the divisional manager, not to the hotel managers. He'd be running the lot with the centralized buying of ship's chandlery and so on. How would you like the job?'

His eyebrows rose. 'Divisional manager?'

'Yes. You'd get the pay that goes with the job.'

Sam took a deep breath. 'Mr Mangan, that's a job I've been praying for.'

I smiled. 'It's yours from the first of the month – that's in two weeks. And as divisional manager you get to call me Tom.' We talked about his new job for some time, settling lines of demarcation, his salary, and other details. Then I said, 'And I want you to beef up on security in the marinas. How many boats have you had stolen, Sam?'

'From the Sea Gardens?' He scratched his head. 'One this year, two last year, and two the year before. The one this year was recovered on Andros, found abandoned. I think someone just took it for a joyride.'

Five in three years did not sound many out of all the boats Sam had handled, but multiply that by the number of marinas in the Bahamas and it was a hell of a lot. I began to appreciate Perigord's point of view. I said, 'Go back over the records of all our marinas for the last five years. I want to know how many boats went missing. And, Sam, we don't want to lose any more.'

'I don't see we're responsible,' said Sam. 'And there's a clause in the marina agreement which says so. You know boat people. They reckon they've gotten the freedom of the seas. Maybe they have because no one has gotten around to licensing them yet, but some are downright irresponsible.'

I winced because Sam had hit a raw nerve; I had been a boat owner. 'Nevertheless, beef up security.'

'It'll cost,' Sam warned. 'That means watchmen.'

'Do it.'

Sam shrugged. 'Anything more, Mr . . . er . . . Tom?'

'I think that's all.'

He stood up, then hesitated. 'Excuse me, but I've been wondering. What are you doing with those pictures of Jack Kayles?'

'Who?'

Sam pointed to the black-and-white photographs. 'There. That's Jack Kayles.'

'*You know this man?*'

'Not to say know like being friends, but he's been in and out of the marina.'

'Sam, you've just earned yourself a bonus.' I pushed a photograph across the desk. 'Now, sit down and tell me everything you know about him.'

Sam picked it up. 'Not a good picture,' he commented. 'But it's Kayles, all right. He's a yacht bum; got a sloop – a twenty-seven footer, British-built and glass fibre. Usually sails single-handed.'

'Where does he keep her?'

'Nowhere and everywhere. She's usually where he happens to be at the time. Kayles can pitch up anywhere, I reckon. He was in New Providence two years ago and told me he'd comes up from the Galapagos, through the Panama Canal, and had worked his way through the islands. He was going on to look at the Florida keys. He's pretty handy with a boat.'

'What's she called?'

Sam frowned. 'Now that's a funny thing – he changed her name, which is mighty unusual. Most folk are superstitious about that. Two years ago she was called *Seaglow*, but when I saw her last she was *Green Wave*.'

'Maybe a different boat,' I suggested.

'Same boat,' said Sam firmly.

I accepted that; Sam knew his boats. 'When was he last in your marina?'

'About three months ago.'

'How does Kayles earn his living?'

Sam shrugged. 'I don't know. Maybe he crews for pay. I told you; he's a yacht bum. There's plenty like Kayles about. They live on their boats and scratch a living somehow.' He thought for a moment. 'Come to think of it, Kayles never seemed short of cash. He paid on the nail for everything. A few bits of chandlery from the shop, fuel, marina fees and all that.'

'Credit card?'

'No. Always in cash. Always in American dollars, too.'

'He's an American?'

'I'd say so. Could be Canadian, but I don't think so. What's all this about, Tom?'

'I have an interest in him,' I said uninformatively. 'Any more you can tell me?'

'Not much to tell,' said Sam. 'I just put diesel oil in his boat and took his money. Not much of that, either. He has a pint-sized diesel engine which he doesn't use much; he's one of those guys who prefers the wind – a good sailor, like I said.'

'Anything at all about Kayles will be useful,' I said. 'Think hard, Sam.'

Sam ruminated. 'I did hear he was awful quick-tempered, but he was always civil to me and that's all I cared about. He never made trouble in the marina but I heard he got into a fight in Nassau. Like all yachtsmen he carries a knife, and he used it – he cut a guy.'

'Were the police in on that?'

Sam shook his head. 'It was a private fight,' he said dryly. 'No one wanted police trouble.'

I was disappointed; it would be useful if Kayles already had a police record. 'Did he have any particular friends that you know of?'

'No, I'd say Kayles is a loner.'

'When he left your marina three months ago did he say where he was going?'

'No.' Sam suddenly snapped his fingers. 'But when I met him last month in the International Bazaar he said he was going to Florida. I forgot about that.' Then he added, 'The International Bazaar here – not the one in Nassau.'

I stared at Sam. 'Are you telling me you saw Kayles here on Grand Bahama a month ago?'

'Not a month ago,' corrected Sam. 'Last month. It would be a little over two weeks ago. I'd brought a boat over for a client to give to Joe Cartwright here.' Sam tugged his ear. 'Chances are that Kayles had his boat here, too. I didn't see her, but I wasn't looking. He knew about the discount.'

We had a system whereby a yachtsman using one of our marinas got a ten per cent discount in any of the others; it helped keep the money in the family. I rang my secretary. 'Jessie, get Joe Cartwright up here fast. I don't care what he's doing but I want him here.' I turned back to Sam. 'Did Kayles say how he was going to Florida?'

'He didn't tell me and I didn't ask. I assumed he'd be going in *Green Wave*.'

I hammered at Sam for quite a while, but could get nothing more out of him. Presently Joe Cartwright arrived. He was the marina manager for the Royal Palm. 'You wanted me, Mr Mangan?' He flicked his hand in a brief salute. 'Hi, Sam!'

I pushed forward the photograph. 'Did this man bring a boat into the marina about two weeks ago?'

Sam said, 'His name is Kayles.'

'The face and the name mean nothing to me,' said Joe. 'I'd have to look at the records.'

I pointed to the telephone. 'Ring your office and have someone do it now.'

As Joe spoke into the mouthpiece I drummed my fingers restlessly on the desk. At least I had something for Perigord and I hoped it would prove to be a firm lead.

Joe put down the telephone. 'He was here, but I didn't see him. He came in a British sloop with a red hull.'

'Green,' said Sam.

'No, it was red. Her name was *Bahama Mama*.'

'He changed the name again,' said Sam in wonder. 'Now why would a man do that?'

My upraised hand silenced him. I said to Joe, 'Is the boat still here?'

'I'll find out.' Joe picked up the telephone again and I held my breath. If the boat was still here then Kayles, in all likelihood, was dead with Julie, Sue and Pete. If not . . .? Joe said, 'She left on the twenty-fifth – Christmas Day.'

I let out my breath with a sigh. That was six days after *Lucayan Girl* had disappeared. Joe said, 'No one saw her leave; suddenly she wasn't there.' He shrugged. 'It didn't bother anyone; the marina fee had been paid in advance to the end of the month. We made a profit on that one.'

I said, 'I want both of you to wait in the outer office until you're wanted.' They left and I rang Perigord. 'I've got a name and a face for you. That crewman.'

He did not sound surprised. All he said was 'Who?'

I told him.

'Where are you?'

'My office at the Royal Palm.'

'Ten minutes,' he said, and rang off.

6

Perigord put Sam Ford and Joe Cartwright through the wringer, but did not get much more out of them than I had, then he took the negative and photographs and departed. But he did not take all of them; I had retained some, locked in the office safe. I spoke to Sam and Joe. 'If you see or hear of this man I want to know, but don't alarm him – just contact me.'

Sam said, 'What's all this about, Tom?'

I hesitated, half inclined to tell him, but said briefly, 'You don't have to know. It's a police matter.' I changed the subject. 'We're organizing the marinas into a division, Joe; and Sam will be boss. Spread the word that we're expanding. There'll be no firings and a lot of hirings. Sam will tell you all about it. All right, that's it.'

And that was that.

Jack Kayles did not come to the surface, not then, but Billy Cunningham arrived a couple of weeks later with a platoon of lawyers and accountants and they started to go through the books of West End Securities, finding not much wrong and a lot that was right. After a few days Billy came to me and said with a crooked smile, 'You under-estimated your value by about a quarter-million – but you're still not going to get more than a fifth of Theta stock.'

'Suits me.'

'The Corporation will be set up by the end of the week; I've had the Nassau lawyers working on it. Then we can sign papers.'

'You'd have done better to have consulted me on that,' I said.

'Perhaps, but I thought that maybe you weren't in any condition to think straight.'

'You could have been right,' I admitted.

He stood up and stretched. 'Gee, it's been a hard week. I could do with a drink. Where do you keep your office bottle?'

I opened the cabinet, poured drinks, and handed him a glass. 'Here's to the Theta Corporation.'

We drank the toast, and Billy said, 'You sure put a burr under Debbie's saddle. What the hell did you do?'

'Just a bit of fatherly advice.'

Billy's lips quirked. 'Fatherly!' He sat down. 'My revered uncle, Jack Cunningham, Chairman of the Cunningham Corporation and something of a prime bastard, thinks you're some kind of subversive nut. He says you've been putting leftist ideas into his daughter's head.'

'What do you think?'

'I think it's the best thing that ever happened to her,' he said frankly. 'She's been spoiled silly all her life and it's time she thought of something other than herself. Maybe this will do it.'

'I hope so.'

He hesitated. 'She told me about Sue, and the funeral. Why didn't you let me know?'

'Not your problem.' I tasted the whisky. 'Did she tell you about the photograph?'

'What photograph?'

So Debbie was keeping her promise to Perigord; she had not even told her family. I was not as honourable. 'I'll tell you about it, but keep it under your hat.'

So I told him and it was long in the telling, and when I had finished he said, 'Jesus, I've never heard of anything like that!' He picked up the photograph I had taken from the safe. 'You mean this son of a bitch killed your family?'

'That's the general theory. If he's still alive he did, and if he's dead who took his boat from the marina here?'

'This is a crummy picture,' said Billy. 'I think we can do better than this?'

'How?'

'You know we have the Space Center in Houston. I know a lot of the guys there because we do business with NASA.

When they shoot pictures back from space they're pretty blurred so they put them through a computer which sharpens them up; makes a computer-enhanced image, as they call it.' He tapped the photograph. 'I think they could do the same with this, and if they can't you're no worse off. Mind if I take this back to Houston?'

I thought it was a good idea. 'Take it.'

Three days later we signed papers and I was President of a $50 million corporation.

Time passed.

I had a heavy workload as I buckled down to making the Theta Corporation work. I began by activating some of the suggestions I had outlined to Billy, beginning with the construction division. Jack Foster was a childless widower who ran a construction company based in Nassau. He was past sixty and wanted to get out, not seeing the point of working himself into the grave when he had no one to leave the company to, so I flew to Nassau and we did a deal, and I got the company for a quarter-million less than I expected to pay. Since this was the company that was building the hotel on Eleuthera things started to move faster there because I saw to it that the Theta Corporation got first choice of materials and manpower. The sooner the hotel was completed the sooner the cash flow would turn from negative to positive.

The quarter-million I saved I put into a geographical and economic survey of the Bahamas, hiring an American outfit to do it. I did not expect them to come up with anything that would surprise me, but what they found would buttress my ideas with the Cunninghams.

I flew to Abaco at least once a week to see Karen, even if only to stay an hour. She seemed to have settled down completely and seemed none the worse for her bereavement. I wished I had her resilience; I stopped myself from brooding only by hard work and keeping occupied. But there were times in the small hours . . .

I discussed the question of taking Karen home but Peggy counselled against it. 'Tom, you're working all the hours God sends. How do you expect to look after a little girl? Let her stay here until things ease off for you. She's no trouble.'

Peggy and Bob were over the moon because I was funding them to a golf course to compete with the one at Treasure Cay. I also told them I was having joint meetings with the Ministry of Finance, the Ministry of Tourism and the Department of Public Works to see if anything could be done about the God-awful road between Marsh Harbour and Treasure Cay. I told them I had produced the Pilot's Bahamas Aviation Guide – the bit where it says that if anyone wants to get from Treasure Cay to Marsh Harbour they'd better fly. 'I asked them, "What sort of tourist advertising is that?" I think we'll get our improved road.'

'It would help our lunch trade a lot,' said Bob. 'People coming on day tours from Treasure Cay.'

'The hell with lunch. You'll be running a car hire service.'

So I was keeping busy and the time passed a little less painfully.

I made a point of dropping in to see Perigord from time to time. The computer-enhanced pictures of Kayles came back from NASA and I gave them to him. He took one look at them and blinked. 'How did you do this?' he demanded.

'Ask no questions,' I said. 'Remember discretion.'

There was no sign of Kayles. 'If he's still alive he could be anywhere,' said Perigord. 'Yachtsmen are mobile and there's no control over them at all. For all I know he's in Cape Town right now.'

'And he'll have changed the name of his boat again.'

'And perhaps his own,' said Perigord.

'He'd surely have passport difficulties there.'

Perigord looked at me a little sorrowfully. 'It may come as a surprise to you to know that the skipper of a boat, no matter how small the boat, doesn't need a passport; all he needs are ship's papers and those are easily forged. In any case, getting a passport is easy enough if you know where to look.'

Perigord was stymied.

Three months passed and Debbie came back bringing with

her two black American girls of about her own age. She blew into my office like a refreshing breeze and introduced them. 'This is Cora Brown and Addy Williams; they're both teachers, and Addy has nursing qualifications. We're an advance scouting party.'

'Then I'd better fix you up with rooms.' I stretched for the telephone.

'No need,' she said airily. 'I made reservations.'

I made a mental note to tell Jack Fletcher to inform me any time Debbie Cunningham made a reservation. 'So you're going ahead.'

They told me about it, extensively and in detail. They were going to bring twenty children each month for a two-week stay. 'I had a bit of trouble with the school boards about that,' said Debbie. 'But I pointed out that both Cora and Addy are teachers and the whole thing is one big geography lesson, anyway – with sport thrown in. They went for it.'

Cora and Addy were to give the kids lessons in basic arithmetic and English, and they were to learn the history of the Bahamas in relationship to the United States. That took care of the education bit. Debbie said tentatively, 'You said something about the Family Islands. I thought a week here and a week on one of those . . .'

'Sure,' I said. 'That's easy. While they're here those kids who can swim can go along to the Underwater Exploration Society and learn scuba-diving. They'll give you a low rate. Those who can't swim can have lessons here in the hotel pool. We have an instructor.'

'That's great,' said Cora. 'I can't swim – maybe I'll take lessons, too.'

And so it went with much enthusiasm. I took time off to introduce them to people I thought they ought to know and then let them loose in Freeport. Before they went back to the States I took Debbie to dinner at the Xanadu Princess. I had engineered that tête-à-tête by sending Cora and Addy to Abaco with an introduction to Peggy.

As we got out of the car Debbie looked up at the hotel. 'Does this belong to the Theta Corporation?'

I laughed. 'No, I just like to keep tabs on what the opposition is up to.'

Over cocktails I said, 'I like Cora and Addy. Where did you find them?'

'Oh, I just asked around and came up with the jackpot.' She smiled. 'Neither of them is married. From what I've observed in the last few days they could very well marry Bahamian boys. Your menfolk sure move in fast.' The smile left her face and she said soberly, 'How are you doing, Tom?'

'All right. The Theta Corporation is keeping me busy. So much so that I'm thinking of selling the house. I don't spend much time there now; usually I sleep at the hotel.'

'Oh, you mustn't sell that beautiful house,' she said impulsively.

'I rattle around in it. And there are too many memories.'

She put her hand on mine. 'I hope it's not too bad.' We were quiet for a while, then she said, 'Billy talked to me. He said you'd told him about Kayles. Any more news?'

'Nothing. Kayles seems to have vanished completely. If it weren't for all the inconsistencies I'd be inclined to believe he went down with *Lucayan Girl* – that it was a genuine accident.'

I changed the subject deliberately and we talked of other and lighter matters, and it was pretty late when I took her back to the Royal Palm. As we walked towards the parking lot, something flashed out of the darkness and Debbie ducked, and gasped, 'What was that!'

'Don't worry, it's harmless – it won't hurt you. It was just a bat. We call them money bats.'

Debbie looked up doubtfully and I could see she did not altgether believe my claim that the bats were harmless. 'That's an odd name? Why *money* bats?'

I chuckled. 'Because the only time you see them is when they're flying away from you.'

That night, lying sleepless in bed, I had a curious thought. Could the mind play tricks on one? Had I given Debbie Cunningham the idea of bringing American kids to the

Bahamas just so I could see more of her? It had not been a conscious decision, of that I was sure. With Julie and Sue just dead a week I would not, could not, have made such a decision. But the mind is strange and complex, and perhaps it had put those words in my mouth, the idea into Debbie's mind, for reasons of its own.

All the same I felt happier than I had felt for a long time, knowing that I would be seeing Debbie Cunningham monthly for the foreseeable future.

The months went by. Seven months after I became President of the Theta Corporation we had the Grand Opening of the Rainbow Bay Hotel on Eleuthera. I invited a crowd of notables: Government ministers, a couple of film stars, a golf champion and so on. I also invited Deputy-Commissioner Howard Perigord and his wife, Amy. And the Cunninghams came; Billy and his father, Billy One; Jack Cunningham, who looked upon me with some mistrust, and, of course, daughter Debbie.

To make sure that everything went like clockwork I pulled the best of the staff from the other three hotels. The service in those hotels might have suffered a little at that time, but not much because, in general, the quality of our staff was high. In the event all went well.

Before we flew to Eleuthera the Cunninghams and I had an informal board meeting. I handed out copies of the survey made by the American company, and added my report with its detailed recommendations. 'You're not expected to read all this now, but I'll give you a brief summary.'

I ticked off the points on my fingers. 'We go into the Family Islands . . .' I paused, and said in parentheses, 'They used to be known as the Out Islands but the Minister of Tourism thinks that the Family Islands sounds more cosy.'

'He's right,' said Billy. 'And Shakespeare was wrong. There's a lot to names.'

'Anyway, the future lies in the Family Islands. We go into real estate in a big way on Crooked Island, Acklins Island, Mayaguana and Great Inagua. And we buy a couple of cays in the Ragged Island Range. All this is undeveloped and we get in there first, especially before the Swiss moneymen move in and send the prices up.'

I tapped another finger. 'We put together our own package deals and farm them out to travel agents in the States and in Europe. In order to do that we either make deals with a couple of airlines or charter planes ourselves to fly our customers into Grand Bahama or New Providence. From there we'll either have to do a deal with Bahamasair or set up our own islands airline.'

Another finger went up. 'Next I want one really top-class luxury hotel; not for the package tourist but for the people with money.' I grinned. 'Simple folks like yourselves. Ten per cent of the visitors to the Islands come in their own aircraft and I want to capture that market.'

'Sounds good,' said Billy.

Billy One said, 'Yeah, it seems to make sense.'

Jack Cunningham had been flipping through the pages of my report. 'What's this about you wanting to start a school?'

I said, 'If we're building hotels we'll need staff to run them. I want to train them my way.'

'The hell with that!' said Jack roundly. 'We pay for training, then they leave and go to some other goddamn hotel like a Holiday Inn. No way are we doing that.'

'The Ministry of Tourism is putting up half the cost,' I said.

'Oh, well,' said Jack grudgingly. 'That may be different.'

Billy said, 'Jack, I'm Chairman of this corporation and as far as I'm concerned you're the seventeenth Vice-President in Charge of Answering Stupid Questions. Don't stick your oar in here.'

'Don't talk to your uncle like that,' said Billy One. But his voice was mild.

'I've gotten my money in here,' snapped Jack. 'And I don't want this guy throwing it away. He's already filled Debbie's head with a lot of communistic nonsense.'

Billy grinned. 'Show me another commie with over ten million bucks.'

'Two million of which we gave him,' snapped Jack. He tossed the report aside. 'Billy, you damn near swore a Bible oath that the Government of the Bahamas was stable.' He pointed at me. 'You believed him. He gives us a report which makes nice reading, but I've been reading other words – in newspapers, for instance. There was a goddamn riot in Nassau three days ago. What's so stable about that?'

I knew about the riot and was at a loss to account for it. It had flashed into being from nowhere and the police had had a hard time in containing the disturbance. I said, 'An American outfit pulled out and closed down a factory. They did it too damned fast and without consultation. People don't like being fired, especially when it's done without so much as a by-your-leave. I think that started the trouble. It's just a local difficulty, Jack.'

He grunted. 'It had better be. Some American tourists got hurt, and that's not doing the industry any good; an industry, I might point out, which we're into for fifty million dollars.'

I could see that any relationship I had with Jack would be uneasy and I determined to steer clear of him as far as I could. As for the riot, I had given a glib enough explanation, but I was not sure it was the right one.

Billy One said, 'Let's cool it, shall we?' He looked at me. 'Would you happen to have any sour mash around?'

So it was smoothed over and next day we flew to Eleuthera. Eleuthera is 120 miles long but at the place where I had built the hotel it was less than two miles wide, so that from the hotel one could see the sea on both sides. Billy One looked at this in wonder. 'I'll be goddamned!'

I said, 'We get two beaches for the price of one. That's why I built here.'

Even Jack was impressed.

During the course of the day I had a few words with Perigord and asked him about the riot in Nassau. 'What caused it?' I asked.

He shrugged. 'I don't really know. It's not in my jurisdiction. It's in Commissioner Deane's lap – and he's welcome to it.'

'Any chance of a similar occurrence on Grand Bahama?'

He smiled grimly. 'Not if I have anything to do with it.'

'Was it political?'

He went opaque on me and deliberately changed the subject. 'I must congratulate you on this very fine hotel. I wish you every success.'

That reaction worried me more than anything else.

But the Grand Opening was a tremendous success and I danced with Debbie all night.

And so it went. The Theta Corporation was a success after its first year although more money was going out than coming in. After all, that was the point – we were still in the stage of expansion. Billy was satisfied with the way I was handling things and so, largely, was Billy One. How Jack felt I did not know; he kept his nose out of things and I did not care to ask. Everything was going fine in my business life, and my private life was perking up, too, to the point where I asked Debbie to marry me.

She sighed. 'I thought you'd never ask.'

So I took her to bed and we were married three weeks later over the protests of Jack, whose open objection concerned the disparity in our ages, but he did not like me, something I knew already. Billy and, I think, Billy One were for it, but Debbie's brother, Frank, followed Jack's line. Various members of the family took sides and the clan was split to some extent on this issue. But none of them could say that I was a fortune-hunter marrying her for her money – I had enough of my own. As for my own feelings about it, I was marrying Debbie, not Jack.

We married in Houston in a somewhat tense atmosphere and then went back to the Bahamas to honeymoon briefly at the new Rainbow Bay Hotel. Then we went back to Grand Bahama via Abaco where we picked up Karen who seemed dubious about having a new mother. Debbie and Karen moved into the house at Lucaya and I went back to running the Corporation. Two months later she told me she was pregnant which made both of us very happy.

But then things began to go wrong again because people who were coming to the Bahamas on vacation were going home to die.

7

Legionella pneumophila.

I learned a lot about that elusive bug with the pseudo-Latin name in the next few months. Anyone connected with the hotel industry had to learn, and learn fast. At first it was not recognized for what it was because those afflicted were not dying in the Bahamas but back home in the States or in England or Switzerland or wherever else they came from. It was the World Health Organization that blew the first warning whistle.

Most people might know it as Legionnaires' disease because it was first discovered at the convention of the American Legion held at the Bellevue-Stratford Hotel in Philadelphia in 1976 where there was an almost explosive outbreak of pneumonia among those who had attended. Altogether 221 people became ill and thirty-four of them died. Naturally, Legionnaires' disease is bad news for any hotelier. No one is likely to spend a carefree vacation in a resort hotel from which he may be carried out feet first, and the problem is compounded by the fact that even those hotels which are well kept and disease-free feel a financial draught. Once the news gets around that a particular holiday resort is tainted then everybody gets hurt.

So it was that a lot of people, me among them, were highly perturbed to hear that Legionnaires' disease was loose in the Parkway Hotel in Nassau. I flew to New Providence to talk to Tony Bosworth, our Corporation doctor. He had his base at the Sea Gardens Hotel because New Providence is fairly central and he could get to our other hotels reasonably quickly, using a Corporation plane in an emergency. A company doctor was another of my extravagances of which Jack Cunningham did not approve, but he earned his salary on this, and other, occasions.

When I told him what was happening at the Parkway he gave a low whistle. 'Legionellosis! That's a bad one. Are you sure?'

I shrugged. 'That's what I hear.'

'Do you know which form? It comes in two ways – Pontiac fever and Legionnaires' disease.'

That was the first time I had heard of Pontiac fever, but not the last. I shook my head. 'I wouldn't know. You're the doctor, not me.'

'Pontiac fever isn't too bad,' he said. 'It hits fast and has a high attack rate, about ninety-five per cent, but usually there are no fatalities. Legionnaires' disease is a killer. I'll get on to the Department of Public Health. Give me fifteen minutes, will you?'

I went away to look at the kitchens. I often make surprise raids on the kitchens and other departments just to keep the staff up to the mark. All departments are equally important but, to paraphrase George Orwell, the kitchen is more equal than others. Every hotelier's nightmare is an outbreak of salmonella. It was nearer half an hour before I got back to Tony and he was still nattering on the telephone, but he laid it down a couple of minutes after my arrival.

'Confirmed,' he said gloomily. 'Legionnaires' disease. Suspected by a smart young doctor in Manchester, England, it was confirmed by the Communicable Disease Surveillance Centre. The World Health Organization has identified a man dead in Paris and two more in Zurich; there's a couple of cases in Buenos Aires and a rash of them across the States.'

'All these people stayed at the Parkway?'

'Yes. How many rooms there?'

I had all the statistics of my competition at my fingertips. 'A hundred and fifty.'

'What would you say the year-round occupation rate is?'

I considered. 'It's a reasonably good hotel. I'd say between seventy-five and eighty per cent.'

Tony's lips moved silently as he made a calculation.

'They'll have to contact about 12,000 people, and they're spread all over the bloody world. That's going to be a job for someone.'

I gaped at him. 'Why so many?'

'There's been some work done on this one since 1976. Studies have shown that this deadly little chap can live in water for over a year, so that's how far back it's standard to check. One will get you ten that the bacteria are in the air-conditioning cooling tower at the Parkway, but we don't know how long they've been in there. Look, Tom, this is pretty serious. The attack rate among those exposed is between one and five per cent. Let's split the difference and call it two-and-a-half. That means three hundred casualties. With a death rate among them of fifteen per cent that gives us forty-five deaths.'

In the event he was not far out. When the whole scare was over the final tally came to 324 casualties and 41 deaths.

'You seem to know a lot about it.'

He gave me a lopsided grin. 'I'm a hotel doctor; this is what I get my salary for. Those casualties who don't die won't be good for much for a few months, and there's a grave risk of permanent lung damage, to say nothing of the kidneys and the liver.'

I took a deep breath. 'All right, Tony; what do we do?'

'Nothing much. These outbreaks tend to be localized – usually restricted to a single building. They've turned off the air-conditioning at the Parkway so there'll be nothing blown out.'

'So you think our hotels are safe?'

He shrugged. 'They should be.'

'I'd like to make sure.'

'Testing for *L. pneumophila* is a finicky business. You need a well-equipped laboratory with livestock – guinea pigs, fertilized eggs and so on. That's why the damned creature only turned up as late as 1976. And it takes a long time, too. I'll tell you what; I'll take samples of the water from the air-conditioners in the four hotels and send them to Miami – but don't expect quick results.'

'What about the room conditioners?' I asked. The lobby and the public rooms of the Sea Gardens were handled by a central air-conditioner, but each room had its own small one which could be set individually by the occupier. The same system worked at the Royal Palm because those two were our older hotels. The Abaco Sands and the brand-new Rainbow Bay had completely centralized air-conditioning.

Bosworth raised his eyebrows. 'You're taking this a bit far, aren't you?' He turned and took a fat medical book from a shelf next to his desk and flipped through the pages. 'We haven't developed an anti-bacterial agent for this one yet; nothing specific, anyway. Heavy chlorination would appear to be the answer.'

'Tell me how it's done.'

So he told me and I got busy. In the two hotels we had 360 rooms and that meant 360 air-conditioners to be emptied, filled with chlorinated water, left to soak for twenty-four hours, emptied again and refilled with guaranteed pure water. A big job.

I did not wait for Bosworth to report on the samples he sent to Miami, but got working on the big air-conditioners in each hotel, taking them out of service one at a time and using the same technique. But there was a difference. An air-conditioner in a moderately big hotel can handle up to 1000 gallons of water a minute and the cooling is effected by evaporation as the water pours over splash bars and has air blown through it.

A cooling tower will lose about ten gallons of water a minute as water vapour and there is another gallon a minute lost in what is known technically in the trade as 'drift'; very finely divided drops of water. Attempts are made to control the emission of drift by drift eliminators, but some always gets out. Tony Bosworth told me that any infectious bacteria would probably be escaping in the drift. I chlorinated that water to a fare-thee-well.

I supervised it all myself to make sure it was done properly. It might seem odd that the boss would do it personally but I had to make sure it was done in the right way. There was a lot riding on this, apart from the fact that I did not want anyone to die just because he had patronized one of my hotels. *L. pneumophila* had a nasty habit of not only killing people, but hotels, too.

Tony Bosworth was also pretty busy flitting from island to island attending suspected cases of Legionnaires' disease which turned out to be the common cold. Our hotels were clean but the tourists were jittery and the whole of the Bahamas ran scared for a little while. It was not a good year for either the Bahamas or the Theta Corporation, and the Ministry of Tourism and I sat back to watch the people stay away. Tourism fell off by fifteen per cent in the next three months. The Parkway Hotel was cleaned up and certified safe, but I doubt if the room occupancy even reached ten per cent in the months that followed. The company that owned it later went broke.

Another thing it meant was that I was away from home more often than I was there. Debbie grew fractious and we had our first rows. It had never been that way with Julie but now, with hindsight, I remember that when Julie was expecting Sue I had been always careful to stay close. That had been my first baby, too.

So, perhaps, in a sense our quarrels were equally my fault even if I did not recognize it at the time. As it was I took umbrage. I was working very hard, not only protecting against this damned disease which was worrying the hell out of me, but also taking the usual workload of the President of the Theta Corporation, and I did not see why I should have to be drained of my energies at home, too. So the quarrelling became worse. It is not only jealousy that feeds on itself.

Debbie was still doing her thing with Cora, Addy and the Texan kids, but operating mainly from the Bahamian end. But then I noticed that she was spending more and more time back home in Texas. Her excuse was that Cora and Addy were hopeless at organization and she had to go back to iron out problems. I accepted that, but when her visits became more frequent and protracted I had the feeling I was losing a wife. It was not good for young Karen, either, who had lost one mother and looked like losing the surrogate. It was a mess and I could not see my way out of it.

My feelings were not improved when I saw the headlines in the *Freeport News* one morning. There had been a fire in Nassau and the Fun Palace had burned down. The Fun Palace was a pleasure complex built, I think, to rival Freeport's International Bazaar as a tourist trap. It contained cinemas, restaurants and sporting facilities and had been a shade too gaudy for my taste. As modern as the day, it had a cheap feel to it of which I did not approve.

And now it was gone. Analysing the newspaper report it would seem that the firemen never had a chance; the place had gone up in flames like a bonfire almost as though it had been deliberately built to burn easily, and it took eighty-two lives with it, most of them tourists and a lot of them children. That, coming on top of Legionnaires' disease, would certainly not help the image of the Bahamas. Come to the Islands and die! Take your pick of method!

Over the next few days I followed the newspaper reports and listened to people talking. There were muttered rumours of arson but that was to be expected; after any big fire there is always talk of arson. The Chief of the Fire Brigade in Nassau was eloquent in his damning of the construction of the Fun Palace and the materials used in its construction. In order to give it a light and airy appearance a lot of plastic had been used and most of the victims had died, not of burning, but of asphyxiation caused by poisonous fumes. He also condemned the use of polyurethane foam as furniture upholstery. 'This is a real killer,' he said. I made a note to check on what we were using in our hotels, and also to tighten up on fire precautions.

And it was at this point that Jack Kayles popped into sight.

8

Storm signals flew over the breakfast table next morning but I was too preoccupied to notice them until Debbie said, 'I suppose you're going back to the office again today.'

I poured myself a cup of tea. 'I had thought of it.'

'I never see you any more.'

I added sugar. 'You do in bed.'

She flared up. 'I'm a wife – not a harlot. When I married a man I expected all of him, not just his penis.'

It was then I became aware that this was not a mere storm in a tea-cup. 'I'm sorry,' I said. 'Things have been really tough lately.' I reflected. 'I suppose I don't really have to go in today, or even tomorrow. In fact, I can take the rest of the week off. Why don't we take one of Joe Cartwright's sailboats from the marina and cruise to one of the Family Islands? That would take us to the weekend and we could fly back.'

She lit up like a Christmas tree. 'Could we?' Then she frowned. 'But we're going nowhere near any of your damned hotels,' she warned. 'This isn't a disguised business trip.'

'Cross my heart and hope to die.' I was drinking my tea as the telephone rang.

It was Jessie. 'I think you'd better come in early this morning; we've got trouble.'

'What kind of trouble?'

'Something to do with baggage at the airport. I don't really know what it is, but the lobby sounds like a hive of bees. Mr Fletcher's at the dentist and the under-manager isn't coping very well.'

That was all I needed. 'I'll be in.' I hung up and said to Debbie, 'Sorry, darling, but duty calls.'

'You mean you're going in spite of what you just promised? Damn you!'

I left the house with recriminations clanging in my ears, and arrived at the Royal Palm to find that a minor bit of hell had broken loose.

I sat in Jack Fletcher's office listening to him moan. 'Two hundred and eight of them, and without a damned toothbrush between them, not to mention other necessities. All they have is their hand baggage and what they stand up in.'

I winced. 'What happened? Did they arrive here and their baggage end up in Barcelona?'

He looked at me with mournful eyes. 'Worse! You know that new baggage-handling carousel at the airport?' I nodded. It was an innovation for which we had been pressing for a long time. With increased flights of wide-bodied jets the airport had developed a baggage-handling bottleneck which the carousel was intended to alleviate.

Fletcher said, 'It couldn't have done a better job if it had been designed for the purpose.'

'A better job of what?'

'Opening the baggage without benefit of keys. The baggage was put on the conveyor, and somewhere in that underground tunnel something ripped open every suitcase. What spewed out on to the carousel were smashed suitcases and mixed-up contents.'

'Didn't they try to turn it off when they saw what was happening?'

'They tried and couldn't. Apparently it wouldn't stop. And the telephone link between the carousel and the loading point outside hasn't been installed yet. By the time they'd fiddled around and sent someone outside to stop the loading it was too late. They'd pushed in the lot – the whole plane-load of baggage.'

I nodded towards the lobby. 'Who is this crowd?'

'LTP Industries convention from Chicago. They're already raising hell. If you want a slice of gloom just go out into the lobby – you can cut it with a knife. One good thing; the Airport Authority carries the can for this – not us.'

The Airport Authority might carry ultimate responsibility but the airport people did not have on their hands over 200 unhappy and discontented Americans – and when Americans are discontented they let it be known, loud and clear. Their unhappiness would spread through the hotel like a plague.

Jack said, 'That Boeing was full, every seat filled. We're not the only people with grief; Holiday Inn, Atlantik Beach, Xanadu – we've all got troubles.'

That did not make me feel any better. 'What's the Airport Authority doing about it?'

'Still trying to make up their minds.'

'Oh, for God's sake!' I said. 'You go out there and give them a pacifier – $50 each for immediate necessities. I'll ring the airport to tell them I'll be sending them the bill. And make it a public relations service on the part of the hotel. Let them know clearly that we don't have to do it, but we're full of the milk of human kindness. We have to make some profit out of this mess.'

He nodded and left, and I rang the airport. There followed a short but tempestuous conversation in which threats of legal action were issued. As I put down the telephone it rang under my hand. Jessie said, 'Sam Ford wants to see you. By the way he's acting the matter is urgent.'

'I'll be along.' I went back to my office via the lobby, testing the atmosphere as I went. Fletcher had made an announcement and the tension had eased. A queue had already formed at the cashier's desk to receive their dole. I walked through Jessie's office, beckoning to Sam as I went, and sat behind my desk. 'I thought you were down by Ragged Island.'

The Ragged Island project was something I had developed by listening to Deputy-Commissioner Perigord. What he had said about the Ragged Island Range and the Jumento Cays had remained with me. My idea was to buy a couple of the cays and set up camps for those tourists who preferred to rough it for a few days on a genuine desert island. It was my intention to cater for all tastes and, being in the low tourist season, I had sent Sam Ford down in a boat to scout a few locations.

'I was,' said Sam. 'But something came up. You remember that fellow you wanted to know about?'

'Who?'

'Kayles. Jack Kayles.'

I jerked. 'What about him? Have you seen him?' It had been over a year and I had almost forgotten.

'No, but I've seen his boat.'

'Where?'

'In the Jumentos – lying off Man-o'-War Cay. Now called *My Fair Lady* and her hull is blue.'

I said, 'Sam, how in hell can you be sure it's the same boat?'

'Easy.' Sam laughed. 'About a year and a half ago Kayles wanted a new masthead shackle for his forestay. Well, it's a British boat and I only had American fittings, so I had to make an adaptor. It's still there.'

'You got that close to her?'

''Bout a cable.' That was 200 yards. 'And I put the glasses on her. I don't think Kayles was on board or he'd have come out on deck. They usually do in those waters because there are not that many boats about and folks get curious. He must have been ashore but I didn't see him.' He looked at me seriously. 'I thought of boarding her but I remembered what you said about not wanting him scared off, so I just passed by without changing course and came back here.'

'You did right. When was this?'

'Yesterday. Say, thirty hours ago. I came back real fast.'

He had indeed; it was over 300 miles to the Jumentos. I pondered for a while. To get there quickly I could fly, but the only place to land was at Duncan Town and that was quite a long way from Man-o'-War Cay and I would have to hire a boat, always supposing there was one to be hired with a skipper willing to make a 100-mile round trip. For the first time I wished we had a seaplane or amphibian.

I said, 'Are you willing to go back now?'

'I'm pretty tired, Tom. I've been pushing it. I haven't had what you'd call a proper sleep for forty-eight hours. I had young Jim Glass with me but I didn't trust his navigation so all I got were catnaps.'

'We'll go by air and see if he's still there, and you can sleep at Duncan Town. Okay?'

He nodded. 'All right, Tom, but you'll get no words from me on the way. I'll be asleep.'

I had completely forgotten about Debbie.

I took the first plane and the first pilot handy, and we flew south-east to the Jumentos, the pilot being Bill Pinder. I sat in the co-pilot's seat next to Bill, and Sam sat in the back. I think he was asleep before take-off. I had binoculars handy and a camera with a telephoto lens. I wanted firm identification for Perigord although how firm it would be was problematical because Kayles's boat changed colour like a bloody chameleon.

Although I use aircraft quite a lot, flying being the quickest way for a busy man to get around the islands, I find that it bores me. As we droned over the blue and green sea, leaving the long chain of the Exumas to port, my eyes grew heavier and I must have fallen asleep because it took a heavy dig in the ribs from Bill to rouse me. 'Man-o'-War Cay in ten minutes,' he said.

I turned and woke Sam. 'Which side of the cay was he?'

Sam peered from a window. 'This side.'

'We don't want to do anything unusual,' I told Bill. 'Come down to your lowest permitted altitude and fly straight just off the west coast of the cay. Don't jink about or circle – just carry on.'

We began to descend and presently Bill said, 'That little one just ahead is Flamingo Cay; the bigger one beyond is Man-o'-War.'

I passed the binoculars back to Sam. 'You know Kayles. Take a good look as we fly past and see if you can spot him. I'll use the camera.'

'There's a boat,' said Bill.

I cocked the camera and opened the side window, blinking as the air rushed in. The sloop was lying at anchor and I could see distinctly the catenary curve of the anchor cable under clear water. 'That's her,' said Sam and I clicked the shutter. I recocked quickly and took another snapshot. Sam said, 'And that's Kayles in the cockpit.'

By then the sloop was disappearing behind us. I twisted my neck to see it but it was gone. 'Did he wave or anything?'

'No, just looked up.'

'Okay,' I said. 'On to Duncan Town.'

Bill did a low pass with his landing gear down over the scattered houses of Duncan Town, and by the time we had landed on the air strip and taxied to the ramp a battered car was already bumping towards us. We climbed out of the Navajo and Sam said, nodding towards the car, 'I know that man.'

'Then you can do the dickering,' I said. 'We want a boat to go out to Man-o'-War – the fastest you can find.'

'That won't be too fast,' he said. 'But I'll do my best.'

We drove into Duncan Town and I stood by while Sam bargained for a boat. I had never been to Duncan Town and I looked around with interest. It was a neat and well-maintained place of the size Perigord had said – less than 200 population, most of them fishermen to judge by the boats. There were signs of agriculture but no cash crops, so they probably grew just enough food for themselves. But there were evaporation pans for the manufacture of salt.

Sam called me, and then led me to a boat. 'That's it.'

I winced at what I saw. It was an open boat about eighteen feet long and not very tidily kept. A tangled heap of nets was thrown over the engine casing and the thwarts were littered with fish-scales. It smelled of rotting fish, too, and would have broken Pete Albury's heart. 'Is this the best you can do?'

'Least it has an inboard engine,' said Sam. 'I don't think it'll break down. I'll come with you, Tom. I know Kayles by sight, and I can get six hours sleep on the way.'

'Six hours!'

'It's forty miles, and I don't reckon this tub will do more than seven knots at top speed.' He looked up at the sun. 'It'll be about nightfall when we get there.'

'All right,' I said resignedly. 'Let's get a seven-knot move on.'

Five minutes later we were on our way with the owner and skipper, a black Bahamian called Bayliss, at the tiller. Sam made a smelly bed of fish nets and went to sleep, while I brooded. I was accustomed to zipping about the islands in a Navajo and this pace irked me. I judged the length of the boat and the bow wave and decided we were not even doing six knots. I was impatient to confront Kayles.

We came to Man-o'-War Cay just as the sun was setting and I woke Sam. 'We're coming to the cay from the other side. How wide is it?'

''Bout half a mile.'

'What's the going like?'

'Not bad.' He peered at me. 'What's all this about, Tom?'

'Personal business.'

He shook his head. 'A year back when I asked why you were interested in Kayles you damn near bit my head off. And then you brought the police in – Commissioner Perigord, no less. This is more than personal business. What are you getting me into?'

It was a fair enough question. If we were going to confront a man I believed to be a murderer then Sam had a right to know. I said, 'How close were you to Pete Albury?'

'I knew him all my life. You know we both came from Abaco. I remember him and you together when I was a little nipper, not more than four years old. You'd be twelve or thirteen then, I reckon.'

'Yes, he was my friend,' I said quietly. 'What about you?'

'Sure, he was my friend. We used to go turtling together. Biggest we ever caught was a 200-pounder. He taught me how to catch bush bugs with a crutch-stick.'

That was Abaconian vernacular for catching land crabs with a forked stick. I said, 'Kayles was on *Lucayan Girl* when she disappeared.'

Sam went very still. 'You mean . . .'

'I don't know what I mean, but I will when I get to the

other side of that damn cay. Right now I'm working out the best way to go about it.'

'Wait a minute.' Sam called out to Bayliss, 'Slow down,' then turned back to me, the whites of his eyes reddened by the light of the setting sun. 'If Kayles was on *Lucayan Girl*, if that's Kayles on that boat, then that means murder.' Sam was as quick as any other Bahamian at adding up the facts of life – and death – at sea. 'I read about the inquest in the *Freeport News*. It seemed to me then there was something left out.'

'Perigord put the lid on it; he didn't want to frighten Kayles away. The picture of Kayles you saw was taken by my daughter, Sue, just before the *Girl* left for Miami. Perigord reckons Kayles is a cocaine smuggler. Anyway, that's not the point, Sam. I want to talk to Kayles.'

'And you're thinking of walking across the island.' He shook his head. 'That's not the way. That boat is anchored nearly a cable offshore. You'd have to swim. It wouldn't look right. What we do is to go around and get next to him in a neighbourly way like any other honest boat would.' He pointed to the water keg in the bows. 'Ask him for some water.'

'Are you coming?'

'Sure I'm coming,' said Sam promptly.

'He'll recognize you,' I said doubtfully.

Sam was ironic. 'What do you want me to do? Put on a white face? It doesn't matter if he knows me or not – he's not afraid of me. But he might know your face and that would be different. You'd better keep your head down.'

So we went around Man-o'-War Cay with the engine gently thumping and made a few final plans. Although Sam had seen Kayles from the air through binoculars, it had been but a quick flash and firm identification would only be made when he talked to the man on the sloop. If Sam recognized Kayles he was to ask for water; if it wasn't Kayles he was to ask for fish. From then on we would have to play it by ear.

When we drifted alongside the sloop there was very little light. I took off the engine casing and stood with my back to

My Fair Lady apparently tinkering with the engine. Bayliss took the way off and Sam bellowed, 'Ahoy, the sloop!' He stood in the bows and held us off with a boathook.

A voice said, 'What do you want?' The accent was American.

I think Sam went more by the voice than by what he could see. 'We've run us a mite short of water. Can you spare us a few drops?'

A light stabbed from the cockpit and played on Sam. 'Don't I know you?' said Kayles. There was a hint of suspicion in his voice.

'You could,' said Sam easily. 'I run a marina in New Providence. I know a lot of yachtsmen and they know me. Maybe you've been to my place – at the Sea Gardens Hotel, west of Nassau. I'm Sam Ford.' He held his hand to shade his eyes, trying to see beyond the bright light.

'I remember you. You want water?'

'I'd appreciate it. We're damn thirsty.'

'I'll get you some,' said Kayles. 'Got anything to put it in?'

Sam had taken the piecaution of emptying the water keg. He passed it up toKyles who went below. 'He'll know if we go aboard,' Sam whispered. 'The sloop will rock. If we're going to take him it'll have to be when he comes up now. Get ready to jump him when I shout.'

'You're sure it is Kayles?'

'Damn sure. Anyway, any ordinary yachtsman would have asked us aboard.'

'All right, then.'

The sound of a hand pump came from the sloop and after a few minutes it stopped. 'Ready, now!' said Sam in a low voice.

The sloop rocked as Kayles came up into the cockpit. Sam said cheerfully, 'This is kind of you, sir.' He had shortened his grip on the boathook and when Kayles leaned over the side to hand down the keg, instead of taking it Sam gripped Kayles's wrist and pulled hard. With the other hand he thrust the end of the boathook into Kayles's stomach like a spear.

I heard the breath explode out of Kayles as I jumped for

the sloop. Kayles stood no chance; he lay half in and half out of the cockpit fighting for breath and with Sam holding on to his wrist with grim tenacity. I got both knees in the small of his back, grinding his belly into the cockpit coaming. 'Come aboard, Sam,' I said breathily.

Bayliss shouted, 'What's going on there?'

'Stick to your own business,' said Sam, and came aboard. He switched on the compass light which shed a dim glow into the cockpit. 'Can you hold him?'

Kayles's body writhed under mine. 'I think so.'

'I'll get some rope; plenty of that on a boat.' Sam plucked the knife from Kayles's belt and vanished for a moment.

Kayles was recovering his breath. 'You . . . you bastard!' he gasped, and heaved under me and nearly threw me off so I thumped him hard at the nape of the neck with my fist – the classic rabbit punch – and he went limp. I hoped I had not broken his neck.

Sam came with the rope and we tied Kayles's hands behind his back, and I knew Sam knew enough about seaman's knots to let him do it. When we had Kayles secure he said, 'What do we do now?'

Bayliss had allowed his boat to drift off a little way in the gathering darkness. Now I heard his engine rev up and he came alongside again. 'What you doin' to that man?' he asked. 'I'm havin' nothin' to do with this.'

I said to Sam, 'Let's get him below, then you can talk to Bayliss. Cool him down because we might need him again.'

We bundled Kayles below and stretched him on a bunk. He was breathing stertorously. Sam said, 'What do I tell Bayliss?'

I shrugged. 'Why not tell him the truth?'

Sam grinned. 'Who ever believes the truth? But I'll fix him.' He went into the cockpit and I looked around. Sam had been right about Kayles being a good seaman because it showed. Everything was neat and tidy and all the gear was stowed; a place for everything and everything in its place. Nothing betrays a bad seaman more than sloppiness, and if everything below was trim it would be the same on deck. That is the definition of shipshape. Given five minutes' notice Kayles could pull up the hook and sail for anywhere.

But a good seaman is not necessarily a good man; the history of piracy in the Bahamas shows that. I turned and looked at Kayles who was beginning to stir feebly, then switched on the cabin light to get a better look at him. I got a good sight of his face for the first time and was relieved to see that Sam had made no mistake – this definitely was the man whose picture had been taken by Sue.

I sat at the chart table, switched on the gooseneck lamp, and began going through drawers. A good seaman keeps a log, an honest seaman keeps a log – but would Kayles have kept a log? It would be useful to have a record of his movements in the past.

There was no log to be found so I started going through the charts. In recording a yacht's course on a chart it is usual to use a fairly soft pencil so that in case of error it can be easily erased and corrected, or when the voyage is over the course line can be erased and the chart used again. Most yachtsmen I know tend to leave the course on the chart until it is needed for another voyage. A certain amount of bragging goes on amongst boat people and they like to sit around in a marina comparing voyages and swapping lies.

Kayles had charts covering the eastern seaboard of the Americas from the Canadian border right down to and including Guyana, which is pretty close to the equator, and they covered the Bahamas and the whole of the Caribbean. On many of them were course lines and dates. It is normal to pencil in a date when you have established a position by a midday sun sight and you may add in the month, but no one I know puts in the year. So were these the records of old or recent voyages?

Sam came below and looked at Kayles. 'Still sleeping?' He went into the galley, unclipped an aluminium pan, and filled it with water. He came back and dumped it in Kayles's face. Kayles moaned and moved his head from side to side, but his eyes did not open.

I said, 'Sam, take a look at these charts and tell me if they mean anything.' We changed places and I stood over Kayles. His eyes opened and he looked up at me, but there was no comprehension in them and I judged he was suffering from concussion. It would be some time before he would be able to talk so I went exploring.

What I was looking for I do not know but I looked anyway, opening lockers and boxes wherever I found them. Kayles's seamanship showed again in the way he had painted on the top of each food can a record of the contents. I found the cans stowed in lockers under the bunks and he had enough to last a long time. If water gets into the bilges labels are washed off cans, and Kayles had made sure that when he opened a can of beef he was not going to find peaches.

I opened his first-aid box and found it well-equipped with all the standard bandages and medications, including two throwaway syringes already loaded with morphine. Those were not so standard but some yachtsmen, especially single-handers, carry morphine by special permission. If so, the law requires that they should be carried in a locked box and these were not. There were also some unlabelled glass ampoules containing a yellowish, oily liquid. Unlike the morphine syringes they carried no description or maker's name.

I picked up one of them and examined it closely. The ampoule itself had an amateur look about it as though it was home-made, the ends being sealed as though held in a flame, and there was nothing etched in the glass to tell the nature of the contents. I thought that if Kayles was in the drug-running scene he could very well be an addict and this was his own supply of dope. The notion was reinforced by the finding of an ordinary reuseable hypodermic syringe. I left everything where it was and closed the box.

I went back to Sam who was still poring over the charts. He had come to much the same conclusion that I had, but he said, 'We might be able to tell when all this happened by relating it to weather reports.'

'We'll leave that to Perigord,' I said.

Sam frowned. 'Maybe we should have left it all to the Commissioner. I think we should have told him about this man before we left. Are we doing right, Tom?'

'Hell, I didn't *know* it was Kayles before we left. It was just a chance, wasn't it?'

'Even so, I think you should have told Perigord.'

I lost my temper a little. 'All right, don't drive it home, Sam. So I should have told Perigord. I didn't. Maybe I wasn't thinking straight. Everything has been going to hell in a handcart recently, from Legionnaires' disease at the Parkway to the fire at the Fun Palace. And we could do without those bloody street riots, too. Do you know what I was doing when you came to my office?'

'No – what?'

'Straightening out a mess caused by the Airport Authority. Their baggage-handling machinery ripped a plane-load of suitcases into confetti and I had over 200 Americans in the lobby looking for blood. Any more of this and we'll all go out of business.' I swung around as Kayles said something behind me. 'What was that?'

'Who the hell are you?' Kayles's voice was stronger than I expected and I suspected he had been feigning unconsciousness for some time while working on his bonds. I did not worry about that – I had seen the knots.

'You know me, Mr Kayles,' said Sam, and Kayles's eyes widened as he heard his own name. 'You're carrying no riding lights. That's bad – you could be run down.' His voice was deceptively mild.

'Goddamn yacht-jackers!' said Kayles bitterly. 'Look, you guys have got me wrong. I can help you.'

'Do you know much about yacht-jacking?' I asked.

'I know it happens.' Kayles stared at me. 'Who are you?'

I did not answer him, but I held his eye. Sam said casually, 'Ever meet a man called Albury? Pete Albury?'

Kayles moistened his lips, and said hoarsely. 'For God's sake! Who are you?'

'You know Sam here,' I said. 'You've met him before. I'm Tom Mangan. You might have heard of me – I'm tolerably well-known in the Bahamas.'

Kayles flinched, but he mumbled, 'Never heard of you.'

'I think you have. In fact I think you met some of my family. My wife and daughter, for instance.'

'And I think you're nuts.'

'All right, Kayles,' I said. 'Let's get down to it. You were hired over a year ago by Pete Albury as crew on *Lucayan Girl* to help take her from Freeport to Miami. Also on board were my wife and daughter. The boat never got to Miami; it vanished without trace. But my daughter's body was found. How come you're still alive, Kayles?'

'I don't know what you're talking about. I don't know you, your wife or your daughter. And I don't know this guy, Albury.' He nodded towards Sam. 'I know him because I put my boat in his marina, that's all. You've got the wrong guy.'

Sam said, 'Maybe we have.' He looked at me. 'But it's easily provable, one way or the other.' He regarded Kayles again. 'Where's your log-book?'

Kayles hesitated, then said, 'Stowed under this bunk mattress.'

Sam picked up Kayles's knife which he had laid on the chart table. 'No tricks or I'll cut you good.' He advanced on Kayles and rolled him over. 'Get it, Tom.'

I lifted the mattress under Kayles, groped about and encountered the edge of a book. I pulled it out. 'Okay, Sam.' Sam released Kayles who rolled over on to his back again.

As I flipped through the pages of the log-book I said, 'All you have to do is to prove where you were on a certain date.' I tossed the book to Sam. 'But we won't find it in there. Where's your last year's log?'

'Don't keep a log more'n one year,' said Kayles sullenly. 'Clutters up the place.'

'You'll have to do better than that.'

'That's funny,' said Sam. 'Most boat folk keep their old log-books. As souvenirs, you know; and to impress other boat people.' He chuckled. 'And us marina people.'

'I'm not sentimental,' snarled Kayles. 'And I don't need to impress anyone.'

'You'll have to bloody well impress me if you expect me to turn you loose,' I said. 'And if I don't turn you loose you'll have to impress a judge.'

'Oh, Christ, how did I get into this?' he wailed. 'I swear to God you've got the wrong guy.'

'Prove it.'

'How can I? I don't know when your goddamn boat sailed, do I? I don't know anything about your boat.'

'Where were you just before last Christmas but one?'

'How would I know? I'll have to think about it.' Kayles's forehead creased. 'I was over in the Florida keys.'

'No, you weren't,' said Sam. 'I met you in the International Bazaar in Freeport, and you told me you were going to Miami. Remember that?'

'No. It's a hell of a long time ago, and how can I be expected to remember? But I did sail to Miami and then on down to Key West.'

'You sailed for Miami, all right,' I said. 'In *Lucayan Girl*.'

'I sailed in my own boat,' said Kayles stubbornly. 'This boat.' He jerked his head at me. 'What kind of a boat was this *Lucayan Girl*?'

'A trawler – fifty-two feet – Hatteras type.'

'For God's sake!' he said disgustedly. 'I'd never put foot on a booze palace like that. I'm a sailing man.' He nodded towards Sam. 'He knows that.'

I looked towards Sam who said, 'That's about it. Like I told you, he has this tiddy little diesel about as big as a sewing machine which he hardly ever uses.'

For a moment I was disconcerted and wondered if, indeed, we had the wrong man; but I rallied when Sam said, 'Why do you keep changing the name of your boat?'

Kayles was nonplussed for a moment, then he said, 'I don't.'

'Come off it,' I scoffed. 'We know of four names already – and four colours. When this boat was in the marina of the Royal Palm in Freeport just over a year ago she was *Bahama Mama* and her hull was red.'

'Must have been a different boat. Not mine.'

'You're a liar,' said Sam bluntly. 'Do you think I don't know my own work? I put up the masthead fitting.'

I thought back to the talk I had had with Sam and Joe Cartwright in my office a year previously. Sam had seen Kayles in the International Bazaar but, as it turned out, neither Sam nor Joe had seen the boat. But he was not telling Kayles that; he was taking a chance.

Kayles merely shrugged, and I said, 'We know you're a cocaine smuggler. If you come across and tell the truth it might help you in court. Not much, but it might help a bit.'

Kayles looked startled. 'Cocaine! You're crazy – right out of your mind. I've never smuggled an ounce in my life.'

Either he was a very good actor or he was telling the truth, but of course he would deny it so I put him down as a good actor. 'Why did you go to Cat Island?'

'I'm not saying another goddamn word,' he said sullenly. 'What's the use? I'm not believed no matter what I say.'

'Then that's it.' I stood up and said to Sam, 'Where do we go from here?'

'Sail this boat back to Duncan Town and hand him over to the local Government Commissioner. He'll contact the police and they'll take it from there. But not until daylight.'

'Scared of sailing in the dark?' jeered Kayles.

Sam ignored him, and said to me, 'I'd like a word with you on deck.'

I followed him into the cockpit. 'What did you tell Bayliss?'

'Enough of the truth to shut him up. He'd heard of the disappearance of *Lucayan Girl* so he'll stick around and cooperate.' He picked up the flashlamp Kayles had used and swept a beam of light into the darkness in a wide arc. There came an answering flicker from a darker patch of blackness about 200 yards to seaward. 'He's there.'

'Sam, why don't we sail back now? I know it's not true what Kayles said.'

'Because we can't,' said Sam, and there was a touch of wryness in his voice. 'I was a mite too careful. I was figuring on what might happen if Kayles got loose and I wanted to hamstring him, so I got some of Bayliss's fish net and tangled it around the propeller. That engine will never turn over now. Then I cut all the halliards so Kayles couldn't raise sail. Trouble is neither can we. I'm sorry, Tom.'

'How long will it take to fix?'

'Splicing the halliards and re-reeving will take more than an hour – in daylight. Same with the engine.'

'We could take Kayles back in Bayliss's boat, starting right now.'

'I don't think he'd do it,' said Sam. 'Fishermen aren't the same as yachtsmen who sail for fun. They don't like sailing around at night because there's no call to do it, so they don't have the experience and they know it.' He pointed south. 'There are a lot of reefs between here and Duncan Town, and Bayliss would be scared of running on to one. You don't know these folk; they don't work by charts and compasses like pleasure boat people. They navigate by sea colour and bird flight – things they can see.'

'You'd be all right on the tiller,' I said.

'But Bayliss wouldn't know that. It's his boat and he wouldn't want to lose her.'

'Let's ask him anyway,' I said. 'Call him in.'

Sam picked up the lamp and flashed it out to sea. There were a couple of answering winks and I heard the putt-putt of the engine as Bayliss drew near. He came alongside, fending off with the boathook, and then passed his painter up to Sam who secured it around a stanchion. Sam leaned over the edge of the cockpit still holding the light. 'Mr Mangan wants to know if you'll take us back to Duncan Town now.'

Bayliss's face crinkled and he looked up at the sky. 'Oh, no,' he said. 'Might if there was a full moon, but tonight no moon at all.'

I said, 'Sam here is willing to navigate and take the tiller, too. He's a good man at sea.'

It was just as Sam had predicted. Bayliss became mulish. 'How do I know that? This the only boat I got – I don't want to lose her. No, Mr Mangan, better wait for sunrise.'

I argued a bit but it was useless; the more I argued the more

Bayliss dug in his heels. 'All right,' I said in the end. 'We wait for sunrise.'

'Jesus!' said Sam suddenly. 'The knife – I left it on the chart table.' He turned and looked below. 'Watch it!' he yelled. 'He's coming through the forehatch.'

I looked forward and saw a dark shape moving in the bows, then there was a flash and a flat report and a *spaaaang* as a bullet ricocheted off metal. Sam straightened and cannoned into me. 'Over the side!'

There was no time to think but it made immediate sense. You could not fight a man with a gun on a deck he knew like the back of his own hand. I stepped on to the cockpit seat and jumped, tripping on something as I did so and because of that I made a hell of a splash. There was another splash as Sam followed, and then I ducked under water because a light flashed from the sloop and the beam searched the surface of the water and there was another muzzle flash as Kayles shot again.

It was then I thanked Pete Albury for his swimming lessons on the reefs around Abaco. Scuba gear had just been introduced in those days and its use was not general; anyway, Pete had a hearty contempt for it. He had taught me deep diving and the breath control necessary so that I could go down among the coral. Now I made good use of his training.

I dribbled air from my mouth, zealously conserving it, while conscious of the hunting light flickering over the surface above. I managed to kick off my shoes, being thankful that I was not wearing lace-ups, and the swimming became easier. I was swimming in circles and, just before I came up for more air, I heard the unmistakeable vibrations of something heavy entering the water and I wondered what it was.

I came to the surface on my back so that just my nose and mouth were above water. Filling my lungs I paddled myself under again, trying not to splash. I reckoned I could stay underwater for two minutes on every lungful of air, and I came up three times – about six minutes. The last time I came up I put my head right out and shook the water from my ears.

Then I heard the regular throb of the engine of Bayliss's boat apparently running at top speed. Ready to duck again if it came my way I listened intently, but the noise died away in the distance and presently there was nothing to be heard. The sound of a voice floated softly over the water. 'Tom!'

'That you, Sam?'

'I think he's gone.'

I swam in what I thought was Sam's direction. 'Gone where?'

'I don't know. He took Bayliss's boat.'

'Where's Bayliss?' I saw the ripples Sam was making and came up next to him.

'I don't know,' said Sam. 'I think he went overboard, too. He may still be in the boat, though.'

'Let's not jump to conclusions,' I said. 'That might have been Bayliss running away, and Kayles might still be around.'

Sam said, 'I was bobbing under the bows and Kayles was swearing fit to bust a gut. First, he tried to start the engine and it seized up. Then he tried to hoist sail and found he couldn't. I think it's fairly certain he took Bayliss's boat.'

'Well, if we're going to find out, let's do it carefully,' I said.

We made a plan, simple enough, which was to come up simultaneously on both sides of the sloop, hoping to catch Kayles in a pincer if he was still there. On execution we found the sloop deserted. Sam said, 'Where's Bayliss?'

We shouted for a long time and flashed the light over the water but saw and heard nothing. Sam said, 'It's my fault, Tom. I botched it. I forgot the knife.'

'Forget it,' I said. 'Which way do you think Kayles went?'

'I don't know, but in his place I'd head north. He has fifty miles of fuel and maybe more, and there are plenty of cays up there to get lost in. He might even have enough fuel to get to Exuma.' He took a deep breath. 'What do we do now?'

I had been thinking about that. 'We wait until sunrise, do the repairs, find Bayliss if we can, go back to Duncan Town and report to the Government Commissioner, and have Bill Pinder make an air search for that son of a bitch.'

It was an uneasy night and a worse morning because, while Sam was repairing the halliards, I went under the stern to cut the fish net from around the propeller and found Bayliss jammed in there. He had been shot through the head and was very dead.

That broke up Sam Ford more than anything else and it did not do me much good.

9

Deputy-Commissioner Perigord was thunderous and gave the definite impression that invisible lightning was flashing around his head. 'You had Kayles and you let him go!' he said unbelievingly.

'Not deliberately,' I said. 'There wasn't much we could do about it – he had the gun.'

'But you did go off half-cocked. I warned you about that. Why, in God's name, didn't you tell me you knew where Kayles was?'

'I didn't know where he was. I thought I knew where his boat was. And I wasn't even sure of that. I know that Sam Ford knows his boats but I couldn't be entirely sure. I went down to the Jumentos to make the identification.'

'Instead of which you made a stinking mess,' said Perigord cuttingly. 'Mr Mangan, I told you that this is a professional matter and you were not to butt in. You are responsible for the death of a man; an innocent bystander whom you casually took along on a hunt for a murderer. Fred Bayliss was a married man with a wife and four children. What of them?'

I felt like hell. 'I'll look after the family,' I muttered.

'Oh, you will? Big deal. You know what it's like to lose your family. How do you suppose Mrs Bayliss is feeling now? Do you think you can cure her grief with a few dollars?'

Perigord was a man who knew how to go for the jugular. 'Christ, what can I say beyond that I'm sorry?'

'Neither your sorrow or your money is of much help. And now I have an armed man loose in the Bahamas who knows he is being hunted, and it is my men who will have to do the hunting. How much sorrow will you feel if one of them is killed in the process?'

'Jesus, Perigord, enough is enough!'

He nodded. 'I think so, too. Go back to running your hotels, Mr Mangan. Go back to making money – but stay out of this business.' He paused. 'I may want to question you and Sam Ford further – I'll let you know. That's all.'

I left Perigord's office feeling so low I could walk under a snake's belly wearing a top hat. He was a man who knew how to use words as weapons, and the hell of it was that I knew I had it coming. I had been irresponsible. When Sam had come with the news of Kayles's boat I should have taken him to Perigord immediately and let the police handle it.

My disposition did not improve when I returned to my office and telephoned home. Luke Bailey answered. 'Is Mrs Mangan at home?'

'No, Mr Mangan.'

'Have you any idea where she is?'

'She left for Houston this morning.'

'Thanks, Luke.' I put down the telephone feeling more depressed than ever.

A few days later Perigord asked to see me and Sam Ford and we met him, not in his office, but in the Customs Department at the harbour. He had had Kayles's sloop brought up from Duncan Town and, as I thought he might, he had enlisted the aid of Customs officers to give it a real going-over.

The boat had been taken out of the water and put into a warehouse where she looked enormous. It is surprising how much larger a sailing boat looks out of the water than in; one tends to forget that most of a boat is under water. The Customs officers had taken most of the gear out of her and it was stacked on the floor of the warehouse and on tables in small heaps, each heap labelled as to where it was found. Again, it is surprising how much you can cram into a twenty-seven footer.

Perigord took us into a small glassed-in office in a corner of the warehouse and put us through the hoops again, this time with a tape recorder on the desk. It was a gruelling interrogation and it hit Sam hard because he blamed himself for everything, knowing that if he had not left the knife on the chart table then Bayliss might still be alive.

It was a two-hour grilling, occasionally interrupted by a Customs officer who would come in to show Perigord something or other. At last he switched off the recorder and took us out into the warehouse where he had Sam show him the masthead fitting by which he was able to identify the boat, even with its name and colour changed.

I said, 'Have you found anything useful?'

'Nothing of interest.' There was that in Perigord's voice which told me that even if he had found something he was not going to inform me.

'Not the drugs?' I asked in surprise.

His interest sharpened. 'What drugs?'

'The stuff in the first-aid box.'

He beckoned to a Customs man and the box was produced. It was empty. The Customs man said, 'We've laid out the contents over there.' We walked over to the trestle table and I scanned through the articles. The morphine syringes were there but there were no glass ampoules.

I described them, and said, 'I thought if Kayles was a drug-runner he might be a user, too, and that this was his personal stock.'

'Yes,' said Perigord thoughtfully. 'If he was a user he would certainly take it along, no matter in how much of a hurry he was. It was a liquid, you say?'

'That's right; a faintly yellowish liquid.' I described the ampoules and told of the home-made look they had.

The Customs officer picked up the reuseable hypodermic syringe. 'It's funny he didn't take this.' He shook his head. 'A yellow liquid. That's new to me.'

'They're always coming up with something new to blow their minds,' said Perigord. 'So now we've got a hopped-up gunman. It gets worse, doesn't it, Mr Mangan? Once his supplies run out he might start raiding pharmacies to resupply. Another headache.'

'Have you any idea where he might be?' I asked.

Bayliss's boat had not been found and, according to

Perigord's gloomy prediction, it never would be. He thought it had been sunk. A small sailing yacht had been stolen from George Town in the Exumas. 'And it could be anywhere now, with a change of name and colour,' said Perigord. 'If Kayles has any sense he'll be getting clear of the Bahamas.'

I was about to turn away, but thought of something. 'There are rumours floating around that the fire at the Fun Palace was due to arson. Is there anything in that?'

'Not to my knowledge,' he said. 'Squash those rumours, if you can.'

'I do,' I said. 'It's in my interest to do so.'

So I went home and found that Debbie had returned.

She was spoiling for a fight. I was greeted with: 'Where were you? You're never here when I want you.'

'I could say the same for you,' I returned acidly. 'In point of fact I was being shot at down in the Jumentos.'

'Shot at!' I could see her disbelief. 'Who by?'

'A man called Kayles – remember him? He killed a man down there, and damn near killed me and Sam Ford.'

'Who is Sam Ford?'

'If you took more interest in me and my doings you'd know damn well who Sam Ford is. He's boss of the marinas division.'

'So you found Kayles.'

'Sam did, and you're looking at a damn fool. I tried to take him myself and got a poor bloody fisherman killed. I'm beginning to sicken myself.' I poured myself a stiff drink and sat down. 'Commissioner Perigord doesn't think a great deal of me these days. Just about as much as you seem to do.'

'And whose fault is that?' she flared. 'What interest are you taking in me? You're never around any more.'

'My God, you know the problems I've had recently, what with one thing and another. And a new one has just come up – the Fun Palace fire. There's a meeting of the Hoteliers' Association and the Ministry of Tourism in Nassau tomorrow. I'll have to leave early.'

'That was bad,' she said. 'I read about it in the Houston papers.'

'You would. If you were in Timbuctu you'd have read about it. That's the problem.'

'But what has it got to do with you? Why should you fly to Nassau?'

I looked at Debbie thoughtfully and decided to cool it. She was in a worse temper than I had ever seen, but even though she was being unreasonable she deserved an explanation. 'Because I'm in the business,' I said patiently. 'It affects the Theta Corporation. The Bahamas seems to have become a disaster area lately and we're trying to figure out ways of minimizing the damage. My guess is that the Ministry of Tourism will propose a levy on the industry to fund a new advertising campaign.'

'Oh, I see.'

I adopted a more conciliatory tone. 'Debbie, I know I haven't been around much lately, and I'm sorry – truly I am. I'll tell you what. Let me get straightened out here and we'll take a holiday. Maybe go to Europe – London and Paris. We've never had a holiday together, not a real one.'

'A second honeymoon so soon after the first?' she said ruefully. 'But will you get straightened out? Won't there be something else come along to need your personal attention? And then something else? And something else? Won't it be like that?'

'No, it won't be like that. No man is indispensable in a decently run organization, not even the boss. And this run of bad luck can't go on for ever.'

She shook her head slowly. 'No, Tom. I'm going away to think this out.'

'Think what out, for God's sake?'

'Us.'

'There's nothing wrong with us, Debbie. And can't you do your thinking here?'

'I'd rather go home – be among my own family.'

I took a deep breath. 'I wish you wouldn't, Debbie, I really do, but if you must I don't suppose I can stop you.'

'No, you can't,' she said, and left the room.

I poured myself another drink, again a stiff one. As I sat down I reflected that although I had told Debbie I had been shot at, never once had she asked if I had been hurt. We had gone so far down the line. The Mangan marriage appeared to be another part of the Bahamian disaster area.

Bobby Bowen flew me to Nassau early next morning and I spent the day arguing the toss with Ministry of Tourism officials and a crowd of apprehensive and tight-wadded hoteliers. Everyone agreed that something must be done; the argument was about who was going to pay for it. The argument went on all day and ended as I had predicted; there would be a levy on the industry and the Government would put up dollar for dollar.

I got home at about seven in the evening to find that Debbie had gone, but had left a note.

'Dear Tom,

I meant what I said yesterday. I have gone back to Houston and will stay until the baby has come. I don't want to see you until then, but I suppose you will want to come just before the birth. That's all right with me, but I don't want to see you until then.

I have not taken Karen with me because I think it would be unfair to take her from her school and her friends and into what is a foreign country. Besides, she is your daughter.

I can't see clearly what has gone wrong between us, but I will be thinking hard about it, and I hope you do the same. It's funny but I still love you, and so I can end this note with

Love,
Debbie.'

I read that letter five times before putting it into my wallet, and then sat down to write my own letter asking her to come back. I had no great hopes that she would.

10

The week after Debbie left we lost Bill Pinder.

He was taking four American fishermen to Stella Maris on Long Island which they were going to use as a base for hunting marlin and sailfish off Columbus Point and on the Tartar Bank in Exuma Sound. I was going with them, not because I am particularly charmed by American fishermen, but because Bill was flying me on to Crooked Island, 100 miles further south, where I was to look at some property on behalf of the Theta Corporation.

As it chanced I did not go because the previous evening I slipped in the bathroom and broke a toe which proved to be rather painful. To look at property and to walk a few miles on Crooked Island in that condition was not a viable proposition, so I cancelled.

Bill Pinder took off in a Navajo early next morning with the Americans. He was flying over Exuma Sound and was filing his intentions with Nassau radio when suddenly he went off the air in mid-sentence, so we know exactly when it happened. What happened I know now but did not know then. The Bahamas may be the Shallow Sea but there are bits like the Tongue of the Ocean and Exuma Sound which are very deep; the Tartar Bank rises to within seven fathoms of the surface in Exuma Sound but the rest is deep water.

The Navajo was never found, nor any wreckage, and Bill Pinder disappeared. So did the four Americans, and two of them were so influential on Wall Street that the event caused quite a stir, more than I and the Bahamas needed. After a couple of weeks some bits and pieces of clothing were washed up on one of the Exuma cays and identified as belonging to one of the Americans.

The death of Bill Pinder hit me hard. He was a good man,

and the only better light plane pilot I know is Bobby Bowen. It is hard for blacks like Bill and Bobby to achieve a commercial pilot's ticket, or at least it was when they pulled off the trick. I suppose it is easier now.

There was a memorial service which I attended and to which many of the Corporation employees came, as many as could be spared without actually closing down the hotels. A lot of BASRA pilots were there, too. After the service I had a word with Bobby Bowen; I had not had a chance to talk to him much because, being an aircraft short, he was an overworked man. I said, 'What happened, Bobby?'

He shrugged. 'Who knows? There'll be no evidence coming out of Exuma Sound.' He thought for a moment. 'He was filing with Nassau at the time so he'd be flying pretty high, about 10,000 feet, to get radio range. But why he fell out of the sky . . .?' He spread his hands. 'That was a good plane, Tom. It had just had its 300-hour check, and I flew it myself three days earlier.' He grimaced a little. 'You'll hear talk of the Bermuda Triangle; pay no heed – it's just the chatter of a lot of screwy nuts who don't know one end of an airplane from the other.'

I said, 'We'll need another plane and another pilot.'

'You won't get one like Bill,' said Bobby. 'He knew these Islands right well. About another plane – something bigger?' he said hopefully.

'Perhaps. I'll have to talk it over with the board. I'll let you know.'

We watched the Pinder family walking away from the church. Bobby said, 'It's bad for Meg Pinder. Bill was a good husband to her.'

'She'll be looked after,' I said. 'The pension fund isn't broke yet.'

'Money won't cure what's wrong with her,' said Bobby, unconsciously echoing what Perigord had said about Bayliss's wife, and I felt a stab of shame.

But how could I know that someone was trying to kill me?

Billy Cunningham paid a flying visit. He came without

warning at a weekend and found me at the house where I was packing a few things to take to my suite at the Royal Palm. We talked about Bill Pinder and he said the usual conventional things about what a tragedy it was, and we talked about getting another aircraft. He appeared to be a little nervous so I said, 'Stop pussy-footing, Billy. Sit down, have a drink, and get it off your chest. Are you an emissary?'

He laughed self-consciously. 'I guess so. I've had obligations laid on me.'

'Cunningham obligations?'

'Score one for you – I never did think you were stupid. You had that subtle look in your eye when you were inspecting us back home when you married Debbie. I suppose you didn't miss much.'

'A tight-knit bunch,' I observed.

'Yeah. The advantages are many – one for all and all for one – that stuff. A guy always has someone guarding his back. But there are disadvantages, like now. Old Jack's not been feeling too well lately so he couldn't come himself.'

'I'm sorry to hear that,' I said sincerely.

Billy waved his hand. 'Nothing serious. Frank had a business meeting in California – important. So I was elected.'

I said, 'Tell me one thing. Does Debbie know about this? Does she know you're here?'

He shook his head. 'No. It's just that Jack wants to know what the hell is going on. Personally, I think it's none of our business, but . . .'

'But the Cunninghams look after their own.'

'That's about it. Hell, Tom, I told Jack that interfering between man and wife is pure poison, but you think he'd listen? You know the old man.'

'Not too well,' I said coolly. 'What do you want to know?'

'It's not what I want to know – it's what Jack wants to know. Jack and Frank both. They're both mad at you.' Billy paused, then said meditatively, 'If Frank had come on this mission he might have taken a poke at you. Very protective is Frank.'

'Why should he do that?' I demanded. 'I don't beat up his little sister every Friday night as a regular routine.'

He grinned crookedly. 'It might have been better if you had. The Cunningham women . . .' He stopped short. 'Anyway, Jack wants to know why his little girl has come running home looking as blue as a cold flounder.'

'Didn't he ask her?'

'She clammed up on him – and on Frank. Me – I didn't bother to ask. What is it, Tom?'

'I don't know,' I said. 'It appears that she wants me to stay home and hold her hand. Says I'm neglecting her. But, God, you know what's been happening here. If it hasn't been one bloody thing it's been another. Did she tell you about Kayles?'

'No. What about him?'

I told Billy in some detail, and said, 'I know I made a damn fool of myself and I'm sorry a man was killed – but Debbie didn't even ask if I'd been hurt.'

'Self-centred,' observed Billy. 'She always was, and I've told her so to her face, many times. So where do you go from here?'

I took out my wallet and showed Billy the note Debbie had left and he made a sour face. 'If she wasn't family I'd call her a bitch,' he said. 'What are you doing about Karen?'

'She's staying with me at the hotel for the moment. I doubt if it's good for her but it's the best I can do right now.'

'Do you want me to talk with Debbie?'

'No,' I said. 'Keep out of it. She must work this thing through herself. And tell Jack and Frank to keep out of it, too.'

He shrugged. 'I've already told them, but I'll pass on the message from you.'

'Do that.'

And so we left it there and began to discuss our problems in the Bahamas. Billy said, 'The way things are going you'd better start another division – staffed by morticians. It should show a profit.'

'Not if the bodies aren't found,' I said. 'Anyway, the Theta

Corporation was only directly involved in one of these incidents, the air crash.'

'We don't want another like that,' warned Billy. 'The waves are still rocking the New York Stock Exchange. Those guys who were killed weren't ready to die; their financial affairs weren't exactly in order. I hear the Securities and Exchange Commission might start an investigation and that'll cause grief all round. Tom, the name of the Bahamas is coming up too often in headlines and it's beginning to stink. And don't give me that crap about any publicity being good publicity as long as they get the name right.'

'It's just a streak of bad luck. It'll come right.' I told him of the deal made between the Hoteliers' Association and the Ministry of Tourism, ending with, 'So we're doing something about it.'

'You'd better do something about it. Jack's getting worried; he's talking about pulling out.'

'Is he chicken-livered? We've had a run of three bad incidents and Jack runs scared?'

'Three incidents and 128 dead,' said Billy. 'Jack's been counting; he's keeping score.' He sighed. 'Trouble is he never really wanted to come into the Bahamas anyway. It was my idea and Billy One backed me. Jack went along but his heart was never really in it.'

'On top of which he's never cottoned on to me,' I said a little bitterly.

'He thinks you run a loose ship,' said Billy frankly. 'That you give too much away. According to Jack at best you're a do-gooder; at worst, when his bile really starts to rise, you're an agent of the Kremlin.'

I gave Billy a level look. 'What do you think?'

'I think Jack is a fossilized dinosaur. Times are changing but he isn't. As for me I'm willing to play along with your plans of operation as long s they show a profit – a reasonable return on a fifty million buck investment, a return comparable to what we'd get anywhere else. I know you're a Bahamian and you want to help your own people; all I ask is that you don't do it *too* much at corporate expense.'

'Fair enough. But, Billy, all those things which Jack thinks are giveaways – the pension fund, the hotel doctor, the hotels' school, and so on – all those are investments for the Corporation. They'll pay off in staff service and corporate loyalty, and that's hard to buy.'

'You're probably right,' acknowledged Billy. 'But Jack's an old-time Texan. He even accused Nixon of being a commie when he pulled out of Vietnam. Sometimes I think he's a nut. But look at you from his side of the fence. You're a foreigner who first subverted his daughter into mixing with black kids, then took her away, and now she's back home looking goddamn unhappy. Add all that together and you'll see he's just looking for an excuse to pull out of here. It won't take much.'

'How much of the Theta Corporation does he control?'

'As an individual, nothing; our eighty per cent of Theta is owned by the Cunningham Corporation. But he has some clout in there. With some fast talking he could line up enough proxies to vote for a pull-out from the Bahamas.'

'That would be a personal disaster for me,' I said slowly. 'I'm too deeply committed now.'

'I know. That's why you'd better pray there isn't an earthquake here next week, or an outbreak of infectious dandruff. No more headlines, Tom.'

As though I did not have enough to worry about I now had Jack Cunningham gunning for me. And, as Billy had said, all I could do was pray.

11

That was on Saturday. Billy stayed to lunch and then departed, saying that he was going to Miami on business for the Cunningham Corporation, and from there to New York. He gave me telephone numbers where I could find him. On Sunday I caught up with paperwork.

Monday was – well, Monday was Monday – one of those days when nothing goes really wrong but nothing goes really right; a day of niggling futilities and a rapidly shortening temper. I suppose we all have days like that.

I dined in the restaurant and went to my room early, after seeing Karen to bed, intending to go to bed myself and to scan some managerial reports before sleeping. I have never known why one is supposed to be vertical while working, and I can read perfectly well while flat on my back. I had just got settled when the telephone rang and a voice said in my ear, as clear as a bell, 'Mangan? Is that you?'

'Yes. Who's speaking?'

'Jack Cunningham here. Is Debbie there?'

'No, I thought she was with you. Where are you?'

'Houston.' His voice suddenly receded although he was still speaking. I caught a few scattered words and concluded he was consulting with someone else. '. . . not there . . . must be right . . . Billy . . .' He came back full strength. 'Is young Billy there?'

'No,' I said. 'He was here on Saturday. He'll be in Miami if he hasn't gone on to New York.'

Again he withdrew and I heard incomprehensible bits of a conversation nearly 1000 miles away. '. . . Miami . . . airplane . . . both . . .' then Jack said loudly, 'Tom, you pack a bag and be ready to get your ass over here.'

I resented that rasping tone of command. 'Why? What's happening?'

'I'm not going to talk about it now. There's a satellite up there spraying this conversation all over the goddamn planet.'

'I don't see . . .'

'Damn it! Do as I say and don't argue. There'll be a jet at Freeport International in about two hours. Don't keep it waiting, and be prepared to stay over awhile.' The connection broke and silence bored into my ear.

I checked the time. It was 9.30 in the evening.

Much against my will I got out of bed and dressed, impelled by the fizzing urgency in Jack Cunningham's voice. Then I thought of Karen, asleep in the next room. Damn Jack Cunningham! Damn the whole blasted family! I rang the desk and asked the clerk to find Kitty Symonette and send her up to my suite, then I started to pack a bag.

I was just finishing a letter when Kitty Symonette tapped at the door and I let her in. 'Sit down, Kitty. I have problems and I want you to help me.'

She looked slightly surprised. 'I'll do what I can.'

Kitty was the hotel nurse and I liked her very much, and so did Karen. She was totally unflappable and equally reliable. 'I'm not interrupting anything, am I?'

'No. I was going to have an early night.'

'Good. I have to go away and I don't know for how long. Tomorrow I want you to take Karen to stay with my sister on Abaco. I've just spoken to Peggy and Karen is expected.' I scribbled my signature. 'These are instructions for Bobby Bowen to take you.'

'No problem there,' said Kitty.

'Karen is asleep in that room there. I don't want her to wake alone so you'd better sleep in my room tonight.'

'You're going right away?'

'This minute. I don't want to wake Karen now, but you tell her I'll be back as soon as I can make it.'

Kitty stood up. 'I'll collect some things from my room.'

I gave her the key to the suite, picked up my bag, and went to my office where I collected my passport from the office safe. As an afterthought I took the packet of 2000 American dollars which I kept there for an emergency and put them in my wallet.

The wait at the airport was long and boring. I drank coffee until it sickened me, then had a couple of scotches. It was after midnight when the public address speakers said, 'Will Mr Mangan please go to the enquiry desk?'

I was met by a pretty girl dressed in a yellow uniform trimmed with black and with a badge on her lapel, two letters 'C' intertwined in a monogram. The outfit made her look waspish, about as waspish as I was feeling. 'Mr Mangan?'

'Yes,' I said shortly.

'This way, sir.' She led the way from the concourse and through a side door. Standing on the apron not very far away was a Lockheed JetStar in gold with black trim; on the tailfin was the Cunningham monogram. Around it was a collection of airport vehicles like workers around a queen bee. I followed her up the gangway and paused as she stopped inside the door to take my bag. 'Glad to have you with us, Mr Mangan.'

I could not reciprocate her feelings, but I murmured, 'Thank you,' and passed on into the main cabin.

Billy Cunningham said explosively, 'Now, will you, for Christ's sweet sake, tell me what's going on?'

From Freeport to Houston is about 1000 miles across the Gulf of Mexico. We droned across the Gulf at 500 miles an hour and Billy was morose – sore because he had been yanked out of Miami as unceremoniously as I had from Freeport – and he was irritated when he found I could tell him nothing. 'What bugs me,' he said, 'is that for the first time in my life I'm going somewhere in an airplane and I don't know why. What the hell's got into Jack?'

'I don't know,' I said slowly. 'I think it's something to do with Debbie.'

'Debbie! How come?'

'The first thing Jack asked was if she was with me – in Freeport.'

'He knew she wasn't,' said Billy. 'She was in Houston.'

I shrugged. 'Air travel is wonderful. A girl can get around fast.'

'You think she's taken off again?' He snorted. 'That girl wants her ass spanked – and if you won't do it, then I will. It's time she settled down and learned how to behave.'

There was nothing more to say so we did not say it.

There was a car waiting at Houston airport and an hour later I was at the start of a Cunningham conference. At least it was the start for me; the others had evidently been arguing the toss for a long time – and it showed. Jack Cunningham was at the head of the table, his silver hair making him look senatorially handsome as usual, and Billy One sat next to him. Debbie's brother, Frank, eyed me with arrogant and ill-concealed hostility. As background there were half a dozen other collateral Cunninghams, most of whom I did not know, ready to take their cue from the powerful tribal bosses. This was the Cunningham clan in full deliberation and, predictably, there was not a woman in sight.

Our arrival brought instant silence which did not last long. Billy flipped a hand at his father, surveyed the gathering, and drawled, 'Morning, y'all.' Uproar broke out, everybody talking at once and I could not distinguish a word until Jack hammered the long table with a whisky bottle and yelled, 'Quiet!'

It could have been the traditional smoke-filled room but for the air-conditioning and, indeed, they did look like a crowd of old-time political bosses carving up next year's taxes. Most had their jackets off and had loosened their neckties and the room smelled of good cigars. Only Jack had kept on his coat, and his tie was securely knotted at his neck. Even so he looked decidedly frayed around the edges, and there was a persistent twitch in his left cheek.

He said, 'Tom, do you know what's happened to Debbie?'

The question could have had two meanings – he really wanted to know if I knew, or it was rhetorical – and there was no way of knowing from the inflection of his voice. I said, 'How would I know? She left me.'

'He admits it,' said Frank.

'Admit! I admit nothing – I'm *telling* you, if she hasn't told you already. She's her own woman and she ran away.'

'Ran away from what? That's what I'd like to know.'

Billy casually walked up to the table and picked up a whisky bottle. 'Any clean glasses around?' Then he swung on Frank. 'Button up your mouth.'

'You can't . . .'

'Shut it,' said Billy quietly, but there was a cutting edge to his voice. 'Your sister's a brat. Everything she ever wanted she got, but she wouldn't know a man when she saw one, not a real man. When she found she couldn't handle him she picked up her marbles and wouldn't play any more.' He looked at Jack. 'Nobody's going to hold a kangaroo court on Tom. Hear?'

Billy One stirred. 'Quiet, boy.'

'Sure,' said Billy easily. 'I've said the core of it, y'all know that.' He dropped into a chair. 'Come sit here, Tom; you look as though you need a drink.'

I suppose I did; we both did. And it was half past three in the morning. I took the chair he offered and accepted the drink, then I said, 'If you want to know what happened to Debbie why don't you ask her?'

I was now facing Billy One across the table. He laid his hands flat. 'That's just it, son. She's not around to be asked.'

'Jesus!' said Billy, and stared at Jack. 'Your little girl runs away again, and you jerk me from making the sweetest deal you ever saw?'

The tic convulsed Jack's cheek; he looked defeated. 'Tell him, Billy One,' he said in an old man's voice.

Billy One stared at the back of his hands. He said slowly, 'We weren't sure at first, not really, not even this afternoon when . . .' He looked up at me. 'Now you're here we're pretty sure Debbie's been kidnapped.'

Suddenly it all did not seem real. My head swam for a moment as a host of questions crowded in. I picked the first at random. 'Who by?'

'Who the hell knows?' said Frank disgustedly. 'Kidnappers don't hand out business cards.'

He was right; it was a stupid question. Billy said, 'When?'

'Saturday, we think; maybe Sunday early.' And today was late Monday or, rather, very early Tuesday. Billy One nodded down the table. 'Last one of us to see her was Joe's wife.'

'Yeah,' said Joe. 'Linda and Debbie went shopping Saturday morning – Sakowitz and Niernan-Marcus. They lunched together.'

'Then what?' asked Billy.

Joe shrugged. 'Then nothing. Linda came home.'

'Did she say what Debbie was going to do Saturday afternoon?'

'Debbie didn't tell her.'

This did not seem to be getting anywhere. I cleared my throat, and said, 'How do you know she's been kidnapped? Billy, here, jumped to the conclusion that she'd taken off again. So did I. So how do you *know*?'

'Because the goddamn kidnappers told us,' said Frank.

Billy One said, 'We got a letter this . . . last afternoon – least, Jack did. Tell the truth I don't think we believed it at first, neither of us. Thought it was some kind of hoax until we discovered she really wasn't around.'

'Where was Debbie staying?'

'At my place,' said Jack. He looked at me reproachfully. 'My girl was very unhappy.'

'She was last seen by the family at midday on Saturday and it took you until Monday to find out she'd disappeared?' I looked at Jack. 'Wasn't her bed slept in?'

'Take it easy, Tom,' said Billy One. 'We thought she'd gone back to you.'

'She'd have left word,' I said. 'She may be irresponsible, but she's not that irresponsible. When she left me she at least had the decency to leave a note telling me where she'd gone, if not why. What about her clothes? Didn't you check to see if any were missing? Or, more to the point, not missing?'

'Oh, Christ!' said Frank. 'She'd been living away. Who knew what clothes she had?' He waved an impatient hand. 'This is wasting time.'

'I agree,' I said emphatically. 'Have you notified the police?'

There was silence around the table and Jack evaded my eye. Finally Billy One said quietly, 'Kidnapping is a federal offence.'

I knew that; it had been a federal offence ever since the stink caused by the Lindbergh kidnapping. 'So?'

He tented his fingers. 'If it was just a matter for the State Police we'd be able to keep control – we draw a lot of water here in Texas. But once the Federal Government gets into the act – and that means the FBI – then anything could happen. Since Watergate every Government department has been as leaky as a goddamn sieve, and that damn fool, Carter, calls it open government.' In his voice was the contempt of the old-line Republican for a Democratic administration. 'The FBI is no exception, and if the newspapers get hold of this I wouldn't give a bent nickel for our chances of getting Debbie back safely.'

'We can control our press down here, but those newspapers back east would really screw things up,' said Frank.

'To say nothing of the professional bleeding hearts on TV,' Joe commented.

'So you haven't told the police,' I said bleakly.

'Not yet,' said Billy One.

'Hell, we can pay,' said Billy. He grinned sardonically. 'And stop it out of Debbie's allowance when we get her back.'

'If we get her back,' said Jack. There was agony in his voice. 'You know what kidnappers are like.'

'Right,' said Billy. 'But if you don't call the cops you don't get her back unless you pay – so let's start opening the coffers.'

'It's not as easy as that,' said Billy One. 'Not by a long shot. There are . . . difficulties.'

'What difficulties? These guys want dough, we want Debbie. We give them how many dollars they want and we get Debbie.' Billy's voice turned savage. 'Then we go hunting and we get the money back and maybe some scalps. But I don't see any difficulty.'

'You brought one with you,' said Frank.

'What the hell do you mean by that?'

'I mean that this son of a bitch . . .'

'Shut up!' said Billy One. He sighed. 'These guys don't want money, Billy. They want him.' He was pointing at me. 'He's the ransom.'

12

Dawn was breaking as I got to bed that morning but I did not sleep much. I just lay there in bed, staring into the darkness of the curtained room, and thinking. The trouble was that I could not think very well; fugitive thoughts chittered about in my skull like bats in an attic. Nothing seemed to connect.

I moved restlessly in bed and again saw the face of Billy One and the finger pointing directly at me. That finger had been a little unsteady; it trembled with age or fatigue – or possibly both. 'Don't ask me why,' said Billy One. 'But they want Tom for Debbie – an even deal.'

'Bullshit!' said Billy. He did not believe it, and neither did I. It made no sense.

'Show him the ransom note,' said Frank.

Jack took a folded letter and tossed it on to the table. I grabbed it and read it with Billy peering over my shoulder. It was in typescript, addressed to Mr John D. Cunningham, and written with a stilted formality which contrasted oddly with the rawness of the contents.

'Dear Mr Cunningham,

You will have difficulty in believing this but we have in our possession the person of your daughter, Deborah Mangan. In short, we have kidnapped her. In the belief that you will want her back unharmed we now give you our terms. They are not subject to negotiation.

You will cause your so n-in-law, Thomas Mangan, to travel to Houston. How you do this is your concern. We will know when he has arrived. Our price for your daughter's safety and, possibly, her life is the person of Thomas Mangan delivered to us intact and unhurt. Your daughter will then be returned in fair exchange.

You will be notified as to the manner of this transaction upon the arrival of Mr Mangan in Texas.

It goes without saying that the police should not be informed of these arrangements nor should any of those steps be taken which might seem obvious in such a dramatic situation as this.

You will understand my motives in not signing this communication.'

'For Christ's sake!' said Billy. He looked at me with a baffled expression. 'Who'd . . .' He stopped and shook his head in wonder.

'I don't know.' What I did know was the reason for Jack Cunningham's peremptory summons to Houston.

'You must be quite a guy,' said Frank, his tone belying his words. He looked around the table. 'Any hoodlum knows a Cunningham woman is worth hard cash money. How much? Quarter of a million dollars? Half a million? A million? Christ, we'd pay five million if we had to. Course, any hoodlum with sense would know he wouldn't live long enough to spend it, no matter which way the ball bounced. But this guy would rather have Mangan than the dough.' He eyed me challengingly. 'So what the hell makes you so valuable?'

'Cut it out,' said Billy.

Billy One said pointedly, 'We want to make friends and influence people.'

'Yeah,' said Billy. 'Tom hasn't said much yet. He hasn't said he wants any part of this.'

'He's not a man if he runs out,' said Frank hotly.

'Oh, I don't know,' said Billy in a detached voice. 'How much would you do for a wife who's run out on you?'

For some reason that seemed to hit Frank where it hurt. He flushed and was about to say something, but thought better of it and sat back in his chair, drumming his fingers on the table. From which I gathered that Frank had marital troubles of his own.

There was a long silence. Jack Cunningham sat at the head

of the table, looking along its length with dead eyes; Billy pulled the letter closer and read it again; Frank fidgeted while Billy One studied him with watchful eyes. The rest, the family underlings, said nothing.

Billy One sat upright, apparently satisfied that Frank had shot his bolt, at least temporarily. 'Okay, Tom.' His voice was neutral but not unfriendly. 'Frank has a point, you know. What makes you so valuable that someone would kidnap a Cunningham to get you?'

That was a good question and I did not have an answer. 'I don't know,' I said flatly. 'You know who I am and what I do. Jack had me thoroughly investigated, didn't he? Twice. Once before the merger and again before the wedding. You don't think I can't recognize private detectives when they're floating around my hotels?'

Billy One smiled slightly. 'You checked out fine,' he said. 'Both times.'

'It wasn't necessary,' I said. 'All you had to do was to come to me and ask. My life is a pretty open book. But I thought that if that's the way you operate, then that's the way you operate, and there was nothing I could do about it. Which isn't to say I liked it.'

'We didn't give a damn if you liked it or not,' said Frank.

Jack said, 'That will be enough, Frank.'

'Jack was dead against the marriage,' said Billy One. 'He had his reasons. Frank was, too; but Billy was for it – he thought you were a right guy. Me, I had no druthers either way. As it turned out, what we all thought didn't matter a damn because Debbie got her own way, as always.'

He reached out and poured a measure of whisky into a glass. 'Now, we've gotten two things here, both separate – I think. Debbie left you, and she's been kidnapped. Can you think of any connection?'

'No,' I said. 'As you know, I've had my hands full lately – you've read the reports – and perhaps I couldn't, or didn't, give Debbie enough of my time. That's what she thought, anyway, so she quit. But I don't know why she should be kidnapped with me as ransom. That fits nowhere.'

'Has anything out of the ordinary happened lately?'

'Yes,' said Billy. 'Tell him about Kayles.'

So I told the story of me and Kayles. When I had finished Frank said, 'And this guy is still loose?'

'Yes – so far.'

'That's it, then,' he said. 'There's your answer.'

'What would Kayles want with me?' I demanded, and prodded at the ransom demand on the table. 'I've met and talked with Kayles – he wouldn't and couldn't write a thing like this. It's way above his head – he's not that much educated.'

Billy One said, 'And where does that leave us? What makes you so goddamn valuable, Tom?'

'I have no idea,' I said tiredly. 'And does it matter? The point at issue here is what to do about Debbie.'

'Mangan, I'd say you lose wives awful easy,' said Frank nastily.

'That does it,' said Billy, and hit Frank before I could get my own hands on him. It was a backhander across the jaw which caught Frank by surprise. He went over backwards and his chair went with him, and he sprawled on the floor with Billy standing over him. He looked up, rubbing his jaw, and Billy said, 'Cousin Frank, I've always been able to whip your ass, and if you don't stay off Tom's back I'm ready to do it again right now.'

Billy One glanced at Jack who was silent. He said, 'That was uncalled for, Frank. Now, you'll stand up and apologize to Tom or you leave this room right now, and maybe you won't be back – ever. Understand? Help him up, Billy.'

Billy hoisted Frank to his feet. Frank rubbed his mouth and looked at the blood on the back of his hand. 'I guess I'm sorry,' he mumbled, then looked at me directly. 'But what are you going to do about my sister?'

'I'm going to make the exchange.' I looked at the expression on his face, and then at Billy One. 'Did you have any doubt I would?'

A suppressed chuckle came from Billy. 'You're damn right they had doubts.'

Billy One exhaled a long sigh. 'Maybe I misjudged you, Tom,' he said quietly.

'Well, now we can plan,' said Billy. He sat down and picked up the letter. 'Frank was talking about hoodlums, but Tom's right; this wasn't written by any illiterate jerk. But he used a typewriter – they can be traced.'

'Typewriters are cheap,' said Frank as he picked up his chair. 'That one is probably at the bottom of Galveston Bay by now.' He sat down. 'And what's to plan? This guy is doing the planning. We can't do a goddamn thing until we get instructions on how we do the deal.'

'You're wrong,' said Billy. 'What's the use of having a security section in the Corporation if we don't use it? Those guys know all about bugs.'

Billy One lifted a shaggy eyebrow. 'So?'

'So we bug Tom. A transmitter in the heel of a shoe, maybe. In a ballpoint pen or sewn into his pants. We bug him until he's crawling.'

'And then?'

'Then we . . .'

Billy One had a sudden thought. He held up his hand and looked about the table. 'Hold it! There are too many damn people in here. Let's do some pruning. Tom stays, of course – and Billy. Jack stays, too, if he wants.' He peered at the far end of the table. 'Jim, you stay. The rest of you clear out.'

There was a general murmur of disapproval but no one objected overtly except Frank. 'What the hell!' he said tightly. 'We're talking about my sister. I'm staying.'

Billy One scowled at him. 'Okay. But quit riding Tom; we're talking about his wife and that's a closer relationship.' He turned to Jack. 'It's after four in the morning and you look beat. You sure you want to stay? You've been grinding at this all night.'

'So has Frank. So have you.'

'Yeah, but Frank is a young guy – and I'm not as close to it as you. I'm more objective. Why don't you catch some sleep and come up tomorrow full of the old moxie?'

'Maybe you're right,' said Jack. His face was grey with

fatigue as he stood up slowly. 'Frank, fill me in tomorrow morning. Hear?'

'I'll do that.' A frown creased Frank's forehead as he watched his father walk to the door.

I had a sudden insight into the workings of the Cunningham Corporation. It operated remarkably like the Kremlin – collective leadership. Everybody had a vote but some votes were heavier than others. Every so often the old bulls at the top would do battle over some issue and the weaker would be tossed out. I had the idea that this was happening now; that Billy One was in the process of tossing out Jack, just as Brezhnev had got rid of Podgorny.

Billy and Frank were fighting for second place. Where Jim Cunningham came into this I did not know; probably Billy One was sea ling an alliance with a faction of the clan. Jim was lucky – he had been promoted to top table.

This was confirmed when, as the door closed, Billy One called, 'Jim, come sit up here.' He glowered at us under white eyebrows. 'From now on we operate on "need to know", and what they don't know won't hurt us, or Debbie. Hell, it only needs Joe to drop a loose word at home and Linda would spread it over half Houston. She's a gossip.'

Frank said, 'If she shoots her mouth off about what's happened to Debbie she'll wish she never married a Cunningham. I'll see to it if Joe doesn't.'

Billy One nodded. 'Jim, you know more about the security angle than any of us. Got any ideas on this?'

Jim was a young chap of about twenty-five, dressed casually in jeans. He had a sleepy look about him which was deceptive because he was as sharp as a tack. He said, 'Billy is right.' He turned to me. 'I'll need your clothes – coat, pants, everything you wear down to socks and underwear. The outfit you'll use when you go to make this lousy deal. We'll have you radiating right through the electromagnetic spectrum.' To Billy One he said, 'We'll need cars, light airplanes and maybe choppers. Better lay on a couple of fast boats, too; Tom might be taken out to sea.'

'We'll use my boat,' said Frank. 'Nothing faster in Texas.'

'No!' said Jim quickly. 'We use nothing Cunningham. We rent everything.'

'My job,' said Billy.

I said, 'But no one makes a move until Debbie's safe.'

'That's understood,' said Billy One. 'What about a gun?'

I shook my head. 'No gun. I don't want to kill anybody.'

He looked disappointed; my way was not the Texan way. 'You might need a gun to stop someone killing *you*.'

'A gun wouldn't stop them – not the way I use one,' I said dryly. 'Anyway, they'll search me. The joker who wrote this ransom note doesn't sound like a damn fool.'

Jim agreed. 'Finding a gun might make him nervous; nervous guys are dangerous.'

A telephone beeped discreetly in a corner of the room. Billy One jerked his head and Jim got up to answer it. Even though he had got to the inner cabinet he knew his place on the totem pole; he was still a messenger boy. Presently he said, 'It's the Security Officer speaking from the lobby. He says an envelope has been handed in addressed to Jack.'

Billy One grunted. 'Have him bring it up.'

'Our security force might need beefing up,' said Billy. 'The way this is turning out we might be spread thin. What about a detective agency?'

'I'll fix that,' said Billy One. 'I know a good one.'

Frank said, 'We might not have time for all that. I have a gut feeling trouble is coming up in the elevator right now.'

Billy One looked at his watch. 'If you're right, it's bad news.' He picked up the ransom letter. 'I know this guy said he'd know when Tom arrives, but Tom's been here not much over an hour.'

'Good intelligence service,' said Billy.

'Too goddamn good.' Frank frowned. 'Inside information? From this building, maybe?'

'Who knows?' Billy One irritably threw down the sheet of paper. 'We'll wait and see.'

If the information of my arrival had come from the inside of the building then it was bad news indeed, because we were sitting in the penthouse of the slab-sided glass tower that was the Cunningham Building, the latest addition to the Houston skyline. It would mean the Cunningham Corporation itself had been penetrated.

The long moments dragged by. Billy One must have parallelled my train of thought because he ceased his finger-tapping and said, 'Jim, have security check this room for bugs first thing in the morning.'

'Will do.'

There was a discreet tap at the door and Jim got up. After a brief colloquy he came back carrying a large envelope which he laid on the table. Billy One bent forward to read the superscription, then pulled the ransom letter towards him and compared. 'Could be the same typewriter. Probably is.'

'The guy has confidence,' said Billy with a sideways glance at Frank.

'Lot of stuff in here,' said Billy One, hefting the envelope. 'Who delivered it?'

'A guy who said he'd been given five bucks in a bar.' As Billy One picked up a paper-knife Jim said sharply, 'Let's do this right. Let's not get our fingers all over what's in there.'

'You do it.'

Jim slit open the envelope and shook its contents on to the table. Most of it appeared to be eight-by-ten glossy black-and-white photographs, but there were also a couple of sheets of paper covered with typescript, single-spaced. Jim took a ballpoint pen and separated it all out, being careful not to touch anything with his fingers. He said, 'I'll have these put in glassine envelopes later. You can look at them now, but don't touch.'

The two pages of typescript were complicated instructions of what to do and when to do it. The photographs were of places where certain actions had to be done, and had been annotated with a red fibre pen. On one, for instance, were the instructions, 'Wait here exactly four minutes. Flash headlamps twice at end of each minute.' There were eleven photographs, each numbered, and the eleventh showed the edge of a road with open country beyond and trees in the distance. A red dashed line traced a path from the road to the trees, and an inscription read, 'Mangan goes this way alone. Deborah Mangan comes out same way ten minutes later. No tricks, please.'

It was all very complicated.

Billy was studying the first typed page. 'What a nerve! This one begins: "Mr Thomas Mangan, welcome to Houston, the fastest growing city in America".'

Frank said, 'Well, he gives us until Thursday – three days. Enough time to get ready for the son of a bitch.'

Billy One grunted, but said nothing.

Jim looked down at the photographs. 'I don't think this guy is American. Look here, Billy.' His finger hovered an inch over the table. 'An American wouldn't refer to headlamps – he'd say headlights.'

'Yeah, could be. European usage, maybe.'

'Why not come right out and say British?' Frank looked at me unsmilingly. 'What do you say in the Bahamas, Mangan? Headlamps or headlights?' He could not resist needling me.

I shrugged. 'I use them interchangeably. Both usages are valid. We're being penetrated by the American language because most of our tourists are American.'

Billy One yawned. 'Since we have time to spare I'm going home to bed. I want y'all in my office downstairs at ten a.m. Jim, don't forget to have this room debugged. Where are you sleeping tonight, Tom? I don't believe Jack made arrangements.'

'Come home with me,' said Billy. He rubbed his eyes wearily. 'Jesus, but I'm tired.'

13

Tuesday morning, early but not very bright. I had had about three hours' sleep and my body felt as heavy as my spirits, and even the forceful shower in the guest bathroom did not help. Knowing Houston I dressed lightly; it's like living in a permanent sauna and it was fairly steamy even so early in the morning.

Breakfast was on the patio outside the house, a low rambling structure of stone, timber and glass. I do not know if Billy's wife, Barbara, knew anything about the kidnapping of Debbie; she made no reference to it as she served breakfast so I concluded that probably Billy had not told her. It is a characteristic of Texans, and Cunninghams in particular, not to involve their womenfolk.

Over breakfast we talked of the weather, of baseball, and other mundane matters. A couple of times I caught Barbara giving me a sidelong glance and I knew what she was thinking – why was I there and not at Jack's place with Debbie? The gossiping close-knit Cunningham women would know, of course, that the marriage was in trouble, but Barbara was too disciplined to refer to it and hid her curiosity well if not entirely.

After breakfast I went with Billy to his study where he picked up a red telephone and depressed a button. 'Hi, Jo-Ann; anything I ought to know?' I realized he had a direct line to his office in the Cunningham Building. He listened for a while then said abruptly. 'Cancel all that.' Standing ten feet away I was able to hear the cry of expostulation which came from the earphone.

'No, I can't tell you,' he said. 'But it'll be a week. Damn it, don't argue with me, Jo-Ann. Here's what you do. I want to see Harry Pearson of Texas Aviation and Charlie Alvarez of the Gulf Fishing Corporation – both this morning – *not* at the Cunningham Building, some place else. Sure, the Petroleum Club will do fine. You can tell me when you see me –half an hour.'

He put down the telephone and grinned. 'I have a strong-minded secretary – but efficient.' He became serious. 'If we want helicopters and fast boats to be used in the way we want them used I'll have to tell Harry and Charlie the reason. No chopper jockey or boat skipper will do what we want without their bosses' say-so – we may have to skirt the law. So Harry and Charlie have to know. They'll keep their mouths shut, I promise.'

'I don't mind,' I said. 'It's my skin you're protecting. Just so you don't take action before you have Debbie safe.'

'Right,' he said. 'Have you got the clothing Jim wants?'

'All packed.'

'Then let's go downtown.'

Houston.

Not so much a city as a frame of mind – a tribute to the dynamism of American technology. Too far from the sea? Bring the sea fifty miles to the city and make Houston the third biggest port in the United States. Want to produce gasoline? Build seven refineries and produce a flood of fifteen billion gallons a year. Want to go to the moon? Spend ten years, forty billion dollars, and make Houston the nerve centre of the operation. Want to play baseball when it is too hot and steamy to move? Put a roof over a stadium which holds 52,000 people and cool it to a constant 74°F. – cool for Houston – using 7000 tons of air-conditioning machinery. The grass in the stadium won't grow? For Christ's sake, man; design a special plastic grass.

The latest proposal was to roof over the entire business quarter of the city – much simpler than to air-condition individual buildings.

Houston – Baghdad-on-the-Bayou. I hated the place.

We went downtown in Billy's car which he drove with the

casual ease which comes to Americans by second nature, through the air they breathe – conditioned, of course. We went from his house to his office in the Cunningham Building without once taking a breath of the nasty, polluted, natural stuff outside. Billy's secretary, I was interested to note, was a middle-aged lady with a face like a prune. As we passed through the outer office she said quickly, 'Mr Pearson and Mr Alvarez – eleven o'clock – Petroleum Club.'

Without breaking stride Billy said, 'Right. Find Cousin Jim – might be in security.' We went into his office and he picked up a telephone and stabbed a button. 'Pop, we're in and ready to go.' He listened for a moment and his expression changed. 'Oh, God, no!' Pause. 'Yeah, I guess so. Okay.'

He put down the telephone. 'Jack had a heart attack an hour ago. He's being taken to the Texas Medical Center. Frank is with him and Pop is going there now. Of all the times . . .'

'Because of the times,' I said. 'It probably wouldn't have happened if Debbie hadn't been kidnapped. He wasn't looking too good last night.'

He nodded. 'That leaves you, me and Jim to plan and execute this operation. Not enough – I'll draft a couple more.'

Jim came in and Billy told him about Jack. 'Tough,' said Jim. 'Poor old guy.'

'Well, let's get to it,' said Billy. 'Tom's outfit is in that grip there.'

'Fine.' Jim frowned. 'I've been worrying about something. What happens if they strip Tom? His bugged clothes might be going one way and Tom in another direction.'

'That's a chance we have to take,' said Billy.

Jim smiled. 'Not so. I've got something, if Tom will go for it.' He produced a capsule of plastic, about an inch long, three-eighths of an inch in diameter, and with rounded ends. 'You have to swallow it.'

'What!'

'It's a transponder – it returns a signal when interrogated by a pulsed transmitter; not a powerful signal but good enough to get a direction finder on it. It goes into action when the gastric juices work on it, so you swallow it at the last minute.'

Billy inspected it critically. 'Looks like one of those pills they blow down a horse's throat through a tube.'

Jim laughed. 'That's all right if the horse doesn't blow first. How about it, Tom?'

I looked at it distastefully. 'All right – if I have to. Where did you get it?'

'I have a pipeline into the CIA. I borrowed it.'

'Borrowed!' said Billy, grimacing. 'Anyone going to use it afterwards?'

Jim said, 'It's good for thirty-six to forty-eight hours before peristalsis gets rid of it.'

'Just don't crap too much, that's all,' said Billy. 'Anything else?'

'I had the contents of the second letter checked for fingerprints. Result negative. No dice, Billy.'

'Okay,' said Billy. 'I have things to do. Tom, why don't you go along with Jim and watch him ruin your coat and pants? I'm going out to round up some transport.'

So I went with Jim to the security section in the Cunningham Building which meant having my photograph taken in colour by a Polaroid camera and wearing a plastic lapel badge with my name, signature and aforesaid photograph. Jim wore one too, as did everybody else.

I was introduced to an electronics genius called Ramon Rodriguez who displayed and discussed his wares, all miracles of micro-miniaturization. 'Do you wear dentures, Mr Mangan?' he asked.

'No.'

'A pity.' He opened a box and displayed a fine set of false gnashers. 'These are good; they'll transmit anything you say – range over a mile. If you keep your mouth a little open they'll also catch what the guy you're talking to is saying – those two front top incisors are microphones.' He put them away.

'We'll put a bug in the car you'll be driving,' said Jim.

'Two,' said Rodriguez. 'Know anything about bugs, Mr Mangan?'

'Not a thing.'

'There are many kinds. Most fall into one of two categories – active and passive. The active bugs are working all the time, sending out a signal saying, "Here I am! Here I am!" The passive bugs only transmit when asked by a coded impulse, like the dohickey Mr Cunningham showed me this morning.'

Jim chuckled. 'The pill.'

'That's to economize on power where space is limited. Those bugs send out an unmodulated signal, either steady or pulsed. When it comes to modulation, a voice transmission, it becomes a little harder. You'll be wired up with every kind of bug we have.'

Rodriguez put a familiar-looking box on the bench. 'Pack of cigarettes; genuine except for those two in the back right corner. Don't try to light those or the sparks will fly.' Something metallic went next to the cigarette pack. 'Stick-pin for your necktie – will pick up a conversation and transmit it a quarter-mile. Belt to hold up your pants – bug in buckle, but will transmit a mile because we have more room to play with. Try to face the man you're talking with, Mr Mangan.'

'I'll remember that.'

Two identical objects joined the growing heaps. 'These go in the heels of your shoes. This one sends a steady signal so we can get a direction finder on it. But this one has a pressure transducer – every time you take a pace it sends out a beep. If you're being hustled along on foot we'll know it – we might even be able to calculate how fast. And if it stops we know you're static – if you're not in an automobile, that is. Now, this is important. You know the rhythm of shave-and-a-haircut?'

I smiled and knocked it out with my knuckles on the bench.

'Good. If you're being taken for a ride tap it out once for a car, twice for a boat, three times for an airplane. Repeat at five minute intervals. Got that?'

I repeated his instructions. 'Just tap it out with my heel? Which one?'

'The right heel.' Rodriguez picked up my jacket and trousers. 'I'm giving you two antennae – one in your coat sewn into the back seam, the other in your pants. Don't worry; they won't show. And there'll be a few other things – I'll give you a new billfold and there'll be the coins in your pockets – anything I can cook up between now and Thursday. You don't have to know about them, just be glad they're there.'

The Cunninghams were going to a great deal of trouble and it occurred to me that if they had all this stuff ready to hand then they were probably up to their necks in industrial espionage. I wondered if they had used it on me in the course of their admitted investigations.

Rodriguez looked at his watch. 'I have to make a phone call. I won't be long, Mr Cunningham.' He walked away into his office.

Jim said, 'That man once said he could make a working microphone out of three carpenter's nails, a foot of copper wire, and a power cell. I bet he couldn't. I lost.' He laughed. 'He even made his own power cell from a stack of pennies and nickels, a piece of blotting paper and some vinegar.'

'He seems a good man.'

'The best,' said Jim, and added casually, 'Ex-CIA.'

I looked longingly at the packet of cigarettes on the bench. I had run out and I knew Jim did not smoke. 'I'll be back in a minute,' I said. I remembered there was a stand in the lobby of the Cunningham Building which sold cigarettes among other things, so I went down in the elevator to street level.

There was a short line waiting for service but I bought two packets of cigarettes within minutes. As I turned, opening one of them, I bumped heavily into a man. 'Watch it, buster!' he said nastily, and walked past me.

I shrugged and headed towards the elevator. In a climate like that of Houston anyone was entitled to be short-tempered. I stood waiting for the elevator and looked at the half-opened packet in my hand while absently rubbing my thigh. The health warning on the side of the packet shimmered strangely.

'You okay, mister?' The elevator starter was looking at me oddly.

I said distinctly, 'I'm per-fect-ly all right.'

'Hey!' He grabbed my arm as I swayed. Everything was swimming and my legs felt like putty. Slowly and majestically I toppled forward like a falling tree, and yelled 'Timber!' at the top of my voice. Oddly enough, not a sound passed my lips.

The next thing I knew was that I was being turned over. I looked at the ceiling and heard someone say, 'Just fell down right there.' Someone else said, 'A drunk, I guess.' And again: 'At this time of day!'

I tried to speak. My brain worked all right in a somewhat crazy manner – but there seemed to be interference with the connection to my voice box. I experimented with 'Mary had a little lamb', but nothing came through. It was weird.

From a distance a man said, 'I'm a doctor – let me through.' He bent over me and I stared up at him, past a big nose and into his eyes, yellow flecks in green irises. He felt my pulse then put his hand over my heart. 'This man is having a heart attack,' he said. 'He must be taken to hospital immediately.' He looked up. 'Someone help me – my car is outside.'

I was lifted bodily and carried to the entrance, shouting loudly that this was no bloody heart attack and this was no bloody doctor, either. My brain told me I was shouting loudly but not a sound did I hear from my lips, and neither could I move a muscle. They put me on the back seat of a limousine and off we went. The man in the front passenger seat twisted around and took my limp arm. I saw the flash of glass and felt the prick of a needle, and soon the bright world began to go grey.

Just before I passed out I reflected that all the Cunninghams' organization and the painstaking work of Ramon Rodriguez was going for nothing. The kidnappers had jumped the gun.

14

It was dark when I woke up. I was lying on my back and staring into blackness and feeling no pain, at least not much. When I stirred I found that I was naked – lying on a bed and covered by a thin sheet – and my left thigh ached a little. I turned my head and saw a rectangular patch of dim light which, when I propped myself up on one elbow, appeared to be a window.

I tossed aside the sheet, swung my legs out of bed, and tentatively stood up. I seemed to be in no immediate danger of falling so I took a step towards the window, and then another. The window was covered with a coarse-fibred cloth which I drew aside. There was nothing much to see outside, just the darker patches of trees silhouetted against a dark sky. From the west came the faint loom of the setting moon. There were noises, though; the chirping of cicadas and the distant, deeper croaking of bull-frogs.

There were bars on the window.

The breeze which blew through the unglazed window was warm and smelled of damp and rotting vegetation. Even so, I shivered as I made my way back to the bed, and I was glad to lie down again. That brief journey had taken the strength out of me; maybe I could have lasted two seconds with Mohammed Ali, but I doubted it. I pulled the sheet over my body and went back to sleep.

When next I woke I felt better. Perhaps it was because of the sunlight slanting through the room, making a yellow patch at the bottom of the bed. The window was now uncurtained and next to the bed a tray was laid on a table which contained a pitcher of orange juice, an empty glass, a pile of thick-cut bread slices, a pot of butter and a crude wooden spatula with which to spread it.

The orange juice went down well and my spirits rose when I saw the pot of honey which had been hidden behind the pitcher. I breakfasted stickily, sitting on the edge of the bed with the sheet draped around me, and doing an inventory of the room. Against one wall was another table holding a basin and a water jug together with a piece of kitchen soap. And there was a chair with clothing draped over it – not mine. And that, apart from the bed and the bedside table, was all.

After breakfast I washed, but first looked through the uncurtained window. There was nothing much to see – just trees baking under a hot sun. The air was humid and dank and smelled of vegetable corruption.

After washing I turned to the clothing – a pair of jeans, a tee-shirt with the words HOUSTON COUGARS emblazoned across the chest, and a pair of dirty white sneakers. As I was putting on the jeans I examined the bruise on the outside of my thigh; it was livid and there seemed to be a small pin hole in the middle of it. It did not hurt much so I put on the jeans, then the shirt, and sat on the bed to put on the shoes. And there I was – dressed and almost in my right mind.

I might have hammered on the door then, demanding in highfalutin terms to be released, and what the devil is the meaning of this, sir? I refrained. My captors would see me in their own time and I needed to think. There is a manoeuvre in rugby football known as 'selling the dummy', a feint in which the ball goes in an unexpected direction. The Cunningham family had been sold the dummy and I would bet that Billy Cunningham would be spitting bullets.

I mentally reviewed the contents of the first and second ransom letters. The object of the first was to get me to Houston. The second was so detailed and elaborate that no one thought it would be the dummy we were being sold. It was a fake all the way through.

One thing was certain: the Cunninghams would be incensed beyond measure. To kidnap a Cunningham was bad enough, but to add a double-cross was to add insult to injury. Right at that moment the Cunningham Building would be like a nest of disturbed rattlesnakes; all hell would be breaking loose and, perhaps, this time they would bring in the police. Not that it would help me, I thought glumly, or Debbie.

Which brought me to Debbie. Was she here or not? And where the devil was here? There was a frustrating lack of information. I went to the window again and looked out through the bars and again saw nothing but trees. I tested the bars; steel set firmly in concrete, and immoveable.

I turned at a metallic noise at the door. The first man to enter held a shotgun pointing at my belly. He was dressed in jeans and a checkered shirt open almost to the waist, and had a lined grim face. He took one pace inside the room and then stepped sideways, keeping the gun on me. 'On the bed.' The barrel of the gun jerked fractionally.

I backed away and sidled sideways like a crab to the bed. The muzzle of that gun looked like an army cannon.

Another man came into the room and closed the door behind him. He was dressed in a lightweight business suit and could have been anybody. He had hair, two eyes and a mouth, with a nose in the middle – a face-shaped face. He was nobody I had seen before or, if I had, I had not noticed him. He was my most forgettable character.

'Good morning, Mr Mangan. I hope you had a quiet night and slept well.'

English – not American, I thought. I said, 'Where's my wife?'

'First things first.' He gestured sideways. 'This man is armed with an automatic shotgun loaded with buckshot. Anything that will kill a deer will kill a man – men die more easily. At ten feet he couldn't miss; he could put five rounds into you in five seconds. I think you'd be chopped in half.'

'Two seconds,' said the shotgunner flatly and objectively.

I was wrong about him being English; at the back of those perfectly modulated tones was the flavour of something I could not pin down. I repeated, 'Where's my wife?'

'She's quite safe,' he said reassuringly.

'Where? Here?'

He shrugged. 'No harm in you knowing. Yes, she's here.'

'Prove it. I want to see her.'

He laughed. 'My dear Mr Mangan, you are in no position to make demands. Although . . .' He was pensive for a moment. 'Yes, my dear chap, that might be a good idea. You shall see her as soon as we have finished our initial conversation. I trust you are fit and well. No ill effects from the curious treatment we were forced to administer?'

'I'm all right,' I said shortly.

He produced a small cylinder from his pocket and held it up; it looked like a shotgun cartridge. 'It was one of these that did the trick. Issued to NATO soldiers for use in nerve-gas attacks. You put one end against the arm or leg – so – and push. A spring-loaded plunger forces a hypodermic needle right through the clothing and into the flesh, then injects atropine. I admit that the needle going through clothing is not hygienic; there's a small risk of tetanus – but that is preferable to heart failure from nerve gas, so the risk is acceptable. I don't think you even felt the prick of the needle.'

'I didn't.'

'Of course we used something other than atropine,' he said. 'A muscle relaxant derived from curare, I believe; used when giving electric shock therapy. You're lucky I wasn't a Middle Eastern guerilla; they use something totally lethal. Very useful for street assassinations.'

'Very interesting,' I said. 'But I can do without the technical lecture.'

'It has a point,' he said, and laughed. 'Just like the needle. It's to tell you we're most efficient. Remember that efficiency, Mr Mangan, should you be thinking of trying anything foolish.'

'Who are you?'

'Does it matter?' He waved his hand. 'Very well, if you must call me something call me . . . Robinson.'

'Okay, Robinson. Tell me why.'

'Why you're here? Rest assured I shall do so, but in my own time.' He looked at a point over my head. 'I was about to begin your interrogation immediately, but I have changed my mind. Don't you think it is a mark of efficiency to be flexible?'

He had a formal, almost pedantic, way of speech which fitted well with the tone of the ransom letters, and could very well have typed 'headlamps' instead of 'headlights'. I said, 'I couldn't give a damn. I want to see my wife.'

His gaze returned to me. 'And so you shall, my dear chap. What is more, you shall have the privilege of seeing her alone so that you may talk freely. I am sure she will be able to tell you many things of which you are, as yet, unaware. And vice versa. It will make my later interrogation so much easier – for both of us.'

'Robinson, quit waffling and get her.'

He studied me and smiled. 'Quite a one for making demands, aren't you? And in the vernacular, too. But I shall accede to . . . er . . . shall we call it your request?'

He put his hand behind him, opened the door, and backed out. The man with the shotgun went out, gun last, and the door closed. I heard it lock.

I thought about it. The man with the shotgun was local, a Texan. He had spoken only a total of five words but the accent was unmistakeable. Robinson was something else. Those cultured tones, those rolling cadences, were the product of a fairly long residence in England, and at a fairly high social level.

And yet . . . and yet . . . there was something else. As a Bahamian, class differences, as betrayed by accent, had been a matter of indifference to me, but my time in England had taught me that the English take it seriously, so I had learned the nuances. It is something hard to explain to our American cousins. But Robinson did not ring a true sound – there was a flaw in him.

I looked with greater interest at my prison. The walls were of concrete blocks set in hard mortar and whitewashed. There was no ceiling so I could look up into the roof which was pitched steeply and built of rough timbers – logs with the bark still on – and covered with corrugated iron. The only door was in a gable end.

From the point of view of escape the wall was impossible. I had no metal to scrape the mortar from between the blocks, not even a belt buckle; and they had carefully not put a knife on the tray with which to spread the butter, just a flat piece of wood. As Robinson had said – efficiency. A careful examination of the furniture told me that I was probably in a rural area. The whole lot had not a single nail in them, but were held together by wooden pegs.

Not that I was intending to escape – not then. But I was looking at the roof speculatively when I heard someone at the door. I sat on the bed and waited, and the door opened and Debbie was pushed in, then it slammed behind her quickly.

She staggered, regained her balance, then looked at me unbelievingly. '*Tom*! Oh, Tom!' The next moment she was in my arms, dampening the front of my Houston Cougars' tee-shirt.

It took some time to get her settled down. She was incoherent with a mixture of relief, remorse, passion and, when she understood that I, too, was a prisoner, amazement, consternation and confusion. 'But how did you get here?' she demanded. 'To Texas, I mean. And why?'

'I was drawn into it by bait,' I said. 'You were the bait. We were all fooled.'

'The family,' she said. 'How are they?'

'Bearing up under the strain.' There were a few things I was not going to tell Debbie. One was that her father had just suffered a heart attack. Others would doubtless occur to me. 'How were you snatched?'

'I don't know. One minute I was looking in the window of a store on Main Street, then I was here.'

Probably Robinson had used his NATO gadget; but it did not matter. 'And where is here? You're the local expert.'

She shook her head. 'I don't know. Somewhere on the coast, I think.'

I disentangled myself, stood up, and turned to look at her. The dress she was wearing certainly had not come from a plushy Main Street store – –it was more reminiscent of Al Capp's Dogpatch and went along with my jeans and tee-shirt. From where I stood it seemed to be the only thing she was wearing. 'All right, Daisy-Mae, has anyone told you why you were kidnapped?'

'Daisy-M . . .?' She caught on and looked down at herself, then involuntarily put a hand to her breast. 'They took my clothes away.'

'Mine, too.'

'I must look terrible.'

'A sight for sore eyes.' She looked up at me and flushed, and we were both silent for a moment. Then we both started to talk at the same time, and both stopped simultaneously.

'I've been a damned fool, Tom,' she said.

'This is not the time – nor place – to discuss our marital problems,' I said. 'There are better things to do. Do you know why you were kidnapped?'

'Not really. He's been asking all sorts of questions about you.'

'What sort of questions?'

'About what you were doing. Where you'd been. Things like that. I told him I didn't know – that I'd left you. He didn't believe me. He kept going on and on about you.' She shivered suddenly. 'Who is this man? What's happening to us, Tom?'

Good questions; unfortunately I had no answers. Debbie looked scared and I did not blame her. That character with the automatic shotgun had nearly scared the jeans off me and I had just arrived. Debbie had been here at least three days.

I said gently, 'Have they ill-treated you?'

She shook her head miserably. 'Not physically. But it's the way some of them look at me.' She shivered again. 'I'm scared, Tom. I'm scared half to death.'

I sat down and put my arm around her. 'Not to worry. How many are there?'

'I've seen four.'

'Including a man whose name isn't Robinson? An English smoothie with a plummy voice?'

'He's the one who asks the questions. The others don't say much – not to me. They just look.'

'Let's get back to these questions. Was there anything specific he wanted to know?'

Debbie frowned. 'No. He asked general questions in a roundabout way. It's as though he wants to find out something without letting me know what it is. Just endless questions about you. He wanted to know what you'd told the police. He said you seemed to spend a lot of time in the company of Commissioner Perigord. I said I didn't know about anything you might have told Perigord, and that I'd only met Perigord once, before we were married.' She paused. 'There was one thing. He asked when I'd left you, and I told him. He then commented that it would be the day after you'd found Kayles.'

I sat upright. '*Kayles*! He mentioned him by name?'

'Yes. I thought he'd ask me about Kayles, but he didn't. He went off on another track, asking when we were married. He asked if I'd known Julie.'

'Did he, by God! What did you say?'

'I told him the truth; that I'd met her briefly but hadn't known her well.'

'What was his reaction to that?'

'He seemed to lose interest. You call him Robinson – is that his name?'

'I doubt it; and I don't think he's English, either.' I was thinking of the connection between Robinson and Kayles and sorting out possible relationships. Was Robinson the boss of a drug-running syndicate? If so then why should he kidnap Debbie and me? It did not make much sense.

Debbie said, 'I don't like him, and I don't like the way he talks. The others frighten me, but he frightens me in a different way.'

'What way?'

'The others are ignorant white trash – corn-crackers – but they look at me as a woman. Robinson looks at me as an object, as though I'm not a human being at all.' She broke down into sobs. 'For God's sake, Tom; who are these people? What have you been doing to get mixed up in this?'

'Take it easy, my love,' I said. 'Hush, now.'

She quietened again and after a while said in a small voice, 'It's a long time since you've called me that.'

'What?'

'Your love.'

I was silent for a moment, then said heavily, 'A pity. I ought to have remembered to do it more often.' I was thinking of a divorce lawyer who had told me that in a breaking marriage there were invariably faults on both sides. I would say he was right.

Presently Debbie sat up and dried her eyes on the hem of her dress. 'I must look a mess.'

'You look as beautiful as ever. Cheer up, there's still hope. Your folks will be skinning Texas to find us. I wouldn't like to be anyone who gets on the wrong side of Billy One.'

'It's a big state,' she said sombrely.

The biggest – barring Alaska – and I could not see the Cunninghams finding us in a hurry. The thought that chilled me was that Robinson had made no attempt at disguise. True, his face was not memorable in the normal way, but I would certainly remember it from now on, and so would Debbie. The rationale behind that sent a grue up my spine – the only way he could prevent future identification was by killing us. We were never intended to be released.

It was cold comfort to know that the Cunninghams were roused and that sooner or later, with the backing of the Cunningham Corporation, Robinson would eventually be run down and due vengeance taken. Debbie and I would know nothing of that.

Debbie said, 'I'm sorry about the way I behaved.'

'Skip it,' I said. 'It doesn't matter now.'

'But you could be a son of a bitch at times – a real cold bastard. Sometimes you'd act as though I wasn't there at all. I began to think I was the invisible woman.'

'There was no one else,' I said. 'There never was.'

'No one human.'

'Nor a ghost, Debbie,' I said. 'I accepted Julie's death a long time ago.'

'I didn't mean that – I meant your goddamn job.' She

looked up. 'But I ought to have known because I'm a Cunningham.' She smiled slightly. '"For men must work and women must weep." And the Cunningham men do work. I thought it might be different with you.'

'And the sooner it's over, the sooner to sleep.' I completed the quotation, but only in my mind; it was too damned apposite to say aloud. 'Why should it have been different? The Cunningham men haven't taken out a patent on hard work. But maybe I did go at it too hard.'

'No,' she said thoughtfully. 'You did what you had to, as all men do. The pity is that I didn't see it. Looking back, I know there's a lot I didn't see. Myself, for one thing. My God, you married an empty-headed ninny.'

That was a statement it would be politic not to answer. I said, 'You had your problems.'

'And piled them on your back. I swear to God, Tom, that things will be different. I'll make an effort to change if you will. We've both, in our own ways, been damned fools.'

I managed a smile. The likelihood that we would have a future together was minimal. 'It's a bargain,' I said.

She held out her hand and drew me down to her. 'So seal it.' I put my hands on her and discovered that, indeed, she wore nothing beneath the shift. She said softly, 'It won't hurt him.'

So we made love, and it was not just having sex. There is quite a difference.

15

Robinson gave us about three hours together. It was difficult to judge time because neither of us had a watch and all I could do was to estimate the hour by the angle of the sun. I think we had three hours before there was a rattle at the door and the Texan came in, gun first.

He stepped sideways, as before, and Robinson came in with another man who could have been the Texan's brother and possibly was. He was armed with a pistol. Robinson surveyed us and said benignly, 'So nice to see young people getting together again. I hope you have acquainted your husband with the issue at hand, Mrs Mangan.'

'She doesn't know what the hell you want,' I said. 'And neither do I. This is bloody ridiculous.'

'Well, we'll talk about that later,' he said. 'I'm afraid I must part you lovebirds. Come along, Mrs Mangan.'

Debbie looked appealingly at me, but I shook my head gently. 'You'd better go.' I could see the man's finger tightening on the trigger of the shotgun.

And so she was taken from me and escorted from the room by the man with the pistol. 'We won't starve you,' said Robinson. 'That should be an earnest of my good intentions – should you doubt them.'

He stood aside and a woman came in with a tray which she exchanged for the breakfast tray. She was a worn woman with sagging breasts and hands gnarled and twisted with rheumatics. I pointed to the pitcher and basin on the other side of the room. 'What about some fresh water?'

'I see no reason why not. What about it, Leroy?'

The Texan said, 'Belle, git th' water.'

She took the pitcher and basin outside, and I had a couple more names, for what they were worth. Robinson looked at the tray from which steam rose gently. 'Not the best of cuisine, I'm afraid, but edible . . . edible. And it's very much a case of fingers being made before forks. I think you'll need the water.'

I said, 'What about coming to the point?'

He wagged a finger at me. 'Later . . . I said later. There is something which I must think over rather carefully. There's really plenty of time, my dear chap.'

Belle came back, put the basin on the table and stood the pitcher in it. When she left Robinson said, '*Bon appetit,*' and backed out, followed by Leroy.

The meal was fish or, rather, wet cotton wadding mixed with spiky bones. I ate with my fingers and the flesh tasted of mud. When I had eaten rather less than my fill, but could stomach no more, I walked over to the water pitcher and was about to pour water into the basin to wash my slimy hands when I stopped and looked at it thoughtfully. I did not pour the water but dabbled my hands in the pitcher, then wiped them dry on my jeans.

The pitcher held more than two gallons. That, plus the weight of the pitcher itself, would be about twenty-five pounds. I was beginning to get ideas. I went back to the bed, spread butter on a thick slice of bread, and munched while looking at the pitcher, hoping it would tell me what to do. The first faint tendrils of an idea began to burgeon.

Robinson came back about two hours later with his usual bodyguard, and Leroy took his position just to the left of the door. Robinson closed the door and leaned on it. 'I'm sorry to learn of your marital troubles, Mr Mangan,' he said suavely. 'But from what I heard I gather you are on your way to solving them.' He smiled at my startled expression. 'Oh, yes, I listened to your conversation with your wife with great interest.'

I cursed silently. Ramon Rodriguez had shown me what could be done with bugs, and I might have known that Robinson would have the place wired. 'So you're a voyeur, too,' I said acidly.

He sniggered. 'I even recorded your love-play. Though not

my main interest it was very entertaining. If set to music it could hit the top twenty.'

'You bastard!'

'Now, now,' he said chidingly. 'That's not the way to speak when you're at the wrong end of a gun. Let us come to more serious matters – the case of Jack Kayles. I noted when listening to the tape that you showed interest when your wife mentioned his name. My interest is in how you tracked him down. I would dearly like to know the answer to that.'

I said nothing but just looked at him, and he clicked his tongue. 'I advise you to be cooperative,' he said. 'In your own interest – and that of your wife.'

'I'll answer that if you tell me why he killed my family.'

Robinson regarded me thoughtfully. 'No harm in that, I suppose. He killed your family because he is a stupid man; how stupid I am only now beginning to find out. In fact, it is essential that I now find the measure of his stupidity, and that is why you are here.'

He took a pace forward and stood with his hands in his pockets. 'Kayles was supposed to sail from the Bahamas to Miami in his own boat. There was a deadline, but Kayles was having problems – something technical to do with boats.' Robinson waved the technicality aside. 'At any rate he found he could not meet the deadline. When he heard that a skipper needed a crewman to help take a boat to Miami the next day he jumped at the chance. Do you follow me?'

'So far.'

'Now, Kayles was carrying something with him, something important.' Robinson waved his hand airily. 'There is no necessity for you to know what it was. As I say, he is stupid and he let your skipper find it, so Kayles killed him with the knife he invariably carries. His intention was to conveniently lose that poor black man overboard but, unfortunately, the killing was seen by your little girl and then . . .' He sighed and shrugged. '. . . then one thing led to another. Now, Mr Mangan, I don't mind telling you that I was very angry about this – very angry, indeed. It was a grievous setback to my plans. Disposing of your boat was a great problem, to begin with.'

'You son of a bitch,' I said bitterly. 'You're talking about my wife, my daughter and my friend.' I stuck my finger out at him. 'And you've no need to be coy about what Kayles was carrying. It was a consignment of cocaine.'

Robinson stared at me. 'Dear me! You do jump to conclusions. Now, I wonder . . .' He broke off and looked up at the roof, deep in thought. After a while his gaze returned to me. 'Well, we can take that up later, can't we? I've answered your question, Mangan. Now answer mine. How did you trace the idiot?'

I saw no reason not to answer, but I was becoming increasingly chilled. If Robinson saw no reason not to gossip about three murders then it meant that he thought he was talking to a dead man, or a man as good as dead. I said, 'I had a photograph of him,' and explained how it had come about.

'Ah!' said Robinson. 'So it *was* the little girl's camera. That really worried Kayles. He was pretty sure she had taken his photograph, but he couldn't find the camera on your boat. Of course, it was a big boat and he couldn't search every nook and cranny, but it still worried him. So he solved his problem – as he thought – by sinking your boat, camera and all. But it wasn't there, was it? You had it. I suppose you gave the photograph to the police.'

'There'll be a copy of it in every police office in the Bahamas,' I said grimly.

'Oh dear!' said Robinson. 'That's bad, very bad. Isn't it, Leroy?'

Leroy grunted, but said nothing. The shotgun aimed at me had not quivered by as much as a millimetre.

Robinson took his hands from his pockets and clasped them in front of him. 'Well, to return to the main thrust of our conversation. You tracked Kayles to the Jumentos. How did you do that? I must know.'

'By his boat.'

'But it was disguised.'

'Not well enough.'

'I see. I told you the man is an idiot. Well, the idiot escaped and reported back to me. He told me a strange story which I found hard to credit. He told me that you knew all my plans. Now, isn't that odd?'

'Remarkable, considering that I don't know who the hell you are.'

'I thought so, too, but Kayles was most circumstantial. Out it all came, information which even he was not supposed to know about – and all quite accurate.'

'And I told him all this?' I said blankly.

'Not quite. He eavesdropped while you were talking to the man, Ford. I must say I was quite perturbed; so much so that I acted hastily, which is uncharacteristic of me. I ordered your death, Mr Mangan, but you fortuitously escaped.' Robinson shrugged. 'However, the four Americans were quite a bonus – I believe the Securities and Exchange Commission is causing quite a stir on Wall Street.'

'The four Am . . .' I broke off. 'You caused that crash? You killed Bill Pinder?'

Robinson raised an eyebrow. 'Pinder?' he enquired.

'The pilot, damn you!'

'Oh, the pilot,' he said uninterestedly. 'Well, by then I had time to think more clearly. I needed to interrogate you in a place of my own choosing – and so here you are. It would have been difficult getting near to you on Grand Bahama; for one thing, you were tending to live in Commissioner Perigord's pocket. But that worried me for other reasons; I want to know how much information you have passed on to him. I must know, because that will influence my future actions.'

'I don't know what you're talking about,' I said, wishing I did.

'I will give you time to think about it; to think and remember. But first I will do you a favour.' He turned and opened the door, saying to Leroy, 'Watch him.'

A couple of minutes later the pistol carrier came in. He jerked his head at Leroy. 'He wants you.' Leroy went out and I was left facing the muzzle of a pistol instead of a shotgun. Not a great improvement.

Presently Robinson came back. He looked at me sitting on the bed, and said, 'Come to the window and see what I have for you.'

'The only favour I want from you is to release my wife.'

'I'm afraid not,' he said. 'Not for the moment. But come here, Mangan, and watch.'

I joined him at the window and the man with the pistol moved directly behind me, standing about six feet away. There was nothing to be seen outside that was new, just the trees and hot sunlight. Then Leroy came into view with another man. They were both laughing.

'Kayles!' I said hoarsely.

'Yes, Kayles,' said Robinson.

Leroy was still carrying the shotgun. He stooped to tie the lace of his shoe, gesturing for Kayles to carry on. He let Kayles get ten feet ahead and then shot him in the back from his kneeling position. He shot again, the two reports coming so closely together that they sounded as one, and Kayles pitched forward violently to lie in a crumpled heap.

'There,' said Robinson. 'The murderer of your family has been executed.'

I looked at Kayles and saw that Robinson was right – buckshot does terrible things to a man's body. Kayles had been ripped open and his spine blown out. A pool of blood was soaking into the sandy earth.

It had happened so suddenly and unexpectedly that I was numbed. Leroy walked to Kayles's body and stirred it with his foot, then he reloaded the shotgun and walked back the way he had come and so out of sight.

'It was not done entirely for your benefit,' said Robinson. 'From being an asset Kayles had become a liability. Anyone connected with me who has his photograph on the walls of police stations is dangerous.' He paused. 'Of course, in a sense the demonstration *was* for your benefit. An example – it could happen to you.'

I looked out at the body of Kayles and said, 'I think you're quite mad.'

'Not mad – just careful. Now you are going to tell me what I want to know. How did you get wind of what I am up to, and how much have you told Perigord?'

'I've told the police nothing, except about Kayles,' I said. 'I know nothing at all about what other crazy ideas you might have. I know nothing about you, and I wish I knew less.'

'So do I believe you?' he mused. 'I think not. I can't trust you to be honest with me. So what to do about it? I could operate on you with a blunt knife, but you could be stubborn. You could even know nothing, as you say, so the exercise would be futile. Even if your wife saw the operation with the blunt knife there would be no profit in it. You see, I believe she knows nothing and so torturing you could not induce her to speak the truth. In fact, anything she might say I would discount as a lie to save you.'

I said nothing. My mouth was dry and parched because I knew what was coming and dreaded it.

Robinson spoke in tones of remote objectivity, building up his ramshackle structure of crazy logic. 'No,' he said. 'We can discard that, so what is left? Mrs Mangan is left, of course. Judging from the touching scene of reconciliation this morning it is quite possible that you still have an attachment for her. So, we operate on Mrs Mangan with a blunt knife – or its equivalent. Women have soft bodies, Mr Mangan. I think you will speak truly of what you know.'

I nearly went for him then and there, but the gunman said sharply, 'Don't!' and I recoiled from the gun.

'You son of a bitch!' I said, raging. 'You utter bastard!'

Robinson waved his hand. 'No compliments, I beg of you. You will have time to think of this – to sleep on it. I regret we can waste no more good food on you. But that is all for the best – the digestion of food draws blood from the brain and impedes the thought processes. I want you in a condition in which you think hard and straight, Mr Mangan. I will ask you more questions tomorrow.'

He went out, followed by the gunman, and the door closed and clicked locked, leaving me in such despair as I had never known in my life.

16

The first thing I did when I had recovered the power of purposive thought was to find and rip out that damned microphone. A futile gesture, of course, because it had already fulfilled Robinson's purpose. It was not even very well hidden, not nearly as subtle as any of Rodriguez's gadgets. It was an ordinary microphone such as comes with any standard tape recorder and was up in the rafters taped to a tie-beam, and the wire led through a small hole in the roof. Not much sense in it, but it gave me savage satisfaction in the smashing of it.

As I hung from the tie-beam, my feet dangling above the floor preparatory to dropping, I looked at the door at the end of the room and then at the roof above it. My first thought was that if I was up in the roof when Leroy came in I might drop something on to his head. That idea was discarded quickly because I had seen that every time he entered he had swung the door wide so that it lay against the wall. That way he made sure that, if I was not in sight, then I would not be hiding behind the door. If he did not see me in that bare room he would know that the only place I could be was up in the roof, and he would take the appropriate nasty action.

If there was anyone watching what I did next he would have thought I had gone around the bend. I stood with my back to the door, imitating the action of a tiger – the tiger being Leroy. I had no illusions about him; he was as deadly as any tiger – possibly more dangerous than Robinson. I do not think that Robinson was the quintessential man of action; he was more the cerebral type and thought too much about his actions. Leroy, however vacant in the head, would act automatically on the necessity for action.

So I imitated Leroy coming in. He booted the door wide

open; I had to imagine that bit. The door swung and slammed against the wall. Leroy looked inside and made sure I was on the bed. Satisfied he stepped inside, fixing me with the shotgun. I stood, cradling an imaginary shotgun, looking at an imaginary me on the bed.

Immediately behind came Robinson. In order that he could enter I had to cease blocking the doorway, so I took a step sideways, still holding the gun on the bed. That was what Leroy had done every time – the perfect bodyguard. I looked above my head towards the roof and was perfectly satisfied with what I saw.

Then I studied the water pitcher and basin. I had seen a piece of a similar basin before. As part of my education I had studied the English legal system and, on one Long Vacation, I had taken the opportunity of attending a Crown Court to see what went on. There had been a case of a brawl in a seamen's hostel, the charge being attempted murder. I could still visualize the notes I took. A doctor was giving evidence:

Prosecutor: Now, Doctor, tell me; how many pints of blood did you transfuse into this young man?

Doctor: Nine pints in the course of thirty hours.

Prosecutor: Is that not a great quantity of blood?

Doctor: Indeed, it is.

Judge (breaking in): How many pints of blood are there in a man?

Doctor: I would say that this man, taking into account his weight and build, would have eight pints of blood in him.

Judge: And you say you transfused nine pints. Surely, the blood must have been coming out of him faster than you were putting it in?

Doctor (laconically): It was.

The weapon used had been a pie-shaped fragment of such a basin as this, broken in the course of the brawl, picked up at random, and used viciously. It had been as sharp as a razor.

I next turned my attention to the window curtain, a mere flap of sackcloth. I felt the coarse weave and decided it would serve well. It was held in place by thumb tacks which would also be useful, so I ripped it away and spent the rest of the daylight hours separating the fibres rather like a nineteenth-century convict picking oakum.

While I worked I thought of what Robinson wanted. Whatever Kayles had told him was a mystery to me. I went back over the time I had spent with Kayles, trying to remember every word and analysing every nuance. I got nowhere at all and began to worry very much about Debbie.

I slept a little that night, but not much, and what sleep I had was shot with violent dreams which brought me up wide awake and sweating. I was frightened of over-sleeping into the daylight hours because my preparations were not yet complete and I needed at least an hour of light, but I need not have worried – I was open-eyed and alert as the sun rose.

An hour later I was ready – as much as I could be. Balanced on a tie-beam in the roof was the pitcher full of water, held only in place by the spatula with which I had spread my butter. I had greased it liberally so that it would slide away easily at the tug of the string I had made from the sackcloth. The string ran across the roof space, hanging loosely on the beams to a point in the corner above my bed where it dropped close to hand. Lacking a pulley wheel to take care of the right-angle bend I had used two thumb tacks and I hoped they would hold under the strain when I pulled on the string.

The pitcher was just above the place where Leroy usually stood, and I reckoned that a weight of twenty-five pounds dropping six feet vertically on to his head would not do him much good. With Leroy out of action I was fairly confident I could take care of Robinson, especially if I could get hold of the shotgun.

Making my hand weapon had been tricky but fortunately I was aided by an existing crack in the thick pottery of the basin. Afraid of making a noise, and thankful that I had destroyed the microphone, I wrapped the basin in the bed sheet and whacked it hard with a leg I had taken from the table. It had not been difficult to dismantle the table; the wooden pegs were loose with age.

It took six blows to break that damned basin and after each one I paused to listen because I was making a considerable row. On the sixth blow I felt it go and unwrapped the bed sheet to find I had done exactly what I wanted. I had broken a wedge-shaped segment from the basin, exactly like the fortuitous weapon I had seen in that distant courtroom in England. The rim fitted snugly into the palm of my hand and the pointed end projected forward when my arm was by my side. The natural form of use would be an upward and thrusting slash.

Then, after gently pulling on the string to take up the slack I sat on the bed to wait. And wait. And wait.

The psychologists say that time is subjective, which is why watched pots never boil. I now believe them. I do not know whether it would have been better to have had a watch; all I know is that I counted time by the pace of shadows creeping across the floor infinitesimally slowly and by the measured beat of my heart.

Debbie had said there were four of them. That would be Leroy, Robinson, Kayles and the man with the pistol – I did not think Debbie had counted Belle. Kayles was now dead and I reckoned that if the pitcher took care of Leroy and I tackled Robinson I would have a chance. I would have the shotgun by then and only one man to fight – I did not expect trouble from Belle. The only thing which worried me was Leroy's trigger finger; if he was hit on the head very hard there might be a sudden muscular contraction, and I wanted to be out of the way when that shotgun fired.

Time went by. I looked up at the pitcher poised on the beam and worked equations in my head. Accelerating under the force of gravity it would take nearly two-thirds of a second to fall six feet, by which time it would be moving at twenty-two feet a second – say, fifteen miles an hour. It might seem silly but that is what I did – I worked out the damned equations. There was nothing else to do.

The door opened with a bang and the man who came in was not Leroy but the other man. He had the shotgun, though. He stood in the doorway and just looked at me, the gun at the ready. Robinson was behind him but did not come into the room. 'All right,' he said. 'What did you tell Perigord?'

'I still don't know what you're talking about.'

'I'm not going to argue,' he said. 'I'm done with that. Watch him, Earl. If you have to shoot, make sure it's at his legs.'

He went away. Earl closed the door and leaned his back against it, covering me with the shotgun. It was all going wrong – he was in the wrong place. A break in the pattern was ruining the plan.

I said, 'What did he say your name was?' My mouth was dry.

'Earl.' The barrel of the shotgun lowered a fraction.

I slid sideways on the bed about a foot, going towards him. 'How much is he paying you?'

'None of your damn business.'

Another foot. 'I think it is. Maybe I could pay better.'

'You reckon?'

'I know.' I moved up again, nearly to the end of the bed. 'Let's talk about it.'

I was getting too close. He stepped sideways. 'Get back or I'll blow yo' haid off.'

'Sure.' I retreated up the bed to my original position. 'I'm certain I could pay better.' I was cheering silently because friend Earl had been manoeuvred into the right place. I leaned back casually against the wall and felt behind me for the string. 'Like to talk about it?'

'Nope.'

I groped and could not find the bloody string. The pottery knife was hidden by my body ready to be grasped by my right hand, but the string had to be tugged with my left hand, and not too obviously, either. I had to be casual and in an apparently easy posture, an appearance hard to maintain as I groped behind me.

As my fingertips touched the string there came a scream from outside, full-throated and ending in a bubbling wail. All my nerves jumped convulsively and Earl jerked the gun warningly. 'Steady, mister!' He grinned, showing brown teeth. 'Just Leroy havin' his fun. My turn next.'

Debbie screamed again, a cry full of agony. 'Christ damn you!' I whispered and got my index finger hooked around the string.

'Let's have your hands in sight,' said Earl. 'Both of 'em.'

'Sure.' I put my left hand forward, showing it to him empty – but I had tugged that string.

I dived forward just as the shotgun blasted. I think Earl had expected me to move up the bed as I had before, but I went at right-angles to that expectation. My shoulder hit the ground with a hell of a thump and I rolled over, struggling to get up before he could get in a second shot. There was no second shot. As I scooped up the fallen shotgun I saw that nearly 600 foot-pounds of kinetic energy had cracked his skull as you would crack an egg with a spoon. A fleeting backward glimpse showed the mattress of the bed ripped to pieces by the buckshot.

I had no time for sightseeing. From outside Debbie screamed again in a way that raised the hair on my neck, and there was a shout. I opened the door and nearly ran into a man I had not seen before. He looked at me in astonishment and began to raise the pistol in his right hand. I lashed out at him with my home-made knife and ripped upwards. A peculiar sound came from him as the breath was forcibly ejected from his lungs. He gagged for air and looked down at himself, then dropped the pistol and clapped both hands to his belly to stop his entrails falling out.

As he staggered to one side I ran past him, dropping the pottery blade, and tossed the shotgun from my left hand to my right. It was then I realized I had made a dreadful mistake; this was no small crowd of four people – I could see a dozen, mostly men. I had a hazy impression of clapboard houses with iron roofs arranged around a dusty square, and a mongrel cur was running towards me, snapping and barking. The men were running, too, and there were angry shouts.

Someone fired a gun. I do not know where the bullet went, but I lifted the shotgun and fired back, but nothing happened because I had forgotten to pump a round into the breech. There was another shot so I ducked sideways and ran like hell for the trees I saw in the middle distance. This was no time to stop and argue – I had probably killed two men and their buddies would not be too impressed by exhortations from Robinson to shoot at my legs.

And, as I ran for my life, I thought despairingly of Debbie.

17

They chased me; by God, how they chased me! The trouble was that I did not know the country and they did. And damned funny country it was, too; nothing like anything I had heard of in Texas. Here were no rolling plains and barren lands but foetid, steaming swamp country, lush with over-ripe growth, bogs and streams. I had no woodcraft, not for that kind of country, and my pursuers had probably grown up in the place. I think that had it been the Texas we all know from Hollywood movies I would not have stood a chance, but here was no open ground where a man could see for miles, and that saved me.

At first I concentrated on sheer speed. There would be confusion back there for a while. They would find Earl and the other man and there would be a lot of chatter and waste of time if I knew human nature. Those first few minutes were precious in putting distance between me and my nemesis. As I ran I tried not to think of Debbie. Giving myself up would not help her, and I doubted if I *could* give myself up. Leroy would just as soon kill me as step on a beetle – there had been a close resemblance between him and Earl.

So I pressed on through this strange wilderness, running when I could and glad to slow down when I could not run. I considered myself to be a reasonably fit man, but this was the equivalent of going through an army battle course and I soon found I was not as fit as I thought.

My clothing was not really up to the job as I found when I inadvertently plunged into a brier patch. Sharp spines raked my arms and ripped the tee-shirt, and I cursed when I had to go back again, moving slowly. My shoes, too, were not adequate; the rubber soles slipped on mud and one of the sneakers was loose on my foot and I tended to lose it. This also slowed me down because to lose even one shoe would be fatal; my feet were not hardened enough for me to run barefoot.

And so I plunged on. My problem was that I did not know where I was going; I could just as well be running away from help as towards it. What I wanted to find was a house, preferably with a telephone attached to it. Then I could find out where I was and ring Billy Cunningham so that he could send one of his lovely helicopters for me – to ring the police and then go and beat the bejasus out of Robinson. There were no houses. There were no roads which would lead to houses. There were no telephone lines or power lines I could follow. Nothing but tall stands of trees interspersed with boggy meadows.

After half an hour I stopped to get my breath back. I had travelled about three miles over the ground, I reckoned, and was probably within two miles of the place where I had been held captive. I fiddled with the shotgun and opened the magazine to find out what I had – four full rounds and one fired. I reloaded, pushed one up the spout, and set the safety catch.

Then I heard them, a distant shout followed by another. I went on, splashing up a shallow stream in the hope of leaving no trail. Presently I had to leave the stream because it was curving back in just the direction I did not want to go. I jumped on to the bank and ran south, as near as I could estimate by the sun.

I went through a patch of woodland, tall trees dappling the ground with sun and shadow, then I came to a river. This was no brook or stream; it was wide and fast-flowing, too deep to wade and too dangerous to swim. If I was spotted half-way across I would be an easy target. I ran parallel with it for some way and then came to a wide meadow.

There was no help for it so I ran on and, half-way over, heard a shout behind me and the flat report of a shot. I turned in the waist-high grass and saw two men coming from different angles. Raising the shotgun I aimed carefully, banged off two shots, and had the satisfaction of seeing them drop, both of them. I did not think I had hit them because the shouts were not those of pain, but nobody in his right mind would stand up against buckshot. As they dropped into the cover of the grass I turned and ran on, feeling an intolerable itch between my shoulder blades. I was not in my right mind.

I got to the cover of the trees and looked back. There was movement; the two men were coming on and others were emerging on to the meadow. I ejected a spent cartridge and aimed and fired one shot. Again both men dropped into cover but the rest came on so I turned and ran.

I ran until my lungs were bursting, tripping over rocks and fallen trees, slipping into boggy patches, and cannoning off tree trunks. My feet hurt. In this last mad dash I had lost both shoes and knew I was leaving a bloody trail. I was climbing a rise and the pace was too much. I threw myself to the ground beneath a tree, sobbing with the rasping agony of entraining air into my lungs.

This was it. One last shot and they would be upon me. I put my hand out to where the shotgun had fallen and then stopped because a foot pinned down my wrist. I twisted around and looked up and saw a tall man dressed in faded denims. He had a shotgun under his arm.

'All right,' I said, defeated. 'Get it over with.'

'Get what over with?' He turned his head and looked down the hill at the sound of a shout. 'You in trouble?'

Someone else moved into sight – a busty brunette in skin-tight jeans and a shirt knotted about her middle. I suddenly realized these were not Leroy's people. 'They're going to kill me,' I said, still gasping for breath. 'Chased me to hell and gone.'

He showed polite interest. 'Who are?'

'Don't know all the names. Someone called Leroy. Torturing my wife.'

He frowned. 'Whichaway was this?'

I pointed with my free arm. 'That way.'

He turned to the girl. 'Could be the Ainslees.'

'It is.' She was looking down the hill. 'I see Trace.'

The man released my wrist, then picked up my shotgun. 'Any load in this?'

'One round of buckshot.'

'Enough. Can you climb a tree?' He was looking at my feet.

'I can try.'

'If you admire yo' skin you better climb this tree,' he advised. He tossed my shotgun to the girl. 'Over there, behind that rock. Watch my signal.'

'Okay, Pop.'

The man gave me a boost into the tree. For a skinny old man he was surprisingly strong. 'Stay on the upslope side an' keep yo' haid down.' I managed the rest by myself and got lost in the leafy branches. I could not see down the hill but I had a good view to one side, and I saw him walk out and look towards my pursuers. I heard heavy breathing as someone came up the hill fast, and the old man said sharply, 'Just hold it there, son.'

'Hell, Dade . . .'

'I mean it, Trace. You stop right there.' The shotgun Dade carried was held steady.

Trace raised his voice in a shout. 'Hey, Leroy; here's old Dade.'

There was the sound of more movement and presently Leroy said breathily, 'Hi, there, Dade.'

'What you huntin', Leroy?' asked Dade. 'T'ain't razorback hog 'cause you ain't gotten dogs. An' yo' makin' too much damn noise for deer.'

'Ah'm huntin' one son of a bitch,' said Leroy. He came into sight.

'I don't care what yo' huntin',' said Dade. 'I told you before. If you came huntin' on my land agin I'd kick yo' ass. I don't care if yo' huntin' a man or Hoover hog – you git offen my land.'

'You don't understand,' said Leroy. 'This guy kilt Earl – smashed his haid in like a water melon. An' Tukey – he's like to die; he ain't hardly got no belly left. Belle's tendin' to him, but ah don't know . . .'

'If Belle's tendin' him he's sure to die,' said Dade flatly. 'Now git the hell outta here.'

Leroy looked around. 'You reckon you can make us?'

'Think I'm crazy?' said Dade. 'I've gotten six of my boys within spittin' distance.'

Leroy eyed him speculatively. 'Prove it.'

'Sure.' Dade took an apple from his pocket. 'I was goin' to enjoy this, an' that's somethin' else I have agin you, Leroy.' He suddenly tossed the apple into the air, and shouted, 'Hit it!'

There was a shotgun blast from the rock behind me and the apple disintegrated in mid-air. Wetness splattered against my cheek.

'Could have been yo' haid, Leroy,' said Dade. 'It's bigger. Mighty fine target is a swelled haid.' His voice sharpened. 'Now, you heard me tellin' you, an' you know I tells no one twice. Move yo' ass.' His hand pointed down the hill. 'That's the shortest way offen my land.'

Leroy looked uncertainly at the shotgun pointing at his belly, then he laughed shortly. 'Okay, Dade. But, listen, old man; you ain't heard the last.'

'An' yo' not the last to tell me that. Better men, too.' Dade spat at Leroy's feet.

Leroy turned on his heel and went out of sight and I heard the sound of many men going down the hill. Dade watched them go, his sparse grey hair moving in the slight breeze. He stood there for a long time before he moved.

From somewhere behind me the girl said, 'They're gone, Pop.'

'Yeah.' Dade came up to the tree. He said, 'I'm Dade Perkins an' this is my girl, Sherry-Lou. Now, suppose you come down outta that tree an' tell me just who the hell you are.'

18

It nearly went sour even then.

I climbed down from the tree, wincing as the rough bark scraped my bruised and bloody feet. As I reached the ground I said, 'Where's the nearest telephone? I need help.'

Sherry-Lou laughed. She looked me up and down, taking in my bleeding arms, the tattered tee-shirt with its incongruous inscription, the ripped jeans and my bare feet. 'You sure do,' she said. 'You look like you tangled with a cougar.' She saw the expression on my face and the laughter vanished. 'Got a telephone back at the house,' she offered.

'How far?'

'Two – three miles.'

'You won't make that in under an hour,' said Dade. 'Yo' feet won't. Can Sherry-Lou go ahead an' talk for you?'

I was not feeling too well. I leaned against the tree, and said, 'Good idea.'

'Who do I talk with?' she asked. 'What number?'

I had forgotten the number and had no secretary handy to ask. 'I don't know – but it's easy to find. Houston – the Cunningham Corporation; ask for Billy Cunningham.'

There was an odd pause. Sherry-Lou seemed about to speak, then hesitated and looked at her father. He glanced at her, then looked back at me. 'You a Cunningham?' he asked, and spat at the ground. That ought to have warned me.

'Do I sound like a Cunningham?' I said tiredly.

'No,' he admitted. 'You talk funny. I reckoned you was from Californy – some place like that.'

'I'm a Bahamian,' I said. 'My name's Mangan – Tom Mangan.'

'What's the Cunninghams to you?'

'I married one,' I said. 'And Leroy's got her.' Perkins said nothing to that. I looked at his expressionless face and said desperately, 'For Christ's sake, do something! She was screaming her head off when I busted out this morning. I couldn't get near her.' I found I was crying and felt the wetness of tears on my cheek.

Sherry-Lou said, 'Those Ainslees . . .'

'Cunningham or Ainslee – dunno which is worst,' said Dade. 'Ainslee by a short haid, I reckon.' He nodded abruptly. 'Sherry-Lou, you run to the house an' talk to Billy Cunningham.' He turned to me. 'The young sprout or Billy One?'

'Young Billy would be best.' I thought he would be better able to make quick decisions.

Dade said, 'Tell young Billy he'll need guns, as many as he can get. An' tell him he'd better be fast.'

'How far are we from Houston?' I did not even know where I was.

'Mebbe hundred miles.'

That far! I said, 'Tell him to use helicopters – he'll have them.'

'An' tell him to come to my place,' said Dade. 'He sure knows where it is. Then come back an' bring a pair of Chuck's sneakers so as Tom here can walk comfortable.'

'Sure,' said Sherry-Lou, and turned away.

I watched her run up the hill until she was lost to sight among the trees, then I turned to look about. 'Where is this place?'

'You don't know?' said Dade, surprised. 'Close to Big Thicket country.' He pointed down the hill to the right. 'Neches River down there.' His arm swung in an arc. 'Big Thicket that way, an' Kountze.' His thumb jerked over his shoulder. 'Beaumont back there.'

I had never heard of any of it, but it seemed I had just come out of Big Thicket.

Dade said, 'Seems I remember Debbie Cunningham marryin' a Britisher a few months back. That you?'

'Yes.'

'Then it's Debbie Leroy's got,' he said ruminatively. 'I think you'd better talk.'

'So had you,' I said. 'What have you got against Cunninghams?'

'The sons of bitches have been tryin' to run me offen my own land ever since I can remember. Tried to run my Paw off, too. Been tryin' a long time. They fenced off our land an' big city sportsmen came in an' shot our hogs. They reckoned they was wild; we said they belonged to people – us people. We tore down their fences an' built our own, an' defended 'em with guns. They ran a lot of folks offen their land, but not us Perkinses.'

'The Cunninghams don't want your land just to hunt pigs, do they?'

'Naw. They want to bring in bulldozers an' strip the land. A lot of prime hardwood around here. Then they replant with softwoods right tidy, like a regiment of soldiers marchin' down Pennsylvania Avenue in Washington like I seen on TV once. Ruinin' this country.'

Dade waved his arm. 'Big Thicket was three million acres once. Not much left now an' we want to keep it the way it is. Sure, I cut my timber, but I do it right an' try not to make too many big changes.'

I said, 'I can promise you won't have trouble with the Cunninghams ever again.'

He shook his head. 'You'll never get that past Jack Cunningham – he's as stubborn as a mule. He'll never let go while there's a dollar to be made outta Big Thicket.'

'Jack will be no trouble; he had a heart attack a couple of days ago.'

'That so?' said Dade uninterestedly. 'Then it's Billy One – that old bastard's just as bad.'

'I promised,' I said stubbornly. 'It'll hold, Dade.'

I could see he was sceptical. He merely grunted and changed the subject. 'How come you tangled with Leroy Ainslee?'

'Debbie was kidnapped from Houston,' I said. 'So was I. Next thing I knew I was at the Ainslee place locked up in a hut with Leroy on guard with a shotgun. That one,' I added, pointing to the shotgun leaning against the tree where Sherry-Lou had left it.

'Kidnappin'!' said Dade blankly. He shook his head. 'Ainslees have mighty bad habits, but that ain't one of 'em.'

'They didn't organize it. There was an Englishman; called himself Robinson, but I doubt if that's his real name. I think all the Ainslees provided was muscle and a place to hide. Who are they, anyway?'

'A no account family of white trash,' said Dade. 'No one around here likes 'em. An' they breed too damn fast. Those Ainslee women pop out brats like shelling peas.' He scratched his jaw. 'How much did they ask for ransom?'

'They didn't tell me.' I was not about to go into details with Dade; he would never believe me.

'Did you really kill Earl? An' gut Tukey?'

'Yes.' I told him how I had done it and he whistled softly. I said, 'And Debbie was screaming all the time and I couldn't get near her.' I found myself shaking.

Dade put his hand on my arm. 'Take it easy, son; we'll get her out of there.' He looked down at my feet. 'Think you can walk a piece?'

'I can try.'

He looked down the hill. 'Them Ainslees might take it into their haids to come back. We'll go over the rise an' find us a better place to be.' He picked up Leroy's shotgun and examined it. 'Nice gun,' he said appreciatively.

'You can have it,' I said. 'I doubt if Leroy will come calling for it.'

Dade chuckled. 'Ain't that so.'

Just over an hour later Dade nudged me. 'Here's Sherry-Lou. Got Chuck with her, too.' He put two fingers in his mouth and uttered a peculiar warbling whistle, and the two distant figures changed course and came towards the tumble of rocks where Dade and I were sitting.

Sherry-Lou had brought more than footwear. She produced a paper bag full of chunky pork sandwiches and I suddenly realized I had not eaten for about twenty-four hours. As I ate them she rubbed my feet with a medicament and then bandaged them.

More important than this was the news she brought. When Billy had heard her story he exploded into action and promised all aid short of the US Navy as fast as humanly possible. 'He's flyin' here direct,' she said. 'I told him to bring a doctor.' She avoided my eyes and I knew *my* hurts were not in her mind when she said that.

'What's all this about?' asked Chuck.

I let Dade tell the story – I was too busy eating. When he had finished Chuck said, 'I always knew the Ainslees were bad.' He shook his head. 'But this . . .' He stared at me. 'An' you kilt Earl?'

'He's dead, unless he can walk around with his brains leaking out,' I said sourly.

'Jeez! Leroy will be madder than a cornered boar. What's to do, Pop?'

Dade said, 'Did Billy Cunningham say how long he'd be?'

''Bout three o'clock,' said Sherry-Lou.

Dade hauled out an old-fashioned turnip watch and nodded. 'Chuck, you get back to the house right smartly. When Billy drops by in his whirlybird you show him the big meadow near Turkey Creek. We'll be there. No reason for Tom to walk more'n he has to.'

'Jeez!' said Chuck with enthusiasm. 'Never flown in one of them things.' He loped away. I thought that Dade Perkins's kids could stand a chance in the Olympics marathon; they did everything on the dead run.

Sherry-Lou snorted. 'He's never been in the air in his life – in anythin'.' She finished knotting a bandage over the deepest gash on my arm. 'You all right, Tom?'

'I'll be better when I know Debbie's all right.'

She veiled her eyes. 'Sure.'

Dade stood up. 'Take us fifteen minutes to get down to the creek. Might as well start.'

When the helicopter came down in the meadow Billy had the

door open before the shock absorbers had taken up the weight, and came running across the grass towards us, stooping as people always do when they know rotors are turning overhead. He took in my condition in one swift glance. 'Christ! How are you? How's Debbie?'

Dade and Sherry-Lou moved tactfully to one side, out of earshot, and were joined by Chuck who was talking nineteen to the dozen and windmilling his arms wildly. I gave Billy the gist of it, leaving out everything unimportant; just outlining the 'whats' and ignoring the 'hows' and 'whys'. He winced. 'Torturing her!' he said incredulously.

'She was screaming,' I said flatly. 'I was being shot at – I had to move fast.' I paused. 'I should have stayed.'

'No,' said Billy, 'you did the best you could.' He looked back at the helicopter. 'The State Police and some of our own security men are coming up behind. We'd better get back to the Perkins place.'

'One more thing,' I said. 'Seems Dade Perkins doesn't like Cunninghams, and from what little he told me I know why. Now, he just saved my life, so from now on you haul off your dogs.'

'It's not up to me,' said Billy. 'Jack won't . . .'

'Jack doesn't matter any more and you know it.'

'Yeah, but Dad won't be buffaloed either.' He frowned. 'Let me think about it. Come on.'

A few minutes later we dropped next to the Perkins's family residence and to two more helicopters with State Police markings. More were in the sky coming in. When all six were on the ground we had a conference – a council of war.

Dade Perkins was in on it, and outlined on a table what the Ainslee place was like, using match books and tobacco tins. Then there was a brief argument when Sherry-Lou announced that she was coming along.

The senior police officer was Captain Booth who was inclined to want to know the whys and wherefores until he was cut down by Billy. 'For Christ's sake, Captain, quit yammering! We can hold the inquest after we've gotten my cousin out of there.' It was a measure of Cunningham influence that Booth stopped right then and there.

Now he said decidedly, 'No place for a woman. There might be shooting.'

'Miz Mangan will need a woman if she's . . .' Sherry-Lou swallowed the words 'still alive', and continued, 'I know Leroy Ainslee.'

Dade turned red in the face. 'Has he interfered with you?'

'No, he hasn't!' she retorted. 'Not since I laid a rock against his head an' then got me a gun an' told him I'd perforate him.'

Dade glowered, and Booth said thoughtfully, 'There'll be one chopper in the air all the time. They might scatter and we'll want to see where they go. I reckon Miss Perkins could be in that one.'

We left in the helicopters and descended like a cloud of locusts on the Ainslee place less than five minutes later with the precision of a military operation. I was in the chopper which dropped right in the middle. No one shot at us because there was no one there to shoot. All the Ainslee menfolk were absent and only the women and a few kids were left. The children were excited by the sudden invasion but the slatternly women merely looked at us with apathetic eyes.

Billy had a gun in his hand when he jumped out, and Dade carried Leroy's shotgun. I looked about and saw cops closing in from all sides. Billy holstered his pistol. 'They're not here.'

'Still out lookin' for Tom, I reckon,' said Dade. He squinted up at the helicopter hovering overhead. 'They'll know somethin's wrong. Been nothin' like this since I seen the Vietnam war on TV. They won't be back in a hurry.'

I said, 'For God's sake, let's find Debbie.' I picked out the biggest house, a ruinous shack, and began to run.

It was Billy who found her. He came out of a smaller shack bellowing, 'A doctor! Where is that goddamn doctor?' He caught me by the shoulders as I tried to go in. 'No, Tom. Let the doctor see to her first. Will you quit struggling?'

A man ran past us carrying a bag and the door of the shack

slammed shut. Billy yelled at me, 'She's alive, damn it! Let the doctor tend to her.'

I sagged in his arms and he had to hold me up for a moment, then I said, 'Okay, Billy, I'm all right now.'

'Sure,' he said. 'I know you are.' He turned and saw Booth. 'Hey, Captain, better get the Perkins girl down here.'

'Right, Mr Cunningham.' Booth spoke to one of the pilots standing by, then came over to us. 'Mr Mangan, I'd like you to come with me.' I nodded and was about to follow him, but he was looking at Billy. 'You okay, Mr Cunningham?'

Billy had developed a curious greenish pallor and beads of sweat stood out on his forehead. He sat down on the stoop of the shack. 'I'll be all right. You go with the Captain, Tom.'

I followed Booth to the shack in which I had been held prisoner. Earl's body had been laid out parallel to the wall and beneath the window. The big pitcher was lying on its side, still intact, and a pool of water lay on the floor, as yet unevaporated. Tukey lay on the bed; he was dead and stank of faeces.

Booth said, 'Know anything about this?'

'Yes. I killed them.'

'You admit it,' he said in surprise. I nodded, and he said, 'You'd better tell me more.'

I thought about that, then shook my head. 'No, I'll say what I have to say in a courtroom.'

'I don't think I can accept that,' he said stiffly. 'Not in a case of murder.'

'Who said anything about murder?' I asked. 'When you lift Tukey you'll find the bed has been ripped up by buckshot. I happened to be sitting there when Earl pulled the trigger. I stabbed Tukey when he was going to shoot me. Don't prejudge the case, Captain; it's for a court to decide if it was murder.' He made a hesitant movement, and I said, 'Are you going to arrest me?'

He rubbed his chin and I heard a faint rasping sound. 'You're not an American, Mr Mangan. That's the problem. How do I know you'll stay in State jurisdiction?'

'You can have my passport, if you can find it,' I offered. 'I had it on me when I was snatched. It may be around here somewhere. Anyway, Billy Cunningham will guarantee I'll stay, if you ask him.'

'Yeah, that'll be best.' Booth seemed relieved.

'There *was* a murder.' I nodded towards the window. 'It happened out there. Leroy Ainslee shot a man in the back. I saw it.'

'There's no body.'

'Then have your men look for a new-dug grave.' I turned on my heel and walked out of that stinking room into the clean sunlight. The hovering helicopter had come down, and I saw Sherry-Lou hurrying into the shack the doctor had gone into. I felt curiously empty of all feeling, except for a deep thankfulness that Debbie was still alive. My rage was muted, dampened down, but it still smouldered deep in my being, and I knew it would not take much for it to erupt.

I went over and stood in the shade of a helicopter. Presently I was found by Chuck Perkins. 'Jeez, you sure kilt Earl,' he said. His face sobered. 'Tukey died bad.'

'They deserved it.'

'Pop's been looking for you.' He jerked his thumb. 'He's over there.'

I walked around the helicopter and saw Dade talking to Sherry-Lou. His face was serious. As I approached I heard Sherry-Lou say, '. . . tore up real bad.'

He put his hand on her arm in a warning gesture as he saw me. He swallowed. 'Sherry-Lou's got something to tell you,' he said. 'I'm sorry, Tom, real sorry.'

I said, 'Yes, Sherry-Lou?'

'Did you know Miz Mangan was pregnant?'

'Yes.' I knew what was coming.

'She lost the baby. I'm sorry.'

I stared blindly into the sky. 'Rape?'

'An' worse.'

'God damn their souls to hell!' I said violently.

She put out her hand to me. 'Some women are hurt more in birthin' a baby,' she said. 'She'll be all right.'

'In her body, maybe.'

'She'll need a lot of love . . . lot of attention. She'll need cherishin'.'

'She will be. Thanks, Sherry-Lou.'

They brought her out on a stretcher, the doctor walking alongside, and a nurse holding up a bottle for an intravenous drip. All that could be seen of her was her face, pale and smudgy about the eyes. I wanted to go with her in the helicopter back to Houston, but the doctor said, 'There's no use in it, Mr Mangan. She'll be unconscious for the next twenty-four hours – I guarantee it. Then we'll wake her up slowly. We'll want you there then.'

So the helicopter lifted without me aboard and I turned to find Captain Booth standing close by talking to Dade. I said bitterly, 'If I find Leroy Ainslee before you, Captain, I can guarantee you'll have a murder case.'

'We'll get him,' Booth said soberly, but from the way Dade spat on the ground I judged he was sceptical.

Billy came up. He had recovered something of his colour. 'Dade Perkins, I want to talk with you. You too, Tom.'

Dade said, 'What do you want?'

Billy glanced at Booth, then jerked his head. 'Over here.' He led us out of earshot of Booth. 'I know we've been putting pressure on you, Dade.'

Dade's face cracked in a slow smile. 'An' not gettin' far.'

'All I want to say is that it stops right now,' said Billy.

Dade glanced at me then looked at Billy speculatively. 'Reckon you big enough to make yo' Paw eat crow?'

'This crow he'll eat with relish,' said Billy grimly. 'But there's something I want from you.'

'Never did know the Cunninghams give anything away free,' observed Dade. 'What is it?'

'I want the Ainslees out of here,' said Billy. 'I don't want to feel there's folks like that dirtying up the place.'

'The cops'll do that for you,' said Dade. 'Why pick me?'

'Because I saw your face when Sherry-Lou said what she did about Leroy back at your place. Where do you suppose Leroy is now?'

'Easy. Hidin' out in Big Thicket.'

'Think the cops will find him there?'

'Them!' Dade spat derisively. 'They couldn't find their own asses in Big Thicket.'

'See what I mean.' Billy stuck his forefinger under Dade's nose. 'I don't want that son of a bitch getting away. I'd be right thankful if he didn't.'

Dade nodded. 'There's a whole passel of folks round here that don't like the Ainslees. Never have – but never gotten stirred up enough to do anythin'. This might do it. As for Leroy – well, if the devil looks after his own, so does the Lord. So let's leave it to the Lord.' Dade spat again, and said thoughtfully, 'But mebbe he could do with a little help.'

Billy nodded, satisfied. 'That make you happy?' he said to me.

'It'll do – for now.' I was thinking of Robinson.

'Then let's go home.'

I said goodbye to the Perkinses, and Dade said, 'Come back some time, you hear? Big Thicket ain't all blood. There's some real pretty places I'd like to show you.'

'I'll do that,' I said and climbed up into the helicopter. I slid the door closed and we rose into the sky and I saw Big Thicket laid out below. Then the chopper tilted and there was nothing but sky as we slid west towards Houston.

19

Medical science made Debbie's wakening mercifully easy, and when she opened her eyes mine was the first face she saw. She was not fully conscious, lapped in a drug-induced peace, but enough so to recognize me and to smile. I held her hand and she closed her eyes, the smile still on her lips, and slipped away into unconsciousness again. But her fingers were still tight on mine.

I stayed there the whole afternoon. Her periods of semi-consciousness became more frequent and longer-lasting, monitored by a nurse who adjusted the intravenous drip. 'We're bringing her out slowly and smoothly,' the nurse said in a low voice. 'No sudden shocks.'

But Debbie did have the sudden shock of remembrance. In one of her periods of wakefulness her eyes widened and she gave a small cry. 'Oh! They . . . they . . .'

'Hush, my love,' I said. 'I'm here, and I won't leave. It's finished, Debbie, it's all over.'

Her eyes had a look of hazy horror in them. 'They . . .'

'Hush. Go back to sleep.'

Thankfully she closed her eyes.

Much later, when she was more coherent, she tried to talk about it. I would not let her. 'Later, Debbie, when you're stronger. Later – not now. Nothing matters now but you.'

Her head turned weakly on the pillow. 'Not me,' she said. 'Us.'

I smiled then because I knew that she – we – would be all right.

I talked with her doctor and asked bluntly if Debbie would be able to have another baby. His answer was almost the same as Sherry-Lou's. 'Women are stronger than most men think, Mr Mangan. Yes, she'll be able to have children. What your wife has suffered, in terms of physical damage, is no more than some women suffer in childbirth. Caesarean section, for instance.'

'Caesarean section is usually done more hygienically,' I said grimly. 'And with anaesthetics.'

He had the grace to look abashed. 'Yes, of course,' he said hurriedly. 'She may need a great deal of care of the kind that is out of my field. If I could recommend a psychiatrist . . .?'

Sherry-Lou had said Debbie would need cherishing, and I reckoned that was my department; the cherishing that comes from a psychiatrist is of an arid kind. I said, 'I'll be taking her home.'

'Yes,' said the doctor. 'That might be best.'

I was hedged about by the law. The Cunninghams retained a good lawyer, the best trial lawyer in Texas I was assured. His name was Peter Heller and his only command was that I keep my mouth shut. 'Don't talk to anyone about the case,' he said. 'Not to the police and especially not to newsmen.'

One thing troubled him. 'The reef we're going to run on is that of intent,' he said. 'You see, Mr Mangan, you made certain preparations, way ahead of the event, to kill one of the Ainslees – and you did kill Earl Ainslee and, subsequently, Tukey. Now, we might just get away with Tukey because you could have had no knowledge he'd be there when you opened the door, but Earl is a different matter – that was deliberately planned. That pitcher did not walk up into the roof by itself. The jury might not like that.'

Ten days after we came out of Big Thicket Leroy Ainslee's body was found by the track of the Southern Pacific railroad. Apparently he had been run over by a train.

'Where exactly did it happen?' I asked Billy.

'Just north of Kountze. Little town which might be described as the capital of Big Thicket.'

'"Leave him to the Lord",' I quoted ironically.

'I got the pathologist's report,' said Billy. 'Most of the

injuries were consistent with tangling with a freight train.'

'Most?'

Billy shrugged. 'Maybe the Lord had help. Anyway the cops have written it down as accidental death. He's being buried in Kountze.'

'I see.' I saw that Texas could be a pretty rough place.

'It's best this way,' said Billy. 'Oh, by the way, Dade Perkins sends his regards.'

The case did not come to trial or, at least, not to the kind of trial we have in the Bahamas where the law is patterned after the British style. It went to the Grand Jury which was supposed to establish if there was a case to be answered at all. I never did get to the bottom of the intricacies of the American legal system, but I suspect that a considerable amount of string-pulling was done by the Cunninghams behind the scenes.

Because it involved kidnapping, a federal offence, the argument before the Grand Jury was not conducted by a local District Attorney from Houston but by a State Attorney from Austin, the State capital. I was represented by Heller and, as far as I could judge, he and the State Attorney – a man called Riker – had no adverse relationship at all. The whole hearing was conducted in such a way as to get a cool assessment of the facts.

There was a tricky moment when I was on the stand and Riker was interrogating me. He said, 'Now, Mr Mangan; you have stated that you made certain preparations – and quite elaborate preparations – involving a pitcher of water to kill Earl Ainslee.'

'No,' I said. 'I thought it would be Leroy Ainslee.'

'I see,' he said thoughtfully. 'Did you have anything against Leroy Ainslee?'

I smiled slightly. 'Apart from the fact that he was keeping me prisoner at gun point, and that he was keeping my wife from me – nothing at all.' There was a rumble of amusement from the jury. 'I'd never met the man before.'

'Yes,' said Riker. 'Now, to return to the man you actually

killed – Earl Ainslee. He actually had you at gun point at that time?'

'Yes. It was a 12-bore shotgun.'

Riker looked puzzled. 'Twelve what?'

'I'm sorry,' I said. 'It would be called 12-gauge here.'

'I see. Did you know the gun was loaded?'

'I had been so informed. Robinson said buckshot.'

'The mysterious Mr Robinson said that?'

'Yes. I found his information to be accurate when Earl pulled the trigger.'

'Earl fired a shot at you?'

'That's right. The buckshot ripped up the bed I was sitting on.'

'Now, I want you to answer this question very carefully, Mr Mangan. Did Earl Ainslee pull that trigger involuntarily as a result of being struck on the head with the heavy pitcher, or did he shoot first?'

'I don't know,' I said. 'I was too busy getting out of the way.' Again there came a murmur from the jury.

'But, at all events, you did pull the string which released the pitcher?'

'Yes.'

'Why?'

Into the sudden silence I said, 'My wife was screaming.' I moistened my lips. 'Earl said Leroy was having fun, and that it was his turn next.'

Riker waited until the stir had died away. 'Mr Mangan, had your wife not screamed would you have pulled that string?'

Again there was silence.

'I don't know. I honestly don't know.'

Heller put up his hand. 'Objection. The witness can testify only as to matters of fact. That is a hypothetical question.'

'I withdraw the question,' said Riker.

And that was the worst of it as far as I was concerned. There were more questions concerning the death of Tukey and the chase through Big Thicket, but Heller steered me past all the pitfalls. Then I retired because I was not allowed to hear other witnesses giving evidence.

Debbie told me afterwards that they handled her gently and considerately, and her time on the stand was brief. I believe the evidence of the doctor who had attended Debbie at the Ainslee place, and that of Sherry-Lou, damned Leroy thoroughly.

Anyway the whole thing was tossed out as being no case of murder or culpable homicide to answer at trial. There appeared to be a slight incredulity mixed with gratification that a Britisher, as I was popularly supposed to be, could be as red-blooded as any American and, I suppose, the unwritten law had a lot to do with it. Anyway, it was over and I was a free man.

Afterwards, Heller said, 'I know I objected to that hypothetical question, but I'm damned glad Riker asked it. You'll notice I objected only *after* you had answered it.'

'Yes.'

He grinned. 'I had my heart in my mouth waiting for your answer. I was taking a hell of a chance on that.'

'So was I,' I said dryly.

He looked a bit startled at that, and said, 'You know, Mr Mangan, you're no man's fool. That was a perfect answer. Have you studied law?'

'Not in any depth.'

'Well, there's a peculiar grey area that's not covered in any of the law books, and that answer of yours was right in the middle of it. You did all right.'

Before I went home to Grand Bahama Billy One convened another conference. Again it was confined to his kitchen cabinet; present were Billy, Frank and young Jim. Jack was absent; although out of hospital he was still confined to his home. I was there, too, and waiting to find out why.

Billy One started by saying to Frank, 'Your Pa is a sick man and I don't reckon he'll be attending to business for some time. But decisions have to be made and someone has to make them, and I think it's up to me. Of course, it'll be put to a full meeting of the board as soon as we get around to it, but we don't have time to wait on that.' He looked around the table. 'Any objections?'

Billy smiled and Jim merely shrugged – he was not going to argue with the man who had promoted him to top table – but Frank said, 'I think it should be put to the board.'

'No time,' said Billy One. 'Joe's in Scotland wrapping up that North Sea oil deal and I don't want to pull him from that. Besides, I'd want to have Jack at the meeting and he's not up to it yet.'

Frank nodded and accepted defeat. 'Okay – but what's he doing here?' His finger stabbed at me.

'He's here because he's a Cunningham,' said Billy One flatly. 'And because I want him here.' He ignored Frank's perplexed look and turned to me. 'How's Debbie today?'

'Not too bad,' I said. 'She's mended in body but . . .' I shrugged. 'She has nightmares.'

'Tom, I know you want to get back to her, but this won't take long.' Billy One leaned back and surveyed us. 'I want to remind you young fellows of some history – family history. We Cunninghams originally came from Scotland. Two brothers, Malcolm and Donald, settled here in tidewater Texas when it was still Mexico. They were piss-poor but it was a goddamn sight better than crofting back home.'

He clasped his hands. 'Over the years the family prospered. We helped Sam Houston take Texas from the Mexicans, and the family were among the leaders who pressurized Tyler into admitting Texas to the Union. We grew rich and strong and now we're not only powerful in Texas but over the whole goddamn world. And the way we did it was this.' He raised his clasped hands before him, the knuckles white under firm pressure. 'The family stays together and works as a team.'

Frank said in a bored voice, 'We know all that.'

'Sure,' said Billy One mildly. 'But I want Tom to know the score. It was Billy's idea to bring him into the Bahamas deal. Me, I was neutral but willing to go along. I didn't think all that much of Tom but I had nothing against him. Same when he married Debbie.'

'He cut himself a fair slice in that Bahamas deal,' said Frank.

'Sure he did,' agreed Billy One. 'And my respect for him went up a notch.' He looked at me. 'Why did you set it up that way?'

'I like my independence.'

'That can be good – but solidarity can be better. How would you like to join the Cunningham Corporation?'

'As what?'

'You'll be on the board making policy.'

'The hell he will!' said Frank outraged.

Billy One swung on him. 'You've still got a sister and Jack's still got a daughter on account of this guy, and he killed two men making it that way. He's shed blood and lost some of his own. In my book that makes him family – a Cunningham.' He stared Frank down and then sighed. 'Okay, Tom, what do you think?'

It was a handsome offer but there had to be a catch. As Dade Perkins had remarked, the Cunninghams were not notorious for offering free handouts. There had to be a catch in spite of Billy One's rhetoric, and he confirmed it by saying, 'Before being appointed to the board there's something you'll have to do.'

'And that is?'

'Well, there's something I want. Another thing about us Cunninghams is that we take insults from nobody. Now, my brother nearly died in that damn hospital, and my niece – your wife – was raped, and that's the biggest insult you can offer a woman.' His voice trembled. 'I want this guy, Robinson, and I want him real bad.'

Jim said, 'The State Police haven't gotten far on it.'

'They don't have our reasons,' snapped Billy One. He stared at me. 'You'll have the whole family right behind you, and that means the Cunningham Corporation. You can have any resources we have and, believe me, that's plenty.'

I said, 'Wow!' but not aloud. I did not know how many

billions of dollars the Cunningham Corporation controlled, but it was a respectable chunk of the GNP. It was not the biggest corporation in the United States, but it was not the smallest, either, not by a long way.

'It might not be a question of money,' I said. 'In any case, I have plenty of that.' I held Billy One's eye. 'And I don't need any reasons from you why I should find Robinson; I have plenty of my own.' I leaned back. 'The problem is that we have a total lack of information.'

Jim said, 'We have a pretty fair intelligence unit; you can put that to work.' I nodded, thinking of the ready way Rodriguez had hustled up bugging devices.

'Anything you want you get through Billy or Jim,' said Billy One. 'You'll liaise with them.'

'What about me?' said Frank.

'You and me have the Corporation to run. Have you any immediate ideas, Tom?'

'I think the answer lies in the Bahamas,' I said. 'That's the reason why your State Police have come up with nothing. I don't think Robinson is in Texas, or even in the United States. I think he's in the Bahamas. That's where I'm going to look for him, anyway. I'm leaving tomorrow with Debbie.'

'With Debbie?' said Frank. 'Wouldn't it be better if she stays here?'

I said deliberately, 'We've had enough of separate lives – both of us.' I turned to Jim. 'But I'd like a twenty-four-hour bodyguard on her until this thing is settled. Can you arrange that?'

'Sure, no problem. We have some dandy bodyguards – Treasury-trained.'

I did not see the point of that remark. 'What's that got to do with anything?'

Billy said, 'The Department of the Treasury bodyguards the President of the United States. Those guys are very good.' He smiled. 'We get to hire them because we pay better than the Treasury. But I've had an idea, Tom. I know you did a photofit of Robinson for the cops, but they've gotten no place with it. I have a kissing cousin who is a pretty fair portrait painter. Maybe she can produce something better.'

So it was that I was introduced to Cassie Cunningham, aged about twenty-five and unmarried, who came armed with a sketching block, pencils and water colours. She was quite a good portraitist and, after a few false starts, I began to feel hopeful of success. When we had done Robinson for good measure I asked Cassie to do another of the fake doctor who had whipped me from the lobby of the Cunningham Building.

The next day we flew to Freeport in the Cunningham Corporation JetStar. Apart from Debbie and myself there were six large men with bulges under their arms. 'Six!' I said to Jim Cunningham. 'I'm not going to start a bloody war.'

'Billy thought you ought to have a bodyguard, too. Anyway, allocate them as you choose.'

After thinking that one over I thought that Billy could very well be right. 'One thing,' I said. 'They're not employed by me. The Bahamian Government is very strict about firearms, and if these men are caught they're on their own.'

So we went home and I installed Debbie back in the house, with Kitty Symonette as attendant and companion. After making arrangements to bring Karen back from Abaco I went to see how the Theta Corporation had fared in my enforced absence. But it was just going to be a quick look because I was not going to leave Debbie for long. I had learned that lesson well.

20

The boss of the bodyguarding team was Steve Walker and he went with me to the office. I introduced him to Jessie in the outer office, then we went into my own. Walker looked around. 'Two doors,' he commented. 'Where does that one lead?'

'To the corridor.'

The key was in the lock so he turned it, locking the door. 'I'd rather you use just the one door,' he said. 'Can I have a desk in the corner of your secretary's office?'

'Sure. I'll have Jessie set it up.' So I did, much to her mystification, and when Walker had settled down I sat behind my own desk to do some heavy thinking.

I went over everything Robinson had said and latched on to something. He had said that Kayles had reported that I knew all about his plans, whatever they were, and that I had not told Kayles directly, but that Kayles had overheard a conversation between me and Sam Ford.

I thought back to the affray on *My Fair Lady*. Kayles could have listened when Sam and I were talking in the cockpit, but we had not talked about any mysterious plans, only about how to get Kayles back to Duncan Town. Anyway, Kayles would have been too busy cutting himself free and grabbing his gun to listen to us.

The only other time he could have listened to Sam and me was when he was tied up on the bunk. I vaguely remembered that I had a notion he had been feigning unconsciousness at the time, so what had I said to Sam about anyone's plans? I remembered I had been a bit irritable and had blown my top about something, but what it was I could not remember – a lot had happened since then. But perhaps Sam would know.

I snapped on the intercom. 'Jessie, get Sam Ford on the

telephone. I don't know where he'll be; you'll have to track him down.'

'But didn't you know?' she said.

'Know what?'

'He's in hospital in Nassau. A boat fell on him.'

'Come in here and tell me more.'

It appeared that Sam had been supervising the removal of a yacht from the water. Half-way up the slip it had fallen sideways from the cradle, and Sam happened to be in the way. It was a ten-ton ketch. 'He's in the intensive care unit of the Princess Margaret Hospital,' said Jessie. 'He was still in a coma the last I heard.'

'When did this happen?'

'About a week ago.'

I was filled with a cold rage. If Robinson had tried to kill me because of what Kayles overheard he would certainly not leave out Sam. This was as much of an ordinary accident as the disappearance of Bill Pinder. I said, 'Ask Mr Walker to come in.'

Jessie stood up, then hesitated. 'Who is he?' she asked. 'He's just sitting there reading magazines. And he asked me to give him a signal if a stranger comes in.'

'Don't worry about him, but do as he says. And I'd appreciate it if you didn't talk about him – to anyone.'

All the same she looked a bit worried as she left. When Walker came in I said, 'We have another bodyguard job,' and filled in the details. 'I don't want anyone getting to Sam.'

Walker tugged his ear. 'That might be tricky. Do we get the cooperation of the hospital?'

'I'll see what I can do about that. In the meantime have a couple of your men on alert, ready to fly to Nassau.'

He nodded and left, and I was about to ask Jessie to put me through to the hospital in Nassau when she buzzed me. 'Commissioner Perigord to see you.'

I had been expecting Perigord but not as soon as this. He was quick off the mark. 'Send him in.'

Perigord came in, as trim and elegant as ever in his well-cut uniform. 'What can I do for you?' I asked. 'Please sit down.'

He took off his cap and laid it on the desk, together with the swagger stick he always carried, and sat in the chair opposite. He regarded me with dark brown eyes set in a dark brown face, and said quietly, 'Don't be bland with me, Mr Mangan. You have much to tell me. When a Bahamian of some eminence is kidnapped in Texas and kills two men in the act of escaping it tends to make headlines in the newspapers. You are a man of some notoriety.'

I should have expected that but it had not occurred to me. True, Jessie had looked at me with big eyes when I had walked into the office, but I had kept her on the run and we had not had time to be chatty. 'I must get the clippings for my scrapbook,' I said ironically.

'Captain Booth of the Texas State Police telephoned me. He wanted to know about you, naturally enough. Your status in the community, had you a criminal record, and so forth. I gave you a clean bill of health.'

'Thanks for the testimonial.'

'We also talked about our common problems – drug-running, for instance. Texas has a long border with Mexico.'

'Do you still think this case has to do with drugs? I'm beginning to wonder about that.'

Perigord shrugged. 'I'm keeping an open mind. I read the transcript of the Grand Jury hearing with great interest.'

I was surprised. 'You did? That hearing was held in private.'

Perigord's lips quirked into a smile. 'Like you, I have friends in Texas. It made . . . how shall I put it? . . . empty reading. For example, there was the mysterious Mr Robinson, your kidnapper, floating about the case with no visible means of support – never found. And there was the body of Kayles which, again, has never been found.'

'It wouldn't be too hard to make a body vanish in Big Thicket,' I said. 'You could toss it into any swamp.'

'True, but Captain Booth is moderately unhappy. You see, he only has your word for it that there was a third body or even a Robinson. He couldn't ask Leroy Ainslee because he was inconsiderately killed by a train.'

I said, 'My wife never saw Kayles, but she did see Robinson. You must have read her evidence.' I took a glossy colour photograph from my desk drawer. 'Meet Mr Robinson.'

Perigord took it from my fingers and examined it critically. 'You did better with Kayles,' he said. 'That was a photograph. This is a photograph of a painting.' He dropped it on to the desk. 'Not what one would call hard evidence for the existence of Robinson.'

'Are you saying you don't believe me – or Debbie?' I demanded.

'No – but I'm dissatisfied. Like Captain Booth I'm moderately unhappy.' He then said what Frank Cunningham had said before Billy hit him, but in a way that robbed it of offence. 'You seem to have problems with your wives, Mr Mangan. I was very sorry when the first Mrs Mangan died because I had a regard for her, and I was equally sorry when I heard what had happened to your present wife. I ask myself if these events are related in any way, and if your problems are going to continue. Too much has happened around you in the last year or so.' He leaned forward. 'Now let us talk about Robinson.'

So we talked about Robinson for a long time. At last I said, 'I've been racking my brains to think of what Kayles overheard between me and Sam Ford, and I can't ask Sam.' I told him about that, and added pointedly, 'And I don't think that was an accident, either.'

Perigord looked grave. 'I'll ring Commissioner Deane in Nassau, and we'll have that incident investigated.'

'And put a guard on Sam,' I said.

He nodded and picked up the picture of Robinson. 'How accurate is this?'

'I really don't know,' I said candidly. 'But it's the best Cassie Cunningham and I could do. She said it's difficult for a painter to depict an image in someone else's mind's eye.'

'Very well put.' Perigord picked up his hat. 'Now, there is just one last matter. You came back from Texas without a passport. Well, that's all right because we know the reason. But you came back with six Americans, two of whom are in your home though not, I suspect, as house guests; three are billeted in the Royal Palm Hotel, and the sixth is sitting in your outer office at this moment. We checked *their* passports very carefully and what did we find on further enquiry? All six are members of the security section of the Cunningham Corporation. Mr Mangan, if you have fears for your own safety or the safety of your wife you should come to me, and not import a private army.'

'My wife is dear to me.'

'I understand that.' He stood up. 'But I would like to see Mr Walker now.'

I eyed Perigord with respect; he even had the identification down pat. I called in Walker and introduced them. Perigord said, 'Mr Walker, we encourage Americans to come to our island; you are our bread and butter. But we don't like firearms. Are you armed, sir?'

Walker said, 'Uh . . .' He glanced at me.

'Tell him,' I said.

'Well . . . er . . . yes, I am.'

Perigord held out his hand without saying a word and Walker took a pistol from a holster clipped to his belt and handed it over. Perigord put it into his pocket where it made an unsightly bulge and spoiled the line of his uniform. He picked up his swagger stick. 'You and your friends may stay, Mr Walker, even though I have the power to deport you. But all your firearms must be delivered to my office before midday today.' He raised the swagger stick in a semi salute. 'Good day, Mr Mangan. I'll let you know of any developments.'

As the door closed Walker said, 'A swagger stick, yet! Is he for real?'

'He had you tagged the moment you got off the JetStar. He knows who you are and what you do. I wouldn't underestimate Perigord.'

'What do we do about the guns?'

'You do exactly as he says. What have you got? A pistol each?'

'Yeah. And a couple of Armalite rifles.'

'My God! Let Perigord have the lot. You'll get them back

when you leave.' I had the impression that Walker and his friends would feel stripped naked.

While not neglecting Debbie I buckled down to getting the Theta Corporation back into shape. Not that there was much wrong – I had a good staff – but when the boss takes an enforced vacation things tend to loosen and the system becomes sloppy. So I did the necessary tightening here and there to tune the organization.

One of the things I did was to transfer Jack Fletcher to the Sea Gardens Hotel on New Providence. The manager there had broken his leg and was out of action, and Philips, the under manager, was a new boy, so I thought it wise to send Fletcher. The point is that I went with him to introduce him to the staff. It was to be a quick trip because I did not want to spend time away from Debbie. Although Cora and Addy had brought over a crowd of kids and were company for Debbie I wanted to get back quickly.

Bobby Bowen flew us to Nassau and Steve Walker came along, too. During this period he was never more than ten feet away from me at any moment, and there would be only one door between us, if that. If Jack Fletcher noticed that Walker stuck closer to me than my shadow he made no comment.

After the round of introductions were over we sat in the manager's office to tidy up a few last details. There were minor differences in running the two hotels and I wanted to be sure that Fletcher knew of them. The manager's office at the Sea Gardens is immediately behind the reception desk in the lobby and one wall is of glass – glass with a difference.

From the customer's point of view when standing in the lobby the wall behind the reception desk is fitted with a big mirror. Mirrors are important in hotel design because they give a sense of space, spurious though it may be. But this mirror is of trick, one-way glass so that the manager, sitting at his desk, can see what is happening in the lobby while being unobserved himself.

So it was that, while chatting with Fletcher, I happened to look out idly at the reception desk and beyond. There was the usual scene, a combination of idleness and bustle. Small groups of tourists stood about chatting, and bellhops were bringing in the baggage of a newly arrived tour group. Philips said they had just come from Italy. Everything was normal. At the cashier's desk there was a short queue of departing visitors doing what the whole business was about – they were paying.

There was something about the third man in the queue that interested me. I thought I knew him but could not recollect ever having met him. He was tall with greying hair and had a neatly trimmed moustache and a short beard. I stood up, went closer to the window, and stared at him. He did what many do – he looked at his reflection in the mirror and straightened his tie. For a moment he stared directly into my eyes; his own were green flecked with yellow, and I had looked into those eyes before when lying helpless in the lobby of the Cunningham Building.

I swung around. 'Jack, see that man with the beard? I want him held up – delayed until I can find out who he is.'

Fletcher looked surprised. 'How?'

'Double his bill. Say it's a computer error and spend a long time rectifying it. But keep him there.' Fletcher shot off, and I said to Philips, 'Go with him. I want the man's name, room number, home address, where he came from, where he's going, and anything else you can find out about him. But be tactful. And quick.'

Walker joined me at the window. 'What's the panic?'

'That's one of Robinson's friends,' I said grimly. 'He had no beard when I last saw him, but there's no disguising those eyes and that big nose. When he leaves I want you to stick close to him.' I thought for a moment. 'How much money have you got on you?'

'I don't really know. A couple of hundred bucks, maybe.'

'You might need more. There's no knowing where he might go.' I took a cash voucher from the desk, scribbled a figure and added my signature. 'The cashier will honour this.'

Walker took the slip and gave a low whistle. 'Five thousand dollars!'

'He might be flying to Europe, damn it! Ask for American dollars or you might be stuck with Bahamian.'

'If I'm going to tail the guy I'd better not join that line at the desk,' he said.

'True. Stay here until Philips comes back. He can get the cash from behind the desk.'

We watched the comedy at the cashier's desk. My friend, the phoney doctor, moved up to the counter and presented his room key with a smile. There was a bit of dumb show and then the bill was presented. He glanced at it, then frowned, prodded at it with his forefinger, and pushed it back across the counter. The cashier made some chat and called over Jack Fletcher who now came into sight.

Walker said, 'If he pays by credit card we can trace him through the number.'

I nodded. Fletcher was making voluble apologies with much gesturing. He held up one hand in a placatory manner and disappeared from view. Two minutes later he walked into the office followed by Philips. 'His name is Carrasco – Dr Luis Carrasco.'

'So he really is a doctor,' I commented. 'Nationality?'

'Venezuelan.'

'Where is he going?'

'I don't know,' said Fletcher. 'I've only spoken to him for about three minutes. He said he had a plane to catch and would I make it short.'

'I know where he's going,' said Philips. 'He used our inter-hotel booking service. He's flying to Freeport and he's staying at the Royal Palm. He's booked in for a week.'

'Damned cheek!' I said, and looked at Carrasco. He was standing at the desk wearing a preoccupied expression and tapping restlessly with his fingers.

'He'll probably be flying Bahamasair,' said Fletcher, glancing at his watch. 'There's a flight in an hour.'

'He booked a hire car to await him at Freeport International,' said Philips.

'One of ours?'

'Yes.'

I looked at Walker. 'Can we bug that car? I mean, do we have the facilities handy?'

Walker shook his head. 'No, but we can have Rodriguez in Freeport in under four hours.'

'Make the phone call, direct to Billy Cunningham. Tell him it's bloody urgent.'

Walker picked up the telephone, and Fletcher said curiously, 'What's all this about, Tom?'

'Something that Commissioner Perigord will want to know about.' I had made one mistake with Perigord and another was unthinkable. 'What room did Carrasco have?'

Philips said, 'Three-one-six.'

'Have it locked and sealed. We can get fingerprints.' Walker heard that and nodded vigorously. I picked up the voucher which Walker had laid on the desk and tore it up; he would not need that now.

'How long do we keep Carrasco hanging about?' asked Fletcher.

'You can let him go as soon as Walker has finished his call and got a Bahamasair ticket to Freeport.' There was a travel agency in the lobby, so I said to Philips, 'Get that now and debit it to hotel expenses.'

Carrasco had interrupted a transaction between another client and the cashier; he was obviously arguing and was tapping his wristwatch meaningfully. Walker put down the telephone. 'Fixed,' he said. 'Rodriguez is coming over in the JetStar with a bag of gadgets.'

The minutes ticked by and Carrasco was becoming increasingly irritable. When I saw Philips walking across the lobby with an air ticket in his hand I said, 'Okay, let him go now. Many apologies, and tell him his taxi fare to the airport is on us as compensation for the trouble we've caused him. Do a grovel.'

Fletcher shrugged and left as Philips came in and gave Walker the ticket. 'Get a taxi for Mr Walker and have it standing by,' I said, and picked up the telephone to ring Perigord.

As I waited for him to come on the line I saw Jack Fletcher

doing his obsequious act in a smarmy manner and I hoped he was not laying it on too thick. He escorted Carrasco to the door and Walker nodded to me and left without saying a word.

I got Perigord and told him what was happening. I said, 'I don't want this man alarmed because we haven't got Robinson yet. Carrasco could lead us to him.'

'At last you are using the brains you undoubtedly possess,' said Perigord, and promised to have a discreet escort awaiting Carrasco at the airport.

I told him that Walker was on the same flight, then said, 'One last thing; there'll be an American called Rodriguez coming in on the Cunningham JetStar later today. I don't want the Customs holding him up by taking a too close interest in his bags. Can you arrange that?'

'Not if he's bringing firearms,' said Perigord. 'You know that.'

'No firearms – my guarantee,' I promised. 'He's an electronics expert – I'll tell you about him later.'

Perigord agreed. I told him I'd be flying back immediately, then hung up and sat at Fletcher's desk and pondered. Was I right? I had seen him only for a matter of seconds, and I had been in a drugged condition at the time. But it had been very close up. Was I right in staking that he was Carrasco? Staking everything on the colour of a man's eyes and the size of his nose?

I thought I was right. The recent painting session with Cassie Cunningham had clarified my mind and etched that face into my mind's eye. But if I was wrong and Perigord laid on an elaborate operation to no good purpose then he would have an even lower opinion of me than ever.

Fletcher came back, and I asked, 'What's Carrasco's credit card number?'

'He paid cash. Just dug out his wallet and paid in hundred dollar bills, American. It didn't empty the wallet, either.'

'How much was the bill?'

'A little over 1100 dollars. He used the restaurant a lot and his bar bill wasn't small. Then there was the car rental charge.'

I leaned back in the chair. 'Jack, you've been in this business quite a time. When was the last time you can remember that a bill like that was paid in cash?'

'It's happened a few times,' he said. 'Not many, though. Usually when a man has cleaned up at the casino – he gets paid out in cash so he pays his bill in cash. But that's usually in Bahamian dollars.'

'I don't think Carrasco is a gambler,' I said meditatively. 'Not that kind, anyway. I'll take a copy of the bill with me.' I felt much more confident and happy.

21

I flew back to Freeport and went to see Perigord immediately. He had Inspector Hepburn with him, and he came quickly to the point. 'Tell us more about this man Carrasco.'

I did not do that. Instead, I looked at Inspector Hepburn, and asked, 'Do you still think this is about cocaine?'

Perigord said, 'Yes, we do.'

'Well, I don't. Both Kayles and Robinson seemed surprised when I brought up the subject.'

'They would,' said Hepburn. 'They were not likely to admit it, were they?'

I said, 'To my mind their surprise was genuine. It took them aback.'

'But we don't have your mind,' said Perigord. 'I doubt if you would consider yourself an expert on the way criminals behave when confronted.'

I saw I was getting nowhere pursuing that line; their minds were made up. 'What do you want to know about Carrasco?'

'Everything,' Perigord said succinctly.

'He kidnapped me from the Cunningham Building,' I said. 'And . . .'

Perigord held up his hand. 'You're sure it's the same man?'

I hesitated. 'Not one hundred per cent, but near enough. I don't trust people who pay large bills in cash.' I told them of what had happened and put a copy of the bill on Perigord's desk.

Perigord, too, found that odd. We thrashed it out a bit, then he said, 'Mr Mangan, can we trust your American friends?'

'In what way?'

'Can we trust them to stick to surveillance, but not to take action in the matter of Carrasco? Our police force is relatively small and I would welcome their help in keeping tabs on Carrasco, but not to the extent of their taking violent action. That I can't permit.'

'They'll do exactly as I tell them.'

'Very well. I have talked to Mr Walker and he has Carrasco under observation at this moment; and is to report to my man at your hotel. Why is Rodriguez coming, and what is he carrying?' I told him and he smiled. 'Yes, I think we can do with scientific aid.'

Hepburn said, 'There's something I don't understand. If Carrasco kidnapped you in Houston isn't he taking a risk by walking openly about your hotels? He could bump into you at any time. In fact, you *did* spot him – or so you think.' He glanced at Perigord. 'To my mind this may be a case of mistaken identification. Mr Mangan admits he only saw the man in Houston for a few seconds.'

'What do you say to that?' asked Perigord.

'It's been puzzling me, too,' I said. 'But I'm ninety-five per cent convinced it's the same man.'

'Nineteen chances out of twenty in favour of you being correct,' he mused. 'Those are odds I can live with. We'll watch Dr Carrasco.'

Driving from the police station to the hotel I thought of what Hepburn had said, and came to the conclusion that it could cut both ways. If Carrasco had been the man in Houston then perhaps he was willing to take the chance of me seeing him *because* I had seen him for only a few seconds. In those circumstances perhaps he thought a beard and moustache were sufficient disguise. As I switched between alternatives my mind felt like a yo-yo.

A good hotel has two circulatory systems, one for the clientèle which is luxuriously furnished, and the other for the staff which has a more spartan décor; and in the best hotels the two systems are mutually exclusive because one does not want maintenance traffic to erupt into the public rooms. When I got back to the hotel I stuck to the staff system because I wanted to keep out of the way of Carrasco.

Walker reported on Carrasco and related affairs. 'He's holed up in his room; probably unpacking. Rodriguez will be here in about two hours; I'll have a man at the airport to meet him. Perigord has a man here in the hotel, and he assigned another to your house to guard your wife.' He scratched the angle of his jaw, and added sourly, 'They're both armed.'

'They're entitled to be,' I said. 'You're not.' It was good of Perigord to think of Debbie. 'You're not to lay a finger on Carrasco. Just watch him and report on who he talks to.'

'Can we tap his room telephone?'

'It's probably illegal but we'll do it. I'll have a word with the switchboard operator. Carrasco might speak Spanish; do we have anyone who can cope with that?'

'One – two when Rodriguez comes.'

'That should be enough. Any problems, let me know.' We knocked it around a bit more, trying to find angles we had forgotten, did not find any and left it at that.

For the next three days nothing happened. Carrasco had no visitors to his room and used his telephone only for room service and for restaurant bookings. Rodriguez bugged his car and his room, and put a tape recorder on the telephone tap so that we had a record of his conversations, but we got little joy out of that. A search of Carrasco's possessions brought nothing; he carried with him just what you would expect of a man on holiday.

Debbie wondered audibly about the muscular young black who had been imported into the house to help Luke Bailey, who did not need it, and who was making good time with Addy Williams. She knew about Walker's crew and I saw no reason to keep from her the knowledge that this addition to the household was one of Perigord's cops. 'I'd like you to keep to the house as much as possible,' I said.

'How long will we have to live like this?' she said desolately. 'Being in a state of siege isn't exactly fun.'

I did not know the answer to that, but I said, 'It will blow over soon, I expect.' I told her about Carrasco. 'If we can use him to nail Robinson I think it will be finished.'

'And if we can't?'

I had no answer to that, either.

I had not expected to go back to New Providence for some time. Jack Fletcher was an experienced manager and did not need his hand held, which is why I had put him into the Sea Gardens. But when he telephoned four days after I had left him in charge he was in a rare panic. 'We've got big trouble, Tom,' he said without preamble. 'Our guests are keeling over in all directions – dropping like flies. Tony Bosworth has his hands full.'

'What is it? Does he know?'

'He's closed down the big air-conditioner.'

'He thinks it's Legionnaires' disease?' I thought quickly. 'But it doesn't work that way – it didn't at the Parkway. Let me talk to him.'

'You can't. He's in a conference with officials from the Department of Public Health.'

'I'll be right over,' I said. 'Have a car waiting for me at the airport.'

During the flight I was fuming so much that I expect steam was blowing out of my ears. After all the trouble I had taken to ensure the hotels were clean, this had to happen. Surely Tony must be wrong; the symptoms seemed quite different to me. This would be enough to give Jack Cunningham another heart attack.

Fletcher met me at Nassau Airport himself. As we drove to the Sea Gardens I said, 'How many people ill?'

His answer appalled me. 'A hundred and four – and I'm not feeling too good myself.' He coughed.

'My God!' I glanced at him. 'Are you really not feeling well, Jack? Or was that just a figure of speech?'

'I'm feeling lousy. I'm running a temperature and I have a hell of a headache.'

He was not the only one. I said, 'You're going to bed when we get back. I'll have Tony look you over. How many of that figure you gave me are staff?'

'As of this morning we had three on the sick list – four with me now.' He coughed again convulsively.

‘Stop the car,’ I said. ‘I’ll drive.’ I found it puzzling that the number of staff casualties should be so low. As I drove off again I said, ‘How many registrations have you got?’

‘Something over three hundred; I’ll let you know when we get to my office.’

‘Never mind,’ I said. ‘I’ll ask Philips. You go to bed.’ What he had told me meant that about one-third of the clientèle had gone down sick. ‘Any deaths?’

‘Not yet,’ he said ominously.

We got to the Sea Gardens and I packed Fletcher off to his staff flat and then went to look for Philips. I found him helping out at the cashier’s desk where there was a long line of tourists anxious to leave as quickly as they could – like money bats. The buzz of conversation in the queue was low and venomous as though coming from a disturbed hive of bees. I was in no mood to placate the rats leaving the sinking ship, to mix the metaphor even further, and I hauled him out of there. ‘Someone else can do that. Jack Fletcher’s gone down sick, so you’re in charge. Where’s Bosworth?’

Philips jerked his thumb towards the ceiling. ‘Doing his rounds.’

‘Has he any help?’

‘A load of doctors from Nassau and some nursing staff from the hospital.’

‘Track him down; I want to see him in Fletcher’s office five minutes ago.’

When I saw Tony Bosworth he looked tired and drawn, his eyes were reddened as though he had not slept, and he swayed a little on his feet. I said, ‘Sit down before you fall down, and tell me what the hell we’ve got.’

He sighed as he sat down. ‘The tests aren’t through yet, but I’m fairly certain it’s legionellosis.’

‘Damn!’ I mopped the sweat from my brow and loosened my tie. It was hot and humid and I realized why. The air-conditioning in the public rooms was not working. ‘It’s hitting faster this time, isn’t it?’

‘It’s the Pontiac fever form, I think. It hits sooner and harder, in the sense that more people exposed to it contract the symptoms – ninety-five per cent is the usual rate.'

'My God!' I said. 'Then we still have a long way to go. Did you see what was happening in the lobby as you came through?'

He nodded. 'I'm not sure it's wise to allow those people to leave. They could go away and still come down with the bug.'

'I don't see how we can stop them. You can't expect people to stay in what they think is a pest house. What's the position of the Public Health Department?'

'They're still making up their minds.' Tony's eyes met mine. 'I think they'll close you down.'

I winced. 'How could this happen?' I demanded. 'You know the precautions we took.'

'Tom, I don't know.' He, too, took out a handkerchief and wiped his brow, then ran it around the edge of his collar. 'What's puzzling me is the spotty spread. We're not getting an incidence of ninety-five per cent – it's more like thirty per cent.'

'Then perhaps it's not Pontiac fever.'

'All the symptoms check.' Tony scratched his head. 'But *all* the Italians have gone down, seventy-five per cent of the Americans, but only twenty-five per cent of the British.'

I blinked at that. 'You mean it's attacking by nationality selectively? That's crazy!' I had a thought. 'It's tending to give Bahamians a miss, too. Only four of the staff have gone down.'

'Four? Who's the fourth?'

'Jack Fletcher – I've just packed him off to bed. I'd like you to look at him when you have time. Who are the other three?' He named them, and I said slowly, 'They all live here in the hotel.' Most of the staff had homes of their own, but a select few of the senior staff, like Fletcher, had staff flats.

It was as though I had goosed Bosworth. He jerked visibly and sat up straight from his slumped position, and I could see the Big Idea bursting from him. Someone has christened it the Eureka Syndrome. He leaned forward and grabbed the telephone. A minute later he was saying, 'Nurse, I want you to go to every patient and ask a question – Do you habitually take tub baths or a shower? Make a tabulated list and bring it to the manager's office. Yes, nurse, I'm serious. Get someone to help you; I want it fast.'

He put down the telephone, and I said dryly, 'I'm not surprised the nurse asked if you were serious. What is this?'

'National habits,' he said. 'Do you know the Russians don't have plugs in their wash hand basins? They don't like washing their hands in dirty water so they let the taps run.'

For a moment I thought Tony had gone completely round the bend. 'What the hell have the bloody Russians to do with this?' I said explosively.

He held up both his hands to quieten me. 'I once talked with an Italian doctor. He told me the Italians consider the English to be a dirty race because they bathe in their own filth. He said most Italians take showers. Now, every Italian in the hotel has gone down with this bug – every last one of them.'

'And seventy-five per cent of the Americans, but only twenty-five per cent of the English.'

'Whereas, if the infection had been coming from the air-conditioner as at the Parkway, it should have been ninety-five per cent overall. You know what this means, Tom; it's in the water supply, not the air-conditioner.'

'That's bad.' I sat and thought about it. If the water supply was contaminated the hotel was sure to be shut down. I said, 'It won't work, Tony. Everybody has been drinking the damn water, and they sure as hell don't drink their shower water.'

'But that's the point. You can drink a gallon of water loaded down with this bug and it'll do no harm in the gut. To be infective it must be inhaled into the lungs. At the Parkway the air in the lobby and on the pavement outside was filled with drift from the air-conditioner – an aerosol loaded with *L. pneumophila* which was inhaled. Exactly the same thing happens when you take a shower; the water is broken up into very fine droplets and you inhale some of it.'

'Jack Fletcher takes showers,' I said. 'I was in his apartment once and his wife said he was in the shower. I could hear him; he has a fine bathroom baritone.' I blew out my cheeks. 'So what do I tell those people out there? That everything is okay as long as they don't take a shower? I really don't think that would work.'

'I'm sorry,' said Tony. 'But I really think you'll have to close if my theory turns out to be right. I'll lay in some sodium hypochlorite to flush out the system.'

Three-quarters of an hour later we had the answer; all the patients, without exception, had taken showers. Tony had sent some of the older people to the Princess Margaret Hospital and they were interrogated, too. Same answer. 'That does it,' he said. 'It's in the water supply.'

I said, 'We have to retrieve something out of this mess, so we'll turn it into a public relations exercise. I'll notify the Department of Public Health that we're closing before they tell me I must.' I grinned at Tony and quoted, '"His cause is just who gets his blow in fust." Then there are the customers. We'll get them into other hotels, preferably our own, and stand the expense.' It would break Jack Cunningham's heart, but would be good business in the long run.

'What about all the people still here and sick?'

'They can stay if you and the other medicos can look after them. My worry is how many of them are going to die here.'

'None,' said Tony. 'No one has been known to die of Pontiac fever yet. They'll be up and about in a few days – a week at most.'

'Thank God for that!' I said fervently. 'Now for the big question. I know we can get this bacterium out of the water system. What I want to know is how it got in.'

'I'll check into that,' said Tony. 'I'll need your maintenance engineer, and I think we should have one of the Public Health people along.'

'And you'll have me,' I said. 'I want to know exactly what happened so I can make sure it never happens again.'

We began the investigation that night. All afternoon I had been helping Philips and the rest of the managerial staff to organize the future wellbeing of our departing guests. It took a lot of telephoning around but it got done, and although my competitors were pleased enough to take the business they did not really like it. We all knew it would be bad for trade in the future.

Then I had to quell a minor revolt on the part of the staff. Word had somehow got around that there was something wrong with the hotel water and I was in danger of losing some of my best people. It took some straight talking on the part of Tony Bosworth, including a demonstration in which he drank a full glass of water straight from the tap – and so did I. I was glad he believed his own theories but I was not so sure, and it took some effort to drink that water without gagging.

Four of us gathered together at eight that evening – myself, Tony Bosworth, Bethel, the hotel maintenance engineer, and Mackay from Public Health. Tony had a dozen sterilized sample bottles. 'Where do you want to start?' asked Bethel. 'Bottom up or top down?'

'We're nearer to the bottom,' said Tony. 'Might as well begin there.'

So we went down into the basement where the boilers were. A hotel needs a lot of hot water and we had three calorifiers, each of a capacity of three million British Thermal Units. The huge drums of the calorifiers were connected by a tangle of pipes coloured red, blue and green, with arrows neatly stencilled to indicate the direction of flow. Tony asked questions and I looked about. The place was spotless and dry.

Bethel was explaining something technical to Tony when I broke in. 'This place is as dry as a bone, Tony; there have been no leaks recently.' I turned to Bethel. 'When did you last strip down any of this?'

He frowned. 'Must have been eight months ago, Mr Mangan. A normal maintenance check. This equipment is efficient; hardly ever goes wrong.'

'Where does the water come from?'

'Out of the mains supply.' He nodded towards Mackay.

'Mr Mackay can tell you more about that.'

'Then why should we be the only building hit?' I asked Tony.

'That's not exactly true,' said Mackay. 'Isn't the mains water piped into tanks somewhere at the top of the building?'

'That's right,' said Bethel. 'Right at the top to give it a good head.'

'So it could have been contaminated in the tanks after it left the mains,' I said. 'I don't think it could have happened down here. Everything is as tight as a drum.'

'Let's go to the top,' proposed Tony, so we went up in the service elevator.

The water tanks were on the roof and they were big. 'Twenty-five thousand gallons,' said Bethel. 'Five thousand in each tank.' He pointed out the mains piping rising up the side of the hotel. 'The water comes up there and is distributed by this manifold into the tanks. Each tank has a ball valve to control the water level.' He shrugged. 'The whole system is just the same as the one you'll have in your own home; it's just that this is bigger.'

'I've never seen mine,' I said.

Bethel grinned. 'I don't come up here too often myself. The system is automatic.' He pointed. 'You can see that the tanks are all interconnected by that manifold at the bottom.'

That meant that water would flow freely between the tanks. 'Why five?' I asked. 'Why not one big tank?'

'Well, if something happens – a tank springs a leak, say – we can isolate it and go on using the other four.' Bethel was very good at answering stupid questions from a layman.

'And the tanks are sealed?'

'Sure. There's a manhole on the top of each so we can get at a sticky valve if we have to, but the lids are bolted down on a mastic seal.'

'Let's take a look,' said Tony, and began to climb the steel ladder on the side of the nearest tank.

We all followed him. On top of the tank Bethel squatted on his haunches. 'Here's the manhole. I had the tanks repainted about three months ago and we just painted over the manhole covers, bolts and all. You can see this hasn't been opened since then – the paint seal isn't cracked.'

I looked at Mackay. 'Then how did the bug get into the system? It *must* be in the mains water.' Something bright on the roof shot a sun reflection into my eye and I turned slightly to get rid of it.

'Impossible!' said Mackay positively. 'Not if this is the only building affected. Look.' He unrolled the chart he was carrying which proved to be a water distribution map. 'All those houses take the same water. Even the airport is on the same water main.'

'People normally don't shower in airports,' said Tony.

'They do in houses,' retorted Mackay. 'It can't be in the mains water. Of that I'm certain.'

Bethel had wandered away and was standing on the next tank. 'Hey!' he called, and again the reflection stabbed my eye as I turned. 'This one's been opened.' We crossed to the tank and stood around the manhole cover. 'The paint has cracked around the bolts.'

'Opened some time in the last three months,' said Tony.

'Later than that,' said Bethel confidently. He pointed to where bright metal showed where paint had flaked away. 'It hasn't started to rust. I'd say some time in the last week.'

'That adds up,' said Tony.

'Who would have opened it?' I asked.

'I didn't,' said Bethel. 'Harry Crossman might have, but if he did he didn't tell me.'

Crossman was Bethel's assistant. 'It will be on his work sheets,' I said. 'I want to see them. I want to see them now.'

Bethel stood up. 'They're in my office.'

'Bring back a wrench,' said Tony. 'I want to take samples from here.'

There was no point in me watching Tony take samples so I went with Bethel. We climbed down on to the roof and walked towards the elevator motor housing, and I kicked something which rolled away and came to a stop with a clink at the edge of a water tank. I stooped and picked it up and found the object that had been sending reflections into my eye.

But it was more than that – much more. It was a cylindrical glass tube broken at one end. The other end was pointed as though it had been sealed in a flame, and I had seen others like it in Jack Kayles's first-aid box on *My Fair Lady*. Suddenly ideas came slamming into my head so hard and so fast that they hurt. Whole areas of mystification suddenly became clear and made sense; a weird and unnatural sense, it is true, but conforming to logic.

I turned and yelled, 'Tony, come down here.'

He clambered down the ladder. 'What's the matter?'

I held out the glass tube. 'Could you take a swab from the inside of there and test it for your damned bug?'

He looked surprised. 'Sure, but . . .'

'How long will it take?'

'Not long. After the last scare they set up a testing facility in the hospital here. Say, four days.'

'I can't wait that long, but take care of it and do your test.' I turned and ran for the staircase.

Five minutes later I was talking to Walker at the Royal Palm on Grand Bahama. He said, 'Where are you, Mr Mangan? I'm supposed to be bodyguarding you.'

'I had to leave in a hurry, but never mind that. I want you to send a man on to the roof. No one is to get near the water tanks up there.'

'The water tanks!' he echoed. 'What the . . .'

'Never mind arguing, just do it,' I said sharply. 'And put another man near the air-conditioning cooling tower. Nobody is to get near that, either. Nobody at all.'

'Not your maintenance crew?'

'Nobody,' I said flatly. I did not know if Carrasco had local assistance or not, but I was taking no chances. 'Where's Carrasco?'

'He spent the day sightseeing in West End,' said Walker a shade wearily. 'Right now he's having dinner at the Buccaneer Club out at Deadman Reef. I have two men with him – Rodriguez and Palmer.'

'You'll probably have police to help you at the hotel as soon as I've talked to Perigord. And after that I'm flying back.'

As I rang off Bethel came in. 'Nothing in Harry's work sheets, Mr Mangan.'

'I know. He didn't do it. Do you know Bobby Bowen, my pilot?' Bethel nodded. 'Chase him up, will you? Tell him we'll be flying to Freeport. Oh, and tell Dr Bosworth he'll be coming with me. Mackay can take the samples to the hospital.' Bethel turned to go, and I added, 'And thanks. You've been a great help.'

When he had gone I rang Perigord. He was not in his office, not entirely unnaturally considering the time of day, but neither was he at home. The telephone was answered by his daughter who told me in a piping voice that Mummy and Daddy were out. Where were they? She was vague about that. They had gone out to dinner. Could be the Stoned Crab or the Captain's Charthouse or possibly the Japanese Steak House in the International Bazaar or the Lobster House in the Mall. Or was it the Lucayan Country Club? I sighed and thanked her, then reached for the Grand Bahama telephone directory.

I found him in none of those places but finally ran him to earth in the Mai Tai. It took me some time to convince him of my sanity and even longer to move him to action. I think I ruined his dinner.

22

Tony Bosworth and I walked into the lobby of the Royal Palm and I noticed immediately the two uniformed policemen, one standing by the elevators, the other at the foot of the staircase. I crossed to the desk. 'Is Commissioner Perigord here?'

'In the manager's office.'

I jerked my head at Tony and we went in. Perigord, in plain clothes, was talking on the telephone, and Walker sat on a settee. Perigord said into the mouthpiece, 'I quite agree; I'll check it out thoroughly. I can expect you tomorrow, then.' He looked up. 'He's here now; I'll have it in more detail by then. Yes, I'll meet you. Goodbye.' He put down the telephone. 'Now, Mangan, you'll have to explain – '

I cut him short. 'First things first. I'd like you to get those coppers out of the lobby and out of sight. I don't want Carrasco scared off.'

He leaned forward. 'If your story is correct then Carrasco is the most dangerous man in the Bahamas.'

'No, he's not,' I contradicted. 'Robinson is, and he's the joker I want. He's the boss.' I pulled up a chair and sat down. 'Besides, you can't charge Carrasco with anything. You need hard proof and you've got none. But scare him and he'll skip, and Robinson will send someone else in his place – someone we don't know. Besides, I don't like uniformed policemen cluttering up the public rooms in my hotels. It lowers the tone.'

Perigord nodded and stood up. 'We may be guarding an empty stable,' he said sourly. 'Carrasco may not be back. Your men have lost him.' He walked out.

I turned on Walker. 'For God's sake! Is that true?'

He said heavily, 'He went into the john at the Buccaneer Club and didn't come out. Rodriguez thinks he left by the window. His car is still there but no Carrasco.'

I thought for a moment. 'Maybe he's in Harry's Bar; that's not far from the Buccaneer.'

'No – Palmer checked that out.'

I thought of the topography of Deadman Reef. 'A boat,' I said. 'He's meeting a boat. Have your men thought of that?'

Walker said nothing but reached for the telephone as Perigord came back. He glanced at Tony. 'Who is this?'

'Dr Bosworth. He identified the disease and has been of great help.'

Perigord nodded briefly and sat down. 'Are you really trying to tell me that Carrasco is a maniac – the stereotyped mad doctor of the "B" movies – who is poisoning the water in hotels in these islands?'

'I don't believe him to be mad, but that's what he's doing. And Robinson is directing him.'

'But why?'

'I've had a few thoughts in that direction which I'll come to in a minute. Let's look at the evidence.'

'That I'd be pleased to do,' said Perigord sardonically.

'I know it's all circumstantial, but so is most evidence of murder. When I found that glass tube it all came together suddenly. One, I'd seen others like it on Kayles's boat. Two, I remembered what Kayles must have heard me saying to Sam Ford.'

'Which was?'

'I was blowing my top about the chain of disasters which had hit the Bahamas. Rioting in the streets of Nassau, Legionnaires' disease at the Parkway, the burning of the Fun Palace, even the shredding of the luggage at the airport. Now, I'd knocked Kayles cold and he was just coming to his senses. He must have been muzzy – dislocated enough in his mind to think I was actually describing Robinson's doings to Sam. So when he escaped he reported to Robinson that I knew all.'

I frowned. 'And what convinced Robinson was that there was at least one item on that list that Kayles wasn't privy to. That indicated to Robinson that I did indeed know about his plans – he told me so – and he was as worried as hell because I might have told you.'

Perigord said, 'Are you telling me that Robinson burned down the Fun Palace? And sabotaged the carousel at the airport?'

'Yes, I think he did – but not personally. Another thing: when Robinson admitted to trying to have me killed in an air crash he made a curious remark. He said the death of the Americans was an unexpected bonus, and he went on to say that Wall Street was a bit rocky about it. The idea seemed to please him.'

'Come to the point you are so circuitously making.'

'It was all pulled into place by a remark made by Billy Cunningham,' I said. 'When we put together the Theta Corporation Billy did some research in the course of which he talked to Butler of the Ministry of Tourism. He learned that eighty per cent of the economy and two-thirds of the population are supported by tourism. Billy said to me that it was too many eggs in one basket, and it worried him a little. And that's your answer.'

'Spell it out,' said Perigord.

'Robinson is trying to sabotage the economy of the Bahamas.' Perigord regarded me expressionlessly, and I said, 'How many tourists have we lost since all this began? Ask Butler, and I guarantee the answer will startle you. And it's not long since Billy Cunningham warned me that if this series of disasters continued the Cunningham Corporation would think seriously of pulling out. The company which runs the Parkway in Nassau is already nearly bankrupt.'

'It's all too thin,' complained Perigord. 'Too speculative. The only hard evidence we have is the glass tube you found, and that won't be evidence if it's clean. How long will it take you to make the tests, Dr Bosworth?'

'The hospital in Nassau is doing the testing, and it will take four days.'

'Not sooner?'

'This bacterium is very elusive,' said Tony. 'The samples have to go through a guinea pig and then be cultured on an agar medium supplemented by cysteine and iron. Then – '

Perigord flapped his hand. 'Spare me the technical details,' he said irritably. 'All right – four days.'

'I'll tell you something, Commissioner,' said Tony. 'If that capsule gives a positive result it means someone has found a way of culturing *Legionella pneumophila* in quantity, and that implies a well-equipped biological laboratory. It's not something you can whip up in a kitchen.'

Perigord absorbed that in silence. Walker stirred and said, 'There's something you ought to know. This morning one of my guys found Carrasco in a place he shouldn't be – on one of the back stairs used by the cleaning staff. He said he'd got lost; taken a wrong turning and gone through the wrong door.'

I slapped the desk with the flat of my hand. 'Perigord, what more do you want?' I turned on Walker. 'So Carrasco has given you the slip before. I hope to God he didn't doctor the water tanks here.'

'No way,' said Walker, stung. 'And he didn't give us the slip. He dropped out of sight and my guy went looking for him. He wasn't out of sight for more than three minutes.'

'I could bear to know a lot about who and why,' said Perigord.

'There's a proverb to the effect that fishing is best done in troubled waters,' I said. 'The CIA know it as destabilization. They've been pretty good at it in the past.'

He looked startled. 'You're not suggesting the CIA is behind this?'

'I don't know who is behind it – I didn't say it was the CIA. It's not in the American interest to destabilize a sound capitalist economy in this part of the world. Others do come to mind, though.'

'Five will get you ten that Carrasco is a Cuban,' said Walker. 'Venezuelan my ass.' The telephone rang and he picked it up. 'I'm expecting this.' He held a short con versation, his end of it consisting of monosyllables. As he laid down the handset he said, 'You were right; Carrasco went out in a boat. He's just come back and he's in the

Buccaneer Club now, having a drink. We have a picture of him landing on the beach.'

'Taken at night,' I said scornfully. 'A fat lot of good that will be. And what good is a picture? We already know what he looks like.'

'There was another guy in the boat,' said Walker reasonably. 'We might like to know who he is. As for picture quality, if anyone can come up with something good it's Rodriguez; he has some kind of gismo on his camera. That guy is gadget-happy. He says Carrasco came back in a small boat that's probably a tender to a big yacht. After landing Carrasco, the boat went out to sea again.'

'A night rendezvous,' said Perigord. 'I'll have a police boat take a look at Deadman Reef.' He reached for the telephone.

When he had finished we continued to kick the problem around for quite a while. No, Perigord had not investigated the catastrophe of the airport carousel; it had not been considered a police matter at the time. He would look into it next day. The fire at the Fun Palace in Nassau had been investigated for arson, but no firm evidence had come up. It might be possible to borrow a deep-diving submersible from the Americans to look for the remains of Pinder's Navajo in Exuma Sound. Evidence of sabotage would be useful.

'Useful for what?' I asked. 'That's in the past and I'm worried about the future. I'm wondering what Robinson's department of dirty tricks will come up with next.'

It was agreed that Carrasco was our only lead and that he would be closely watched. I looked hard at Walker. 'And don't lose him again.'

'I'll assign some of my own men to him,' said Perigord. 'There are too many whites watching him now. My blacks will blend into the background better.' He looked at his watch. 'Nearly midnight. I suggest that Dr Bosworth will sleep better in a bed than in that chair. And I'm for bed, too.'

I turned and found Tony asleep. I woke him up. 'I'll find you a room. Come on.'

We went into the lobby, but Walker stayed behind to wait for the call which would tell us that Carrasco had left the

Buccaneer. He would not have long to wait because the Buccaneer closes at midnight. There were quite a few returning revellers in the lobby and I waited at the desk for a few moments while they collected their keys.

Perigord walked towards the entrance, but turned and came back. 'I forgot to tell you that I have informed Commissioner Deane in Nassau of these developments, and he is flying across to see me tomorrow. He will certainly want to see you. Shall we say my office at ten tomorrow morning?'

Perigord may have been the top copper on Grand Bahama, but there was a bigger gun in Nassau. I said, 'That will be okay.'

The man next to me asked for his key. 'Room two-three-five.'

Carrasco!

I should not have looked at him but I did, in an involuntary movement. He picked up his key and turned towards me. He certainly recognized me because I saw the fractional change in his expression, and he must have seen the recognition in my eyes because he dropped the key, whirled, and ran for the entrance.

'Stop him!' I yelled. 'Stop that man!'

Carrasco turned on me and there was a gun in his hand. He levelled it at me and I flung myself sideways as he fired. Then there was another shot from behind me, and another. When I next looked, Carrasco was pitching forward to fall on the floor. I looked back and saw Perigord in the classic stance – legs apart with knees bent, and his arms straight out with both hands clasped on the butt of the revolver he held.

I picked myself up shakily and found I was trembling all over, and my legs were as limp as sticks of cooked celery and about as much use in holding me up. Perigord came forward and put his hand under my elbow in support. 'Are you all right? Did he hit you?'

'I don't think so. I don't feel anything. He threw a bloody scare into me, though.'

Somewhere in the middle of all that I had heard a woman scream and now there was a babble of excited voices.

Perigord's uniformed men appeared from where he had hidden them, and he motioned them forward to break up the mob which was surrounding Carrasco's body. He raised his voice. 'All right, everybody; it's all over. Please clear the lobby and go to your rooms. There's nothing more to see.'

I beckoned to the nearest bellboy. 'Get something to cover the body – a tablecloth or a blanket.' I saw Walker standing in the doorway of the manager's office, and strode over to him. 'What the hell happened?' I was as mad as a hornet. 'How did he get here without warning?'

Walker was bewildered. 'I don't know, but I'll find out. There's Rodriguez.' He ran towards the entrance of the lobby where Rodriguez had just appeared.

Perigord was standing over the body and Tony Bosworth was on his knees beside it. Tony looked up and said something and Perigord nodded, then came over to me. 'He's dead,' he said. 'I didn't want to kill him but I had no option. There were too many innocent bystanders around to have bullets flying. Where can we put him?'

'In the office will be best.'

The policemen carried the body into the office and we followed. 'Where did his bullet go?' I asked. 'Anyone hurt?'

'You'll probably find a hole in the reception desk,' said Perigord.

'Well, thanks. That was good shooting.' Walker returned and I stuck my finger under his nose. 'What happened? He damn near killed me.'

Walker spread his hands. 'The damnedest thing. Rodriguez was in the bar watching Carrasco, and Palmer was in the car outside with the engine running. When Carrasco made his move to go, Rodriguez went to the public phone to make his call and found that some drunken joker had cut the cord. It had been working earlier because I'd talked to him about a possible boat. He didn't have much time because Carrasco was already outside, in his car, and on the move. So he made a judgement – he went after Carrasco.'

Perigord said, 'Perhaps Carrasco knew he was being watched. Perhaps he cut the telephone cord.'

'No way,' said Walker. 'Rodriguez said that Carrasco never went near the public phone when he came back from his sea trip. It was just plain dumb luck.'

'There was no reason for Carrasco to cut the cord,' I said. 'He wasn't going anywhere mysterious; he was coming back here. And now he's dead, and we've lost our lead to Robinson.'

'Well, let's have a look at him,' said Perigord. He stripped away the tablecloth which covered the body, knelt beside it, and began going through the pockets, starting with the inner breast pocket. 'Passport – Venezuelan.' He opened it. 'Dr Luis Carrasco.' He laid it aside. 'Wallet with visiting cards in the name of Dr Luis Carrasco; address – Avenida Bolivar, 226, Caracas. And money, more than a man should decently carry; there must be 4000 dollars here.'

There were several other items: a billfold containing a few dollars in both American and Bahamian currency, coins, a pen knife, a cigar case containing three Havana cigars – all the junk a man usually carries in his pockets.

From a side pocket of the jacket Perigord took a flat aluminium box. He opened it and there, nestling in cotton wool, were three glass ampoules filled with a yellowish liquid. He held it up. 'Recognize them?'

'They're exactly like those I saw in Kayles's boat,' I said. 'And like the broken one I found on the roof of the Sea Gardens Hotel. My bet is that he picked them up tonight when he went on his little sea trip. He wouldn't want to carry those about too long, and they weren't in his room when we searched it.'

He closed the box and stood up. 'I think you're beginning to make your case. Commissioner Deane will definitely want to see you tomorrow morning.'

I glanced at the clock. 'This morning.' I was feeling depressed. Later, when the body was removed on a stretcher I reflected gloomily that Carrasco had advanced his bloody cause as much in the manner of his death as in life. A shoot-out in the lobby of a hotel could scarcely be called an added attraction.

23

The morning brought news – bad and good.

When I got home I told Debbie what had happened because there was no way of keeping it from her; it was certain to be on the front page of the *Freeport News* and on the radio. She said incredulously, 'Shot him!'

'That's right. Perigord shot him right there in the lobby of the Royal Palm. A hell of a way to impress the guests.'

'And after he shot at you. Tom, you could have been killed.'

'I haven't a scratch on me.' I said that lightly enough, but secretly I was pleased by Debbie's solicitude which was more than she had shown after my encounter with Kayles in the Jumentos.

She was pale. 'When will all this stop?' Her voice trembled.

'When we've caught up with Robinson. We'll get there.' I hoped I put enough conviction into my voice because right then I could not see a snowball's chance in hell of doing it.

So I slept on it, but did not dream up any good ideas. In the morning, while shaving, I switched on the radio to listen to the news. As might have been predicted the big news was of the shooting of an unnamed man in the lobby of the Royal Palm by the gallant and heroic Deputy-Commissioner Perigord. It was intelligent of Perigord to keep Carrasco's name out of it, but also futile; if Robinson was around to hear the story he would be shrewd enough to know who had been killed.

The bad news came with the second item on the radio. An oil tanker had blown up in Exuma Sound; an air reconnaissance found an oil slick already twenty miles long, and the betting was even on whether the oil would foul the beaches of Eleuthera or the Exuma Cays, depending on which way it drifted.

The Bahamas do not have much going for them. We have no minerals, poor agriculture because of the thin soil, and little industry. But what we do have we have made the most of in building a great tourist industry. We have the sea and sun and beaches with sand as white as snow – so we developed water sports; swimming, scuba-diving, sailing – and we needed oiled water and beaches as much as we needed *Legionella pneumophila*.

I could not understand what an oil tanker was doing in Exuma Sound, especially a 30,000 tonner. A ship that size could not possibly put into any port in any of the surrounding islands – she would draw far too much water. I detected the hand of Robinson somewhere; an unfounded notion to be sure, but this was another hammer blow to tourism in the Bahamas.

I dressed and breakfasted, kissed Debbie goodbye, and checked into my office before going on to see Perigord. Walker, my constant companion, had not much to say, being conscious of the fiasco of the previous night, and so he was as morose as I was depressed. At the office I gave him a job to do in order to take his mind off his supposed shortcomings. 'Ring the Port Authority and find out all you can about the tanker that blew up last night. Say you're enquiring on my behalf.' Then I got down to looking at the morning mail.

At half past nine Billy Cunningham unexpectedly appeared. 'What's all this about a shoot-out at the OK Corral?' he demanded without preamble.

'How do you know about it?'

'Steve Walker works for me,' he said tersely. 'He keeps me informed. Was Debbie involved in any way?'

'Didn't Walker tell you she wasn't?'

'I forgot to ask when he rang last night.' Billy blew out his cheeks and sat down. 'I haven't told Jack about this, but he's sure to find out. He's not in good shape and bad news won't do him any good. We've got to get this mess cleared up, Tom. What's the pitch?'

'If you've talked to Walker you know as much as I do. We've lost our only lead to Robinson.' I held his eye. 'Have you flown a thousand miles just to hold my hand?'

He shrugged. 'Billy One is worried. He reckons we should get Debbie out of here, both for her own sake and Jack's.'

'She's well enough protected,' I said.

'Protected!' Billy snorted. 'Steve Walker is pissed off with your cops; he tells me they've taken his guns. How can he protect her if his guys are unarmed?'

'Perigord seems to be doing all right,' I said. 'And there's an armed police officer at the house.'

'Oh!' said Billy. 'I didn't know that.' He was silent for a moment. 'How will you find Robinson now?'

'I don't know,' I said, and we discussed the problem for a few minutes, then I checked the time. 'I have an appointment with Perigord and his boss. Maybe they'll come up with something.'

It was then that Rodriguez and the good news came in. 'I've got something for you,' he said, and skimmed a black-and-white photograph across the desk.

It was a good photograph, a damned good photograph. It showed Carrasco hopping over the bows of a dory which had its prow dug into a sandy beach. The picture was as sharp as a pin and his features showed up clearly. In the stern of the dory, holding on to the tiller bar of an outboard motor, was another man who was equally sharply delineated. I did not know him.

'You took this last night?' Rodriguez nodded. 'You were crazy to use a flash. What did Carrasco do?'

'He did nothing. And who said anything about a flash? That crazy I'm not.'

I stared at him then looked at the picture. 'Then how . . .?'

He laughed and explained. The 'gismo' mentioned by Walker was a light amplifier, originally developed by the military for gunsights used at night but now much used by naturalists and others who wished to observe animals. 'And for security operations,' Rodriguez added. 'You can take a pretty good picture using only starlight, but last night there was a new moon.'

I looked at the photograph again, then handed it to Billy. 'All very nice, but it doesn't get us very far. All that shows is Carrasco climbing from a boat on to a beach. We might get somewhere by looking for the man in the stern, but I doubt it. Anyway, I'll give it to Perigord; maybe he can make something of it.'

'I took more than one picture,' said Rodriguez. 'Take a look at this one – especially at the stern.' Another photograph skimmed across the desk.

This picture showed the dory again which had turned and was heading out to sea. And it was a jackpot because, lettered across the stern, were the words: 'Tender to *Capistrano*'.

'Bingo!' I said. 'You might have made up for losing Carrasco last night.' I looked at Billy. 'That's something for you to do while I'm with Perigord. Ring around the marinas and try to trace *Capistrano*.'

Five minutes later I was in Perigord's office. Also present was Commissioner Deane, a big, white Bahamian with a face the colour of mahogany, and the authority he radiated was like a blow in the face. I knew him, but not too well. We had been at school together in Nassau, but I had been a new boy when he was in his last year. I had followed him to Cambridge and he had gone on to the Middle Temple. Returning to the Bahamas he had joined the Police Force, an odd thing for a Bahamian barrister to do, because mostly they enter politics with the House of Assembly as prime target. He was reputed to be tough and abrasive.

Now he said raspily, 'This is a very strange business you've come up with, Mangan.'

'We'd better discuss it later.' I tossed the pictures before Perigord. 'Carrasco probably made a rendezvous with a boat called *Capistrano*. Rodriguez took those last night.'

A little time was wasted while we discussed how Rodriguez could possibly have taken photographs at night without a flash, then Perigord twitched an eyebrow at Deane. 'With your permission?'

'Yes,' said Deane. 'Get busy. But you have a watching brief, that's all.'

Perigord left, and Deane said, 'As I started to say, you have come up with an oddity. You have suggested a crime, or a series of crimes, with no hard evidence – merely a chain of suppositions.'

'No evidence! What about the ampoules taken from Carrasco?'

'Those won't be evidence until we find what is in them, and Perigord tells me that will take four days. We flew an ampoule to Nassau during the night. So far the whole affair is very misty. A lot of strange things have been happening around you, and don't think my deputy has not kept me informed. Now, these events are subject to many interpretations, as all subjective evidence is.'

'Subjective!' I said incredulously. 'My first wife disappeared and my daughter was found dead; there's nothing bloody subjective about that. My second wife and I were kidnapped; I suppose we dreamed it up. There have been two cases of disease in hotels and that's fact, Commissioner, bloody hard fact.'

'What is subjective is your interpretation of these events,' said Deane. 'You have brought in a number of events – the breakdown of a baggage carousel at the airport, a fire, an air crash, and a number of other things, and the only connection you can offer is your interpretation. Just give me one piece of hard evidence, something I can put before a court – that's all I ask.'

'You've got it – the ampoules.'

'I've got nothing, until four days from now. And what's in the ampoules might prove to be a cough cure.'

'You can prove it right now,' I said. 'Just take one of those ampoules, break it, and inhale deeply. But don't ask me to be in the same room when you do it.'

Deane smiled unexpectedly. 'You're a stubborn man. No, I won't do that because you may be right. In fact, I think you *are* right.' He stood up and began to pace the room. 'Your interpretation of events dovetails with a number of mysteries which have been occupying my mind lately.'

I sighed. 'I'm glad to hear it.'

'A lot of telephoning was done during the night. We now know that Dr Luis Carrasco is unknown at 226 Avenida Bolivar in Caracas.'

That was disappointing. 'Another lead gone,' I said dejectedly.

'Negative findings can be useful,' observed Deane. 'It tells us, for instance, that he was bent, that he had something to hide.' He added casually, 'Of course, now we know his real name all becomes clear.'

I sat up. '*You know who he is?*'

'When you sealed his hotel room you did well. We could make nothing of the fingerprints so we passed them on to the Americans, and their report came on that telephone just before you arrived here. Carrasco turns out to be one Serafin Perez.'

That meant nothing to me. 'Never heard of him.'

'Not many people have,' said Deane. 'He liked his anonymity. Perez is – was – a Cuban, a hardline communist and Moscow-trained. He was with Che Guevara when Guevara tried to export the revolution, but he broke with Guevara because he thought Guevara was mishandling the business. As it turned out Perez proved to be right and Guevara wrong. Since then he's been busy and a damn sight more successful than Che. He's been pitching up all over the place – Grenada, Nicaragua, Martinique, Jamaica. Notice anything about that list?'

'The hot spots,' I said. 'Grenada has gone left, so has Nicaragua. Jamaica is going, and the French are holding on to Martinique with their finger tips.'

'I believe Perez was here during the riots in Nassau. There was a certain amount of justification for that trouble, but not to the length of riot. Many of the rioters had no direct connection and I smelled a rent-a-mob. Now I know who rented it.'

'So much for Carrasco-Perez,' I said. 'A white ant.'

Deane looked puzzled. 'What do you mean?'

'When I was at Cambridge I knew a South African. He once said something which had me baffled and I asked him to explain it. He said he had been white-anted; apparently it's a common South African idiom. A white ant is what we would call a termite, Commissioner.'

Deane grunted. 'Don't talk to me about termites,' he said sourly. 'I've just discovered that my house is infested. It's going to cost me five thousand dollars – probably more.'

I said, 'You take a wooden post or a beam in a house. It looks good and solid until you hit it, then it collapses into a heap of powder – the termites have got into it. When the South African said he'd been white-anted he meant he'd been undermined without his knowledge. In his case it was student politics – something to do with the student union. Commissioner, the Bahamas are being white-anted. We're being attacked at our most vulnerable point – tourism.'

'A good analogy,' said Deane thoughtfully. 'It's true that the Ministry of Tourism is perturbed about the fall in the number of visitors lately. So is the Prime Minister – there was a special Cabinet meeting last week. And there's more political unrest. Fewer tourists means more unemployment, and that is being exploited. But we need evidence – the Prime Minister demands it. Any crack-down without evidence would lead to accusations of police interference in political matters. The Prime Minister doesn't want the Bahamas to have the reputation of being a police state – that wouldn't do much for tourism, either.'

'Then investigate the sinking of that tanker in Exuma Sound last night. The report mentioned a twenty-mile oil slick only eight hours after she went down. If that's true the oil came out awfully fast. If I were you I'd question the skipper closely – if he's still around. Don't wait for the official inquiry; regard it as a police matter.'

'By God!' said Deane. 'I hadn't made *that* connection.'

'And find Robinson,' I said. 'What do you know about *him*?'

'Nothing at all. Your Mr Robinson is an unknown quantity.'

Perigord came in. '*Capistrano* just left Running Mon marina, heading east along the coast.'

East! 'Making for the Grand Lucayan Waterway and the north coast,' I said. 'Florida next stop.'

'What kind of a boat is she?' asked Deane.

'Sixty-foot motor yacht, white hull,' said Perigord. 'I don't think she's all that fast, she's a displacement type according to the management of Running Mon. She put into the marina during the night with engine trouble. Had it fixed this morning.'

I looked at Deane who was sitting immobile. 'What are we waiting for? You have a fast police launch, and *Capistrano* is still in Bahamian waters.'

'So we put men aboard, search her, and find nothing. Then what?' Deane stood up. 'I'll tell you what would happen next. We'd have to let her go – with profuse apologies. If your Mr Robinson is as clever as you say we would certainly not find anything because there would be nothing to be found.'

'But you might find Robinson,' I said. 'He could be aboard and he's wanted for kidnapping in Texas.'

'Not so,' contradicted Deane. 'A man calling himself Robinson is wanted for questioning concerning a kidnapping in Texas. He cannot possibly be extradited merely for questioning. We would have to let him go. He has committed no crime in the Bahamas for which we have evidence – as yet.'

'Robinson might not be on board, anyway,' said Perigord.

'Then aren't you going to do *anything*?' I demanded desperately.

'Oh, yes,' said Deane blandly. He lifted his eyebrows interrogatively at Perigord. 'I hope your contingency planning is working well.'

'It is. A fast Customs boat will pass *Capistrano* and enter the Lucayan Waterway ahead of her. There'll be another behind. Once she's in the Waterway she's bottled up. Then we put the Customs officers aboard her.'

‘But I thought you said . . .’ I was bewildered.

‘We might as well try,’ said Deane smoothly. ‘Who knows what the Customs officers might find if they search thoroughly enough. Cocaine, perhaps?’

I opened my mouth again, then shut it firmly. If this pair was about to frame Robinson by planting cocaine on his boat they would certainly not admit it to me, but it seemed that Deane was a hard case who was not above providing his own evidence. After all, all he had to do was to keep Robinson in the Bahamas for four days.

‘We had better be on hand,’ Deane said casually. ‘You’ll come, too – you can identify Robinson.’ He picked up the photograph of Carrasco-Perez. ‘And I shall certainly want to question those on board about their association with Perez. We rendezvous at the Casuarina Bridge in thirty minutes.’

‘I’ll be there,’ I said.

Hoping and praying that Robinson would be aboard *Capistrano* I drove the few hundred yards to the Royal Palm knowing that Billy Cunningham would want to be in at the kill. As soon as he saw me he said, ‘*Capistrano* was in a marina called Running Mon, but she’s gone now.’

I said, ‘I know. The police are going to pick her up.’

‘Is Robinson on board?’

‘I hope so. I’m joining Perigord and Deane. They want me to identify Robinson. Want to come along?’

‘Try stopping me,’ he said. ‘I’m looking forward to meeting that son of a bitch.’

I made a decision. ‘We’ll go by boat. Let’s go down to the marina.’

We found Joe Cartwright in the marina office. I popped my head around the door, and said, ‘I want the rescue boat, Joe; with a full tank.’

Cartwright looked up. ‘Can’t be done, Mr Mangan. Got the engine out of her. Tuning her up for the BASRA Marathon next month.’

‘Damn! What else have we got that’s fast and seaworthy?’

‘What about the inflatable?’ he suggested. ‘She’s not bad.’

'Get her ready.'

Within minutes we were at sea, roaring east along the south coast towards the Lucayan Waterway. Some people feel uncomfortable about being in a blow-up boat but they are very good. They are unsinkable, and the British even use them as lifeboats for inshore rescue. And they are damned fast even if they do tend to skitter a bit on the surface of the water.

I told Billy about the plan of attack, and presently I pointed. 'There's the Waterway, and that's the Customs launch just turning in. We've got *Capistrano* trapped.'

I slowed as we entered the Waterway. The Casuarina Bridge was nearly two miles ahead, and in the distance I could see the Customs launch lying next to a white-hulled boat. 'They've got her.' We motored on and drew alongside the Customs launch where I tossed the painter to a seaman and cut the engine. 'Let's go aboard.'

As we stepped on to *Capistrano*'s deck I was accosted by a Customs officer. 'Who are you?'

'Tom Mangan.' I looked up at the bridge and saw Perigord and Deane looking down. 'I'm with Commissioner Deane.' Three men stood on the after deck. None of them was Robinson. 'That the crew?'

'Yes; skipper, engineer and seaman-cum-cook.'

'No one else?'

'We're still looking. I've got men searching below.'

One of the three men approached us. 'Hell, Captain, this is crazy. We're not carrying anything illegal. We're just on a cruise.' He was an American.

'Then you have nothing to worry about,' said the Customs man.

'Well, I've gotta get back before the bad weather blows up. Did you hear the weather report? If you don't let me go I'll have to see the American consul here.'

'I'll give you his address,' said the officer blandly.

Another Customs man emerged from a hatch. 'No one below,' he reported.

'Are you sure?' I said.

'We opened up every compartment big enough to hold a man.'

'It's a bust,' said Billy disgustedly.

Deane and Perigord had come down from the bridge and were picking their way along the shore towards us. I looked around the deck of *Capistrano* and stiffened as I noticed that the stern davits were empty. I swung around to face the skipper. 'Where's the dory – your tender?'

'Mr Brown took it.'

'Brown? Who's he?'

'The guy who chartered this boat back in Fort Lauderdale.'

'When was this?'

'Just as soon as we entered this canal. He said he'd have a final spin and he'd meet us at the other end at the north shore.'

'Christ, he's given us the slip.' I looked at the Customs man. 'You must have been following him too closely and he took fright – or an insurance policy. If you weren't going to stop *Capistrano* there'd be no harm done and he'd rejoin her on the north shore. But you did and his insurance has paid off.'

'He won't get far. He'll run into the boat at the other end.'

'I wouldn't bet on it,' said Billy. 'This guy plays real cute.' He gave an exasperated snort. 'Brown, for God's sake!'

The skipper said, 'Will someone tell me what the hell's going on?'

I turned and stepped on to the Customs launch. 'Come on. Let's go after him.' Billy followed me.

We dropped down into the inflatable, and just before I started the engine I heard Deane bellow, 'Mangan, come back!' I ignored him and drowned his voice in a staccato roar as I twisted the throttle. We shot under the bridge and I looked back to see Deane on the deck of *Capistrano*. He was waving frantically.

Billy chuckled. 'I guess he's wondering what will happen to Robinson if we get to him first.' He suddenly had an automatic pistol in his hand.

'Put that damn thing away,' I said. 'If Deane knows you have it you're for the chop. And we don't want murder.'

'Not murder,' said Billy. 'Execution.' But he put the gun back into its holster.

The Lucayan Waterway stretched ahead of us and there was nothing to be seen on its surface. On either side there were occasional inlets leading to the proposed residential estates on which no houses had yet been built – the water maze. It all went by in a blur as I cranked up to top speed.

'Something ahead – coming this way,' said Billy.

It was a small dot in the middle of the Waterway which rapidly grew in size under the influence of our combined speeds. 'The dory!' I said.

'And something coming up behind it,' said Billy. 'The other Customs launch?'

'I hope not,' I said.

There was no time to explain why because I was busy trying to ram the approaching boat. I pulled on the tiller but the dory went the other way in an evading manoeuvre, and as it flashed past I saw the man at the wheel pointing at me. Something hit the side with a thwack and there was the hiss of escaping air.

'Goddamn!' said Billy.

I twisted the boat in the water and cut speed. 'This boat is compartmented. One hole won't make much difference.' I looked around. There was no sign of the dory.

'I didn't mean that,' said Billy. 'But if I'm shot at I'm going to shoot back and to hell with Deane.' The gun was in his hand again.

I could not argue with that. 'It was Robinson; I saw him. Where did he go?'

Billy pointed to an inlet on the port side. 'He shot down that rabbit hole.'

The boat that had chased Robinson from the north shore was almost upon us. I stood up and waved with both hands, and as it approached it slowed. A Customs officer leaned from the wheelhouse, and I yelled, 'Get back to the north shore, you damn fool. Keep the cork in the bloody bottle. If he gets past he can lose you.'

'Who are you to give orders?'

'If you want to argue do it with Commissioner Deane. Now, get the hell back and guard that bloody entrance.'

The officer withdrew and the launch began to turn in the water. There was a metallic click as Billy put a round into the breech of his pistol. 'How to make friends and influence people.' He snapped off the safety catch. 'What do we do now?'

'I don't know.' I wished I had a map. 'Winkling him out of there won't be easy, but if we don't he can ditch the dory and make an escape overland. He could lose himself in the pine barrens to the east, and it would take a damned army to find him.'

Billy pointed down the Waterway. 'A boat's coming. Your friend the Commissioner, no doubt.'

I slipped the clutch on the idling engine and we began to move slowly. 'We're going in – but easy.'

I took the boat into the inlet, the engine putt-putting quietly, and we immediately came to a cross canal. 'Which way?' said Billy.

I tossed a mental coin. 'To starboard,' I said. 'It doesn't really matter.' We turned to the right and went on for about a hundred yards and came to another junction. Straight on or turn to the left? This was impossible – worse than Hampton Court Maze – and there were forty-five miles of it.

From behind came the noise of a rapidly accelerating engine, and Billy shouted, 'We went the wrong way! Go back!'

I spun the throttle and slammed over the tiller, and I was in time to see Robinson's dory shooting across the canal and into the main artery of the Waterway. As it went Billy popped off a shot and then was thrown back as the boat picked up speed and the bow rose into the air.

We slalomed round the corner and nearly ran into a Customs boat in the Waterway, scooting under its stern and missing by the thickness of a playing card. I twisted the throttle to slow, and kicked over the tiller so as to avoid hitting the opposite bank, then I looked around. The damned dory had disappeared again so I hailed the launch. 'Where did he go?'

Deane was on deck. 'Mangan, get out of here, and take your friend. This is no place for heroics from civilians.'

I repeated, 'Where did he go?'

The launch moved so as to be between me and an inlet. 'He moved in here – but it's no business of yours. Perigord is organizing reinforcements. *Is* he Robinson?'

'Yes.'

'Who's your friend?'

'If you want to know, why don't you ask me?' said Billy. 'I'm Billy Cunningham and I want that bastard, Robinson.'

'Mr Cunningham, I see you're holding a gun. You'd better not have it on your person when we meet again. You'd better drop it over the side.'

'In a pig's eye,' said Billy. He pointed to the hole in the rubber and fabric side of the boat. 'Robinson came out shooting.'

'Suit yourself,' said Deane. 'We have excellent jails. Mangan, go away. I want to see you going back down the Waterway.'

'Let's go,' I said quietly, and turned the boat away.

'Your goddamn cops!' said Billy disgustedly. 'You'd think he'd want our help, even thank us for it.'

'Be quiet!' I said. 'I'm thinking.'

Again I wished I had a map. I had used the Waterway many times when I had *Lucayan Girl*, but I had always stuck to the main channel and had not bothered to explore the maze. Now I wished I had. I had a map of Freeport-Lucaya in my office and I tried to visualize the layout of the Waterway.

We went on a mile down the Waterway and came to another inlet on the same side as the one blocked by the Customs launch. I said, 'We're going in here.'

'Is there a through connection?'

'No.'

'Then what's the use?'

I said, 'Billy, every section of this water-riddled bit of real estate has but one connection with the main channel, like the one we're in now. Deane knows that and he's sitting there like a terrier outside a rabbit hole waiting for Robinson to come out. Robinson may *not* know that and if he doesn't he'll be looking for another way out. So what happens when he can't find one?'

'He'll leave the boat and take to land.'

'Yes. And he's on the town side this time. It wouldn't be too hard for him to steal a car, and he stands a sporting chance of getting away. I think Deane is counting on Robinson wasting enough time looking for an exit to allow Perigord to bring up his reinforcements, and I think he's taking a hell of a chance.'

'So?'

'So we're going in to chase him into Deane's arms.'

'How in hell are we going to do that if there's no interconnection?'

'Portage,' I said. 'Now I'm glad we came in this boat and not the other.'

I had timed the minutes we had taken to get from one inlet to the other, and had kept a constant speed. Now we were going back, parallelling the Waterway on a minor canal. I reckoned that when we got half-way that would be the place to go overland. Presently I said, 'This should be it. We put ashore straight ahead.'

I cut the engine and we drifted until the boat nosed the bank. 'Keep your voice down,' I said. 'Robinson could very well be just on the other side of here.'

We went ashore and hauled out the inflatable. 'We'll take a look across there before carrying the boat over. And keep your head down.' We walked over limestone rubble and then over an unused paved road, built for the traffic that had never come. On the other side of the road I dropped into a crouch and then on to my belly as I neared the edge of the next canal.

I peered over the bank and everything was peaceful. A light breeze ruffled the surface of the water and there was no sign of Robinson's dory. I caught a movement out of the corner of my eye and looked to the left. In the middle distance was a half-constructed house, and a man was working on the roof. I returned my attention to the canal. 'Okay. Let's bring up the boat.'

Billy looked back. 'A long haul,' he said. 'Nearly two hundred yards.'

'We'll unship the engine,' I said. 'And the inflatable has carrying straps.'

It was hot and heavy work but we finally made the portage and were sitting in the boat with the engine resecured on the transom. I was about to start up when Billy said, 'Listen!'

Someone in the half-built house was using a hammer, but under the rhythmic knocking I heard the faraway growl of an outboard engine. It grew louder, and I said, 'He's coming this way. Let's move it.'

I started the engine, hoping that Robinson would not hear it over the noise of his own, and we moved off. I kept the pace slow and, when we had gone about 200 yards and come to a junction, I killed the engine. Again we heard the sound of another outboard motor, this time distinctly louder. Billy was moving his head from side to side to locate the direction. 'To the left,' he said, and took out his gun.

I restarted the engine and pushed over the tiller, and we moved to the left and towards the house in the distance. There was a bend ahead and I moved to the inside curve, still travelling slowly because I wanted to keep quiet. Over the sound of our own engine I heard the noise of another.

'There he is,' said Billy, and I saw the dory coming towards us on the other side of the canal on the outside of the bend. I twisted the throttle and the boat bucked at the sudden application of power. Then we were on to him and Billy was shooting, but so was Robinson. Even as Billy fired, a bullet impacted inboard close to my hand and again there was the hiss of escaping air. Robinson was too damn good with his shooting; he had fired but two shots and had hit us both times, and although I had told Billy the inflatable was compartmented Robinson had punctured two air chambers out of the five.

Then he was past us and I slammed over the tiller, already feeling the difference in the behaviour of the boat; she was slow to come about and not as easily controlled. But Billy shouted, 'He's stopped. I hit his engine.'

I twisted and looked back. The dory was drifting into the bank and, as it touched, Robinson leapt ashore and began to run. He paused and snapped one shot at us before disappearing behind one of the heaps of grey limestone rubble, the spoil left from the dredging of the canal.

'Let's get after him,' urged Billy.

I needed no urging. Already I was heading for the bank and standing, ready to jump. Our feet hit the ground simultaneously, and Billy said, 'We'll tackle him from two sides.' He gestured with his pistol. 'You go that way and keep your head down.' He ran in the other direction.

I ran to the nearest heap of limestone and dropped flat before peering around it cautiously. There was no sign of Robinson. From behind I heard the sound of engines so I looked back to see the Customs launch coming up the canal, fairly boiling along at top speed. Deane must have heard the shots and decided to come in.

I ignored it and turned again to look for Robinson. We were quite close to the house and there were now two men on the roof, and one of them was pointing at something. I followed the direction of his arm, got to my feet, and began to run. Skidding around another heap of rubble I came across Robinson about ten yards away. He had his back to me, and beyond him I saw Billy come into sight.

I was late in the tackle. Before I could get to him Robinson fired and Billy dropped in his tracks. But then I was on to him and I had no mercy. His pistol went flying and it took Deane and two of his men to prise my hands from Robinson's neck.

Deane hauled me to my feet and pushed me away, standing between me and Robinson. 'That's enough!' he said curtly.

I heard a car door slam and saw Perigord walking over from a police car near the house. I regained my breath, and said, 'Then get the bastard out of my sight before I kill him.' I turned and walked towards Billy.

He was sitting up, his hand to his head, and when he took it away it was red with blood. 'He creased me!' he said blankly. 'Jesus, but it hurts!' There was an unfocused look to his eyes, a sign of concussion. I stooped, picked up his gun, and walked to the water's edge and tossed it into the canal. Then I went back and helped him to his feet.

'You're lucky you're not dead,' I said. 'Be glad it hurts; it means you'll live.'

Already he was looking better. He glanced across at Deane and saw Robinson still prostrate on the ground. 'Well, we've got him.'

'Yes,' I said shortly. Deane would not now need any excuse for holding Robinson. Any man who popped off a gun was automatically his prey – including Billy. Still, Deane had not seen Billy shoot, so, as we walked towards him, I said, 'I ditched your gun in the canal.'

'Thanks.'

Robinson sat up and Deane was addressing him in fast, fluent Spanish. Among the spate of words I heard the name Perez, repeated several times. Robinson shook his head and replied in Spanish, and then switched into English, with the same plummy accent I had come to know in Texas. 'I'm a soldier of the revolution,' he said pompously. 'And now a prisoner of war. I will answer no questions.' He got to his feet.

'Prisoner of war?' said Billy unbelievingly. 'The guy's nuts!'

'He's a bloody murderer,' I said.

'But that's for a court to decide, Mr Mangan,' said Perigord.

Deane took out handcuffs and then paused, looking at Billy expressionlessly. 'Search this man,' he said.

Billy grinned widely as Perigord's hands expertly patted his body. 'What gun?' he said. 'I took your advice. It was good.'

It was then that Robinson made his break. He thumped the nearest Customs officer in the gut, sending him to the ground writhing and retching, and took off, running towards the house. He took us all by surprise. Deane dropped the handcuffs and broke into a run, with me at his heels.

The builders at the house had stopped work and were now all on the roof, a good vantage point to view the morning's unexpected entertainment. The sole exception was the driver of a truck which had just arrived. He had got out, leaving the door open and the engine idling, and was calling to the men on the roof. Robinson clouted him in passing and he staggered back to collide with Deane and they both went down in a tangle of arms and legs.

By that time Robinson was in the cab and the engine of the truck roared. I leaped over the sprawled bodies of Deane and the driver and jumped for the cab, but it was too late and the truck was moving. I missed and fell to the ground. By the time I had picked myself up the truck was speeding up the road.

I saw Perigord getting into his car so I ran and piled in next to him just as he drove off with a squeal of rubber and a lot of wheel spin. He drove with one hand while unhooking the microphone of his radio from its bracket. He began to give brief but precise instructions, and I gathered that he was remarshalling his forces.

The truck was still in sight and we were gaining on it. It turned left on to East Sunrise Highway, and I said, 'He'll be going on to Midshipman Road, by the Garden of the Groves.'

'Yes,' said Perigord, and spoke into the microphone again.

The Garden of the Groves is one of the more sedate of our tourist attractions, the name being a punning one because the 100-acre gardens are dedicated to the memory of Wallace Groves, the founder of Freeport. There were always tourists wandering about that area and the chances were that Robinson could kill someone, travelling at the speed he was.

We sped down East Sunrise and turned on to Midshipman, and by then we were within fifty yards of the truck. A car shot out of a side road and hit the truck a glancing blow and Perigord braked hard as it crashed into a palm tree. I fumbled for the door handle as I saw Robinson jump from the cab and run towards the Garden.

Perigord was out before me, and he did something surprising – he threw his swagger stick at Robinson. It flew straight as an arrow and hit Robinson at the nape of the neck and he fell in a tumbled heap in the road.

Perigord was about to go to him but jumped back as a big double-decker London bus came around the corner. The driver swerved to avoid the crashed truck and his brakes squealed, but it was too late. The bus brushed past Perigord but one wheel went over Robinson's head.

Epilogue

After the immediate discussion that followed that incident I did not see Perigord to talk with seriously for nearly a month. He was a very busy man, and so was Commissioner Deane over in Nassau. But he did telephone to tell me that the ampoules found on Carrasco-Perez proved to contain a culture of *L. pneumophila*, enough to poison the water in every hotel in the Bahamas.

On the occasion of the annual BASRA Swimming Marathon I invited him and his family back to the house for drinks. Both our daughters had been competitors and Karen, like Sue before her, had won a second prize in her class. Full of pride and ice-cream she cavorted in the pool with Ginnie Perigord, and there did not seem to be much difference between a tanned white hide and a natural brown hide.

Debbie laughed and said to Amy Perigord, 'Where do they get the energy? You wouldn't think they've just swum two miles. Would you like a drink?'

'I'd rather have tea,' said Mrs Perigord. 'I'm not really a drinker.'

'We won't bother Luke,' said Debbie. 'Come into the kitchen and chat while I make it.'

I smiled at Perigord as they went away. Because he had attended the Marathon in his official capacity he was in full fig, swagger stick and all. I said, 'I propose something stronger. What will you have?'

He sat down and laid his cap and swagger stick by the chair. 'Some people think because I'm a black Bahamian that I exist on a liquid diet of rum, but I prefer scotch.'

I went to the poolside bar and held up a bottle of Glenlivet. 'This do?'

He grinned. 'That will do very well.'

I poured two drinks and put a bottle of iced water at his elbow. I said, 'Billy Cunningham rang me this morning. He says he's growing a streak of white hair where that bullet grazed him. He thinks it makes him look distinguished.'

'Did he really lose that pistol in the water?' asked Perigord curiously.

'I'll answer that by asking you a question,' I said. 'Would Deane really have framed the crew of *Capistrano* by planting cocaine?'

Perigord smiled. 'I see.' He ignored the water and sipped the scotch. 'Very good,' he observed.

'Now, tell me – who was Robinson?'

'We sent his fingerprints to the States and the Americans told us, but we could have found out ourselves once we began to dig. He was an Anglo-Cuban, educated in England. His name was Rojas and he was Perez's brother-in-law.'

I contemplated that information which did not mean much to me. 'So what happens now? Do we live in a permanent state of siege?'

'I don't think so,' said Perigord. 'An attempt was made – a covert attack on the Bahamas – and it failed. We have investigated every unusual occurence since Rojas was killed and have found nothing to indicate that the attack is continuing. In my opinion, an opinion now shared by Commissioner Deane and the Government, the whole idea was conceived, planned and executed by Perez and Rojas. Probably Castro knew nothing about it.'

'You think not?'

'I think it was rather like Henry II and Becket. You know the story?'

'Henry said, "Who will rid me of this turbulent priest?" and the four knights went and slaughtered Becket in the cathedral.'

'Henry did penance for it afterwards,' said Perigord. 'I know Fidel Castro is no saint, but I don't think he'd stoop to what that pair did. He's too vulnerable himself. No, there's been bad blood between Cuba and the Bahamas ever since their jet planes shot up our fishery patrol vessel and killed four men, and matters haven't become any easier since. I think Castro wondered aloud how to solve the Bahamian question, and Perez and Rojas decided to take action.'

'So you now think we can live like reasonable human beings.'

'I would say so.' He smiled. 'But didn't someone say that eternal vigilance is the price of liberty. It has taught us a lesson from which we have benefited. At a cost.'

'I'm not going to relax the security measures in the hotels,' I said.

'Very wise. We also have instituted security measures; they are unobtrusive but they are there.' He held up his hand. 'Don't ask me what they are.'

I grinned at him. 'I wouldn't dream of it.' We sat in silence for a while and Perigord savoured his whisky. I said, 'You know the funniest thing in the whole damn business?'

'What?'

'When you threw that swagger stick. You looked so damned silly, but it worked.'

'Ah, the swagger stick. Do you know the history of this?'

'No.'

'It's the lineal descendent of the ash plant carried by the Roman centurion over two thousand years ago. He used it to discipline his men, but then it became a staff of office. The line split quite early; one way led to the field marshal's baton, the other to the officer's cane. Catch!' He suddenly tossed it to me.

I grabbed it out of the air and nearly dropped it because it was unexpectedly heavy. I had thought it to be merely a cane encased in leather, but this one was loaded with lead at both ends. Perigord said suavely, 'Not only a staff of office but a weapon against crime. It has saved my life twice.'

I returned the weapon against crime, and he said, 'Amy confided in me this afternoon that your wife is expecting a baby. Is that so?'

'Yes – in about six months.'

'I'm glad she wasn't permanently harmed by what happened in Texas. In view of what I know about your family history may I offer the hope that it will be a boy?'

And six months later Karen had a brother.

The Enemy

To all the DASTards

especially

Iwan and Inga
Jan and Anita
Hemming and Annette

We have met the enemy, and he is ours.

OLIVER HAZARD PERRY
Heroic American Commodore

We have met the enemy, and he is us.

WALT KELLY
Subversive Sociological Cartoonist

1

I met Penelope Ashton at a party thrown by Tom Packer. That may be a bit misleading because it wasn't the kind of party that gets thrown very far; no spiked punch or pot, and no wife-swapping or indiscriminate necking in the bedrooms at two in the morning. Just a few people who got together over a civilized dinner with a fair amount of laughter and a hell of a lot of talk. But it did tend to go on and what with Tom's liberal hand with his after-dinner scotches I didn't feel up to driving, so when I left I took a taxi.

Penny Ashton came with Dinah and Mike Huxham; Dinah was Tom's sister. I still haven't worked out whether I was invited as a makeweight for the odd girl or whether she was brought to counterbalance me. At any rate when we sat at table the sexes were even and I was sitting next to her. She was a tall, dark woman, quiet and composed in manner and not very forthcoming. She was no raving beauty, but few women are; Helen of Troy may have launched a thousand ships but no one was going to push the boat out for Penny Ashton, at least not at first sight. Not that she was ugly or anything like that. She had a reasonably good figure and a reasonably good face, and she dressed well. I think the word to describe her would be average. I put her age at about twenty-seven and I wasn't far out. She was twenty-eight.

As was usual with Tom's friends, the talk ranged far and wide; Tom was a rising star in the upper reaches of the medical establishment and he was eclectic in his choice of dining companions and so the talk was good. Penny joined in but she tended to listen rather than talk and her interjections were infrequent. Gradually I became aware that when she did speak her comments were acute, and there was a sardonic cast to her eye when she was listening to something she didn't agree with. I found her spikiness of mind very agreeable.

After dinner the talk went on in the living-room over coffee and brandy. I opted for scotch because brandy doesn't agree with me, a circumstance Tom knew very well because he poured one of his measures big enough to paralyse an elephant and left the jug of iced water convenient to my elbow.

As is common on these occasions, while the dinner-table conversation is general and involves everybody, after dinner the party tended to split into small groups, each pursuing their congenial arguments and riding their hobby-horses hard and on a loose rein. To my mild surprise I found myself opting for a group of two – myself and Penny Ashton. I suppose there were a dozen of us there, but I settled in a corner and monopolized Penny Ashton. Or did she monopolize me? It could have been six of one and half-a-dozen of the other; it usually is in cases like that.

I forget what we talked about at first but gradually our conversation became more personal. I discovered she was a research biologist specializing in genetics and that she worked with Professor Lumsden at University College, London. Genetics is the hottest and most controversial subject in science today and Lumsden was in the forefront of the battle. Anyone working with him would have to be very bright indeed and I was suitably impressed. There was a lot more to Penny Ashton than met the casual eye.

Some time during the evening she asked, 'And what do you do?'

'Oh, I'm someone in the City,' I said lightly.

She got that sardonic look in her eye and said reprovingly, 'Satire doesn't become you.'

'It's true!' I protested. 'Someone's got to make the wheels of commerce turn.' She didn't pursue the subject.

Inevitably someone checked his watch and discovered with horror the lateness of the hour, and the party began to break up. Usually the more congenial the party the later the hour, and it was pretty late. Penny said, 'My God – my train!'

'Which station?'

'Victoria.'

'I'll drop you,' I said and stood up, swaying slightly as I felt Tom's scotch. 'From a taxi.'

I borrowed the telephone and rang for a taxi, and then we stood around making party noises until it arrived. As we were driven through the brightly-lit London streets I reflected that it had been a good evening; it had been quite a while since I had felt so good. And it wasn't because of the quality of Tom's booze, either.

I turned to Penny. 'Known the Packers long?'

'A few years. I was at Cambridge with Dinah Huxham – Dinah Packer she was then.'

'Nice people. It's been a good evening.'

'I enjoyed it.'

I said, 'How about repeating it – just the two of us? Say, the theatre and supper afterwards.'

She was silent for a moment, then said, 'All right.' So we fixed a time for the following Wednesday and I felt even better.

She wouldn't let me come into the station with her so I kept the taxi and redirected it to my flat. It was only then I realized I didn't know if she was married or not, and I tried to remember the fingers of her left hand. Then I thought I was a damned fool; I hardly knew the woman so what did it matter if she was married or not? I wasn't going to marry her myself, was I?

On the Wednesday I picked her up at University College at seven-fifteen in the evening and we had a drink at a pub near the theatre before seeing the show. I don't like theatre crush bars; they're too well named. 'Do you always work as late as this?' I asked.

She shook her head. 'It varies. It's not a nine-to-five job, you know. When we're doing something big we could be there all night, but that doesn't happen often. I laboured tonight because I was staying in town.' She smiled. 'It helped me catch up on some of the paperwork.'

'Ah; the paperwork is always with us.'

'You ought to know; your job is all paperwork, isn't it?'

I grinned. 'Yes; shuffling all those fivers around.'

So we saw the show and I took her to supper in Soho and then to Victoria Station. And made another date for the Saturday.

And, as they say, one thing led to another and soon I was squiring her around regularly. We took in more theatres, an opera, a couple of ballets, a special exhibition at the National Gallery, Regent's Park Zoo, something she wanted to see at the Natural History Museum, and a trip down the river to Greenwich. We could have been a couple of Americans doing the tourist bit.

After six weeks of this I think we both thought that things were becoming pretty serious. I, at least, took it seriously enough to go to Cambridge to see my father. He smiled when I told him about Penny, and said, 'You know, Malcolm, you've been worrying me. It's about time you settled down. Do you know anything about the girl's family?'

'Not much,' I admitted. 'From what I can gather he's some sort of minor industrialist. I haven't met him yet.'

'Not that it matters,' said my father. 'I hope we've gone beyond snobberies like that. Have you bedded the girl yet?'

'No,' I said slowly. 'We've come pretty close, though.'

'Um!' he said obscurely, and began to fill his pipe. 'It's been my experience here at the college that the rising generation isn't as swinging and uninhibited as it likes to think it is. Couples don't jump bare-skinned into a bed at the first opportunity – not if they're taking each other seriously and have respect for each other. Is it like that with you?'

I nodded. 'I've had my moments in the past, but somehow it's different with Penny. Anyway, I've known her only a few weeks.'

'You remember Joe Patterson?'

'Yes.' Patterson was head of one of the departments of psychology.

'He reckons the ordinary man is mixed up about the qualities he wants in a permanent partner. He once told me that the average man's ideal wife-to-be is a virgin in the terminal stages of nymphomania. A witticism, but with truth in it.

'Joe is a cynic.'

'Most wise men are. Anyway, I'd like to see Penny as soon as you can screw up your courage. Your mother would have been happy to see you married; it's a pity about that.'

'How are you getting on, Dad?'

'Oh, I rub along. The chief danger is of becoming a university eccentric; I'm trying to avoid that.'

We talked of family matters for some time and then I went back to London.

It was at this time that Penny made a constructive move. We were in my flat talking over coffee and liqueurs; she had complimented me on the Chinese dinner and I had modestly replied that I had sent out for it myself. It was then that she invited me to her home for the weekend. To meet the family.

2

She lived with her father and sister in a country house near Marlow in Buckinghamshire, a short hour's spin from London up the M4. George Ashton was a widower in his mid-fifties who lived with his daughters in a brick-built Queen Anne house of the type you see advertised in a full-page spread in *Country Life*. It had just about everything. There were two tennis courts and one swimming pool; there was a stable block converted into garages filled with expensive bodies on wheels, and there was a stable block that was still a stable block and filled with expensive bodies on legs – one at each corner. It was a Let's-have-tea-on-the-lawn sort of place; The-master-will-see-you-in-the-library sort of place. The good, rich, upper-middle-class life.

George Ashton stood six feet tall and was thatched with a strong growth of iron-grey hair. He was very fit, as I found out on the tennis court. He played an aggressive, hard-driving game and I was hard put to cope with him even though he had a handicap of about twenty-five years. He beat me 5–7, 7–5, 6–3, which shows his stamina was better than mine. I came off the court out of puff but Ashton trotted down to the swimming pool, dived in clothed as he was, and swam a length before going into the house to change.

I flopped down beside Penny. 'Is he always like that?'

'Always,' she assured me.

I groaned. 'I'll be exhausted just watching him.'

Penny's sister, Gillian, was as different from Penny as could be. She was the domestic type and ran the house. I don't mean she acted as lady of the house and merely gave orders. She *ran* it. The Ashtons didn't have much staff;

there were a couple of gardeners and a stable girl, a houseman-cum-chauffeur called Benson, a full-time maid and a daily help who came in for a couple of hours each morning. Not much staff for a house of that size.

Gillian was a couple of years younger than Penny and there was a Martha and Mary relationship between them which struck me as a little odd. Penny didn't do much about the house as far as I could see, apart from keeping her own room tidy, cleaning her own car and grooming her own horse. Gillian was the Martha who did all the drudgery but she didn't seem to mind and appeared to be quite content. Of course, it was a weekend and it might have been different during the week. All the same, I thought Ashton would get a shock should Gillian marry and leave to make a home of her own.

It was a good weekend although I felt a bit awkward at first, conscious of being on show; but I was soon put at ease in that relaxed household. Dinner that evening, cooked by Gillian, was simple and well served, and afterwards we played bridge. I partnered Penny and Ashton partnered Gillian, and soon I found that Gillian and I were the rabbits. Penny played a strong, exact and carefully calculated game, while Ashton played bridge as he played tennis, aggressively and taking chances at times. I observed that the chances he took came off more often than not, but Penny and I came slightly ahead at the end, although it was nip and tuck.

We talked for a while until the girls decided to go to bed, then Ashton suggested a nightcap. The scotch he poured was not in the same class as Tom Packer's but not far short, and we settled down for a talk. Not unexpectedly he wanted to know something about me and was willing to trade information, so I learned how he earned his pennies among other things. He ran a couple of manufacturing firms in Slough producing something abstruse in the chemical line and another which specialized in high-impact plastics. He employed about a thousand men and was the sole owner, which impressed me. There are not too many organizations like that around which are still in the hands of one man.

Then he enquired, very politely, what I did to earn my bread, and I said, 'I'm an analyst.'

He smiled slightly. 'Psycho?'

I grinned. 'No – economic. I'm a junior partner with McCulloch and Ross; we're economic consultants.'

'Yes, I've heard of your crowd. What exactly is it that you do?'

'Advisory work of all sorts – market surveys, spotting opportunities for new products, or new areas for existing products, and so on. Also general economics and financial advice. We do the general dogsbodying for firms which are not big enough to support their own research group. ICI wouldn't need us but a chap like you might.'

He seemed interested in that. 'I've been thinking of going public,' he said. 'I'm not all that old, but one never knows what may happen. I'd like to leave things tidy for the girls.'

'It might be very profitable for you personally,' I said. 'And, as you say, it would tidy up the estate in the event of your death – make the death duties bit less messy.' I thought about it for a minute. 'But I don't know if this is the time to float a new issue. You'd do better to wait for an upturn in the economy.'

'I've not entirely decided yet,' he said. 'But if I do decide to go public then perhaps you can advise me.'

'Of course. It's exactly our line of work.'

He said no more about it and the conversation drifted to other topics. Soon thereafter we went to bed.

Next morning after breakfast – cooked by Gillian – I declined Penny's invitation to go riding with her, the horse being an animal I despise and distrust. So instead we walked where she would have ridden and went over a forested hill along a broad ride, and descended the other side into a sheltered valley where we lunched in a pub on bread, cheese, pickles and beer, and where Penny demonstrated her skill at playing darts with the locals. Then back to the house where we lazed away the rest of the sunny day on the lawn.

I left the house that evening armed with an invitation to return the following weekend, not from Penny but from Ashton. 'Do you play croquet?' he asked.

'No, I don't.'

He smiled. 'Come next weekend and I'll show you how. I'll have Benson set up the hoops during the week.'

So it was that I drove back to London well contented.

I have given the events of that first weekend in some detail in order to convey the atmosphere of the place and the family. Ashton, the minor industrialist, richer than others of his type because he ran his own show; Gillian, his younger daughter, content to be dutifully domestic and to act as hostess and surrogate wife without the sex bit; and Penny the bright elder daughter, carving out a career in science. And she *was* bright; it was only casually that weekend I learned she was an MD although she didn't practise.

And there was the money. The Rolls, the Jensen and the Aston Martin in the garage, the sleek-bodied horses, the manicured lawns, the furnishings of that beautiful house – all these reeked of money and the good life. Not that I envied Ashton – I have a bit of money myself although not in the same class. I mention it only as a fact because it was there.

The only incongruity in the whole scene was Benson, the general factotum, who did not look like anyone's idea of a servant in a rich household. Rather, he looked like a retired pugilist and an unsuccessful one at that. His nose had been broken more than once in my judgement, and his ears were swollen with battering. Also he had a scar on his right cheek. He would have made a good heavy in a Hammer film. His voice clashed unexpectedly with his appearance, being soft and with an educated accent better than Ashton's own. I didn't know what to make of him at all.

Something big was apparently happening in Penny's line of work that week, and she rang to say she would be in the laboratory all Friday night, and would I pick her up on Saturday morning to take her home. When she got into the car outside University College she looked very tired, with dark smudges under her eyes. 'I'm sorry, Malcolm,' she said. 'This won't be much of a weekend for you. I'm going to bed as soon as I get home.'

I was sorry, too, because this was the weekend I intended to ask her to marry me. However, this wasn't the time, so I grinned and said, 'I'm not coming to see you – I'm coming for the croquet.' Not that I knew much about it – just the bit from Alice and an association with vicars and maiden ladies.

Penny smiled, and said, 'I don't suppose I should tell you this, but Daddy says he can measure a man by the way he plays croquet.'

I said, 'What were you doing all night?'

'Working hard.'

'Doing what. Is it a state secret?'

'No secret. We transferred genetic material from a virus to a bacterium.'

'Sounds finicky,' I remarked. 'With success, I hope.'

'We won't know until we test the resulting strain. We should know something in a couple of weeks; this stuff breeds fast. We hope it will breed true.'

What I know about genetics could be measured with an eye-dropper. I said curiously, 'What good does all this do?'

'Cancer research,' she said shortly, and laid her head back, closing her eyes. I left her alone after that.

When we got to the house she went to bed immediately. Other than that the weekend was much the same as before. Until the end, that is – then it changed for the worse. I played tennis with Ashton, then swam in the pool, and we had lunch on the lawn in the shade of a chestnut tree, just the three of us, Ashton, Gillian and me. Penny was still asleep.

After lunch I was introduced to the intricacies of match-play croquet and, by God, there *was* a vicar! Croquet, I found, is not a game for the faint-hearted, and the way the Reverend Hawthorne played made Machiavelli look like a Boy Scout. Fortunately he was on my side, but all his tortuous plotting was of no avail against Gillian and Ashton. Gillian played a surprisingly vicious game. Towards the end, when I discovered it's not a game for gentlemen, I quite enjoyed it.

Penny came down for afternoon tea, refreshed and more animated than she had been, and from then on the weekend took its normal course. Put down baldly on paper, as I have done here, such a life may be considered pointless and boring, but it wasn't really; it was a relief from the stresses of the working week.

Apparently Ashton did not get even that relief because after tea he retired to his study, pleading that he had to attend to paperwork. I commented that Penny had complained of the same problem, and he agreed that putting unnecessary words on paper was the besetting sin of the twentieth century. As he walked away I reflected that Ashton could not have got where he was by idling his time away playing tennis and croquet.

And so the weekend drifted by until it was nearly time for me to leave. It was a pleasant summer Sunday evening. Gillian had gone to church but was expected back at any moment; she was the religious member of the family – neither Ashton nor Penny showed any interest in received religion. Ashton, Penny and I were sitting in lawn chairs arguing a particularly knotty point in scientific ethics which had arisen out of an article in the morning newspaper. Rather, it was Penny and her father doing the arguing; I was contemplating how to get her alone so I could propose to her. Somehow we had never been alone that weekend.

Penny was becoming a little heated when we heard a piercing scream and then another. The three of us froze, Penny in mid-sentence, and Ashton said sharply, 'What the devil was that?'

A third scream came. It was nearer this time and seemed to be coming from the other side of the house. By this time we were on our feet and moving, but then Gillian came into sight, stumbling around the corner of the house, her hands to her face. She screamed again, a bubbling, wordless screech, and collapsed on the lawn.

Ashton got to her first. He bent over her and tried to pull her hands from her face, but Gillian resisted him with all her strength. 'What's the matter?' he yelled, but all he got was a shuddering moan.

Penny said quickly, 'Let me', and gently pulled him away. She bent over Gillian who was now lying on her side curled in a foetal position, her hands still at her face with the fingers extended like claws. The screams had stopped and were replaced by an extended moaning, and once she said, 'My eyes! Oh, my eyes!'

Penny forced her hand to Gillian's face and touched it with her forefinger, rubbing gently. She frowned and put the tip of her finger to her nose, then hastily wiped it on the grass. She turned to her father. 'Take her into the house quickly – into the kitchen.'

She stood up and whirled towards me in one smooth motion. 'Ring for an ambulance. Tell them it's an acid burn.'

Ashton had already scooped up Gillian in his arms as I ran to the house, brushing past Benson as I entered the hall. I picked up the telephone and rang 999 and then watched Ashton carry his daughter through a doorway I had never entered, with Penny close behind him.

A voice said in my ear, 'Emergency services.'

'Ambulance.'

There was a click and another voice said immediately, 'Ambulance service.' I gave him the address and the telephone number. 'And your name, sir?'

'Malcolm Jaggard. It's a bad facial acid burn.'

'Right, sir; we'll be as quick as we can.'

As I put down the phone I was aware that Benson was staring at me with a startled expression. Abruptly he turned on his heel and walked out of the house. I opened the door to the kitchen and saw Gillian stretched on a table with Penny applying something to her face. Her legs were kicking convulsively and she was still moaning. Ashton was standing by and I have never seen on any man's face such an expression of helpless rage. There wasn't much I could do there and I'd only be in the way so I closed the door gently.

Looking through the big window at the far end of the hall, I saw Benson walking along the drive. He stopped and bent down, looking at something not on the drive but on the wide grass verge. I went out to join him and saw what had attracted his attention; a car had turned there, driving on the grass, and it had done so at speed because the immaculate lawn had been chewed up and the wheels had gouged right down to the soil.

Benson said in his unexpctedly gentle voice, 'As I see it, sir, the car came into the grounds and was parked about there, facing the house. When Miss Gillian walked up someone threw acid in her face here.' He pointed to where a few blades of grass were already turning brown. 'Then the car turned on the grass and drove away.'

'But you didn't see it.'

'No, sir.'

I bent and looked at the wheel marks. 'I think this should be protected until the police get here.'

Benson thought for a moment. 'The gardener made some hurdles for the new paddock. I'll get those.'

'That should do it,' I agreed.

I helped him bring them and we covered the marks. I

straightened as I heard the faint hee-haw of an ambulance, becoming louder as it approached. That was quick – under six minutes. I walked back to the house and rang 999 again.

'Emergency services.'

'The police, please.'

Click. 'Police here.'

'I want to report a criminal assault.'

3

They got Gillian into the ambulance very quickly. Penny used her authority as a doctor and went into the ambulance with her, while Ashton followed in a car. I judged he was in no condition to drive and was pleased to see Benson behind the wheel when he left.

Before he went I took him on one side. 'I think you ought to know I've sent for the police.'

He turned a ravaged face towards me and blinked stupidly. 'What's that?' He seemed to have aged ten years in a quarter of an hour.

I repeated what I'd said, and added, 'They'll probably come while you're still at the hospital. I can tell them what they need to know. Don't worry about it. I'll stay here until you get back.'

'Thanks, Malcolm.'

I watched them drive away and then I was alone in the house. The maid lived in, but Sunday was her day off, and now Benson had gone there was no one in the house but me. I went into the living-room, poured myself a drink and lit a cigarette, and sat down to think of just what the hell had happened.

Nothing made sense. Gillian Ashton was a plain, ordinary woman who lived a placid and unadventurous life. She was a homebody who one day might marry an equally unadventurous man who liked his home comforts. Acid-throwing wasn't in that picture; it was something that might happen in Soho or the murkier recesses of the East End of London – it was incongruous in the Buckinghamshire countryside.

I thought about it for a long time and got nowhere.

Presently I heard a car drive up and a few minutes later I was talking to a couple of uniformed policemen. I couldn't tell them much; I knew little about Gillian and not much more about Ashton and, although the policemen were polite, I sensed an increasing dissatisfaction. I showed them the tracks and one of them stayed to guard them while the other used his car radio. When I looked from the window a few minutes later I saw he had moved the police car so he could survey the back of the house.

Twenty minutes later a bigger police gun arrived in the person of a plain clothes man. He talked for a while with the constable in the car, then walked towards the house and I opened the door at his knock. 'Detective-Inspector Honnister,' he said briskly. 'Are you Mr Jaggard?'

'That's right. Won't you come in?'

He walked into the hall and stood looking around. As I closed the door he swung on me. 'Are you alone in the house?'

The constable had been punctilious about his 'sirs' but not Honnister. I said, 'Inspector, I'm going to show you something which I shouldn't but which, in all fairness to yourself, I think you ought to see. I'm quite aware my answers didn't satisfy your constable. I'm alone in Ashton's house, admit to knowing hardly anything about the Ashtons, and he thinks I might run away with the spoons.'

Honnister's eyes crinkled. 'From the look of it there's a lot more to run away with here than spoons. What have you to show me?'

'This.' I dug the card out of the pocket which my tailor builds into all my jackets and gave it to him.

Honnister's eyebrows rose as he looked at it. 'We don't get many of these,' he commented. 'This is only the third I've seen.' He flicked at the plastic with his thumbnail as he compared me with the photograph. 'You'll realize I'll have to test the authenticity of this.'

'Of course. I'm only showing it to you so you don't waste

time on me. You can use this telephone or the one in Ashton's study.'

'Will I get an answer this time on Sunday?'

I smiled. 'We're like the police, Inspector; we never close.'

I showed him into the study and it didn't take long. He came out within five minutes and gave me back the card. 'Well, Mr Jaggard; got any notions on this?'

I shook my head. 'It beats me. I'm not here in a professional capacity, if that's what you mean.' From his shrewd glance I could see he didn't believe me, so I told of my relationship with the Ashtons and all I knew of the attack on Gillian which wasn't much.

He said wryly, 'This is one we'll have to do the hard way, then – starting with those tracks. Thank you for your co-operation, Mr Jaggard. I'd better be getting on with it.'

I went with him to the door. 'One thing, Inspector, you never saw that card.'

He nodded abruptly and left.

Ashton and Penny came back more than two hours later. Penny looked as tired as she had the previous morning, but Ashton had recovered some of his colour and springiness. 'Good of you to stay, Malcolm,' he said. 'Stay a little longer – I want to talk to you. Not now, but later.' His voice was brusque and he spoke with authority; what he had issued was not a request but an order. He strode across the hall and went into the study. The door slammed behind him.

I turned to Penny. 'How's Gillian?'

'Not very good,' she said sombrely. 'It was strong acid, undiluted. Who would do such a barbarous thing?'

'That's what the police want to know.' I told her something of my conversation with Honnister. 'He thinks your father might know something about this. Does he have any enemies?'

'Daddy!' She frowned. 'He's very strong-minded and single-minded, and people like that don't go through life without treading on a few toes. But I can't think he'd make the kind of enemy who would throw acid into his daughter's face.'

Somehow I couldn't, either. God knows some funny things go on in the economic and industrial jungles, but they rarely include acts of gratuitous violence. I turned as Benson came out of the kitchen carrying a tray on which were a jug of water, an unopened bottle of whisky and two glasses. I watched him go into the study then said, 'What about Gillian?'

Penny stared at me. 'Gillian!' She shook her head in disbelief. 'You're not suggesting Gillian could make that kind of enemy? It's preposterous.'

It was certainly unlikely but not as impossible as Penny thought. Quiet homebodies have been known to lead exotic and secret lives, and I wondered if Gillian had done anything else on her shopping trips into Marlow besides buying the odd pound of tea. But I said tactfully, 'Yes, it's unlikely.'

As I helped Penny get together a scratch meal she said, 'I tried to neutralize the acid with a soda solution, and in the ambulance they had better stuff than that. But she's in the intensive care unit at the hospital.'

We had rather an uncomfortable meal, just the two of us because Ashton wouldn't come out of the study, saying he wasn't hungry. An hour later, when I was wondering if he'd forgotten I was there, Benson came into the room. 'Mr Ashton would like to see you, sir.'

'Thank you.' I made my excuses to Penny and went into the study. Ashton was sitting behind a large desk but rose as I entered. I said, 'I can't tell you how sorry I am that this awful thing should have happened.'

He nodded. 'I know, Malcolm.' His hand grasped the whisky bottle which I noted was now only half full. He glanced at the tray, and said, 'Be a good chap and get yourself a clean glass.'

He was silent for a while, then he said, 'You could do better by changing your job. I have an opening which is ideal for a man like yourself. Initially you'd have to spend at least one year in Australia getting things off the ground, but that wouldn't hurt a couple of youngsters like you and Penny. The only trouble is that it must be now – almost immediately.'

He was going too fast for me. 'Hold on a moment,' I protested. 'I don't even know if she'll marry me.'

'She will,' he said positively. 'I know my daughter.'

He evidently knew her better than I did because I wasn't nearly so certain. 'Even so,' I said. 'There's Penny to consider. Her work is important to her. I can't see her throwing it up and going to Australia for a year just like that. And that's apart from anything I might think about the advisability of making a change.'

'She could take a sabbatical. Scientists do that all the time.'

'Maybe. Frankly, I'd need to know a lot more about it before making a decision.'

For the first time Ashton showed annoyance. He managed to choke it down and disguise it, but it was there. He thought for a moment, then said in conciliatory tones, 'Well, a decision on that might wait a month. I think you'd better pop the question, Malcolm. I can fix a special licence and you can get married towards the end of the week.' He tried to smile genially but the smile got nowhere near his eyes which still had a hurt look in them. 'I'll give you a house for a dowry – somewhere in the South Midlands, north of London.'

It was a time for plain speaking. 'I think you're going a bit too fast. I don't see the necessity for a special licence. In fact, it's my guess that Penny wouldn't hear of it, even if she does agree to marry me. I rather think she'd like to have Gillian at the wedding.'

Ashton's face crumpled and he seemed to lose what little composure he had. I said evenly, 'It was always in my

'I'd rather not drink any more this evening. I still have to drive back to town.'

He put down the bottle gently and came from behind the desk. 'Sit down,' he said, and thus began one of the weirdest interviews of my life. He paused for a moment. 'How are things with you and Penny?'

I looked at him consideringly. 'Are you asking if my intentions are honourable?'

'More or less. Have you slept with her yet?'

That was direct enough. 'No.' I grinned at him. 'You brought her up too well.'

He grunted. 'Well, what are your intentions – if any?'

'I thought it might be a good idea if I asked her to marry me.'

He didn't seemed displeased at that. 'And have you?'

'Not yet.'

He rubbed the side of his jaw reflectively. 'This job of yours – what sort of income do you make out of it?'

That was a fair question if I was going to marry his daughter. 'Last year it was a fraction over £8000; this year will be better.' Aware that a man like Ashton would regard that as chickenfeed I added, 'And I have private investments which bring in a further £11,000.'

He raised his eyebrows. 'You still work with a private income?'

'That £11,000 is *before* tax,' I said wryly, and shrugged. 'And a man must do something with his life.'

'How old are you?'

'Thirty-four.'

He leaned back in his chair and said musingly, '£8000 a year isn't bad – so far. Any prospects of advancement in the firm?'

'I'm bucking for it.'

He then asked me a couple of questions which were a damned sight more personal than digging into my finances but, again, in the circumstances they were fair and my answers seemed to satisfy him.

mind to buy a house when I married. Your offer of a house is very generous, but I think the kind of house it should be – and where it should be – are matters for Penny and me to decide between us.'

He stood up, walked to the desk, and poured himself a drink. With his back to me he said indistinctly, 'You're right, of course. I shouldn't interfere. But will you ask her to marry you – now?'

'Now! Tonight?'

'Yes.'

I stood up. 'Under the circumstances I consider that entirely inappropriate, and I won't do it. Now, if you'll forgive me, I have to go back to town.'

He neither turned nor made an answer. I left him there and closed the study door quietly behind me. I was at a loss to understand his driving insistence that Penny and I should marry quickly. That, and the offer of the job in Australia, had me worried. If this was the way he engaged his staff, not to mention picking a son-in-law, I was surprised how he'd got to where he was.

Penny was telephoning when I entered the hall. She replaced the receiver and said, 'I've been talking to the hospital; they say she's resting easier.'

'Good! I'll be back tomorrow evening and we'll go to see her. It might make her feel better to have someone else around, even a comparative stranger like me.'

'I don't know if that's a good idea,' said Penny, doubtfully. 'She might be . . . well, self-conscious about her appearance.'

'I'll come anyway and we can decide then. I have to go now – it's late.' She saw me to my car and I kissed her and left, wondering what kind of bee was buzzing in Ashton's bonnet.

4

Next morning, when I walked into the office I shared with Larry Godwin, he looked up from the Czechoslovakian trade magazine he was reading and said, 'Harrison wants to see you.' Harrison was our immediate boss.

'Okay.' I walked straight out again and into Harrison's office, sat in the chair before the desk, and said, 'Morning, Joe. Larry said you wanted to see me.'

Harrison was a bit of a stuffed shirt, very keen on formality, protocol and the line of authority. He didn't like me calling him Joe, so I always did it just to needle him. He said stiffly, 'On checking the weekend telephone log I found you had disclosed yourself to a police officer. Why?'

'I was at a house-party over the weekend. There was a nasty incident – one of the daughters of the house had acid thrown in her face. She was taken to hospital and, when the police pitched up, I was alone in the house and they started to get off on the wrong foot. I didn't want them wasting time on me, so I disclosed myself to the officer in charge.'

He shook his head disapprovingly and tried to hold me in what he supposed to be an eagle-like stare. 'His name?'

'Detective-Inspector Honnister. You'll find him at the copshop in Marlow.' Harrison scribbled in his desk book, and I leaned forward. 'What's the matter, Joe? We're *supposed* to co-operate with the police.'

He didn't look up. 'You're not supposed to disclose yourself to all and sundry.'

'He wasn't all and sundry. He was a middle-ranking copper doing his job and getting off to a bad start.'

Harrison raised his head. 'You needn't have done it. He would never seriously suspect you of anything.'

I grinned at him. 'The way you tell it co-operation is a one-way street, Joe. The cops co-operate with us when we need them, but we don't co-operate with them when all they need is a little setting straight.'

'It will be noted in your record,' he said coldly.

'Stuff the record,' I said, and stood up. 'Now, if you'll excuse me I have work to do.' I didn't wait for his permission to leave and went back to my office.

Larry had switched to something in Polish. 'Have a good weekend?'

'A bit fraught. Who's pinched our *Who's Who*?'

He grinned. 'What's the matter? Wouldn't she play?' He fished out *Who's Who* from among the piles of books which cluttered his desk and tossed it to me. Our job called for a lot of reading; when I retired I'd be entitled to a disability pension due to failing eyesight incurred in the line of duty.

I sat at my desk and ran through the 'A's and found that Ashton was not listed. There are not many men running three or more factories employing over a thousand men who are not listed in *Who's Who*. It seemed rather odd. On impulse I took the telephone directory and checked that, and he was not listed there, either. Why should Ashton have an ex-directory number?

I said, 'Know anything about high-impact plastics, Larry?'

'What do you want to know?'

'A chap called Ashton runs a factory in Slough, making the stuff. I could bear to know a little more about him.'

'Haven't heard of him. What's the name of the firm?'

'I don't know.'

'You don't know much. There might be a trade association.'

'Great thinking.' I went to our library and an hour later knew there were more associations of plastic manufacturers than I wotted of – there was even one devoted to high-impact plastics – but none of them had heard of George Ashton. It seemed unnatural.

Gloomily I went back to my office. It's a hard world where a man can't check up on his prospective father-in-law. Ashton, as of that moment, knew a hell of a lot more about me than I knew about him. Larry saw my face and said, 'No luck?'

'The man keeps a bloody low profile.'

He laughed and waved his hand across the room. 'You could ask Nellie.'

I looked at Nellie and grinned. 'Why not?' I said lightly, and sat at the console.

You don't have to cuddle up to a computer to ask it questions – all you need is a terminal, and we called ours Nellie for no reason I've ever been able to determine. If you crossed an oversized typewriter with a television set you'd get something like Nellie, and if you go to Heathrow you'll see dozens of them in the booking hall.

Where the computer actually was no one had bothered to tell me. Knowing the organization that employed me, and knowing a little of what was in the monster's guts, I'd say it was tended by white-coated acolytes in a limestone cavern in Derbyshire, or at the bottom of a Mendip mine-shaft; anywhere reasonably safe from an atomic bomb burst. But, as I say, I didn't really know. My crowd worked strictly on the 'need to know' principle.

I snapped a couple of switches, pushed a button, and was rewarded by a small green question mark on the screen. Another button push made it ask:

IDENTIFICATION?

I identified myself – a bit of a complicated process – and Nellie asked:

CODE?

I answered:

GREEN

Nellie thought about that for a millionth of a second, then came up with:

INPUT GREEN CODING

That took about two minutes to put in. We were strict about security and not only did I have to identify myself but I had to know the requisite code for the level of information I wanted.

Nellie said:

INFORMATION REQUIRED?

I replied with:

IDENTITY
MALE
ENGLAND

The lines flicked out as Nellie came back with:

NAME?

I typed in:

ASHTON, GEORGE

It didn't seem to make much difference to Nellie how you put a name in. I'd experimented a bit and whether you put in Percy Bysshe Shelley – Shelley, Percy Bysshe – or even Percy Shelley, Bysshe – didn't seem to matter. Nellie still came up with the right answer, always assuming that Bysshe Shelley, Percy was under our eagle eye. But I always put the surname first because I thought it would be easier on Nellie's overworked little brain.

This time she came up with:

ASHTON, GEORGE – 3 KNOWN
PRESENT ADDRESS – IF KNOWN?

There could have been two hundred George Ashtons in the country or maybe two thousand. It's a common name and not surprising that three should be known to the department. As I typed in the address I reflected that I was being a bit silly about this. I tapped the execute key and Nellie hesitated uncharacteristically. Then I had a shock because the cursor scrolled out:

THIS INFORMATION NOT AVAILABLE ON CODE GREEN
TRY CODE YELLOW

I looked pensively at the screen and tapped out:

HOLD QUERY

Dancing electronically in the guts of a computer was a whole lot of information about one George Ashton, my future father-in-law. And it was secret information because it was in Code Yellow. I had picked up Larry Godwin on a joke and it had backfired on me; I hadn't expected Nellie to find him at all – there was no reason to suppose the department was interested in him. But if he had been found I would have expected him to be listed under Code Green, a not particularly secretive batch of information. Practically anything listed under Code Green could have been picked up by an assiduous reading of the world press. Code Yellow was definitely different.

I dug into the recesses of my mind for the coding of yellow, then addressed myself to Nellie. 'Right, you bitch; try again!' I loaded in the coding which took four minutes, then I typed out:

RELEASE HOLD

Nellie's screen flickered a bit and the cursor spelled out:

THIS INFORMATION NOT AVAILABLE ON CODE YELLOW
TRY CODE RED

I took a deep breath, told Nellie to hold the query, then sat back to think about it. I was cleared for Code Red and I knew the information there was pretty much the same as the code colour – redhot! Who the hell was Ashton, and what was I getting into? I stood up and said to Larry, 'I'll be back in a minute. Don't interfere with Nellie.'

I took a lift which went down into the guts of the building where there lived a race of troglodytes, the guardians of the vaults. I presented my card at a tungsten-steel grille, and said, 'I'd like to check the computer coding for red. I've forgotten the incantation.'

The hard-faced man behind the grille didn't smile. He merely took the card and dropped it into a slot. A machine chewed on it for a moment, tasted it electronically, and liked the flavour but, even so, spat it out. I don't know what would have happened if it hadn't liked the flavour; probably I'd have been struck down by a bolt of lightning. Strange how the real world is catching up with James Bond.

The guard glanced at a small screen. 'Yes, you're cleared for red, Mr Jaggard,' he said, agreeing with the machine. The grille swung open and I passed through, hearing it slam and lock behind me. 'The coding will be brought to you in Room Three.'

Half an hour later I walked into my office, hoping I could remember it all. I found Larry peering at Nellie. 'Do you have red clearance?' I asked.

He shook his head. 'Yellow is my top.'

'Then hop it. Go to the library and study *Playboy* or something elevating like that. I'll give you a ring when I'm finished.'

He didn't argue; he merely nodded and walked out. I sat at the console and loaded Code Red into Nellie and it took nearly ten minutes of doing the right things in the right order. I wasn't entirely joking when I called it an incantation. When faced with Nellie I was always reminded of the medieval sorcerers who sought to conjure up spirits; everything had to be done in the right order and all the right words spoken or the spirit wouldn't appear. We haven't made much progress since then, or not too much. But at least our incantations seem to work and we do get answers from the vasty deep, but whether they're worth anything or not I don't know.

Nellie accepted Code Red or, at least, she didn't hiccough over it.

I keyed in:

RELEASE HOLD

and waited with great interest to see what would come out. The screen flickered again, and Nellie said:

THIS INFORMATION NOT AVAILABLE ON CODE RED
TRY CODE PURPLE

Purple! The colour of royalty and, possibly, of my face at that moment. This was where I was stopped – I was not cleared for Code Purple. I was aware it existed but that's about all. And beyond purple there could have been a whole rainbow of colours visible and invisible, from infra-red to ultra-violet. As I said, we worked on the 'need to know' principle.

I picked up the telephone and rang Larry. 'You can come back now; the secret bit is over.' Then I wiped Nellie's screen clear and sat down to think of what to do next.

5

A couple of hours later I was having a mild ding-dong with Larry. He wasn't a bad chap but his ideals tended to get in the way of his job. His view of the world didn't exactly coincide with things as they are, which can be a bit hampering because a man can make mistakes that way. A spell of field work would have straightened him out but he'd never been given the chance.

My telephone rang and I picked it up. 'Jaggard here.'

It was Harrison. His voice entered my ear like a blast of polar air. 'I want you in my office immediately.'

I put down the phone. 'Joe's in one of his more frigid moods. I wonder how he gets on with his wife.' I went to see what he wanted.

Harrison was a bit more than frigid – he could have been used to liquefy helium. He said chillily, 'What the devil have you been doing with the computer?'

'Nothing much. Has it blown a fuse?'

'What's all this about a man called Ashton?'

I was startled. 'Oh, Christ!' I said. 'Nellie *is* a tattle-tale, isn't she? Too bloody gossipy by half.'

'What's that?'

'Just talking to myself.'

'Well, now you can talk to Ogilvie. He wants to see us both.'

I think I gaped a bit. I'd been with the department for six years and I'd seen Ogilvie precisely that number of times; that's to talk with seriously. I sometimes bumped into him in the lift and he'd exchange pleasantries courteously enough and always asked to be remembered to my father. My monkeying with Nellie must have touched a nerve so sore that the whole firm was going into a spasm.

'Well, don't just stand there,' snapped Harrison. 'He's waiting.'

Waiting with Ogilvie was a short, chubby man who had twinkling eyes, rosy cheeks and a sunny smile. Ogilvie didn't introduce him. He waved Harrison and me into chairs and plunged *in medias res*. 'Now, Malcolm; what's your interest in Ashton?'

I said, 'I'm going to marry his daughter.'

If I'd said I was going to cohabit with the Prince of Wales I couldn't have had a more rewarding reaction. The clouds came over Mr Nameless; his smile disappeared and his eyes looked like gimlets. Ogilvie goggled for a moment, then barked, '*What's that?*'

'I'm going to marry his daughter,' I repeated. 'What's the matter? Is it illegal?'

'No, it's not illegal,' said Ogilvie in a strangled voice. He glanced at Mr Nameless as though uncertain of what to do next. Mr Nameless said, 'What reason did you have for thinking there'd be a file on Ashton?'

'No reason. It was suggested jokingly that I try asking Nellie, so I did. No one was more surprised than I when Ashton popped up.'

I swear Ogilvie thought I was going round the twist. 'Nellie!' he said faintly.

'Sorry, the computer.'

'Was this enquiry in the course of your work?' he asked.

'No,' I said. 'It was personal and private. I'm sorry about that and I apologize for it. But some odd things have been going on around Ashton over the weekend and I wanted to check him out.'

'What sort of things?'

'Someone threw acid into his daughter's face and . . .'

Mr Nameless cut in. 'The girl you intend to marry?'

'No – the younger girl, Gillian. Later on Ashton behaved a bit strangely.'

'I'm not surprised,' said Ogilvie. 'When did this happen?'

'Last night.' I paused. 'I had to disclose myself to a copper, so it came through on the weekend telephone log. Joe and I discussed it this morning.'

Ogilvie switched to Harrison. 'You *knew* about this?'

'Only about the acid. Ashton wasn't mentioned.'

'You didn't ask me,' I said. 'And I didn't know Ashton was so bloody important until Nellie told me afterwards.'

Ogilvie said, 'Now let me get this quite right.' He stared at Harrison. 'A member of your staff in this department reported to you that he'd been involved in police enquiries into an acid-throwing attack, and you didn't even ask who was attacked. Is that it?'

Harrison twitched nervously. Mr Nameless paused in the act of lighting a cigarette and said smoothly, 'I think this is irrelevant. Let us get on with it.'

Ogilvie stabbed Harrison with a glance which told him that he'd hear more later. 'Of course. Do you think this is serious?'

'It could be very serious,' said Mr Nameless. 'But I think we're very lucky. We already have an inside man.' He pointed the cigarette at me just as Leonard Bernstein points his baton at the second violins to tell them to get scraping.

I said, 'Now, hold on a minute. I don't know what this is about, but Ashton is going to be my father-in-law. That's bringing things very close to home. You can't be seriously asking me to . . .'

'You're not being asked,' said Mr Nameless coolly. 'You're being told.'

'The hell with that,' I said roundly.

Momentarily he looked startled, and if ever I thought those eyes had twinkled it was then I changed my mind. He glanced at Ogilvie, and said, 'I know this man has a good record, but right now I fail to see how he achieved it.'

'I've said it once this morning, but I'll say it again,' I said. 'Stuff my record.'

'Be quiet, Malcolm,' said Ogilvie irritably. He turned to Harrison. 'I don't think we need you any more, Joe.'

Harrison's expression managed to mirror simultaneously shock, outrage, curiosity and regret at having to leave. As the door closed behind him Ogilvie said, 'I think a valid point has been made. It's not good for an agent to be emotionally involved. Malcolm, what do you think of Ashton?'

'I like him – what I know of him. He's not an easy man to get to know, but then I haven't had much chance yet; just a couple of weekends' acquaintanceship.'

'A point has been made,' conceded Mr Nameless. He twinkled at me as though we were suddenly bosom friends. 'And in rather unparliamentary language. But the fact remains that Mr Jaggard, here, is on the inside. We can't just toss away that advantage.'

Ogilvie said smoothly, 'I think that Malcolm will investigate the circumstances around Ashton as soon as it is properly explained to him why he should.'

'As to that,' said Mr Nameless, 'you mustn't overstep the limits. You know the problem.'

'I think it can be coped with.'

Mr Nameless stood up. 'Then that's what I'll report.'

When he had gone Ogilvie looked at me for a long moment, then shook his head. 'Malcolm, you really can't go about telling high-ranking civil servants to get stuffed.'

'I didn't,' I said reasonably. 'I told him to stuff my record. I didn't even tell him where to stuff it.'

'The trouble about people like you who have private incomes is that it makes you altogether too bloody independent-minded. Now that, while being an asset to the department, as I told his lordship before you came in, can make things difficult for your colleagues.'

His lordship! I didn't know if Ogilvie was being facetious or not.

He said, 'Will you take things a bit easier in future?'

That wasn't asking too much, so I said, 'Of course.'

'Good. How's your father these days?'

'I think he's a bit lonely now that Mother's dead, but he bears up well. He sends you his regards.'

He nodded and checked his watch. 'Now you'll lunch with me and tell me everything you know about Ashton.'

6

We lunched in a private room above a restaurant at which Ogilvie seemed to be well known. He made me begin right from the beginning, from the time I met Penny, and I ended my tale with the abortive checking out of Ashton and my confrontation with Nellie. It took a long time to tell.

When I had finished we were over the coffee cups. Ogilvie lit a cigar and said, 'All right; you're supposed to be a trained man. Can you put your finger on anything unusual?'

I thought a bit before answering. 'Ashton has a man called Benson. I think there's something peculiar there.'

'Sexually, you mean?'

'Not necessarily. Ashton certainly doesn't strike me as being double-gaited. I mean it's not the normal master-and-servant relationship. When they came back from the hospital last night they were closeted in Ashton's study for an hour and a half, and between them they sank half a bottle of whisky.'

'Um,' said Ogilvie obscurely. 'Anything else?'

'The way he was pressuring me into marrying Penny was bloody strange. I thought at one time he'd bring out the traditional shotgun.' I grinned. 'A Purdy, of course – for formal weddings.'

'You know what I think,' said Ogilvie. 'I think Ashton is scared to death; not on his own behalf but on account of his girls. He seems to think that if he can get your Penny away from him she'll be all right. What do you think?'

'It fits all right,' I said. 'And I don't like one damned bit of it.'

'Poor Ashton. He didn't have the time to polish up a scheme which showed no cracks, and he sprang it on you too baldly. I'll bet he pulled that Australian job out of thin air.'

'Who *is* Ashton?' I asked.

'Sorry; I can't tell you that.' Ogilvie blew a plume of smoke. 'I talked very high-handedly to that chap this morning. I told him you'd take on the job as soon as you knew what was involved, but he knew damned well that I can't tell you a thing. That's what he was objecting to in an oblique way.'

'This is bloody silly,' I said.

'Not really. You'll only be doing what you'd be doing anyway, knowing what you know now.'

'Which is?'

'Bodyguarding the girl. Of course, I'll ask you to bodyguard Ashton, too. It's a package deal, you see; one automatically includes the other.'

'And without knowing the reason why?'

'You know the reason why. You'll be guarding Penelope Ashton because you don't want her to get a faceful of sulphuric acid, and that should be reason enough for any tender lover. As for Ashton – well, our friend this morning was right. A commander can't tell his private soldiers his plans when he sends them into battle. He just tells them where to go and they pick up their feet.'

'The analogy is false, and you know it,' I said. 'How can I guard a man if I don't know who or what I'm guarding him against? That's like sending a soldier into battle not only without telling him where the enemy is, but *who* the enemy is.'

'Well, then,' said Ogilvie tranquilly. 'It looks as though you'll have to do it for the sake of my bright blue eyes.'

He had me there and I think he knew it. I had an idea that Mr Nameless, whoever he was, could be quite formidable and Ogilvie had defused what might have been a nasty situation that morning. I owed him something for it. Besides, the cunning old devil's eyes were green.

'All right,' I said. 'But it isn't a one-man job.'

'I'm aware of that. Spend this afternoon thinking out your requirements – I want them on my desk early tomorrow morning. Oh, by the way – you don't disclose yourself.'

I opened my mouth and then closed it again slowly before I swore at him. Then I said, 'You must be joking. I have to guard a man without telling him I'm guarding him?'

'I'm sure you'll do it very well,' he said suavely, and rang for the waiter.

'Then you'll be astonished at what I'll need,' I said acidly.

He nodded, then asked curiously, 'Hasn't it disturbed you that you'll be marrying into a rather mysterious family?'

'It's Penny I'm marrying, not Ashton.' I grinned at him. 'Aren't you disturbed for the same reason?'

'Don't think I'm not,' he said seriously, and left me to make of that what I could.

7

When I got back to the office Larry Godwin looked me up and down critically. 'I was just about to send out a search party. The griffin is that you've been given a real bollocking. I was just about to go down to the cellar to see if they really do use thumbscrews.'

'Nothing to it,' I said airily. 'I was given the RSPCA medal for being kind to Joe Harrison – that's all.'

'Very funny,' he said acidly, and flapped open a day-old copy of *Pravda*. 'The only time you'll get a medal is when you come with me when I get my knighthood.' He watched me putting a few things in a bag. 'Going somewhere?'

'I won't be around for a couple of days or so.'

'Lucky devil. I never get out of this bloody office.'

'You will one day,' I said consolingly. 'You have to go to Buck House to get a knighthood.' I leaned against the desk. 'You really should be in Slav Section. Why did you opt for General Duties?'

'I thought it would be more exciting,' he said, and added sourly, 'I was wrong.'

'With you around, the phrase "as happy as Larry" takes on an entirely new meaning.' I thought he was going to throw something at me so I ducked out fast.

I drove to Marlow and found the police station. My name presented to the desk sergeant got me Honnister in jig time. He shared an office with another inspector and when I indicated a desire for privacy Honnister shrugged and said, 'Oh, well; we can use an interview room. It's not as comfortable as here, though.'

'That's all right.'

The other copper closed a file and stood up. 'I'm going,

anyway. I don't want to pry into your girlish secrets, Charlie.' He gave me a keen glance as he went out. He'd know me again if he saw me.

Honnister sat at his desk and scowled. 'Secretive crowd, your lot.'

I grinned. 'I don't see you wearing a copper's uniform.'

'I had one of your blokes on the blower this morning – chap by the name of Harrison – threatening me with the Tower of London and unnameable tortures if I talk about you.'

I sat down. 'Joe Harrison is a silly bastard, but he means well.'

'If anyone knows how to keep secrets it's a copper,' said Honnister. 'Especially one in the plain clothes branch. I know enough local secrets to blow Marlow apart. Your chap ought to know that.' He sounded aggrieved.

I cursed Harrison and his ham-fisted approach; if he'd queered my pitch with the local law I'd string him up by the thumbs when I got back. I said, 'Inspector, I told you last night I had no official connection with Ashton. It was true then, but it is no longer true. My people now have a definite interest.'

He grunted. 'I know. I've been asked to make an extra copy of all my reports on the Ashton case. As though I don't have enough to do without producing a lot of bloody bumf for people who won't even give me the time of day without consulting the Official Secrets Act.' His resentment was growing.

I said quickly. 'Oh, hell; you can forget that nonsense – just as long as I can see your file copies.'

'You got authority for that?'

I smiled at him. 'A man has all the authority he can take. I'll carry the can if there's a comeback.'

He stared at me and then his lips curved in amusement. 'You and me will get on all right,' he said. 'What do you want to know?'

'First, how's the girl?'

'We haven't been allowed to talk to her so she must be pretty bad. And I need a description. I don't even know the sex of the assailant.'

'So that means no visitors.'

'None except the family. Her sister has been at the hospital most of the day.'

I said, 'I think I might be able to help you there. Suppose I got Penny to ask Gillian for a description. That would do to be going on with until you can ask her yourself.' He nodded. 'I won't be seeing her until later. Where will you be tonight?'

'Theoretically off duty. But I'll be sinking a couple of pints in the Coach and Horses between nine and ten. I'm meeting someone who might give me a lead on another case. You can ring me there. Doyle, the landlord, knows me.'

'Okay. Now, how have you got on with the acid?'

Honnister shrugged. 'About as far as you'd expect. It's battery acid, and the stuff's too common. There are filling stations all around here, and then it might have come from somewhere else.' He leaned back in his chair. 'To me this has the smell of a London job.'

'Have you seen Ashton?'

'Oh, yes, I've seen Ashton. He says he can think of absolutely no reason why his daughter should be attacked in such a manner. No reason whatsoever. It was like talking to a bloody stone wall.'

'I'll be talking to him myself tonight. Maybe I'll get something.'

'Does he know who – and what – you are?'

'No, he doesn't; and he mustn't find out, either.'

'You blokes lead interesting lives,' said Honnister, and grinned crookedly. 'And you wanting to marry his daughter, too.'

I smiled. 'Where did you get that?'

'Just pieced it together from what you told me last night, and from what one of the uniformed boys picked up when talking over a cuppa with the Ashtons' maid. I told you I hear secrets – and I'm not a bad jack, even though I say it myself.'

'All right,' I said. 'Tell me a few secrets about Ashton.'

'Not known to the police. Not criminally. The CPO had a few words with him.'

'CPO?'

'Crime Prevention Officer. There are a lot of big houses around here full of expensive loot worth nicking. The CPO calls in to check on the burglar-proofing. You'd be surprised how stupid some of these rich twits can be. A man will fill his house with a quarter of a million quids' worth of paintings and antiques and balk at spending a couple of thousand on keeping the stuff safe.'

'How is Ashton's burglar-proofing?'

Honnister grinned. 'It might rate second to the Bank of England,' he conceded.

That interested me. 'Anything more on Ashton?'

'Nothing relevant. But he wasn't the one who was attacked, was he?' He leaned forward. 'Have you thought of the possibility that Gillian Ashton might have been sleeping in the wrong bed? There are two things I think of when I hear of an acid attack on a woman; the first is that it could be a gangland punishment, and the other is that it's one woman taking revenge on another.'

'I've thought of it. Penny discounts it, and I don't go much for it myself. I don't think she's the kind.'

'Maybe, but I've been doing a bit of nosing around. I haven't come up with anything yet, but I can't discount it.'

'Of course you can't.'

I stood up, and Honnister said, 'Don't expect too much too quickly. In fact, don't expect anything at all. I've no great hopes of this case. Anyway, we've not gone twenty-four hours yet.'

That was so, and it surprised me. So much had happened that day that it seemed longer. 'Okay,' I said. 'I'll be in touch tonight.'

8

I drove in the direction of Ashton's house and cruised around slowly, making circuits on the country roads and looking for anything out of the ordinary such as cars parked on the verge with people in them doing nothing in particular. There was nothing like that so after an hour of futility I gave up and drove directly to the house.

The gates were locked but there was a bell-push which I pressed. While I waited I studied the gates in the light of what Honnister had said about Ashton's burglar-proofing. They were of ornamental wrought-iron, about ten feet high, very spiky on top, and hung on two massive stone pillars. They barred an opening in an equally high chain-mesh fence, unobtrusive because concealed by trees, which evidently circled the estate. All very good, but the gates hadn't been closed the day before.

Presently a man came down the drive, dressed in rough country clothes. I hadn't seen him before. He looked at me through the gates and said curtly, 'Yes?'

'My name is Malcolm Jaggard. I'd like to see Mr Ashton.'

'He's not in.'

'Miss Ashton?'

'They're not in, either.'

I tugged thoughtfully at my ear. 'What about Benson?'

He looked at me for a moment, then said, 'I'll see.' He stepped to one side behind one of the stone pillars and I heard a click and the whirr of a telephone dial. There's a phrase for what was happening; it's known as closing the stable door after the horse has gone.

The man came back into sight and wordlessly began to unlock the gate, so I got back into the car and drove up to the house. Benson, in his courtly Boris Karloff manner, ushered me into the living-room, and said, 'I don't expect Miss Penelope will be long, sir. She rang to say she would be back at five.'

'Did she say how Gillian is?'

'No, sir.' He paused, then shook his head slowly. 'This is a bad business, sir. Disgracefully bad.'

'Yes.' I had always been taught that it is bad form to question servants about their masters, but I had no compunction now. Benson had never struck me as being one of your run-of-the-mill servants, least of all at that very moment because, unless he'd developed a fast-growing tumour under his left armpit, he was wearing a gun. 'I see you have a guard on the gate.'

'Yes; that's Willis. I'll give him your name so he will let you in.'

'How is Mr Ashton taking all this?'

'Remarkably well. He went to his office as usual this morning. Would you care for a drink, sir?'

'Thank you. I'll have a scotch.'

He crossed the room, opened a cabinet, and shortly came back with a tray which he put on a small table next to my elbow. 'If you will excuse me, sir.'

'Thank you, Benson.' He was not staying around to be questioned, but even if he had I doubted if I could have got much out of him. He tended to speak in clichés and bland generalities, but whether he thought that way was quite another matter.

I had not long to wait for Penny and was barely half way through the drink when she came into the room. 'Oh, Malcolm; how good to see you. What a blessed man you are.' She looked tired and drawn.

'I said I'd come. How's Gillian?'

'A little better, I think. She's getting over the shock.'

'I'm very glad to hear it. I had a talk with Honnister, the police inspector in charge of the case. He wants to interview her.'

'Oh, Malcolm; she's not ready for that. Not yet.'

She came to me and I took her in my arms. 'Is it that bad?'

She laid her head on my chest for a moment, and then looked up at me. 'I don't think you know how bad this sort of thing is for a woman. Women seem to care more for their appearance than men – I suppose we have to because we're in the man-catching business, most of us. It's not just the physical shock that's hit Gillian; there's the psychological shock, too.'

'Don't think I'm not aware of it,' I said. 'But put yourself in Honnister's place. He's in a jam – he needs a description. Right now he doesn't even know if he's looking for a man or a woman.'

Penny looked startled. 'I hadn't even thought of that. I assumed it would be a man.'

'Honnister hasn't made that assumption. He hasn't made any assumptions at all because he has damn-all to go on. Is Gillian talking to you?'

'A little, this afternoon.' Penny made a wry face. 'I've kept off the subject of acid-throwing.'

'Could you go to the hospital tonight and see what you can get out of her? Honnister is really at his wits' end about this. Your father couldn't help him and he's stuck.'

'I suppose I could try.'

'Better you than Honnister; he might not have your understanding. I'll come with you; not into the ward, but I'll come along.'

'Will eight o'clock be all right for you? Not too late?'

'All my time is at your disposal.' I didn't tell her that was literally true, by courtesy of one Ogilvie and paid for by the taxpayer. 'You look as though you could do with a drink.'

'I could stand a gin and tonic. Bring it into the kitchen, will you? I have to do something about dinner – Daddy will be home soon.'

She went away and I fixed the drink and took it into the

kitchen. I offered to help but she laughed, and said, 'You'd just be in the way. Mary is coming down to help.'

'Mary who?'

'The maid – Mary Cope. You find yourself something to do.'

I went away reflecting that what I really wanted to do was to give Ashton's study a good shake-down. But if it's bad form to question the servants I don't know what the devil it would be called to be found searching through your host's private papers in his *sanctum sanctorum*. Moodily I walked out into the garden.

I was knocking croquet balls about on the lawn when Ashton pitched up. There was a worn and honed look about him as though he was being fined down on some spiritual grindstone. His skin had not lost its tan but he looked paler than usual, and there was still that hurt look in his eyes. It was the look of a little boy who had been punished for something he hadn't done; the anguished look of the injustice of the world. It's hard to explain to a small boy that the world isn't necessarily a just place, but Ashton had been around long enough to know it.

I said, 'Penny's in the kitchen, if you want her.'

'I've seen her,' he said shortly.

'She tells me Gillian's better this evening.'

He looked down, kicking the turf with the toe of his shoe. He didn't speak for some time and I began to think he'd misheard me. But then he looked up and said abruptly, 'She's blind.'

'Christ; I'm sorry to hear that.'

He nodded. 'I had a specialist in this afternoon.'

'Does she know? Does Penny know?'

'Neither of them know. I had it kept from them.'

'I can understand not telling Gillian, but why keep it from Penny?'

'Unlike many sisters they've always been very close even though they are so unalike in temperament – perhaps because of it. I think if Penny knew, Gillian would get it out of her, and she couldn't stand the shock now.' He looked me in the eye. 'Don't tell her.'

Now that was all very logical and carefully thought out, and he had just given me a direct order, there was no doubt about that. 'I won't tell her,' I said. 'But she might find out anyway. She's medically trained and nobody's fool.'

'Just so that it comes later rather than sooner,' he said.

I thought I'd better start to earn my pay. 'I saw Honnister this afternoon. He tells me he didn't get much change out of you this morning. Don't you have any idea why Gillian should be attacked?'

'No,' he said colourlessly.

I studied him carefully. His jacket was much better cut than Benson's but no amount of fine tailoring could hide the slight bulge under his arm. 'You haven't had threatening letters or anything like that?'

'Nothing like that,' he said impatiently. 'I'm at a loss to understand it.'

I felt like asking him, 'Then why carry a gun?' My problem was that I didn't know why he was on our files. Men were listed for many reasons and to be listed did not make them villains – far from it. The trouble was that no one would tell me which class Ashton came into, and that made this job damned difficult. Difficult to know how to push at him; difficult to identify the cranny into which to push the wedge that would crack him.

But I tried. I said practically, 'Then the reason must lie somewhere in Gillian's own life. Some crowd she's been mixed up with, perhaps.'

He became instantly angry. 'Nonsense!' he said sharply. 'That's a monstrous suggestion. How could she get mixed up with types like that without me knowing? The type who could do such a dreadful thing?'

I was acting the part of the impartial onlooker. 'Oh, I don't know,' I said judiciously. 'It happens all the time judging by what we read in the newspapers. The police arrest a kid and uncover a whole series of offences, from mainlining on heroin to theft to get the cash to feed the habit. The parents are shocked and plead ignorance; they had no idea that little Johnny or little Mary was involved. I believe them, too.'

He took a deep breath. 'For one thing, Gillian isn't a kid; she's a grown woman of twenty-six. And for another, I know my family very well. You paid me a compliment last night; you said I'd brought up Penny too well. That goes for Gillian, too.' He drove his toe viciously into the turf. 'Would you think that of Penny?'

'No, I don't think I would.'

'Then why should you think it of Gillian? It's bloody ridiculous.'

'Because Penny didn't have acid thrown in her face,' I reminded him. 'Gillian did.'

'This is a nightmare,' he muttered.

'I'm sorry; I didn't mean to hurt you. I hope you'll accept my apology.'

He put his hands to his face, rubbing at closed eyelids. 'Oh, that's all right, Malcolm.' His hand dropped to his side. 'It's just that she was always such a good little girl. Not like Penny; Penny could be difficult at times. She still can. She can be very wilful, as you'll find out if you marry her. But Gillian . . .' He shook his head. 'Gillian was never any trouble at all.'

What Ashton said brought home to me some of the anguish parents must feel when things go wrong with the kids. But I was not so concerned with his agony that I didn't note his reference to *if* I married Penny, not *when* I married her. Evidently the fixation of the previous night had left him.

He disillusioned me immediately. 'Have you given any thought to what we discussed last night?'

'Some.'

'With what conclusion?'

'I'm still pretty much of the same mind,' I said. 'I don't think this is the time to present Penny with new problems, especially if the girls are as close as you say. She's very unhappy, too, you know.'

'I suppose you're right,' he said dispiritedly, and kicked at the grass again. He was doing that shoe no good at all, and it was a pity to treat Lobb's craftsmanship so cavalierly. 'Are you staying to dinner?'

'With your permission,' I said formally. 'I'm taking Penny to the hospital afterwards.'

He nodded. 'Don't tell her about Gillian's eyes. Promise me that.'

'I already have.'

He didn't answer that, but turned on his heel and walked away towards the house. As I watched him go I felt desperately sorry for him. It didn't matter to me then if Nellie had him listed as a hero or a villain; I still felt sorry for him as a simple human being in the deepest of distress.

Penny and I got to the hospital at about half past eight. I didn't go in with her but waited in the car. She was away quite a long time, more than an hour, and I became restive because I had promised to call Honnister. When she came out she said quietly, 'I've got what you wanted.'

I said, 'Will you tell it to Honnister? I have an appointment with him.'

'All right.'

We found Honnister standing at the bar of the Coach and Horses looking broodily into a glass of beer. When we joined him he said, 'My man's been and gone. I've been hanging on waiting for your call.'

'Inspector Honnister – this is Penny Ashton. She has something to tell you.'

He regarded her with gravity. 'Thank you, Miss Ashton. I don't think you need me to tell you that we're doing the best we can on this case, but it's rather difficult, and we appreciate all the help we can get.'

'I understand,' she said.

He turned to me. 'What'll you have?'

'A scotch and . . .' I glanced at Penny.

'A gin and tonic.'

Honnister called to the man behind the bar. 'Monte, a large scotch and a gin and tonic.' He turned and surveyed the room. 'We'd better grab that table before the last-minute crowd comes in.'

I took Penny over to the table and presently Honnister joined us with the drinks. He wasted no time and even before he was seated, he said, 'Well, Miss Ashton, what can you tell me.'

'Gillian says it was a man.'

'Aah!' said Honnister in satisfaction. He had just eliminated a little more than half the population of Britain. 'What sort of man? Young? Old? Anything you tell me will be of value.'

He led her through the story several times and each time elicited a further nugget of information. What it boiled down to was this: Gillian had walked back from church and, coming up the drive towards the house, had seen a car parked with the bonnet open and a man peering at the engine. She thought he was someone who had broken down so she approached with the intention of offering assistance. As she drew near the man turned and smiled at her. He was no one she knew. She was about to speak when he slammed down the bonnet with one hand and simultaneously threw the acid into her face with the other. The man didn't speak at any time; he was about forty, with a sallow complexion and sunken eyes. She did not know the make of car but it was darkish in colour.

'Let's go back a bit,' said Honnister yet again. 'Your sister saw the man looking at the engine with the bonnet open. Did she mention his hands?'

'No, I don't think so. Is it important?'

'It might be,' said Honnister noncommittally. He *was* a good jack; he didn't put his own ideas into the mouth of his witnesses.

Penny frowned, staring at the bubbles rising in her glass,

and her lips moved slightly as she rehearsed her thoughts. Suddenly she said, 'That's it, Inspector. Gillian said she walked up and the man turned and smiled at her, then he took his hands out of his jacket pockets.'

'Good!' said Honnister heartily. 'Very good indeed!'

'I don't see the importance,' said Penny.

Honnister turned to me. 'Some cars have a rod on a hinge to hold up the bonnet; others have a spring-loaded gadget. Now, if he had his hands in his pockets he couldn't have been holding the bonnet open manually; and if he took them out of his pockets to close the bonnet and throw the acid at the same time then that bonnet was spring-loaded. He wouldn't have time to unhook a rod. It cuts down considerably on the makes of car we have to look for.' He drained his glass. 'Anything more to tell me?'

'I can think of nothing else, Inspector.'

'You and your sister have done very well,' he said as he stood up. 'Now I have to see a man about a dog.' He grinned at me. 'I really mean that – someone pinched a greyhound.'

Penny said, 'You'll let us know if . . .'

'You'll be first to know when something breaks,' promised Honnister. 'This is one villain I really want to get my hands on.'

As he walked out I said, 'He's a good copper.'

'It seems so,' said Penny. 'I wouldn't have thought of the significance of the way a car bonnet is held open.'

I stared into my glass. I was thinking that if I got hold of that acid-throwing bastard first there wouldn't be much left of him for Honnister to deal with. Presently Penny said, 'I can't say, "A penny for your thoughts", or you might get the wrong idea; but what are you thinking?'

I said it automatically; I said it without moving my mind. I said, 'I'm thinking it would be a good idea if we got married.'

'Malcolm!'

I'm pretty good at detecting nuances but there were too

damn many in that single two-syllable word to cope with. There was something of surprise and something of shock; something, I was afraid, of displeasure and something, I hoped, of delight. All mixed up together.

'Don't *you* think it's a good idea?' I watched her hunt for words. 'But don't say, "This is so sudden!"'

'But it *is* so damned sudden,' she said, and waved her hand at the room. 'Here, of all places.'

'It seems a good pub to me,' I said. 'Does the place matter?'

'I don't suppose it does,' she said quietly. 'But the time – and the timing – does.'

'I suppose I could have picked a better time,' I agreed. 'But it just popped out. I'm not the only one who thinks it's a good idea. Your father does, too; he wanted me to ask you last night.'

'So you two have been discussing me behind my back. I don't know that I like that.'

'Be reasonable. It's traditional – and courteous, too – for a man to inform his prospective father-in-law of his intentions.' I refrained from saying that it had been Ashton who had brought up the subject.

'What would you have done if he had been against it?'

'I'd have asked you just the same,' I said equably. 'I'm marrying you, not your father.'

'You're not marrying anyone – yet.' I was thankful for the saving grace of that final monosyllable. She laid her hand on mine. 'You idiot – I thought you'd never ask.'

'I had it all laid on, but circumstances got in the way.'

'I know.' There was melancholy in her voice. 'Oh, Malcolm; I don't know what to say. I've been so unhappy today, thinking about Gillian, and seeing her in such pain. And then there was that awful task you laid on me tonight of questioning her. I saw it had to be done, so I did it – but I don't like one bit of it. And then there's Daddy – he doesn't say much but I think he's going through hell, and

I'm worried about him. And now you come and give me more problems.'

'I'm sorry, Penny; I truly am. Let's put the question back in the deep freeze for a while. Consider yourself unasked.'

'No,' she said. 'You can't unask a question. In a way that's what my work is all about.' She was silent for a while. I didn't know what she meant by that but I had sense enough to keep my mouth shut. At last she said, 'I will marry you, Malcolm – I'd marry you tomorrow. I'm not one for non-essentials, and I don't want a white wedding with all the trimmings or anything like that. I want to marry you, but it can't be now, and I can't tell you when it will be. We've got to get this matter of Gillian sorted out first.'

I took her hand. 'That's good enough for me.'

She gave me a crooked smile. 'It won't be the usual kind of engagement, I'm afraid, I'm in no mood for romantic frivolities. Later, perhaps; but not now.' She squeezed my hand. 'Do you remember when I asked you to come here and meet Daddy? It was the night we had the Chinese dinner in your flat.'

'I remember.'

'It was a diversion. I had to stop myself from doing something.'

'Doing what, for God's sake?'

'Marching into your bedroom and getting into your bed.' She disengaged her hand and finished her drink. 'And now you'd better take me home before I change my mind and we start behaving badly.'

As I escorted her to the car my heart was like a singing bird and all the other guff poets used to write about. They don't any more; they leave it to the writers of pop songs, which is a pity. I drove her home and stopped the car before the gates, and we had five minutes' worth of love before she got out. She had no key and had to press the button for someone to come.

I said, 'We won't announce the engagement, but I think your father ought to know. It seems to be on his mind.'

'I'll tell him now.'

'Are you going to London tomorrow?'

She shook her head. 'Lumsden has given me a few days off. He's very understanding.'

'I'll pop out to see you.'

'But what about your job?'

I grinned. 'I have an understanding boss, too.'

There was a rattle at the gate and it swung open, pushed by Willis, the dour and unfriendly type who had let me in that afternoon. Penny kissed me and then slipped inside and the gate clanged shut. I stepped up to it, and said to Willis, 'Escort Miss Ashton up to the house, see her safe inside, and make sure the house door is locked.'

He looked at me for a moment in silence, then smiled, and it was like an ice floe breaking up. 'I'll do that, sir.'

9

I was in the office early next morning and first I had an extended chat with Nellie. I had just moved to the typewriter when Larry came in with a pile of newspapers which he dumped on his desk. 'Thought you were out on a job.'

'I am,' I said. 'I'm not here. I'm a figment of your imagination.'

I finished my list and took it in to Ogilvie, and wasted no time in getting down to the bones of it. I said, 'I don't mind fighting with one hand tied behind my back, but I object to having both hands tied. I'll need a list of Ashton's present overt activities and affiliations.'

Ogilvie smiled and pushed a file across the desk. 'I anticipated you.'

In return he got my sheet of paper. 'That's more of what I need.'

He scanned it. 'Six men, six cars, telephone ta . . .' He broke off. 'Who do you think we are – the CIA?'

I looked studiously at the back of my hands. 'Have you ever been in the field, sir?'

'Of course I've . . .' I looked up and found him smiling sheepishly. The smile disappeared as he said irritably, 'I know; you people think we desk-bound types have lost touch. You could be right.' He tapped the paper. 'Justify this.'

'I have to do a twenty-four-hour secret surveillance of three – perhaps four – people. It'll be . . .'

He caught me up on that. 'Which three or four?'

'First Ashton and Penny Ashton. Then Gillian Ashton. Just because she's been attacked once doesn't give her a lifelong exemption. I might be able to arrange with Honnister to have one of his chaps at the hospital if I ask him nicely enough. That'll take some of the load off us.'

'And the fourth?'

'Benson. I pushed the lot of them through the computer until I lost them in Code Purple.'

'Benson, too?' Ogilvie thought about it. 'You know, the computer might be going by the address only. Anyone living there might be classed with Ashton.'

'I thought of that and it won't wash. Mary Cope, the maid, lives in and I put her through as a control. Nellie has never heard of her. If Ashton is so damned important then he's six-man-important.'

'I agree – but you can't keep an eye on four people with six men. I'll let you have eight.' He smiled slightly. 'I must be going soft-headed. If Harrison was handling this he'd cut you down to four.'

I was taken aback but rallied enough to discuss who we were going to use on the operation. I said, 'I'd like to take Laurence Godwin.'

'You think he's ready?'

'Yes. If we don't use him soon he'll go sour on us. I've been keeping an eye on him lately; he's been right more times than he's been wrong, which is not bad going in this trade.'

'Very well.' Ogilvie returned to my list. 'I agree that Ashton's telephones should be tapped. If he's being threatened we want to know about it. I'll have to get authorization from upstairs, though; but I'll be as quick as I can. As for the postal surveillance, that's trickier but I'll see what I can do.' He put his finger down. 'This last item worries me. You'll have to have a damned good reason for wanting a pistol.'

'Benson's carrying a gun in his oxter, and Ashton is carrying another. If they are expecting that sort of action I think we should be prepared.'

'You're sure of this?'

'Dead certain. I'd like to know if they have gun permits.'

Ogilvie considered it. 'Under the circumstances, Ashton might. I don't know about Benson. I'll check.' I'd have given a lot to know what those circumstances were but I didn't ask because I knew he wouldn't tell me.

We settled a few more minor details, then Ogilvie said, 'Right, that's it. Round up your boys and brief them. I want a recording made of the briefing, the tape to be given to me personally before you leave. Get on with it, Malcolm.' As I was leaving he added, 'I'll authorize two pistols.'

I went back and gave Larry a list of names. 'Get on the blower. I want those men in my office ten minutes ago.' I paused. 'And put yourself on the bottom of the list.'

His expression was a study in pure delight. 'You mean . . .'

I grinned. 'I mean. Now get busy.' I sat at my desk and opened the file on Ashton. It was very thin. The names and addresses of his firms were given, but his other associations were few, mostly professional men – lawyers, accountants and the like. He was a member of no club, whether social, sporting or intellectual. A millionaire hermit.

The team assembled and I switched on the tape-recorder. The briefing didn't take long. I outlined the problem and then told how we were going to handle it, then allocated jobs and shifts. One pistol would be carried by the man overseeing Ashton, whoever he happened to be at the time; the other I reserved for myself.

I said, 'Now we have radios so we use them. Stay on net and report often so everyone is clued up all the time. Those off-shift to be findable and near a telephone. You might be needed in a hurry.'

Simpson asked, 'Do off-shift men go home?' He'd just got back from his honeymoon.

'No. Everyone books into hotels in or near Marlow.' There was an audible groan. 'As soon as you've done it report which hotel together with its phone number so we can find you. I'm at the Compleat Angler.'

Brent said, 'Living it up on the expense account.'

I grinned, then said soberly, 'I don't think we'll have much time for that on this exercise. I might add that this is an important one. You can judge its importance by the fact that Ogilvie raised the team from six to eight on his own initiative and without me having to needle him. In the light of our staff position that says a lot. So don't lose any of these people – and keep your own heads down. Right; that's all.' I switched off the recorder and rewound the tape.

Larry said, 'You haven't given me a job.'

'You stick with me. I'll be back in a minute – I'm going to see Ogilvie.'

As I walked into his outer office his secretary said, 'I was about to ring you, Mr Jaggard. Mr Ogilvie wants to see you.'

'Thanks.' I went on in, and said, 'Here's the tape of the briefing.'

He was frowning and said directly, 'Did you cancel a request given to Inspector Honnister for copies of his reports on the Ashton case?'

I put the cassette on his desk. 'Yes.'

'Why?'

'Because I thought it was a lot of bull,' I said bluntly. 'It was getting in the way of good relations. What Harrison did was bad enough.'

'Harrison? What did Joe do?'

I related Harrison's flat-footed approach and Honnister's reaction to it, and then his views on providing extra copies of his reports. I added, 'If we're going to ask Honnister to provide a guard at the hospital we need to keep in his good books.'

'Very good thinking,' said Ogilvie heavily. 'But for one thing. This department did not request those copies. It came from elsewhere, and someone has just been chewing my ear off by telephone.'

'Oh,' I said, rather inadequately, and then, 'Who?'

'Need you ask?' said Ogilvie acidly. 'The gentleman you met yesterday is sticking his oar in – which, I might add, he is perfectly entitled to do.' He rubbed his jaw and amended the statement. 'As long as he restricts himself to requests for information and does not initiate any action.'

He pondered for a moment, then said, 'All right, Malcolm, you can go. But don't take any precipitate action without referring back to me.'

'Yes. I'm sorry, sir.'

He waved me away.

10

There was nearly an hour of bureaucracy to get through before Larry and I could drive to Marlow. On the way I gave him the score up to that point, and his reaction was emphatic. 'This is downright stupid! You mean Ogilvie won't tell you what's behind all this?'

'I think his hands are tied,' I said. 'This is real top-level stuff. He has a character from Whitehall like a monkey on his back.'

'You mean Cregar?'

I glanced sideways at Larry. 'Who?'

'Lord Cregar. Short, chubby little chap.'

'Could be. How did you get on to him? Did you bug Ogilvie's office?'

He grinned. 'I went to the loo yesterday and saw him coming out of Ogilvie's room while you were in there.'

I said musingly, 'Ogilvie did refer to him as "his lordship" but I thought he was joking. How did you know he was Cregar?'

'He got divorced last week,' said Larry. 'His photograph was splashed on the middle inside pages of the *Telegraph*.'

I nodded. The *Daily Telegraph* takes a keen interest in the marital ups-and-downs of the upper crust. 'Do you know anything more about him, other than that he's wifeless?'

'Yes,' said Larry. 'He's not womanless – *that* came out very strongly in the court case. But beyond that, nothing.'

We crossed the Thames at Marlow, and I said, 'We'll check the hospital first, then go to the police station and I'll introduce you to a good copper. How good are you at grovelling? I might need a few lessons.'

The hospital car park was full so I put the car illicitly

into a doctor's slot. I saw Jack Brent, who was trailing Penny, so that meant she was in the hospital; he was talking to someone over his radio. I was about to go over to him when someone hailed me, and I turned to find Honnister at my elbow.

He seemed quite cheerful as I introduced Larry. I said, 'I got some wires crossed yesterday. My people didn't ask for reports; the request came from elsewhere.'

He smiled. 'I thought the Super was a bit narky this morning. Not to worry, Mr Jaggard. A man can't do more than his best.'

'Any progress?'

'I think we have the make of car. A witness saw a Hillman Sceptre close to Ashton's place on Saturday afternoon. The driver fits the description of the suspect. A dark blue car and spring-loaded bonnet, so it fits.' He rubbed his hands. 'I'm beginning to think we stand a chance on this one. I want to get this man before Miss Ashton for a firm identification.'

I shook my head. 'You won't get it. She's blind.'

Honnister looked stricken. 'Christ!' he said savagely. 'Wait till I lay my hands on this whoreson!'

'Stand in line. There's a queue.'

'I'm just going up to see her. The doctor says she's fit to talk.'

'Don't tell her she's blind – she doesn't know yet. And don't tell her sister.' I pondered for a moment. 'We have reason to believe another attack may be made on her. Can you put a man in the hospital?'

'That's asking something,' said Honnister. He paused, then asked, 'Do you know what's wrong with the bloody force? Too many chiefs and not enough Indians. If there's a multiple smash on the M4 we'd be hard put to it to find four uniformed men for crowd control. But go into the nick in Slough and you can't toss a pebble in any direction without it ricocheting off three coppers of the rank of chief inspector or higher.' He seemed bitter. 'But I'll see what I can do.'

I said, 'Failing that, give the hospital staff a good briefing. No stranger to get near Gillian Ashton without authority from you, me or the Ashton family. Pitch it to them strongly.'

Brent left his car and joined us and I introduced him to Honnister. 'Everything okay?'

'She's inside now; that's her car over there. But this town is hell on wheels. She went shopping before she came here and led me a devil of a dance. There's nowhere to park – I got two tickets in half an hour.'

'Hell, we can't have that.' I could imagine Penny being abducted while my man argued the toss with a traffic warden. I said to Larry, 'I want CD plates put on all our cars fast.'

'Oh, very tricky!' said Honnister admiringly.

Larry grinned. 'The Foreign Office won't like it.'

'Nothing to do with the Foreign Office,' observed Honnister. 'It's just a convention with no legal significance. A copper once stopped a car with CD plates and found a Cockney driver, so he asked him what CD stood for. The bloke said, "Cake Deliverer". And he was, too.' He shrugged. 'There was nothing he could do about it.' He nudged me. 'Coming in?'

'I'll join you inside.'

Jack Brent waited until Honnister was well out of earshot before saying, 'I thought it best not to talk in front of him, but Ashton and Benson haven't been found.'

'Ashton isn't at his office?'

'No, and he isn't at home, either.'

I thought about it. In the course of his business Ashton might be anywhere in the Home Counties; he might even have gone to London. And there was nothing to say that Benson was a prisoner in the house; he had to go out some time. All the same, I didn't like it.

I said, 'I'm going to the house. Come on, Larry.' I turned

to Brent. 'And you stick close to Penny Ashton. For Christ's sake, don't lose her.'

I drove a little faster than I should on the way to Ashton's place, and when I got there I leaned on the bell-push until Willis arrived wearing an annoyed expression. 'There's no one in,' he said abruptly.

'I want to make sure of that. Let me in.' He hesitated and then opened the gate reluctantly and I drove up to the house.

Larry said, 'He's a surly devil.'

'But reliable, I'd say.' I stopped before the front door, got out, and rang the bell. It was a fair time before the door opened and I was confronted by the maid who looked surprised to see me. 'Oh, Mr Jaggard, Miss Penny's not here. She's at the hospital.'

'I know. Mr Ashton's not in?'

'No, he's out, too.'

'What about Benson?'

'I haven't seen him all morning.'

I said, 'Mind if we come in? I'd like to use the telephone.'

In response she opened the door wider. Larry and I walked into the hall, and I said, 'You're Mary Cope, aren't you?'

'Yes, sir.'

'Have you seen either Mr Ashton or Benson at all today?'

'No, sir.'

'When was the last time you saw them?'

'Well, not really to see,' she said. 'But they were in the study last night; I heard them talking. That would be about nine o'clock. Just before, really, because I was going up to my room to catch the nine o'clock news and I switched on five minutes early.' She paused, wondering if she was right in talking of the doings of the family. After all, I hadn't been around all that long. She said nervously, 'Is this anything to do with what happened to Miss Gillian?'

'It could be.'

'Mr Ashton's bed wasn't slept in,' she volunteered.

I glanced at Larry who raised his eyebrows. 'What about Benson's bed?'

'I haven't looked – but he always makes up his own bed.'

'I see. I'll use the telephone if I may.'

I rang the hospital, asking for Penny, and told the operator she'd be in or near the intensive care unit. It was a long time before she came on the line. 'I hope you haven't waited long,' she said. 'I slipped away for a cup of tea. Gillian's much better, Malcolm; she's talking to Honnister now, and she doesn't mind a bit.'

I said, 'Did you tell your father about us last night?'

'No. He'd gone to bed when I got in.'

'Did you tell him this morning?'

'No. I slept late and he'd gone out when I got up. I expect Mary made breakfast for him.'

I didn't comment on that. 'When did you last see Benson?'

Her voice was suddenly wary. 'What's the matter, Malcolm? What's going on?'

I said, 'Look, Penny, I'm at your house. I'd like you to come home because I want to talk to you about something. I expect Honnister will be at the hospital for quite some time, and there's nothing you can do there.'

'There's something wrong, isn't there?' she said.

'Not really. I'll tell you when I see you.'

'I'm coming now.' She rang off.

I put down the receiver and looked around to see Mary Cope regarding me curiously from the other end of the hall. I jerked my head at Larry and gave him my keys. 'In the special compartment of my car you'll find a file on Ashton. There's a list of cars he owns – on page five, I think. Nip round to the garage and see what's missing. Then go down to the gate and ask Willis what time Ashton and Benson left here.'

He went quickly and I walked into Ashton's study. On his desk were two envelopes; one addressed to Penny and the other to me. I picked up mine and broke the seal.

The note might have been enigmatic to anyone else, but to me it was as clear as crystal. It read:

My dear Malcolm,
You are far too intelligent a man not to have seen what I was driving at in our more recent conversations. You may be acquainted with the French proverb: *Celui qui a trouvé un bon gendre a gagné un fils; mais celui qui en a recontré un mauvais a perdu une fille.*

Marry Penny with my blessing and make her happy – but, for her sake, be a bad son-in-law.

Yours
George Benson.

I sat down heavily and had a queasy feeling in the pit of my stomach because I knew we'd botched the job. I picked up the telephone to ring Ogilvie.

11

I didn't wrap it up for him. 'Our pigeons have flown the coop,' I said baldly.

He was incredulous. 'What! All of them?'

'Just the two cock birds.'

He was silent for a moment, then said slowly, 'My fault, I'm afraid. I ought to have given you your team yesterday. How certain are you?'

'He left me a note.' I read it out.

Ogilvie put the French into English. '"He who has found a good son-in-law has gained a son, but he who has picked up a bad one has lost a daughter." What the hell is that supposed to mean?'

I said, 'It may be my fault that he's cut and run. He tackled me again last evening about marrying Penny, and I gave him another refusal. I think that since he couldn't get her to cut loose from him, he has cut loose from her. If you read the note in that context you'll see what I mean.'

'Um. What was his attitude last evening?'

'He was a walking disaster,' I said flatly.

'How much start have they had?'

I sorted through the details I had picked up, then checked the time. 'I don't know about Benson, but for Ashton say fifteen hours maximum. I might get to know a bit more in the next few minutes.'

'We don't know that he went,' said Ogilvie objectively. 'He might have been taken. That note to you may be a fraud. Either case is serious, of course.'

'I don't think he was taken. The note is too accurately pointed, and this house is well protected.'

'Yes, it would be.' Ogilvie knew enough of the background to make a statement like that. 'How's the girl taking it?'

'She doesn't know yet. Ashton left her a note, too. I haven't opened it – I'll let her do that. I'll let you know anything that's relevant.'

'Think she'll tell you?'

'Yes. It's a funny thing, sir, but I did ask her to marry me last night and she accepted. She was going to tell Ashton when she got home but she said he'd gone to bed. I think he'd already left. If he'd waited another couple of hours he might have decided not to go.'

'Yes,' said Ogilvie meditatively. 'But don't blame yourself for that.' I looked up as Larry came into the study. Ogilvie said, 'Did you disclose yourself to her?'

'No.'

There was a pause. 'You take your duties very seriously, don't you, Malcolm?'

'I try to. Hang on a minute.' I looked up at Larry. 'Well?'

'There's an Aston Martin short, and both Benson and Ashton left last night at about half past nine, and didn't come back.'

The Aston Martin was Penny's car. I said to Ogilvie, 'We've got a pretty firm time. They left together at nine-thirty last night, probably in a hired car.' He seemed to be a long time digesting that, so I said, 'What's the next step?'

'There's going to be a row, of course,' he said, not sounding too perturbed. 'But I'll handle that. What you do is to go through that house like a dose of salts. See if you can find anything to indicate where Ashton has gone. Anything you don't understand bring here for evaluation.'

I said, 'That will blow my cover with Penny. I can't search the house without giving her an explanation.'

'I know.'

'Hold on.' I turned to Larry. 'Get on the radio – I want everyone here as soon as possible.'

'Off-shift boys included?'

'Yes. And go to the gate to make sure they can get in.'

Before speaking to Ogilvie again I glumly contemplated the explanation I'd have to give Penny. It was a hell of a thing to tell a girl you've just proposed to, and I had the feeling that our relationship was about to alter for the worse.

I pushed it out of my mind, and said, 'Do we bring the police in on this?'

I could almost hear Ogilvie's brains creaking as he thought that one out. At last he said, 'Not at this stage. I'll have to push it upstairs for a ruling. Police security is not too good on this sort of thing – they have too many reporters watching them. How long do you think you'll be there?'

'I don't know. It's a big house and I can see at least one safe from here. If we can't find keys we may have to take extreme measures. I'll give you a ring in an hour. I'll have a better idea by then.'

'I can't hold this for an hour. If you look towards London in fifteen minutes you'll see flames rising from Whitehall. Do your best.' He rang off.

I put down the telephone and looked thoughtfully at the letter addressed to Penny, then crossed to the safe. It had a combination lock and the door didn't open when I turned the handle. I went back to the desk and gave it a quick once-over lightly in the hope of finding something useful immediately. There was nothing. Five minutes later I heard a car draw up outside and, thinking it might be Penny, I went outside.

It was Peter Michaelis, one of the team. He came over with an enquiring look on his face, and I said, 'Stick around.' He had given Larry a lift from the gate, so I called him over. 'Take Ashton's file and start ringing around – his office, factories, every address you find in there. If Ashton is seen he's to ring his home immediately.' I shrugged. 'It won't work but we must cover it.'

'Okay.'

An Aston Martin was coming up the drive so I braced myself. 'Use the telephone in the hall. I want to use the study.'

Larry walked towards the house as Penny's car came to a fast halt, braked hard. She tumbled out, looking uncertainly at Michaelis, then ran towards me. 'I'm being followed,' she said, and whirled around, pointing at the car coming up the drive. 'He followed me into the grounds.'

'It's all right,' I said, as Brent's car stopped. 'I know who he is.'

'What's happening?' she demanded. 'Who are these men?' Her voice caught. 'What's happened to Daddy?'

'As far as I know he's all right.' I took her elbow. 'I want you to come with me.'

I took her into the house and she paused in the hall as she saw Larry at the telephone, then quickened her pace again. We went into the study and I picked up the letter from the desk. 'You'd better read this.'

She looked at me uncertainly before glancing at the superscription. 'It's from Daddy,' she said, and ripped open the envelope. As she read the note she frowned and her face paled. 'But I don't . . . I don't understand. I don't . . .'

'What does he say?'

Wordlessly she handed the letter to me, then walked over to the window and looked out. I watched her for a moment, then bent my head and read:

My dearest Penny,

For reasons I cannot disclose I must go away for a while. The reasons are not disreputable, nor am I a criminal, although that imputation may be made. My affairs are all in order and my absence should not cause you any trouble financially. I have made all the necessary arrangements: for legal advice consult Mr Veasey of Michelmore, Veasey and Templeton; for financial advice go to Mr Howard of Howard and Page. They have been well briefed for this eventuality.

I do not know for how long I shall have to be away. You will be doing me a great service if you make no attempt at all to find me and, above all, I do not wish the police to be brought into this matter if that can be avoided. I assure you again that my reasons for leaving in this manner are purely private and personal. I will come to no harm because my old friend, Benson, will be looking after me.

It would give me the greatest peace of mind if you would marry your Malcolm as soon as is practically possible. I know that you love him and I know that he wants to marry you very much, and I have a great respect for the intelligence and character of the man you have chosen. Please do not let the matter of poor Gillian impede your plans to marry and, on the occasion, please put a notice in *The Times*.

I have the greatest confidence that the two of you will be very happy together, and I am equally sure that you will both look after Gillian. Forgive me for the abrupt manner of my depature but it is in the best interests of all of us.

Your loving father,
George.

I looked up. 'I'm sorry, Penny.'

'But I don't understand,' she cried desolately. 'Oh, Malcolm, what's *happened* to him?'

She came into my arms and I held her close. 'I don't know – but we'll find out.'

She was still for a while, but pushed herself away as two cars arrived in quick succession. She stared from the window at the gathering knot of men. 'Malcolm, who are all those men? Have you told the police? Daddy said not to.'

'No, I haven't told the police,' I said quietly. 'Sit down, Penny; I have a lot to tell you.' She looked at me wonderingly, and hesitated, but sat in the chair behind the desk. I hesitated, too, not knowing where to begin, then thought it best to give it to her straight and fast.

'I work for the firm of McCulloch and Ross, and I've told no lies about what the firm does. It does everything I've said it does, and does it very well, too. Our clients are most satisfied, and they ought to be because of the amount of public money going into their service.'

'What are you getting at?'

'McCulloch and Ross is a cover for a sort of discreet government department dealing mainly with economic and industrial affairs in so far as they impinge on state security.'

'State security! You mean you're some sort of secret agent. A spy?'

I laughed and held up my hands. 'Not a spy. We're not romantic types with double-o numbers and a licence to kill – no nonsense like that.'

'But you were watching and investigating my father like a common spy.' Anger flamed in her. 'And was I just a means to an end? Did you snuggle up to me just to get to know him better?'

I lost the smile fast – this was where the crunch came. 'Christ, no! I didn't know a damned thing about him until yesterday, and I don't know much more now. Believe me when I say it was something I stumbled into by accident.'

She was disbelieving and contemptuous. 'And just what did you *stumble* into?'

'I can't tell you that because I don't know myself.'

She shook her head as though momentarily dizzy. 'That man in the hall – those men outside: are they in your department, too?'

'Yes.'

'Then I'd like to talk to the man in charge.' She stood up. 'I'd like to tell him just what I think of all this. I knew Daddy was under pressure. Now I know where it was coming from.'

I said deliberately, 'You're talking to the man in charge, and you're dead wrong.'

That stopped her. She sat down with a bump. '*You* are in charge?'

'That's right.'

'And you don't know what you're doing?' she laughed hysterically.

'I know what I'm doing, but I don't know why. There's a hierarchy of levels, Penny – wheels within wheels. Let me tell you how I got into this.'

So I told her. I told her everything, holding nothing back. I told her about Nellie and the colour codes; I told her about Ogilvie and Lord Cregar. I told her a damned sight more than I ought to have done, and to hell with the Official Secrets Act.

She heard me out, then said thoughtfully, 'Your people aren't very trusting, are they?'

'They're not in the trust business.' I lit a cigarette. 'The pressure didn't come from us, Penny. We threw no acid. We came into it after that, and my brief was to watch over your father and protect him – your father, you and Gillian, and Benson, too, if I thought it necessary.' I walked over to the window and looked at the cars. The gang had all arrived. 'I've not done a very good job so far.'

'It's not your fault that Daddy went away.' Her words hung heavily in the air, and she seemed to take another look at her father. 'That he *ran* away.'

I turned to her. 'Don't start blaming him without knowing what you're blaming him for.'

She said pensively, 'I wonder if he'd still want me to marry you, if he knew what I know now?'

'I'll ask him as soon as I catch up with him,' I said grimly.

'You're not going after him?' She picked up her letter. 'He said . . .'

'I know what he said. I also know he's regarded by my people as a very important man, and he may be going into danger without knowing it. I still have my job to do.'

'But he doesn't want . . .'

I said impatiently, 'What he wants or doesn't want is immaterial.' I plucked the letter from her fingers and scanned it. 'He says he doesn't want you to go looking for him. Well, you won't – I will. He says not to involve the police. Right; they haven't been told. He says, "I will come to no harm because my old friend, Benson, will be looking after me." Good God, Penny, how old is Benson? He must be pushing sixty-five. He's in no position to protect himself, let alone anyone else.'

She started to weep. She didn't sob or make an outcry, but the tears welled in her eyes and ran down her cheeks. She cried silently and helplessly, and she was shivering as though suddenly very cold. I put my arm around her and she clung to me with a fierce grip. One of the worst things that can happen is when a hitherto cosy and secure world falls apart. An icy wind seemed to be blowing through that pleasant panelled study from the greater and more vicious world outside.

'Oh, Malcolm, what am I to do?'

I said very quietly, 'You must do what you think is best. If you trust me you will help me find him, but I wouldn't – I couldn't – blame you if you refuse. I haven't been open with you – I should have told you about this yesterday.'

'But you were under orders.'

'A common plea,' I said. 'All the Nazis made it.'

'Malcolm, don't make it harder for yourself than you have to.' She put my arm aside, stood up, and went to the window. 'What are your men waiting for?'

I took a deep breath. 'For your decision. I want to search the house, and I can't do that without your permission.'

She came back to the desk and read her father's letter again. I said, 'He wrote to me, too,' and produced the letter. 'You can read it if you like.'

She read it, then gave it back to me. 'Bring in your men,' she said tonelessly.

12

We found a number of surprising things in that house but nothing that did us much good, at least, not then. In the basement there was a remarkably well-equipped workshop and chemical laboratory, way beyond amateur standard. There was also a small computer with a variety of input and output peripherals including an X–Y plotter. Still on the plotter was a sketch which had been drawn under computer control; it seemed to be a schematic of a complicated molecule and it made no sense to me, but then I'm no expert. For bigger problems with which the little computer couldn't cope there was a modem and an acoustic coupler so that the little chap could be used as a terminal to control a big computer by way of the post office land lines.

In the workshop was a bench on which a thingamajig was under construction. Whatever it was intended to do it was going to do under computer control because there were no fewer than fifteen integrated-circuit microelectronic chips built into it, and that's a fair amount of computing power. Also coupled into it was a laser, a cathode ray tube, a lot of laboratory glassware and a couple of gadgets I didn't recognize.

I didn't snap any switches or push any of the unlabelled buttons because I didn't know what would happen if I did. Instead I said to Larry, 'Any of Ashton's firms connected with electronics or computers?'

'No, just chemicals and plastics moulding. Some of the chemical processes might be computer-controlled, though.'

I grunted and had the entire basement sealed. The boffins from the department would have to check it out, and I wasn't going to touch anything until they had done so.

Penny had the combination for the safe in the study, and I knew by that we were unlikely to find anything of consequence in it. I was right. There was a bit of money, less than £50, which was not much considering Ashton's resources – I suppose it was emergency pocket money. There were some account books on which I wasted some time until I discovered they related to the running of the household, the stables and the cars. All very orderly. There was a whole sheaf of balance sheets headed with the name of the firm of accountants, Howard and Page. A quick glance at the bottom lines told me that George Ashton was doing very nicely, thank you, in spite of the economic recession.

And that was all.

Ashton's own quarters were a bit more productive. He had a suite – bedroom, bathroom, dressing-room and sitting-room which were as clean as a whistle. He seemed to live somewhat spartanly; there was less than the usual amount of junk which a man tends to accumulate and it was all very clean and tidy. There was nothing at all in any of the pockets of the clothes hanging in the wardrobes; whoever did his valeting – Benson probably – did a good job.

But a considerable amount of panel-tapping discovered a tambour which, when slid aside after a complicated procedure involving switching on certain lights in all four rooms thus releasing an electrically-controlled lock, revealed a massive metal door of armour-plated steel. The way I've described that might make you think we were lucky to find it, but it wasn't luck. The boys were good at their jobs.

Not good enough to open that vault door, though. After Simpson had done some architectural measuring with a tape I knew that beyond that door was not merely a safe but a sizeable room, big enough to swing a kitten in, if not a cat. Now, any man who would put a door like that as entrance to a room would be sure to take other precautions.

The walls, floor and ceiling would be very thick concrete, well reinforced with toughened steel, and the whole package would weigh a lot even when empty. It was on the second floor which meant that a special underpinning structure must have been built to support it. I made a note to look up Ashton's architect.

When the vault door was shown to Penny she was as surprised as anyone. She had never suspected its existence.

All this doesn't mean that I was prowling about the house personally knocking on walls. I left that to the boys and only inspected the results when they came in. I supervised the search of Ashton's study in Penny's presence, then settled down to talk to her because I assumed she would know more about her father than anyone else.

'Benson,' I said. 'How long have you known Benson?'

She looked surprised. 'He's always been around.'

'That's a long time. How long is always?'

'Always is always, Malcolm. I can't remember a time when there wasn't Benson.'

'As long as that? Twenty-five or twenty-six years?'

Penny smiled. 'Longer than that. He was with Daddy before I was born.'

'Always is a long time,' I agreed. 'He does the faithful family retainer bit very well, I must say. But he's more than that, isn't he?'

She crinkled her brow. 'I don't know. That's difficult to assess. When a man has been with a family as long as Benson he tends to become regarded as more of a friend than a servant.'

'To the extent that your father would share a bottle of whisky with him?'

'I don't think he ever did that.'

'He did on Sunday night,' I observed. 'Has Benson always been a personal servant to your father?'

She thought for a moment. 'We moved into the house in 1961 – I was twelve then. It was then Benson moved in here as Daddy's valet and dogsbody. Before that we had a house in Slough; just a little one, nothing as grand as this. Benson worked in one of Daddy's factories, but he visited the house quite often – at least once a week.' She smiled. 'He was one of our favourites. He used to bring us sweets – forbidden fruit because Daddy didn't like us to eat too many sweets. Benson used to smuggle them to us.'

'What was Benson doing in the factory?'

'I don't know. I was only a little girl.'

'When did your mother die, Penny?'

'When I was four.'

I thought that was bad luck on Ashton, having to bring up two small daughters. Still, he hadn't made a bad job of it. It seemed he didn't make a bad job of anything. I said, 'Do you know how your father got started? I mean, how did he start in business? Did he have inherited money, for instance?'

She shook her head vigorously. 'Daddy never talked much about his early life but I know he didn't inherit anything because he was an orphan brought up in a foundling home. He was in the army during the war and when he came out he met my grandfather and they set up in business together. They didn't have much money at the time, so my grandfather said before he died. He said Daddy's brains made it a success.'

'What was he in the army?' I asked idly.

'Just a private.'

That surprised me. Ashton would have been twenty-six or twenty-seven when he was demobbed and it was strange that a man of his drive and character should still have been a private soldier. Perhaps his army record would bear looking into.

'Did your father ever carry a gun?'

She misunderstood me. 'He did rough shooting at times, but not often.'

'I don't mean a shotgun. I mean a revolver or automatic pistol.'

'Lord, no! He hasn't got such a thing.'

'Would you know?'

'Of course I would.'

'You didn't know about that strong room upstairs.'

She was silent and bit her lips, then said, 'You think he's armed?'

I was saved from answering that because Larry popped his head around the door. 'Can I have a word, Malcolm?' I nodded and joined him in the hall. He said, 'Gillian Ashton's rooms are clean, nothing there of consequence. I read her diaries; she seems to live a quiet, upper-middle-class life – theatre, ballet, opera and so on. She reads a lot, too.'

'Not any more. Any liaisons?'

'Nothing very strong; a string of men who appeared one at a time and then petered out after a while.' He grinned. 'No mysterious assignations with people referred to by only their initials, nothing like that.'

'What about Penny's rooms? Have you checked there?'

Larry looked at me a bit queerly. 'But I thought . . .'

'I don't care what you thought,' I said evenly. 'Do it.'

'Okay.' He went downstairs again, and I thought that young Larry still had a lot to learn.

I was about to return to the study when Michaelis came through the hall. I said, 'Found anything?'

'Nothing for us. But in an attic there's the damndest thing – the biggest model railway set-up I've seen in my life.'

'Model railway!' I said incredulously.

'It's a real enthusiast's job,' he said. 'I'm a bit keen, myself, but I've never seen anything like this. There must be over a mile of HO-gauge track up there – it's like a bloody spider web. You'd have to do some smart scheduling to keep that lot runing smoothly.'

It was a facet of Ashton I wouldn't have dreamed of, but it didn't have a thing to do with the matter at hand. I dismissed it. 'Where's Jack Brent?'

'Giving the outbuildings a going-over – the garages and stables.'

'Tell him I want to see him when he's finished.' I went back into the study and thought it was time to try to find Ogilvie again. I'd been ringing every hour on the hour but each time he'd been out of the office so I'd passed my stuff on to Harrison. I put my hand out to dial again but the telephone shrilled before I got there.

It was Ogilvie. 'What have you got?' he said abruptly.

'I've passed it all to Harrison. Have you spoken to him?'

'No. As you may have gathered the balloon went up on schedule and I've been busy the last few hours. Give me the gist of it.'

'We've got a bloody big vault here,' I said. 'Not a safe, but a professional bank vault. We'll need experts to open it, and it'll probably take *them* a week.'

'It had better not,' said Ogilvie. 'You'll have them within the hour. What else?'

'I'd like some boffins – electronic and chemical. There's a cellar full of scientific stuff to look at. And you'd better send someone competent in computers.' I grinned. 'And maybe a model railway expert.'

'What's that?' he barked.

'Ashton has a model railway lay-out in his attic. I haven't seen it but I'm told it's quite something.'

'This is no time to be funny,' said Ogilvie acidly. 'What else?'

'Damn all. Nothing of use to us.'

'Keep looking,' he said sharply. 'A man can't live fifteen years in a house and not leave something of his personality lying around. There'll be *some* indication of where he's gone.' He thought for a moment. 'But I want you back here. Put someone else in charge.'

'That'll be Gregory,' I said. 'I still have a few things to wrap up – I'll be back in two hours.' I rang off and said to Penny, 'Well, that's it, love. The boss wants me back.'

She said, 'Just before you went out you said something about Daddy having a gun. What did you mean?'

'He's armed,' I said.

She shook her head disbelievingly but, since so many strange things had occurred that day, she could not combat my statement. 'And will you find him?'

'Oh, we'll find him. What's worrying me is that perhaps someone else is looking for him who will find him first. And the hell of it is we aren't sure, one way or another.'

Brent came in. 'You want me?'

I waved him out and joined him in the hall. As I stripped off my jacket, I said, 'Find anything?'

'Nothing.'

I unhitched the shoulder-holster from under my left armpit. 'Take this; you might need it.' I waited until he'd put it on, then took him into the study. 'Penny, this is Jack Brent; he's your guardian angel from now on. He sticks with you everywhere you go, excepting the loo and the bedroom – and he inspects those first.'

Penny looked at me as though she suspected me of joking. 'Are you serious?'

'You'll have to find a room for Jack – he'll be living here as long as you do.' I turned to Brent. 'Make yourself acquainted with the burglar precautions here, and make sure the damn things work.'

He nodded, and said, 'Sorry about this, Miss Ashton; I have to do as I'm told.'

'Another man under orders,' she said tightly. There were pink anger spots in her cheeks. 'Do you really mean that this man goes everywhere I go?'

'As long as you want to keep your schoolgirl complexion.'

Maybe I was a bit brutal about it, but the force of what I said hit her hard. She went very pale. 'My God, Malcolm. What *is* my father?'

'I don't know; but I'm going to wring it out of Ogilvie if it's the last thing I do.'

Jack Brent gave me a look as though he thought it would

be the last thing I did. Twisting the boss's arm in any organization is not the way to promotion and that indexed pension.

I said, 'I have things to do. I'll see you before I go, Penny.' I went to brief Gregory on the latest developments and to hand over to him. I found him with Simpson going over Benson's quarters which were a bit more opulent than you'd expect of a house servant – a three-roomed suite. Gregory and Simpson had torn the place apart on my instructions because I was particularly interested in Benson. 'Any luck?'

Gregory grunted. 'Not much. There's this.' He pointed to a small can of oil. 'Recommended for gun actions. And we found a single round of ammunition – unfired. It had rolled under the bed and dropped into a crack near the wall.'

It was a 9 mm parabellum round, popular with the military and the police. 'We know he was armed,' I said. 'Now we know what with – not that it helps. Anything else?'

'Not yet.'

I told Gregory the score and then went to check the activities of the rest of the team. I had to find *something* to take to Ogilvie. In the attic I found two of the boys playing trains. 'Oh, Jesus!' I said. 'Cut it out. We're here on business.'

Michaelis grinned. 'This is business – all in the line of duty. If you want this place searched thoroughly we'll have to look inside every engine, carriage and truck in this lay-out. The only way to do it is to bring them to this central control point a trainload at a time.'

I examined the lay-out and saw he had a point. You might have found a more complicated system in an international model engineering exhibition but I doubted it. There were about ten levels of track and a complexity of points and sidings which was baffling, and the whole lot was controlled from a central console which looked like the flight deck of Concorde. Michaelis seemed to have got the hang of it; maybe he was a budding genius.

'How many trucks and carriages are there?'

'We've looked at about three hundred so far,' he said. 'I reckon that's about a quarter. We're lucky there's an automatic coupling and uncoupling system. See those trucks in the siding over there?' He pointed to a spot about eight yards inside the spider's web of rails. 'We'd never be able to get in there without smashing the lot up – so we send an engine in to pull them out. Like this.'

He flicked switches and an engine about five inches long moved into the siding and attached itself to a line of trucks with a slight click. It reversed slowly, drawing out the train of trucks, and Michaelis smiled with pleasure. 'Now the problem is – how do we get it from there to here?'

My God! I thought. What we have to do in the line of duty.

I snorted and left them to it, and went in search of Penny to make my farewells. Somebody said she was in her bedroom. She answered when I tapped on the door, and she was as angry as I'd ever seen her. 'Come in,' she said impatiently, so I did and she slammed the door behind me with a crash, 'Someone has been searching my room.'

'I know. *All* rooms in the house have been searched.'

'On your instructions?'

'Yes.'

'Oh, no! I thought I deserved better of you than that. You were right when you said you people don't deal in trust. Last night you asked me to marry you, and less than twenty-four hours later you show just how much you trust me. What sort of a man are you that you would send someone in here to paw over my things?'

'It's not a question of trusting or not trusting,' I said. 'I do my job the way I was taught.'

'So you go by the book! It's not the kind of book I'd want to read.'

And so we had a flaming row – our first. I got so boiling

mad that in the end I stormed out of the house and jumped into my car. I left a bit of rubber on the drive and got to the office in record time, being lucky not to be picked up by the police for speeding.

I wasn't in the best of moods when I confronted Ogilvie. He said immediately, 'Got anything more?'

I dropped the round of ammunition on his desk. 'Benson has something which shoots these.'

'All right, Malcolm,' he said. 'Let's begin at the beginning.'

So we talked. I told him in detail everything that had happened and we discussed the implications. Or rather, Ogilvie did. I didn't know enough about Ashton to see any implications. At one point in the discussion I said, 'It's obvious that Ashton had been prepared for this a long time. He told Penny that his lawyer and accountant had been well briefed, and he couldn't have done that in a day. I don't know if he expected acid-throwing, but he was certainly ready to jump. Someone has put the frighteners on him.'

Ogilvie made no comment on that. He said. 'You may know – or not know – that there's an inter-departmental committee for organizations like ours which sits to straighten out any demarcation disputes.'

'I don't know, but it sounds a good idea.'

'There was a special meeting called for this afternoon, and I had to talk very hard and very fast. There was considerable opposition.'

'From Lord Cregar?'

Ogilvie's eyebrows rose. 'How did you identify him?'

'He gets his pictures in the papers,' I said sardonically.

'I see. Do you know anything of the early history of this department?'

'Not much.'

He leaned forward and tented his fingers. 'The British way of intelligence and security is rather strange. Over the years we've acquired a reputation for being good at it, good and rather subtle. That is the considered assessment of our American and Russian rivals. They're wrong, of course. What they mistake for subtlety is merely that our right hand hardly ever knows what our left hand is doing.'

He took out a case and offered me a cigarette. 'The politicians are deathly afraid of a centralized intelligence outfit; they don't want anything like the CIA or the KGB because they've seen what happens when such a group becomes too big and too powerful. And so, in the classic way of divide and rule, intelligence work in Britain is broken down among relatively small groups.'

He accepted a light. 'That has its drawbacks, too. It leads to amateurism, rivalry between departments, overlapping functions, the building of empires and private armies, lack of co-operation, a breakdown of the lines of communication – a whole litany of petty vices. And it makes my job damned difficult.'

His tone was a mixture of bitterness and resignation. I said, 'I can imagine.'

'In the early 1950s the risks of industrial espionage became noticeable. We weren't really bothered about one firm stealing secrets from another, and we're still not, unless it affects state security. The whole problem was that our friends to the east have no private firms, so any industrial espionage from that direction was *ipso facto* state inspired, and that we couldn't have. In our inimitable British fashion a new department was set up to cope. This department.'

'I know what we're doing, but I didn't know how we got started.'

Ogilvie drew on his cigarette. 'There's an important point. In an attempt to cut down on duplication of effort, several other departments had to hand over large chunks of their *raison d'être* and were closed down completely. They were only small fry, though. But it all led to jealousy and bad blood which exists in a dilute form to this day. And that's how we inherited the problem of Ashton.'

I said, 'Who did we pinch Ashton from?'

'Lord Cregar's department.' Ogilvie leaned forward. 'This afternoon the Minister came down on our side. Ashton is still our baby and we have to find him. You are still inside man, and that means *you* find him. Any help you need just ask for.'

'That suits me,' I said. 'I want clearance for Code Purple.'

Ogilvie shook his head. 'Not that.'

I blew up. 'For Christ's sake! How can I look for a man when I don't know anything about him? Back in Marlow I had an interesting lecture on trust which has soured me to the belly, and this job has already interfered too much with my private life. Now you either trust me or you don't – and the crunch comes here. I get clearance for Code Purple or my resignation will be on your desk at nine tomorrow morning.'

He said sadly, 'I have warned you about being impetuous. To begin with, I couldn't get you clearance in that time, and even if you did you wouldn't find what you're looking for because Ashton is in Code Black.' His voice was grim. 'And you couldn't be cleared for Code Black inside three months – if ever.'

Code Black sounded as though it was the end of the rainbow and Ashton was the pot of gold. There was a silence which I broke by saying diffidently, 'That's it, then. I'd better go along to my office and type my resignation.'

'Don't be a young fool!' snapped Ogilvie. He drummed on the desk, then said, 'I've come to a decision. If it gets out I could be fired. Wait here.'

He got up and went to an unobtrusive door behind his desk and disappeared. I waited a long time and wondered what I'd done. I knew I'd laid my career on the line. Well, I was prepared for that and with my financial backing I could stand it. Maybe I wouldn't have done it if I had only my pay to depend on. I don't know. And I'd pushed

Ogilvie into doing something he might be sorry for, and that was bad because I liked him.

Presently he opened the door and said, 'Come in here.' I followed him into a small room where there was one of the ubiquitous computer terminals. 'I'm cleared for Code Black,' he said. 'The information on Ashton is coming on line. If you sit there you'll know what you need to know. The computer won't know who is pushing the buttons.' He checked the time. 'I'll be back in two hours.'

I was a bit subdued. 'All right, sir.'

'I want your word,' he said. 'I don't want you roving at random in Code Black. I want to know that you'll stick to Ashton and only to Ashton. There are other matters in Code Black that are better for you not to know – for your own peace of mind.'

I said, 'You can make sure of that just by sitting in here with me.'

He smiled. 'You made a point just now about trust. Either I trust you or I don't, and there's an end to it.'

'You have my word.'

He nodded abruptly and left, closing the door behind him.

I glanced at Nellie who was staring at me with an interrogative bright green question mark, and then glanced around the small room which was really more of a cubicle. On one side of the terminal was a small plotter, very much like the one in Ashton's cellar; on the other side was a line printer.

I sat at the console and reflected that if Ashton was so important and had been around and of interest since before the department had started then there was probably reams of stuff about him in Nellie's guts. This idea was reinforced by the two hours Ogilvie had allowed for reviewing the information, so I switched on the printer, and typed:

OUTPUT MODE – PRINTER

Nellie had an attack of verbal diarrhoea. She came back at me with:

PRINTER OUTPUT NEGATIVED UNDER CODE BLACK
NOTE WELL: NO WRITTEN RECORD TO BE MADE UNDER CODE BLACK
NOTE WELL: NO TAPE-RECORDED TRANSCRIPTIONS TO BE MADE UNDER CODE BLACK
NOTE WELL: NO PHOTOGRAPHS TO BE TAKEN OF THE CRT UNDER CODE BLACK

I sighed and switched off the printer.

I've described before how one juggles with Nellie so there's no point in going into that again. What I haven't said is that Nellie is accommodating; if she's going too fast you can slow her down, and if she's producing something of no interest you can speed her up. You can also skip about in the record, going back to items forgotten or neglected. She's quite a toy.

I did quite a bit of skipping when swanning around in Ashton's life. He'd lived quite a bit.

13

Aleksandr Dmitrovitch Chelyuskin was born to poorish, but respectable parents in the small town of Tesevo-Netyl'skiy, just to the north of Novgorod in Russia. The year was 1919. Both parents were schoolteachers; his mother taught in an infants' school and his father taught mathematics and allied subjects to older boys.

These were the years of revolution, and whether the Whites or the Reds were to come on top had not yet been decided in 1919. Armies of foreigners – British, French, American – were on Russian soil, and it was a time of turmoil and conflagration. Little Aleksandr was very nearly snuffed out just after birth as the waves of war swept over the country. In fact, his elder brother and his two sisters did die during this period as the family was buffeted in the storm; the record did not disclose just how they died.

Eventually, in 1923, the family Chelyuskin came to haven in the town of Aprelevka, just outside Moscow. The family had been reduced to three and, since Aleksandr had been a late child and his mother was now apparently barren, there were to be no more children and he was brought up as an only child. His father found a job teaching mathematics and they settled down to a life of relative security.

Although Dmitri Ivanovitch Chelyuskin was a teacher of mathematics he was not a good mathematician himself in the sense that he produced original work. His role in life was to teach small boys the elements of arithmetic, algebra and geometry, which he did largely by rote, a sarcastic tongue and a heavy hand. But he was good enough at his job to notice that he did not have to tell young Aleksandr anything twice, and when the time came that he found he did not have to tell the boy once and that his son was beginning to ask unanswerable questions it was then that he thought he might have an infant prodigy on his hands.

Aleksandr was about ten years old at the time.

He played chess very well and joined the chess club in Aprelevka where he proceeded to lick the pants off his elders and betters. The elder Chelyuskin forgot about the mathematics and thought of the possibility of having a Grand Master in the family, a great honour in Russia.

One Suslov, a member of the chess club, disagreed. He persuaded Chelyuskin *père* to write to a friend of his in Moscow, a member of the Board of Education. Letters and months passed, and eventually, after a series of supposedly gruelling examinations which Aleksandr went through without so much as a qualm, he was admitted to a Lycée in Moscow at the hitherto unheard-of age of twelve years and ten months. Whether the fact that Suslov had been the undisputed chess champion of Aprelevka until the appearance of Aleksandr had anything to do with that, is not known. At least, Suslov said nothing for the record but went on to win the club championship the following year.

In Britain the left wing decries elitism; in Russia the communists foster it. When a bright youngster is found he is whisked away to a special school where his mind is stretched. He can no longer count on having an easy time walking nonchalantly through the school subjects without effort, coming out on top while his duller brethren work like hell plodding along behind. Aleksandr was subjected to a forced draught of education.

He liked it. He had the cast of mind which loves grappling with the abstruse and difficult, and he found much to his liking in pure mathematics. Now, mathematics at its purest is a game for adults and need have no relationship at all to the real physical world, and the fact that it sometimes does is a bit of luck. The pure mathematician is concerned with the concept of number at its most abstract, and Aleksandr played happily among the abstractions for quite a while. At the age of sixteen he wrote a paper, 'Some Observations on the Relationship between Mathieu Functions and Weierstrass Elliptic Functions.' It consisted of three paragraphs of written text and ten pages of mathematical formulae, and was rather well received. He followed it up with another paper the following year, and that brought him under the eye of Peter Kapitza and led to the second great change in his life.

It was 1936 and Kapitza was the white hope of Russian physics. He was born in Kronstadt and studied in Kronstadt and Petrograd, as it was then. But in 1925 he made a change which was rather odd for a Russian at the time. He went to Cambridge, then the leading university dealing with physics. He became a fellow of Trinity College, and assistant director of research at the Cavendish Laboratory under Rutherford. He was elected a Fellow of the Royal Society in 1929, and managed to pick up about every scientific honour that was not absolutely screwed down except the Nobel Prize which he missed. In 1936 he went back to Russia, supposedly on a sabbatical, and never left again. Stalin is reputed to have lowered the portcullis on him.

This, then, is the man who extended his influence over Aleksandr Chelyuskin. Perhaps he looked at the youth and was reminded of himself at the age of seventeen. At any rate, he diverted Aleksandr from his playground of pure mathematics and showed him that there were real problems to be solved in the world. Kapitza introduced him to theoretical physics.

Physics is an experimental science, and most physicists are good mechanics and have broken fingernails caused by putting bits and pieces of equipment together. But there are a few – a very few – who do nothing but think. They tend to sit around, gazing into space, and their favourite weapons are blackboard and chalk. After a few hours, days or years of thought they diffidently suggest that an experiment should be made.

The realm of the theoretical physicist is the totality of the universe, and there are very few good ones around at any one time. Aleksandr Chelyuskin was one of them.

He studied magnetism and low temperature physics under Peter Kapitza and, applying quantum theory to the earlier work of Kammerlingh Onnes, did important work relating to phase II of liquid helium, and the new field of superconductivity got under way. But this was just one of the many things he thought about. His work was astonishingly wide-ranging and eclectic, and he published profusely. He did not publish everything he thought because he liked to have things wrapped up tidily, but some of his work, reproduced in the record from his notebooks written at this time, clearly anticipated the cosmological theories of Fred Hoyle in the '50s and '60s. Other work from his notebooks included thoughts on the nature of catalytic action and a brief sketch extending these thoughts into the organic field of enzymes.

In 1941 the war came to Russia, but the brain the state had so carefully nurtured was considered too valuable to risk having a bullet put through it, and Chelyuskin never saw a shot fired in anger. For most of the war he sat behind the Urals and thought his thoughts. One of the many things he thought about was the fine structure of metals. The resultant improvement in Russian tank armour was quite noticeable.

In March 1945 he was visited by a high official and told to give careful consideration to the atomic structure of certain rare metals. Stalin had just come back from the Yalta Conference where he had been informed of the existence of the atomic bomb.

In the period immediately following the war Chelyuskin became increasingly dissatisfied, mainly because, although the war was over, he was still constrained to involve himself in weapons research. He did not like what he was doing and deliberately slowed his pace. But a mind cannot stop thinking and he turned to other things than physics – to sociology, for example. In short, he stopped thinking about things and began to think about people.

He looked at the world immediately about him and did not like what he saw. This was the time when Stalin was conducting an extended post-mortem on the mistakes made during the war. Returning Russians who had been taken prisoner were hardly given time to sneeze before being whisked into Siberian camps, and hundreds of former officers mysteriously dropped out of sight. He reflected that continuous purging is as bad for society as it is for a body, and he knew that the infamous army purge of 1936 had so weakened the army that it had contributed largely to the startling defeats at the beginning of the war. And yet the process was continuing.

He was determined, on moral grounds, not to continue with atomic research, and beyond that he was sure he did not want to put such weapons into the hands of a man like Stalin. But he was equally determined not to end up in a forced labour camp as some of his colleagues had done, so he was presented with quite a problem which he solved with characteristic neatness and economy.

He killed himself.

It took him three months to plan his death and he was ruthless in the way he went about it. He needed the body of a man about his own age and with the same physical characteristics. More complicatedly, he needed the body before it had died so that certain surgical and dental work could be done and given time to age. This could not be done on a corpse.

He found what he wanted on a visit to Aprelevka. A boyhood friend of his own age was afflicted with leukaemia and there was much doubt about his survival. Chelyuskin visited the hospital and chatted to his friend, at first in generalities and then, more directly and dangerously, about politics. He was fortunate in that he found his friend to have much the same convictions as himself, and so he was encouraged to ask the crucial question. Would his friend, in the terminal stages of a killing illness, donate his body for Chelyuskin's survival?

The record does not disclose the name of Chelyuskin's friend but, in my opinion, he was a very brave man. Chelyuskin pulled strings and had him transferred to another hospital where he had the co-operation of a doctor. File entries were fudged, papers were lost and bureaucracy was baffled; it was all very efficiently inefficient and ended up with the fact that Chelyuskin's friend was effectively dead as far as anyone knew.

Then the poor man had his leg broken under surgical and aseptic conditions and suffered a considerable amount of dental work. The fracture in the leg corresponded exactly with a similar fracture in Chelyuskin's leg and the dental structure duplicated Chelyuskin's mouth exactly. The bone knitted together, and all he had to do was to wait for his friend to die.

Meanwhile, going through underground channels, he had contacted British Intelligence and requested political asylum. We were only too glad to oblige, even on his terms. To wave a defecting Russian scientist like a flag is not necessarily a good ploy, and we were quite happy to respect his terms of secrecy as long as we got him. The necessary arrangements were made.

It took a long time for Chelyuskin's friend to die. In fact, for a period there was a marked improvement in his condition which must have infuriated my masters. I doubt if it worried Chelyuskin very much. He went about his work as usual, attending the committees which were an increasing and aggravating part of his life, and soldiered on. But his friends did comment that he appeared to be doing his best to drown himself in the vodka bottle.

Seven months later the Russian scientific community was saddened to learn that Academician A. D. Chelyuskin had been burnt to death when his *dacha*, to which he had retired for a short period of relaxation, had caught fire. There was a post-mortem examination and an enquiry. The rumour got around that Chelyuskin had been smoking in bed when in his cups and that vodka added to the flames had not helped him much. That was a story everybody could believe.

A month later Chelyuskin slipped over the Iranian border. Three days later he was in Teheran and the following day he was put down at RAF Northolt by courtesy of Transport Command. He was given an enthusiastic welcome by a select group who turned out to welcome this genius who was then at the ripe age of twenty-eight. There would be a lot of mileage left in him.

The powers-that-be were somewhat baffled by Chelyuskin's comparative youth. They tended to forget that creative abstract thought, especially in mathematics, is a young man's game, and that Einstein had published his Special Theory of Relativity when only nineteen. Even the politicians among them forgot that Pitt was Prime Minister at twenty-four.

They were even more baffled and irritated by Chelyuskin's attitude. He soon made it clear that he was a Russian patriot and no traitor, and that he had no intention of disclosing secrets, atomic or otherwise. He said he had left Russia because he did not want to work on atomics, and that to communicate his knowledge would be to negate the action he had taken. Conversations on atomic theory were barred.

The irritation grew and pressure was applied, but authority found that it could neither bend nor break this man. The more pressure was applied the more stubborn he became, until finally he refused to discuss *any* of his work. Even the ultimate threat did not move him. When told that he could be disclosed to the Russians even at that late stage he merely shrugged and indicated that it was the privilege of the British to do so if they wished, but he thought it would be unworthy of them.

Authority changed its tack. Someone asked him what he wanted to do. Did he want a laboratory put at his disposal, for instance? By now Chelyuskin was wary of the British and their motives. I suppose, in a way, he had been naïve to expect any other treatment, but naïvety in a genius is comparatively normal. He found himself surrounded, not by scientists whom he understood, but by calculating men, the power brokers of Whitehall. Mutual incomprehensibility was total.

He rejected the offer of a laboratory curtly. He saw quite clearly that he was in danger of exchanging one intellectual prison for another. When they asked him again what it was he wanted, he said something interesting. 'I want to live as an ordinary citizen,' he said. 'I want to sink and lose myself in the sea of Western capitalism.'

Authority shrugged its shoulders and gave up. Who could understand these funny foreigners, anyway? A dog-in-the-manger attitude was adopted; if we couldn't get at the man's brain then the Russians didn't have it, either, and that was good enough. He could always be watched and, who knows, he might even declare a dividend in the future.

So Chelyuskin got exactly what he asked for.

An REME soldier called George Ashton had been killed in a traffic accident in Germany. He was twenty-seven and had been brought up in a foundling home. Unmarried and with neither kith nor kin to mourn him, he was the perfect answer. Chelyuskin was flown to Germany, put in the uniform of a private in the British Army, and brought back to England by train and sea, accompanied discreetly at all times. He went through a demobilization centre where he was given a cheap suit, a small amount of back pay and a handshake from a sombre unrecruiting sergeant.

He was also given an honorarium of £2000.

He asked for, and was given, something else before he was cast adrift. Because of the necessity for scientific study he had learned English in his youth and read it fluently. But he never had occasion to speak it, which might have been an advantage when he was put through a six months' total immersion course in conversational English, because he had no bad habits to unlearn. He came out of it with a cultured generalized Home Counties accent, and set out to sink or swim in the capitalist world.

Two thousand pounds may not seem much now, but it was quite a sizeable piece of change back in 1947. Even so, George Ashton knew he must conserve his resources; he put most of it in a bank deposit account, and lived very simply while he explored this strange new world. He was no longer an honoured man, an Academician with a car and a *dacha* at his disposal, and he had to find a way of earning a living. Any position requiring written qualifications was barred to him because he did not have the papers. It was a preposterous situation.

He took a job as a book-keeper in the stores department of a small engineering firm in Luton. This was in the days before computers when book-keeping was done by hand as in the days of Dickens, and a good book-keeper could add a triple column of pounds, shillings and pence in one practised sweep of the eye. But there weren't many of those around and Ashton found himself welcome because, unlike the popular myth, he was an egghead who could add and *always* got his change right. He found the job ridiculously easy if monotonous, and it left him time to think.

He struck up an acquaintanceship with the foreman of the toolroom, a man called John Franklin who was about 50 years of age. They got on very well together and formed the habit of having a drink together in the local pub after work. Presently Ashton was invited *chez* Franklin for Sunday dinner where he met Franklin's wife, Jane, and his daughter, Mary. Mary Franklin was 25 then, and as yet unmarried because her fiancé had been shot down over Dortmund in the final days of the war.

All this time Ashton was being watched. If he was aware of it he gave no sign. Other people were watched, too, and the Franklin family came in for a thorough rummaging on the grounds that those interested in Ashton were *per se* interesting in themselves. Nothing was discovered except the truth; that Jack Franklin was a damned good artisan with his brains in his fingertips, Jane Franklin was a comfortable, maternal woman, and Mary Franklin had suffered a tragedy in her life.

Six months after they met, Ashton and Franklin left the engineering firm to strike out on their own. Ashton put up £1500 and his brains while Franklin contributed £500 and his capable hands. The idea was to set up a small plastics moulding shop; Franklin to make the moulds and the relatively simple machines needed, and Ashton to do the designing and to run the business.

The small firm wobbled along for a while without overmuch success until Ashton, becoming dissatisfied with the moulding powders he was getting from a big chemical company, devised a concoction of his own, patented it, and started another company to make it. After that they never looked back.

Ashton married Mary Franklin and I dare say a member of some department or other was unobtrusively present at the wedding. A year later she gave him a daughter whom they christened Penelope, and two years later another girl whom they called Gillian. Mary Ashton died a couple of years later in 1953, from childbirth complications. The baby died, too.

All his life Ashton kept a low profile. He joined no clubs or trade associations; he steered clear of politics, national or local, although he voted regularly, and generally divided his life between his work and his home. This gave him time to look after his two small girls with the help of a nanny whom he brought into the small suburban house in Slough, where he then lived. From the record he was devoted to them.

About 1953 he must have opened his old notebooks and started to think again. As Chelyuskin he had never published any of his work on catalysts and I suppose he thought it was safe to enter the field. A catalyst is a substance which speeds up the chemical reactions between other substances, sometimes by many thousands of times. They are used extensively in chemical processing, particularly in the oil industry.

Ashton put his old work to good use. He devised a whole series of new catalysts tailored to specialized uses. Some he manufactured and sold himself, others he allowed to be made under licence. All were patented and the money began to roll in. It seemed as though this odd fish was swimming quite well in the capitalist sea.

In 1960 he bought his present house and, after fifteen months of extensive internal remodelling, he moved in with his family. After that nothing much seemed to happen except that he saw the portent of North Sea oil, opened another factory in 1970, took out a lot more patents and became steadily richer. He also extended his interest to those natural catalysts, the enzymes, and presumably the sketchy theory presented in the early notebook became filled out.

After 1962 the record became particularly flat and perfunctory, and I knew why. Authority had lost interest in him and he would exist only in a tickler file to remind someone to give an annual check. It was only when I set the bells jangling by my inadvertent enquiry that someone had woken up.

And that was the life of George Ashton, once Aleksandr Dmitrovitch Chelyuskin – my future father-in-law.

14

What I have set down about Ashton-Chelyuskin is a mere condensation of what was in the computer together with a couple of added minor assumptions used as links to make a sustained narrative. Had I been able to use the printer it would have churned out enough typescript to make a book the size of a family bible. To set down in print the details of a man's life needs a lot of paper. Yet I think I have presented the relevant facts.

When I finished I had a headache. To stare at a cathode ray screen for two and a half hours is not good for the eyes, and I had been smoking heavily so that the little room was very stuffy. It was with relief that I emerged into Ogilvie's office.

He was sitting at his desk reading a book. He looked up and smiled. 'You look as though you need a drink.'

'It would go down very well,' I agreed.

He got up and opened a cabinet from which he took a bottle of whisky and two glasses; then he produced a jug of iced water from a small built-in refrigerator. The perquisites of office. 'What do you think?'

'I think Ashton is one hell of a man. I'm proud to have known him.'

'Anything else?'

'There's one fact that's so damned obvious it may be overlooked.'

'I doubt it,' said Ogilvie, and handed me a glass. 'A lot of good men have checked that file.'

I diluted the whisky and sat down. 'Do you have all of Ashton in there?'

'All that we know is there.'

'Exactly. Now, I've gone through Ashton's work in some detail and it's all in the field of applied science – technology, if you like. All the things he's been doing with catalysts is derived from his earlier unpublished work; there's nothing fundamentally new there. Correct me if I'm wrong.'

'You're quite right, although it took a man with Ashton's brains to do it. We've given our own top chemists photocopies of those notebooks and their attitude was that the stuff was all right from a theoretical point of view but it didn't seem to lead anywhere. Ashton made it lead somewhere and it's made him rich. But, in general, your point is good; it's all derivative of earlier work – even his later interest in enzymes.'

I nodded. 'But Chelyuskin was a theoretician. The point is this – did he stop theorizing and, if not, what the hell has he been thinking about? I can understand why you want that bloody vault opened.'

'You're not too stupid,' said Ogilvie. 'You've hit the nail smack on the head. You're right; you can't stop a man thinking, but what he's been thinking about is difficult to figure. It won't be atomic theory.'

'Why not?'

'We know what he reads; the magazines he subscribes to, the books he buys. We know he's not been keeping up with the scientific literature in any field except catalytic chemistry, and no one thinks in a vacuum. Atomic theory has made great strides since Ashton came out of Russia. To do any original work a man would have to work hard to keep ahead of the pack – attend seminars and so on. Ashton hasn't been doing it.' He tasted his whisky. 'What would you have done in Ashton's position and with a mind like his?'

'Survival would come first,' I said. 'I'd find a niche in society and look for security. Once I'd got that perhaps I'd start thinking again – theorizing.'

'What about? In your struggle for survival the world of thought has passed you by; you've lost touch. And you daren't try to regain touch, either. So what would you think about?'

'I don't know,' I said slowly. 'Perhaps, with a mind like his, I'd think about things other people haven't been thinking about. A new field.'

'Yes,' said Ogilvie thoughtfully. 'It makes one wonder, doesn't it?'

We sat for a few moments in silence. It was late – the light was ebbing from the summer sky over the City – and I was tired. I sipped the whisky appreciatively and thought about Ashton. Presently Ogilvie asked, 'Did you find anything in the file to give you a clue about where he's gone?'

'Nothing springs to mind. I'd like to sleep on it – let the unconscious have a go.' I finished the whisky. 'Where does Cregar fit into this?'

'It was his crowd Ashton approached when he wanted to leave Russia. Cregar went into Russia himself to get him out. He was a young man then, of course, and not yet Lord Cregar – he was the Honourable James Pallton. Now he heads his department.'

I'd come across the name Pallton in reading the file, but I hadn't connected it with Cregar. I said, 'He mishandled Ashton right from the start. He approached him with all the sensitivity of a fifty-pence whore. First he threatened, then he tried to bribe. He didn't understand the type of man he'd come across, and he put Ashton's back up.'

Ogilvie nodded. 'That's one element in the mixture of his resentment. He always thought he could retrieve Ashton; that's why he was so annoyed when the Ashton case was transferred to us. That's why he's sticking his oar in now.'

'What steps have already been taken to find Ashton?'

'The usual. The Special Branch are on the watch at sea ports and airports, and they're checking passenger lists for the past twenty-four hours. You'd better liaise with Scotland Yard on that tomorrow.'

'I'll do that. And I'll have a go from the other end. There's one thing I'd like to know.'

'What's that?'

'Who threw such a scare into Ashton? Who threw that bloody acid?'

I was overtired that night and couldn't get to sleep. As I tossed restlessly Penny was very much on my mind. It was evident from what she had said that she knew nothing of Ashton in the larval stage, before he changed from Chelyuskin. Her account of his early life fitted that of the REME soldier killed in Germany.

I wondered how it would be with Penny and me. I had been damned insensitive that afternoon. Her room had to be searched, but if anyone had done it then it ought to have been me, preferably in her presence. I didn't blame her for blowing her top and I wondered how I could retrieve the situation. I felt very bad about it.

Most people, when they have had a burglary, are not so much concerned about the articles stolen as about the intrusion into the heart of their lives, the home which is so peculiarly their own. It is the thought that strange hands have been delving among their innermost secrets, rummaging in drawers, opening doors in the private parts of the house – all this is profoundly shocking. I knew all that and ought to have applied it to Penny.

At last I sat up in bed, checked the time, then stretched for the telephone. Although it was late I was going to talk to her. Mary Cope answered my call. 'Malcolm Jaggard here; I'd like to talk to Miss Ashton.'

'Just a moment, sir,' she said. She wasn't away long. 'Miss Ashton isn't in, sir.' There was a hint of nervousness in her voice as though she thought I wouldn't believe her. I didn't, but there was nothing I could do about it.

It was early morning when I finally slept.

* * *

I spent most of the forenoon at Scotland Yard with a Special Branch officer. I had no great hope of success and neither had he but we went through the motions. His crowd had been busy but even so the reports were slow to come in. A lot of people leave from Heathrow in twenty-four hours and that is only one exit from the country.

'Ashton and Benson,' he said morosely, as he ticked off a name. 'Bloody near as bad as Smith and Robinson. Why the hell do people we're interested in never have names like Moneypenny or Gotobed?'

Six Bensons and four Ashtons had left from Heathrow. Half could be eliminated because of sex and the Ashtons were a family of four. But two of the Bensons would have to be followed up; one had gone to Paris and the other to New York. I got busy on the telephone.

Heathrow may be large but it is still only one place and there are other airports, more than the average person realizes. And there were the sea ports of which islanded Britain had a plenitude. It was going to be a long job with nothing but uncertainty guaranteed.

The Special Branch man said philosophically, 'And, of course, they may have left under other names. Getting a spare passport is dead easy.'

'They may not have left at all,' I said. 'Tell your chaps to keep their eyes open.'

I lunched in a commissary at the Yard and then went back prepared for a slogging afternoon. At three o'clock Ogilvie rang me. 'They'll be opening that vault later today. I want you there.'

A drive to Marlow would be a lot more refreshing than checking passenger lists. 'All right.'

'Now, these are my exact instructions. When that door is opened you will be present, and the head of the safe-cracking team. No one else. Is that clear?'

'Perfectly clear.'

'Then you send him out of the room and check the contents. If they are removeable you bring them here under guard. If not, you close and lock the door again, first making sure we can open it again more easily.'

'How long are you staying at the office?'

'All night, if necessary.' He hung up.

So I drove to Marlow and to Ashton's place. I was wearing grooves in that road. Simpson was the gate man and he let me in and I drove up to the house. I met Gregory in the hall. 'Found anything useful?'

He shrugged. 'Not a thing.'

'Where's Miss Ashton?'

'At the hospital. Jack Brent is with her.'

'Good enough.' I went up to Ashton's quarters and found the safe-cracking team at work. I don't know where the department kept its experts when not in use, but they were always available when needed. The chief safe-cracker was a man I'd met before by the name of Frank Lillywhite. 'Afternoon, Frank,' I said. 'How much longer?'

He grunted. 'An hour.' He paused. 'Or two.' There was a longer pause as he did something intricate with a tool he held. 'Or three.'

I grinned. 'Or four. Is this a tricky one?'

'They're all tricky. This is a twenty-four-hour safe, that's all.'

I was curious. 'What do you mean?'

Lillywhite stepped away from the vault door and an underling moved in. 'Safe manufacturers don't sell security – they sell time. Any safe made can be cracked; all the manufacturer guarantees is the length of time needed to crack it. They reckon this is a twenty-four-hour job; I'm going to do it in twenty – with a bit of luck. The tricky part comes in circumventing the booby traps.'

'What booby traps?'

'If I do the wrong thing here, twelve bloody big tungsten steel bars will shoot out all round the door. Then only the maker will be able to open it.'

'Then why didn't we get the maker on the job in the first place?'

Lillywhite sighed, and said patiently, 'The whole vault would have to be ripped out and taken to the factory. They've got a bloody big tin-opener there that weighs a thousand tons. Of course the vault wouldn't be good for much after that.'

I contemplated the awful possibility of taking the whole vault out. 'Neither would this house. I'll stop asking silly questions. Don't open the door unless I'm here.'

'Message received and understood.'

I went down to the cellar where I found a couple of studious-looking types being baffled by Ashton's contraption. Their conversation, if you could call it that, was in English, but that's to use the word loosely; it was technical jargon-ridden and way over my head, so I left them to it. Another man was packing tape cassettes into a box ready to take away. I said, 'What are those?'

He indicated the little computer. 'Program and data tapes for this thing. We're taking them to the lab for analysis.'

'You're listing everything, I hope. You'll have to give a receipt to Miss Ashton.' He frowned at that, and I said acidly, 'We're not thieves or burglars, you know. It's only by courtesy of Miss Ashton that we're here at all.' As I left the cellar he was taking cassettes out of the box and stacking them on a table.

An hour and a half later Gregory found me in Ashton's study. 'They'll be opening the vault in about fifteen minutes.'

'Let's go up.'

We left the study and encountered Lord Cregar in the hall; with him was a big man with the build of a heavyweight boxer. Cregar looked brisk and cheerful but his cheerfulness, if not his briskness, evaporated when he saw me. 'Ah, Mr Jaggard,' he said. 'A fine mess has been made of things, I must say.'

I shrugged. 'Events moved faster than we anticipated.'

'No doubt. I understand there's a vault here which is being opened this afternoon. Has it been opened yet?'

I wondered where he'd got his information. 'No.'

'Good. Then I'm in time.'

I said, 'Am I to understand that you wish to be present when the vault is opened?'

'That's correct.'

'I'm sorry,' I said. 'But I'll have to take that under advisement.'

He looked at me thoughtfully. 'Do you know who I am?'

'Yes, my lord.'

'Very well,' he said. 'Make your telephone call.'

I jerked my head at Gregory and we went back into the study. 'There's no need for a call,' I said. 'Ogilvie's instructions were very precise, and they didn't include Cregar.'

'I know that big chap,' said Gregory. 'His name is Martins. A bad chap to tangle with.' He paused. 'Maybe you'd better check with Ogilvie.'

'No. He told me what to do and I'm going to do it.'

'So what if Cregar won't take it? A bout of fisticuffs with a member of the House of Lords could have its repercussions.'

I smiled. 'I doubt of it will come to that. Let's tell his lordship the bad news.'

We went back into the hall to find that Cregar and Martins had vanished. 'They'll be upstairs,' said Gregory.

'Come on.' We ran upstairs and found them in Ashton's room. Cregar was tapping his foot impatiently as I stepped forward and said formally, 'My lord, I regret to inform you that you will not be permitted to be present when the vault is opened.'

Cregar's eyes bulged. 'Did Ogilvie say that?'

'I have not spoken to Mr Ogilvie recently. I am merely following instructions.'

'You take a lot upon yourself,' he commented.

I turned to Lillywhite. 'How much longer, Frank?'

'Give me ten minutes.'

'No – stop work now. Don't start again until I tell you.'

I turned back to Cregar. 'If you would like to speak to Mr Ogilvie yourself you may use the telephone here or in the study.'

Cregar actually smiled. 'You know when to pass the buck. You're quite right; it's better if I speak to Ogilvie. I'll use the study.'

'Show his lordshp where it is,' I said to Gregory, and the three of them left the room.

Lillywhite said, 'What was all that about?'

'A bit of inter-departmental nonsense; nothing to do with humble servants like ourselves. You can carry on, Frank. That vault must be opened come what may.'

He went back to his job and I strolled over to the window and looked down at the drive. Presently Cregar and Martins came out of the house, got into a car, and drove away. Gregory came into the room. 'Cregar was a bit sour when he came out of the study,' he remarked. 'Ogilvie wants to talk to you.'

I walked over and picked up the telephone next to Ashton's bed. 'Jaggard here.'

Ogilvie said quickly: 'On no account must Cregar know what's in that vault. Don't let him pull rank on you – it's got nothing to do with him.'

'He won't,' I said. 'He's gone.'

'Good. When will you open it?'

'Another five minutes.'

'Keep me informed.' He rang off.

Gregory held out a packet of cigarettes and we smoked while Lillywhite and his two assistants fiddled with the door. At last there was a sharp click and Lillywhite said, 'That's it.'

I stood up. 'All right. Everybody out except me and Frank.' I waited until they left then went to the vault. 'Let's get at it.'

'Right.' Lillywhite put his hand to a lever and pulled it down. Nothing happened. 'There you are.'

'You mean it's open now?'

'That's right. Look.' He pulled and the door began to open. It was nearly a foot thick.

'Hold it,' I said quickly. 'Now, can it be locked again and opened easily?'

'Sure. Nothing to it now.'

'That's all I need to know. Sorry, Frank, but I'll have to ask you to leave now.'

He gave a crooked smile. 'If what's in here can't even be seen by a member of the House of Lords it's certainly not for Frank Lillywhite.'

He went out and closed the door emphatically.

I opened the vault.

15

Ogilvie gaped. 'Empty!'

'As bare as Mother Hubbard's cupboard.' I considered that. 'Except for a layer of fine dust on the floor.'

'You checked all the shelves and cabinets?'

'There were no cabinets. There were no shelves. It was just an empty cube. I didn't even go inside; I just stuck my head in and looked around. Then I closed the door again and had it relocked. I thought I'd better leave it as it was in case you want the forensic chaps to have a look at it. My bet is that it's never been used since it was built fifteen years ago.'

'Well, my God!' Ogilvie stopped then. He seemed at a total loss for words, but he was thinking furiously. I stepped over to the window and looked down into the empty street. It was late and the bowler-hatted tide had receded from the City leaving it deserted except for a few stragglers. There is no other urban area in the world that can look so empty as the City of London.

Ogilvie said thoughtfully, 'So only you, the chief of the safe-opening team, and now me, know about this.'

I turned. 'Even your Chief Burglar doesn't know. I sent Lillywhite out of the room before I opened the vault.'

'So it's only you and me. Damn!'

He swore so explosively that I said, 'What's wrong?'

'It's backfired on me. Cregar will never believe me now when I tell him the truth about that damned vault. I wish now he'd been there.'

Personally I didn't care what Cregar believed or didn't believe. I took a sheet of paper from my wallet, unfolded it, and laid it on the desk. 'This is the new combination for opening the vault. Lillywhite reset it.'

'This is the only copy?'

'Lillywhite must have a record of it.'

Ogilvie wagged his head. 'This will bear a lot of thinking about. In the meantime you carry on looking for Ashton and Benson, and don't forget they might have split up. Made any progress?'

'Only by elimination, if you call that progress.'

'All right,' said Ogilvie tiredly. 'Carry on.' I had my hand on the doorknob when he said, 'Malcolm.'

'Yes.'

'Watch out for Cregar. He makes a bad enemy.'

'I'm not fighting Cregar,' I said. 'He's nothing to do with me. What's between you and him is way over my head.'

'He didn't like the way you stood up to him this afternoon.'

'He didn't show it – he was pleasant enough.'

'That's his way, but he'll only pat you on the back to find a place to stick a knife. Watch him.'

'He is nothing to do with me,' I repeated.

'Maybe,' said Ogilvie. 'But Cregar may not share your view.'

After that nothing happened for a while. The Special Branch investigation petered out with no result although their men at the exits were still keeping a sharp watch in case our pair made a late dash for it. Honnister had nothing to offer. On my third enquiry he said tartly, 'Don't ring us – we'll ring you.'

I spent two and a half days reading every word of the bushel or so of miscellaneous papers Gregory had brought back from Ashton's house – appointment books, financial records, business diaries, letters and so on. As a result of that many enquiries were made but nothing of interest turned up. Ashton's companies were given a thorough going-over with like result.

A week after Ashton's disappearance my team was cut in half. I kept Brent with Penny and Michaelis looked after Gillian, leaving two to do the legwork. I was doing a lot of legwork myself, going sixteen hours a day, running like hell like the Red Queen to stay in the same place. Larry Godwin was back at his desk reading the East European journals. His fling at freedom had been brutally brief.

The boffins had nothing much to report. The computer tapes showed nothing out of the ordinary except some very clever program designing, but what the programs did was nothing special. The prototype whatsit Ashton had been tinkering with caused a flood of speculation which left a thin sediment of hard fact. The consensus of opinion was that it was a pilot plant of a process designed to synthesize insulin; very ingenious and highly patentable but still in an early stage of design. It told me nothing to my purpose.

The day after we opened the empty vault I had telephoned Penny. 'Is this to tell me you've found Daddy?' she asked.

'No, I've nothing to tell you about that. I'm sorry.'

'Then I don't think we've much to talk about, Malcolm,' she said, and rang off before I could get in another word. Right at that moment I didn't know whether we were still engaged or not.

After that I kept in touch with her movements through Brent. She went back to doing her work at University College, London, but tended to use her car more instead of the train. She didn't seem to resent Brent; he was her passenger in her daily journeys to and from London, and she always kept him informed of her proposed movements. He was enjoyng his assignment and thought she was a very nice person. He didn't think she knew he was armed. And, no, she never talked of me.

Gillian was moved to Moorfields Eye Hospital and I went to see her. After checking with Michaelis I had a few words with her doctor, a specialist called Jarvis. 'She's still heavily bandaged,' he said. 'And she'll need cosmetic plastic surgery, but that will be later and in another place. Here we are concerned only with her eyes.'

'What are the odds, Doctor?'

He said carefully, 'There may be a chance of restoring some measure of sight to the left eye. There's no hope for the right eye at all.' He looked straight at me. 'Miss Ashton doesn't know that yet. Please don't tell her.'

'Of course not. Does she know that her father has – er – gone away?'

'She does, and it's not making my job any easier,' said Jarvis waspishly. 'She's very depressed, and between us we have enough problems without having to cope with a psychologically depressed patient. It's most insensitive of the man to go on a business trip at this time.'

So that's what Penny had told Gillian. I suppose it was marginally better than telling her that Daddy had done a bolt. I said, 'Perhaps I can cheer her up.'

'I wish you would,' Jarvis said warmly. 'It would help her quite a lot.'

So I went to talk to Gillian and found her flat on her back on a bed with no pillow and totally faceless because she was bandaged up like Claude Rains in the film, *The Invisible Man*. The nursing sister gently told her I was there, and went away. I steered clear of the reasons she was there, and asked no questions about it. Honnister was probably a better interrogator than I and would have sucked her dry. Instead I stuck to trivialities and told her a couple of funny items I had read in the papers that morning, and brought her up-to-date on the news of the day.

She was very grateful. 'I miss reading the papers. Penny comes in every day and reads to me.'

Brent had told me of that. 'I know.'

'What's gone wrong between you and Penny?'

'Why, nothing,' I said lightly. 'Did she say there was anything wrong?'

'No, but she stopped talking about you, and when I asked, she said she hadn't seen you.'

'We've both been busy,' I said.

'I suppose that's it,' said Gillian. 'But it's the way she said it.'

I changed the subject and we chatted some more and when I left I think she was a little better in outlook.

Michaelis found his job boring, which indeed it was. As far as the hospital staff were concerned, he was a policeman set to guard a girl who had been violently attacked once. He sat on a chair outside the ward and spent his time reading paperbacks and magazines.

'I read to Miss Ashton for an hour every afternoon,' he said.

'That's good of you.'

He shrugged. 'Nothing much else to do. There's plenty of time to think on this job, too. I've been thinking about that model railway in Ashton's attic. I've never seen anything to beat it. He was a schedules man, of course.'

'What's that?'

'There's a lot of variety in the people who are interested in model railways. There are the scenic men who are bent on getting all the details right in miniature. I'm one of those. There are the engineering types who insist their stuff should be exact from the engineering aspect; that's expensive. I know a chap who has modelled Paddington Station; and all he's interested in is getting the trains in and out according to the timetable. He's a schedules man like Ashton. The only difference is that Ashton was doing it on a really big scale.'

Hobbies are something that people really do become fanatical about, but Ashton hadn't struck me as the type. Still, I hadn't known that Michaelis was a model railwayman, either. I said, 'How big a scale?'

'Bloody big. I found a stack of schedules up there which made me blink. He could duplicate damn nearly the whole of the British railway system – not all at once, but in sections. He seemed to be specializing in pre-war stuff; he had schedules from the old LMS system, for instance; and the Great Western and the LNER. Now that takes a hell of a lot of juggling, so you know what he'd done?'

Michaelis looked at me expectantly, so I said, 'What?'

'He's installed a scad of microprocessors in that control board. You know – the things that have been called a computer on a chip. He could program his timetables into them.'

That sounded like Ashton, all right; very efficient. But it wasn't helping me to find him. 'Better keep your mind on the job,' I advised. 'We don't want anything happening to the girl.'

Two weeks after Ashton bolted Honnister rang me. Without preamble he said, 'We've got a line on our man.'

'Good. When are you seeing him?' I wanted to be there.

'I'm not,' said Honnister. 'He's not in my parish. He's a London boy so he's the Met's meat. A chap from the Yard will be seeing him tonight; Inspector Crammond. He's expecting you to ring him.'

'I'll do that. What's this character's name, and how did you get on to him?'

'His name is Peter Mayberry, aged about forty-five to fifty, and he lives in Finsbury. Apart from that I know damn-all. Crammond will pick it up from there. Mayberry hired the car for the weekend – not from one of the big hire-car firms, but from a garage in Slough. The bobbies over there came across it as a matter of routine and asked a few questions. The garage owner was bloody annoyed; he said someone had spilled battery acid on the back seat, so that made us perk up a bit.'

I thought about that. 'But would Mayberry give his real name when he hired the car?'

'The bloody fool did,' said Honnister. 'Anyway, he'd have to show his driving licence. This one strikes me as an amateur; I don't think he's a pro. Anyway, Crammond tells me there's a Peter Mayberry living at that address.'

'I'll get on to Crammond immediately. Thanks, Charlie. You've done very well.'

He said earnestly, 'You'll thank me by leaning bloody hard on this bastard.' I was about to ring off, but he chipped in again. 'Seen anything of Ashton lately?'

It was the sort of innocuous question he might be expected to ask, but I thought I knew Honnister better than that by now; he wasn't a man to waste his time on idle chit-chat. 'Not much,' I said. 'Why?'

'I thought he'd like to know. Every time I ring him he's out, and the beat bobby tells me there's been some funny things going on at the house. A lot of coming and going and to-ing and fro-ing.'

'I believe he went away on a business trip. As for the house I wouldn't know – I haven't been there lately.'

'I suppose that's your story and you're sticking to it,' he said. 'Who's going to tell the Ashton sisters – you or me?'

'I will,' I said. 'After I've made sure of Mayberry.'

'All right. Any time you're down this way pop in and see me. We can have another noggin at the Coach and Horses. I'll be very interested in anything you can tell me.' He rang off.

I smiled. I was sure Honnister would be interested. Something funny was going on in his parish which he didn't know about, and it irked him.

I dialled Scotland Yard and got hold of Crammond. 'Oh, yes, Mr Jaggard; it's about this acid-throwing attack. I'll be seeing Mayberry tonight – he doesn't get home until about six-thirty, so his landlady tells us. I suggest you meet me here at six and we'll drive out.'

'That's fine.'

'There's just one thing,' Crammond said. 'Whose jurisdiction applies here – ours or yours?'

I said slowly, 'That depends on what Mayberry says. The acid-throwing is straightforward criminal assault, so as far as that's concerned he's your man and you can have him and welcome. But there are other matters I'm not at liberty to go into, and we might like to question him further before you charge him. Informally, of course.'

'I understand,' said Crammond. 'It's just that it's best to get these things straight first. See you at six, Mr Jaggard.'

Crammond was properly cautious. The police were not very comfortable when mixing with people like us. They knew that some of the things we did, if strictly interpreted, could be construed as law-breaking, and it went against the grain with them to turn a blind eye. Also they tended to think of themselves as the only professionals in the business and looked down on us as amateurs and, in their view, they were not there to help amateurs break the law of the land.

I phoned Ogilvie and told him. All he said was, 'Ah well, we'll see what comes of it.'

I met Crammond as arranged. He was a middling-sized thickset man of nondescript appearance, very useful in a plain clothes officer. We went out to Finsbury in his car, with a uniformed copper in the back seat, and he told me what he knew.

'When Honnister passed the word to us I had Mayberry checked out. That was this morning so he wasn't at home. He lives on the top floor of a house that's been broken up into flats. At least, that's what they call them; most of them are single rooms. His landlady described him as a quiet type – a bit bookish.'

'Married?'

'No. She thinks he never has been, either. He has a job as some kind of clerk working for a City firm. She wasn't too clear about that.'

'He doesn't sound the type,' I complained.

'He does have a police record,' said Crammond.

'That's better.'

'Wait until you hear it. One charge of assaulting a police officer, that's all. I went into it and the charge should never have been brought, even though he was found guilty. He got into a brawl during one of the Aldermaston marches a few years ago and was lugged in with a few others.'

'A protester,' I said thoughtfully. 'Amateur or professional?'

'Amateur, I'd say. He's not on our list of known rabble-rousers and, in any case, he has the wrong job for it. He's not mobile enough. But his appearance fits the description given by Honnister's witness. We'll see. Who does the asking?'

'You do,' I said. 'I'll hang about in the background. He'll think I'm just another copper.'

Mayberry had not arrived home when we got there so his landlady accommodated us in her front parlour. She was plainly curious and said archly, 'Has Mr Mayberry been doing anything naughty?'

'We just want him to help us in our enquiries,' said Crammond blandly. 'Is he a good tenant, Mrs Jackson?'

'He pays his rent regularly, and he's quiet. That's good enough for me.'

'Lived here long?'

'Five years – or is it six?' After much thought she decided it was six.

'Has he any hobbies? What does he do with his spare time?'

'He reads a lot; always got his head in a book. And he's religious – he goes to church twice every Sunday.'

I was depressed. This sounded less and less like our man. 'Did he go to church on the Sunday two weekends ago?' asked Crammond.

'Very likely,' she said. 'But I was away that weekend.' She held her head on one side. 'That sounds like him now.'

Someone walked along the passage outside the room and began to ascend the stairs. We gave him time to get settled then went after him. On the first landing Crammond said to the uniformed man, 'Wait outside the door, Shaw. If he makes a break grab him. It's not likely to happen, but if he is an acid-throwing bastard he can be dangerous.'

I stood behind Crammond as he tapped on Mayberry's door and noted that Shaw was flat against the wall so

Mayberry couldn't see him. It's nice to see professionals at work. Mayberry was a man in his late forties and had a sallow complexion as though he did not eat well. His eyes were sunk deep into his skull.

'Mr Peter Mayberry?'

'Yes.'

'We're police officers,' said Crammond pleasantly. 'And we think you can help us. Do you mind if we come in?'

I saw Mayberry's knuckles whiten a little as he gripped the edge of the door. 'How can I help you?'

'Just by answering a few questions. Can we come in?'

'I suppose so.' Mayberry held open the door.

It wasn't much of a place; the carpet was threadbare and the furniture was of painted whitewood and very cheap; but it was clean and tidy. Along one wall was a shelf containing perhaps forty or fifty books; anyone with so many would doubtless be a great reader to Mrs Jackson who probably got through one book a year, if that.

I glanced at the titles. Some were religious and of a decidedly fundamentalist slant; there was a collection of environmental stuff including some pamphlets issued by Friends of the Earth. For the rest they were novels, all classics and none modern. Most of the books were paperbacks.

There were no pictures in the room except for one poster which was stuck on the wall by sticky tape at the corners. It depicted the earth from space, a photograph taken by an astronaut. Printed at the bottom were the words: I'M ALL YOU'VE GOT; LOOK AFTER ME.

Crammond started by saying, 'Can I see your driving licence, Mr Mayberry?'

'I don't have a car.'

'That wasn't what I asked,' said Crammond. 'Your driving licence, please.'

Mayberry had taken off his jacket which was hanging on the back of a chair. He bent down and took his wallet from the inside breast pocket, took out his licence and gave it to

Crammond who examined it gravely and in silence. At last Crammond said approvingly, 'Clean; no endorsements.' He handed it to me.

'I always drive carefully,' said Mayberry.

'I'm sure you do. Do you drive often?'

'I told you – I don't have a car.'

'And I heard you. Do you drive often?'

'Not very. What's all this about?'

'When did you last drive a car?'

Mayberry said, 'Look, if anyone says I've been in an accident they're wrong because I haven't.' He seemed very nervous, but many people are in the presence of authority, even if innocent. It's the villain who brazens it out.

I put the licence on the table and picked up the book Mayberry had been reading. It was on so-called alternative technology and was turned to a chapter telling how to make a digester to produce methane from manure. It seemed an unlikely subject for Finsbury.

Crammond said, 'When did you last drive a car?'

'Oh, I don't know – several months ago.'

'Whose car was it?'

'I forget. It was a long time ago.'

'Whose car do you usually drive?'

There was a pause while Mayberry sorted that one out. 'I don't *usually* drive.' He had begun to sweat.

'Do you ever hire a car?'

'I have.' Mayberry swallowed. 'Yes. I have hired cars.'

'Recently?'

'No.'

'Supposing I said that you hired a car in Slough two weekends ago, what would you say?'

'I'd say you were wrong,' said Mayberry sullenly.

'Yes, you might say that,' said Crammond. 'But would I be wrong, Mr Mayberry?'

Mayberry straightened his shoulders. 'Yes,' he said defiantly.

'Where were you that weekend?'

'Here – as usual. You can ask Mrs Jackson, my landlady.'

Crammond regarded him for a moment in silence. 'But Mrs Jackson was away that weekend, wasn't she? So you were here all weekend. In this room? Didn't you go out?'

'No.'

'Not at all? Not even to church as usual?'

Mayberry was beginning to curl up at the edges. 'I didn't feel well,' he muttered.

'When was the last time you missed church on Sunday, Mr Mayberry?'

'I don't remember.'

'Can you produce one person to testify to your presence here in this room on the whole of that Sunday?'

'How can I? I didn't go out.'

'Didn't you eat?'

'I didn't feel well, I tell you. I wasn't hungry.'

'What about the Saturday? Didn't you go out then?'

'No.'

'And you didn't eat on the Saturday, either?'

Mayberry shifted his feet nervously; the unending stream of questions was getting to him. 'I had some apples.'

'You had some apples,' said Crammond flatly. 'Where and when did you buy the apples?'

'On the Friday afternoon at a supermarket.'

Crammond let that go. He said, 'Mr Mayberry, I suggest that all you've told me is a pack of lies. I suggest that on the Saturday morning you went to Slough by train where you hired a Hillman Sceptre from Joliffe's garage. Mr Joliffe was very upset by the acid damage to the back seat of the car. Where did you buy the acid?'

'I bought no acid.'

'But you hired the car?'

'No.'

'Then how do you account for the fact that the name and address taken from a driving licence – this driving licence – ' Crammond picked it up and waved it under Mayberry's nose – 'is your name and address?'

'I can't account for it. I don't have to account for it. Perhaps someone impersonated me.'

'Why should anyone want to impersonate you, Mr Mayberry?'

'How would I know?'

'I don't think anyone would know,' observed Crammond. 'However, the matter can be settled very easily. We have the fingerprints from the car and they can be compared with yours quite easily. I'm sure you wouldn't mind coming to the station and giving us your prints, sir.'

It was the first I'd heard of fingerprints and I guessed Crammond was bluffing. Mayberry said, 'I'm . . . I'm not coming. Not to the police station.'

'I see,' said Crammond softly. 'Do you regard yourself as a public-spirited citizen?'

'As much as anybody.'

'But you object to coming to the police station.'

'I've had a hard day,' said Mayberry. 'I'm not feeling well. I was about to go to bed when you came in.'

'Oh,' said Crammond, as though illuminated with insight. 'Well, if that's your only objection I have a fingerprint kit in the car. We can settle the matter here and now.'

'You're not taking my fingerprints. I don't have to give them to you. And now I want you to leave.'

'Ah, so that's your true objection.'

'I want you to leave or I'll – ' Mayberry stopped short.

'Send for the police?' said Crammond ironically. 'When did you first meet Miss Ashton?'

'I've never met her,' said Mayberry quickly. Too quickly.

'But you know of her.'

Mayberry took a step backwards and banged into the table. The book fell to the floor. 'I know nobody of that name.'

'Not personally, perhaps – but you do know of her?'

I stopped to pick up the book. A thin pamphlet had fallen from the pages and I glanced at it before putting the book on the table. Mayberry repeated, 'I know nobody of that name.'

The pamphlet was a Parliamentary Report issued by the Stationery Office. Beneath the Royal coat-of-arms was the title: *Report of the Working Party on the Experimental Manipulation of the Genetic Composition of Micro-organisms*.

A whole lot of apparently unrelated facts suddenly slotted into place: Mayberry's fundamentalist religion, his environmental interests, and the work Penny Ashton was doing. I said, 'Mr Mayberry, what do you think of the state of modern biological science?'

Crammond, his mouth opened to ask another question, gaped at me in astonishment. Mayberry jerked his head around to look at me. 'Bad,' he said. 'Very bad.'

'In what way?'

'The biologists are breaking the laws of God,' he said. 'Defiling life itself.'

'In what way?'

'By mixing like with unlike – by creating monsters.' Mayberry's voice rose. '"And God said, 'Let the earth bring forth the living creature after his kind."' That's what He said – *after his kind*. "Cattle, and creeping thing, and beast of the earth after his kind." *After his kind!* That is on the very first page of the Holy Bible.'

Crammond glanced at me with a mystified expression, and then looked again at Mayberry. 'I'm not sure I know what you mean, sir.'

Mayberry was exalted. 'And God said unto Noah, "Of fowls after their kind" – *after their kind* – "and of cattle after their kind" – *after their kind* – "of every creeping thing of the earth after his kind" – *after his kind* – "two of every sort shall come unto thee, to keep them alive." She's godless; she would destroy God's own work as is set down in the Book.'

I doubted if Crammond knew what Mayberry was saying, but I did. I said, 'How?'

'She would break down the seed which God has made,

and mingle one kind with another kind, and so create monsters – chimaeras and abominations.'

I had difficulty in keeping my voice even. 'I take it by "she" you mean Dr Penelope Ashton?'

Crammond's head jerked. Mayberry, still caught up in religious fervour, said thoughtlessly, 'Among others.'

'Such as Professor Lumsden,' I suggested.

'Her master in devilry.'

'If you thought she was doing wrong why didn't you talk to her about it? Perhaps you could have led her to see her error.'

'I wouldn't foul my ears with her voice,' he said contemptuously.

I said, 'Doesn't it say in the Bible that God gave Adam dominion over the fish of the sea, the fowls of the air, and every beast or thing that creeps on the earth? Perhaps she's in the right.'

'The Devil can quote scripture,' said Mayberry, and turned away from me. I felt sick.

Crammond woke up to what was happening. 'Mr Mayberry, are you admitting to having thrown acid into the face of a woman called Ashton?'

Mayberry had a hunted look, conscious of having said too much. 'I haven't said that.'

'You've said enough.' Crammond turned to me. 'I think we have enough to take him.'

I nodded, then said to Mayberry, 'You're a religious man. You go to church every Sunday – twice, so I'm told. Do you think it was a Christian act to throw battery acid into the face of a young woman?'

'I am not responsible to you for my actions,' said Mayberry. 'I am responsible to God.'

Crammond nodded gravely. 'Nevertheless, I believe someone said, "Render unto Caesar the things that are Caesar's." I think you'll have to come along with me, Mr Mayberry.'

'And may God help you,' I said. 'Because you got the

wrong girl. You threw the acid in the face of Dr Ashton's sister who was coming back from church.'

Mayberry stared at me. As he had spoken of being responsible to God he had worn a lofty expression but now his face crumpled and horror crept into his eyes. He whispered, 'The wrong . . . wrong . . .' Suddenly he jerked convulsively and screamed at the top of his voice.

'Oh, Christ!' said Crammond as Shaw burst into the room.

Mayberry collapsed to the floor, babbling a string of obscenities in a low and monotonous voice. When Crammond turned to speak to me he was sweating. 'This one's not for the slammer. He'll go to Broadmoor for sure. Do you want any more out of him?'

'Not a thing,' I said. 'Not now.'

Crammond turned to Shaw. 'Phone for an ambulance. Tell them it's religious mania and they might need a restraining jacket.'

16

By the time we'd got Mayberry into an ambulance Ogilvie had left the office and gone home. I didn't bother ringing his home, but I did ring Penny because I thought she ought to know about Mayberry. Mary Cope answered again and said that Penny wasn't in, but this time I pushed it harder. She said Penny had gone to Oxford to attend a lecture and wouldn't be back until late. I rang off, satisfied I wasn't being given another brush-off.

Before seeing Ogilvie next morning I rang Crammond. 'What's new on Mayberry?'

'He's at King's College Hospital – under guard in a private ward.'

'Did he recover?'

'Not so you'd notice. It seems like a complete breakdown to me, but I'm no specialist.'

'A pity. I'll have to talk to him again, you know.'

'You'll have to get through a platoon of assorted doctors first,' warned Crammond. 'It seems he's suffering from everything from ingrowing toenails to psychoceramica.'

'What the hell's that?'

'It means he's a crack-pot,' said Crammond sourly. 'The head-shrinkers are keeping him isolated.'

I thanked him for his help and went to see Ogilvie. I told him about Mayberry and his face was a study in perplexity. 'Are you sure Mayberry isn't pulling a fast one?'

I shook my head. 'He's a nutter. But we've got him, and a psychiatrist will sort him out for us.'

'I'll buy that – for the moment.' Ogilvie shook his head. 'But I wouldn't call psychiatry an exact science. Have you noticed in court cases that for every psychiatrist called for the defence there's another called for the prosecution who'll give an opposing opinion? Still, supposing Mayberry is established as a religious maniac without doubt, there are a few questions which need asking.'

'I know. Why did he pick on Penny – or the girl he thought was Penny? Did he act of his own volition or was he pointed in the right direction and pushed? I'll see he gets filleted as soon as he can be talked to. But you're avoiding the big problem.'

Ogilvie grunted, and ticked points off on his fingers. 'Supposing Mayberry *is* crazy; and supposing he *wasn't* pushed – that he did it off his own bat, and that Penelope Ashton was a more or less random choice among the geneticists. That leaves us up a gum tree, doesn't it?'

'Yes.' I put the big question into words. 'In that case why did Ashton do a bunk?'

I was beginning to develop another headache.

I'd had second thoughts about ringing Penny; it wasn't the sort of thing to tell her on the telephone. But before going to University College I rang Honnister and told him the score. He took it rather badly. His voice rose. 'The wrong girl! The inefficient, crazy bastard picked the wrong girl!' He broke into a stream of profanity.

'I thought you ought to know. I'll keep you informed on future developments.'

I went to University College and was about to enquire at the reception desk when I saw Jack Brent standing at the end of a corridor. I went up to him. 'Any problems?'

'Nary a one.'

'Where's Penny Ashton?'

He jerked his thumb at a door. 'With her boss. That's Lumsden's office.'

I nodded and went in. Penny and Professor Lumsden looked very professional in white laboratory coats, like the chaps who sell toothpaste in TV ads. They were sitting at a desk, drinking coffee and examining papers which looked like computer print-outs. Lumsden was much younger than I expected, not as old as I was; pioneering on the frontiers of science is a young man's game.

Penny looked up. A look of astonishment chased across her face and then she became expressionless, but I noted the tightening of muscles at the angle of her jaw and the firmly compressed lips. I said, 'Good morning, Dr Ashton – Professor Lumsden. Could I have a word with you, Penny?'

'Well?' she said coolly.

I glanced at Lumsden. 'It's official, I'm afraid. In your office, perhaps?'

She said shortly, 'If it is official . . .' and regarded me distrustfully.

'It is,' I said, matching her curtness.

She made her excuses to Lumsden and we left his office. I said to Brent, 'Stick around,' then followed Penny who led me along another corridor and into her office. I looked around. 'Where's the microscope?'

Unsmilingly she said, 'We're working on things you can't see through microscopes. What do you want? Have you found Daddy?'

I shook my head. 'We've found the man who threw the acid.'

'Oh.' She sat on her desk. 'Who is he?'

'A man called Peter Mayberry. Ever heard of him?'

She thought for a moment. 'No, I can't say that I have. What is he?'

'A clerk in a City office – and a religious maniac.'

She frowned, then said questioningly, 'A religious maniac? But what would he have to do with Gillian? She's an Anglican – and you can't get more unmaniacal than that.'

I sat down. 'Brace yourself, Penny. The acid wasn't intended for Gillian. It was intended for you.'

'*For me!*' Her forehead creased and then she shook her

head as though she wasn't hearing aright. 'You did say . . . for me?'

'Yes. Are you sure you haven't heard of this man?'

She ignored my question. 'But why would a religious maniac . . . ?' She choked on the words. 'Why me?'

'He seemed to think you are tampering with the laws of God.'

'Oh.' Then: 'Seemed? He's dead?'

'No, but he's not doing much thinking right now. He's gone off into some kind of fugue.'

She shook her head. 'There have been objections to what we've been doing, but they've been scientific. Paul Berg, Brenner, Singer and a few others objected very strongly to . . .' Suddenly it hit her. 'Oh, my God!' she said. 'Poor Gillian!'

She sat rigidly for a moment, her hands clasped together tightly, and then she began to shake, the tremors sweeping across her body. She moaned – a sort of keening sound – and then fell forward across her desk, her head pillowed on her arms. Her shoulders shook convulsively and she sobbed stormily. I located a hand basin in the corner of the office and filled a glass with water and returned quickly to the desk, but there wasn't much I could do until the first shock had abated.

Her sobbing lessened in intensity and I put my arm around her. 'Steady on. Drink this.'

She raised her head, still sobbing, and showed a tear-stained face. 'Oh, Gillian! She'd be . . . all right . . . if I . . . if I hadn't . . .'

'Hush,' I said. 'And stop that. Drink this.'

She gulped down some water, then said, 'Oh, Malcolm; what am I to do?'

'Do? There's nothing to do. You just carry on as usual.'

'Oh, no. How can I do that?'

I said deliberately, 'You can't possibly blame yourself for what happened to Gillian. You'll tear yourself apart if you try. You can't hold yourself responsible for the act of an unbalanced man.'

'Oh, I wish it had been me,' she cried.

'No, you don't,' I said sharply. 'Don't ever say that again.'

'How can I tell her?'

'You don't tell her. Not until she's well – if then.' She began to cry again, and I said, 'Penny, pull yourself together – I need your help.'

'What can *I* do?'

'You can tidy yourself up,' I said. 'Then you can get Lumsden in here, because I want to ask you both some questions.'

She sniffled a bit, then said, 'What sort of questions?'

'You'll hear them when Lumsden comes in. I don't want to go through it all twice. We still don't know why your father went away, but it seemed to be triggered by that acid attack, so we want to find out as much about it as we can.'

She went to the hand basin and washed her face. When she was more presentable she rang Lumsden. I said, 'I'd rather you don't say anything about your father before Lumsden.' She said nothing to that, and sat at the desk.

When Lumsden came in he took one glance at Penny's reddened eyes and white face, then looked at me. 'What's happened here? And who are you?'

'I'm Malcolm Jaggard and I'm a sort of police officer, Professor.' To divert him from asking for my warrant card I added, 'I'm also Penny's fiancé.'

Penny made no objection to that flat statement, but Lumsden showed astonishment. 'Oh, I didn't know . . .'

'A recent development,' I said. 'You know, of course, of the acid attack on Penny's sister.'

'Yes, a most shocking thing.'

I told him about Mayberry and he became very grave. 'This is bad,' he said. 'I'm deeply sorry, Penny.' She nodded without saying anything.

'I want to know if you or anyone in your department has

been threatened – anonymous letters, telephone calls, or anything like that.'

He shrugged. 'There are always the cranks. We tend to ignore them.'

'Perhaps that's a mistake,' I said. 'I'd like some specifics. Do you keep any such letters? If so, I want them.'

'No,' he said regretfully. 'They are usually thrown away. You see . . . er . . . Inspector?'

'Mister.'

'Well, Mr Jaggard, most of the crank letters aren't threatening – they just tend to ramble, that's all.'

'About what?'

'About supposed offences against God. Lots of biblical quotations, usually from *Genesis*. Just what you might expect.'

I said to Penny, 'Have you had any of these letters?'

'A couple,' she said quietly. 'No threats. I threw them away.'

'Any telephone calls? Heavy breathers?'

'One about six months ago. He stopped after a month.'

'What did he say?'

'What Lummy has described. Just what you might expect.'

'Did you get the calls here or at home?'

'Here. The telephone at home is unlisted.'

I turned to Lumsden. 'You've both used the same phrase – "Just what you might expect". What might I expect, Professor Lumsden?'

'Well, in view of our work here . . .' He threw out his hands expressively.

We were still standing. I said, 'Sit down, Professor, and tell me of your work, or about as much as you can without breaking the Official Secrets Act.'

'Breaking the Official Secrets Act! There's no question of that – not here.'

'In that case, you won't object to telling me, will you?'

'I don't suppose so,' he said doubtfully, and sat down.

He was silent for a moment, marshalling his thoughts, and I knew what was happening. He was hunting for unaccustomed simple words to explain complex ideas to an unscientific clod. I said, 'I can understand words of three syllables – even four syllables if they're spoken slowly. Let me help you. The basis of inheritance is the chromosome; inside the chromosome is an acid called DNA. A thing called a gene is the ultimate factor and is very specific; there are distinct genes for producing the different chemicals needed by the organism. The genes can be thought of as being strung along a strand of DNA like beads on a spiral string. At least, that's how I visualize them. That's where I get lost so you'd better go on from there.'

Lumsden smiled. 'Not bad, Mr Jaggard; not bad at all.' He began to talk, at first hesitantly, and then more fluently. He ranged quite widely and sometimes I had to interrupt and bring him back on to the main track. At other times I had him explain what he meant in simpler terms. The basic concepts were rather simple but I gathered that execution in the laboratory was not as easy as all that.

What it boiled down to was this. A strand of DNA contains many thousands of genes, each gene doing its own particular job such as, for instance, controlling the production of cholinesterase, a chemical which mediates electrical action in the nervous system. There are thousands of chemicals like this and each has its own gene.

The molecular biologist had discovered certain enzymes which could cut up a strand of DNA into short lengths, and other enzymes which could weld the short lengths together again. They also found they could weld a short length of DNA on to a bacteriophage, which is a minute organism capable of penetrating the wall of a cell. Once inside, the genes would be uncoupled and incorporated into the DNA of the host cell.

Put like that it sounds rather simple but the implications are fantastic, and Lumsden was very emphatic about this. 'You see, the genes you incorporate into a cell need not come from the same kind of animal. In this laboratory we have bacterial cultures which contain genetic material from mice. Now a bacterium is a bacterium and a mouse is a mammal, but our little chaps are part bacterium and part mammal.'

'Breaking down the seed, mingling one kind with another, creating chimaeras,' I mused.

'I suppose you could put it that way,' said Lumsden.

'I didn't put it that way,' I said. 'Mayberry did.' At that stage I didn't get the point. 'But what's the use of this?'

Lumsden frowned as though I was being thick-witted, as I suppose I was. Penny spoke up. 'Lummy, what about *Rhizobium*?'

His brow cleared. 'Yes, that's a good example.'

He said that although plants need nitrogen for their growth they cannot take it from the air, even though air is 78 per cent nitrogen. They need it in the form of nitrates which, in man-planted cash crops, are usually spread as artificial fertilizer. However, there is a range of plants, notably the legumes – peas, beans and so on – which harbours in its roots the *Rhizobium* bacterium. This organism has the power of transforming atmospheric nitrogen into a form the plant can use.

'Now,' said Lumsden. 'All plants have bacteria in their roots and some are very specific. Supposing we take the *Rhizobium* bacterium, isolate the gene that controls this nitrogen-changing property, and transfer it into a bacterium that is specific to wheat. Then, if it bred true, we'd have self-fertilizing wheat. In these days of world food shortages that seems to me to be a good thing to have around.'

I thought so, too, but Penny said, 'It can be pretty dangerous. You have to be damned sure you've selected the right gene. Some of the *Rhizobium* genes are tumour-causing. If you get one of those you might find the world wheat crop dying of cancer.'

'Yes,' said Lumsden. 'We must be very sure before we let loose our laboratory-changed organisms. There was a hell of a row about that not long ago.' He stood up. 'Well, Mr Jaggard, have you got what you wanted?'

'I think so,' I said. 'But I don't know if it's going to do me a damned bit of good. Thanks for your time, Professor.'

He smiled. 'If you need more information I suggest you ask Penny.' He glanced at her. 'I suggest you take the day off, Penny. You've had a nasty shock – you don't look too well.'

She shivered. 'The thought that there are people in the world who'd want to do that to you is unnerving.'

'I'll take you home,' I said quietly. 'Jack Brent can follow in your car.' She made no objection, and I turned to Lumsden. 'I suggest that any crank letters – no matter how apparently innocuous – should be forwarded to the police. And telephone calls should be reported.'

'I agree,' he said. 'I'll see to it.'

So I took Penny home.

17

My relationship with Penny improved although neither of us referred to marriage. The shock of Mayberry's error had been shattering and I stuck around and helped her pick up the pieces; from then on propinquity did the rest. She was persuaded by Lumsden to stay with her work and her life took a triangular course – her home, her work, and whatever hospital Gillian happened to be in at the time.

Mayberry was thoroughly investigated by a band of psychiatrists and by Mansell, the department's best interrogator, a soft-spoken man who could charm the birds from the trees. They all came to the same conclusion: Mayberry was exactly what he appeared to be – a nut case. 'And a bit of a coward, too,' said Mansell. 'He was going for Lumsden at first, but thought a woman would be easier to handle.'

'Why did he pick on Lumsden's crowd?' I asked.

'A natural choice. Firstly, Lumsden is very well known – he's not as averse to talking to newspaper reporters as a lot of scientists are. He gets his name in the papers. Secondly, he hasn't been reticent about what he's been doing. If you wanted a handy geneticist Lumsden would be the first to spring to mind.'

Mayberry was the deadest of dead ends.

Which caused the problem Ogilvie and I had anticipated. If the acid attack had been fortuitous why should Ashton have bolted? It made no sense.

Once Mayberry had been shaken down the guards were taken from Penny and Gillian, and my legmen were put to other work. Ogilvie had little enough manpower to waste and the team investigating the Ashton case was cut down to one – me, and I wasted a lot of time investigating mistaken identities. Ashton's bolt-hole was well concealed.

And so the weeks – and then the months – went by. Gillian was in and out of hospital and finally was able to live at home, managing on a quarter of her normal eyesight. She and Penny were making plans to go to the United States where she would undergo plastic surgery to repair her ravaged face.

Once, when I persuaded Penny to dine with me, she asked, 'What did you find in that big vault of Daddy's?'

It was the first time she had shown any interest. 'Nothing.'

'You're lying.' There was an edge of anger.

'I've never lied to you, Penny,' I said soberly. 'Never once. My sins have been those of omission, not commission. I may have been guilty of *suppressio veri* but never *suggestio falsi*.'

'Your classical education is showing,' she said tartly, but she smiled as she said it, her anger appeased. 'Strange. Why should Daddy build such a thing and not use it? Perhaps he did and found it too much trouble.'

'As far as we can make out it was never used,' I said. 'All it contained was stale air and a little dust. My boss is baffled and boggled.'

'Oh, Malcolm, I wish I knew why he disappeared. It's been over three months now.'

I made the usual comforting sounds and diverted her attention. Presently she said. 'Do you remember when you told me of what you really do? You mentioned someone called Lord Cregar.'

'That's right.'

'He's been seeing Lumsden.'

That drew my interest. 'Has he? What about?'

She shook her head. 'Lummy didn't say.'

'Was it about Mayberry?'

'Oh, no. The first time he came was before you told us

about Mayberry.' She wrinkled her brow. 'It was two or three days after you opened the vault.'

'Not two or three weeks?'

'No – it was a matter of days. Who is Lord Cregar?'

'He's pretty high in government, I believe.' I could have told her that Cregar had smuggled her father out of Russia a quarter of a century earlier, but I didn't. If Ashton had wanted his daughters to know of his Russian past he would have told them, and it wasn't up to me to blow the gaff. Besides, I couldn't blab about anything listed under Code Black; it would be dangerous for me, for Ogilvie and, possibly, Penny herself. I wasn't supposed to know about that.

All the same it was curious that Cregar had been seeing Lumsden before we knew about Mayberry. Was there a connection between Ashton and Lumsden – apart from Penny – that we hadn't spotted?

I caught the eye of a passing waiter and asked for the bill. As I drained my coffee cup I said, 'It's probably not important. Let's go and keep Gillian company.'

Ogilvie sent for me next morning. He took an envelope, extracted a photograph, and tossed it across the desk. 'Who's that?'

He wore a heavy coat and a round fur hat, the type with flaps which can be tied down to cover the ears but which never are. Wherever he was it was snowing; there were white streaks in the picture which was obviously a time exposure.

I said, 'That's George Ashton.'

'No, he isn't,' said Ogilvie. 'His name is Fyodr Koslov, and he lives in Stockholm. He has a servant, an elderly bruiser called Howell Williams.' Another photograph skimmed across the desk.

I took one look at it, and said. 'That be damned for a tale. This is Benson. Where did you get these?'

'I want you to make quite sure,' said Ogilvie. He took a

sheaf of photographs and fanned them out. 'As you know, we had a couple of bad pictures of Ashton and none at all of Benson. You are the only person in the department who can identify them.'

Every one of the photographs showed either Ashton or Benson, and in two of them they were together. 'Positive identification,' I said flatly. 'Ashton and Benson.'

Ogilvie was pleased. 'Some of our associated departments are more co-operative than others,' he remarked. 'I had the pictures of Ashton circulated. These came back from a chap called Henty in Stockholm. He seems to be quite good with a camera.'

'He's very good.' The pictures were unposed – candid camera stuff – and very sharp. 'I hope he's been circumspect. We don't want them to bolt again.'

'You'll go to Stockholm and take up where Henty left off. He has instructions to co-operate.'

I looked out at the bleak London sky and shivered. I didn't fancy Stockholm at that time of year. 'Do I contact Ashton? Tell him about Mayberry and persuade him to come back?'

Ogilvie deliberated. 'No. He's too near Russia. It might startle him to know that British Intelligence is still taking an interest in him – startle him into doing something foolish. He had a low opinion of us thirty years ago which may not have improved. No, you just watch him and find out what the hell he's doing.'

I took the sheet of paper with Henty's address in Stockholm and his telephone number, then said, 'Can you think of any connection between Cregar and Professor Lumsden?' I told him Penny's story.

Ogilvie looked at the ceiling. 'I hear backstairs gossip from time to time. There could be a connection, but it's nothing to do with Ashton. It *can't* have anything to do with Ashton.'

'What is it?'

He abandoned his apparent fascination with the electric

fittings and looked at me. 'Malcolm, you're getting to know too damned much – more than is good for you. However, I'll humour you because, as I say, this is only servants' hall rumour. When this department was set up we took a sizeable chunk from Cregar which diminished his outfit considerably, so he began to empire-build in a different direction. The story is that he's heavily involved in CBW – that would explain any interest he has in Lumsden.'

By God it would! Chemical and bacteriological warfare and what Lumsden was doing fitted together like hand in glove. 'Is he still in security?'

'No, he's executive. He mediates between the Minister and the scientists. Of course, with his experience he also handles the security side.'

I could just imagine Cregar happily contemplating some previously inoffensive microbe now armed for death and destruction by genetic engineering. 'Is he in with the Porton Down crowd?'

'The Ministry of Defence is closing down Porton Down,' said Ogilvie. 'I don't know where Cregar does his juggling with life and death. Microbiology isn't like atomics; you don't need a particle accelerator costing a hundred million and a power plant capable of supplying energy for a fair-sized city. The physcal plant and investment are both relatively small, and Cregar may have a dozen laboratories scattered about for all I know. He doesn't talk about it – not to me.'

I contemplated this, trying to find a link with Ashton, and failed. There was only Penny, and I said so. Ogilvie asked, 'Has Cregar talked to her?'

'No.'

'I told you it can't have anything to do with Ashton,' he said. 'Off you go to Sweden.'

There was something else I wanted to bring up. 'I'd like to know more about Benson. He's probably filed away in Code Black.'

Ogilvie looked at me thoughtfully then, without speaking, got up and went into the room behind his desk. When he came back he was shaking his head. 'You must be mistaken. Benson isn't listed – not even under Code Green.'

'But I took him up as far as Code Purple,' I said. 'Someone is monkeying around with that bloody computer.'

Ogilvie's lips tightened. 'Unlikely,' he said shortly.

'How unlikely?'

'It's not easy to suborn a computer. It would need an expert.'

'Experts are ten a penny – and they can be bought.'

Ogilvie was palpably uneasy. He said slowly, 'We aren't the only department on line with this computer. I've been pressing for our own computer for several years but without success. Some other department . . .' He stopped and sat down.

'Who determines what material is added to the files – or removed?'

'There's an inter-departmental review committee which meets monthly. No one is authorized to add or subtract without its approval.'

'Someone has subtracted Benson,' I said. 'Or, more likely, he's been blocked off. I'll bet someone has added a tiny sub-program which would be difficult to find – if Benson is asked for say there's no one here of that name.'

'Well, it's for me to deal with,' said Ogilvie. 'There's a meeting of the review committee on Friday at which I'll raise a little bit of hell.' He stuck his finger out at me. 'But you know nothing about this. Now, go away. Go to Sweden.'

I got up to leave but paused at the door. 'I'll leave you with a thought. I got into the Ashton case by asking Nellie about Ashton. Two hours later I was on the carpet in your office with you and Cregar asking awkward questions. Did Cregar come to you with it?'

'Yes.'

'In two hours? How did he know who was asking questions about Ashton unless the computer tipped him off? I don't think you have far to look for the chap who is monkeying around with it.'

I left leaving Ogilvie distinctly worried.

18

It was dark and cold in Stockholm at that time of year. All the time I was in Sweden it didn't stop snowing; not heavily most of the time, but there was a continual fall of fine powder from leaden-grey clouds as though God up there was operating a giant flour sifter. I was booked into the Grand, which was warm enough, and after I had made my call to Henty I looked out over the frozen Strömmen to the Royal Palace. Edward VII didn't like Buckingham Palace, and called it 'that damned factory'. It's not on record if he said anything about the Palace in Stockholm, but that afternoon it looked like a dark satanic mill.

There were swans on the Strömmen, walking uneasily on the ice and cuddling in clusters as though to keep warm. One was on an ice floe and drifting towards Riddarfjärden; I watched until it went out of sight under the Ström bridge, then turned away feeling suddenly cold in spite of the central heating. Sweden in winter has that affect on me.

Henty arrived and we swapped credentials. 'We don't have much to do with your mob,' he commented as he handed back my card. He had a raw colonial accent.

'We don't move out of the UK much,' I said. 'Most of our work is counter-espionage. This one is a bit different. If you can take me to George Ashton I'll buy you a case of Foster's.'

Henty blinked. 'Good beer, that. How did you know I'm Australian? I've not been back for twenty years. Must have lost the accent by now.'

I grinned. 'Yes, you've learned to speak English very well. Where's Ashton?'

He went to the window and pointed at the Royal Palace. 'On the other side of that. In Gamla Stan.'

Gamla Stan – the Old Town. A warren of narrow streets threading between ancient buildings and the 'in' place to live in Stockholm. Cabinet ministers live there, and film directors – if they can afford it. The Royal Palace is No. 1, Gamla Stan. I said, 'How did you find him?'

'I got a couple of crummy pictures from London, and the day I got them I walked slam-bang into this character on the Vasabron.' Henty shrugged. 'So it's a coincidence.'

'By the laws of statistics we've got to get lucky some time,' I observed.

'He has a flat just off Västerlånggatan. He's passing himself off as a Russian called Fyodr Koslov – which is a mistake.'

'Why?'

Henty frowned. 'It's a tip-off – enough to make me take the pictures and send them back. There's something about the way he speaks Russian – doesn't sound natural.'

I thought about that. After thirty years of non-use Ashton's Russian would be rusty; it's been known for men to forget completely their native language. 'And Benson is with him in the flat?'

'Benson? Is that who he is? He calls himself Williams here. An older man; looks a bit of a thug. He's definitely British.'

'How can I get a look at them?'

Henty shrugged. 'Go to Gamla Stan and hang around outside the flat until they come out – or go in.'

I shook my head. 'Not good enough. They know me and I don't want to be seen. What's your status here?'

'Low man on the bloody totem,' said Hentry wryly. 'I'm junior partner in an import-export firm. I have a line into the Embassy, but that's for emergency use only. The diplomats here don't like boys like us, they reckon we cause trouble.'

'They could be right,' I said drily. 'Who do I see at the Embassy?'

'A Second Secretary called Cutler. A toffee-nosed bastard.' The iron seemed to have entered Henty's soul.

'What resources can you draw on apart from the Embassy?'

'Resources!' Henty grinned. 'You're looking at the resources – me. I just have a watching brief – we're not geared for action.'

'Then it will have to be the Embassy.'

He coughed, then said, 'Exactly who is Ashton?' I looked at him in silence until he said, 'If it's going to be like that . . .'

'It always is like that, isn't it?'

'I suppose so,' he said despondently. 'But I wish, just for once, that I knew why I'm doing what I'm doing.'

I looked at my watch. 'There's just time to see Cutler. In the meantime you pin down Ashton and Benson. Report to me here or at the Embassy. And there's one very important thing – don't scare them.'

'Okay – but I don't think you'll get very much change out of Cutler.'

I smiled. 'I wouldn't want either you or Cutler to bet on that one.'

The Embassy was on Skarpögatan, and Cutler turned out to be a tall, slim, fair-haired man of about my age, very English and Old School Tie. His mamnner was courteous but rather distant as though his mind was occupied by other, and more important, considerations which a non-diplomat could not possibly understand. This minor Metternich reminded me strongly of a shop assistant in one of the more snob London establishments.

When I gave him my card – the special one – his lips tightened and he said coolly, 'You seem to be off your beat, Mr Jaggard. What can we do for you?' He sounded as though he believed there was nothing he could possibly do for me. I said pleasantly, 'We've mislaid a bit of property and we'd like it back – with your help. But tact is the watchword.' I told him the bare and minimum facts about Ashton and Benson.

When I'd finished he was a shade bewildered. 'But I don't see how . . .' He stopped and began again. 'Look, Mr Jaggard, if this man decides to leave England with his man-servant to come to Sweden and live under an assumed name I don't see what we can do about it. I don't think it's a crime in Swedish law to live under another name; it certainly isn't in England. What exactly is it that you want?'

'A bit of manpower,' I said. 'I want Ashton watched. I want to know what he does and why he does it.'

'That's out of the question,' said Cutler. 'We can't spare men for police work of that nature. I really fail to see what your interest is in the man on the basis of what you've told me.'

'You're not entitled to know more,' I said bluntly. 'But take it from me – Ashton is a hot one.'

'I'm afraid I can't do that,' he said coldly. 'Do you really think we jump when any stranger walks in off the street with an improbable story like this?'

I pointed to my card which was still on the blotter in front of him. 'In spite of that?'

'In spite of that,' he said, but I think he really meant because of it. 'You people amaze me. You think you're James Bonds, the lot of you. Well, I don't think I'm living in the middle of a highly coloured film, even if you do.'

I wasn't going to argue with him. 'May I use your telephone?' He frowned, trying to think of a good reason for denial, so I added, 'I'll pay for the call.'

'That won't be necessary,' he said shortly, and pushed his telephone across the desk.

One of our boffins once asked me what was the biggest machine in the world. After several abortive answers I gave up, and he said. 'The international telephone system. There are 450 million telephones in the world, and 250 million of them are connected by direct dialling – untouched by hand in the exchanges.' We may grouse about the faults of local systems, but in under ninety seconds I was talking to Ogilvie.

I said, 'We have Ashton but there's a small problem. There's only one of Henty, and I can't push in too close myself.'

'Good. Get on to the Embassy for support. We want him watched. Don't approach him yourself.'

'I'm at the Embassy now. No support forthcoming.'

'What's the name of the obstruction?'

'Cutler – Second Secretary.'

'Wait a moment.' There was a clatter and I heard the rustle of papers in distant London. Presently Ogilvie said, 'This will take about half an hour. I'll dynamite the obstruction. For God's sake, don't lose Ashton now.'

'I won't,' I said, and hung up. I stood up and picked my card from Cutler's blotter. 'I'm at the Grand. You can get me there.'

'I can't think of any circumstances in which I should do so,' he said distantly.

I smiled. 'You will.' Suddenly I was tired of him. 'Unless you want to spend the next ten years counting paper clips in Samoa.'

Back at the hotel there was a curt note from Henty: 'Meet me at the Moderna Museet on Skeppsholmen.' I grabbed a taxi and was there in five minutes. Henty was standing outside the main entrance, his hands thrust deep into his pockets and the tip of his nose blue with cold. He jerked his head at the gallery. 'Your man is getting a bit of culture.'

This had to be handled carefully. I didn't want to bump into Ashton face to face. 'Benson there too?'

'Just Ashton.'

'Right. Nip in and locate him – then come back here.'

Henty went inside, no doubt glad to be in the warm. He

was back in five minutes. 'He's studying blue period Picassos.' He gave me a plan of the halls and marked the Picasso Gallery.

I went into the Museum, moving carefully. There were not many people in the halls on the cold winter's afternoon, which was a pity because there was no crowd to get lost in. On the other hand there were long unobstructed views. I took out my handkerchief, ready to muffle my face in case of emergency, turned a corner and saw Ashton in the distance. He was contemplating a canvas with interest and, as he turned to move on to the next one, I had a good sight of his face.

To my relief this *was* Ashton. There would have been a blazing row if I had goosed Cutler to no purpose.

19

Cutler jumped like a startled frog. An hour later, when I was unfreezing my bones in a hot bath and feeling sorry for Henty who was still tagging Ashton, the telephone rang to announce that he was waiting in the hotel foyer. 'Ask him to come up.' I dried myself quickly and put on a dressing-gown.

He brought two men whom he introduced as Askrigg and Debenham. He made no apologies for his previous attitude and neither of us referred to it. All the time I knew him he maintained his icily well-bred air of disapproval; that I could stand so long as he did what he was told and did it fast, and I had no complaints about that. The only trouble was that he and his people were lacking in professionalism.

We got down to business immediately. I outlined the problem, and Askrigg said, 'A full-time surveillance of two men is a six-man job.'

'At least,' I agreed. 'And that's excluding me and Henty. Ashton and Benson know me, so I'm out. As for Henty, he's done enough. He spotted Ashton for us and has been freezing his balls off ever since keeping an eye on him. I'm pulling him out for a rest and then he'll be in reserve.'

'Six men,' said Cutler doubtfully. 'Oh, well, I suppose we can find them. What are we looking for?'

'I want to know everything about them. Where they go, what they eat, who they see, do they have a routine, what happens when they break that routine, who they write to – you name it, I want to know.'

'It seems a lot of fuss over a relatively minor industrialist,' sniffed Cutler.

I grinned at him, and quoted, '"Yours not to reason why, Yours but to do or die." Which could happen because they're probably armed.'

That brought a moment of silence during which Cutler twitched a bit. In his book diplomacy and guns didn't go together. I said, 'Another thing: I want to have a look inside Ashton's apartment, but we'll check their routine first so we can pick the right moment.'

'Burglary!' said Cutler hollowly. 'The Embassy mustn't be involved in that.'

'It won't be,' I said shortly. 'Leave that to me. All right; let's get organized.'

And so Ashton and Benson were watched, every movement noted. It was both wearisome and frustrating as most operations of this nature are. The two men led an exemplary life. Ashton's was the life of a gentleman of leisure; he visited museums and art galleries, attended the theatre and cinemas, and spent a lot of time in bookshops where he spent heavily, purchasing fiction and non-fiction, the non-fiction being mostly biographies. The books were over a spread of languages, English, German and Russian predominating. And all the time he did not do a stroke of what could reasonably be called work. It was baffling.

Benson was the perfect manservant. He did the household shopping, attended to the laundry and dry-cleaning, and did a spot of cooking on those occasions when Ashton did not eat out. He had found himself a favourite drinking-hole which he attended three or four times a week, an *ölstuga* more intellectual than most because it had a chess circle. Benson would play a couple of games and leave relatively early.

Neither of them wrote or received any letters.

Neither appeared to have any associates other than the small-change encounters of everyday life.

Neither did a single damned thing out of the ordinary

with one large and overriding exception. Their very presence in Stockholm was out of the ordinary.

At the beginning of the third week, when their routine had been established, Henty and I cracked the apartment. Ashton had gone to the cinema and Benson was doing his Bobby Fischer bit over a half-litre of Carlsberg and we would have an hour or longer. We searched that flat from top to bottom and did not find much.

The main prize was Ashton's passport. It was of Israeli issue, three years old, and made out in the name of Fyodr Antonovitch Koslov who had been born in Odessa in 1914. I photographed every page, including the blank ones, and put it back where I found it. A secondary catch was the counterfoil stub of a cheque-book. I photographed that thoroughly, too. Ashton was spending money quite freely; his casual expenses were running to nearly £500 a week.

The telephone rang. Henty picked it up and said cautiously, '*Vilket nummer vill ni ha?*' There was a pause. 'Okay.' He put down the receiver. 'Benson's left the pub; he's on his way back.'

I looked around the room. 'Everything in order?'

'I reckon so.'

'Then let's go.' We left the building and sat in Henty's car until Benson arrived. We saw him safely inside, checked his escort, then went away.

Early next morning I gave Cutler the spools and film and requested negatives and two sets of prints. I got them within the hour and spent quite a time checking them before my prearranged telephone call from Ogilvie. It had to be prearranged because he had to have a scrambler compatible with that at the Embassy.

Briefly I summarized the position up to that point, then said, 'Any breakthrough will come by something unusual – an oddity – and there are not many of those. There's the Israeli passport – I'd like to know if that's kosher. I'll send you the photographs in the diplomatic bag.'

'Issued three years ago, you say.'

'That's right. That would be about the time a bank account was opened here in the name of Koslov. The apartment was rented a year later, also in the name of Koslov; it was sublet until four months ago when Ashton moved in. Our friend had everything prepared. I've gone through cheque stubs covering nearly two months. Ashton isn't stinting himself.'

'How is he behaving? Psychologically, I mean.'

'I've seen him only three times, and then at a distance.' I thought for a moment. 'My impression is that he's more relaxed than when I saw him last in England; under less of a strain.' There didn't seem much else to say. 'What do I do now?'

'Carry on,' said Ogilvie succinctly.

I sighed. 'This could go on for weeks – months. What if I tackled him myself? There's no need to blow my cover. I can get myself accredited to an international trade conference that's coming up next week.'

'Don't do that,' said Ogilvie. 'He's sharper than anyone realizes. Just keep watching; something will turn up.'

Yes, Mr Micawber, I thought, but didn't say it. What I said was, 'I'll put the negatives and prints into the diplomatic bag immediately.'

Two more weeks went by and nothing happened. Ashton went on his way serenely, doing nothing in particular. I had another, more extended, look at him and he seemed to be enjoying himself in a left-handed fashion. This was possibly the first holiday he'd ever had free from the cares of the business he had created. Benson pottered about in the shops and markets of Gamla Stan most mornings, doing his none-too-frugal shopping, and we began to build up quite a picture of the culinary tastes of the *ménage* Ashton. It didn't do us one damned bit of good.

Henty went about his own mysterious business into which I didn't enquire too closely. I do know that he was in some form of military intelligence because he left for a week and went north to Lapland where the Swedish Army was holding winter manoeuvres. When he came back I saw him briefly and he said he'd be busy writing a report.

Four days later he came to see me with disturbing information. 'Do you know there'a another crowd in on the act?'

I stared at him. 'What do you mean?'

'I've got a bump of curiosity,' he said. 'Last night, in my copious spare time, I checked to see whether Cutler's boys were up to snuff. Ashton is leading quite a train – our chap follows Ashton and someone else follows him.' I was about to speak but he held up his hand. 'So I checked on Benson and the same is happening there.'

'Cutler's said nothing about this.'

'How would he know?' said Henty scathingly. 'Or any of them. They're amateurs.'

I asked the crucial question. 'Who?'

Henty shrugged. 'My guess is Swedish Intelligence. Those boys are good. They'd be interested in anyone with a Russian name, and even more interested to find out he's under surveillance. They'll have made the connection with the British Embassy by now.'

'Damn!' I said, 'Better not let Cutler know or he'll have diplomatic kittens. I think this is where we join in.'

Next morning, when Ashton took his morning constitutional, we were on the job. Ashton appeared and collected the first segment of his tail who happened to be Askrigg. Henty nudged me and pointed out the stranger who fell in behind. 'That's our joker. I'll cross the road and follow him. You stay on this side and walk parallel, keeping an eye on both of us.'

By God, but Henty was good! I tried to watch both him and the man he was following but Henty was invisible half the time, even though I knew he was there. He bobbed back and forth, letting the distance lengthen and then closing up, disappearing into shop entrances and reappearing in unexpected places and, in general, doing his best not to be there at all. Two or three times he was even in front of the man he was shadowing.

It was one of Ashton's book mornings. He visited two bookshops and spent about three-quarters of an hour in each, then he retired with his plunder to a coffee-house and inspected his purchases over coffee and Danish pastries. It was pretty funny. The coffee-house was on the corner of a block. Askrigg waited outside while, kitty-corner across the street, his follower stamped his feet to keep warm while ostensibly looking into a shop window. The third corner held Henty, doing pretty much the same, while I occupied the fourth corner. My own wait was made risible by the nature of the shop in which I was taking an intent interest. Henty was outside a camera shop. Mine sold frilly lingerie of the type known pungently as passion fashion.

Out came Ashton and the train chugged off again, and he led us back to where we had started, but going home by the Vasabron just to make a variation. So far the whole was a bust, but better times were coming. Our man went into a tobacconist's shop and I followed. As I bought a packet of cigarettes I heard him speaking in low tones on the telephone. I couldn't hear what he said but the intonation was neither English nor Swedish.

He left the shop and walked up the street while I followed on the other side. A hundred yards up the street he crossed, so I did the same; then he reversed direction. He was doing what he hoped was an unobtrusive patrol outside Ashton's flat.

Fifteen minutes later the event we'd waited for – his relief arrived. The two men stood and talked for a few moments, their breath steaming and mingling in the cold air, then my man set off at a smart pace and I followed. He turned the corner which led around the back of the Royal Palace, and when I had him in sight he was dickering with a taxi-driver.

I was figuring out how to say, 'Follow that car!' in Swedish when Henty pulled up alongside in his car. I scrambled in, and Henty said in satisfaction, 'I thought he might do that. We've all had enough walking for the day.' I've said he was good.

So we followed the taxi through Stockholm, which was not particularly difficult, nor did he take us very far. The taxi pulled up outside a building and was paid off, and our man disappeared inside. Henty carried on without slackening speed. 'That does it!' he said expressively.

I twisted in my seat and looked back. 'Why? What is that place?'

'The bloody Russian Embassy.'

20

I expected my report on that to bring action but I didn't expect it to bring Ogilvie. I telephoned him at three in the afternoon and he was in my room just before midnight, and four other men from the department were scattered about the hotel. Ogilvie drained me dry, and I ended up by saying, 'Henty and I did the same this evening with the man following Benson. He went back to a flat on Upplandsgatan. On checking, he proved to be a commercial attaché at the Russian Embassy.'

Ogilvie was uncharacteristically nervous and indecisive. He paced the room as a tiger paces its cage, his hands clasped behind his back; then he sat in a chair with a thump. 'Damn it all to hell!' he said explosively. 'I'm in two minds about this.'

I waited, but Ogilvie did not enlarge on what was on either of his minds, so I said diffidently, 'What's the problem?'

'Look, Ashton hasn't given us what we expected when we sprung him from Russia. Oh, he's done a lot, but in a purely commercial way – not the advanced scientific thought we wanted. So why the hell should we care if he plays silly buggers in Stockholm and attracts the attention of the Russians?'

Looked at in a cold and calculating way that was a good question. Ogilvie said, 'I'd wash my hands of him – let the Russians take him – but for two things. The first is that I don't *know* why he ran, and the hell of it is that the answer might be quite unimportant. It's probably mere intellectual curiosity on my part, and the taxpayer shouldn't be expected to finance that. This operation is costing a packet.'

He stood up and began to pace again. 'The second thing is that I can't get that empty vault out of my mind. Why did he build it if he didn't intend to use it? Have you thought of that, Malcolm?'

'Yes, but I haven't got very far.'

Ogilvie sighed. 'Over the past months I've read and reread Ashton's file until I've become cross-eyed. I've been trying to get into the mind of the man. Did you know it was he who suggested taking over the persona of a dead English soldier?'

'No. I thought it was Cregar's idea.'

'It was Chelyuskin. As I read the file I began to see that he works by misdirection like a conjuror. Look at how he got out of Russia. I'm more and more convinced that the vault is another bit of misdirection.'

'An expensive bit,' I said.

'That wouldn't worry Ashton – he's rolling in money. If he's got something, he's got it somewhere else.'

I was exasperated. 'So why did he build the safe in the first place?'

'To tell whoever opened it that they'd reached the end of the line. That there are no secrets. As I say – misdirection.'

'It's all a bit fanciful,' I said. I was tired because it was late and I'd been working hard all day. Hammering the ice-slippery streets of Stockholm with my feet wasn't my idea of pleasure, and I was past the point of coping with Ogilvie's fantasies about Ashton. I tried to bring him to the point by saying, 'What do we do about Ashton now?' He was the boss and he had to make up his mind.

'How did the Russians get on to Ashton here?'

'How would I know?' I shrugged. 'My guess is that they got wind of a free-spending fellow-countryman unknown to Moscow, so they decided to take a closer look at him. To their surprise they found he's of great interest to British Intelligence. That would make them perk up immediately.'

'Or, being the suspicious lot they are, they may have been keeping tabs on the British Embassy as a matter of routine and been alerted by the unaccustomed activity of Cutler and his mob, who're not the brightest crowd of chaps.' Ogilvie shrugged. 'I don't suppose it matters how they found out; the fact is that they have. They're on to Koslov but have not, I think, made the transition to Ashton – and certainly not to Chelyuskin.'

'That's about it. They'll never get to Chelyuskin. Who'd think of going back thirty years?'

'Their files go back further, and they'll have Chelyuskin's fingerprints. If they ever do a comparison with Koslov's prints they'll know it wasn't Chelyuskin who died in that fire. They'd be interested in that.'

'But is it likely?'

'I don't know.' He scowled in my direction but I don't think he saw me; he was looking through me. 'That Israeli passport is quite genuine,' he said. 'But stolen three years ago. The real Koslov is a Professor of Languages at the University of Tel Aviv. He's there right now, deciphering some scrolls in Aramaic.'

'Do the Israelis know about Koslov? That might be tricky.'

'I shouldn't think so,' he said absently. Then he shook his head irritatedly. 'You don't think much of my theories about Ashton, do you?'

'Not much.'

The scowl deepened. 'Neither do I,' he admitted. 'It's just one big area of uncertainty. Right. We can do one of two things. We can pull out and leave Ashton to sink or swim on his own; or we can get him out ourselves.' Ogilvie looked at me expectantly.

I said, 'That's a policy decision I'm not equipped to make. But I do have a couple of comments. First, any interest the Russians have in Ashton has been exacerbated by ourselves, and I consider we have a responsibility towards him because of that. For the rest – what I've seen of Ashton I've liked and, God willing, I'm going to marry his daughter. I have a personal reason for wanting to get him out which has nothing to do with guessing what he's been doing with his peculiar mind.'

Ogilvie nodded soberly. 'Fair enough. That leaves it up to me. If he really has something and we leave him for the Russians then I'll have made a big mistake. If we bring him out, risking an international incident because of the methods we may have to use, and he has nothing, then I'll have made a big mistake. But the first mistake would be bigger than the second, so the answer is that we bring him out. The decision is made.'

21

Ogilvie had brought with him Brent, Gregory, Michaelis and, to my surprise, Larry Godwin, who looked very chipper because not only had he got away from his desk but he'd gone foreign. We had an early morning conference to discuss the nuts and bolts of the operation.

Earlier I had again tackled Ogilvie. 'Why don't I approach Ashton and tell him the Russians are on to him? That would move him.'

'In which direction?' asked Ogilvie. 'If he thought for one moment that British Intelligence was trying to manipulate him I wouldn't care to predict his actions. He might even think it better to go back to Russia. Homesickness is a Russian neurosis.'

'Even after thirty years?'

Ogilvie shrugged. 'The Russians are a strange people. And have you thought of his attitude to you? He'd immediately jump to wrong conclusions – I won't risk the explosion. No, it will have to be some other way.'

Ogilvie brought the meeting to order and outlined the problem, then looked about expectantly. There was a lengthy pause while everyone thought about it. Gregory said, 'We have to separate him from the Russians before we can do anything at all.'

'Are we to assume he might defect to Russia?' asked Brent.

'Not if we're careful,' said Ogilvie. 'But it's a possibility. My own view is that he might even be scared of the Russians if he knew they were watching him.'

Brent threw one in my direction. 'How good are the Russians here?'

'Not bad at all,' I said. ' A hell of a lot better than Cutler's crowd.'

'Then it's unlikely they'll make a mistake,' he said glumly. 'I thought if he knew the Russians were on to him he might cut and run. That would give us the opportunity for a spoiling action.'

Ogilvie said, 'Malcolm and I have discussed that and decided against it.'

'Wait a minute,' I said, and turned to Larry. 'How good is your conversational Russian?'

'Not bad,' he said modestly.

'It will have to be better than not bad,' I warned. 'You might have to fool a native Russian.' I didn't tell him Ashton *was* a Russian.

He grinned. 'Which regional accent do you want?'

Ogilvie caught on. 'I see,' he said thoughtfully. 'If the Russians don't make a mistake we make it for them. I'll buy that.'

We discussed it for a while, then Michaelis said, 'We'll need a back-up scheme. If we're going to take him out against his will we'll need transport, a safe house and possibly a doctor.'

That led to another long discussion in which plans were hammered out and roles allocated. Kidnapping a man can be complicated. 'What about Benson?' asked Gregory. 'Is he included in the deal?'

'I rather think so,' said Ogilvie. 'I'm becoming interested in Benson. But the primary target is Ashton. If it ever comes to a choice between taking Ashton or Benson, then drop Benson.' He turned to Michaelis. 'How long do you need?'

'If we use Plan Three we don't need a house, and the closed van I can hire inside an hour. But I'll have to go to Helsingborg or Malmo to arrange for the boat and that will take time. Say three days.'

'How long to cross the strait to Denmark?'

'Less than an hour; you can nearly spit across it. But

someone will have to organize a receiving committee in Denmark.'

'I'll do that.' Ogilvie stood up and said with finality, 'Three days, then; and we don't tell Cutler anything about it.'

Three days later the operation began as planned and started well. The situation in Gamla Stan was becoming positively ridiculous: two of Cutler's men were idling away their time in antique shops ready for the emergence of Ashton and Benson and unaware that they were being watched by a couple of Russians who, in their turn, were not aware of being under the surveillance of the department. It could have been a Peter Sellers comedy.

Each of our men was issued with a miniature walkie-talkie with strict instructions to stay off the air unless it was absolutely necessary to pass on the word. We didn't want to alert the Swedes that an undercover operation was under way; if they joined in there'd be so many secret agents in those narrow streets there'd be no room for tourists.

I sat in my car, strategically placed to cover the bridges leading from Gamla Stan to the central city area, and kept a listening watch. Ogilvie stayed in his room in the hotel next to the telephone.

At ten-thirty someone came on the air. 'Bluebird Two. Redbird walking north along Västerlånggatan.' Ashton was coming my way so I twisted in my seat to look for him. Presently he rounded the corner and walked up the road next to the Royal Palace. He passed within ten feet of me, striding out briskly. I watched him until he turned to go over Helgeandsholmen by way of Norrbro, then switched on the car engine. Ahead I saw Larry slide out of his parking place and roll along to turn on to Norrbro. His job was to get ahead of Ashton.

I followed behind, passing Ashton who was already carrying a tail like a comet, crossed Norrbro and did a couple of turns around Gustav Adolfs Torg, making sure that everything was in order. I saw Gregory leave his parking place to make room for Larry; it was important that Larry should be in the right place at the right time. Michaelis was reserving a place further west should Ashton have decided to go into town via the Vasabron. I switched on my transmitter and said to him, 'Bluebird Four to Bluebird Three; you may quit.'

At that point I quit myself because there was nothing left to do – everything now depended on Larry. I drove the short distance to the Grand Hotel, parked the car, and went to Ogilvie's room. He was nervous under his apparent placidity. After a few minutes' chat he said abruptly, 'Do you think Godwin is up to it? He's not very experienced.'

'And he never will be if he's not given the chance.' I smiled. 'He'll be all right. Any moment from now he'll be giving his celebrated imitation of an inexperienced KGB man. From that point of view his inexperience is an asset.'

Time wore on. At twelve-thirty Ogilvie had smörgåsbord sent up to the room. 'We might as well eat. If anything breaks you'll be eating on the run from now on.'

At five to one the telephone rang. Ogilvie handed me a pair of earphones before he picked up the receiver. It was Brent, who said, 'Redbird is lunching at the Opera – so am I and so is everyone else concerned. He's looking a bit jumpy.'

'How did Godwin handle first contact?'

'Redbrid went into that corner bookshop on the Nybroplan. Godwin was standing next to him when he barked his shin on a shelf; Larry swore a blue streak in Russian and Redbird jumped a foot. Then Larry faded out as planned.'

'And then?'

'Redbird wandered around for a bit and then came here. I saw him get settled, then signalled Larry to come in. He took a table right in front of Redbird who looked worried when he saw him. Larry has just had a hell of a row with a waiter in very bad, Russian-accented Swedish – all very noisy. Redbird is definitely becoming uncomfortable.'

'How are the others taking it?'

'The real Russians look bloody surprised. Cutler's chap . . . wait a minute.' After a pause Brent chuckled. 'Cutler's chap is heading for the telephones right now. I think he wants to report that the Russians have arrived. I think I'll let him have this telephone.'

'Stay with it,' said Ogilvie. 'Stick to Ashton.' He replaced the receiver and looked up. 'It's starting.'

'Everything is ready,' I said soothingly. I picked up the telephone and asked the hotel operator to transfer my calls to Ogilvie's room.

We had not long to wait. The telephone rang and I answered. Cutler said, 'Jaggard, there may be an important development.'

'Oh,' I said seriously. 'What's that?'

'My man with Ashton seems to think the Russians are interested.'

'In Ashton?'

'That's right.'

'Oh. That's bad! Where is Ashton now?'

'Lunching at the Opera. Shall I put someone on to the Russian? There may be time.'

Ogilvie had the earphone to his ear and shook his head violently. I grinned, and said, 'I think not. In fact I think you'd better pull out all your men as soon as you can get word to them. You don't want the Russians to know you're on to Ashton, do you?'

'My God, no!' said Cutler quickly. 'We can't have the Embassy involved. I'll do as you say at once.' He rang off, seemingly relieved.

Ogilvie grunted. 'The man's an idiot. He's well out of it.'

'It does clear the field,' I said, and put on my jacket. 'I'm going over to Gamla Stan for the beginning of the second act. If Larry does his stuff we should get a firm reaction from Ashton.' I paused. 'I don't like doing it this way, you know. I'd much prefer we talk to him.'

'I know,' said Ogilvie sombrely. 'But your preferences don't count. Get on with it, Malcolm.'

So I got on with it. I went to Gamla Stan and met Henty in a bar-restaurant in Västerlånggatan, joining him in a snack of herring and aquavit. He had been watching the flat, so I said, 'Where's Benson?'

'Safe at home. His Russian is still with him but Cutler's boy has vanished. Maybe Benson lost him.'

'No. Cutler is no longer with us.' I described what had happened.

Henty grinned. 'Something should break any moment then.' He finished his beer and stood up. 'I'd better get back.'

'I'll come with you.' As we left I said, 'You're our Swedish expert. Supposing Ashton makes a break – how can he do it?'

'By air from Bromma or Arlanda, depending on where he's going. He can also take a train. He doesn't have a car.'

'Not that we know of. He could also leave by sea.'

Henty shook his head. 'At this time of the year I doubt it. There's a lot of ice in the Baltic this year – the Saltsjön was frozen over this morning. It plays hell with their schedules. If I were Ashton I wouldn't risk it; he could get stuck on a ship which didn't move for hours.'

The bone conduction contraption behind my ear came to life. 'Bluebird Two. Redbird by Palace heading for Västerlånggatan and moving fast.' Bluebird Two was Brent.

I said to Henty, 'He's coming now. You go on ahead, spot him and tag that bloody Russian. I don't want Ashton to see me.'

He quickened his pace while I slowed down, strolling from one shop window to the next. Presently there came the news that Ashton was safely back home, and then

Henty came back with Larry Godwin. Both were grinning, and Henty remarked, 'Ashton's in a muck-sweat.'

I said to Larry, 'What happened?'

'I followed Ashton from the Opera – very obviously. He tried to shake me; in fact, he did shake me twice, but Brent was able to steer me back on course.'

Henty chuckled. 'Ashton came along Västerlånggatan doing heel-and-toe as though he was in a walking race, with Godwin trying hard for second place. He went through his doorway like a rabbit going down a hole.'

'Did you speak to him, Larry?'

'Well, towards the end I called out, '*Grazhdaninu* Ashton – *ostanovites!*' as though I wanted him to stop. It just made him go faster.'

I smiled slightly. I doubt if Ashton relished being called 'citizen' in Russian, especially when coupled with his English name. 'The ball is now in Ashton's court, but I doubt he'll move before nightfall. Larry, go and do an ostentatious patrol before Ashton's flat. Be a bit haphazard – reappear at irregular intervals.'

I had a last word with Henty, and then did the rounds, checking that every man was in his place and the Russians were covered. After that I reported by telephone to Ogilvie.

Larry caught up with me in about an hour. 'One of those bloody Russians tackled me,' he said. 'He asked me what the hell I thought I was doing.'

'In Russian?'

'Yes. I asked him for his authority and he referred me to a Comrade Latiev in the Russian Embassy. So I got a bit shirty and told him that Latiev's authority had been superseded, and if Latiev didn't know that himself he was even more stupid than Moscow thought. Then I said I didn't have time to waste and did a quick disappearing act.'

'Not bad,' I said. 'It ought to hold Comrade Latiev for a while. Any reaction from the flat?'

'A curtain did twitch a bit.'

'Okay. Now, if Ashton makes his break I don't want him

to see you – we don't want to panic him more than necessary. Take over Gregory's car, ask him what the score is, and send him to me.'

It was a long wait and a cold wait. The snow came down steadily and, as darkness fell, a raw mist swept over Gamla Stan from the Riddarfjärden, haloing the street lights and cutting down visibility. I spent the time running over and over in my mind the avenues of escape open to Ashton and wondering if my contingency planning was good enough. With Henty there were six of us, surely enough to take out the two Russians and still keep up with Ashton wherever he went. As the mist thickened I thought of the possibility of taking Ashton there and then, but thought better of it. A quiet kidnapping in a major city is hard enough at the best of times and certainly not the subject for improvisation. Better to follow the plan and isolate Ashton.

It happened at ten to nine. Gregory reported Ashton and Benson on Lilla Nygatan moving south, and both had bags. Michaelis chipped in and said that both Russians were also on the move. I summoned up my mental map of Gamla Stan and concluded that our targets were heading for the taxi rank on the Centralbron, so I ordered the cars south ready to follow. More interestingly, on the other side of the Centralbron, in the main city, was Stockholm's Central Railway Station.

Then I ordered Michaelis and Henty, our best strong-arm men, to take the Russians out of the game. They reported that, because of the mist, it was easy and that two Russians would have sore heads the following morning.

After that things became a bit confused. When Ashton and Benson reached the taxi rank they took separate cabs, Benson going over the Centralbron towards the railway station, and Ashton going in the dead opposite direction towards Södermalm. Larry followed Benson, and Brent went after Ashton. I got busy and ordered the rest of the team to assemble at the railway station which seemed the best bet under the circumstances.

At the station I stayed in the car and sent in Henty to find out if Larry was around. He came back with Larry who got into the car, and said, 'Benson bought two tickets for Göteborg.'

They were heading west. From my point of view that was a relief; better west than east. I said, 'When does the train leave?'

Larry checked his watch. 'In a little over half an hour. I bought us four tickets – and I got a timetable.'

I studied the timetable and thought out loud. 'First stop – Södertälje; next stop – Eskilstuna. Right.' I gave a ticket each to Gregory and Henty. 'You two get on that train; spot Ashton and Benson and report back by radio. Then stick with them.'

They went into the station, and Larry said, 'What do we do?'

'You and I lie as low as Br'er Rabbit.' I turned to Michaelis. 'Scout around in the station and see if you can spot Ashton. Make sure he's on that train when it leaves, then come back here.'

He went away and I wondered how Brent was getting on. Presently Gregory radioed in. 'We're on the train – spotted Redbird Two – but no Redbird One.'

We'd lost Ashton. 'Stay with it.'

The time ticked by. At five minutes to train-time I became uneasy, wondering what had happened to Ashton. At two minutes to train-time Brent pitched up. 'I lost him,' he said hollowly.

'Where did he go?'

'He went bloody island-hopping – Södermalm – Långholmen – Kungsholmen; that's where I lost him. He seemed to be heading in this general direction at the time so I took a chance and came here.'

'We haven't seen him and he's not on the train so far. Benson is, though; with two tickets to Göteborg.'

'When does it leave?'

I looked over his shoulder and saw Michaelis coming towards the car. He was shaking his head. I said, 'It's just left – and Ashton wasn't on it.'

'Oh, Christ! What do we do now?'

'The only thing we can do – stick with Benson and pray. And this is how we do it. Get yourself a timetable like this one, and check the stops of that train. You and Michaelis take the first stop – that's Södertälje, you check with Gregory and Henty on the train and you team up if Benson gets off. You also report to Ogilvie. In the meantime Larry and I will be heading for the next stop at Eskilstuna – same procedure. And we leapfrog up the line until the train arrives at Göteborg or anything else happens. Got that?'

'Okay.'

'Reporting to Ogilvie is very important because he can keep us all tied in. I'm going to ring him now.'

Ogilvie wasn't at all pleased but he didn't say much – not then. I told him how I was handling it and he just grunted. 'Carry on – and keep me posted.'

I went back to the car, slumped into the passenger's seat, and said to Larry, 'Drive to Eskilstuna – and beat that train.'

22

From Stockholm to Eskilstuna is about 100 kilometres. The firt 40 kilometres are of motorway standard and we were able to make good time, but after that it became more of an ordinary road with opposing traffic and our average speed dropped. It was very dark – a moonless night – but even if there had been a moon it wouldn't have helped because there was a thick layer of cloud from which descended a heavy and continuous fall of snow.

Like all modern Swedish cars ours was well equipped for this kind of weather. The tyres had tungsten-steel studs for traction and the headlights had wipers to clear the encrusting snow, but that didn't mean fast driving and I suppose we didn't average more than 70 KPH and that was a shade fast for the conditions. Neither Larry nor I could be classed as rally drivers, and I was very much afraid the train would be faster. Fortunately, I saw by the map that it had further to go, the track sweeping round in a loop. Also it would stop at Södertälje.

After an hour I told Larry to pull into a filling station where he refuelled while I phoned Ogilvie. When I got back to the car I was smiling, and Larry said, 'Good news?'

'The best. I'll drive.' As we pulled away I said, 'Ashton tried to pull a fast one. When Brent lost him he wasn't on his way to the railway station in Stockholm; he took a taxi ride to the Södertälje station and got on the train there. We've got them both now.'

Thus it was that I was quite happy when we pulled up outside the railway station at Eskilstuna to find the train standing on the platform. I switched on my transmitter, and said, 'Any Bluebirds there? Come in, Bluebirds.'

A voice in my ear. 'Redbird and friend jumped train.'

'What the hell?'

Henty said, 'What do you want me to do?'

'Get off that bloody train and come here. We're parked outside the station.' Even as I spoke the train clanked and began to move slowly. I was beginning to wonder if Henty had made it when I saw him running towards the car. I wound down the side window. 'Get in and tell me what, for Christ's sake, happened.'

Henty got into the back seat. 'The train pulled up at some bloody whistle-stop called Akers-styckebruk, and don't ask me why. Nothing happened until it began to move out, then Ashton and Benson jumped for it. Gregory went after them but it was too late for me – and the way he went he was like to break a leg.'

I got out the road map and studied it. 'Akers-styckebruk! The place isn't even on the map. Have you reported to Ogilvie?'

'No. I was just going to when you called me.'

'Then I suppose I have to.'

I went into the station and rang Stockholm, and Ogilvie said testily, 'What the devil's going on? I've just had a call from Gregory in some God-forsaken place. He's either broken or sprained his ankle and he's lost Ashton. He thinks they've gone to somewhere called Strängnäs.'

Strängnäs was back along the road; we'd skirted around the edges. I said, 'We'll be there in an hour.'

'An hour may be too late,' he snapped. 'But get on with it.'

I ran back to the car. 'Get weaving, Larry – back where we came from.' He moved over into the driving seat and I hadn't closed the door before he took off. I twisted around and said to Henty, 'What can you tell me about Strängnäs? Anything there we ought to know about?'

He snapped his fingers. 'Of course! There's a spur-line going into Strängnäs from Akers-styckebruk – no passenger trains, just the occasional *räslbuss*.'

'What's that?'

'A single coach on the railway – diesel driven.'

'You say it's a spur-line. You mean the rail stops at Strängnäs?'

'It has to, or it would run into Lake Mälaren.'

I contemplated that. 'So it's a dead end.'

'For the railway, but not for cars. There's a road which goes by way of the islands to the north shore of Mälaren. But it's late. I wouldn't bet they'll be able to hire a car at this time of night.'

'True,' I said. 'But step on it, Larry.' I watched the road unwinding out of the darkness against the hypnotic beat of the wipers as they cleared snow from the windscreen. The headlights brightened as Larry operated the light wipers. 'Anything else about Strängnäs?'

'It's not much of a place,' said Henry. 'Population about twelve thousand; a bit of light industry – pharmaceuticals, penicillin, X-ray film – stuff like that. It's also a garrison town for a training regiment, and it's HQ, East Military Command.' His interest sharpened. 'Is Ashton connected with the soldier boys?'

'No,' I said.

Henty persisted. 'You'd tell me if he is? That's my line of country, and I've helped you enough.'

'Definitely not,' I said. 'His interestes aren't military, and neither are mine. We're not poaching on your patch.'

'Just as long as I know.' He seemed satisfied.

We didn't bother going back all the way to Akersstyckebruk; finding Ashton was more important than finding the state of Gregory's ankle. We came to the outskirts of Strängnäs and coasted gently through the snow-covered streets towards the lake edge and the centre of town. A few turns around the town centre proved one thing – there was only one hotel – so we pulled up on the other side of the street from the Hotel Rogge and I sent Henty in to find out the form.

He was away about five minutes and when he came back

he said, 'They're both there – booked under the names of Ashton and Williams.'

'So he's reverted,' I said. 'Using his own passport. Koslov has suddenly become too hot.'

'I booked in for the three of us.'

'No; you stay, but Larry and I are going to find Gregory. I'll ring Ogilvie now and ask him to retrieve Brent and Michaelis from wherever the hell they are now – they can have the other two beds here. We'll be back at six tomorrow morning and I want a concentration inside and outside the hotel. Where are Ashton and Benson now?'

'Not in any of the public rooms,' said Henty. 'I'd say they're in bed.'

'Yes, they're getting pretty old for this sort of thing,' I said pensively. 'Come to think of it, so am I.'

23

Gregory had sensibly waited at the railway station at Akersstyckebruk for someone to pick him up. He said he was stiff, cold, tired, and that his ankle hurt like hell, so we all booked into a hotel. At five the next morning Larry and I were on our way back to Strängnäs, but Gregory was able to sleep in because I decided to send him back to Stockholm. He'd be no good to us because his ankle really was bad, but he had the satisfaction of knowing that, because of him, we'd pinned down Ashton and Benson.

Just before six I parked the car around the corner from the Hotel Rogge, and at six on the button I went on the air. 'Hello,' I said brightly. 'Any Bluebirds awake?'

Henty said disgruntedly into my ear, 'Don't be so bloody cheerful.'

'Did the other two arrive?'

'Yes, at two this morning. They're still asleep.'

'And Redbird and his friend?'

'They're definitely here – I made sure of that – they're asleep, too.' He paused. 'And I wish to Christ I was.'

'Come out here. We're just around the corner on – ' I craned my neck to find a street sign – 'on Källgatan.'

He said nothing but the transmission hum stopped so I switched off. He did not appear for a quarter of an hour so Larry and I made small talk. There was nothing much to say because we'd talked the subject to death already. When Henty did arrive he was newly shaven and looked in reasonably good shape even though his manner was still a little shaggy. 'Morning,' he said shortly, as he got into the car.

I passed a vacuum flask over my shoulder. 'Be gruntled.'

He unscrewed the top and sniffed appreciatively. 'Ah, scotch coffee!' He poured a cupful and was silent for a moment before he said, 'That's better. What's the drill?'

'What time is breakfast?'

'I don't know. Say, from seven o'clock – maybe seven-thirty. These country hotels all differ.'

'I want the three of you in the breakfast room as soon as it opens; you at one table, Michaelis and Brent at another. They are to talk to each other and one of them has to give a running commentary over the air about Ashton and Benson as soon as they come in to beakfast. I want to know exactly how Ashton is acting – and reacting.'

'We can do that,' said Henty. 'But I don't get the reason.'

I said, 'Half way through breakfast I'm going to send Larry in to do a replay of his Russian act.'

'Jesus! You'll give Ashton a heart attack.'

'We've got to keep the pressure on,' I said. 'I don't want to give them time to hire a car, and I want to herd them out of the town pretty early. Where's the closed van Michaelis has been driving?'

Henty pointed across the darkened street. 'In the hotel car park.'

'Good enough. I want him inside it and ready to go as soon as Ashton moves. I want this whole bloody thing cleaned up before eight o'clock if possible. Now you can go in and wake the sleeping beauties.'

When Henty had gone Larry regarded me curiously. 'I know you've been keeping out of sight,' he said. 'But if what you're doing ever comes out you're not going to be popular with the Ashton family.'

'I know,' I said shortly. 'But this is the way Ogilvie wants it done. And I'm making bloody sure I do stay out of sight, not for Ogilvie's reasons but my own.' Christ! I thought. If Penny ever got to know about this she'd never forgive me in a thousand years.

The time passed and we shared the flask of scotch coffee between us. Strängnäs began to wake up and there was movement in the streets, and we occasioned a couple of curious glances from passers-by. I suppose it was strange for a couple of men to be sitting in a parked car so early in the morning so I told Larry to drive into the hotel car park which was more secluded.

The hotel breakfast started at seven-thirty. I knew that because Jack Brent came on the air with a description of the breakfast he was eating. He described the herring and the boiled eggs and the cheese and the coffee and all the trimmings until I began to salivate. He was doing it deliberately, the bastard.

Because I made no response he tired of the game and switched off, but at seven-fifty he said, 'They're here now – Ashton and Benson. Just sitting down – two tables away. Benson looks sour but Ashton seems cheerful enough.'

No one would know Brent was broadcasting; apparently he would be chatting animatedly to Michaelis, but every word was picked up by the throat microphone concealed beneath the knot of his tie. The throat microphone gave a peculiarly dead quality to the broadcast; there was no background noise – no clatter of cutlery or coffee cups to be heard – just Brent's voice and the rasp of his breathing greatly magnified. Even if he spoke in a whisper every word would come across clearly.

I listened to his description and felt increasingly uneasy. Not about Ashton who, according to Brent, seemed fairly relaxed; I was uneasy about myself and my role in this charade. I would have given a lot to be able to walk into the Hotel Rogge, sit down at Ashton's table, and have a down-to-earth chat with him. I was convinced I could get him back to England just by talking to him, but Ogilvie wouldn't have that. He didn't want our cover blown.

I was depressed when I turned to Larry, and said quietly, 'All right. Go in and have your breakfast.' He got out of the car and walked into the hotel.

Brent said, 'Ashton's just poured himself another cup of

coffee. He hasn't lost his appetite, that's for certain. Ho ho! Larry Godwin has just walked in. Ashton hasn't seen him yet, nor has Benson. Larry's talking to the waitress by the door. God, how he's mangling his Swedish – can hear him from here. So can Ashton. He's turned and he's looking at Larry. I can't see his face. He's turned back again and now he's nudging Benson. He's as white as a sheet. The waitress is coming forward with Larry now – showing him to a table. Larry is passing Ashton's table – he turns and speaks to him. Ashton has knocked over his coffee cup. Benson is looking bloody grim; if ever I saw a man capable of murder it's Benson right now. He's no oil painting at the best of times but you should see him now. Ashton wants to get up and leave, but Benson is holding him back.'

I switched channels on my transmitter and Brent's voice abruptly stopped. I said, 'Henty, finish your breakfast and leave. Cover the front of the hotel. Michaelis, same for you, but get in your van and cover the back.'

I reversed out of the hotel car park and drove a little way up Källgatan and parked where I could see the front entrance of the hotel. When I switched back to Brent he was saying '. . . looks pretty shattered and Benson is talking to him urgently. I think he's having a hard job keeping control. You'd think it would be the other way round because Benson is only Ashton's servant. Anyway, that's what it looks like from here – Ashton wants to make a break and Benson is stopping him. Larry isn't doing much – just eating his breakfast – but every now and then he looks across at Ashton and smiles. I don't think Ashton can take much more of it. I'll have to stop now because Michaelis is leaving and I'll look bloody funny talking to myself.'

He stopped speaking and the transmission hum ceased. I keyed my transmitter. 'Larry, when Ashton and Benson leave follow them from behind with Brent.' I saw Henty come out of the hotel and walk across the street. Michaelis came next and walked around to the car park where he disappeared from sight.

Ten minutes later Ashton and Benson appeared, each carrying a bag. They stepped out on to the pavement and Ashton looked up and down the street uncertainly. He said something to Benson who shook his head, and it looked as though there was a difference of opinion. Behind them Larry appeared in the hotel entrance.

I said, 'Larry, go and talk to Ashton. Ask him to follow you. If he agrees, take him to the van and put him in the back.'

'And Benson?'

'Him too – if possible.'

Ashton became aware that Larry was watching him and pulled at Benson's arm. Benson nodded and they began to walk away but stopped at Larry's call. Larry hurried over to them and began talking and, as he did so, Brent came out and stood close to them.

I heard the one-way conversation. Larry talked fast in Russian and twice Ashton nodded, but Benson made interjections, each time accompanied by a headshake, and tried to get Ashton away. At last he succeeded and the pair of them walked off, leaving Larry flat. They were coming straight towards me so I ducked out of sight.

While I was down on the car floor I spoke to Larry. 'What happened?'

'Ashton nearly came, but Benson wouldn't have it. He spoiled it.'

'Did Benson speak Russian?'

'No, English; but he understood my Russian well enough.'

'Where are they now?'

'Going up the street – about thirty yards past your car.'

I emerged from hiding and looked in the mirror. Ashton and Benson were walking away quickly in the direction of the railway station.

After that it all became a little sick because we literally herded them out of town. They found the railway station blocked by Brent, and when they tried to duck back to the town centre they were confronted by Larry and Henty. They soon became aware that they had a quartet of opponents and, twist and turn as they might, they found themselves being driven to the edge of town. And all the time I orchestrated the bizarre dance, manipulating them like puppets. I didn't like myself at all.

At last we got to the main Stockholm-Eskilstuna road and they plunged across, Benson nearly being hit by a speeding car which went by with a wailing blast of horn. There were no more streets or houses on the other side – just an infinity of pine trees. I had Michaelis go back and pick up the van, and sent the other three into the forest while I parked my car before following. It seemed as though the chase was nearly over – you can't be more private than in a Swedish forest.

They made better time over rough country than I would have expected of two elderly men. Ashton had already proved his fitness to me, but I hadn't expected Benson to have the stamina because he was a few years older than Ashton. Once in the trees you couldn't see far and they kept foxing us by changing direction. Twice we lost them; the first time we picked them up by sheer luck, and the second time by finding their abandoned bags. And all the time I was leading from the rear, directing the operation by radio.

We had gone perhaps three kilometres into the forest and the going was becoming rougher. Where the ground was not slippery with snow and ice it was even more slippery with pine needles. The ground rose and fell, not much but enough to take your breath away on the uphill slopes. I paused at the top of one such slope just as Brent said in my ear, 'What the hell was that?'

'What?'

'Listen!'

I listened, trying to control my heavy breathing, and heard a rattle of shots in the distance. They seemed to come from somewhere ahead, deeper in the forest.

'Someone hunting,' said Larry.

Brent said incredulously, 'With a machine-gun!'

'Quiet!' I said. 'Is Ashton spotted?'

'I'm standing looking into a little valley,' said Henty. 'Very few trees. I can see both Ashton and Benson – they're about four hundred yards away.'

'That's all very well, but where the hell are you?'

'Just keep coming ahead,' said Henty. 'It's a long valley – you can't miss it.'

'Everybody move,' I said. Again came the sound of firing, this time a sporadic rattling of badly-spaced single shots. Certainly not a machine-gun as Brent had suggested. It could have been the shoot-out at the OK Corral, and I wondered what was happening. Hunters certainly didn't pop off like that.

I pressed on and presently came to a crest where I looked down into the valley. Henty was right; it was relatively treeless and the snow was thicker. In the distance I saw Ashton and Benson moving very slowly; perhaps they were hampered by the snow, but I thought the chase was telling on them. Henty was at the valley bottom below me, and Brent and Larry were together, bounding down the hill-side, closing in on our quarry from an angle.

Again came firing and, by God, this time it was machine-gun fire, and from more than one machine-gun. Then there came some deeper coughs, followed by thumping explosions. In the distance, not too far ahead, I saw a haze of smoke drifting above the trees on the far side of the valley.

Henty had stopped. He looked back at me and waved, and said over the radio, 'I know what it is. This is an army exercise area. They're having war games.'

'Live ammunition?'

'Sounds like it. Those were mortars.'

I began to run, bouncing and slithering down the slope. When I got to the bottom I saw that Brent and Larry were within fifty yards of Ashton and gaining on him fast.

Ashton switched direction, and I yelled, 'Brent – Larry – fall back!'

They hesitated momentarily but then went on, caught in the lust of the chase. I shouted again. 'Fall back! Don't drive him into the guns.'

They checked, but I ran on. I was going to speak to Ashton myself, regardless of what Ogilvie had said. This was a sick game which had to be stopped before somebody was killed. Ashton was climbing the other side of the valley, heading towards the trees on the crest, but going very slowly. Benson was nowhere to be seen. I ran until I thought my chest would burst, and gained on Ashton.

At last I was close enough, and I shouted, 'Ashton – George Ashton – stop!'

He turned his head and looked back at me as a further burst of firing came, and more explosions of mortar bombs. I took off the fur hat I was wearing and threw it away so that he could get a good look at me. His eyes widened in surprise and he hesitated in his upward climb, then stopped and turned around. Brent and Larry were coming in on my left and Henty on the right.

I was about to call out to him again when there was another single shot, this time from quite close, and Ashton tumbled forward as though he had tripped. I was within ten yards of him and heard him gasp. Then there was another shot and he whirled around and fell and came rolling down the slope towards me to stop at my feet.

I was aware that Henty had passed me and momentarily saw a gun in his fist, then I bent over Ashton. He coughed once and blood trickled from the corner of his mouth. His eyes still held surprise at the sight of me, and he said, 'Mal . . . colm . . . what . . .'

I said, 'Take it easy, George,' and put my hand inside his coat. I felt a warm wetness.

He scrabbled in his pocket for something, and said, 'The . . . the . . .' His hand came up before my face with the fist clenched. 'The . . . the . . .' Then he fell back, his eyes still open and looking at the sky with deeper surprise. A snowflake fell and settled on his left eyeball, but he didn't blink.

In the distance mortars thumped and machine-guns rattled, and there were more single shots, again from quite close. I looked down at Ashton and cursed quietly. Brent crunched over the snow. 'Dead?'

I withdrew my hand and looked at the blood. Before wiping it clean on the snow I said, 'You try his pulse.'

I stood up as Brent knelt and thought of the unholy mess we – *I* – had made of the operation. The snow around Ashton's body was changing colour from white to red. Brent looked up at me. 'Yes, he's dead. From the amount of blood here the aorta must have been cut. That's why he went so fast.'

I had never felt so bad in all my life. We had driven Ashton towards the guns as beaters drive an animal. It was so stupid a thing to do. I didn't feel very human at that moment.

Henty came crunching down the slope, carrying a pistol negligently in his right hand. 'I got him,' he said matter-of-factly.

I could smell the faint reek of cordite as he came closer. 'Got who, for Christ's sake?'

'Benson.'

I stared at him. '*You shot Benson!*'

He looked at me in surprise. 'Well, he shot Ashton, didn't he?'

I was stupefied. 'Did he?'

'Of course he did. I saw him do it.' Henty turned and looked up the slope. 'Maybe you couldn't see him from this angle – but I did.'

I was unable to take it in. '*Benson* shot Ashton!'

'He bloody nearly shot me,' said Henty. 'He took a crack at me as soon as I showed myself up there. And if anyone shoots at me I shoot back.'

It had never occurred to me to ask Henty if he was

armed. Nobody else was on Ogilvie's instructions, but Henty was from another department. I was still gaping at him when there was a grinding rattle from above and a tank pointed its nose over the crest and began to come down into the valley. Its nose was a 105 mm high-velocity tank gun which looked like a 16-incher as the turret swivelled to cover our small group. They wouldn't have bothered to use that, though; the machine-gun in the turret of that Centurion was capable of taking care of us much more economically.

As the tank stopped I dropped to my knees next to Ashton's body. The turret opened and a head popped out, followed by a torso. The officer raised his anti-flash goggles and surveyed us with slightly popping eyes. Henty moved, and the officer barked, '*Stopp!*' With a sigh Henty tossed his pistol aside in the snow.

I opened Ashton's clenched fist to look at what he had taken from his pocket. It was a crumpled railway timetable of the route from Stockholm to Göteborg.

24

I don't know what sort of heat was generated at a higher level but the Swedes never treated me with anything less than politeness – icy politeness. If I had thought about it at all that cold correctitude would have been more frightening than anything else, but I wasn't thinking during that period – I was dead inside and my brains were frozen solid.

The Swedes had found two dead men and four live on army territory. One of the dead men had two passports, one stolen and the other genuine; the other had three passports, all false. The passports of the four live men were all genuine. It was claimed that one of the dead men had shot the other and, in turn, was shot and killed by one of the live men, an Australian living and working in Sweden. He had no permit for a gun.

It was all very messy.

Ogilvie was out of it, of course, and so were Michaelis and Gregory. Michaelis had waited with the van at the road, but when a squad of infantry in full battle order debouched from the forest and systematically began to take my car to pieces he had tactfully departed. He drove back into Strängnäs and rang Ogilvie who pulled him back to Stockholm. And what Ogilvie heard from the Embassy made him decide that the climate of London was more favourable than the chilliness of Stockholm. The three of them were back in London that night and Cutler was saying, 'I told you so.'

The four of us were taken to the army barracks in Strängnäs, HQ the Royal Södermanland Regiment and HQ East Military Command. Here we were searched and eyebrows were lifted at the sight of our communication equipment. No doubt conclusions were duly drawn. We weren't treated badly; they fed us, and if what we ate was representative of army rations then the Swedish Army does a damned sight better than the British Army. But we were not allowed to talk; a stricture reinforced by two hefty Swedes armed with sub-machine guns.

After that I was led into an empty room and, just as I thought the interrogation was about to begin, a civilian arrived and began being nasty to the military. At least, that's the impression I had judging by the rumble of voices from the office next door. Then an army colonel and a civilian came in to see me and, having seen me, went away without saying a word, and I was transferred into a cell in which I spent the next three weeks apart from an hour's exercise each day. During that time I didn't see the others at all, and the Swedes wouldn't give me the time of day, so I ought to have been pretty lonely, but I wasn't. I wasn't anything at all.

I was awakened one morning at three a.m., taken into an ablutions block and told to take a shower. When I came out I found my own clothes – the army fatigues I had been wearing had disappeared. I dressed, checked my wallet and found everything there, and put on my watch. The only things missing were my passport and the radio.

I was marched smartly across the dark and snow-covered parade ground and shown into an office where a man dressed in civilian clothes awaited me. He wasn't a civilian, though, because he said, 'I am Captain Morelius.' He had watchful grey eyes and a gun in a holster under his jacket. 'You will come with me.'

We went outside again to a chauffeur-driven Volvo, and Captain Morelius didn't say another word until we were standing on the apron of Arlanda Airport over three hours later. Then he pointed to a British Airways Trident, and said, 'There is your aircraft, Mr Jaggard. You realize you are no longer welcome in Sweden.' And that is all he said.

We walked to the gangway and he handed a ticket to a

steward who took me inside and installed me in a first-class seat. Then they let on the common herd and twenty minutes later we were in the air. I had good service from that steward who must have thought I was a VIP, and I appreciated the first drink I had had for nearly a month.

When we landed at Heathrow I wondered how I was going to get by without a passport; I certainly didn't feel like going into tedious explanations. But Ogilvie was waiting for me and we walked around Passport Control and Customs. Once in his car he asked, 'Are you all right, Malcolm?'

'Yes.' I paused. 'I'm sorry.'

'Not to worry,' he said. 'We'll leave the explanations for later.'

Going into town he talked about everything except what had happened in Sweden. He brought me up-to-date on the news, talked about a new show that had opened, and generally indulged in light chit-chat. When he pulled up outside my flat he said, 'Get some sleep. I'll see you in my office tomorrow.'

I got out of the car. 'Wait! How's Penny?'

'Quite well, I believe. She's in Scotland.'

'Does she know?'

He nodded, took out his wallet, and extracted a newspaper cutting. 'You can keep that,' he said, and put the car into gear and drove away.

I went up to the flat and its very familiarity seemed strange. I stood looking around and then realized I was holding the newspaper cutting. It was from *The Times*, and read:

KILLED IN SWEDEN

Two Englishmen, George Ashton (56) and Howard Greatorex Benson (64) were killed near Strängnäs, Sweden, yesterday when they wandered on to a firing range used by the Swedish army. Both men died instantaneously when they were caught in a shell explosion.

A Swedish army spokesman said that the area was adequately cordoned and that all roads leading into it were signposted. Announcements of the proposed firing of live ammunition were routinely made in the local newspapers and on the radio.

The dateline of the story was five days after Ashton and Benson died.

25

When I walked into my office Larry Godwin was sitting at his desk reading *Pravda* and looking as though he had never left it. He looked up, 'Hello, Malcolm.' He didn't smile and neither did I. We both knew there was nothing to smile about.

'When did you get back?'

'Three days ago – the day after Jack Brent.'

'Henty?'

He shook his head. 'Haven't seen him.'

'How did they treat you?'

'Not bad. I felt a bit isolated, though.'

'Has Ogilvie debriefed you?'

Larry grimaced. 'He emptied me as you'd empty a bottle of beer. I still feel gutted. It'll be your turn now.'

I nodded, picked up the telephone, and told Ogilvie's secretary I was available. Then I sat down to contemplate my future and couldn't see a damned thing in the fog. Larry said, 'Someone knew the right strings to pull. I tell you, I wasn't looking forward to a stretch in a Swedish jail. They'd have put us in their version of Siberia – up in the frozen north.'

'Yes,' I said abstractedly. I wondered what *quid pro quo* the Swedes had claimed for our release and their silence.

Ogilvie called me in twenty minutes later. 'Sit down, Malcolm.' He bent to his intercom. 'No more calls for the rest of the morning, please,' he said ominously, then looked at me. 'I think we have a lot to talk about. How are you feeling?'

I felt he really wanted to know, so I said, 'A bit drained.'

'The Swedes treat you all right?'

'No complaints.'

'Right. Let's get to the crux. Who killed Ashton?'

'Of my own knowledge I don't know. At the time I thought he'd caught a couple from the Swedes – there was a lot of shooting going on. Then Henty told me Benson had shot him.'

'But you didn't see Benson shoot him.'

'That's correct.'

Ogilvie nodded. 'That fits with what Godwin and Brent told me. Now, who killed Benson?'

'Henty said he did it. He said he saw Benson shooting at Ashton so he drew his own gun and went after him. Apparently Benson was at the top of the slope in the trees. He said that Benson shot at him, too, so he shot back and killed him. I didn't even know Henty was armed.'

'Have you thought why Benson should have killed Ashton? It's not the normal thing for an old family retainer to do to his master.'

A humourless thought crossed my mind: in the less inventive early British detective stories it was always the butler who committed the murder. I said, 'I can think of a reason but it doesn't depend on Benson's status as a servant.'

'Well?'

'Henty was coming up on my right, and Brent and Godwin angling in from the left. Ashton was just above, but there was a big boulder screening me from the top of the slope. I didn't see Benson and I don't think he saw me. But he did see Larry, and Larry was a Russian, remember. When Ashton stopped and turned, and showed signs of coming down, then Benson shot him.'

'To prevent him falling into the hands of the Russians. I see.'

I said, 'And that makes him something more than a family servant.

'Possibly,' said Ogilvie. 'But I've been going into the history of Howard Greatorex Benson and the man is as pure as the driven snow. Born in Exeter in 1912, son of a solicitor; normal schooling but flunked university entrance to his father's disappointment. Did clerical work for a firm in Plymouth and rose to be the boss of a rather small department. Joined the army in 1940 – rose to be a sergeant in the RASC – he was an ideal quarter-master type. Demobilized in 1946, he went to work for Ashton, running the firm's office. There he ran into the Peter Principle; he was all right as long as the firm remained small but, with expansion, it became too much for him. Remember he never rose to be more than a sergeant – he was a small-scale man. So Ashton converted him into a general factotum which would seem to be ideal for Benson. There'd be nothing too big for him to handle, and he was glad to be of service. Ashton probably got his money's worth out of him. He never married. What do you think of all that?'

'Did you get that from the computer?'

'No. The brains are still baffled. They're telling me now Benson can't be in the data bank.'

'They're wrong,' I said flatly. 'He popped up when I asked Nellie.'

Ogilvie looked at me doubtfully, then said, 'But what do you think of his history as I've related it?'

'There's nothing there to say why he should kill Ashton. There's nothing there to say why he should be carrying a gun in the first place. Did he have a pistol permit?'

'No.'

'Have you traced the gun?'

Ogilvie shrugged. 'How can we? The Swedes have it.' He pondered for a moment, then opened a quarto-sized, hard-backed notebook and took the cap off his pen. 'I wanted to go for the main point first, but now you'll tell me, in detail, everything that happened right from the time Ashton and Benson left their flat in Stockholm.'

That took the rest of the morning. At quarter to one Ogilvie recapped his pen. 'That's it, then. Now you can go home.'

'Am I suspended from duty?'

He looked at me from lowered eyebrows. 'There are a few people around who would like to see you fired. Others favour a transfer to the Outer Hebrides so you can counter industrial espionage into the production of Harris Tweed; they're talking about a twenty-year tour of duty. Have you any idea of the trouble this enterprise of ours has caused?'

'I have a good imagination.'

He snorted. 'Have you? Well, imagine how the Swedes felt about it, and imagine their reaction when we began to put on the pressure at a high level. It got up to the Cabinet, you know, and the Ministers aren't at all happy. They're talking about bungling amateurs.'

I opened my mouth to speak, but he held up his hand. 'No, you're not suspended from duty. What you did was under my instruction, and I can't see that you could have done differently given the circumstances. Neither of us expected Benson to kill Ashton, so if anyone carries the can it's me, as head of the department. But this department is now under extreme pressure. There's an inter-departmental meeting tomorrow morning at eleven at which the screws will begin to turn. You will be required to attend. So you will go away now and come back here at ten-fifteen tomorrow, rested and refreshed, and prepared to have a hard time. Do you understand?'

'Yes.'

'And I would be obliged if you do not disclose to the committee that you are aware of the Ashton file in Code Black. We're in enough trouble already.'

I stood up. 'All right, but I'd like to know one thing – what happened to the bodies?'

'Ashton and Benson? They were brought back to England two weeks ago. There was a funeral service in Marlow and they are buried in adjoining graves in the cemetery.'

'How did Penny take it?'

'As you might expect. Both the daughters were hit rather badly. I wasn't there myself, of course, but I was informed of the circumstances. I managed to have word passed to Miss Ashton that you were in America but were expected back in the near future. I thought that advisable.'

Advisable and tactful. 'Thanks,' I said.

'Now go away and prepare your thoughts for tomorrow.' I walked towards the door, and he added, 'And Malcolm: regardless of how the meeting goes, I want you to know there is much still to be explained about the Ashton case – and it will be explained. I am becoming very angry about this.'

As I left I thought that Ogilvie angry might be formidable indeed.

I was left to my own thoughts for a long time while the committee meeting was in progress; it was twelve-fifteen before an usher entered the ante-room and said, 'Will you come this way, Mr Jaggard.' I followed him and was shown into a large, airy room overlooking an inner courtyard somewhere in Westminster.

There was a long, walnut table around which sat a group of men, all well-dressed and well-fed, and all in late middle-age. It could have been the annual meeting of the directors of a City bank but for the fact that one of them wore the uniform of a Commander of the Metropolitgan Police and another was a red-tabbed colonel from the General Staff. Ogilvie twisted in his chair as I entered and indicated I should take the empty seat next to him.

Chairing the meeting was a Cabinet Minister whose politics I didn't agree with and whose personality I had always thought of as vacillating in the extreme. He showed no trace of vacillation that morning, and ran the meeting like a company sergeant-major. He said, 'Mr Jaggard, we have been discussing the recent Swedish operation in which you were involved, and in view of certain differences of opinion Mr Ogilvie has suggested that you appear to answer our questions yourself.'

I nodded, but the colonel snorted. 'Differences of opinion is putting it mildly.'

'That has nothing to do with Mr Jaggard, Colonel Morton,' said the Minister.

'Hasn't it?' Morton addressed me directly. 'Are you aware, young man, that you've lost me my best man in Scandinavia? His cover is blown completely.'

I concluded that Morton was Henty's boss.

The Minister tapped the table with his pen and Morton subsided. 'The questions we shall ask are very simple and we expect clear-cut, unequivocal answers. Is that understood?'

'Yes.'

'Very well. Who killed Ashton?'

'I didn't see who shot him. Henty told me it was Benson.'

There was a stir from lower down the table. 'But you don't know that he did, other than you have been told so.'

I turned and looked at Lord Cregar. 'That is correct. But I have, and still have, no reason to disbelieve Henty. He told me immediately after the event.'

'After he had killed Benson?'

'That's right.'

Cregar regarded me and smiled thinly. 'Now, from what you know of Benson, and I'm assuming you had the man investigated, can you give me one reason why Benson should kill the man he had so faithfully served for thirty years?'

'I can think of no sound reason,' I said.

His lip curled a little contemptuously. 'Can you think of any unsound reasons?'

Ogilvie said tartly, 'Mr Jaggard is not here to answer stupid questions.'

The Minister said sharply, 'We shall do better if the questions are kept simple, as I suggested.'

'Very well,' said Cregar. 'Here is a simple question. Why did you order Henty to kill Benson?'

'I didn't,' I said. 'I didn't even know he was armed. The

rest of us weren't; those were Mr Ogilvie's instructions. Henty was in a different department.'

Colonel Morton said, 'You mean Henty acted on his own initiative?'

'I do. It all happened within a matter of, say, twenty seconds. At the time Benson was killed I was trying to help Ashton.'

Morton leaned forward. 'Now, think carefully, Mr Jaggard. My men are not in the habit of leaving bodies carelessly strewn about the landscape. What reason did Henty give for shooting Benson?'

'Self-defence. He said Benson was shooting at him, so he shot back.'

Colonel Morton leaned back and appeared satisfied, but Cregar said to the company at large, 'This man, Benson, seems to be acting more and more out of character. Here we have an old age pensioner behaving like Billy the Kid. I find it unbelievable.'

Ogilvie dipped his fingers into a waistcoat pocket and put something on the table with a click. 'This is a round of 9 mm parabellum found in Benson's room in Marlow. It would fit the pistol found with Benson's body. And we know that the bullet recovered from Ashton's body came from that pistol. We got that from the Swedes.'

'Precisely,' said Cregar. 'All you know is what the Swedes told you. How much is that really worth?'

'Are you suggesting that Benson did not kill Ashton?' asked Morton. There was a note of sourness in his voice.

'I consider it highly unlikely,' said Cregar.

'I don't employ men who are stupid enough to lie to me,' said Morton, in a voice that could cut diamonds. 'Henty said he saw Benson kill Ashton, and I believe him. All the evidence we have heard so far does not contradict that.'

Ogilvie said, 'Unless Lord Cregar is suggesting that my department, Colonel Moreton's department and Swedish Army Intelligence are in a conspiracy to put the blame for

Ashton's death on Benson and so shield the killer.' His voice was filled with incredulity.

The uniformed commander guffawed and Cregar flushed. 'No,' he snapped. 'I'm just trying to get to the bottom of something damned mysterious. Why, for instance, *should* Benson shoot Ashton?'

'He is not here to be asked,' said the Minister coolly. 'I suggest we stop this chasing of hares and address ourselves to Mr Jaggard.'

The Commander leaned forward and talked to me around Ogilvie. 'I'm Pearson – Special Branch. This Swedish operation isn't my bailiwick but I'm interested for professional reasons. As I take it, Mr Ogilvie did not want Ashton to become aware that British Intelligence was taking note of him. Do you know why?'

That was a tricky one because I wasn't supposed to know who Ashton really was. I said, 'I suggest you refer that question to Mr Ogilvie.'

'Quite so,' said the Minister. 'It involves information to which Mr Jaggard is not privy.'

'Very well,' said Pearson. 'At the same time he wanted Ashton out of Sweden because the Russians had become attracted, so he put pressure on Ashton by having a man pretend to be Russian and thus "explode Ashton out of Sweden", as he has put it. What I don't understand is why this kidnapping attempt in Strängnäs was necessary. Why did you try it?'

I said, 'They took tickets from Stockholm to Göteborg. That was all right with me. I intended to shepherd them along and, if they took ship from Göteborg to find out where they were going. The important thing was to get them out from under the Russians in Sweden. But when they gave us the slip and went to Strängnäs it became something more complex than a discreet escort operation. Stronger measures were necessary as sanctioned by Mr Ogilvie.'

'I see,' said Pearson. 'That was the point I misunderstood.'

'I misunderstood something, too,' said Cregar. 'Are we to assume that your instructions precluded the disclosure of yourself to Ashton?'

'Yes.'

'Yet according to what I've been told you did so. We have been informed by Mr Ogilvie this morning that you showed yourself to him. Deliberately. It was only when he saw you that he turned back. Is that not so?'

'That's correct.'

'So you disobeyed orders.'

I said nothing because he hadn't asked a question, and he barked, 'Well, didn't you?'

'Yes.'

'I see. You admit it. Now, with all respect to Colonel Morton's trust in the truthfulness of his staff, I'm not satisfied by the somewhat misty evidence presented here that Benson shot Ashton; but the fact remains that Ashton was shot by someone, and it is highly likely that he was shot *because* he turned back. In other words, he died because you disobeyed an order not to disclose yourself.' His voice was scathing. 'Why did you disobey the order?'

I was seething with rage but managed to keep my voice even. 'The idea was not to kill Ashton but to bring him out alive. At that time he was going into grave danger. There was heavy fire in that part of the forest where he was heading – machine-guns and mortars, together with rifle fire. Just what was going on I didn't know. It seemed imperative to stop him and he did stop and started to come back. That he was shot by Benson came as a complete shock.'

'But *you* don't know he was shot by Benson,' objected Cregar.

The Minister tapped with his pen. 'We have already been over that ground, Lord Cregar.'

'Very well.' Cregar regarded me and said silkily,

'Wouldn't you say that your conduct of this whole operation, right from the beginning, has been characterized by, shall we say, a lack of expertise?'

Ogilvie bristled. 'What Mr Jaggard has done has been on my direct instruction. You have no right or authority to criticize my staff like this. Address your criticisms to me, sir.'

'Very well, I will,' said Cregard. 'Right at the beginning I objected to your putting Jaggard on this case, and all the . . .'

'That's not my recollection,' snapped Ogilvie.

Cregar overrode him '. . . all the events since have proved my point. He let Ashton slip from under his nose at a time when he had free access to Ashton's home. That necessitated the Swedish operation which he has also botched, and botched for good, if I may say so, because Ashton is now dead. As for claiming that all he did was on your direct instructions, you have just heard him admit to disobeying your orders.'

'He used his initiative at a critical time.'

'And with what result? The death of Ashton,' said Cregar devastatingly. 'You have expounded before on the initiative of this man. I wasn't impressed then, and I'm still less impressed now.'

'That will be enough,' said the Minister chillily. 'We will have no more of this. Are there any more questions for Mr Jaggard? Questions that are both simple and relevant, please.' No one spoke, so he said, 'Very well, Mr Jaggard. That will be all.'

Ogilvie said in an undertone, 'Wait for me outside.'

As I walked to the door Cregar was saying, 'Well, that's the end of the Ashton case – after thirty long years. He was a failure, of course; never did come up to expectations. I suggest we drop it and get onto something more productive. I think . . .'

What Cregar thought was cut off by the door closing behind me.

* * *

They came out of committee twenty minutes later. Ogilvie stuck his head into the ante-room. 'Let's have lunch,' he proposed. He didn't seem too depressed at what had happened, but he never did show much emotion.

As we were walking along Whitehall he said, 'What do you think?'

I summoned a hard-fought-for smile. 'I think Cregar doesn't like me.'

'Did you hear what he said as you were leaving?'

'Something about the Ashton case being over, wasn't it?'

'Yes. Ashton is buried and that buries the Ashton case. He's wrong, you know.'

'Why?'

'Because from now on until everything is accounted for and wrapped up you are going to work full time on the Ashton case.' He paused, then said meditatively, 'I wonder what we'll find.'

26

In view of what had been said at the meeting Ogilvie's decision came as a profound surprise. The worst possibility that had come to mind was that I would be fired; drummed out of the department after my special card had been put through the office shredding machine. The best that occurred to me was a downgrading or a sideways promotion. I had the idea that Ogilvie had not been entirely joking when he had spoken of the Hebrides. That he was carrying on with the Ashton case, and putting me in charge, gave me a jolt. I wondered how he was going to make it stick with the Minister.

He told me. 'The Minister won't know a damned thing about it.' He gave me a wintry smile. 'The advantage of organizations like ours is that we really are equipped to work in secret.'

This conversation took place in the privacy of his office. He had refused to speak of the case at all after dropping his bombshell and the luncheon conversation had been innocuous. Back at the office he plunged into the heart of it.

'What I am about to do is unethical and possibly mutinous,' he said. 'But, in this case, I think I'm justified.'

'Why?' I asked directly. If I was going to be involved I wanted to know the true issues.

'Because someone has done a conjuring trick. This department has been deceived and swindled. Who organized the deception is for you to find out – it may have been Ashton himself, for all we know. But I want to know who organized it, and why.'

'Why pick me? As Cregar made plain, I've not done too well up to now.'

Ogilvie raised his eyebrows. 'You think not? You've satisfied me, and I'm the only man who matters. There are several reasons why I've picked you. First, you're the totally unexpected choice. Secondly, you are still the inside man in the Ashton family. Thirdly, I have complete confidence in you.'

I stood up and went to the window. A couple of pigeons were engaged in amorous play on the window ledge but flew away as I approached. I turned and said, 'I'm grateful for your thirdly, but not too happy about your secondly. As you know, I dropped into the middle of the Ashton case sheerly by chance and ever since then my private life has been intolerably disturbed. I have just harried a man to his death and you expect me to be *persona grata* with his daughters?'

'Penelope Ashton doesn't know of your involvement. I made sure of that.'

'That's not the point, and you know it,' I said sharply. 'You're too intelligent a man not to know what I mean. You're asking me to live a lie with the woman I want to marry – if she still wants to marry me, that is.'

'I appreciate the difficulty,' said Ogilvie quietly. 'You mustn't think I don't. But . . .'

'And don't ask me to do it for the good of the department,' I said. 'I hope I have higher loyalties than that.'

Ogilvie quirked his eyebrows. 'Your country, perhaps?'

'Even than that.'

'So you believe with E. M. Forster that if you had to choose between betraying your country and betraying your friend you would hope to have the guts to betray your country. Is that it?'

'I'm not aware that betraying my country comes into this,' I said stiffly.

'Oh, I don't know,' said Ogilvie musingly. 'Betrayal takes many forms. Inaction can be as much betrayal as action, especially for a man who has chosen your work of his own will. If you see a man walking on a bridge which you know to be unsafe, and you do not warn him so that he falls to his death, you are guilty in law of culpable homicide. So with betrayal.'

'Those are mere words,' I said coolly. 'You talk about betrayal of the country when all I see is an interdepartmental squabble in which your *amour propre* has been dented. You loathe Cregar as much as he loathes you.'

Ogilvie looked up. 'How does Cregar come into this? Do you know something definite?'

'He's been trying to poke his nose in, hasn't he? Right from the beginning.'

'Oh, is that all,' said Ogilvie tiredly. 'It's just the nature of the beast. He's a natural scorer of points; it feeds his enormous ego. I wouldn't jump to conclusions about Cregar.' He stood up and faced me. 'But I really am sorry about your opinion of me. I thought I deserved better than that.'

'Oh, Christ!' I said. 'I'm sorry; I didn't really mean that. It's just that this thing with Penny has me all mixed up. The thought of talking to her – lying to her – makes me cringe inside.'

'Unfortunately it goes with the job. We're liars by profession, you and I. We say to the world we work for McCulloch and Ross, economic and industrial consultants, and that's a lie. Do you think my wife and daughters really know what I do? I lie to them every minute of every day merely by existing. At least Penny Ashton knows what you are.'

'Not all of it,' I said bitterly.

'You're not to blame for Ashton's death.'

I raised my voice. 'No? I drove him to it.'

'But you didn't kill him. Who did?'

'Benson did, damn it!'

Ogilvie raised his voice to a shout. 'Then find out why, for God's sake! Don't do it for me, or even for yourself. All her life that girl of yours has been living in the same house as the man who eventually murdered her father. Find out why he did it – you might even be doing it for her sake.'

We both stopped short suddenly and there was silence in the room. I said quietly, 'You might have made your point – at last.'

He sat down. 'You're a hard man to convince. You mean I've done it?'

'I suppose so.'

He sighed. 'Then sit down and listen to me.' I obliged him, and he said, 'You're going to be in disgrace for a while. Everybody will expect that, including the Minister. Some sort of downgrading is indicated, so I'm going to make you a courier. That gives you freedom of action to move around in this country, and even out of it.' He smiled. 'But I'd hesitate about going back to Sweden.'

So would I. Captain Morelius would become positively voluble, even to the extent of speaking three consecutive sentences. And I knew what he'd say.

'We've been making quite a noise in here,' said Ogilvie. 'Had a real shouting match. Well, that will add verisimilitude to an otherwise bald and unconvincing narrative. There's one thing about being in an organization of spies – news gets around fast. You may expect some comments from your colleagues; can you stand that?'

I shrugged. 'I've never worried much about what people think of me.'

'Yes,' he agreed. 'Cregar discovered that when he first met you. All right; you'll have complete autonomy on this job. You'll do it in the way you want to do it, but it will be a solo operation; you'll have all the assistance I can give you short of men. You'll report your results to me and to no one else. And I do expect results.'

He opened a drawer and took out a slim file. 'Now, as for Penny Ashton, I laid some groundwork which will possibly help you. As far as she knows you have been in America for the past few weeks. I hope you didn't write from Sweden.'

'I didn't.'

'Good. She has been tactfully informed that you have been away on some mysterious job that has debarred you from writing to her. Knowing what she thinks she knows about your work it should seem feasible to her. However, you were informed of her father's death through the department, and you sent this cable.'

He passed the slip of paper across the desk. It was a genuine Western Union carbon copy emanating from Los Angeles. The content was trite and conventional, but it would have to do.

Ogilvie said, 'You also arranged for wreaths at the funeral through a Los Angeles flower shop and Interflora. The receipt from the flower shop is in this file together with other bits and pieces which a man might expect to pick up on a visit and still retain. There are theatre ticket stubs for current shows in Los Angeles, some small denomination American bills, book matches from hotels, and so on. Empty your pockets.'

The request took me by surprise and I hesitated. 'Come now,' he said. 'Dump everything on the desk.'

I stripped my pockets. As I took out my wallet Ogilvie delved in the small change I had produced. 'You see,' he said in triumph, and held up a coin. 'A Swedish crown mixed with your English money. It could have been a dead give-away. I'll bet you have a couple of Swedish items in your wallet. Get rid of them.'

He was right. There was a duplicate bar bill from the Grand which had yet to be transferred to my expense account, and a list of pound-kroner exchange rates made when I was trying to keep up with the vagaries of the falling pound sterling. I exchanged them for the Americana, and said, 'You were sure of me, after all.'

'Pretty sure,' he said drily. 'You got back from the States yesterday. Here is your air ticket – you can leave it lying around conspicuously somewhere. Penny Ashton, to the best of my knowledge, is coming back from Scotland tomorrow. You didn't buy any Swedish clothing?'

'No.'

'There are a couple of shirts and some socks in that small case over there. Also some packets of cigarettes. All genuine American. Now, leave here, go back to your office and mope disconsolately. You've just been through the meat grinder and you can still feel the teeth. I expect Harrison will want to see you in about half an hour. Don't try to score any points off him; let him have his little triumph. Remember you're a beaten man, Malcolm – and good luck.'

So I went back to the office and slumped behind my desk. Larry rustled his paper and avoided my eyes, but presently he said, 'I hear you were with the top brass all morning.'

'Yes,' I said shortly.

'Was Cregar there?'

'Yes.'

'Bad?'

'You'll know all about it soon,' I said gloomily. 'I don't think I'll be around here much longer.'

'Oh.' Larry fell silent for a while, then he turned a page and said, 'I'm sorry, Malcolm. It wasn't your fault.'

'Somebody has to get the axe.'

'Mmm. No, what I meant is I'm sorry about you and Penny. It's going to be difficult.'

I smiled at him. 'Thanks, Larry. You're right, but I think I'll make out.'

Ogilvie was right in his prediction. Within the hour Harrison rang and told me to report to his office. I went in trying to appear subdued and for once did not address him as Joe, neither did I sit down.

He kept me standing. 'I understand from Mr Ogilvie that you are leaving this section.'

'I understand so, too.'

'You are to report to Mr Kerr tomorrow.' His eyes glinted with ill-suppressed joy. He had always thought me too big for my britches and now I was demoted to messenger-boy – thus are the mighty fallen. 'This is really very difficult, you know,' he said fretfully. 'I'm afraid I'll have to ask you to clean out your desk before you leave today. There'll be another man coming in, of course.'

'Of course,' I said colourlessly. 'I'll do that.'

'Right,' he said, and paused. I thought for a moment he was going to give me a homily on the subject of mending my ways, but all he said was, 'You may leave, Jaggard.'

I went and cleared out my desk.

27

I trotted in to see Kerr next morning. He was one of several Section heads, but his Section was the only one to make a financial profit because, among other things, it ran the legitimate side of McCulloch and Ross, the bit the public knew about. It made a good profit, too, and so it ought; if it made a loss with all the professional expertise of the other sections behind it then Kerr ought to have been fired. Under Kerr also came several other miscellaneous bits and pieces including the couriers – the messenger-boys.

He seemed somewhat at a loss as to how to deal with me. 'Ah, yes – Jaggard. I think I have something here for you.' He handed me a large, thick envelope, heavily sealed. 'I'm told you know where to deliver that. It appears that . . . er . . . delivery may take some time, so you may be absent for a period.'

'That's so.'

'I see,' he said blankly. 'Will you be needing desk space – an office?'

'No, I don't think so.'

'I'm glad. We're tight for space.' He smiled. 'Glad to have you . . . er . . . with us,' he said uncertainly. I don't know what Ogilvie had told him but evidently he was baffled by my precise status.

In my car I opened the envelope and found £1000 in used fivers. That was thoughtful of Ogilvie but, after all, I could hardly claim expenses in the normal way on this operation. I put the money in the special locker built under the front passenger seat and drove to the police station in Marlow where I asked for Honnister. He came out front to meet me. 'You haven't been around for a while,' he said, almost accusingly. 'I've been trying to get you.'

'I've been in the States for a few weeks. What did you want me for?'

'Oh, just a chat,' he said vaguely. 'You must have been away when Ashton and Benson were killed in Sweden.'

'Yes, but I was told of it.'

'Funny thing, Ashton going away like that.' There was a glint in his eye. 'And then getting messily killed. Makes a man wonder.'

I took out a packet of cigarettes and offered it. 'Wonder what?'

'Well, a man like Ashton makes his pile by working hard and then, when he's still not too old to enjoy it, he suddenly gets dead.' He looked at the packet in my hand. 'No, I don't like American coffin nails. They take good Virginia tobacco, mix it with Turkish, then roast it and toast it and ultra-violet-ray it until it tastes like nothing on God's earth.'

I shrugged. 'Everybody dies. And you can't take it with you, although they tell me Howard Hughes tried.'

'Seen Penelope Ashton?'

'Not yet.' I lit a cigarette although I didn't like them, either. 'I'll be going to the house. I hear she's expected back today. If she's not there I'll see Gillian anyway.'

'And she'll see you,' said Honnister. 'But only barely. I had a talk with Crammond. He tells me Mayberry hasn't been brought to trial, and it's not likely that he will. He's unfit to plead.'

'Yes, I know about that.'

Honnister eyed the desk sergeant and then pushed himself upright from the counter. 'Let's have a noggin,' he proposed. I agreed quickly because it meant he wanted to talk confidentially and I was short of information. On the way to the pub he said, 'You didn't come to chat for old times' sake. What are you after?'

I said, 'When we started investigating we concentrated on Ashton and didn't look too closely at Benson, although at one point it did cross my mind that he might have chucked the acid.'

'Not the act of an old family servant.'

Neither was drilling his master full of holes – but I didn't say that aloud. 'Did you check on him?'

We turned into the Coach and Horses. 'A bit; enough to put him in the clear.' Honnister addressed the landlord. 'Hi, Monte; a large scotch and a pint of Director's.'

'My shout,' I said.

'It's okay – I'm on an expense account.'

I smiled. 'So am I.' I paid for the drinks and we took them to a table. It happened to be the same table at which I'd proposed marriage to Penny; it seemed a lifetime ago. It was early, just before midday, and the pub was quiet. I said, 'I've developed an interest in Benson.'

Honnister sank his nose into his beer. When he came up for air he said, 'There's been something funny going on in the Ashton family. This will have to be tit-for-tat, you know.'

'I'll tell you as much as I'm allowed to.'

He grunted. 'A fat lot of good that'll do me.' He held up his hand. 'All right, I know your lips are sealed and all that bull, and that I'm just a bumbling country copper who doesn't know which end is up – but tell me one thing: was Ashton kidnapped?'

I smiled at Honnister's description of himself which was a downright lie. 'No, he went under his own steam. He specifically asked that the police not be involved.'

'So he thought we might be. That's interesting in itself. And Benson went with him. What do you want to know about him?'

'Anything you can tell me that I don't know already. I'm scraping the bottom of the barrel.'

'Bachelor – never married. Worked for Ashton since the dark ages – butler, valet, handyman, chauffeur – you name it. Age at death, sixty-four, if you can believe *The Times*.'

'Any family – brothers or sisters?'

'No family at all.' Honnister grinned at me. 'As soon as I saw that bit in *The Times* I got busy. The itch in my bump of curiosity was driving me mad. Benson had a bit of money, about fifteen thousand quid, which he left to Dr Barnardo's Homes for Boys.'

'Anything else?' I asked, feeling depressed.

'Ever been in a war?' asked Honnister unexpectedly.

'No.'

'Seen any deaths by violence?'

'A few.'

'So have I, in my professional capacity. I've also seen the results of bombs and shellfire. It was a bit difficult to tell after a pathologist had been at them but I'd say Ashton had been shot in the back twice, and Benson shot through the head from the front. Caught in a shell blast, my arse!'

'*You've seen the bodies!*'

'I made it my business to – unofficially, of course. I went to the mortuary here. I told you my bump of curiosity was itching.'

'Charlie, you keep that under your bloody hat or you'll find yourself in dead trouble. I really mean that.'

'I told you before I can keep secrets,' he said equably. 'Anyway, Sweden isn't in my parish, so there's nothing I can do about it. If they were killed in Sweden,' he added as an afterthought.

'They were killed in Sweden,' I said. 'That's genuine. And they *were* killed in a Swedish battle practice area while manoeuvres were going on.' I paused. 'Probably *The Times* got the report wrong.'

'In a pig's eye,' said Honnister pointedly.

I shrugged. 'Anyone else here seen the bodies?'

'Not that I know of. The coffins arrived here sealed and complete with death certificates, probably signed by one of your department's tame doctors. Christ, talk about medical ethics! Anyway, they're underground now.'

'Any more about Benson?'

'Not much. He lived a quiet life. He had a woman in Slough but he gave that up about five years ago.'

'What's her name?'

'It won't do you any good,' he said. 'She died of cancer eighteen months ago. Benson paid for her treatment in a private ward – for old times' sake, I suppose. Other than that there's nothing I can tell you. There was nothing much to Benson; he was just a sort of old-maid bachelor with nothing remarkable about him. Except one thing.'

'What was that?'

'His face. He'd taken a hell of a beating at one time or other. Nature didn't make him like that – man did.'

'Yes,' I said. I was bloody tired of coming up against dead ends. I thought about it and decided that my best bet would be to look into Benson's army career but I wasn't sanguine that anything would come of that.

'Another drink?'

'No, thanks, Charlie. I want to see the Ashtons.'

'Give them my regards,' he said.

I drove to the Ashton house and, to my surprise, bumped into Michaelis who was just leaving. Under his arm he carried a loose-leaf ledger about as big as two bibles. 'What the devil are you doing here?'

He grinned. 'Playing puff-puffs. You know I'm interested and Miss Ashton gave me permission to mess about in the attic pretty nearly any time I like. It really is a fascinating set-up.'

I suppose it wasn't too weird that a counter-espionage agent should be nuts on model railways. I indicated the big book. 'What's that?'

'Now this is really interesting,' he said. 'Let me show you.' He rested the book on the bonnet of my car. The leters 'LMS' were inscribed on the leather-bound cover in gilt. 'This is a set of timetables for the old LMS – the London Midland and Scottish railway that was before nationalization. Effectively speaking, the railways were nationalized in 1939 and all the trains were steam in those days.'

He opened the book and I saw column after column of figures. 'Ashton was duplicating the LMS timetable, but I haven't figured out which year he was using so I'm taking this home to check against some old Bradshaws I have. Ashton's system up there in the attic isn't what you'd call standard practice in the model world – most of us can't afford what he'd got. I told you about those microprocessors he can program. These figures give the settings needed to the control panel to duplicate parts of the LMS timetable. He'd also got similar books for other pre-war railway companies – the London and North-Eastern, the Great Western and so on. It's bloody remarkable.'

'Indeed it is,' I said. 'Which Miss Ashton gave you permission?'

'Gillian. I talked to her a lot in hospital, about her father at the beginning, but one thing led to another. She was lonely, you know, being all bandaged up like that. I used to read books and newspapers for her. Anyway, I talked about the model railway and she found I was interested so she said I could come and play.'

'I see.'

'Gillian's a very nice girl,' he said. 'We get on very well.' He paused. 'I don't spend all my time in the attic.'

I studied Michaelis in a new light. It occurred to me that he was unmarried like myself and, if all went well with both of us, I was probably talking to my future brother-in-law. 'Is Gillian home now?'

'Yes – and she's expecting Penny for lunch.' He slammed the ledger closed. 'I heard on the grapevine what's happened to you. I think it's a bloody disgrace. Who the hell was to know . . .'

I interrupted. 'The less said about it the better, even in private. Don't talk about it at all – ever. That way nothing will slip out accidentally.' I consulted my watch. 'If you're so chummy with Gillian I thought you might be staying for lunch.'

He shook his head. 'I don't feel like facing Penny so I made an excuse. You see, Penny hasn't told Gillian about us – the department, I mean. She doesn't know anything about it and that makes it easier. But I haven't seen Penny since we came back from Sweden and I haven't the guts to face her yet – not after what happened. I have a weird feeling she might read my mind.'

'Yes,' I agreed. 'It is bloody difficult.'

'You're more involved than I am,' he said. 'How do you feel about it?'

'Pretty much the same as you, but maybe a bit more so. Well, I'll go in and see Gillian. See you around.'

'Yes,' said Michaelis. 'I hope so.'

28

I had forgotten that Gillian was not very pretty to look at and she came as a renewed shock. Her face was puckered and drawn with scar tissue and her right eyelid was pulled almost closed. The first few moments were not at all easy; there was the double embarrassment of condoling on the death of her father and coping with her dreadful appearance, and I hoped my face did not reflect what I felt. But she put me at my ease, gave me a scotch and had a sherry herself.

Of her father she had little to say beyond expressing a puzzled sadness and a total lack of knowledge of his motives. 'What can I say? There *is* nothing to be said, except that I'm deeply sorry and totally bewildered.'

Of herself she had come to terms with her affliction and was prepared to talk about it. 'Of course, it will be better after the plastic surgery. I'm told the best man for that is in America, and Penny wants me to go over. But my face is not so nice now, and I don't go out much.' She smiled lopsidedly. 'I saw you talking to Peter Michaelis outside. Do you know him?'

I said carefully, 'I met him at the hospital.'

'Oh, yes; you would, of course.' She smiled again, and there was a happy sparkle in her good eye. 'One never thinks of policemen as ordinary human beings – just shadows dashing about on television arresting people. Peter is such a delightful man.'

I agreed that a policeman's lot, etc., 'Must cramp their social lives.'

'He just told me about Mayberry. It appears the man is quite insane. Penny told me about . . . about the mistake.'

'So you know.'

'She waited until I'd been home a few days. I suppose she was right to withhold it until then. I wasn't in any condition to take more shocks. But how awful for her. It took a great deal of straight talking from me to make her carry on with Professor Lumsden.'

'I'm glad you did.'

Gillian looked at me closely. 'There's something wrong between you and Penny, isn't there? I think she's unhappy about it. What is it, Malcolm?'

'I don't know if the trouble altogether concerns me,' I said. 'I rather think she's unhappy about what happened to you, and then to your father.'

'No,' she said pensively. 'She appears to involve you in it, and I don't know why. She won't talk about it, and that's unlike her.' She turned her head to the window as a car drew up. 'Here she is now. You'll stay for lunch, of course.'

'Glad to.'

I was pleased to find that Penny was pleased to see me. 'Oh, Malcolm!' she cried, and hurried to meet me. I met her half way across the room, took her in my arms, and kissed her.

'I was very sorry to hear about your father.'

She looked beyond me to where Gillian sat, and said quietly, 'I want to talk to you about that afterwards.'

I nodded. 'Very well.'

'A sherry,' she said. 'A sherry, to save my life. Lummy and I have talked our throats dry this morning.'

So we had lunch, at which we chatted amiably and kept away from controversial subjects. We discussed Gillian's forthcoming trip to the United States, and Penny asked about my experiences there. 'I was told where you were,' she said obliquely.

Later she said, 'Gillian and I have decided to sell the house. It's much too big for the two of us, so we've decided to set ourselves up in a decent flat in town. Gillian will be closer to the theatres and concert halls, and I won't have to commute to the lab.'

'That sounds sensible,' I said. 'When do you move?'

'I'll be going to America with Gillian,' she said. 'We're selecting some of the best pieces from here and the rest will be auctioned, the antiques at Sotheby's and the rest of the stuff from the house. But we'll be in America then. I couldn't bear to stay and see the place sold up. So I suppose the auction will be in about three weeks. I'm making the final arrangements this afternoon.'

And that would put paid to Michaelis's fun and games with the model railway. I wondered if he was preparing to put in a bid.

After lunch Gillian pleaded tiredness and went to rest in her room, but I rather think she wanted to leave us alone together. Penny and I sat before the blazing fire with a pot of coffee and I could tell she was getting set for a serious discussion. 'Malcolm,' she said, 'what's the truth about Daddy?'

I offered her one of my American cigarettes which she took. 'I don't think anyone will ever know.'

'Did he die the way they said? You must know, being who you are, even though you were in America at the time. You were investigating him, after all.'

'My information is that he was in a Swedish army proving ground where they were using live ammunition when he was killed.'

'And that's the truth?' she said steadily. 'You wouldn't lie to me?'

'That's the truth.' But not the whole truth, Jaggard, you bastard!

She was silent for a while, gazing into the flames. 'I don't understand,' she said at last. 'I don't understand any of it. What was he doing in Sweden?'

'Apparently nothing very much, from what I can gather. He was living quietly in Stockholm with Benson to look after him. He read a lot and went to the occasional concert. A quiet and placid life.'

'How do you know this?'

'The department checked, of course.'

'Of course,' she said colourlessly. 'I'm going to Sweden. I want to find out for myself. Will you come with me?'

That was a poser! I could imagine the expression on the face of the colonel of the Royal Södermanland Regiment if I poked my nose into Strängnäs again. I needed no imagination at all to picture the cold grey eyes of Captain Morelius of Swedish Army Intelligence.

'That may not be easy,' I said. 'I've just been transferred and my time isn't my own.'

'Transferred from your department?'

'No, just within the department, but I may be office-bound from now on. Still, I'll see what I can do.' Which would be precisely nothing. 'Look, Penny, how would it be if I arranged for you to talk with my chief? He can tell you all that's known about your father in Sweden.' And he can tell my damned lies for me, I thought savagely.

She thought about it, then said, 'Very well. But that doesn't mean I'm not going to Sweden.'

'I'll arrange it.' I rose to pour us some more coffee. 'Penny, what's happening to us? I still want to marry you, but every time I get near the subject you edge away. I'm very much in love with you and it's becoming frustrating. Have you turned off?'

She cried, 'Oh, Malcolm, I'm sorry; I really am. Everything turned topsy-turvy so suddenly. First there was Gillian, then Daddy – and then you. I've been going about looking at people I know and wondering if what I think I know is really so. Even Lummy has come under scrutiny – I'm beginning to worry him, I think. He imagines I'm going paranoid.'

'It's not been too easy for me, either,' I said, 'I didn't want to have anything to do with the Ashton case.'

'The Ashton case,' she repeated. 'Is that what they call it?' When I ndoded, she said, 'That takes the humanity out of it, doesn't it? When it's a "case" it's easy to forget the flesh and blood because a case is mostly dockets and paperwork. How would you like to be referred to as the Jaggard case?'

'Not much,' I said sombrely.

Penny took my hand. 'Malcolm, you'll have to give me time. I think – no – I *know* I love you, but I'm still a bit mixed up; and I don't know that I'm too happy about what you do with your life. That's something else which needs thinking about.'

'My God!' I said. 'You make it sound as though I go about eating live babies. I'm just a dreary counter-espionage man specializing in industry and making sure too many secrets don't get pinched.'

'You mean weapons?'

I shook my head. 'Not necessarily. That's not our pigeon – and we're not interested in the latest toothapste additive, either. But if an engineering firm has ploughed a couple of millions into research and come up with something revolutionary, then we don't want some foreign Johnny nicking it and going into competition with a head start. And, don't forget, the foreign Johnnies from the East are state supported.'

'But these things are patented, aren't they?'

'Patents are a dead giveaway. The really big stuff isn't patented, especially in electronics. If you produce a new electronic chip which does the work of eleventy thousand transistors the opposition can put the thing under a microscope and see what you've done, but how the hell you've done it is quite another thing, and our boys aren't telling. They're certainly not going to disclose the process in a published patent.'

'I see,' she said. 'But that means you're just another sort of policeman.'

'Most of the time,' I said. 'Our problem is that the theft of information, as such, is not illegal in this country. Suppose I stole a sheet of paper from your lab, say, and I was caught. I'd be found guilty of the theft of a piece of paper worth one penny, and I'd suffer the appropriate penalty. The fact that written on that paper was some formula worth a million quid wouldn't count.'

Her voice rose. 'But that's silly.'

'I agree,' I said. 'Do you want to hear something really silly? A few years ago a chap was caught tapping a post office line. The only charge they could get him on was the theft of a quantity of electricity, the property of the Post-master-General. It was about a millionth of a watt.' Penny laughed, and I said, 'Anyway, that's my job, and it doesn't seem all that heinous to me.'

'Nor to me, now you've explained it. But where did Daddy come into this?'

I said, 'You may not realize how important a man your father was. The catalysts he was developing were revolutionizing the economics of the oil industry and helping the economics of the country. When a man like that goes missing we want to know if anyone has been putting pressure on him, and why. Of course, if he's just running away from a shrewish wife then it's his affair, and we drop it. That's happened before.'

'And what conclusions did you come to about Daddy?'

'At first we tied it in with the attack on Gillian,' I said. 'But that's a dead end; we know Mayberry was a loner. As it is, as far as the department could make out, your father was living quietly in Stockholm and apparently taking an extended holiday. There's nothing we could do about that.'

'No,' said Penny. 'We're not yet a police state. What's being done now?'

I shrugged. 'The committee of brains at the top has decided to drop the matter.'

'I see.' She stared into the fire for a long time, then shook her head. 'But you'll have to give me time, Malcolm. Let me go to America. I'd like to get away from here and think. I'd like to . . .'

I held up my hand. 'Point taken – no further argument.

Change of subject. What were you doing in Scotland?' I was damned glad to change the subject; I'd been shaving the truth a bit too finely.

'Oh, that. Acting as adviser in the reconstruction of a laboratory. It's been worrying me because they're only willing to go up to P3 and I'm recommending P4. I was arguing it out with Lumsden this morning and he thinks I'm a bit . . . well, paranoiac about it.'

'You've lost me,' I said. 'What's P3? To say nothing of P4.'

'Oh, I forgot.' She waved her hand at the room. 'I was so used to talking things out here with Daddy that I'd forgotten you're a layman.' She looked at me doubtfully. 'It's a bit technical,' she warned.

'That's all right. Mine is a technical job.'

'I suppose I'd better start with the big row,' she said. 'An American geneticist called Paul Berg . . .'

It seemed that Berg blew the whistle. He thought the geneticists were diddling around with the gene in the same way the physicist had diddled around with the atom in the '20s and '30s, and the potential hazards were even more horrendous. He pointed out some of them.

It seems that the favourite laboratory animal of the geneticists is a bacterium called *Escherichia coli* and it is the most studied organism on earth – more is known about *E.coli* than about any other living thing. It was natural that this creature be used for genetic experimentation.

'There's only one snag about that,' said Penny. '*E.coli* is a natural inhabitant of the human gut, and I don't mean by ones and twos – I mean by the million. So if you start tinkering around with *E.coli* you're doing something potentially dangerous.'

'For example?' I asked.

'You remember Lummy's example of genetic transfer from *Rhizobium* to make an improved wheat. I said we'd have to be careful not to transfer another, more dangerous, gene. Now, consider this. Supposing you incorporated into

E.coli, accidentally or on purpose, the gene specifying the male hormone, testosterone. And supposing that strain of *E.coli* escaped from the laboratory and entered the human population. It would inhabit the digestive tracts of women, too, you know. They might start growing beards and stop having babies.'

'Christ!' I said. 'It would be a catastrophe.'

'Berg and some of his concerned friends called an international conference at Asilomar in California in 1975. It was well attended by the world's geneticists but there was much controversy. Gradually a policy was hammered out involving the concept of biological containment. Certain dangerous experiments were to be banned pending the development of a strain of *E.coli* unable to survive outside the laboratory and unable to colonize the human gut. The specification laid down was that the survival rate of the new strain should not be more than one in a thousand million.'

I smiled. 'That sounds like certainty.'

'It's not,' said Penny soberly, 'considering the numbers of *E.coli* around, but it's close. I think that was the most important conference in the history of science. For the first time scientists had got together to police themselves without having restrictions thrust upon them. I think at the back of all our minds was the bad example set by the atomic physicists.'

Fifteen months later the development of the new strain was announced by the University of Alabama. Penny laughed. 'A writer in *New Scientist* put it very well. He called it "the world's first creature designed to choose death over liberty".'

I said slowly, 'The first creature *designed* . . . That's a frightening concept.'

'In a way – but we've been designing creatures for a long time. You don't suppose the modern dairy cow is as nature intended it to be?'

'Maybe, but this strikes me as being qualitatively different. It's one thing to guide evolution and quite another to bypass it.'

'You're right,' she said. 'Sooner or later there'll be some hack or graduate student who will go ahead with a bright idea without taking the time to study the consequences of what he's doing. There'll be a bad mistake made one day – but not if I can help. And that brings us to Scotland.'

'How?'

'What I've just described is biological containment. There's also physical containment to keep the bugs from escaping. Laboratories are classified from P1 to P4. P1 is the standard microbiological lab; P4 is the other extreme – the whole of the lab is under negative air pressure, there are air locks, showers inside and out, changes of clothing, special pressurized suits – all that kind of thing.'

'And you're running into trouble with your recommendations in Scotland?'

'They're upranking an existing P2 lab. In view of what they want to do I'm recommending P4, but they'll only go to P3. The trouble is that a P4 lab is dreadfully expensive, not only in the building, but in the running and maintenance.'

'Are there no statutory regulations?'

'Not in this field; it's too new. If they were working with recognized pathogens then, yes – there are regulations. But they'll be working with good old *E.coli*, a harmless bacterium. You have about a couple of hundred million of them in your digestive tract right now. They'll stay harmless, too, until some fool transfers the wrong gene.' She sighed. 'All we have are guidelines, not laws.'

'Sounds a bit like my job – not enough laws.'

She ruefully agreed, and our talk turned to other things. Just before I left she said, 'Malcolm; I want you to know that I think you're being very patient with me – patient and thoughtful. I'm not the vapouring sort of female, and I usually don't have much trouble in making up my mind; but events have been getting on top of me recently.'

'Not to worry,' I said lightly. 'I can wait.'

'And then there's Gillian,' she said. 'It may have been

silly of me but I was worrying about her even before all this happened. She's never been too attractive to men and she looked like turning into an old maid; which would have been a pity because she'd make someone a marvellous wife. But now – ' she shook her head – 'I don't think there's a chance for her with that face.'

'I wouldn't worry about that, either,' I advised. 'Michaelis has a fond eye for her.' I laughed. 'With a bit of luck you'll not have one, but two, spies in the family.'

And with that startling thought I left her.

29

The British weekend being what it is I didn't get to the War Office until Monday. Anyone invading these islands would be advised to begin not earlier than four p.m. on a Friday; he'd have a walkover. I filled in the necessary form at the desk and was escorted by a porter to the wrong office. Two attempts later I found the man I needed, an elderly major called Gardner who was sitting on his bottom awaiting his pension. He heard what I had to say and looked at me with mournful eyes. 'Do you realize the war has been over for thirty years?'

I dislike people who ask self-evident questions. 'Yes, I'm aware of it; and I still want the information.'

He sighed, drew a sheet of paper towards him, and picked up a ball point pen. 'It's not going to be easy. Do you know how many millions of men were in the army? I suppose I'd better have the names.'

'I suppose you had.' I began to see why Gardner was still a grey-haired major. 'George Ashton, private in the Royal Electrical and Mechanical Engineers; demobilized 4 January, 1947.'

'In London?'

'Probably.'

'Could have been at Earl's Court; that was used as a demob centre. The other man?'

'Howard Greatorex Benson, sergeant in the Royal Army Service Corps. I don't know where he was demobilized.'

'Is that all you know of these men?'

'That's it.'

Gardner laid down his pen and looked at me glumly. 'Very well, I'll institute a search. You'd better give me your address or a phone number where I can find you.' He sniffed lugubriously. 'It'll take about a month, I should say.'

'That's not good enough. I need the information a damned sight faster than that.'

He waved a languid hand. 'So many records,' he said weakly. 'Millions of them.'

'Don't you have a system?'

'System? Oh, yes; we have a system – when it works.'

I set out to jolly him along and by a combination of sweet talk, name-dropping and unspoken threats got him out of his chair and into action, if one could dignify his speed by such a name. He stood up, regarding me owlishly, and said, 'You don't suppose we keep five million army records here, do you?'

I smiled. 'Shall we take your car or mine?'

I had what I wanted four hours later. At the time I thought I'd been lucky but later decided that luck had nothing to do with it because it had been planned that way thirty years earlier.

We started with the records of Earl's Court, now an exhibition hall devoted to such things as cars and boats, but then a vast emporium for the processing of soldiers into civilians. There they exchanged their uniforms for civilian clothing from the skin out – underwear, shirt, socks, shoes, suit, overcoat and the inevitable trilby or fedora hat of the 1940s. There was also the equivalent of a bank which took in no money but which lashed it out by the million; the serviceman's gratuity, a small – very small – donation from a grateful nation. At its peak the throughput of Earl's Court was 5000 men a day but by early 1947 it had dropped to a mere 2000.

The ledgers for 4 January were comparatively small; they had coped with only 1897 men – it had been a slack day. Infuriatingly, the ledgers were not listed in alphabetical order but by army number, which meant that every name and page had to be scanned. 'What was the name again?' said Gardner.

'Ashton.'

'Ashton,' he muttered, as he started on the first page of a ledger. 'Ashton . . . Ashton . . . Ashton.' I think he had to repeat the name to himself because he had the attention span of a retarded five-year-old.

I took another ledger and started to check it. It was like reading a war memorial with the difference that these were the survivors; a long list of Anglo-Saxon names with the odd quirky foreigner for spice, and even more boring than checking Heathrow passenger lists. Half an hour later Gardner said, 'What was that name again?'

I sighed. 'Ashton. George Ashton.'

'No – the other one.'

'Benson, Howard Greatorex.'

'He's here,' said Gardner placidly.

'*Benson!*' I went to the other side of the table and leaned over Gardner's shoulder. Sure enough, his finger rested under Benson's name, and the rest of the information fitted. Sergeant H. G. Benson, RASC, had been discharged on the same day, and from the same place, as Private G. Ashton, REME. I didn't think coincidence could stretch that far.

'That's a piece of luck,' said Gardner with smug satisfaction. 'Now we have his army number we shall find his file easily.'

'We haven't got Ashton yet,' I said, and we both applied ourselves to the ledgers. Ashton came up three-quarters of an hour later. Gardner scribbled on a piece of paper and drifted away in his somnambulistic manner to organize the search for the files, while I sat down and began to sort out what we'd found.

I tried to figure out the odds against two specific men in the British Army being demobilized on the same day and from the same place, but the mathematics were too much for me – I couldn't keep count of the zeroes, so I gave up.

It was stretching the long arm a bit too far to suggest that it had happened by chance to two men who subsequently lived together as master and servant for the next quarter of a century. So if it wasn't coincidence it must have been by arrangement.

So who arranged it?

I was still torturing my brain cells when Gardner came back an hour later with the files. There was a sticky moment when I said I wanted to take them away; he clung to them as though I was trying to kidnap his infant children. At last he agreed to accept my receipt and I left in triumph.

I studied the files at home, paying little attention to Ashton's file because it had nothing to do with the Ashton I knew, but I went over Benson's file in detail. His career was exactly as Ogilvie had described. He joined the army in 1940 and after his primary training and square-bashing he was transferred to the RASC and his promotions came pretty quickly at first – to lance-corporal, to corporal, and then to sergeant where he stuck for the rest of the war. All his service was in England and he never went overseas. Most of his duties were concerned with storekeeping, and from the comments of his superiors written in the file, he was quite efficient, although there were a few complaints of lack of initiative and willingness to pass the buck. Not many, but enough to block his further promotion.

His pay-book showed that he was unmarried but was contributing to the upkeep of his mother. The payments ceased in 1943 when she died. From that time until his discharge his savings showed a marked increase. I thought that anyone who could save out of army pay in those days must have lived a quiet life.

His medical record was similarly uneventful. Looked at *en masse* it appeared alarming, but closer inspection revealed just the normal ailments which might plague a man over a period of years. There were a couple of tooth extractions, two periods of hospitalization – one for a bout of influenza and the other when he dropped a six-inch shell on his left foot. Luckily the shell was defused.

My attention was caught by the last entry. Benson had complained of aches in his left arm which had been preliminarily diagnosed as twinges of rheumatism and he had been given the appropriate treatment. He was thirty-three then, and rheumatism seemed a bit odd to me, especially since Benson had a cushy billet for a soldier in wartime. Not for him route marches in the pouring rain or splashing about joyfully in the mud; he worked in a warm office and slept every night in a warm bed.

Evidently the medical officer had thought it odd, too, when the treatment didn't work. In a different coloured ink he had appended a question mark after the previous diagnosis of rheumatism, and had scribbled beneath, 'Suggest cardiogram.' The amendment was dated 19 December, 1946.

I went back to the general service file where I struck another oddity, because his immediate superior had written as the last entry, 'Suggested date of discharge – 21 March, 1947.' Underneath another hand had written, 'Confirmed', and followed it with an indecipherable signature.

I sat back and wondered why, if it had been suggested and confirmed that Benson should be discharged in March, 1947, he should have been discharged three months earlier. I consulted the medical record again and then rang Tom Packer.

This account started with Tom Packer because it was at his place I first met Penny. I rang him now because he was a doctor and I wanted confirmation of the idea that was burgeoning. If he didn't know what I wanted he'd be certain to know who could tell me.

After a brief exchange of courtesies, I said, 'Tom, I want a bit of free medical advice.'

He chuckled. 'You and the rest of the population. What is it?'

'Supposing a man complains of a pain in his left arm. What would you diagnose?'

'Hell, it could be anything. Have you got such a pain?'

'This is hypothetical.'

'I see. Could be rheumatism. What's the hypothetical age of this hypothetical chap?'

'Thirty-three.'

'Then it's unlikely to be rheumatism if he's lived a normal civilized life. I say unlikely, but it could happen. Did he say pain or ache?'

I consulted the medical file. 'Actually, he said ache.'

'Um. Not much to go on. Doctors usually have real patients to examine, not wraiths of your imagination.'

I said, 'Supposing the man was treated for rheumatism and it didn't work, and then his doctor thought a cardiogram was indicated. What would you think then?'

'How long has the man been treated for rheumatism?'

'Hang on.' I checked the file. 'Three months.'

Tom's breath hissed in my ear. 'I'm inclined to think the doctor should be struck off. Do you mean to say it took him three months to recognize a classic symptom of ischaemia?'

'What's that?'

'Ischaemic heart disease – *angina pectoris*.'

I suddenly felt much happier. 'Would the man survive?'

'That's an imponderable question – very iffy. *If* he's had that ache in his arm for three months and *if* it is ischaemic and *if* he hasn't had treatment for his heart then he'll be in pretty bad shape. His future depends on the life he's been living, whether he smokes a lot, and whether he's been active or sedentary.'

I thought of Sergeant Benson in an army stores office. 'Let's say he's been sedentrary and we'll assume he smokes.'

'Then I wouldn't be surprised to hear he's dropped dead of a coronary one morning. This *is* hypothetical, isn't it? Nobody I know?'

'No one you know,' I assured him. 'But not quite

hypothetical. There was a man in that condition back in 1946. He died about a month ago. What do you think of that?'

'I think that I think I'm surprised, but then, medicine isn't a predictive sport and the damndest things can happen. I wouldn't have thought it likely he'd make old bones.'

'Neither would I,' I said. 'Thanks for your trouble, Tom.'

'You'll get my bill,' he promised, and rang off.

I depressed the telephone rest, rang Penny, and asked her the name of Benson's doctor. She was faintly surprised but gave it to me when I said my boss wanted to tidy up a few loose ends before I was transferred. 'It's just a matter of firm identification.'

The doctor's name was Hutchins and he was a shade reserved. 'Medical files are confidential, you know, Mr Jaggard.'

'I don't want you to break any confidences, Dr Hutchins,' I said. 'But the man is dead after all. All I want to know is when Benson last had a heart attack.'

'Heart attack!' echoed Hutchins in surprise. 'I can certainly tell you all about that. It's no breach of confidentiality on a doctor's part if he says a man is perfectly well. There was absolutely nothing wrong with Benson's heart; it was in better condition than my own, and I'm a much younger man. He was as fit as a flea.'

'Thank you, Doctor,' I said warmly. 'That's all I wanted to know.' As I put down the telephone I thought I'd handled that rather well.

I sat back and checked off all the points.

ITEM: Sergeant Benson was suffering from heart disease at the end of 1946. His condition, according to Tom Packer, was grave enough so that no one would be surprised if he dropped dead.

HYPOTHESIS: Sergeant Benson had died of heart diease some time after 18 December, 1946 and before 4 January, 1947.

ITEM: Civilian Benson was discharged at Earl's Court on 4 January, 1947 and subsequently showed no trace of a bad heart condition.

HYPOTHESIS: Civilian Benson was a planted substitute for Sergeant Benson, exactly as Chelyuskin was a substitute for Private Ashton. The method was exactly the same and it happened on the same day and in the same place, so the likelihood of a connection was very high, particularly as Benson worked for Ashton for the rest of his life.

COROLLARY: Because the methods used were identical the likelihood was high that both substitutions were planned by the same mind. But Ogilvie had told me that the idea was Chelyuskin's own. Was Benson another Russian? Had two men been smuggled out?

It all hung together very prettily, but it still didn't tell me who Benson was and why he had shot Ashton.

30

Ogilvie was pleased about all that even though it got us no further into cracking the problem of why Benson should kill Ashton. At least we had seen the common linkage and he was confident that by probing hard enough and long enough we – or rather I – would come up with the truth. All the same he coppered his bet by having me do an intensive investigation into the life of Sergeant Benson before he joined the army. Ogilvie was a belt-and-braces man.

So I spent a long time in the West Country looking at school records in Exeter and work records in Plymouth. At Benson's school I found an old sepia class photograph with Benson in the third row; at least, I was assured it was Benson. The unformed young face of that thirteen-year-old gazing solemnly at the camera told me nothing. Some time in the ensuing years Benson had had his features considerably rearranged.

There were no photographs of an older Benson to be found in Plymouth, but I did talk to a couple of people who knew him before the war. The opinion was that he wasn't a bad chap, reasonably good at his job, but not very ambitious. All according to the record. No, he hadn't been back since the war; he had no family and it was assumed there was nothing for him to go back for.

All this took time and I got back to London just as Penny and Gillian were about to leave for America. I drove them to Heathrow myself and we had a drink in the bar, toasting surgical success. 'How long will you be away?' I asked Gillian. She wore a broad-brimmed straw hat with a scarf tied wimple-fashion and large dark glasses; style coming to the aid of concealment.

'I don't know; it depends how the operations go, I suppose.' She sketched a mock shiver. 'I'm not looking forward to it. But Penny will be back next week.'

Penny said, 'I just want to see Gillian settled and to make sure everything is all right, then I'll be back. Lummy wants to go to Scotland with me.'

'So you undermined his certainty.'

'Perhaps,' she said noncommittally.

'Did you arrange for the auction?'

'It's on Wednesday – viewing day on Tuesday. We already have a flat in town.' She took a notebook and scribbled the address. 'That's where you'll find me when I come back, if I'm not in Scotland.'

Gillian excused herself and wandered in the direction of the ladies' room. I took the opportunity of asking, 'How did you get on with Ogilvie?' I had arranged the meeting with Ogilvie as promised. He hadn't liked it but I'd twisted his arm.

Penny's brow furrowed. 'Well enough, I suppose. He told me pretty much what you have. But there was something . . .'

'Something what?'

'I don't know. It was like speaking in a great empty hall. You expect an echo to come back and you're a bit surprised when there isn't one. There seemed to be something missing when Ogilvie talked. I can't explain it any better than that.'

Penny was right – there was a hell of a lot missing. Her psychic antennae were all a-quiver and she perceived a wrongness but had no way of identifying it. Below the level of consciousness her intelligence was telling her there was something wrong but she didn't have enough facts to prove it.

Ogilvie and I *knew* there was something wrong because

we had more facts, but even we were blocked at that moment.

I saw them into the departure lounge, then went home and proceeded to draw up an elaborate chart containing everything I knew about the Ashton case. Lines (ruled) were drawn to connect the *dramatis personae* and representing factual knowledge; lines (dashed) were drawn representing hypotheses.

The whole silly exercise got me nowhere.

About this time I started to develop an itch in my mind. Perhaps it had been the drawing of the chart with its many connections which started it, but I had something buried within me which wanted to come to the surface. Someone had said something and someone else had said something else, apparently quite unrelated and the little man Hunch who lived in the back of my skull was beginning to turn over in his sleep. I jabbed at him deliberately but he refused to wake up. He would do so in his own good time and with that I had to be content.

On the Tuesday I went to the Ashton house for the public viewing. It was crowded with hard-eyed dealers and hopeful innocents looking for bargains and not finding much because all the good stuff had gone to the London flat or to Sotherby's. Still, there was enough to keep them happy; the accumulated possessions of a happy family life of fifteen years. I could see why Penny didn't want to be there.

I wasn't there to buy anything, nor was I there out of mere curiosity. We had assumed Ashton had hidden something and, although we hadn't found it, that didn't mean it wasn't there. When I say 'we' I really mean Ogilvie, because I didn't wholly go along with him on that. But he could have been right, and I was on hand to see if any suspicious-looking characters were taking an undue interest. Of course, it was as futile an exercise as drawing the chart because the normal dealer looks furtive and suspicious to begin with.

During the morning I bumped into Mary Cope. 'Hello, Mary,' I said, 'Still here, then.'

'Yes, sir. I'm to live in the house until it's been sold. I still have my flat upstairs.' She surveyed the throng of inquisitive folk as they probed among the Ashtons' possessions. 'It's a shame, sir, it really is. Everything was so beautiful before . . . before . . .'

She was on the verge of tears. I said, 'A pity, Mary, but there it is. Any offers for the house yet?'

'Not that I know of, sir.'

'What will you do when it's sold?'

'I'm to go to London when Miss Penny and Miss Gillian come back from America. I don't know that I'll like London, though. Still, perhaps it will grow on me.'

'I'm sure it will.'

She looked up at me. 'I wish I knew what was in God's mind when he does a thing like this to a family like the Ashtons. You couldn't wish for better people, sir.'

God had nothing to do with it, I thought grimly; what happened to the Ashtons had been strictly man-made. But there was nothing I could say to answer such a question of simple faith.

'It's not only Mr Ashton, though,' said Mary wistfully. 'I miss Benson. He was such a funny man – always joking and light-hearted; and he never had a wrong word for anyone. He did make us laugh, sir; and to think that he and Mr Ashton should die like that, and in a foreign country.'

'Did Benson ever talk about himself, Mary?'

'About himself, sir? How do you mean?'

'Did he ever tell anecdotes – stories – about his early life, or when he was in the army?'

She thought about it, then shook her head. 'No, Benson was a man who lived in the present. He'd joke about politicians, and what he'd read in the papers or seen on telly. A real comedian, Benson was; had us in stitches a lot of the time. I used to tell him he should have been on the stage, but he always said he was too old.'

A real comedian! What an epitaph for a man whose last macabre joke was to shoot his master. I said, 'You'd better look sharp, Mary, or some of these people will be stealing the spoons.'

She laughed. 'Not much chance of that, sir. The auctioneer has Securicor men all over the place.' She hesitated. 'Would you like a cup of tea? I can make it in my flat.'

I smiled. 'No, thank you, Mary. I don't think I'll be staying long this morning.'

All the same, I was there next day for the actual auction, and why I was there I didn't really know. Perhaps it was the feeling that with the dispersal of the contents of the house the truth about the Ashton case was slipping away, perhaps to be lost forever. At any rate I was there, impotent with ignorance, but on the spot.

And there, to my surprise, was also Michaelis. I didn't see him until late morning and was only aware of him when he nudged me in the ribs. The auctioneer was nattering about a particularly fine specimen of something or other so we withdrew to Ashton's study, now stripped rather bare. 'What a bloody shame this is,' he said. 'I'm glad Gillian isn't here to see it. Have you heard anything yet?'

'No.'

'Neither have I,' he said broodily. 'I wrote to her but she hasn't replied.'

'She's only been gone four days,' I pointed out gently. 'The postal services weren't that good even in their palmy days.'

He grinned and seemed oddly shy. 'I suppose you think I'm making a damned fool of myself.'

'Not at all,' I said. 'No more than me. I wish you luck.'

'Think I have a chance?'

'I don't see why not. In fact, I think you have everything

going for you, so cheer up. What are you doing here anyway?'

'That model railway still interests me. I thought that if it's broken up for sale I might put in a bid or two. Of course, in model railway terms to break up that system would be like cutting up the Mona Lisa and selling bits of it. But it won't be broken up and I won't have a chance. Lucas Hartman is here.'

'Who's he?'

'Oh, everybody in the model railway world knows Hartman. He's a real model railway buff, but he calls it railroad because he's an American. He's also quite rich.'

'And you think he'll buy it as it stands?'

'He's sure to. He's up in the attic gloating over it now.'

'How much do you think it will bring?' I asked curiously.

Michaelis shrugged. 'That's hard to say. It's not exactly standard stuff – there's so much extra built in that it's hard to put a price on it.'

'Have a try.'

'For the rail and rolling stock and normal control instrumentation, all of which is there, it would cost about £15,000 to build from scratch, so let's say it might bring between £7000 and £10,000 at auction. As for the other stuff built in, that's more difficult to assess. I'd say it'll double the price.'

'So you think it will bring somewhere between £15,000 and £20,000.'

'Something like that. Of course, the auctioneer will have a reserve price on it. Any way you look at it, Hartman will get it. He'll outbid the dealers.'

'Ah, well,' I said philosophically. 'It will fall into good hands – someone who appreciates it.'

'I suppose so,' said Michaelis gloomily. 'The bloody thing beat me in the end, you know.'

'What do you mean?'

'Well, you know those schedules I talked about – I showed you one of them.'

'The London, Midland and Scottish, I think it was.'

'That's right. I compared them against old Bradshaws and got nowhere. I even went right back to the mid-1800s and nothing made sense. The system doesn't seem to compare with any normal railway scheduling.'

'Not even when those schedules were clearly labelled "LMS" and so on,' I said slowly.

'They don't fit at any point,' said Michaelis. 'It beats me.'

There was a picture in my mind's eye of Ashton's clenched fist opening to reveal a railway timetable – Stockholm to Göteborg, and it was like a bomb going off in my skull. 'Jesus!'

Michaelis stared at me. 'What's wrong?'

'Come on. We're going to talk to that bloody auctioneer.'

I left the study at a fast stride and went into the crowded hall where the auction was taking place. The autioneer had set up a portable rostrum at the foot of the stairs and, as I elbowed my way through the throng towards it, I took a business card from my wallet. Behind me Michaelis said, 'What's the rush?'

I flattened myself against the wall and scribbled on the card. 'Can't explain now.' I pushed the card at him. 'See the auctioneer gets this.'

Michaelis shrugged and fought his way through to the rostrum where he gave the card to one of the auctioneer's assistants. I walked up the stairs and stood where I could easily be seen. The auctioneer was in mid-spate, selling an eighteen-place Crown Derby dinner service; he took the card which was thrust under his nose, turned it over, looked up at me and nodded, and then continued with hardly a break in his chant.

Michaelis came back. 'What's the panic?'

'We must stop the sale of that railway.'

'I'm all for that,' he said. 'But what's your interest?'

The auctioneer's hammer came down with a sharp crack. 'Sold!'

'It's too complicated to tell you now.' The auctioneer had

handed over to his assistant and was coming towards the stairs. 'It'll have to keep.'

The auctioneer came up the stairs. 'What can I do for you – er – ' He glanced at the card – 'Mr Jaggard.'

'I represent Penelope and Gillian Ashton. The model railway in the attic mustn't be sold.'

He frowned. 'Well, I don't know about that.'

I said, 'Can't we go somewhere a bit more quiet while I explain?'

He nodded and pointed up the stairs, so we went into one of the bedrooms. He said, 'You say you represent the Ashton sisters?'

'That's right.'

'Can you prove that?'

'Not with anything I carry with me. But I can give you written authority if you need it.'

'On your signature?'

'Yes.'

He shook his head. 'Sorry, Mr Jaggard, but that's not good enough. I was engaged by Penelope Ashton to sell the contents of this house. I can't vary that agreement without her authority. If you can give me a letter from her, that's different.'

'She's not easy to get hold of at short notice. She's in the United States.'

'I see. Then there's nothing to be done.' Something in my expression caused him to add quickly, 'Mr Jaggard, I don't know you. Now, I'm a professional man, engaged to conduct this sale. I can't possibly take instructions from any Tom, Dick or Harry who comes here telling me what to do or what not to do. I really don't conduct my business that way. Besides, the railway is one of the plums of the sale. The press is very interested; it makes a nice filler for a columnist.'

'Then what do you suggest? Would you take instruction from Miss Ashton's legal adviser?'

'Her solicitor? Yes, I might do that.' He frowned perplexedly. 'This all appears very odd to me. It seems, from what you say, that Miss Ashton knows nothing about this and it is something you are taking upon yourself. But if I have written instructions from her solicitor, then I'll withdraw the railway.'

'Thank you,' I said. 'I'll get in touch with him. Oh, by the way, what's the reserve price?'

He was affronted. 'I really can't tell you that,' he said coldly. 'And now you must excuse me. There are some important pieces coming up which I must handle myself.'

He turned to walk away, and I said desperately, 'Can you tell me when the railway will come up for sale?'

'Things are going briskly.' He looked at his watch. 'I'd say about three this afternoon.' He walked out.

'A telephone,' I said. 'My kingdom for a telephone.'

'There's one next door in Ashton's bedroom.' Michaelis looked at me a little oddly. 'This sudden interest in model railways doesn't seem kosher to me.'

I had a sudden thought. 'Where are those schedules?'

'In the attic; on a shelf under the control console. There are a dozen.'

'I want you in the attic on the double. Keep an eye on that railway and especially on those schedules. I don't want anything removed and I want note taken of anyone who takes a special interest. Now move.'

I went into Ashton's room and attacked the telephone. For the first time Ogilvie let me down; he wasn't in the office and no one knew where he was or when he'd be back. Neither was he at home. I left messages to say he should ring me at the Ashton house as soon as possible.

There were more frustrations. Mr Veasey of Michelmore, Veasey and Templeton was away in the fastness of Wales talking to a valued but bedridden client. His clerk would not make a decision in the matter, and neither would any of the partners. They did say they would try to get hold of Veasey by telephone and I had to be satisfied with that. I had no great hopes of success – Veasey didn't know me and I had no standing.

I went up to the attic and found Michaelis brooding over the railway. Several small boys were larking about and being chased off by a Securicor guard. 'Any suspects?'

'Only Hartman. He's been checking through those schedules all morning.' He nodded in the direction of the control console. 'There he is.'

Hartman was a broad-shouldered man of less than average height with a shock of white hair and a nut-brown lined face. He looked rather like Einstein might have looked if Einstein had been an American businessman. At that moment he was poring over one of the schedules and frowning.

I said, 'You're sure that *is* Hartman?'

'Oh, yes. I met him three years ago at a Model Railway Exhibition. What the hell are you really up to, Malcolm?'

I looked at the railway. 'You're the expert. Are there any other peculiarities about this other than the schedules?'

Michaelis stared at the spider web of rails. 'It did occur to me that there's an excessive number of sidings and marshalling yards.'

'Yes,' I said thoughtfully. 'There would be.'

'Why would there be?' Michaelis was baffled.

'Ashton was a clever bastard,' I said. 'He wanted to hide something so he stuck it right under our noses. Do you know how a computer works?'

'In a vague sort of way.'

I said, 'Supposing you instruct a computer that A=5. That tells the computer to take that number five and put it in a location marked A. Suppose you gave the instruction C=A+B. That tells the computer to take whatever number is in A, add it to whatever number is in B, and put the result in C.' I jerked my head towards the railway. 'I think that's what this contraption is doing.'

Michaelis gasped. 'A *mechanical* computer!'

'Yes. And those schedules are the programs which run it

– but God knows what they're about. Tell me, how many different kinds of rolling stock are there in the system? I'd say ten.'

'You'd be wrong. I counted sixty-three.'

'Hell!' I thought about it a little more. 'No, by God, I'm right! Ten for the numbers 0 to 9; twenty-six for the letters of the alphabet, and the rest for mathematical signs and punctuation. This bloody thing can probably talk English.'

'I think you're nuts,' said Michaelis.

I said, 'When Ashton was shot he couldn't talk but he was trying to tell me something. He pulled something from his pocket and tried to give it to me. It was a railway timetable.'

'That's pretty thin,' said Michaelis. 'Larry had one, too.'

'But why should a man in his last extremity try to give me, of all things, a railway timetable? I think he was trying to tell me something.'

'I can see why you want the sale stopped,' admitted Michaelis. 'It's a nutty idea, but you may be right.'

'I haven't got very far,' I said gloomily. 'Ashton's law firm won't play and Ogilvie's gone missing. I'd better try him again.'

So I did, but with no joy. I tried every place I thought he might be – his clubs, the restaurant he had once taken me to, then back to the office and his home again. No Ogilvie.

At half past two Michaelis sought me out. 'They're about to start bidding on the railway. What are you going to do?'

'Make another call.'

I rang my bank manager, who said, 'And what can I do for you this afternoon, Mr Jaggard?'

'Later today I'm going to write a largish cheque. There won't be enough funds to cover it, either in my current account or in the deposit account. I don't want it to bounce.'

'I see. How much will the cheque be for?'

'Perhaps £20,000.' I thought of Hartman. 'Maybe as much as £25,000. I don't quite know.'

'That's a lot of money, Mr Jaggard.'

I said, 'You know the state of my financial health, and you know I can cover it, not immediately but in a few weeks.'

'In effect, what you're asking for is a bridging loan for, say, a month.'

'That's it.'

'I don't see any difficulty there. We'll accept your cheque, but try to keep it down; and come in tomorrow – we'll need your signature.'

'Thanks.' I put down the telephone knowing that if I was wrong about the railway I was about to lose a lot of money. I couldn't see Ogilvie dipping into the department's funds to buy an elaborate toy, and the only person who might be happy about it would be Michaelis.

I went into the hall to see a small crowd gathered by the rostrum listening to a man talking. Michaelis whispered, 'They've got old Hempson from *Model Railway News* to give a pep-talk. I suppose they think that'll drive up the price.'

Hempson was saying, '. . . core of the system is the most remarkable console I have ever seen, using the ultimate in modern technology. It is this which makes this example of the art unique and it is to be hoped that the system will be sold as a complete unit. It would be a disaster if such a fine example should be broken up. Thank you.'

He stepped down to a low murmur of agreement, and I saw Hartman nodding in approval. The auctioneer stepped up and lifted his gavel. 'Ladies and gentlemen: you have just heard Mr Hempson who is an acknowledged expert, and his opinion counts. So I am about to ask for bids for the complete system. It would be normal to do this on site, as it were, but even in so large a house the attic is not big enough to hold both the exhibit and the crowd gathered here. However, you have all had the opportunity of examining this fine example of the model-maker's art, and on the table over there is a representative collection of the rolling stock.'

He raised his gavel. 'Now what am I bid for the complete system? Who will start the bidding at £20,000?'

There was a sigh – a collective exhalation of breath. 'Come,' said the auctineer cajolingly. 'You just heard Mr Hempson. Who will bid £20,000? No one? Who will bid £18,000?'

He had no takers at that, and gradually his starting price came down until he had a bid of £8000. 'Eight thousand I am bid – who will say nine? Eight-five I am bid – thank you, sir – who will say nine? Nine I am bid – who will say ten?'

Michaelis said, 'The dealers are coming in, but they won't stand a chance. Hartman will freeze them out.'

I had been watching Hartman who hadn't moved a muscle. The bidding crept up by 500s, hesitated at the £13,500 mark, and then went up by 250s to £15,000 where it stuck. 'Fifteen I am bid; fifteen I am bid,' chanted the auctioneer. 'Any advance on fifteen?'

Hartman flicked a finger. 'Sixteen I am bid,' said the auctioneer. 'Sixteen thousand. Any advance on sixteen?' The dealers were frozen out.

I held up a finger. 'Seventeen I am bid. Any advance on seventeen? Eighteen I am bid – and nineteen – and twenty. I have a bid of £20,000. Any advance on twenty?'

There was a growing rustle of interest as Hartman and I battled it out. At £25,000 he hesitated for the first time and raised his bid by £500. Then I knew I had him. I raised a single finger and the auctioneer said, 'Twenty-six and a half – any advance . . . twenty-seven, thank you, sir – twenty-eight I am bid.'

And so it went. Hartman lost his nerve at thirty and gave up. The auctioneer said, 'Any advance on thirty-one? Any advance on thirty-one? Going once,' *Crack!* 'Going twice.' *Crack!* 'Sold to Mr Jaggard for £31,000.'

Crack!

I was now the proud owner of a railway. Maybe it wasn't British Rail but perhaps it might show more profit. I said to Michaelis, 'I wonder if Ogilvie has that much in the petty cash box?'

Hartman came over. 'I guess you wanted that very much, sir.'

'I did.'

'Perhaps you would be so kind as to let me study the layout some time. I am particularly interested in those schedules.'

I said, 'I'm sorry. I acted as agent in this matter. However, if you give me your address I'll pass it to the owner for his decision.'

He nodded. 'I suppose that will have to do.'

Then I was surrounded by pressmen wanting to know who, in his right mind, would pay that much money for a toy. I was rescued by Mary Cope. 'You're wanted on the telephone, Mr Jaggard.'

I made my escape into Ashton's study. It was Ogilvie. 'I understand you wanted me.'

'Yes,' I said, wishing he had rung half an hour earlier. 'The department owes me £31,000 plus bank charges.'

'*What's that?*'

'You now own a model railway.'

His language was unprintable.

31

I saw Ogilvie at his home that night. His welcome was somewhat cool and unenthusiastic and he looked curiously at the big ledger I carried as he ushered me into his study. I dumped it on his desk and sat down. Ogilvie warmed his coat tails at the fire, and said, 'Did you really spend £31,000 on a toy train set?'

I smiled. 'Yes, I did.'

'You're a damned lunatic,' he said. 'And if you think the department will reimburse you, then I'll get the quacks in and have you certified. No bloody model railway can be worth that much.'

'An American called Hartman thought it worth £30,000,' I observed. 'Because that's how much he bid. You haven't seen it. This is no toy you buy your kid for Christmas and assemble on the floor before the living-room fire to watch the chuff-chuff go round in circles. This is big and complex.'

'I don't care how big and complex it is. Where the hell do you think I'm going to put it in the department budget? The accountants would have *me* certified. And what makes you think the department wants it?'

'Because it holds what we've been looking for all the time. It's a computer.' I tapped the ledger. 'And this is the programing for it. One of the programs. There are eleven more which I put in the office vaults.'

I told him how Michaelis had unavailingly tried to sort out the schedules and how I'd made an intuitive jump based on the timetable in Ashton's hand. I said, 'It would be natural these days for a theoretician to use a computer, but

Ashton knew we'd look into all his computer files and programs. So he built his own and disguised it.'

'It's the most improbable idea I've ever heard,' said Ogilvie. 'Michaelis is the train expert. What does he think?'

'He thinks I'm crazy.'

'He's not far wrong.' Ogilvie began to pace the room. 'I tell you what I think. If you're right then the thing is cheap at the price and the department will pay. If you're wrong then it costs *you* £31,000.'

'Plus bank charges.' I shrugged. 'I stuck out my neck, so I'll take the chance.'

'I'll get the computer experts on it tomorrow.' He wagged his head sadly. 'But where are we to put it? If I have it installed in the department offices it'll only accelerate my retirement. Should the Minister hear of it he'll think I've gone senile – well into second childhood.'

'It will need a big room,' I said. 'Best to rent a warehouse.'

'I'll authorize that. You can get on with it. Where is it now?'

'Still in the Ashtons' attic. Michaelis is locked in with it for the night.'

'Enthusiastically playing trains, I suppose.' Ogilvie shook his head in sheer wonderment at the things his staff got up to. He joined me at the desk and tapped the schedule. 'Now tell me what you think this is all about.'

It took four days to dismantle the railway and reassemble it in a warehouse in South London. The computer boys thought my idea hilarious and to them the whole thing was a big giggle, but they went about the job competently enough. Ogilvie gave me Michaelis to assist. The department had never found the need for a model railway technician and Michaelis found himself suddenly elevated into the rank of expert, first class. He quite liked it.

The chief computer man was a systems analyst called Harrington. He took the job more seriously than most of the others but even that was only half-serious. He installed a computer terminal in the warehouse and had it connected to a computer by post office land lines; not the big chap Nellie was hooked up to, but an ordinary commercial time-sharing computer in the City. Then we were ready to go.

About this time I got a letter from Penny. She wrote that Gillian was well and had just had the operation for the first of the skin grafts. She herself was not coming back immediately; Lumsden had suggested that she attend a seminar at Berkeley in California, so she wouldn't be back for a further week or ten days.

I showed the letter to Michaelis and he said he'd had one from Gillian, written just before the operation. 'She seemed a bit blue.'

'Not to worry; probably just pre-operation nerves.'

The itch at the back of my mind was still there, and so the buried connection was nothing to do with the railway. Little man Hunch was sitting up and rubbing his eyes but was still not yet awake. I badly needed to talk to Penny because I thought it was something she had said that had caused the itch. I was sorry she wasn't coming home for that reason among many.

One morning at ten o'clock Harrington opened the LNER schedule. 'The first few pages are concerned with the placement of the engines and the rolling stock,' he said. 'Now, let's get this right if we can. This is silly enough as it is without us putting our own bugs into the system.'

It took over an hour to get everything in the right place – checked and double checked. Harrington said, 'Page eleven to page twenty-three are concerned with the console settings.' He turned to me. 'If there's anything to your idea at all these Roms will have to be analysed to a fare-thee-well.'

'What's a Rom?'

'A read-only module – this row of boxes plugged in here. Your man, Michaelis, calls them microprocessors. They are pre-programed electronic chips – we'll have to analyse what they're programed to do. All right; let's get on with the setting.'

He began to call out numbers and an acolyte pressed buttons and turned knobs. When he had finished he started again from the beginning and another acolyte checked what the first had done. He caught three errors. 'See what I mean,' said Harrington. 'One bug is enough to make a program unworkable.'

'Are you ready to go now?'

'I think so – for the first stage.' He put his hand on the ledger. 'There are over two hundred pages here, so *if* this thing really is a computer and *if* this represents one program, then after a while everything should come to a stop and the console will have to be readjusted for the next part of the program. It's going to take a long time.'

'It will take even longer if we don't start,' I said tartly.

Harrington grinned and leaned over to snap a single switch. Things began to happen. Trains whizzed about the system, twenty or thirty on the move at once. Some travelled faster than others, and once I thought there was going to be a collision as two trains headed simultaneously for a junction; but one slowed just enough to let the other through and then picked up speed again.

Sidings and marshalling yards that had been empty began to fill up as engines pushed in rolling stock and then uncoupled to shoot off somewhere else. I watched one marshalling yard fill up and then begin to empty, the trains being broken up and reassembled into other patterns.

Harrington grunted. 'This is no good; it's too damned busy. Too much happening at once. If this is a computer it isn't working sequentially like an ordinary digital jog; it's working in parallel. It's going to be hell to analyse.'

The system worked busily for nearly two hours. Trains shot back and forth, trucks were pushed here and there, abandoned temporarily and then picked up again in what seemed an arbitrary manner. To me it was bloody monotonous but Michaelis was enthralled and even Harrington appeared to be mildly interested. Then everything came to a dead stop.

Harrington said, 'I'll want a video-camera up there.' He pointed to the ceiling. 'I want to be able to focus on any marshalling yard and record it on tape. And I want it in colour because I have a feeling colour comes into this. And we can slow down a tape for study. Can you fix that?'

'You'll have it tomorrow morning,' I promised. 'But what do you think now?'

'It's an ingenious toy, but there may be something more to it,' he said, noncommittally. 'We have a long way to go yet.'

I didn't spend all my time in the warehouse but went back three days later because Harrington wanted to see me. I found him at a desk flanked by a video-recorder and a TV set. 'We may have something,' he said, and pointed to a collection of miniature rolling stock on the desk. 'There *is* a number characterization.'

I didn't know what he meant by that, and said so. He smiled. 'I'm saying you were right. This railway is a computer. I think that any of this rolling stock which has red trim on it represents a digit.' He picked up a tank car which had ESSO lettered on the side in red. 'This one, for instance, I think represents a zero.'

He put down the tank car and I counted the trucks; there were nine, but one had no red on it. 'Shouldn't there be ten?'

'Eight,' he said. 'This gadget is working in octal instead of decimal. That's no problem – many computers work in octal internally.' He picked up a small black truck. 'And I think this little chap is an octal point – the equivalent of a decimal point.'

'Well, I'm damned! Can I tell Ogilvie?'

Harrington sighed. 'I'd rather you didn't – not yet. We haven't worked out to our satisfaction which number goes with which truck. Apart from that there is a total of sixty-three types of rolling stock; I rather think some of those represent letters of the alphabet to give the system alpha-numeric capability. Identification may be difficult. It should be reasonably easy to work out the numbers; all that it takes is logic. But letters are different. I'll show you what I mean.'

He switched on the video-recorder and the TV set, then punched a button. An empty marshalling yard appeared on the screen, viewed from above. A train came into view and the engine stopped and uncoupled, then trundled off. Another train came in and the same thing happened; and yet again until the marshalling yard was nearly full. Harrington pressed a button and froze the picture.

'This marshalling yard is typical of a dozen in the system, all built to the same specification – to hold a maximum of eighty trucks.' With his pen he pointed out something else. 'And scattered at pretty regular intervals are these blue trucks.'

'Which are?'

Harrington leaned back. 'If I were to talk in normal computer terms – which may be jargon to you – I'd say I was looking at an alphameric character string with a maximum capacity of eighty characters, and the blue trucks represent the spaces between words.' He jabbed his finger at the screen. 'That is saying something to us, but we don't know what.'

I bent down and counted the blue trucks; there were thirteen. 'Thirteen words,' I said.

'Fourteen,' said Harrington. 'There's no blue truck at the end. Now, there are twelve marshalling yards like this, so the system has a capacity of holding at any one time about a hundred and sixty words in plain, straightforward English – about half a typed quarto sheet. I know it's not much, but it keeps changing all the time as the system runs; that's the equivalent of putting a new page in the typewriter and doing some more.' He smiled. 'I don't know who designed this contraption, but maybe it's a new way of writing a novel.'

'So all you have to do is to find out which truck equals which letter.'

'All!' said Harrington hollowly. He picked up a thick sheaf of colour photographs. 'We've been recording the strings as they form and I have a chap on the computer doing a statistical analysis. So far he's making heavy weather of it. But we'll get it, it's just another problem in cryptanalysis. Anyway, I just thought I'd let you know your hare-brained idea turned out to be right, after all.'

'Thanks,' I said, glad not to be £31,000 out of pocket. Plus bank charges.

Two days later Harrington rang me again. 'We've licked the numbers,' he said. 'And we're coming up with mathematical formulae now. But the alphabet is a dead loss. The statistical distribution of the letters is impossible for English, French, German, Spanish and Latin. That's as far as we've gone. It's a bit rum – there are too many letters.'

I thought about that. 'Try Russian; there are thirty-two letters in the Russian alphabet.' And the man who had designed the railway was a Russian, although I didn't say that to Harrington.

'That's a thought. I'll ring you back.'

Four hours later he rang again. 'It's Russian,' he said. 'But we'll need a linguist; we don't know enough about it here.'

'Now is the time to tell Ogilvie. We'll be down there in an hour.'

So I told Ogilvie. He said incredulously, 'You mean that bloody model railway speaks Russian?'

I grinned. 'Why not? It was built by a Russian.'

'You come up with the weirdest things,' he complained.

'I didn't,' I said soberly. 'Ashton did. Now you can make my bank manager happy by paying £35,000 into my account.'

Ogilvie narrowed his eyes. 'It cost you only £31,000.'

'"Thou shalt not muzzle the ox that treadeth the corn",' I quoted. 'It was a risky investment – I reckon I deserve a profit.'

He nodded. 'Very well. But it's going to look damned funny in the books – for one model railway, paid to M. Jaggard, £35,000.'

'Why don't you call it by its real name? A computing system.'

His brow cleared. 'That's it. Now let's take a look at this incredible thing.' We collected Larry Godwin as an interpreter and went to the warehouse.

The first thing I noticed was that the system wasn't running and I asked Harrington why. 'No need,' he said cheerfuly. 'Now we've got the character list sorted out we've duplicated the system in a computer – put it where it really belongs. We weren't running the entire program, you know; just small bits of it. To run through it all would have been impossible.'

I stared at him. 'Why?'

'Well, not really impossible. But look.' He opened the LNER schedule and flipped through. 'Take these five pages here. They contain reiterative loops. I estimate that to run these five pages on the system would take six days, at twenty-four hours a day. To run through the whole program would take about a month and a half – and this is one of the smaller programs. To put all twelve of them through would take about two years.'

He closed the schedule. 'I think the original programs were written on, and for, a real computer, and then transferred on to this system. But don't ask me why. Anyway, now we've put the system back into a computer we're geared to work at the speed of electrons and not on how fast a model railway engine can turn its wheels.'

Ogilvie said, 'Which computer?'

'One in the City; a time-sharing system.'

Ogilvie looked at me. 'Oh, we can't have that. I want

everything you've put into that computer cleared out. We'll put it in our own computer.'

I said quickly, 'I wouldn't do that. I don't trust it. It lost Benson.'

Although Harrington could not know what we were talking about he caught the general drift. 'That's no problem.' He pointed to the railway. 'As a model railway that thing is very elaborate and complex, but as a computer it's relatively simple. There's nothing there that can't be duplicated in the Hewlett-Packard desk-top job I have in my own office. But I'll need a printer to handle Russian characters and, perhaps, a modified keyboard.'

Ogilvie said, 'That's a most satisfactory solution.' He walked over to the railway and looked at it. 'You're right; it is complex. Now show me how it works.'

Harrington smiled. 'I thought you'd ask that. Can you read Russian?'

Ogilvie indicated Larry. 'We've brought an interpreter.'

'I'm going to run through the program from the beginning; it's set up ready. I want you to keep an eye on that marshalling yard there. When it's full you can read it off because I've labelled each truck with the character it represents. I'll stop the system at the right time.'

He switched on and the trains began to scurry about, and the marshalling yard, which was empty, began to fill up. Harrington stopped the system. 'There you are.'

Ogilvie leaned forward and looked. 'All right, Godwin. What does it say?'

Harrington handed Larry a small pair of opera glasses. 'You'll find these useful.'

Larry took them and focused on the trains. His lips moved silently but he said nothing, and Ogilvie demanded impatiently, 'Well?'

'As near as I can make out it says something like this: "First approximation using toroidal Legendre function of the first kind."'

'Well, I'll be damned!' said Ogilvie.

* * *

Later, back at the office, I said, 'So they're not going to use the railway.'

'And better not,' said Ogilvie. 'We can't wait two years to find out what this is all about.'

'What will you do with it? According to Harrington it's a pretty simple-minded computer. Without the schedules – the programs – it's just an elaborate rich man's toy.'

'I don't know what to do with it,' said Ogilvie. 'I'll have to think about that.'

'Do me a favour,' I said. 'Give it to Michaelis. It was he who figured those schedules were fakes. It'll make his day.'

32

So Harrington put the programs on tape acceptable to his own computer and the Russian character printer began to spew out yards of Russian text and international figures. When Larry translated the Russian it proved to be oddly uninformative – brief notes on what the computer was doing at the time, but not why it was doing it. I mean, if you read a knitting pattern and find 'knit 2, purl 1', that doesn't tell you if you're knitting a body-belt for a midget or a sweater for your hulking Rugby-playing boy-friend. And that's not really such a good analogy because if you're knitting you know you're knitting, while a computer program could be doing damned nearly anything from analysing the use of the subjunctive in Shakespeare's *Titus Andronicus* to designing a trajectory for a space shot to Pluto. The field was wide open so a selection of assorted boffins was brought in.

All this was beyond me so I left them to it. I had other things on my mind, the principal one being that Penny had cabled me, saying that she was returning and giving her flight number and time of arrival at Heathrow. I felt a lot better immediately because it meant she expected me to meet her, and she wouldn't have done it if her decision had not been in my favour.

When I met her she was tired. She had flown from Los Angeles to New York, stopped for a few hours only to see Gillian, and then flown the Atlantic. She was suffering from jet lag and her stomach and glands were about nine hours out of kilter. I took her to the hotel where I had booked her a room; she appreciated that, not wanting to move into an empty flat with nothing in the refrigerator.

I joined her in a coffee before she retired to her room, and she told me that the operation on Gillian was going well and would I pass that message on to Michaelis. She smiled. 'Gillian particularly wants him to know.'

I grinned. 'We mustn't hinder the marriage of true minds.'

She talked briefly about what she had been doing in California and of a visit to the Harvard School of Medical Studies. 'They're doing good work there with PV40,' she said.

'What's that?'

'A virus – harmless to human beings.' She laughed. 'I keep forgetting you're not acquainted with the field.'

I said nothing to her about the model railway, although she would have to be told eventually. We couldn't just expropriate the knowledge to be found there – whatever it was – although the legal position would seem to be confused. The department had bought it, but whether the information it held came under the Copyright Act or not was something to keep the lawyers happy for years. In any case it was for Ogilvie to make the decision.

But she had just said something that had jerked little man Hunch out of bed and he was yelling his head off. I said, 'Did you talk over your work much with your father?'

'All the time,' she said.

'It doesn't seem a subject that would interest a man primarily versed in catalysts,' I said casually. 'Did he know much about it?'

'Quite a lot,' she said. 'Daddy was a man with a wide range of interests. He made one or two suggestions which really surprised Lummy when they worked in the laboratory.' She finished her coffee. 'I'm for bed. I feel I could sleep the clock around.'

I saw her to the lift, kissed her before she went up, then went back to the office at speed. Ogilvie wasn't in, so I went to see Harrington and found him short-tempered and tending to be querulous. 'The man who put these programs together was either quite mad or a genius. Either way we can't make sense out of them.'

Harrington knew nothing about Ashton and I didn't enlighten him beyond saying, 'I think you can discount insanity. What can you tell me about the programs – as a whole?'

'As a whole?' He frowned. 'Well, they seem to fall into two groups – a group of five and a group of seven. The group of seven is the later group.'

'Later! How do you know?'

'When we put them through the computer the last thing that comes out is a date. The first five seem to be totally unrelated to each other, but the group of seven appear to be linked in some way. They all use the same weird system of mathematics.'

I thought hard for some minutes and made a few calculations. 'Let me guess. The first of the group of seven begins about 1971, and the whole lot covers a period finishing, say, about six months ago.'

'Not bad,' said Harrington. 'You must know something I don't.'

'Yes,' I said. 'I rather think I do.'

I sought Ogilvie again and found he had returned. He took one look at my face, and said. 'You look like the cat that swallowed the canary. Why so smug?'

I grinned and sat down. 'Do you remember the time we had a late night session trying to figure what Ashton would have been working on? We agreed he would keep on theorizing, but we couldn't see what he could theorize about.'

'I remember,' said Ogilvie. 'And I still can't. What's more, neither can Harrington and he's actually working on the material itself.'

'You said he wouldn't be working in atomics because he hadn't kept up with the field.'

'He didn't keep up in any field with the exception of

catalytic chemistry, and there he was mainly reworking his old ideas – nothing new.'

'You're wrong,' I said flatly.

'I don't see what he could have kept up in. We know the books he bought and read, and there was nothing.'

I said softly, 'What about the books Penny bought?'

Ogilvie went quite still. 'What are you getting at?'

'Penny said something just before she went to the States which slipped right past me. We were talking about some of the complications of her work and most of it was over my head. We were in her home at the time, and she said she was so used to talking with her father in that room she'd forgotten I was a layman.'

'The implication being that Ashton wasn't?'

'That's it. It came up again just now and this time it clicked. I've just been talking to Harrington, and he tells me there's a group of seven linked programs. I made an educated guess at the period they covered and I got it right first time. They started when Penny first began her graduate work in genetics. I think Ashton educated himself in genetics alongside his daughter. This morning Penny said he'd made suggestions which surprised Lumsden when they worked in the laboratory. Now, Penny works with Lumsden, one of the top men in the field. Everything he knew and learned she could pass on to Ashton. She read the relevant journals – and so did Ashton; she attended seminars and visited other laboratories – and passed everything back to Ashton. She could have been doing it quite unconsciously, glad to have someone near to her with whom she could discuss her work. He was right in the middle of some of the most exciting developments in science this century, and I'm not discounting atomic physics. What's more likely than that a man like Ashton should think and theorize about genetics?'

'You've made your point,' said Ogilvie. 'But what to do about it?'

'Penny must be brought in, of course.'

He shook his head. 'Not immediately. I can't make that decision off the cuff. The problem lies in the very fact that she *is* Ashton's daughter. She's intelligent enought to ask why her father should have considered it necessary to hide what he's doing, and that, as the Americans say, opens up a can of worms, including his early history and how and why he died. I doubt if the Minister would relish an angry young woman laying siege to his office or, much worse, talking to newspaper reporters. I'll have to ask him for a decision on this one.'

I said, 'You can't possibly suppress a thing like this.'

'Who is talking about suppressing it?' he said irritably. 'I'm merely saying we'll have to use tact in handling it. You'd better leave it with me. You haven't said anything to her about it, have you?'

'No.'

'Good. You've done well on this, Malcolm. You'll get the credit for it when the time comes.'

I wasn't looking for credit, and I had an uneasy feeling that Ogilvie wasn't being quite straight with me. It was the first time I had ever felt that about him, and I didn't like it.

I saw Penny the following afternoon, by arrangement, at University College. As I walked down the corridor towards her office the door of Lumsden's office opened and Cregar came out so that I had to sidestep smartly to avoid barging into him. He looked at me in astonishment and demanded, 'What are you doing here?'

Apart from the fact that it wasn't any of his business, I still felt sore enough at the roasting he had given me at the committee meeting to be inclined to give him a sharp answer. Instead I said, mildly enough, 'Just visiting.'

'That's no answer.'

'Perhaps that's because I neither liked the question nor the way it was put.'

He boggled a bit then said, 'You're aware the Ashton case is closed?'

'Yes.'

'Then I'll have to ask you again – what are you doing here?'

I said deliberately, 'The moon will turn into green cheese the day I have to ask your permission to visit my fiancée.'

'Oh!' he said inadequately. 'I'd forgotten.' I really think it had slipped his memory. Something in his eyes changed; belligerence gave way to speculation. 'Sorry about that. Yes, you're going to marry Dr Ashton, aren't you?'

At that moment I didn't know whether I was or not, but I wouldn't give Cregar that satisfaction. 'Yes, I am.'

'When is the wedding to be?'

'Soon, I hope.'

'Ah, yes.' He lowered his voice. 'A word to the wise. You are aware, of course, that it would be most undesirable if Miss Ashton should ever know what happened in Sweden.'

'Under the circumstances I'm the last person likely to tell her,' I said bitterly.

'Yes. A sad and strange business – very strange. I hope you'll accept my apology for my rather abrupt manner just now. And I hope you'll accept my good wishes for your future married life.'

'Of course – and thank you.'

'And now you must excuse me.' He turned and went back into Lumsden's office.

As I walked up the corridor I speculated on Cregar's immediate assumption that my presence in University College was linked to the Ashton case. Granted that he had genuinely forgotten I was to marry Penny, then what possible link could there be?

I escorted Penny to Fortnum's where she restocked her depleted larder. Most of the order was to be sent, but we took enough so that she could prepare a simple dinner for two. That evening, in the flat, as we started on the soup she said, 'I'm going to Scotland tomorrow.'

'With Lumsden?'

'He's busy and can't come. The extra time I spent in America has thrown our schedule out a bit.'

'When will you be back?'

'I don't think I'll be away as much as a week. Why?'

'There's a new play starting at the Haymarket next Tuesday which I thought you might like to see. Alec Guinness. Shall I book seats?'

She thought for a moment. 'I'll be back by then. Yes, I'd like that. I haven't been in a theatre for God knows how long.'

'Still having trouble in Scotland?'

'It's not really trouble. Just a difference of opinion.'

After dinner she made coffee, and said, 'I know you don't like brandy. There's a bottle of scotch in the cabinet.'

I smiled. 'That's thoughtful of you.'

'But I'll have a brandy.'

I poured the drinks and took them over to the coffee table. She brought in the coffee, and then we sat together on the settee. She poured two black coffees, and said quietly, 'When would you like us to get married, Malcolm?'

That was the night the new carpet became badly coffee-stained, and it was the night we went to bed together for the first time.

It had been quite long enough.

33

The rest of the week went slowly. Penny went to Scotland and I booked a couple of seats at the Haymarket Theatre. I also made enquiries into exactly how one gets married; it hadn't come up before. I felt pretty good.

Ogilvie was uncommunicative. He wasn't around the office much during the next few days and, even when he was, he didn't want to see me. He asked how I was getting on with the investigation of Benson and made no comment when I said I was stuck. Twice thereafter he refused to see me when I requested an audience. That worried me a little.

I checked with Harrington to find how he was doing and to see if any genetics experts had been brought in – not by asking outright but by tactful skating around the edges. No new boffins were on the job and certainly no biologists of any kind. That worried me, too, and I wondered why Ogilvie was dragging his heels.

Harrington's temper was becoming worse. 'Do you know what I've found?' he asked rhetorically. 'This joker is using Hamiltonian quaternions!' He made it sound like a heinous offence of the worst kind.

'Is that bad?'

He stared at me and echoed, 'Bad! No one, I repeat – *no one* – has used Hamiltonian quaternions since 1915 when tensor analysis was invented. It's like using a pick and shovel when you have a bulldozer available.'

I shrugged. 'If he used these Hamilton's whatsits he'd have a sound reason.'

Harrington stared at a print-out of the computer program with an angry and baffled expression. 'Then I wish I knew what the hell it is.' He went back to work.

And so did I, but my trouble was that I didn't know what to do. Benson was a dead issue – there seemed to be no possible way of getting a line on him. Ogilvie seemed to have lost interest, and since I didn't want to twiddle my thumbs in Kerr's section, I spent a lot of time in my flat catching up on my reading and waiting for Tuesday.

At the weekend I rang Penny hoping she'd be back but got no answer. I spent a stale weekend and on the Monday morning I rang Lumsden and asked if he'd heard from her.

'I spoke to her on Thursday,' he said. 'She hoped to be back in London for the weekend.'

'She wasn't.'

'Well, perhaps she'll be back today. If she comes in is there a message for her?'

'Not really. Just tell her I'll meet her at home at seven tomorrow evening.'

'I'll tell her,' said Lumsden, and rang off.

I went to the office feeling faintly dissatisfied and was lucky to catch Ogilvie at the lift. As we went up I asked bluntly, 'Why haven't you given Harrington a geneticist to work with him?'

'The situation is still under review,' he said blandly.

'I don't think that's good enough.'

He gave me a sideways glance. 'I shouldn't have to remind you that you don't make policy here,' he said sharply. He added in a more placatory tone, 'The truth is that a lot of pressure is being brought to bear on us.'

I was tired of framing my words in a diplomatic mode. 'Who from – and why?' I asked shortly.

'I'm being asked to give up the computer programs to another department.'

'Before being interpreted?'

He nodded. 'The pressure is quite strong. The Minister may accede to the request.'

'Who the devil would want . . . ?' I stopped and remembered something Ogilvie had let drop. 'Don't tell me it's Cregar again?'

'Why should you think . . .' He paused and reconsidered. 'Yes, it's Cregar. A persistent devil, isn't he?'

'Jesus!' I said. 'You know how he'll use it. You said he was into bacteriological warfare techniques. If there's anything important in there he'll use it himself and hush it up.'

The lift stopped and someone got in. Ogilvie said, 'I don't think we should discuss this further.' On arrival at our floor he strode away smartly.

Tuesday came and at seven in the evening I was at Penny's flat ringing the bell. There was no answer. I sat in my car outside the building for over an hour but she didn't arrive. She had stood me up without so much as a word. I didn't use the tickets for the show but went home feeling unhappy and depressed. I think even then I had an inkling that there was something terribly wrong. Little bits of a complicated jigsaw were fitting themselves together at the back of my mind but still out of reach of conscious reasoning power. The mental itch was intolerable.

The next morning, as early as was decent, I rang Lumsden again. He answered my questions good-humouredly enough at first, but I think he thought I was being rather a pest. No, Penny had not yet returned. No, he had not spoken to her since Thursday. No, it wasn't at all unusual; her work could be more difficult than she expected.

I said, 'Can you give me her telephone number in Scotland?'

There was a silence at my ear, then Lumsden said, 'Er . . . no – I don't think I can do that.'

'Why? Haven't you got it?'

'I have it, but I'm afraid it isn't available to you.'

I blinked at that curious statement, and filed it away for future reference. 'Then can you ring her and give her a message?'

Lumsden paused again, then said reluctantly, 'I suppose I can do that. What's the message?'

'It'll need an answer. Ask her where she put the letters from her father. I need to know.' As far as I knew that would be perfectly meaningless.

'All right,' he said. 'I'll pass it on.'

'Immediately,' I persisted. 'I'll wait here until you ring me back.' I gave him my number.

When I sorted the morning's post I found a slip from British Road Services; they had tried to deliver a package but to no avail because I was out – would I collect said package from the depot at Paddington? I put the slip in my wallet.

Lumsden rang nearly an hour later. 'She says she doesn't know which particular letters you mean.'

'Does she? That's curious. How did she sound?'

'I didn't speak to her myself; she wasn't available on an outside line. But the message was passed to her.'

I said, 'Professor Lumsden, I'd like you to ring again and speak to her personally this time. I . . .'

He interrupted. 'I'll do no such thing. I haven't the time to waste acting as messenger-boy.' There was a clatter and he was cut off.

I sat for a quarter of an hour wondering if I was making something out of nothing, chasing after insubstantial wisps as a puppy might chase an imaginary rabbit. Then I drove to Paddington to collect the package and was rather shattered to find that it was my own suitcase. Captain Morelius had taken his time in sending my possessions from Sweden.

I put it in the boot of my car and opened it. There seemed to be nothing missing although after such a length of time, I couldn't be sure. What was certain was that Swedish Intelligence would have gone over everything with a microscope. But it gave me an idea. I went into Paddington Station and rang the Ashton house.

Mary Cope answered, and I said, 'This is Malcolm Jaggard. How are you, Mary?'

'I'm very well, sir.'

'Mary, has anything arrived at the house from Sweden? Suitcases or anything like that?'

'Why, yes, sir. Two suitcases came on Monday. I've been trying to ring Miss Penny to ask her what to do with them, but she hasn't been at home – I mean in that flat in London.'

'What did you do with them?'

'I put them in a box-room.'

There were traffic jams on the way to Marlow. The congestion on the Hammersmith by-pass drove me to a distraction of impatience, but after that the road was open and I had my foot on the floor as I drove down the M4. The gates of the house stood open. Who would think Mary Cope might need protection?

She answered the door at my ring, and I said immediately, 'Has anyone else asked about those cases?'

'Why, no, sir.'

'Where are they?'

'I'll show you.' She led me upstairs by the main staircase and up another flight and along a corridor. The house was bare and empty and our footsteps echoed. She opened a door. 'I put them in here out of the way.'

I regarded the two suitcases standing in the middle of the empty room, then turned to her and smiled. 'You may congratulate me, Mary. Penny and I are getting married.'

'Oh, I wish you all the best in the world,' she said.

'So I don't think you'll have to stay in London, after all. We'll probably have a house in the country somewhere. Not as big as this one, though.'

'Would you want me to stay?'

'Of course,' I said. 'Now, I'd like to look at this stuff alone. Do you mind?'

She looked at me a shade doubtfully, then made up her mind. So many strange things had happened in that house that one more wouldn't make any difference. She nodded and went out, closing the door behind her.

Both cases were locked. I didn't trouble with lock-picking

but sprung open the catches with a knife. The first case was Ashton's and contained the little he had taken with him on the run from Stockholm. It also contained the clothes he had been wearing; the overcoat, jacket and shirt were torn – but there was no trace of blood. Everything had been cleaned.

It was Benson's case I was really interested in. In this two-cubic-foot space was all we had left of Howard Greatorex Benson, and if I couldn't find anything here then it was probable that the Ashton case would never be truly solved.

I emptied the case and spread everything on the floor. Overcoat, suit, fur hat, underwear, shirt, socks, shoes – everything he had died with. The fur hat had a hole in the back big enough to put my fist through. I gave everything a thorough going-over, aware that Captain Morelius would have done the same, and found nothing – no microfilm, beloved of the thriller writers, no hidden pockets in the clothing, nothing at all out of the usual.

There was a handful of Swedish coins and a slim sheaf of currency in a wallet. Also in the wallet were some stamps, British and Swedish; two newspaper cuttings, both of book reviews in English, and a scribbled shopping-list. Nothing there for me unless smoked salmon, water biscuits and Mocha coffee held a hidden meaning, which I doubted.

I was about to drop the wallet when I saw the silk lining was torn. Closer inspection showed it was not a tear but a cut, probably made by a razor blade. Captain Morelius left nothing to chance at all. I inserted my finger between the lining and the outer case and encountered a piece of paper. Gently I teased it out, then took my find to the window.

It was a letter:

TO WHOM IT MAY CONCERN

Howard Greatorex Benson is the bearer of this letter. Should his *bona fides* be doubted in any way the undersigned should be consulted immediately before further action is taken with regard to the bearer.

Stapled to the letter was a passport-type photograph of Benson, a much younger man than the Benson I remembered but still with the damaged features and the scar on the cheek. He looked to be in his early thirties. Confirmation of this came from the date of the letter – 4 January, 1947. At the bottom of the letter was an address and a telephone number; the address was in Mayfair and the number was in the old style with both letters and digits, long since defunct. The letter was signed by James Pallson.

The itch at the back of my mind was now assuaged, the jigsaw puzzle was almost complete. Although a few minor pieces were missing, enough pieces were assembled to show the picture, and I didn't like what I saw. I scanned the letter again and wondered what Morelius had made of it, then put it into my wallet and went downstairs.

I telephoned Ogilvie but he was out, so after making my farewell to Mary Cope I drove back to London, going immediately to University College. Aware that Lumsden might refuse to see me, I avoided the receptionist and went straight to his office and went in without knocking.

He looked up and frowned in annoyance as he saw me. 'What the devil . . . I won't be badgered like this.'

'Just a few words, Professor.'

'Now look here,' he snapped, 'I have work to do, and I haven't time to play post office between two love-birds.'

I strode to his desk and pushed the telephone towards him. 'Ring Penny.'

'I will not.' He picked up the card I flicked on to the desk, then said, 'I see. Not just a simple policeman, after all. But I can't see this makes any difference.'

I said, 'Where's the laboratory?'

'In Scotland.'

'Where in Scotland?'

'I'm sorry. I'm not at liberty to say.'

'Who runs it?'

He shrugged. 'Some government department, I believe.'

'What's being done there?'

'I really don't know. Something to do with agriculture, so I was told.'

'Who told you?'

'I can't say.'

'Can't or won't?' I held his eye for a moment and he twitched irritably. 'You don't really believe that guff about agriculture, do you? That wouldn't account for the secretive way you're behaving. What's so bloody secret about agricultural research? Cregar told you it was agriculture and you accepted it as a sop to your conscience, but you never really believed it. You're not as naïve as that.'

'We'll leave my conscience to me,' he snapped.

'And you're welcome to it. What's Penny doing there?'

'Giving general technical assistance.'

'Laboratory design for the handling of pathogens,' I suggested.

'That kind of thing.'

'Does she know Cregar is behind it?'

'You're the one who brought up Cregar,' said Lumsden. 'I didn't.'

'What did Cregar do to twist your arm? Did he threaten to cut off your research funds? Or was there a subtly-worded letter from a Cabinet Minister suggesting much the same thing? Co-operate with Cregar or else.' I studied him in silence for a moment. 'That doesn't really matter – but did Penny know of Cregar's involvement?'

'No,' he said sullenly.

'And she didn't know what the laboratory was for, but she was beginning to have suspicions. She had a row with you.'

'You seem to know it all,' said Lumsden tiredly, and shrugged. 'You're right in most of what you say.'

I said, 'Where is she?'

He looked surprised. 'At the laboratory. I thought we'd established that.'

'She was very worried about safety up there, wasn't she?'

'She was being emotioinal about it. And Cregar was pushing Carter hard. He wants results.'

'Who is Carter?'

'The Chief Scientific Officer.'

I pointed to the telephone. 'I'll lay you a hundred pounds to a bent farthing that you won't be able to talk to her.'

He hesitated for a long time before he picked up the telephone and began to dial. Although he was being niggly on secrecy, on security he was lousy. As he dialled I watched his finger and memorized the number. 'Professor Lumsden here. I'd like to speak to Dr Ashton. Yes, I'll hang on.'

He put his hand over the mouthpiece. 'They've gone to call her. They think she's in her room.'

'Don't bet on it.'

Lumsden hung on to the telephone for a long time, then suddenly said, 'Yes? . . . I see . . . the mainland. Well, ask her to ring me as soon as she comes back. I'll be in my office.' He put down the telephone and said dully, 'They say she's gone to the mainland.'

'So it's on an island.'

'Yes.' He looked up and his eyes were haunted. 'They could be right, you know.'

'Not a chance,' I said. 'Something has happened up there. You referred to your conscience; I'll leave you with it. Good day, Professor Lumsden.'

I strode into Ogilvie's outer office, said to his secretary, 'Is the boss in?' and breezed on through without waiting for an answer. There were going to be no more closed doors as far as I was concerned.

Ogilvie was just as annoyed as Lumsden at having his office invaded. 'I didn't send for you,' he said coldly.

'I've cracked Benson,' I said. 'He was Cregar's man.'

Ogilvie's eyes opened wide. 'I don't believe it.'

I tossed the letter before him. 'Signed, sealed and delivered. That was written on the fourth of January, 1947, the day Benson was discharged from the army, and signed by the Honourable James Pallson who is now Lord Cregar. Christ, the man has no honour in him. Do you realize, that when Ashton and Benson skipped to Sweden and Cregar was doing his holier-than-thou bit, he knew where they were all the time. The bastard has been laughing at us.'

Ogilvie shook his head. 'No, it's too incredible.'

'What's so incredible about it? That letter says Benson has been Cregar's man for the past thirty years. I'd say Cregar made a deal with Ashton. Ashton was free to do as he wanted – to sink or swim in the capitalist sea – but only on condition he had a watchdog attached: Benson. And when the reorganization came and Cregar lost responsibility for Ashton he conveniently forgot to tell you about Benson. It also explains why Benson was lost from the computer files.'

Ogilvie drew in his breath. 'It fits,' he admitted. 'But it leaves a lot still to be explained.'

'You'll get your explanation from Cregar,' I said savagely. 'Just before I skin him and nail his hide to the barn door.'

'You'll stay away from Cregar,' he said curtly. 'I'll handle him.'

'That be damned for a tale. You don't understand. Penny Ashton has gone missing and Cregar has something to do with it. It will take more than you to keep me off Cregar's back.'

'What's all this?' He was bewildered.

I told him, then said, 'Do you know where this laboratory is?'

'No.'

I took a card from my wallet and dropped it on the desk. 'A telephone number. The post office won't tell me anything about it because it's unlisted. Do something.'

He glanced at the card but didn't pick it up. He said slowly, 'I don't know . . .'

I cut in. 'I know something. That letter is enough to ruin Cregar, but I can't wait. Don't stop me. Just give me what

I need and I'll give you more than that letter – I'll give you Cregar's head on a platter. But I'm not going to wait too long.'

He looked at me thoughtfully, then picked up the card and the telephone simultaneously. Five minutes later he said two words. 'Cladach Duillich.'

34

Cladach Duillich was a hard place to get to. It was one of the Summer Isles, a scattering of rocks in an indentatiion of the North Minch into Ross and Cromarty. The area is a popular haunt of biological dicers with death. Six miles to the south of Cladach Duillich lies Gruinard Island, uninhabited and uninhabitable. In 1942 the biological warfare boys made a trifling mistake and Gruinard was soaked with anthrax – a hundred years' danger. No wonder the Scots want devolution with that sort of foolishness emanating from the south.

I flew to Dalcross, the airport for Inverness, and there hired a car in which I drove the width of Scotland to Ullapool at the head of Loch Broom. It was a fine day; the sun was shining; the birds singing and the scenery magnificent – all of which left me cold because I was trying to make good speed on a road which is called in Scotland 'Narrow, Class 1 (with passing places)'. I felt with a depressing certainty that time was a commodity which was running out fast.

It was latish in the day when I arrived in Ullapool. Cladach Duillich lay twelve miles further, out in the bay; say a four hour round trip for a local fishing boat. I dickered with a couple of fishermen but none was willing to take me out at that time. The sun was an hour from setting, clouds were building up in the west, and a raw wind blew down the narrow loch, ruffling water which had turned iron grey. I made a tentative deal with a man called Robbie Ferguson to take me out to the island at eight the next morning, weather permitting.

It was not yet the tourist season so I found a room in a

pub quite easily. That evening I sat in the bar listening to the local gossip and putting in a word or two myself, not often but often enough to stake a conversational claim when I decided to do a small quiz on Cladach Duillich.

It was evident that the rising tide of Scottish nationalism was in full rip in the West Highlands. There was talk of English absentee landlords and of 'Scottish' oil and of the ambivalent attitude of the Scottish Labour Party, all uttered in tones of amused and rather tired cynicism as though these people had lost faith in the promises of politicians. There was not much of it, just enough to spice the talk of fishing and the weather, but if I had been a bland habitué of the Westminster corridors of power it would have been enough to scare the hell out of me. Ullapool, it seemed, was further removed from London than Kalgoorlie, Australia.

I finished my half-pint of beer and switched to Scotch, asking the barman which he recommended. The man next to me turned. 'The Talisker's not so bad,' he offered. He was a tall, lean man in his mid-fifties with a craggy face and the soft-set mouth found in Highlanders. He spoke in that soft West Highland accent which is about as far from Harry Lauder as you can get.

'Then that's what I'll have. Will you join me?'

He gave me a speculative look, then smiled. 'I don't see why not. You'll be from the south, I take it. It's early for folk like you.'

I ordered two large Taliskers. 'What sort am I, then?'

'A tourist, maybe?'

'Not a tourist – a journalist.'

'Is it so? Which paper?'

'Any that'll publish me. I'm a freelance. Can you tell me anything about Gruinard Island?'

He chuckled, and shook his head. 'Och, not again? Every year we get someone asking about Gruinard; the Island of Death they used to call it. It's all been written, man; written into the ground. There's nothing new in that.'

I shrugged. 'A good story is still a good story to anyone who hasn't heard it. There's a rising generation which thinks of 1942 as being in the Dark Ages. I've met kids who think Hitler was a British general. But perhaps you're right. Anything else of interest around here?'

'What would interest an English newspaper in Ullapool? There's no oil here; that's on the east coast.' He looked into his whisky glass thoughtfully. 'There's the helicopter which comes and goes and no one knowing why. Would that interest you?'

'It might,' I said. 'An oil company chopper?'

'Could be, could be. But it lands on one of the islands. I've seen it myself.'

'Which island?'

'Out in the bay – Cladach Duillich. It's just a wee rock with nothing much on it. I doubt if the oil is there. They put up a few buildings but no drilling rig.'

'Who put up the buildings?'

'They say the government rented the island from an English lord. Wattie Stevenson went over in his boat once, just to pass the time of day, you know, and to say that when the trouble came there'd always be someone in Ullapool to help. But they wouldn't as much as let him set foot on the rock. Not friendly neighbours at all.'

'What sort of trouble was your friend expecting?'

'The weather, you understand. The winter storms are very bad. It's said the waves pass right over Cladach Duillich. That's how it got its name.'

I frowned. 'I don't understand that.'

'Ah, you haven't the Gaelic. Well, long ago there was a fisherman out of Coigach and his boat sank in a storm on the other side of the island out there. So he swam and he swam and he finally got ashore and thought he was safe. But he was drowned all the same, poor man, because the shore was Cladach Duillich. The water came right over. Cladach Duillich in the English would be the Sad Shore.'

If what I thought was correct it was well named. 'Do the people on Cladach Duillich ever come ashore here?'

'Not at all. I haven't seen a one of them. They fly south in the helicopter and no one knows where it goes or where it comes from. Not a penny piece do they spend in Ullapool. Very secret folk they are. There's just one landing place on Cladach Duillich and they've put up a big notice about trespassers and what will be done to them.'

I noticed that his glass was empty and wondered when he'd sunk the whisky. He must have done it when I blinked. I said, 'Have another, Mr . . . er . . .'

'You'll have one with me.' He signalled to the barman, then said, 'My name is Archie Ferguson and it's my brother who'll be taking you out to Cladach Duillich tomorrow morn.' He smiled sardonically at my evident discomfiture, and added, 'But I doubt if you'll set foot there.'

'I'm Malcolm Jaggard,' I said. 'And I think I will.'

'Malcolm's a good Scots name,' said Ferguson. 'I'll drink to your success, anyway; whatever it may be.'

'There's certainly something odd about the place,' I said. 'Do you think it's another Gruinard?'

Ferguson's face altered and for a moment he looked like the wrath of Almighty God. 'It had better not be so,' he said sternly. 'If we thought it was we would take the fire to it.'

I chewed that over together with my dinner, then made a telephone call – to Cladach Duillich. A voice said, 'How can I help you?'

'I'd like to speak to Dr Ashton. My name is Malcolm Jaggard.'

'Just a moment. I'll see if she's available.'

There was a four minute silence, then another voice said, 'I'm sorry, Mr Jaggard, but I'm told Dr Ashton went to the mainland and is not yet back.'

'Where on the mainland?'

There was a pause. 'Where are you speaking from, Mr Jaggard?'

'From London. Why?'

He didn't answer the question. 'She went to Ullapool – that's our local metropolis. She said she'd like to stretch her legs; there's not much scope for walking where we are. And she wanted to shop for a few things. May I ask how you got our number?'

'Dr Ashton gave it to me. When do you expect her back?'

'Oh, I don't know. The weather has closed in, so I don't think she'll be back until tomorrow morning. You could speak to her then.'

'Where would she stay in Ullapool? I don't know the place.'

'I really couldn't say, Mr Jaggard. But she'll be back tomorrow with the boat.'

'I see. May I ask who I'm speaking to?'

'I'm Dr Carter.'

'Thank you, Dr Carter. I'll ring tomorrow.'

As I put down the telephone I reflected that someone was lying – other than myself – and I didn't think it was Archie Ferguson. But to make sure I went into the bar and found him talking to Robbie, his brother. I joined them. 'Excuse me for butting in.'

'That's all right,' said Ferguson. 'I was just talking over with Robbie your chances of getting out to Cladach Duillich the morrow's morn.'

I looked at Robbie. 'Is there any doubt of it?'

'I think there'll be a wee blow,' he siaid. 'The glass is dropping as the weather forecast said. Have you a strong stomach, Mr Jaggard?'

'Strong enough.'

Archie Ferguson laughed. 'You've been talking to them! How?'

'By telephone – how else?'

'Aye,' said Robbie. 'They had the cable laid.' He shook his head. 'Awful expensive.'

‘A man there told me a woman came ashore today from Cladach Duillich – here in Ullapool. She’s about five feet eight inches, dark hair, age twent . . .’

Robbie interrupted. ‘How did she come?’

‘By boat.’

‘Then she didn’t come,’ he said positively. ‘All the comings and going are by that bluidy helicopter. There’s no boat on Cladach Duillich.’

‘Are you sure?’

‘O’ course I’m sure. I pass the place twice a day, most days. You can take my word – there’s no boat.’

I had to make sure of it. ‘Well, supposing she came anyway. Where would she stay in Ullapool?’

‘Ullapool’s not all that big,’ said Archie. ‘If she’s here at all we can put our hands on her – in a manner o’ speaking, that is. What would be the lassie’s name?’

‘Ashton – Penelope Ashton.’

‘Rest easy, Mr Jaggard. You’ll know within the hour.’ He smiled genially at his brother. ‘Do you not smell something awful romantic, Robbie?’

35

The wind whistled about my ears as I stood on the pier at eight next morning. The sky was slate-grey and so was the loch, stippled with whitecaps whipped up by the wind. Below me Robbie Ferguson's boat pitched violently, the rubber tyre fenders squealing as they were compressed and rubbed on the stone wall. It looked much too fragile to be taken out on such a day, but Robbie seemed unconcerned. He had taken the cover off the engine and was swinging on a crank.

Beside me, Archie Ferguson said, 'So you think the young lady is still on Cladach Duillich?'

'I do.'

He pulled his coat closer about him. 'Maybe we're wrong about the government,' he said. 'Could this be one of those queer religious groups we're importing from America these days? Moonies or some such? I've heard some remarkably funny things about them.'

'No, it's not that.' I looked at my watch. 'Mr Ferguson, could you do me a favour?'

'If I can.'

I estimated times. 'If I'm not back in eight hours – that's by four this afternoon – I want you to get the police and come looking for me.'

He thought about it for a moment. 'No harm in that. What if Robbie comes back and you don't?'

'Same thing applies. They might spin Robbie a yarn, tell him I've decided to stay. They'll be lying, but he's to accept the lie, come back here, and raise the alarm.'

Below, the diesel engine spluttered into life and settled down into a slow and steady thumping. Archie said, 'You know, Malcolm Jaggard, I don't believe you're a journalist at all.'

I took a card from my wallet and gave it to him. 'If I don't come back ring that number. Get hold of a man called Ogilvie and tell him about it.'

He studied the card. 'McCulloch and Ross – and Ogilvie. It seems we Scots have taken over the City of London.' He looked up. 'But you look less like a financier than you do a journalist. What's really going on out there on Cladach Duillich?'

'We spoke about it last night,' I said. 'And you talked of fire.'

A bleakness came over him. 'The government would do that again?'

'Governments are made of men. Some men would do that.'

'Aye, and some men can pay for it.' He looked at me closely. 'Malcolm Jaggard, when you come back you and I are going to have a bit of a talk. And you can tell yon laddies on Cladach Duillich that if you don't come back we'll be bringing the fire to them. A great cleanser is fire.'

'Stay out of it,' I said. 'It's a job for the police.'

'Don't be daft, man. Would the police go against the government? You leave this to me.' He looked down into the boat. 'Away with you; Robbie is waiting. And I'll away and have a talk with a few of my friends.'

I didn't argue with him. I climbed down the iron ladder which was slippery with water and seaweed and tried to time my drop into the boat to coincide with its erratic pitching. I fumbled it but was saved from sprawling full length by Robbie's strong arm.

He looked me up and down, then shook his head. 'You'll freeze, Mr Jaggard.' He turned and rummaged in a locker and brought out a seaman's guernsey. 'This'll keep you warm, and this – ' he gave me a pair of trousers and an anorak, both waterproof – 'this'll keep you dry.'

When I had put them on he said, 'Now sit you down and

be easy.' He went forward, walking as easily in that tossing boat as another man would walk a city pavement. He cast off the forward line, then walked back, seemingly unconcerned that the bow was swinging in a great arc. As he passed the engine he pushed over a lever with his boot, then dexterously cast off the stern line. The throbbing note of the engine deepened and we began to move away from the pier wall. Robbie was standing with the tiller between his knees, looking forward and steering by swaying motions of his body while he coiled the stern line into a neat skein.

The wind strengthened as we got out into the loch and the waves were bigger. The wind was from the north-west and we plunged into the teeth of it. As the bow dipped downwards sheets of spray were blown aft and I appreciated the waterproofing. As it was, I knew I'd be thoroughly drenched by the time we got to Cladach Duillich.

Presently Robbie sat down, controlling the tiller with one booted foot. He pointed, and said, 'The Coigach shore.'

I ducked a lump of spray. 'What sort of man is your brother?'

'Archie?' Robbie thought a bit and then shrugged. 'He's my brother.'

'Would you call him a hot-headed man?'

'Archie hot-headed!' Robbie laughed. 'Why, the man's as cold as an iceberg. I'm the laddie in the family to take the chances. Archie weighs everything in a balance before he does anything. Why do you ask?'

'He was talking about what he'd do if I didn't come back from Cladach Duillich.'

'There's one thing certain about my brother – he does what he says he'll do. He's as reliable as death and taxes.'

That was comforting to know. I didn't know what lay ahead on Cladach Duillich, but I knew I wasn't going to get an easy answer. The knowledge that I had a reliable backstop gave me a warm feeling.

I said, 'If I go missing on that bloody bit of rock you'll

take no for an answer. You'll swallow what they tell you, then go back and see your brother.'

He looked at me curiously. 'Are you expecting to disappear?'

'I wouldn't be surprised.'

He wiped the spray from his face. 'I don't ken what this is about, but Archie seems to like you, and that's enough for me. He's a thinker.'

It was a long haul across Annat Bay towards the Summer Isles. The waves were short and deep, and the pitching was combined with rolling, giving a corkscrew motion which was nauseating. Robbie looked at me and grinned. 'We'd better talk; it'll take your mind off your belly. Look, there's Carn nan Sgeir, with Eilean Dubh beyond. That's Black Island in the English.'

'Where's Cladach Duillich?'

'Away the other side of Eilean Dubh. We've a way to go yet.'

'Why don't they keep a boat there? If I lived on an island it's the first thing I'd think of.'

Robbie chuckled. 'You'll see when we get there – but I'll tell you anyway, just for the talking. There's but one place to land and a chancy place it is. There's no protection for boat or man. You can't just tie up as you can at Ullapool Pier. There'd be no boat when you got back if there was anything of a blow. It would be crushed on the rocks. I won't be waiting there for you, you know.'

'Oh? Where will you be?'

'Lying off somewhere within easy reach. There are more boats wrecked on land than at sea. It's the land that kills boats. I'll be doing a wee bit of fishing.'

I looked at the jumbled sea. 'In this!'

'Och, I'm used to it. You give me a time and I'll be there.'

'I'll tell you now. I want exactly two hours ashore.'

'Two hours you'll get,' he said. 'About the boat they haven't got on Cladach Duillich. When those folk first came they had a boat but it got smashed, so they got another and that was smashed. After they lost the third they began to get the idea. Then they thought that if they could take the boat ashore it would be all right, but it's an awful weary job pulling a boat ashore on Cladach Duillich because there's no beach. So they rigged davits just like on a ship and they could take the boat straight up a cliff and out of the water. Then a wave came one night and took the boat and the davits and they were never seen again. After that they gave up.'

'It sounds a grim place.'

'It is – in bad weather. It won't be too bad today.' I looked at the reeling seas and wondered what Robbie called bad weather. He pointed. 'There it is – Cladach Duillich.'

It was just as Archie Ferguson had described it – a wee bit of rock. There were cliffs all around, not high but precipitous, and the sea boiled white underneath them. Off the island was a scattering of rocks like black fangs and I thought the people on Cladach Duillich had been right when they decided this was no place for a boat.

As we drew nearer Robbie said, 'See that ravine? The landing place is at the bottom.'

There was a narrow crack in the cliff face, at the bottom of which the sea seemed to be calmer – relatively speaking. Robbie swung the tiller over sharply to avoid a rock which slid astern three feet off the port quarter, then he swung hard the other way to avoid another. He grinned. 'This is when you hope the engine doesn't pack in. You'd better get right forrard – you'll have to jump for it, and I won't be able to hold her there long.'

I scrambled forward and stood right in the bows as he brought the boat in. Now I saw that the crack in the rock was wider than at first glance and there was a concrete platform built at the bottom. The engine note changed as Robbie throttled back for the final approach. It was an amazing feat, but in that swirling sea with its cross-currents he brought her in so the bow kissed the concrete with a touch as light as a feather. At his shout I jumped and went sprawling as my feet skidded from under me on the weed-covered surface. When I picked myself up the boat was thirty yards off-shore and moving away fast. Robbie waved and I waved back, and then he applied himself to the task of avoiding rocks.

I looked at my surroundings. The first thing I saw was the notice board Archie Ferguson had mentioned. It was weatherbeaten and the paint was peeling and faded but it was still readable.

GOVERNMENT ESTABLISHMENT
Landing is Absolutely Prohibited
By Order

It did not say who had issued the order.

A path led from the concrete platform up the ravine, so I followed it. It climbed steeply and led to a plateau, sparsely grassed, in the centre of which was a group of buildings. They were low concrete structures which had the appearance of military blockhouses, probably because they were windowless. From what had been said about Cladach Duillich they were the only type of building which could survive there.

I had no more time to study the place because a man was approaching at a run. He slowed as he came closer, and said abruptly, 'Can't you read?'

'I can read.'

'Then clear off.'

'The age of miracles is past, friend. Walking on the water has gone out of fashion. The boat's gone.'

'Well, you can't stay here. What do you want?'

'I want to talk to Dr Carter.'

He seemed slightly taken aback, and I studied him as he thought about it. He was big and he had hard eyes and a stubborn jaw. He said, 'What do you want to talk to Dr Carter about?'

'If Dr Carter wants you to know he'll tell you,' I said pleasantly.

He didn't like that but there wasn't much he could do about it. 'Who are you?'

'Same thing applies. You're out of your depth, friend. Let's go and see Çarter.'

'No,' he said curtly. 'You stay here.'

I looked at him coldly. 'Not a chance. I'm wet through and I want to dry out.' I nodded to the buildings. 'Those look as bloody inhospitable as you behave, but I'm willing to bet they're warm and dry inside. Take me to Carter.'

His problem was that he didn't know me or my authority, but I was behaving as though I had a right to be there and making demands. He did as I thought he would and passed the buck. 'All right, follow me. You see Carter and you go nowhere else.'

36

As we walked towards the buildings I looked around at Cladach Duillich. It was not very big – about a third of a mile long and a quarter-mile across. Life had a poor existence on this rock. What grass had managed to gain a roothold was salt resistant marram, growing in crannies where a poor soil had gathered, and even the dandelions were wizened and sickly growths. The seabirds appeared to like it, though; the rocks were white with their droppings and they wheeled overhead screaming at our movements below.

There were three buildings, all identical, and I noted they were connected by enclosed passages. To one side, on a level bit of ground, was a helicopter pad, empty. I was conducted around the corner to one of the buildings and ushered through the doorway, bidden to wait, and then taken through another doorway. I looked back and realized I had gone through an air lock.

We turned sharply left and into a room where a man in a white coat was sitting at a desk and writing on a pad. He was slightly bald, had a thin face and wore bifocals. He looked up and frowned as he saw me, then said to my escort, 'What's this, Max?'

'I found him wandering about loose. He says he wants to see you.'

Carter's attention switched to me. 'Who are you?'

I glanced sideways at Max, and said smoothly, 'Who I am is for your ears only, Dr Carter.'

Carter sniffed. 'More cloak and dagger stuff. All right, Max. I'll take care of this.'

Max nodded and left, and I stripped off the anorak. 'I

hope you don't mind me getting out of this stuff,' I said, as I began to take off the waterproof trousers. 'Too warm for indoors.'

Carter tapped on the desk with his pen. 'All right. Who are you, and what do you want?'

I tossed the trousers aside and sat down. 'I'm Malcolm Jaggard. I've come to see Dr Ashton.'

'Didn't you ring me last night? I told you she wasn't here – she's on the mainland.'

'I know what you told me,' I said evenly. 'You said she'd be back this morning, so I came to see her.'

He gestured. 'You've seen the weather. She wouldn't come over in this.'

'Why not? I did.'

'Well, she hasn't. She's still in Ullapool.'

I shook my head, 'She's not in Ullapool, and she wasn't there last night, either.'

He frowned. 'Look here, when I asked last night you said you were ringing from London.'

'Did I? Must have been force of habit,' I said blandly. 'Does it make a difference where I rang from?'

'Er . . . no.' Carter straightened and squared his shoulders. 'Now, you're not supposed to be here. This establishment is, shall we say, rather hush-hush. If it became known you were here you could be in trouble. Come to that, so could I, so I'll have to ask you to leave.'

'Not without seeing Penny Ashton. She's supposed to be here. Now isn't that a funny thing. I'm where I'm supposed not to be, and she's not where she's supposed to be. How do you account for it?'

'I don't have to account for anything to you.'

'You'll have to account for a lot, Dr Carter, if Penny Ashton doesn't turn up pretty damn quick. How did she get to Ullapool?'

'By boat, of course.'

'But this establishment doesn't have a boat. All journeys are by helicopter.'

He moistened his lips. 'You appear to be taking an unhealthy interest in this place, Mr Jaggard. I warn you that could be dangerous.'

'Are you threatening me, Dr Carter?'

'For any purpose prejudicial to the safety of the State, to approach, inspect or enter any prohibited place, or to – '

'Don't quote the Official Secrets Act at me,' I snapped. 'I probably know it better than you do.'

'I could have you arrested,' he said. 'No warrant is needed.'

'For a simple scientist you appear to know the Act very well,' I observed. 'So you'll know that to arrest me automatically brings in the Director of Public Prosecutions.' I leaned back. 'I doubt if your masters would relish that, seeing that Penny Ashton is missing from here. I told you, you'll have to account for a lot, Dr Carter.'

'But not to you,' he said, and put his hand on the telephone.

'I hope that's to give instructions to have Dr Ashton brought in here.'

A cool and amused voice behind me said, 'But Dr Carter really can't have her brought in here.' I turned my head and saw Cregar standing at the door with Max. Cregar said, 'Doctor, I'll trouble you for the use of your office for a moment. Max, see to Mr Jaggard.'

Carter was palpably relieved and scurried out. Max came over to me and searched me with quick, practised movements. 'No gun.'

'No?' said Cregar. 'Well, that can be rectified if necessary. What could happen to an armed man who breaks into a government establishment, Max?'

'He could get shot,' said Max unemotionally.

'So he could, but that would lead to an official enquiry which might be undesirable. Any other suggestions?'

'There are plenty of cliffs around here,' said Max. 'And the sea's big.'

It was a conversation I could do without. I said, 'Where's Penny Ashton?'

'Oh, she's here – you were quite right about that. You'll see her presently.' Cregar waved his hands as though dismissing a minor problem. 'You're a persistent devil. I almost find it in me to admire you. I could do with a few men of your calibre in my organization. As it is, I'm wondering what to do with you.'

'You'd better not compound your offences,' I said. 'Whatever you do about me, you've already done for yourself. We've linked you with Benson. I wouldn't be surprised if the Minister hasn't already been informed of it.'

The corners of his mouth turned down. 'How could I be linked with Benson? What possible evidence could there be?'

'A letter dated the fourth of January, 1947, carried by Benson and signed by you.'

'A letter,' said Cregar blankly, and looked through me into the past. Comprehension came into his eyes. 'Are you telling me that Benson still carried that damned letter after thirty years?'

'He'd probably forgotten about it – just as you had,' I said. 'It was hidden in the lining of his wallet.'

'A brown calf wallet with a red silk lining?' I nodded and Cregar groaned. 'I gave Benson that wallet thirty years ago. It would seem I tripped myself.'

He bent his head, apparently studying the liverspots on the backs of his hands. 'Where is the letter?' he asked colourlessly.

'The original? Or the twenty photocopies Ogilvie will have already made?'

'I see,' he said softly, and raised his head. 'What were your first thoughts on seeing the letter?'

'I knew you were linked with Ashton because you brought him out of Russia. Now you were linked with Benson, too. I thought of all the odd things that had happened, such as why a gentleman's gentleman should carry a gun, and why you tried to discount the fact he had shot Ashton when we had the meeting on my return from Sweden. It seemed hard to believe he was still your man after thirty years, but I was forced into it.'

Cregar lounged back in his chair and crossed his legs. 'Benson was a good man once, before the Germans got him.'

He paused. 'Of course he wasn't Benson then, he was Jimmy Carlisle and my comrade in British Intelligence during the war. But he lived and died as Benson, so let him remain so. He was captured in a Gestapo round-up in '44 and they sent him to Sachsenhausen, where he stayed until the end of the war. That's where he got his broken nose and his other brutalized features. They beat him with clubs. I'd say they beat his brains out because he was never the same man afterwards.'

He leaned forward, elbows on the desk. 'He was in a mess after the war. He had no family – his father, mother and sister were killed in an air raid – and he had no money apart from a disability pension. His brains were addled and his earning capacity limited. He'd never be any good in our line of work after that, but he deserved well of us, and by 1947 I pulled enough weight to help him, so I offered him the job of shepherd to Chelyuskin – Ashton as he became. It was a sinecure, of course, but he was pathetically grateful. You see, he thought it meant he wasn't finished in his job.'

Cregar took out a packet of cigarettes. 'Are you finding this ancient history interesting?' He held out the packet.

I took a cigarette. 'Very interesting,' I assured him.

'Very well. We switched him into the person of Benson at the same time we switched Chelyuskin to Ashton, then he hung around for a while. When Ashton got going Benson had a job in Ashton's office, and then later he became Ashton's factotum.'

'And Ashton knew what he was?'

'Oh, yes. Benson was the price Ashton had to pay for freedom. I knew that a man with that calibre of mind would not long be content to fiddle around in industry and I wanted to keep tabs on what he was doing.' He smiled. 'Benson was on to quite a good thing. We paid him a retainer and Ashton paid him, too.'

He leaned forward and snapped a gold lighter into flame under my nose. 'When the reorganization came and I lost Ashton to Ogilvie I kept quiet about Benson. In fact, I paid his retainer out of my own pocket. He didn't cost much; the retainer wasn't raised and the erosion in the value of money made Benson dirt cheap. It was an investment for the future which would have paid off but for you.'

I said, 'Did you know Ashton was into genetics?'

'Of course. Benson caught on to that as soon as it started happening. His job was to *know* what Ashton was doing at all times and, being permanently in the house, he could hardly miss. It was an incredible stroke of luck – Ashton becoming interested in genetics, I mean – because after the reorganization I had moved into the biological field myself.' He waved his hand. 'As you have discovered.'

'Ogilvie told me.'

'Ogilvie appears to have told you too much. From what you have let fall he appears to have given you the run of Code Black. Very naughty of him, and something he may regret. I was fortunate enough to be able to put a block on the computer to cover Benson, but evidently it wasn't enough.' He stopped suddenly, and stared at me. 'Even I appear to be telling you too much. You have an ingratiating way with you.'

'I'm a good listener.'

'And I become garrulous as I grow old, a grave failing in a man of our profession.' He looked at his half-smoked cigarette distastefully, stubbed it out, and put his hands flat on the desk. 'I'm at a loss to know how to dispose of you, young Jaggard. Your revelation that Ogilvie has that letter makes my situation most difficult.'

'Yes, he's in a position to blast hell out of you,' I agreed. 'I don't think the Minister will be pleased. I rather think you've put yourself on the retirement list.'

'Very succinctly put. Nevertheless, I will find a way out of the difficulty. I have surmounted difficulties before and I see no reason why I should fail this time. All it takes is applied thought to the study of men's weaknesses.' He slapped his hands together. 'And that is what I must do immediately. Put him somewhere safe, Max.'

I ignored the hand on my shoulder. 'What about Penny Ashton?'

'You will see her in my good time,' said Cregar coldly. 'And only if I think it advisable.'

In my rage I wanted to lash out at him but I couldn't ignore that tightening hand. Max leaned over me. 'No tricks,' he advised. 'I have a gun. You won't see it but it's there.'

So I rose from the chair and went with him. He took me from the office and along a corridor. Because the place was windowless it was almost like being in a submarine; everything was quiet except that the air shivered with the distant rumble of a generator. At the other end of the corridor I saw movement on the other side of a glass partition as a man walked across. He was wearing totally enveloping overalls and his head was hooded.

I had no time to see more because Max stopped and opened a heavy door. 'In there,' he said curtly, so I walked through and he slammed the door, leaving me in total darkness because he had not seen fit to turn on a light. The first thing I did was to explore my prison and arrived at the conclusion that it was an unused refrigerated room. The walls were thick and solid, as was the door, and I soon came to the conclusion that the only way out was to be let out. I sat on the floor in a corner and contemplated possibilities.

It appeared to have been wise to tell Cregar of the letter. Up to then he had primarily been interested in discussing ways and means of transforming me into a corpse safely, but my disclosure that Ogilvie had the letter had put a stopper on that line of thought. But what a ruthless bastard he had turned out to be.

I don't know what makes men like Cregar tick, but there seem to be enough of the bastards around just as there are many Carters eager to help them. Somewhere in the world, I suppose, is the chemist who lovingly mixed a petroleum derivative with a palm oil derivative to produce napthenic acid palmetate, better known as napalm. To do that required a deliberate intellectual effort and a high degree of technical training, and why a man should put his brain to such a use is beyond me. Supervising that chemist would be an American Cregar whose motives are equally baffling, and at the top are the politicians ultimately responsible. Their motive is quite clear, of course: the ruthless grasp of sheer power. But why so many others should be willing to help them is beyond me.

It's hard to know who to blame. Is it the Lumsdens of the world who know what is going on but turn a blind eye, or is it the rest of us who don't know and don't take the trouble to find out? Sometimes I think the world is like a huge ant heap full of insects all busily manufacturing insecticide.

I was in the black room for a long time. The only light came from the luminous dial of my watch which told me of hours ticking away. I was oppressed by the darkness and became claustrophobic and suffered strange fears. I got up and began to walk around the room, keeping to the walls; it was one way of taking exercise. The silence was solid except for the sound of my own movements and a new fear came upon me. What If Cladach Duillich had been abandoned – evacuated? I could stay in that room until the flesh rotted from my bones.

I stopped walking and sat in the corner again. I may have fallen asleep for a while, I don't remember. The hours I spent there are pretty much blanked out in my memory.

But I was aware when the door opened to let in a flood of light as glaring as from arc lamps. I put my hands to my eyes and saw Cregar at the door. He tut-tutted, and said, 'You didn't leave him a light, Max.'

'Must have forgotten,' said Max indifferently.

The light was quite ordinary light shed from fluorescent tubes in the ceiling of the corridor. I got up and went to the door. 'God damn you!' I said to Max.

He stood back a pace and lifted the pistol he held. Cregar said, 'Calm down. It wasn't intentional.' He saw me looking at the pistol. 'That's to warn you not to do anything silly, as well you might. You wanted to see the girl, didn't you? Well, you can see her now. Come with me.'

We walked along the corridor side by side with Max bringing up the rear. Cregar said conversationally, 'You won't see any of the staff because I've had them cleared out of this block. They're scientific types and a bit lily-livered. The sight of guns makes them nervous.'

I said nothing.

We walked a few more paces. 'I think I've found a way of confounding Ogilvie – there'll be no problem there – but that still leaves you. After we've seen Dr Ashton we'll have a talk.' He stopped at a door. 'In here,' he said, and let me precede him.

It was a strange room because one wall was almost entirely glass but the window looked, not upon the outside, but into another room. At first I didn't know what I was looking at, but Cregar said, 'There's Dr Ashton.' He pointed to a bed in the next room.

Penny was in bed, seemingly asleep. Her face was pale and ravaged, she could have been a woman twice her age. Around the bed were various bits of hospital equipment among which I recognized two drip feeds, one of which appeared to contain blood. I said, 'In God's name, what happened?'

Cregar said, almost apologetically, 'We had . . . er . . . an accident here last week in which Dr Ashton was involved. I'm afraid she's rather ill. She's been in a coma for the last two days.' He picked up a microphone and snapped a switch. Dr Ashton, can you hear me?'

His voice came amplified and distorted from a loud-speaker in the next room. Penny made no movement.

I said tightly, 'What's she got?'

'That's rather hard to say. It's something nobody has ever had before. Something new. Carter has been trying to run it down but without much success.'

I was frightened and angry simultaneously. Frightened for Penny and angry at Cregar. 'It's something you brewed up here, isn't it? Something that got loose because you were too tight-fisted to have a P4 laboratory as she wanted.'

'I see that Dr Ashton has been chattering about my business.' Cregar gestured. 'That's not a proper hospital ward of course; it's one of our laboratories. She had to be put somewhere safe.'

'Not safe for her,' I said bitterly. 'Safe for you.'

'Of course,' said Cregar. 'Whatever she's got we can't have spread about. Carter thinks it's most infectious.'

'Is Carter a medical doctor?'

'His degree is in biology not medicine, but he's a very capable man. She's getting the best of attention. We're transfusing whole blood and glucose, as you see.'

I turned to him. 'She should be in a hospital. This amateur lash-up is no good, and you know it. If she dies you'll be a murderer, and so will Carter and everybody else here.'

'You're probably right,' he said indifferently. 'About the hospital, I mean. But it's difficult to see how we could put her in a hospital and still maintain security.' His voice was remote and objective. 'I pride myself on my ability to solve problems but I haven't been able to solve that one.'

'Damn your security!'

'Coming from a man in your profession that smacks of heresy.' Cregar stepped back as he saw my expression, and gestured to Max who lifted the pistol warningly. 'She's having the best attention we can give her. Dr Carter is assiduous in his duties.'

'Carter is using her as a guinea pig and you damned well know it. She must be taken to a hospital – better still, to Porton. They understand high-risk pathogens there.'

'You're in no position to make demands,' he said. 'Come with me.' He turned his back and walked out.

I took a last look at Penny, then followed him with Max close behind. He walked up the corridor and opened a door on the other side. We entered a small vestibule and Cregar waited until Max had closed the outer door before proceeding. 'We do take precautions, in spite of anything you've been told,' he said. 'This is an air lock. The laboratory through there is under low pressure. Do you know why?'

'If there's a leak air goes in and not out.'

He nodded in satisfaction as though I'd passed a test, and opened the inner door. My ears popped as the pressure changed. 'This is Carter's own laboratroy. I'd like to show it to you.'

'Why?'

'You'll see.' He began a tour, behaving for all the world like a guide in one of those model factories where they show you what they're proud of and hide the bad bits. 'This is a centrifuge. You'll notice it's in an air-tight cabinet; that's to prevent anything escaping while it's in operation. No aerosols – microbes floating in the air.'

We passed on, and he indicated an array of glass-fronted cabinets covering one wall. 'The incubating cabinets, each containing its own petri dish and each petri dish isolated. Nothing can escape from there.'

'Something escaped from somewhere.'

He ignored that. 'Each cabinet can be removed in its entirety and the contents transferred elsewhere without coming into contact even with the air in the laboratory.'

I looked into a cabinet at the circular growth of a culture on a petri dish. 'What's the organism?'

'*Escherichia coli*, I believe. It's Carter's favourite.'

'The genetically weakened strain.'

Cregar raised his eyebrows. 'You seem well informed for a laymen. I don't know; that's Carter's affair. I'm not the expert.'

I turned to face him. 'What's this all about?'

'I'm trying to show you that we do take all possible precautions. What happened to Dr Ashton was purely accidental – a million to one chance. It's very important to me that you believe that.'

'If you'd listened to her it wouldn't have happened, but I believe you,' I said. 'I don't think you did it on purpose. What's so important about it?'

'I can come to an accommodation with Ogilvie,' he said, 'I'll lose some advantage but not all. That leaves you.'

'Have you spoken with Ogilvie?'

'Yes.'

I felt sick. If Cregar could corrupt Ogilvie I wouldn't want to work with him again. I said steadily, 'What about me?'

'This. I can do a deal with Ogilvie all right, but I don't think I could make it stick if anything happened to you. He always was squeamish. That means you have to be around and able to talk for some time to come which, as you will appreciate, presents me with a problem.'

'How to keep my mouth shut without killing me.'

'Precisely. You are a man like myself – we cut to the heart of a problem. When you appeared in the Ashton case I had you investiaged most thoroughly. To my surprise you had no handle I could get hold of, no peccadilloes to be exploited. You seem to be that rarity, the honest man.'

'I won't take compliments from you, damn it!'

'No compliment, I assure you, just a damnable nuisance. I wanted something to hold over you, something with which to blackmail you. There was nothing. So I have to find something else to close you mouth. I think I've found it.'

'Well?'

'It will mean my giving up more of the advantage I have achieved over the years, but I'll retain the most of it. I'll trade the young lady in the next laboratory for your silence.'

I looked at him with disgust. He had said the solution to his problem would lie in the study of man's weaknesses and he had found mine. He said, 'As soon as you agree, the girl can be taken to hospital, in carefully controlled conditions, of course. Perhaps your suggestion that she be taken to Porton is best. I could arrange that.'

I said, 'What guarantee would you have that I won't talk when she's well? I can't think of anything but no doubt you can.'

'Indeed I can – and I have. In Carter's office there's a document I want you to sign. I should say it's a carefully constructed document which took all my ingenuity to concoct. Quite a literary gem.'

'About what?'

'You'll see. Well, do you agree?'

'I'll need to read it first.'

Cregar smiled. 'Of course you may read it, but I think you'll sign it anyway. It's not much to ask – your signature for the life of your future wife.'

'You sicken me,' I said.

A telephone rang, startlingly loud. Cregar frowned, and said to Max, 'Answer it.' He held out his hand. 'I'll have the pistol. I don't trust him yet.'

Max gave him the gun and walked to the other end of the laboratory. Cregar said, 'Sticks and stones, etcetera. I don't care what you think of me as long as I get my way.'

'Show me what you want me to sign.'

'We'll wait for Max.'

Max talked in monosyllables in a low voice, then hung up and came back. 'Carter's got his knickers in a twist. He says a lot of men are landing. He reckons there are twenty boats out there.'

Cregar frowned. 'Who the hell are they?'

'He reckons they're local fishermen.'

'Damned Scots peasants! Go and shoo them away, Max. Put the fear of God into them with the Official Secrets Act. Get rid of them any way you can. Threaten them with the police if you have to.'

'Just threaten or actually send for them?'

'You can send for them if you think the situation warrants it.'

Max nodded towards me. 'That may not be entirely safe.'

'Don't worry about Jaggard,' said Cregar. 'We've reached an agreement.' As Max left he turned to me. 'Is this your doing?'

'How could I start a popular uprising?' I asked. 'They've probably got wind of what you're doing here, and remembering Gruinard, are determined not to let it happen again.'

'Ignorant bastards,' he muttered. 'Max will put them in their place.'

I said, 'I want Penny in hospital fast. How do we get off here?'

'A phone call will bring the helicopter in two hours.'

'You'd better make the call, then.'

He looked down at the floor, rubbing the side of his jaw while he thought about it. It was then I hit him in the belly, knocking the wind out of him. The gun went off and a bullet ricocheted from the wall and there was a smash of glass. I grabbed his wrist as he tried to bring up the gun and chopped him across the neck with the edge of my hand. He sagged to the floor.

When he painfully picked himself up I had the pistol. He glanced at it, then raised his eyes to mine. 'Where do you think this will get you?'

'I don't know about me, but it'll put you in prison.'

'You're a stupid, romantic fool,' he said.

'What's the number to ring for the helicopter?'

He shook his head. 'You don't know how government works, damn it. I'll never go to prison, but you'll be in water so hot you'll wish you'd never heard of Ashton or me.'

I said, 'I don't like hitting old men but I'll hammer hell out of you if I don't get that number.'

He turned his head and froze, then a weird bubbling cry came from him. 'Oh, Christ! Look what you've done!' His hand quivered as he pointed to the wall.

I looked, being careful to step behind him. At first I didn't see it. 'No tricks. What am I supposed to see?'

'The cabinets. Two are broken.' He whirled on me. 'I'm getting out of here.'

Blindly he tried to push past me, ignoring the gun. He was in a frenzy of terror, his face working convulsively. I stiff-armed him but his panic gave him added strength and he got past me and headed for the door. I went after him, reversed the pistol and clubbed him over the head. He went down like a falling tree.

I dragged him away from the door and went back to see the damage. Two of the panes in the incubating cabinets were broken and fragments of the petri dishes were scattered on the floor as were slimy particles of the cultures they had contained.

I whirled round as the door of the laboratory burst open. There stood Archie Ferguson. 'You're right, Mr Jaggard,' he said. 'It's another damned Gruinard.'

'Get out!' I yelled. 'For your life, get out!' He looked at me with startled eyes, and I pointed to the glasss wall at the end of the room. 'Go next door – I'll talk to you there. Move, man!'

The door slammed shut.

37

When I picked up the microphone my hand was shaking almost uncontrollably. I pushed the transmit button and heard a click. 'Can you hear me, Archie?' Ferguson, on the other side of the glass, nodded and spoke but I heard nothing. 'There's a microphone in front of you.'

He looked about him then picked it up. 'What happened here, Malcolm?'

'This place is bloody dangerous. Tell your men not to enter any of the laboratories – especially this one and the one across the corridor. Do that now.'

'I'll have guards on the doors.' He dropped the microphone and left on the run.

I went across to Cregar who was breathing stertorously. His head was twisted in an awkward position so I straightened him out and he breathed easier but showed no signs of coming awake.

'Mr Jaggard – are you there?'

I went back to the window to find Archie and Robbie Ferguson and a third man, one of the biggest I've seen, who was introduced as Wattie Stevenson. Archie said, 'It would seem you have problems. Is the lassie across the corridor the one you looked for?'

'Yes. You haven't been in there, have you?'

'No. I saw her by this arrangement we have here.'

'Good. Keep out of there. What size of an army did you bring? I heard of twenty boats.'

'Who told you that? There's only the six.'

'Have any trouble?'

'Not much. A man has a broken jaw.'

I said, 'How many people are there in this place?'

'Not as many as I would have thought. Maybe a dozen.'

Ogilvie had been right. It didn't take much to run a microbiological laboratory; perhaps half a dozen technical staff and the same number of domestics and bottlewashers. 'Put the lot under arrest. You have my authority for it.'

Archie looked at me speculatively. 'And what authority would that be?' I took out my departmental card and held it against the glass. He said, 'It doesn't mean much to me, but it looks official.'

'It takes you off the hook for invading government property. You did it on my instructions and you're covered. Oh, if you find a character called Max I don't care how roughly he's handled.'

Robbie Ferguson laughed. 'He's the one with the broken jaw. Wattie, here, hit him.'

'Och, it wasna' more than a wee tap,' said Wattie. 'The man has a glass jaw.'

'Wattie won the hammer throwing at the last Highland Games,' said Archie, with a grim smile. 'Besides, it was the man, Max, who sent Wattie away with a flea in his ear when he offered to help. What's to do now?'

'Did you ring Ogilvie as I asked?'

'Aye. He said he already knew about it.'

I nodded. He would have talked with Cregar. 'I want you to ring him again and the call put through to this telephone in here. You'll find a switchboard somewhere.'

'You can't come out?'

'No. You have my permission to listen in when I talk.' There was a groan behind me and I turned to see Cregar stirring. I said, 'Tell your men guarding the laboratories it's just as important that no one comes out. In fact, it's more important. This place being what it is there's probably some guns somewhere. In emergency use them.'

Archie looked grave. 'Is it so fearsome a thing?'

'I don't know,' I said wearily. 'I'm just taking prophylactic measures. Get busy, will you?'

I went back to Cregar, helped him to get up, and sat him

in a chair where he slumped flaccidly. He was dazed and in shock; too old to cope with the rough stuff any more. I said, 'Cregar, can you hear me?' He muttered something indistinguishable, and I slapped his cheek, 'Can you hear me?'

'Yes,' he whispered.

'Don't try to leave. There's a man outside with orders to shoot. Do you understand?'

He looked at me with glazed eyes, and nodded. 'Doesn't matter,' he muttered. 'I'm dead anyway. So are you.'

'We'll all be dead in a hundred years,' I said, and went to look again at the cultures in the broken petri dishes. The stuff looked harmless enough but I was careful not to touch it. Penny had described the elaborate precautions which were taken to prevent the escape of dangerous organisms from laboratories and, according to her, the lab I was now in wasn't up to snuff for what Carter had been doing.

The cultures could have been ordinary *E.coli* and, as such, perfectly harmless. But if they were cultures of *E.coli* which Carter had diddled around with then they could be dangerous in totally unpredictable ways. Cregar wasn't a scientist but he knew what Carter was up to, and the broken dishes had been enough to scare him half to death. From now on no chances would be taken and I hoped there had not been an escape already when Archie had opened the door. I didn't think so – the laboratory had low air pressure and I'd got him out fast.

Twenty minutes later I had Ogilvie on the phone. I wasted no time on politeness and answered none of the questions he shot at me. I said, 'This is a matter for urgency, so get it right the first time. Have you something to write with?'

'I'll record.' I heard a click.

'Cregar's laboratory on Cladach Duillich has run wild. There's one serious case of infection and two suspected. The organism causing it is new to medicine and probably man-made; it's also highly infectious. I don't know if it's a killer but it's highly likely. You'll have to set the alarm ringing and probably Lumsden, Penny's boss, is the best man to do it. Tell him hospitalization for three is needed in P4 – repeat – P4 conditions. He'll know what that means. Tell him I suggest Porton Down, but he might have a better idea.'

'I'll get on to it immediately,' said Ogilvie. 'Who are the three?'

'The serious case is Penny Ashton.'

There was a sharp withdrawal of breath. 'Oh, Christ! I'm sorry, Malcolm.'

I went on, 'The suspected cases are Cregar and myself.'

'For the love of God!' said Ogilvie. 'What's been going on up there?'

I ignored him. 'There's a helicopter pad on Cladach Duillich so Lumsden had better use a chopper. Tell him the man to see here is a Dr Carter. He's the chap who cooked up whatever hellbrew has got loose.'

'I've got that.'

'Then make it quick. I think Penny is dying,' I said bleakly.

38

Cregar and I were in an odd position. Loathing each other beyond all belief, we were condemned to each other's company for an unspecified period. The next few hours were to be extremely uncomfortable, but I tried to make them as comfortable as possible.

Archie Ferguson came back as soon as I had spoken to Ogilvie and the expression on his face was terrifying. He looked like one of the Old Testament prophets might look after inditing one of the more dire chapters of the Bible. 'May their souls rot forever in hell!' he burst out.

'Take it easy,' I said. 'There are practical things to do.' I thought of Ogilvie recording my telephone conversation and it gave me an idea. 'See if you can find a tape-recorder. I'll need it.'

Archie simmered down. 'Aye, I'll see what I can do.'

'And we'll need food in here, but you can give us food once and once only. What you do is this. You open the outer door of the laboratory and put the food on the floor just inside. Tell me when you've closed the door and I'll come out and get it. It can be done once only because I can't risk contamination through the air lock, so you'd better give us enough for three meals. If you can find vacuum flasks for coffee that would be a help.'

Ferguson looked past me. 'Is yon man the Cregar you spoke of?'

'Yes.'

'Then he gets nothing from me.'

'You'll do as I say,' I said sharply. 'We both eat or neither of us eats.'

He took a deep breath, nodded curtly, then laid down

the microphone and went away. Half an hour later he came back. 'Your food's there. I did better than flasks; there's a coffee percolator to make your own.'

'Thanks.' I had another idea. 'Archie, this laboratory is maintained at a lower air pressure than the outside. That means pumps, and pumps mean electricity. Put someone to watch the generator; I don't want it stopping, either by breakdown or lack of fuel. Will you see to that?'

'Aye. It won't stop.'

I went into the air lock and got the food – a pile of sandwiches – and also found a small battery-powered cassette tape-recorder. I put everything on the table next to the telephone. Cregar was apathetic and looked at the sandwiches without interest. I filled the percolator from a tap on one of the benches and got the coffee going. Cregar accepted coffee but he wouldn't eat.

Unobtrusively I switched on the recorder; I wanted Cregar condemned out of his own mouth. I said, 'We've a lot to talk about.'

'Have we?' he said without interest. 'Nothing matters any more.'

'You're not dead yet, and you may not be if Ogilvie does his stuff. When did Benson learn of Ashton's interest in genetics?'

He was silent for a moment, then said, 'Must have been 1971. He saw that Ashton was keeping up with the girl's studies, and then starting to do a lot of work on his own, usually at the weekends – a lot of calculating. He tried to get a look at it, but Ashton kept it locked away.' Cregar brooded. 'Ashton never did like me. I've often wondered if he knew what I was doing.' He waved his hand at the laboratory. 'This, I mean. It's supposed to be secret, but a man with money can usually find out what he wants to know.' He shrugged. 'Anyway, he made damned certain that Benson didn't lay an eye on his work.'

'That empty vault must have come as a shock.'

He nodded. 'Benson knew about the vault but never

managed to get inside. And when Ogilvie told me it was empty I didn't believe him. It was only when he offered to let one of my forensic chaps look at the vault that I accepted that fact.' He looked up. 'You're a clever man. I never thought of the railway. I ought to have done. Ashton wasn't the man to fool about with toy trains.'

Now Cregar had started to talk he positively flowed. I suppose he thought there was no reason to keep his silence. It was a sort of deathbed confession.

I said, 'What I can't understand was how you engineered Mayberry's acid attack – and why. That's the bit that seems senseless.'

'It was senseless,' said Cregar. 'I had nothing to do with it. I didn't even know Mayberry existed until the police tracked him down. Do you remember when you appeared before the inter-departmental committee, Ogilvie said something about you "exploding Ashton out of Stockholm"? Well, I exploded him out of England.'

'How?'

He shrugged. 'Opportunism combined with planning. I'd been wanting to have a dig at Ashton for a long time. I wanted to get him out of that house so I could get into that vault. I thought whatever he had would be ripe. I'd already made preparations – rented the flat and opened the bank account in Stockholm, got the Israeli passport, and so on. All I needed was a trigger. Then along came that maniac, Mayberry – most opportunely. I got Benson to panic Ashton, talking of threats to the other girl, and so on. Benson told him my department couldn't cope with that sort of thing unless Ashton got out, that we were prepared to help and that we had a safe hideaway for him, which of course we had. And after all that the damned vault was empty.'

'But why did Benson kill Ashton?'

'Standing orders from thirty years ago,' said Cregar simply. 'Ashton wasn't to be allowed to go back to the Russians. If there was a chance of him falling into Russian hands Benson was to kill him. Benson had every reason to think you were Russians.'

'Jesus!' I said. 'What sort of man was Benson to kill Ashton after being with him thirty years?'

Cregar gave me a lopsided smile. 'He had gratitude, I suppose; and personal loyalty – to me.'

I remembered my musings in the dark room and, out of curiosity, said, 'Cregar, why did you do all this?'

He looked at me in surprise. 'A man must leave his mark on the world.'

I felt chilled.

There wasn't much I wanted to know after that, but, the dam now broken, Cregar rambled on interminably, and I was glad when the telephone rang. It was Ogilvie. 'There'll be an RAF helicopter on its way with a medical team. Lumsden thinks you're right about Porton and he's made the arrangements.' He paused. 'He also wants me to pass on his apologies – I don't know why.'

'I do. Thank him for me. When will the chopper get here?'

'They're assembling the team now. I'd say six hours. How's Miss Ashton?'

'I don't know,' I said bitterly. 'I can't get to her. She's in a coma. You can tell that to Lumsden, too.'

Ogilvie was inclined to talk but I put him off. I wasn't in the mood for that. Half an hour later the phone rang again and I found Archie Ferguson on the line. 'There's someone called Starkie wants to talk to the man Carter. Shall I let him?'

'Let me talk to Starkie.' The earphone crackled and a deep voice said, 'Richard Starkie here – is that Dr Carter?'

'Malcolm Jaggard here. Who are you?'

'I'm a doctor speaking from Porton Down. Are you one of the infected men?'

'Yes.'

'Any symptoms starting to show?'

'Not yet.'

'If Carter manufactured this bug he'll know more about it than anyone. I need the information.'

'Right,' I said. 'If you don't get satisfaction from him let me know. Are you on the line, Archie?'

'Aye.'

'Let them talk. If Carter wants persuading I'm sure you know what to do.'

They came for us seven hours later, dressed like spacemen in plastic clothing with self-contained breathing apparatus. They put us in plastic envelopes whole and entire, plugged in an air supply and sealed us up. We stopped in the air lock and the envelopes and themselves were drenched with a liquid, then we were carried out to the helicopter where I found Penny already installed in her own envelope. She was still unconscious.

39

A month later I was feeling pretty chipper because Starkie had given me a clean bill of health. 'For three weeks now we've inspected every damned *E.coli* bug that's come out of you and they're all normal. I don't know why you're still lying around here. What do you think this is, a doss house?'

He hadn't always been as cheerful as that. At the beginning I was placed in a sterile room and untouched by human hand for the next two weeks. Everything that was done to me was done by remote control. Later they told me that a team of thirty doctors and nurses was working on me alone.

Penny did better. For her they apparently mobilized the entire medical resources of the United Kingdom, plus sizeable chunks from the United States and the Continent, with a little bit from Australia. The bug she had was different from the one I'd caught, and it was a real frightener. It got the medical world into a dizzy tizzy and, although they were able to cure her, they wanted to make sure that the bug, whatever it was, was completely eradicated. So I came out of Porton Down a month before her.

Starkie once said soberly, 'If she'd have been left another day with the minimal attention she was getting I don't think we could have done it.' That made me think of Carter and I wondered what was being done about him. I never found out.

When I came out of purdah but before I was discharged I went to see her. I couldn't kiss her, or even touch her, but we could speak separated by a pane of glass, and she seemed cheerful enough. I told her something of what had happened, but not everything. Time enough for that when she was better. Then I said, 'I want you out of here pretty damned quick. I want to get married.'

She smiled brilliantly. 'Oh, yes, Malcolm.'

'I can't fix a day because of that bloody man Starkie,' I complained. 'He's likely to keep you in here forever, investigating the contents of your beautiful bowels.'

She said, 'How would you like a double wedding? I had a letter from Gillian in New York. Peter Michaelis flew over and proposed to her. She was lying in bed with her left arm strapped to her right cheek and swaddled in bandages when he asked her. She thought it was very funny.'

'I'll be damned!'

'It will be a little time yet. We all have to get out of our hospitals. Is four months too long to wait?'

'Yes,' I said promptly. 'But I'll wait.'

I didn't ask anyone how Cregar was doing because I didn't care.

On the day I came out of the sterile room Ogilvie came to see me, bearing the obligatory pound of grapes. I received him with some reserve. He asked after my health and I referred him to Starkie, then he said, 'We got the tape cassette after it had been decontaminated. Cregar won't be able to wriggle out of this one.'

I said, 'Had any success with Ashton's computer programs?'

'Oh, my God, they're fantastic. Everyone has claimed the man was a genius and he's proved it.'

'How?'

Ogilvie scratched his head. 'I don't know if I can explain – I'm no scientist – but it seems that Ashton has done for genetics what Einstein did for physics. He analysed the DNA molecule in a theoretical way and came up with a series of rather complicated equations. By applying these you can predict exactly which genes go where and why, and which genetic configurations are possible or not possible. It's a startling breakthrough; it's put genetics on a firm and mathematical grounding.'

'That should make Lumsden happy,' I said.

Ogilvie ate a grape. 'He doesn't know. It's still confidential. It hasn't been released publicly yet.'

'Why not?'

'The Minister seems to feel . . . well, there are reasons why it shouldn't be released yet. Or so he says.'

That saddened me. The bloody politicians with their bloody reasons made me sick to the stomach. The Minister was another Creger. He had found a power lever and wanted to stick to it.

Ogilvie took another grape. 'I asked Starkie when you'd be coming out but he isn't prepared to say. However, when you do I've a new job for you. As you may know, Kerr is retiring in two years. I want to groom you for his job.' Kerr was Ogilvie's second-in-command. He smiled. 'In seven years, when I go, you could be running the department.'

I said bluntly, 'Get lost.'

He was not a man who showed astonishment easily, but he did then. 'What did you say?'

'You heard me. Get lost. You can take Kerr's job and your job and stuff them wherever you like. The Minister's backside might be a good place.'

'What the devil's got into you?' he demanded.

'I'll tell you,' I said. 'You were going to do a deal with Cregar.'

'Who said that?'

'Cregar.'

'And you believed him? The man lies as naturally as he breathes.'

'Yes, I believed him because at that point he had no reason to lie. He did proposition you, didn't he?'

'Well, we talked – yes.'

I nodded. 'That's why you won't get me back in the department. I'm tired of lies and evasions; I'm tired of self-interest masquerading as patriotism. It came to me when Cregar called me an honest man, not as a compliment but as someone to corrupt. I realized then that he was wrong. How could an honest man do what I did to Ashton?'

'I think you're being over-emotional about this,' Ogilvie said stiffly.

'I'm emotional because I'm a man with feelings and not a bloody robot,' I retorted. 'And now you can take your bloody grapes and get the hell out of here.'

He went away moderately unhappy.

40

And they all lived happily ever after. The hero married the principal girl, and second hero got the second girl, and they moved out of the poor woodcutter's cottage into the east wing of the king's palace.

But this is not a fairy tale.

On the day Penny came out of hospital she, Peter Michaelis and I went on a wing-ding in the East End and the three of us became moderately alcoholic and distinctly merry. On the day Gillian arrived back from New York the four of us went on another wing-ding with similar effect. That American plastic surgeon must have been a genius because Gillian's new face was an improvement on the one she had before the acid was thrown. I was very glad for Peter.

The clanging of wedding bells could be heard in the near future. Penny and Gillian were dashing about London denuding the better stores of dresses and frillies for their trousseaux, while I scouted around for a house, introduced it to Penny, and then secured it with a cash deposit against the time the lawyers had finished their expensive wrangling over the deeds. It was all very exhilarating.

Ten days before the wedding I felt it incumbent on me to go back to see Starkie. He heard what I had to say and frowned, then took me into a laboratory where I was subjected to a battery of tests. He told me to go away and return in a week.

On the day I went back I read of Cregar's death in *The Times*. The obituary was sickening. Described as a faithful public servant who had served his country with no thought of self for many years, he was lauded as an example for coming generations to follow. I threw the paper out of the train window and was immediately sorry; that sort of stuff could pollute the countryside very seriously.

Starkie was serious, too, when I saw him, and I said, 'It's bad news.'

'Yes, it is,' he said directly. 'It's cancer.'

It was a blow, but I had half-expected it. 'How long do I have?'

He shrugged. 'Six months to a year, I'd say. Could be longer, but not much.'

I walked to his office window and looked out. I can't remember what I saw there. 'Cregar's dead,' I said. 'Same thing?'

'Yes.'

'How?'

Starkie sighed. 'That damned fool, Carter, was doing shot-gun experiments. That means he was chopping up DNA molecules into short lengths, putting them into *E.coli*, and standing back to see what happened. It's not a bad technique if you know what you're doing and take the proper precautions.'

'He was taking precautions,' I said. 'The stuff got loose because of my own damned foolishness.'

'He wasn't,' snapped Starkie. 'Cregar was putting pressure on him – wanting fast results. He couldn't wait for a consignment of genetically weakened *E.coli* from the States so he used the normal bug. There was no biological containment at all. The stuff went straight into your gut and started to breed happily.'

'To cause cancer?' It didn't seem likely.

'I'll try to explain this as simply as possible,' said Starkie. 'We believe that in the genetic material of all normal cells there are genes which can produce tumour-forming chemicals, but they are normally repressed by other genes. Now, if you do a shotgun experiment and introduce a short length of DNA into *E.coli* you're in danger of introducing a tumour gene without the one that represses it. That's what's happened to you. The *E.coli* in your gut was producing tumour-forming chemicals.'

'But you said the *E.coli* coming out of me was normal,' I objected.

'I know I did, and so it was. One of the most difficult things to do in these experiments is to get a new strain to breed true. They're very unstable. What happened was that this strain began to breed back to normal *E.coli* almost immediately. But it was in your gut long enough to do the damage.'

'I see.' I felt a sudden chill. 'What about Penny?'

'She's all right. That was a different bug entirely. We made sure of that.'

I said, 'Thank you, Dr Starkie. You've been very direct and I appreciate it. What's the next step?'

He rubbed his jaw. 'If you hadn't come to see me I'd have sent for you – on the basis of what happened to Lord Cregar. This is a type of cancer we haven't come across before; at least it hasn't been reported in the literature in this particular form. Cregar went very fast, but that may have been because of his age. Older cellular structures are more susceptible to cancers. I think you have a better chance.'

But not much better, I thought. Starkie spoke in the flat, even tone used by doctors when they want to break the bad news slowly. He scribbled on a sheet of paper. 'Go to this man. He's very good and knows about your case. He'll probably put you on tumour-reducing drugs and, possibly, radiation therapy.' He paused. 'And put your affairs in order as any sensible man should.'

I thanked him again, took the address, and went back to London where I heard another instalment of bad news. Then I told Penny. I had no need to give her Starkie's explanation because she grasped that immediately. It was her job, after all. I said, 'Of course, the marriage is off.'

'Oh, no; Malcolm!'

And so we had another row – which I won. I said, 'I

have no objection to living in sin. Come live with me and be my love. I know a place in the south of Ireland where the mountains are green and the sea is blue when the sun shines, which it does quite often, and green when it's cloudy and the rollers come in from the Atlantic. I could do with six months of that if you're with me.'

We went to Ireland immediately after Peter and Gillian were married. It was not the happy occasion one would have wished; the men were sombre and the women weepy, but it had to be gone through.

At one time I thought of suicide; taking the Hemingway out, to perpetrate a bad pun. But then I thought I had a job to do, which was to write an account of the Ashton case, leaving nothing out and making it as truthful as possible, and certainly not putting any cosmetics on my own blemishes. God knows I'm not proud of my own part in it. Penny has read the manuscript; parts of it have amused her, other parts have shattered her. She has typed it all herself.

We live here very simply if you discount the resident medical staff of a doctor and three nurses which Penny insisted upon. The doctor is a mild young American who plays bad chess and the nurses are pretty which Penny doesn't mind. It helps to have a wealthy woman for a mistress. For the first few months I used to go to Dublin once a fortnight where they'd prod and probe and shoot atoms into me. But I stopped that because it wasn't doing any good.

Now time is becoming short. This account and myself are coming to an end. I have written it for publication, partly because I think people ought to know what is done in their names, and partly because the work of Ashton on genetics has not yet been released. It would be a pity if his work, which could do so much good in the right hands, should be withheld and perhaps diverted to malignant uses in the hands of another Cregar. There are many Cregars about in high office.

Whether publication will be possible at all I don't know. The wrath of the Establishment can be mighty and its instruments of suppression strong and subtle. Nevertheless Penny and I have been plotting our campaign to ensure that these words are not lost.

A wise one-legged American, in adapting the words of a naval hero, once said, 'We have met the enemy, and he is us.'

God help you all if he is right.